Makeshift Girl

The Secret Heritage Trail

Published in Australia in 2023 by
Story Playscapes
Victoria, Australia
ABN 62197863313

publications@storyplayscapes.com
www.storyplayscapes.com

Copyright © Susan Marshall, 2023

All rights reserved. Apart from any fair dealing for the purposes of private study, research, criticism or review as permitted under the Copyright Act, no part of this publication may be translated, adapted, performed, reproduced, stored in a retrieval system or transmitted in any forms by any means, electronic, mechanical, photocopying, recording or otherwise, without the written permission of the publisher.

This book is a work of fiction. The names, characters, places and events are products of the author's imagination and any resemblance to actual persons or events, past or present, is entirely coincidental.

 A catalogue record for this book is available from the National Library of Australia

Title: Makeshift Girl: The Secret Heritage Trail
Series: Makeshift Girl: Book 1
Author: Susan Marshall
ISBN: 9780645404104 (Paperback)
Subject: Fiction: General and Literary

Produced by Story Playscapes
Written by Susan Marshall
Book design, illustration and photography by Ryan Marshall

All images and text are Copyright © Story Playscapes

The opinions expressed in this publication are those of the author and do not necessarily reflect those of the views of Story Playscapes. While all reasonable checks have been made to ensure the accuracy of statements and advice, no responsibility can be accepted for errors, omissions or representations, express or implied. The author and Story Playscapes do not, under any circumstance, accept any responsibility or loss occasioned to any person acting or refraining from action as a result of material in this publication.

Warning: This book contains mature content, including: adult themes, violence, harassment, sexual references and mature language. It is not intended to be read by any persons under 18 years of age.

BOOK ONE
The Secret Heritage Trail

Makeshift Girl

Susan Marshall

For my beautiful daughter, Arlia

Contents

9   The Art of Writing
11   Preface
28   Trekking an Age of Light
30   Redbank City Map

33   Chapter 1
41   Chapter 2
52   Chapter 3
60   Chapter 4
65   Chapter 5
68   Chapter 6
73   Chapter 7
82   Chapter 8
94   Chapter 9
104   Chapter 10
114   Chapter 11
125   Chapter 12
136   Chapter 13
140   Chapter 14
152   Chapter 15
169   Chapter 16
189   Chapter 17
211   Chapter 18
225   Chapter 19
242   Chapter 20

247	Chapter 21	435	Chapter 41
256	Chapter 22	440	Chapter 42
269	Chapter 23	449	Chapter 43
276	Chapter 24	456	Chapter 44
283	Chapter 25	462	Chapter 45
288	Chapter 26	469	Chapter 46
303	Chapter 27	475	Chapter 47
320	Chapter 28	483	Chapter 48
328	Chapter 29	498	Chapter 49
333	Chapter 30	509	Chapter 50
344	Chapter 31	517	Chapter 51
354	Chapter 32	528	Chapter 52
361	Chapter 33	546	Chapter 53
367	Chapter 34	559	Chapter 54
378	Chapter 35		
387	Chapter 36	570	About the Author
393	Chapter 37	572	About the Book Designer
399	Chapter 38	572	About Story Playscapes
413	Chapter 39		
425	Chapter 40		

The Art of Writing

I consider myself as a wanderer who treks the pathways of life. Wherever I go, I am able to discover the simple moments: their energy and vibrancy radiate through my soul. I flesh out such moments, playing with ideas and enabling them to take flight.

Interacting with simple moments in physical spaces enable them to become my playscapes: scapes that inspire my playful story telling. I've learnt to never underestimate a life and the precious trail that it leads ... Our world is full of great stories to discover.

It has been a wonderful journey creating *Makeshift Girl: The Secret Heritage Trail*. I have had the joy of sharing my inspirational playscapes and writing processes with *Story Playscapes'* very dedicated and supportive global readership.

This book celebrates the premiere printed publication for *Story Playscapes* and my debut novel. It is a beautiful paperback edition that I hope brings you much entertainment and a love for reading.

Happy discoveries!

–Susan Marshall,
Founder, Australian Author & Publisher at *Story Playscapes*.

Preface

The Bond Between a Mother and Daughter

I am truly blessed to be a mother to my beautiful daughter. It has been an absolute delight to watch her grow and to become attuned to her needs and instincts. Sharing my life with hers has taught me more about myself. My special bond with her has enriched my heart and soul.

It was on the afternoon of the 7 September 2020, while I sat with my daughter and reflected upon our experiences together, that I came up with the initial ideas for *Makeshift Girl: The Secret Heritage Trail*. I was excited to begin engaging in the makeshift movements and flow of the novel and to focus on the everlasting bond that can exist between a mother and daughter.

Make Shifting as a Human Condition

> Adira: "Exiting the tent, I stand and press my bare feet into the earth. The air swirls around me, caressing the fallen leaves and sending them tumbling across my feet.
>
> If I listen closely enough, I can hear a breath.
>
> It is far away, many footprints from here, expelling a rhythmic energy, a sign of life.
>
> I used to watch Mother wring her hands together while she sighed. Her eyes were dark and intense as they darted around her. Her ears were pricked and alert to any dangerous sounds.
>
> In our hyper vigilant states our hearts did wrestle, determined to live and fight. We were willing to sacrifice contentment for that single, valuable breath.
>
> A sign of existence.

A sign of life.

Now, I inhale the air, the microcosmic particles of the earth and all that I tread upon. I keep inhaling, drawing in the fragments of time that we have both make shifted our ways through. Their presence, their fleeting moments, cannot ever be captured in a single breath.

Exhaling, my breath is strong, trekking an age of light which glows dimly in the distance. Light that bounces across the earth, flashing images of familiar, warm faces, silk and red gum trees. Moments of precious heritage that should be treasured and prolonged."

– *Makeshift Girl: The Secret Heritage Trail*, Susan Marshall, 2023

In the quote above, the protagonist, Adira, reflects on her bond with her mother and the importance of their acts of make shifting through time. The strength and conviction that Adira expresses in the quote are the result of her increased confidence and independence throughout the novel.

F. Opper's (1895) painting: *'The "new woman" and her bicycle – there will be several varieties of her !'* was inspirational in my development of the enduring and independent strength of a woman in this novel. The painting uses a variety of vignettes to show the changing identities and natures of women throughout history.

Central to the painting's image, is a cartoon vignette of the "new woman" looking fiercely determined in her pantaloons and accompanied by three mice. It is this strong image that dominates the painting, encapsulating the woman's bravery and independence, whereas once before she may have been more marginalised in public perception. The vignettes in the background contrast, showing the "old woman" who was perceived to be: scared of mice, riding her bike as a salvation army 'lassy' and a servant girl, just to name a few.

Visually, *'The "new woman" and her bicycle – there will be several varieties of her !'* does give me a sense of the "makeshift" woman who is coping and/or adapting momentarily to her context as well as responding to perceptions of her in society.

On a larger scale, *Makeshift Girl: The Secret Heritage Trail* explores the degrees of independence that women are able to express. Faced with political, social and/or economical stress, they are left to makeshift their ways across adverse terrain and to find ways to face and/or overcome challenging moments. It is not always about being brave. Every woman is different and their experiences will certainly shape who they are.

Adira learns to make shift her way across the perilous terrain of Mira at a young age. She and her mother, Maricelle, use their fighting instincts to discover temporary solutions in order to escape the dark horse (Petoy clan) that is tracking them down.

Throughout the novel, Adira demonstrates a growing heroic prowess in make shifting her ways through adverse terrain and situations. Forcibly separated from her mother at the age of 6, Adira grows up in Redbank. Make shifting is already her instinctive response to any danger that occurs in her life. In Redbank, Adira discovers that she must once again attune herself to the terrain in order to escape the dark horse.

Girl is fleeing from persecution in Mira. However, the Petoys continue to track her down in Redbank. Therefore, with Adira's help, Girl must find her strength and continue to grow and survive under tremendously adverse conditions.

Heritage Trade

Girl (a verse from her song):

> *"Clutch the cloth close to your heart,*
> *let its creation speak its art.*
> *Share its journeys across the land,*
> *away from the dark horse's hand."*
>
> *– Makeshift Girl: The Secret Heritage Trail,*
> Susan Marshall, 2023

I am passionate about heritage trade and its importance in our world. I grew up in a large, multicultural family. Therefore, my ethnic background is: Maltese, Portuguese, English, Turkish and Italian. I was also fortunate to learn how to speak French fluently throughout my schooling. My cultural heritage and experiences have made me more aware of the diverse ways to live in our world and to communicate with others.

My Nanna lived in Gozo before she migrated to Australia. The lace trade is a strong part of Maltese culture there. I have fond memories of a lace table cloth that my Nanna displayed on her kitchen table. It provided me with a sense of family and heritage every time I sat at her table and chatted with her.

Heritage trade bestows identity, preservation and confidence upon a culture. It is also a way of sharing one's wisdom with others and so should be celebrated. In this way, a heritage item far transcends itself as an object, yet falls into the realm of intangible connection.

A heritage item can elicit complex human emotions and a forced loss of connection with it may be considered inhumane for a culture, people or person.

Silk Making and Trade Around the Globe

It was a joy to begin researching the origins of silk making in China. The ancient beliefs and techniques evident in Chinese culture are to be celebrated. In Neolithic China, the Silk Road began its roots, eventually creating a series of trade routes that connected the East to the West over many centuries (Cartwright, M., 2017 and UNESCO, n.d.).

Silk is a natural fibre, which is created by silk worms *(Bombyx mori)*. Raw silk fibre is spun, weaved and dyed. It is used to create apparel, carpets, furnishings, manchester, etc. Such a process is laborious and often undertaken by women. (Cartwright, M., 2017; Science Direct, 2013 and UNESCO, n.d.).

In the world of *Makeshift Girl: The Secret Heritage Trail*, silk itself is used as a catalyst for conflict and discovery of identity. Silk also holds great sentimental value too.

I believe that the Silk Road still breathes its life through the many cultural and trade developments that we see evident in daily life today.

I was inspired by Tomás Skinner's (2016), critical discussions about heritage along the silk road in his article titled: *Urban Heritage of the*

Silk Road. It is here that heritage and the sense of identity derived from it are raised as assets to be manipulated for local, national and international interests.

It is this shifting nature of heritage and its trade: its precious beginnings and importance for a culture, leading to its evolving exploitation through time that I explore in the novel. The fictional cities of Redbank and Mira are both interconnected by their trade routes, which have continually developed and evolved over centuries.

Social, political and economical pressures affect such trade routes, unravelling a secret heritage trail that encompasses past and present decisions regarding heritage.

Developing the Ancient City of Mira

I decided to focus on the significance of heritage when developing Mira. Some big questions I asked were: How did the empire rule Mira throughout history? What ancient heritage practices formed in Mira? Could such practices be transferable to the modern city of Redbank? How did heritage decisions by stakeholders affect Mira socially, politically and economically?

One thing that I found amazing about the Silk Road was its vibrancy of life. Culture, language, medicine, architecture, food, plants, textiles, spices, precious stones and many more aspects of life and trade traveled their journeys across the interconnecting trade routes. There is an amazing map provided by the University of Chicago, titled: *Silk Road and Indian Ocean Traders: Connecting China and the Middle East* which provides details of the silk trade routes and the vibrancy of life shared.

Completing my studies of the Silk Road and ancient silk practices in China, I began to research further.

I was drawn to the beauty of ancient Indian heritage, particularly around the Himalayas. Flora and fauna were abundant in such areas, leading to much trade of animals reared and agriculture. The beautiful aspects of heritage were also evident around the mountains, where culture could and still can flourish harmoniously (UNESCO, n.d.).

I marveled at the wonders of master artisans in Baskal, Azerbaijan, who are involved in the creation of Kelaghayi silk head scarves for women (inscribed on the UNESCO intangible cultural world heritage list). Decorated with symbols that represent the lives, histories and heritage of women, the scarves share their own important stories (The Caspian Post, 2021 and UNESCO, n.d.).

I gleaned the concept of Girl's family scarf and the significant use of heritage totems in silk design from the traditional art of Kelaghayi.

I was taken aback by the beauty of Georgia's Caucasus mountains, which travel from the Black Sea to the Caspian. Historically, the mountain passes consisted of grass land and unmarked dirt roads and were often traveled on foot or by horse and cart (UNESCO, n.d.).

Such rocky terrain, constructed by the Romans, is also present along the Via Egnatia, the ancient highway that exists in Durrës, Albania and links the Silk Road to Istanbul. Archaeologists suggest that there is evidence that parts of the highway still exist. One can imagine feet treading or horse and cart being pushed along its terrain (BBC, 2018).

In *Makeshift Girl: The Secret Heritage Trail,* Girl, herself, is used to traveling on foot across a bumpy terrain:

> Girl: "I used to tread the world freely in Mira," she smiles gently. "My feet would feel the bare earth sifting its way between my toes. I'd push a cart full of wares, hearing it roll along the bumpy terrain, catching stones and flicking them up in the air.
>
> "At times I would stop to take a break, staring out at the shifting clouds in the sky. The route did not seem too long but familiar. It was a path I always took to deliver the silk designs to Emperor Laynton."
>
> –Susan Marshall, *Makeshift Girl: The Secret Heritage Trail,* 2023.

Furthermore, parts of Georgia are isolated, with villagers undertaking farming and agricultural duties themselves. Being self sufficient is important in order to survive. The weather and turbulence involved in living high in the mountains by the sea poses very real challenges to one's existence (BBC, 2018).

Comparably, Mira itself, is a small, isolated city, that sits by the sea. Trade is important to its people in order to survive. I extended my research into the art of tallow candle making, (a practice which was originated by the ancient Roman people), as a self sufficient way to have light and live in Mira during dark and cold times. Furthermore, many people of Mira practice silk making and other craft skills that lead them to the hope of trade and survival.

Venice and its strategic position as a hub in the west with great maritime trade capacity, inspired the concept of desire for progress in the novel. Historically, Venice sacked Constantinople and brought back much loot (including St Mark's Cathedral's bronze horses) and so became the most esteemed centre for trade in the west. Venice also continued to gain more power, forming links with many cities along the Silk Road (UNESCO, n.d.).

Researching the aforementioned historical silk trade routes and more, provided me with ideas for the development of the original trade routes that originate in Mira and extend into Redbank. Such routes are perilous, even in times of ancient trade and help to build the novel's mystery.

The Travels of Marco Polo

The inspirational Marco Polo, the silk merchant, originated from Venice and undertook his travels in trade along the Silk Road.

The Travels of Marco Polo by Marco Polo and Rustichello da Pisa was an inspiration to me. It brought life to the silk trade routes and ways of maritime trade and enabled me to flesh out original ideas for the vibrancy of trade practice in the novel.

The power structures around silk trade became evident to me. As luxurious and exquisite as silk was, it had the power to begin wars over ownership and trade. Reading wider, I immersed myself in the importance of silk for a variety of cultures and the power structures that governed them around the world.

Mira began to develop its own unique social, political and economical world, which I was able to progress from ancient times until the present. I focused on issues such as: the banning of tallow candles, the addition of silk tax and land use tax and how these factors would affect an empire. This led to the development of characters such as Sophie and Hidu Wang, siblings who both had to survive the harsh realities that Mira provided them with. The citizens of Mira also developed their own voices, with many in protest of the decisions made by Emperor Laynton.

As I considered ancient imperial heritage, I discovered that falconry was a popular sport in ancient central Asia. Further research into the sport, led to my interest in what work was being undertaken in order to conserve falcons (birds of prey) around the world historically and today.

Interestingly, many steps were taken to protect falcons through time. An example is the work of Eleanor d'Arborea, the queen of Sicily who developed the Falco eleonorae (International Association of Falconry and Birds of Prey, n.d.).

Arabian falconry places a high demand on saker falcons, which are great hunters. This has led to the falcon being greatly demanded for international trade. In response to this issue and after seven years of research, the International Wildlife Consultants (UK) Ltd and their Mongolian research partners, the Wildlife Science and Conservation Center developed the Mongolian Artificial Nest Project. It aims to conserve the saker falcon via the implementation of artificial nests across the flat and undulating grasslands of the Mongolian steppe (International Wildlife Consultants Ltd., n.d.).

My research into the essential need for protection of falcons, led me to developing Empress Mira's commitment to the life and well being of her late father's falcons. Her decision to ban falconry as a sport leaves her faced with much protest from the barons who once relied upon falconry for sporting and trade opportunities under her father's reign.

Continuing to read *The Travels of Marco Polo*, I became intrigued by the ways in which messages were delivered by imperial leaders. Messengers would travel for miles from one message post to another over strict time frames in order to ensure the secrecy of the message and prompt delivery. This provided me with inspiration for the Petoys' delivery service and its evolving progress. Mitch Cazon's role as a delivery boy in the service helps to shed some light into its mysteries and intricacies.

Makeshift Girl: The Secret Heritage Trail

Cultural Appropriation of Heritage Apparel and Totems

One of the major pressures in *Makeshift Girl: The Secret Heritage Trail*, eventuates from the cultural appropriation of heritage garments and their significant totems.

The novel explores the great weight of silk within its world. Silk is a fibre that led to great desire, conflict, poverty and riches. The narrative contrasts the difference between natural silk found in traditionally made products and sustainable fashion, versus the use of synthetic fibres and dyes in the creation of fast fashion. Major issues arise from the exploitation of silk trade, including: cultural appropriation, identity politics and forced labour, among others.

The novel emphasises the importance of engaging in sustainable fashion practices. It explores the production of fast fashion via toxic materials and what negative impacts such production has on a people's heritage and the environment.

Transport in Trade

I researched the history of transport in trade, from horse back to trucks on land. Ships and boats were also a vital part of maritime trade. It was important to gain historical accuracy of such transport in order to world build Mira and Redbank (ancient versus modern transport types). The transport enabled me to provide great contrasts between the two cities. I was also able to further develop conflicting interests between the Petoy clan and leaders such as: Emperor Laynton of Mira and Mayor Rahi of Redbank.

Gottlieb Daimler's first truck (1896) and its revised edition (Daimler Truck, 2021), also gave me inspiration to develop a more modern transport and motivation for the Petoy clan. It was a great way to show how the clan had continued to exist and progress across the ages.

The range of transport researched also enabled me to create my own map of Redbank, which was vital to have access to as I wrote this novel. The map enabled me to provide consistent navigation across the city; enhance clues and mystery; world build the rules and ways of life existent and to develop detailed dramatic actions within the story.

The Terrain

In *Makeshift Girl: The Secret Heritage Trail*, the terrain constantly shifts through time, seasons and places, unraveling its own diverse identities as the novel progresses. The terrain seems to exist as a character in itself, absorbing the human characters within its worlds and making them work out ways to cope and / or survive its challenges.

Winter solstice was an inspiration to me as it unravelled itself in Australia in 2022 and we officially celebrated the beginning of winter. I considered the earth that we tread upon and its diverse nature. While winter can be fierce, there is also a rugged beauty that reaches out for us to experience too.

I contemplated the darkness of winter in different countries around the world (at different times of year) and how for some, the only access of light is that reflected from a burning candle. In some cases, a candle that one must make him/herself. By exploring the use of tallow and beeswax candles in the novel (discussed in more detail later), I felt that I was able to explore the lifestyle of citizens and leadership in Mira and how such a resource is highly significant to one's ability to live.

The cold weather can be considered a time of hibernation and a refocus on the home and/or village identity that one has. Isolation itself, along with challenges faced, such as getting through a day or coping with laws or rules of leadership can leave one feeling overwhelmed. It is during this time that support is essential for one to be able to continue to live, survive and /or progress.

May your next winter bring you abundance in food; great health and vitality to you and any plants or animals you care for; much light to see; warmth and the love of your own special village as you continue on your own journey.

Tallow Candles

The heritage tallow candle was also of great interest to me. The creation of such a candle was and still is, laborious, involving the rendering of animal fats. A major benefit of the heritage tallow candle was that it was an affordable source of light for families.

In the 16th century, the tallow candle was essential in creating London's compulsory street lighting. Tallow chandlers were greatly affected around 1700, once the spermaceti and paraffin wax replaced tallow. (Medieval Candle Maker, n.d. and Tallow Chandlers' Company, n.d.)

Using my research, I questioned the idea of the tallow candle being replaced by high priced beeswax candles and the impact that this would have on a culture that could not afford such a luxury in Mira. Furthermore, with no electricity available in an empire, how could one gain the relief of light?

Sixteenth Century Letter Writing and Art

Research of historical candle making led to my discovery of the painting: *A Young Woman Writing a Letter* by Frans van Mieris (1670). The art work details a young woman engaged in the intimacy of letter writing. Next to her sits a burning candle, which provides a dim, intimate light to her room.

A bit of history … Leading up to the 12th century, letter writing was an essential mode of communication for merchants, in order to help communications of trade occur and to expand it into global markets. Women also became able to write letters during this time. Using cultural innovation, humanists drew from Greek and Roman antiquity to enable the letter to have its own signature (Shemek, D., 2013).

Around the 16th century, letters became more published, even by leading cultural figures and enabled the letter itself to develop as its own literary form (Shemek, D., 2013). Currently there are many works that study the letters of this period and comment on the social, political and economic structures that were visible through such oral communication of the time.

What I find the most fascinating is the sense of intimacy that letter writing provided women in the 16th century. There was now a way to communicate personal impressions or desires with an audience: the receiver.

The writer could engage in the intricate art of letter locking, in order to keep the message hidden away from prying eyes. The imprisoned Mary Queen of Scots is famously known in 1587 to have engaged in the art of letter locking for her very final letter before death (Fisher, R., 2021).

Frans van Mieris' painting has been inspirational in my development of Empress Celine of Mira. Her modern letters to Maricelle in the late 90s reveal her dark, intimate feelings and thoughts within the palace and the streets of Mira as she learns to makeshift her way across its social, economical and political terrain.

Creating an Epistolary Culture

To create and enhance the epistolary culture of the novel, I drew upon the art of tallow candle making as part of the cultural heritage in Mira. In fact, the tallow candle is a key object of significance in the novel's mystery.

Empress Celine's letters detail how significant the tallow candle was for the lives of the people of Mira. The harsh treatment of this candle by Emperor Laynton is a catalyst for more civilians to join the resistance movement that the Petoy clan had already formed against the empire.

The use of epistolary is also evident in the journal entries written by Aisha, Girl's ancestor. Set in the 1200s, the journal entries share the story of how Aisha make shifted her way across the social, political and economical terrain of Mira. Silk making and trade is highly prevalent to these entries, as well as senses of family, identity and romance in the world. Once again, these entries share an intimacy: they are the voice of Aisha, who engages with her life.

Red Gum Trees

It was a spiritual journey to become attuned to the historical significance of the red gum and river red gum trees and the importance of taking care of them (Environment Victoria, n.d. and The Conversation, 2019).

I was inspired by the historic, successful Australian campaign, which involved environmentalists and traditional owners working together to secure the protection (by ending logging and cattle grazing) of the red gum forests across the Riverina bio region of Victoria and New South Wales. The Aboriginal traditional owners' attainment of the co-management of new national parks as well as the recognition of their ancient and continual relationship with the forests warmed my heart (Mooney, Will, n.d.). There is such spirit, heritage and culture in the life of red gum trees and I wanted to explore such concepts further.

In this novel, the habitats of the red gum and river red gum trees in Redbank are ones to protect. Growling grass frogs reside in Spirit River. They rely on a variety of fauna, such as pond weed and common spike rush (Australian Wildlife Protection Council, 2015 and Statewide Integrated Flora and Fauna Teams, n.d.), which become depleted as the river red gum trees decline in number.

The red gum and river red gum trees speak of ages of wisdom and heritage for the people of Redbank. They are protected by Jacquelyn Botanica, the custodian of the forest, who is passionate about their wellbeing, heritage and their connections with the people.

Adira is accustomed to the red gum and river red gum trees, having grown up in the Redbank Forest and is connected to their presence, the wildlife and river they nurture and the strong wisdom and guidance that they provide for the people.

The novel explores how the people of Redbank fight for justice as the trees become exploited by the Petoy clan in order to further its progress in trade opportunities.

Developing the Petoy Clan

Historically, the Silk Road was travelled by many bandits, who sought their opportunities to threaten and steal trade from merchants.

Similarly to the bandits, in this novel, the Petoy clan is aggressive by nature, stealing trade in order to enhance their resistance and to extend their progress. The clan provides the catalysts for conflict in both Mira and Redbank.

One story that I found useful in developing the ways of the Petoy clan was *Ali Baba and the Forty Thieves*, a folk tale from *The Arabian Nights*, by Albert Goodwin in 1901. The secrecy and greed of riches prevalent in the tale inspired me to develop the motivations of the Petoy clan, who will stop at nothing in order to progress.

The tale also enabled me to consider ways in which the Petoy clan would lure people to defect to their clan and to engage in acts of resistance. I discovered that I could also detail the personal motivations and convictions of characters such as Nick Farago and Naricia Petoy, who were persuaded to work with the Petoys.

Developing Chief Opula of the Petoy clan was a challenging task. I wanted to ensure that his main motivation would be relevant to trade practices. However, I also needed to provide him with a fatal flaw. I found *The Emperor's New Clothes* by Hans Christian Andersen very inspirational in challenging the idea of the finest textiles of the world being equivalent to riches. If one believes in such a philosophy enough, they may even believe that they are wearing such clothing when they are not. The story was very inspirational for the development of the Chief's delusional nature.

Photography, Digital Art & Book Design

I was very blessed to have the opportunity to work with the expertise of Ryan Marshall, who created the photography and digital art for the covers of this novel. He also illustrated the beautiful City of Redbank map. Ryan was very attuned to the story and provided superbly responsive design ideas. His book design and typesetting skills are also high quality, leading to a stunning book for you, the reader to engage with.

Story Playscapes' Readership

It has been a joy to share my writing and to connect with our global audience. Thank you to each and every one of Story Playcapes' dedicated readership who have joined us on our journey in completing *Makeshift Girl: The Secret Heritage Trail*. Some of you have even committed your readership to us from the moment I began writing this novel.

Readers, your encouragement and support have helped me to remain focused on completing this novel. I hope that you enjoy reading and discovering the story of *Makeshift Girl: The Secret Heritage Trail*.

–Susan Marshall, October, 2022.

Preface Bibliography

Andersen, Hans Christian (1837) *The Emperor's New Clothes* in Archer, Mandy (retold) (2015): *The Fairy Tales of Hans Christian Andersen.* Parragon Books Ltd, UK.

Australian Wildlife Protection Council (2015): *Growling Grass Frog Growls for Attention as Melbourne's Growth Corridors Threaten Annihilation.* Accessed at: https://awpc.org.au/growling-grass-frog-growls-for-attention-as-melbournes-growth-corridors-threaten-annihilation/

BBC (2018): *Joanna Lumley's Silk Road Adventure, Episode 1: Venice/Albania/Turkey.* (Television Series).

BBC (2018): *Joanna Lumley's Silk Road Adventure, Episode 2: Georgia/Azerbaijan.* (Television Series).

Cartwright, M. (2017): *Silk in Antiquity.* Accessed at: https://www.worldhistory.org/Silk/

Daimler Truck (2021): *The First Truck in the World was Built by Gottlieb Daimler in 1896.* Accessed at: https://media.daimlertruck.com/marsMediaSite/en/instance/ko/The-first-truck-in-the-world-was-built-by-Gottlieb-Daimler-in-1896.xhtml?oid=49433712

Environment Victoria (n.d): *River Red Gum Forests and Wetlands.* Accessed at: https://environmentvictoria.org.au/river-red-gum-forests-and-wetlands/

Fisher, Richard (2021): *The Clever Folds that Kept Letters Secret.* Accessed at: https://www.bbc.com/future/article/20210616-how-the-forgotten-tricks-of-letterlocking-shaped-history

Goodwin, Albert (1901). *Ali Baba and the Forty Thieves* in Sir Richard F. Burton (trans. ed.) 'The Arabian Nights.' Sterling Publishing Co., Inc., 2016.

International Association for Falconry and Conservation of Birds of Prey (n.d.) *Falconry and Conservation.* Accessed at: https://iaf.org/falconry-and-conservation/

International Wildlife Consultants Ltd., (n.d.) *Mongolian Artificial Nest Project Information.* Accessed at: https://www.falcons.co.uk/conservation-research-and-welfare/the-saker-falcon/mongolian-artificial-nest-project-information/

Marshall, Susan (2023): *Makeshift Girl: The Secret Heritage Trail.* Story Playscapes, Melbourne, Australia.

Medieval Britain (n.d.) *Medieval Candlemaker.* Accessed at: https://medievalbritain.com/type/medieval-life/occupations/medieval-candlemaker/

Mooney, Will at Friends of the Earth, Australia (n.d.): *Saving the River Red Gums: An Historic Conservation Victory.* Accessed at: https://www.foe.org.au/saving-river-red-gums-historic-conservation-victory

Opper, F. (1895): *The "new woman" and her bicycle – there will be several varieties of her /* (painting). Accessed at: https://www.loc.gov/item/2012648801/?loclr=blogflt

Polo, Marco & da Pisa, Rustichello (c1300): *The Travels of Marco Polo* in 'The Travels by Marco Polo': Penguin Classics (trans ed.) (2015), Penguin Random House, UK.

Science Direct (2013): *Silk Filament* from 'Handbook of Sustainable Textile Production,' 2011. Accessed at: https://www.sciencedirect.com/topics/engineering/silk-filament

Shemek, Deanna (2013): *Letter Writing and Epistolary Culture.* Accessed at: https://www.oxfordbibliographies.com/view/document/obo-9780195399301/obo-9780195399301-0194.xml

Skinner, Tomás at International Institute for Asian Studies (2016): *Urban Heritage of the Silk Roa*d (newsletter). Accessed at: https://www.iias.asia/the-newsletter/article/urban-heritage-silk-road

Statewide Integrated Flora and Fauna Teams (n.d.) Growling Grass Frog. Accessed at: https://www.swifft.net.au/cb_pages/sp_growling_grass_frog.php

Tallow Chandlers' Company (n.d.): *Need to Know Facts About the History of Tallow Chandlers.* Accessed at: https://www.tallowchandlers.org/about-us/our-history/historical-narratives/need-to-know-facts-about-the-history-of-the-tallow-chandlers#:~:text=Tallow%20candles%20played%20a%20vital,of%20the%2018th%20c.

The Caspian Post (2021): *The Art of the Kelaghayi – Azerbaijan's Unesco-celebrated Silk Scarf.* Accessed at: https://caspianpost.com/en/post/culture/the-art-of-the-kelaghayi-azerbaijans-unesco-celebrated-silk-scarf

The Conversation (2019): *Beating Around the Bush* (newsletter): *The River Red Gum is an Icon of the Driest Continent.* Accessed at: https://theconversation.com/the-river-red-gum-is-an-icon-of-the-driest-continent-118839

UNESCO (n.d.): *Silk Roads Programme: About the Silk Roads.* Accessed at: https://en.unesco.org/silkroad/about-silk-roads

UNESCO (n.d.): *Silk Roads Programme: Georgia.* Accessed at: https://en.unesco.org/silkroad/countries-alongside-silk-road-routes/georgia#:~:text=Georgia%20and%20the%20Silk%20Roads,is%20today%20Georgia%20as%20well.

UNESCO (n.d.): *Silk Roads Programme: India.* Accessed at: https://en.unesco.org/silkroad/countries-alongside-silk-road-routes/india

UNESCO (n.d.): *Silk Roads Programme: Venice.* Accessed at: https://en.unesco.org/silkroad/content/venice

UNESCO, (n.d.), *Traditional Art and Symbolism of Kelaghayi, Making and Wearing Womens' Silk Headscarves.* Accessed at: https://ich.unesco.org/en/RL/traditional-art-and-symbolism-of-kelaghayi-making-and-wearing-womens-silk-headscarves-00669

University of Chicago (n.d.) *Silk Road and Indian Ocean Traders: Connecting China and the Middle East* (map). Accessed at: https://oi.uchicago.edu/sites/oi.uchicago.edu/files/uploads/managed/slideshows/Silk%20Road_map.jpg

Van Mieris, Frans (1670): *A Young Woman Writing a Letter* (oil painting) in Yeager-Crasselt, Lara: *A Young Woman Writing a Letter* (2022). In "The Leiden Collection Catalogue, 3rd ed." Edited by Arthur K. Wheelock Jr. and Lara Yeager-Crasselt. New York, 2020. Accessed at: https://theleidencollection.com/artwork/a-young-woman-writing-a-letter/

Trekking an Age of Light

A poem by Susan Marshall, inspired by themes in Makeshift Girl: The Secret Heritage Trail *and a night, candle lit playscape.*

The dark shifts across the terrain,
its shadows casting soft images
of silhouettes against the night sky.
Their presence warms my heart
and I extend my arm into the ether.

The wind blows across my skin
in small, gentle gusts of energy.
Its touch, its presence, I feel
as I connect with spirits of an age
that existed long before I breathed
my very presence upon this terrain.

Presently, time does freeze,
capturing a moment of silence.
Shifting silhouettes reach across
the age of wise, ticking time towards
my present being and all it is.

Dressed in white, embodying all ages,
I am a figure of a people who lit their way,
across the dark of night into light's hope.
Right here, right now, I embody
the lasting energy of a people's heritage.

Striking a sulfur match against the fence,
I watch the flame spark its fiery life.
My arm shakes with anxiety.
I hold one very last tallow candle,
an object of great, human desire.

The silhouettes lean towards me,
their voices hoarse whispers
that coast across the night air.
Long live the tallow! They chant.
Bring back our light of life!

Fingers shaking, I hold the candle,
setting wick alight with orange spark.
As the flame glows across the black,
it reveals the warm flesh of faces.
Eyes shine wide with soaring hope,
mouths fall open with anticipation.

The world unravels itself before me,
revealing an age of desired light.
I step gently across the terrain,
passing through a wave of silhouettes
who shift aside to let me see.

Windows do glow with soft candlelight,
as do the streets with rush lights aglow.
Yet the sound of screaming masks the peace,
as a people shout their heartfelt protests.
For some windows are dark, eerie and silent,
awaiting the wash of light to thrive.

Holding the burning tallow in the air,
I watch the orange-yellow sparks fly.
A loyal message I release into the night
and watch it dazzle through dark's cloak,
passing its way through ages of time.

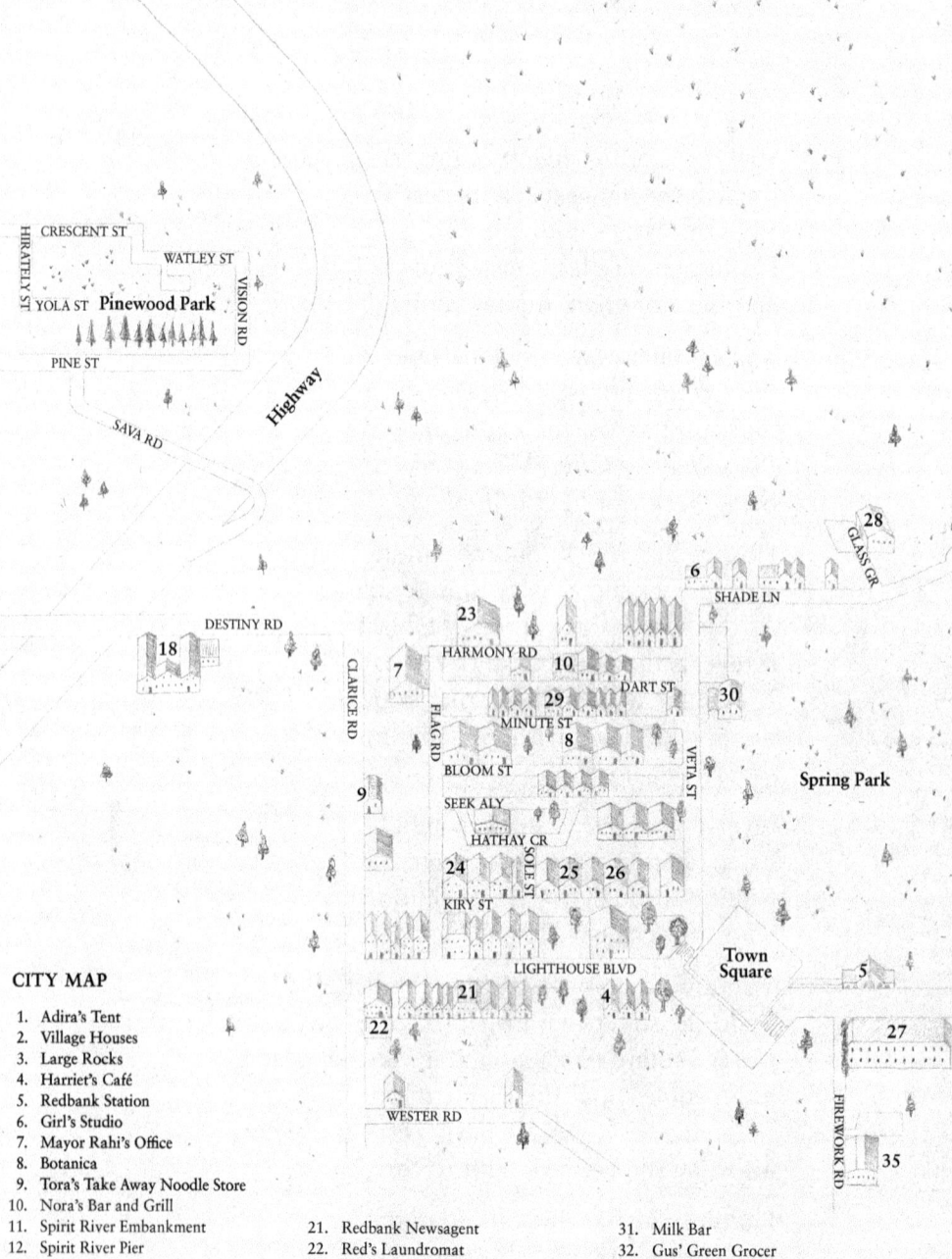

CITY MAP

1. Adira's Tent
2. Village Houses
3. Large Rocks
4. Harriet's Café
5. Redbank Station
6. Girl's Studio
7. Mayor Rahi's Office
8. Botanica
9. Tora's Take Away Noodle Store
10. Nora's Bar and Grill
11. Spirit River Embankment
12. Spirit River Pier
13. Nick's Memorabilia Warehouse
14. A-Z Antiques
15. J.F. Snow Globes
16. Truck Depot
17. Botanica Warehouse
18. Journey Motor Inn
19. Old Elm Tree
20. Concetta's Hideout
21. Redbank Newsagent
22. Red's Laundromat
23. Happy Beats Music Store
24. Oakwood Café
25. Redbank Chemist
26. Lucca's Real Estate Agency
27. Lighthouse Apartment Complex
28. Sophie's Art Gallery
29. Nick's Memorabilia Store
30. Café Chaud et Froid
31. Milk Bar
32. Gus' Green Grocer
33. Wise River Red Gum Tree
34. Sawmill
35. Corporate Building
36. Bownie's Timber Mill
37. Nestle Camp Ground
38. Pierre's Patisserie
39. Spirit River Bank
40. Forest Car Park

REDBANK

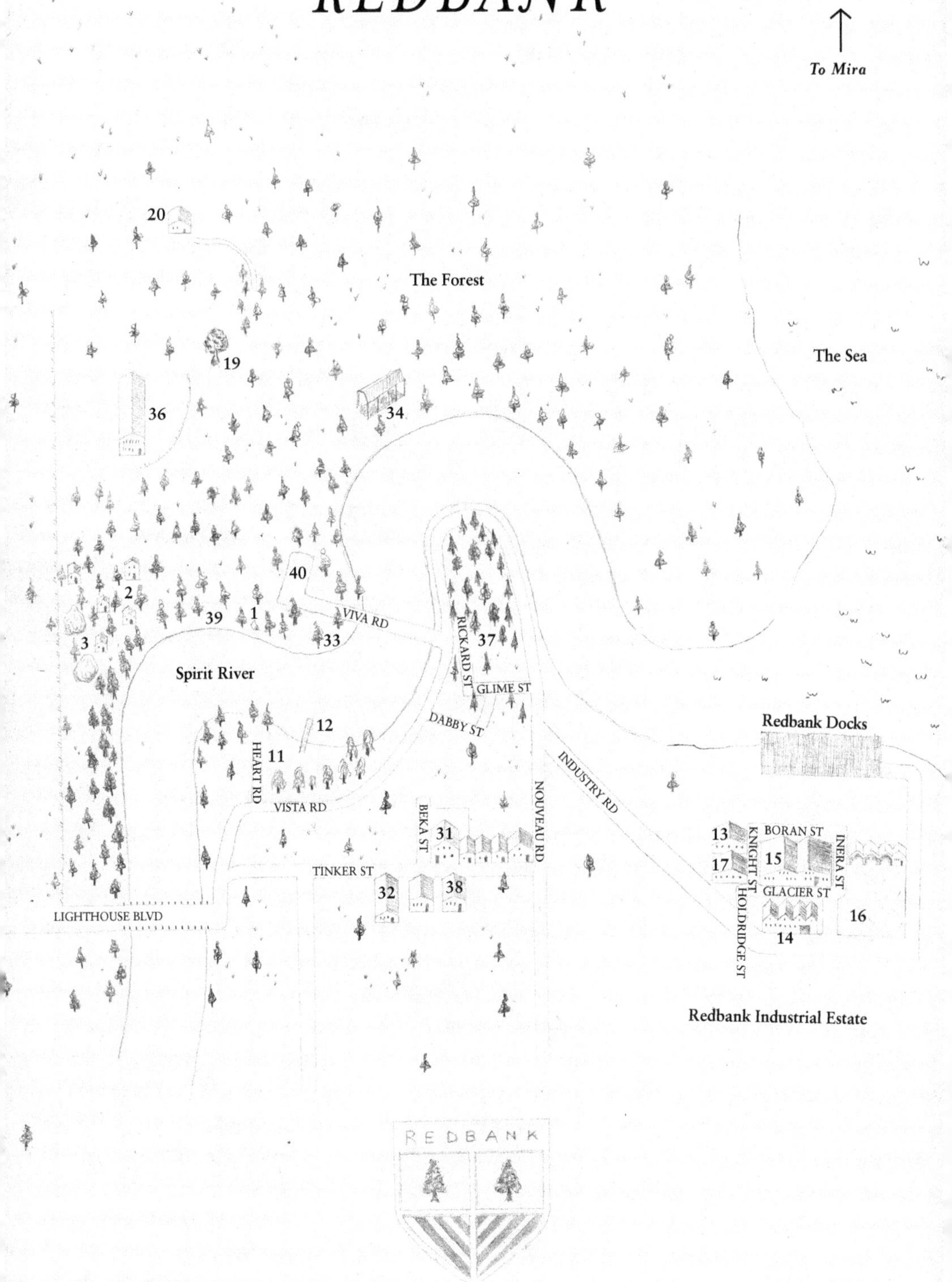

To Mira

The Forest

The Sea

Spirit River

Redbank Docks

Redbank Industrial Estate

Chapter 1

The Redbank forest is crying silently this morning. The red, green and golden leaves of late autumn are separating from their branches like youngsters leaving their nests. Carried by the wind, the leaves toss and turn, trying to gain control over their pathways through the vast, wide terrain of the world.

Staring down, I witness my bare feet treading upon the grassy floor. Small, sharp rocks scatter and cut into my soles but I ignore the pain, trekking across the familiar terrain towards the red gum trees.

Scattered across the forest, the red gum trees soar high, radiating their spirits and wisdom out into the ether. They are a source of guidance and solace to me this evening, as I take the time to remember my mother's birthday. She will be 48 years of age today.

Sitting under a majestic red gum tree, I lean my head against its shedding trunk. As I view long strands of bark hanging precariously, I consider the many years that have passed since I last saw my mother. I was only a child when we were separated and I am now 23.

Digging into my pocket, I retrieve a beautiful, pink rose. Twisting its stem between my thumb and forefinger, I admire its glistening, soft petals that flounce and unfurl in the sunlight. I have had a connection with pink roses since I was a child.

Susan Marshall

At the age of 17, a pink rose helped me to express my feelings about my past experiences in Mira, especially my sudden separation from my mother. I wrote a poem, which is addressed to her. As a ritual, I recite the poem aloud every year on her birthday.

Inhaling a deep breath, I stare at the rose and begin to recite:

> "Sweet new buds, welcome to life.
> I see you glisten with morning's dew.
> May your brightness help me see
> more colour on this very dark trek.
>
> "I have walked these steps each day,
> dodging the serious, watchful gazes,
> who check if a friend or enemy plays
> in this new world of hide and seek.
>
> "Mother, you were lost to my heart,
> which pounded with ferocious fear.
> Burying myself under the ground,
> I stared silently at the pitch black.
>
> "The hole I dug was safe and small,
> protecting me from the other side.
> I huddled, eyes wide and awake,
> ears alert to any sudden sound.
>
> "The drum beats would startle me,
> intruding upon my silent state.
> Hiding in corners of the black,
> I dodged the luring dark horse.
>
> "I ate the very last food scraps,
> starving for the light up above.
> That was when I saw Concetta,
> smiling in the fierce darkness.
>
> "She helped me climb into the light,
> revealing a vibrantly lit space.
> Escaping from the dark shadows,
> I discovered refuge in a forest.

"Its flora displayed a myriad of
colourful bursts of flowers in bloom.
Nestling into a bed of leaves,
I closed my eyes for the first time …
since the world changed.

"Mother, I wonder where you are,
as I stare out towards the horizon.
Plucking a rose petal, I whisper a message
and let it float into the gentle breeze.

"The words will drift out of the forest,
towards paths of Mira we once trekked.
Circling your ground to find your feet,
they might learn about the life you lead.

"May my footsteps lighten as I walk
across the fallen autumn leaves.
In green, gold and red, I feel your spirit,
breathing a breeze and guiding me."

My voice drifts off and I stare once more at the rose in my hand. Placing it carefully into my lap, I turn my attention to my black cloth bag. Digging into it, I discover a tattered and adored photo of my mother that I always carry with me.

My heart burns at the sight of her large hazel eyes, staring directly at me. They hold years of adversity and wisdom, a result of living life on the run. I stroke the photo, running my finger across her long, brown strands of hair, which fly wildly in the air. My mother's lips have formed a small smile, which I know carries the weight of the world. Yet the smile is still there, alighting the tiniest spark of life in her eyes and reminding me of her strong determination.

In her hand, my mother carries a tallow candle, whose flame is blowing gently in the breeze. In my short time with her, I remember her using such candles to provide light as we dashed across the perilous terrain of Mira. If I became lost, I would search for the light of a flame and I would find my mother again …

One early evening, when I was five years old, the sky was yellow and heavy in Mira. Reaching my hands out, I felt sand particles land on my palm. I stared at them for a long while, feeling the grit and rubbing it between my fingers.

A storm was on its way.

Standing still, I watched the world heave and swirl around me in the air. The sandy earth of the beach was making itself visible to my young heart, reminding me that it still lived and breathed. I grounded myself in the granules and refused to let the wind take me away.

I could barely see through the thick yellow sand that smeared the air. It held me entranced within its existence.

My tiny mind wondered if I could tread across the rising sand and climb it higher and higher, way up into the depths of the sky. Up above, I could look down and keep watch over our followers.

"Adira," my name reached me like a soft lullaby. Closing my eyes, I listened acutely. All I could hear was the fierce rage of the wind.

I awaited the sound of my name again.

"Adira, open your eyes." My eyelids fluttered open and my gaze fell upon a dark silhouette flexing in the shifting wind. Peering closer, I noticed a warm light flickering in her hand.

"Mother?" My little heart beat ferociously. I was very scared.

"Yes, I am here." As Mother reached her hand out towards me, the flickering light beckoned, inviting me to step closer.

While the wild wind swayed ferociously, I stumbled across the ground, battling its strength. I felt the cold air strike against my tiny frame and it blew me sideways, landing me flat onto my bottom.

As I stared up, gasping and shivering in the cold, sand particles forced their ways into my eyes. Rubbing my eyelids, I blinked, waiting for the grit to clear.

As my vision returned, my gaze fell upon the silhouette. Light and floating, it shifted closer towards me, seemingly unaffected by the turbulent wind.

For a split moment, time stopped as I was faced with the rugged beauty of my mother. There she stood in her tattered dress, her bare feet almost completely buried in the sand. Across her shoulder lay two skinned rabbits, which she had captured for us to eat. In her hand, she carried a single, tallow candle, which was stubbornly sparking its fire into the sky.

I stood shakily on my two feet, meeting my mother's gaze. She had been gone for a long time, disappearing into the forest to hunt for our dinner. I had felt confused at being abandoned, unsure of what I was to do on my own on the beach.

"Mother," I felt relieved to see her, to know that she was still with me.

"Follow the light, Adira, come to me," my mother's voice was gentle and reassuring.

I stared silently at the flame, allowing it to soothe my pounding heart. It was light, it was life and it was connected to my mother.

Stepping forward slowly, the shaking in my feet began to subside. I let my mother draw me into her arms. The scent of her was familiar and comforting.

Mother smiled and stroked my cheek. "You were very brave," she said to me. "You battled the terrain alone."

"I did?" My eyes widened in surprise.

"Yes," my mother nodded. "See, now the wind is calming down, just like your fear is."

I watched as the gusts of wind dissipated slowly, transforming into a much lighter breeze. The sand dropped from the sky, landing in mounds across the terrain.

"I feel better with you, Mother. I don't like being by myself." I reached out to touch her face, to bond with her.

Mother pulled me close and I buried my head into her shoulder. She smelled of sweat and the earth, familiar scents that calmed my panicked heart.

"Adira," my mother met my gaze with a serious expression. "I only have a few more moments left before this candle goes out. Can you hold it for me?"

"Yes," I said, taking hold of the candle.

Mother placed the skinned rabbits down onto the sand and dug into her pocket. Retrieving a piece of paper and a pencil, she stared into my eyes. "I need to write a letter," she said, wriggling her bottom into the sand until she was comfortable. "Can you hold the candle just over the paper, like this, so I can see?"

"Yes," I nodded, holding the warm candle where she asked. Watching the tallow burn, I became attuned to its strong scent. "Oh, smelly!" I waved my free hand across my nose.

"That's tallow," Mother sighed. "It can have a very strong smell as it comes from the animals of nature." She scrawled her letters across the paper, spelling out words I could not read. After a short while, she stopped writing.

"Have you finished writing, Mother?" I asked her, my fingers feeling very warm, still wrapped around the candle.

"Yes," Mother said, staring at the letter with a thoughtful expression. "I want to read this to you, Adira."

"Okay," I shook my hand, feeling the stinging heat of the flame. "Can I put the candle on the ground?"

"I'll take it," Mother retrieved the candle from my hand and held it over the letter. "Time to read," she said, raising the page closer to her eyes.

"Dear Concetta,

"My beautiful daughter, Adira and I have spent a long time trekking the dangerous terrain of Mira. We have accepted some help from the Empress along the way, who provides us with used tallow candles that we sell in order to continue to eat and to survive.

"The roads here are scattered with members of the dangerous Petoy clan, who constantly hunt us down. We have managed to survive some very dark moments and I worry that time has become our enemy.

"I am thankful for your offer to take care of Adira and to keep her safe in Redbank. It is there that I hope she can rejuvenate and explore her childhood dreams, free from fear.

"I have promised Adira that she and I will reunite when it is safe too.

"Blessings from my very thankful heart,

Maricelle."

Mother met my gaze, her eyes welling with tears. "It is time to prepare for you to leave, Adira," she said softly.

My heart fluttered wildly in my chest as my fear began to return. "Why can't I go with you?" I asked her.

"Because you will definitely be captured," my mother replied without hesitation. "We need to keep you safe, Adira. You know that Chief Opula will not rest until he has us both under his control."

"Is he too hard to run away from, Mother?" I asked, trying to understand her decision to leave me.

"Yes," Mother nodded. "Very." She reached for my hands and squeezed them tightly. "I am so tired, Adira. So are you. This is not how your life should be, always fleeing from the Petoys. Where you are going, you have a chance to live a better life, free of so much fear."

Tears welled up in my eyes. "I want to live with you," I retorted, clenching my fists. "You are my mother."

Mother stared at me and the tears spilled freely down her cheeks. "Yes," she said. "A mother who is doing her best to keep you safe." She tightened her grip on my hands. "Adira, it is best if you leave first, so that the Chief thinks that you are still with me. After a while, I will join you and we can be together again."

The tears began to fall down my cheeks and my throat burned. "I am scared," I choked on my words.

"So am I," Mother's voice cracked and she swiped away at her own tears.

We sat, staring at each other for a long while.

"Please trust me, Adira," Mother finally managed to say.

I took a deep breath. My head was spinning with confusion. I did not know what to trust or to expect.

Bending down, Mother began to dig a fire pit in the sand. "Before we do anything else, we should eat. We'd better make a fire to cook these rabbits, eh?" I watched as she began to dig into the sand with her fingers. "Help me, Adira?"

I grabbed handfuls of the sand and tossed them away, helping to widen the pit. As I worked, a deep sadness filled my heart. I had only ever known life with my mother. I could not imagine my world without her.

As the memory dissipates, I discover that I am staring at the rose flower that lies snugly in my lap. Retrieving it, I breathe in the flower's gorgeous scent. Plucking a petal, I whisper a message and release it into the air. I visualise my mother's brave smile as the pink petal floats gently through the breeze.

Chapter 2

The vibrations beneath my feet startle me. Dropping down onto my knees, I lower my ear to the terrain. Listening closely to the earth, I hear the harsh striking of footsteps approaching me.

Inhaling a sharp breath, I feel the hair rise at the back of my neck.

I am being chased.

Slinging the cloth bag over my shoulder, I tuck the photograph and remaining rose flower deeply inside it. Rising slowly to my feet, I survey my terrain.

The land of the forest spans a few kilometres and consists of bumpy and grassy terrain. The open land is scattered with a range of shrubs, which provide temporary spots to hide behind. They are a distance away from here and I would certainly be exposed as I dashed across the earth.

Only half a metre away from me is my makeshift resting place. It is a small cave in the side of the hill. I crawled into its dark habitat last night and was accompanied by a growling grass frog that had left the river and chosen to explore the terrain. I fell asleep on the firm earth, holding the frog in one hand.

When I awoke this morning, the frog had fallen asleep, snuggled next to my cheek. I patted it gently and directed it to hop outside the cave and across the forest terrain. It warmed my heart to see it jump into the river water and swim towards its natural habitat in the rushes.

Towards the west, a number of small homes are dotted across the plain. The villagers reside there and live in harmony with the forest. Right now many would be heading towards the Redbank Autumn Market, which is being set up in the north.

The terrain is too open and exposed. Running will not save me. I will be discovered quickly.

Experience has taught me to seek a closer place to hide.

Eyes darting across the area, I locate a pile of leaves on the earth nearby. They are the perfect hiding spot.

Dashing across the floor, I jump through the air, landing flat on my stomach onto the leaf pile. Digging madly through the leaves, I form a large gap. Tunnelling myself through it, I bury my body, scattering small bunches of leaves over my back to cover myself.

It is stuffy under here. Inhaling shallow breaths, I try to maintain my oxygen. After a few moments, my breathing settles and I regain my focus.

Pushing my fingers through a small gap in the leaves, I watch the fading light seep in. From this vantage point, I witness the flailing arms and legs of a wild figure bursting into the space.

Slowing to a walk, the tall, olive skinned man gasps for breath. His black headscarf has fallen off his head and catches in the breeze, fluttering around his neck. Pulling it up, he positions it back onto his head, adjusting it to sit properly on top of his familiar aging, grey hair.

My breath catches in my throat at the sight of the gold, rearing horse totem displayed on the man's head scarf.

"Adira," the man's voice is eerie. His eyes scan the environment intensely, searching for me.

My heart pounds with fear. There, shifting across my home terrain, is Chief Opula, the leader of the Petoy clan. His steel grey eyes and sharp cheek bones constantly haunt my dreams. I have spent my whole life hiding away from this terrifying man and the clan that he leads.

"I know you are hiding here," the Chief's voice rings in the air. "I will find you."

I stay still, continuing to inhale small, shallow breaths and trying to calm my pounding heart.

The Chief has discovered my location. I am no longer safe here.

I stay as still as I can, listening acutely to the snapping of twigs beneath the Chief's feet. His breath is rattling after running and this enables me to detect how far away he is.

"Adira," the Chief calls my name again and I realise that he is standing very close. Inhaling a deep breath, I pray that I am not discovered.

The Chief's footsteps continue to shuffle across the terrain, eventually fading away.

I am now immersed in the starkness of silence. Eyes darting from side to side, I exhale a deep sigh of relief as I realise that the Chief has left.

Pushing through the pile of leaves that I am buried under, I form a larger gap and pull myself up. The fresh air is welcoming and I inhale grateful gulps.

The light is bright now, with the deep orange and red streaks of morning.

Glancing around the terrain, I check that all is clear. There is no-one around, just the sound of leaves gently rustling across the forest floor.

Standing slowly, I shake fallen leaves and dirt out of my hair and brush them off my arms and legs. My light blue singlet and grey shorts are streaked with remaining dirt marks and it makes me smile. I find it comforting.

Reaching into my pocket, I retrieve my mobile phone and check the time. It is 8:13 a.m. I have two minutes left to reach the meeting point.

Dashing across the forest floor, I tread upon sharp stones, which cut into my soles. It is a pain that I ignore, focusing on my mission.

I head west, towards the large, grey rocks positioned next to the village houses. As I approach them, I slow to a walk, catching my breath.

Suddenly, a firm hand grabs my shoulder. I gasp as an arm tightens itself around my neck. I am being dragged across the forest floor.

My heart stops. I've been captured.

Struggling to breathe, I wriggle and grasp the arm tightly, trying to release its stranglehold. I am panting and my heart is racing with fear.

"Too slow," the woman's voice is strong as she tightens her grip around my neck and pulls me behind a large grey rock. "You are late."

Grabbing hold of her hands, I pull them away forcefully, twisting myself out of her grasp. "I'm sorry," I step back, trying to catch a breath. Slowly, I meet her gaze. "I wasn't paying attention."

A dark blue head scarf conceals Concetta Mancini's face. She checks over her shoulder every few seconds, ensuring that we aren't being followed.

"Not good enough, Lira," Concetta uses my cover name. She bites her lower lip and stretches her toned arms. Her deep blue eyes burn with intensity. "You know the Petoys have made their way here into Redbank. You'll only have a split second to defend yourself if you're captured."

"I just escaped Chief Opula," I say, crossing my arms over my chest. I feel the need to protect myself. "He has finally discovered where I am hiding."

Concetta's eyes widen. "Really? I was hoping this wouldn't happen so soon." She is silent for a moment, absorbing the news. "We have no choice but to move you away from here quickly. You should venture into the city, Lira."

My mouth drops open in surprise. "The city?"

"Yes," Concetta wraps her arm around me. "Being there will help you to gain some closure."

"Closure?" I am unsure what Concetta means.

Concetta's eyes narrow. "The Petoys have recently begun using the city of Redbank to support and fund their resistance movement against the empire of Mira. Take this chance to investigate their activities Lira. It might just lead you to your mother."

Staring up at Concetta, I feel doubt settling into my heart. "I'm not sure I am courageous enough to face the Petoys yet," I say.

Concetta squeezes my arm gently. "You are Lira. You've spent years in training with me and have become a brilliant detective. Use your acquired skills to help you."

I stare up at the morning sky, which is now streaked with the warming red pallet of sunrise. My mind reels in confusion. I never thought that I would have to walk straight into the lion's den.

The sharp breeze slaps my own red head scarf, sending it flying through the air. Bending down to pick it up, my skirt blows fiercely in the wind, almost toppling me over.

Concetta bends down to retrieve my scarf. "Here, let me help you," she says, covering my head and face and tying the scarf securely.

I meet her gaze. She smiles warmly at me and strokes my cheek. "You will always be my family, Lira. You have been since I took you into my care."

"Thank you," I manage a small smile, feeling touched by Concetta's words. "Any news of my mother?" I ask, my heart soaring with hope.

"Not yet," Concetta says, handing me a folder. "I have waited a long time for this moment to arrive, Lira." She uses my cover name.

My eyes widen with surprise at her announcement.

Concetta digs into her satchel and reveals a grey folder. "You are now ready to receive your mother's missing person case file. In this folder, there are five different letters that she received from Empress Celine during the year that you were born. They will provide you with some insight into your mother's life in Mira and her commitment to help the people."

I stare at the front cover of the folder. It has a portrait photograph of my mother, who has her brown hair tied back into a pony tail. Untamed strands flutter wildly across her serious hazel eyes. Her lips are pressed together tightly, as though she holds a great secret. Below her photo, her name is written in bold, black capitalised letters: Maricelle Vivesque, along with the word: missing.

Seeing my mother's photo strikes my heart with sadness. I feel overcome with a great dizziness.

Concetta taps me lightly on the elbow, gaging my attention. "Are you okay, Lira?" She asks.

I shrug, unable to see. My mind is clouded with memories.

A rustle of leaves.

My ears prick up, afraid. I can't see what is approaching.

"Try to focus now," Concetta whispers. "I invited you here because I wanted you to become aware of a person of interest. She may be able to help you."

Alert and swaying, my gaze darts around me, trying to regain focus. As the colours and shapes re-emerge, I am able to re-establish my surroundings. Placing one hand on the grey rock, I peer around it, staring out at the forest landscape.

The beautiful Jacquelyn Botanica is treading lightly across the fallen twigs. They do not crackle. It soothes me a little. She is the custodian of the forest and has spent the last week setting up for the annual Redbank forest Autumn Market.

Signs are now placed throughout the forest, noting acceptable camping areas across the grounds. Visitors are allowed to pitch their tents or park their caravans a distance away from the red gum trees, which have been declining at a steady rate due to logging. The city of Redbank is in danger of losing its precious resource.

Jacquelyn's head is covered in a multi-coloured scarf, which she holds up with both hands to shield her from the strong wind.

She is stunning, Jacquelyn, her smiling green eyes sparkling.
She swings her dark blonde hair in the wind and it falls in gentle trestles across her shoulders.

In her hands, Jacquelyn carries a cloth, which she places on a trestle table.

It is one of many clothing items that she has made using locally grown organic cotton. As the autumn grows colder, she has been creating gloves, hats, scarves, jumpers and dresses for villagers who need to keep warm. This afternoon, she is selling her wares, along with many other merchants at the annual market.

Jacquelyn sits down on a large wooden cask and begins to thread a needle. Retrieving a spare piece of organic cotton cloth from under the table, she embroiders the material with a pattern.

Concetta nudges me once more. "Suspect approaching," she whispers hoarsely. "On time too, just like my informant said she would be."

My heart begins to race. Bracing myself, I exhale a deep breath and dare to glance in her direction.

She is a tall woman. Her dark brown hair hangs like a thick blanket, touching her shoulders. She stares at Jacquelyn with piercing, dark brown eyes. As she approaches the market stall, she spreads her thick lips into a forced smile, which smudges her heavy red lipstick across her chin.

"Naricia Petoy," Concetta whispers. "She is the sales and marketing manager for the Petoy clan. We know that she has been involved in illegal trade and are yet to prove it."

Naricia lifts a green dress off the table and admires it. "Did you make this dress yourself?" She asks Jacquelyn in a strong voice, which cuts through the peaceful silence.

Jacquelyn tears her eyes away from her cloth and stares at the dress. "Yes," she says. "It's made from local, natural cotton. Would you like to try it on?"

Naricia shakes her head. "No darling, no." She reaches into the pocket of her red jacket and retrieves a business card. "You are very talented, uh, what's your name, darling?" Placing one hand on her hip, she appears impatient to finish the conversation.

"This is how it all begins," Concetta whispers. "True Petoy style, reeling in a new recruit." Retrieving her mobile phone from her pocket, she takes some photos of Naricia in action.

Jacquelyn's gaze softens. "Jacquelyn," she smiles.

Naricia waves her hand in the air. "I'll tell you what, darling, I'll give you my business card. If you would like to gain a larger audience and earn some decent money using your talent, then give me a call."

Jacquelyn's eyes widen, taken aback by Naricia's comments. "Thank you, I'll think about it," she says as she reaches for the card.

"Don't think too long," Naricia sighs. "The job won't be available forever. Let me know by the end of the week, okay darling?"

"Okay," Jacquelyn nods, staring at the card.

A tall man with dark brown hair, tied back into a pony tail, approaches the trestle table. His tattooed, muscular arms are burdened with the weight of heavy red gum planks. He grimaces as he places the load down onto the dirt ground and rubs his back.

A warm smile crosses Jacquelyn's lips. "Hello handsome," she says.

The man kisses Jacquelyn gently on the lips. "Hi wifey," he smiles. "What have you got there?'

Jacquelyn's eyes are shining. "A business card, from …" she glances at the card. "Naricia here," she says, pointing in Naricia's direction. "She's offered me some work."

Naricia is holding onto the trestle table with both hands. "Did you just fell that red gum yourself, Zac?" She asks, her cheeks a little red. She waves her hand in front of her face to cool herself down.

Zac looks uncomfortable as he meets Naricia's gaze. "Yes," he says. "If you lived in the Redbank forest, you'd know that is what we villagers do. We only log the trees when necessary, unlike some of the destructive loggers we've had recently. It's how we preserve the environment."

Redbank is named after the deep, blood-red coloured bark of its red gum trees. The trees are the city's main source of trade and are highly sort after.

"I didn't know you could fell trees, Zac," Naricia's voice is as sweet as sugar. "Your skill will prove very useful indeed." She pauses for effect. After a moment she retreats and walks away, leaving Zac speechless.

"You know her?" Jacquelyn asks, staring at Zac with a puzzled expression.

Zac rolls his eyes. "Yeah, we've met before," he pulls at the collar of his t-shirt nervously.

Concetta grabs my arm and leads me behind the red gum trees. Leaning towards me, she gages my attention. "Zac works for the

Petoys," she says softly, tapping her head. "The man suffers from great inner conflict. On the one hand, he must support his wife's interests in nature. On the other, he is somehow caught in the web of the Petoys' secret operation." She shakes her head, clearly not impressed with Zac.

"What is he doing?" I ask her.

"I'm still gathering evidence," Concetta scratches her head. "Keep an eye on him when you hit the city. Zac loves his wife and sooner or later he will break down from the guilt and pressure. When that happens, we need him to bare all."

"Understood," I say, nodding. "I'll do my best."

Concetta steps on her tiptoes, peering over my head. "The Petoy numbers are increasing," she says, pointing towards Naricia who is suddenly accompanied by three strong looking men. "We need to leave quickly now, before we're discovered here."

I follow Concetta down to the bank of Spirit River. Pushing passed the branches of the red gums, I nearly stumble over a tree trunk.

Once we've gained enough distance, Concetta stops walking and turns to face me. "It's time now Lira," she says firmly. "Are you ready to venture into the city?"

I inhale a deep, focused breath. A spirit of determination is filling my heart after seeing Naricia. "Yes," I say. "I will do all that I can to find my mother."

Concetta nods, understanding. "We have a young woman to protect," she says. "She has been persecuted in Mira by the Petoys and has sought refuge here. If she is captured, the clan will not hesitate to kill her. She poses a threat to their resistance movement against the empire of Mira."

"Right," I say. "Does she know about me?"

"Yes," Concetta's eyes narrow. "Seeing you are venturing into the city, it will be your task to take care of her," she says. "Keep her safe. She has her own wisdom and will be able to help you too."

"Where is she?" I ask, my heart soaring with hope.

Concetta smiles warmly. "Head to the open plain. Girl waits there to meet you."

"Okay," I say, exhaling my breath. "I'll head there now."

"You'll do great," Concetta smiles. "Just remember to remain alert at all times. The Petoys are dangerous." She reaches for me, holding me tight. "You know how to find me."

"I do," I say, remembering all that I have been told.

Concetta rests her head against mine. "You can do this, Lira. It's a journey you know that you must take. Best of luck as you tread your way out there."

"Thanks Concetta," I smile, not sad but grateful. "I will be in touch."

Concetta smiles as she walks away, blowing me a kiss in the air. I watch her gradually shrink into a small speck in the distance.

I am alone again.

Holding the case folder in both hands, I stare once more at the photograph of my mother. It hurts so much to see the pain in her eyes.

I run my shaking fingers across the edges of the folder. It is a big step for me to look inside this file. Once I do, I know that I will discover more about my mother's secrets and her life.

Inhaling a deep breath, I open the folder. There lies the first letter, which is decorated with a border of eagles in flight. Retrieving the paper, I note that it is tattered and dated the year that I was born.

My eyes scan the neat black handwriting scrawled across the page:

Spring 1998

Dear Maricelle,

It is darker than usual in my chamber tonight, not having you here to light the tallow candles as you usually do. I used to find comfort in your warm smile as you would spark light throughout my melancholy space.

I managed to save one single tallow candle and have kept it burning alight all day, while I paced up and down the length of my chamber.

The smell emitting from it is very strong, making me appreciate the work it would have taken for you to render animal fats in order to make such a candle.

With candle light, Maricelle, you have provided me with a newfound freedom to write. I am sitting at my small writing desk with my quill clasped tightly between my fingers. It is sheer joy to be able to dip my nib into fresh, black ink and watch the letters scrawl across the paper in my cursive handwriting. This moment is a chance to confide in you my dear friend, if you wish to receive my epistolary.

The truth is that I feel very disconcerted about the Emperor's indiscretion. I understand that it has brought you great distress and caused you to depart from the palace. As you roam with your husband across the dangerous terrain of Mira, I urge you to keep watch over your footsteps and to check your perimeters. A great enemy lurks in your shadow. The Petoy clan are shrewd hunters and if they find you, they will not hesitate to bring you harm.

Deep in my heart, I feel the need to help you Maricelle. Every Wednesday, I will wait for you by the single gate entrance at the rear of the palace. There you will find me with a bundle of used tallow candles, which I will gift to you to sell off for your necessities. It will warm my heart to feel that I can help provide some relief for all that you are suffering.

My heartfelt blessings to you, my dear friend.

Empress Celine.

It is the first time that I have heard this story and now understand that my mother chose to leave her employment at the palace due to an indiscretion made by the Emperor. I wonder what the indiscretion was?

The Empress' gesture of gifting the tallow candles to my mother as she and my father continued to makeshift their way across Mira was a generous and secret act. I realise that it is also the reason why my mother was able to have a tallow candle handy for light or heat when I also travelled with my parents.

Closing the folder, I place it into my bag. My thoughts turn to the city and I begin to feel some hope.

It is time to meet Girl.

Chapter 3

It takes me a whole day to trek to the open plain. The cold snap of autumn surrounds me, making my breath fog. My fingers feel frozen and I tuck them inside my pant pockets, trying to keep them warm. I kick the scattered, fallen red and golden leaves, my heart aching as I remember my mother.

I carry nothing other than my black cloth bag, which contains all my necessities. Concetta even filled it with biscuits and fruit before leaving it for me to collect from our secret communication place, the old elm tree in the forest.

I munch on the apple now as I approach my destination. There they are, the plywood planks, bolted loosely together. They stand tall, swinging slightly in the early afternoon breeze. A few plywood planks have been placed tightly together across the top of the makeshift structure, providing a roof.

I marvel at Girl's energy and inventiveness. She would have spent a long time building this structure herself.

The front façade holds a simple plywood door, which is shut. As I approach, I notice that a rope has been threaded through a tiny hole in the door and continues through another hole in the side plank. The rope disappears inside the building, where it is most probably tied together to form a lock.

Girl is not taking any chances.

Inhaling a deep breath, I knock six times on the door. It shakes from the force of the hit and the impact reverberates throughout the entire building.

I wait for a long while, scuffing my feet against the dirt. The plain is arid with small tufts of grass scattered here and there across it. It would be very isolating out here. I wonder how Girl manages to exist on her own.

I do not knock again. I am not meant to. Just knock six times and wait, like Concetta told me to.

I seem to have passed the security test.

I watch as the rope is pulled out of the holes and the front doorway is freed from its lock. It swings wide open, waiting for me to enter.

"Hello?" I call, my eyes wide with anticipation.

Silence.

Peering inside the building, I notice how dark it is. Small patches of light filter through the gaps in the plywood planks and shine across the groundsheet flooring.

Girl's two green eyes peer out from behind a dark blue blanket. They do not stare directly at me.

Here hides Girl, existing as a cover name, like me.

Her makeshift setting continues to rock when the wind hits its walls. Cheaply built, it will soon be retired, along with other miscellaneous objects. It's not up to her when that happens. Time is very short here.

Girl must spend a lot of her time locked away in here and hiding in the dark.

Glancing over my shoulder, my gaze rests upon the bright world outside.

If only Girl could see the lightness of the deep blue sky and feel the warmth of the sun.

I watch as she stands slowly and tosses the blanket onto the floor.

It lands with a small *thud* at my feet.

Girl is pale skinned and tired looking. Her long blue hair is a mess with static strands sticking up in the air. Her hands are shaking slightly. Staring ahead, out the door, her green eyes flicker intensely.

What has got her so jittery?

Stretching up high to the timber shelf, Girl grabs a few crumbled biscuits.

I watch her nibbling at them voraciously and wonder what other food she has.

She is very hungry.

After a long while, Girl stares directly into my eyes, giving me her full attention. "You are Lira," she says in a matter of fact tone.

"Yes," I reply, my feet aching. "Do you mind if I sit down? I walked all the way here."

Girl smiles appreciatively. "The things we do," she says. "Yes, make yourself comfortable."

As I sit, the wind slaps against the plywood wall planks again, making the building shake. Girl laughs, tossing her head back into the air. I watch her as she sways her legs and places her hand to her head like a captain.

"I feel like I am at sea in here," she smiles, making swimming motions with her arms.

I nod, agreeing. "Yes, I can understand that," I say. "It must be hard staying here."

"It's only temporary," Girl smiles. "Until now, when you arrive for the next stage." She stops moving. "Have you got the special papers that Concetta organised?" She asks, her eyes widening with anticipation.

"Yes, of course," I dig into my cloth bag, pulling out the folder which holds the confidential special papers that we use to document our findings of the Petoys' illegal activities.

"Thank you," says Girl as she receives the folder. Flicking through the papers, her eyes narrow with concentration. "Naricia was at the Redbank forest Autumn Market yesterday," she says. "That's interesting." Her gaze drifts off into the distance as she considers the information.

"It is?" I ask her, unsure what she means.

Girl's gaze meets mine again. "The woman has been out and about lately, trying to drum up new recruits. I see that she tried to poach a villager." Her eyes narrow with concern. "Do you know if she succeeded?"

"No," I shake my head. "I am worried about Jacquelyn myself. She is such a lovely person. I hope that she is clever enough to stay away."

Girl pulls at her long, blue hair in frustration. Bits of wood shavings fall out of the strands, cascading down onto the floor. "It's never that easy," she sighs. "Naricia will offer just the right incentive to get her on board."

My heart sinks. "I guess we'll soon find out if Naricia was successful," I say.

Girl's eyebrows raise. "She will be," she says. "The Petoys are shrewd. They always get what they desire."

Stepping forward, Girl stares out the doorway, into the sun. "I used to tread the world freely in Mira," she smiles gently. "My feet would feel the bare earth sifting its way between my toes. I'd push a cart full of wares, hearing it roll along the bumpy terrain, catching stones and flicking them up into the air.

"At times I would stop to take a break, staring out at the shifting clouds in the sky. The route did not seem too long but familiar. It was a path that I always took to deliver the silk designs to Emperor Laynton.

"Every time that I left my home in the village to trek the silk route, I wrapped my ancestor, Aisha's scarf around my neck. White in colour, it was stamped with two totems: a wolf's claw, representing my family and a falcon's talon, the symbol of the imperial dynasty. The scarf served as a form of identification for me when I arrived at the palace gates. The soldier on guard knew to look out for it and to let the woman wearing it inside.

"One night, as I pushed my cart along the silk trade route, everything changed. Suddenly, I heard the loud beating of drums. Staring back towards the majestic, grey mountains, I noticed smoke wavering into the air. A few bodies stamped their feet onto the ledge halfway up the summit. They beat heavily into drums and screamed their protests into the night air.

"My heart raced, knowing that it was the Petoy clan, who occupied the mountain. Anxiously, my eyes darted across the earth. There were bound to be some clan members out on the prowl.

"My gaze fell upon a light shining by the path of cedar trees. Squinting, I noticed that it was a single lantern, held by a tall, eerie male figure. The cold air blew gusts of wind, causing me to sway, yet the figure stood still, his steel-like gaze boring a hole into my face. I stopped pushing my cart, feeling the sudden urge to turn around and return home.

"The figure approached, staring at me intensely. Grabbing hold of my chin forcefully, his eyes sparked with detest. "Daughter of the silk Chief," his voice was dark, like a penetrating knife. It sent a deep shiver down my spine. "Tell me why I don't kill you right now."

"I took a deep breath and gathered my strength. I could see the man's black head scarf hanging loosely around his neck. The gold, rearing horse totem was emblazed upon it, gleaming in the moonlight. For some reason, he did not wear the head scarf proudly, like other Petoy men did.

"I had to think fast. Reaching out, I stroked the man's face. "You're beautiful," I said calmly. "A man I'd like to see again. Are you attracted to me too?"

"The man's face softened into a smile and he touched my hair lightly. "Yes," he whispered. "Very." Leaning in, he grazed my cheek with his lips and licked my ear.

"Deep inside, I was shaking with fear but I knew that I had to keep feigning my interest. Reaching up, I grabbed hold of the man's face and kissed him firmly on the lips. His eyes fluttered open in surprise and he parted his lips, deepening our kiss.

"After a moment, I pulled back and grabbed hold of his shoulders. "Two souls in Mira," I sighed. "Stumbling our ways through a city that has lost its way and is left with an uncertain future." I smiled at him. "We need to take our small chances at love in all this mess."

"The man's eyes narrowed into slits and he dug his fingers into my neck, nearly strangling me. I fought to take a breath, to pull his hands away from me but he was too strong and tightened his grip. "Not uncertain," he spat, letting go of me and ripping the scarf away from my neck. "I will not allow myself to care for the likes of you. The future of Mira will not include you and the ancient ways you keep." He pushed me firmly, sending me flying towards my cart. "Run now, before I slit your throat."

"I met his gaze one more time, reading his inner conflict. He had allowed himself a moment to connect with me, to feel his attraction. Yet, he was a Petoy, expected to support the act of resistance that the clan were bestowing upon the Emperor.

"The man stared at me intensely. "Go!" He yelled in a shaky voice.

"Scrambling to my feet, I clutched the handle of my cart and inhaled a sharp breath. Heaving the cart, I spun it around and pushed it firmly, heading back towards my home in the village.

"My heart sank as I thought about my scarf. It was in Petoy hands. They would be able to use it to gain access to the palace and put everyone's lives in danger. I had to get it back before it was too late." Girl continues to stare outside the doorway, wringing her hands.

I remain silent, letting her take her time to reflect and to feel.

After a short while, Girl meets my gaze. "They still have my scarf Lira," she looks troubled. "And they're still after me," her hands are shaking.

"They're after me, too," I say, meeting her gaze.

It is silent as we both realise what we have in common.

"What a mess," Girl says, staring at the floor. Bending down, she retrieves the special papers. "Our existence is full of dates, times and places now," she points at the papers. Shuffling them into a neat pile, she places them back into the folder and hands it to me. "I should return these to you," she sighs.

"Thanks," I say, accepting the folder and storing it safely into my bag.

I watch Girl approach her mirror. Staring at herself, she pulls at her long strands of blue hair. Grabbing some scissors, she chops away at the strands, which fly and land onto the floor. She stares at her shoulder length hair in the mirror, tearing her fingers through it roughly. "That'll do for now," she grunts. "I'm starting to forget what I look like naturally."

I nod, understanding. Life on the run involves changing your appearance and maintaining cover stories. After a while, you forget who you really are.

Girl approaches a small wooden sculpture, which sits on a bench. "What do you think of this piece?" She asks as she runs her hands across the red gum wood.

"It's quite striking," I reply. "I love the sharp edges."

"It's called Beach Crescendo," Girl runs her forefinger across the crests of waves. "It's inspired by my love for the sea."

I nod, understanding. "Is it nearly completed?" I ask her.

Girl's gaze is intense. "Almost," she says. "I haven't stored the assets into the statue yet."

Concetta has informed me about the assets. Top secret, they are essential to Girl's future. "*The* assets? What a great idea," I say, a small smile forming across my lips. "At least they will be out of sight."

"That's exactly right," Girl says. "I'll take this back to my studio in the city when it's ready. Hopefully it will just blend in with the rest of my works."

"You're doing well as a sculptor," I say. "The cover suits you."

"Thanks," says Girl. "I'm keeping myself busy."

Girl takes a chisel out of her pocket. She makes some more small carvings across the wood.

I reach into my bag and retrieve the video camera. "Let me film you at work for a moment," I say, switching it on. Peering through the lens, I begin to film. "Is this okay?"

Girl shrugs, staring down at her sculpture.

Realising that she is uncomfortable, I switch the camera off. "Do you want to see the footage?"

She shakes her head, no. "It's just a bunch of images," she says.

"Important images," I say gently. "Every moment counts."

Girl sighs, staring up.

I try gaging her eye contact. She won't look at me now.

I put the camera away in my bag. I want to say something more but the words sit like big chunks in my mouth, hard to chew. Our communication is too strained.

A few more awkward minutes pass. Still no eye contact.

Silence.

Lots of fidgeting.

It is time for me to leave.

"It was nice to meet you," I blurt. "I might rest outside tonight. Let's leave in the morning, okay?"

Girl keeps her head up, waving a dismissive good bye.

I take four steps, welcoming the bright daylight.

My feelings are mixed as I walk away.

Chapter 4

As my feet tread across the arid plain, I clutch my hands, rubbing them together to keep warm. Closing my eyes, I listen to the beating of drums echoing in my mind. It is a sound that takes me back to a time in my childhood …

One evening at the age of 5, I lay huddled between both my parents in our makeshift tent. While they slept soundly, I tossed and turned, frightened by the sounds outside.

Sitting up, I crawled towards the tent flap and unzipped it. My ears pricked up as I listened to the noise.

It was the sound of drums, thrashing in the night air. It set my heart racing as it seemed so close, like a warning.

Crawling back inside the tent, I zipped the flap closed and was met with Father's worried, hazel gaze. His short, light brown hair was dishevelled and spiky from sleeping.

"What is it, Adira?" He asked with narrowed eyes.

"The loud drums, are they coming for us?" My hands shook with fear.

Father stared up at the tent roof for a moment, as though he was considering what to say. Meeting my gaze once more, he reached for both my hands. "That sound comes from the mountains," he said gently. "The Petoy clan have occupied it, which means they now live there, even though the Emperor has not given them his permission to do so."

"Oh!" My eyes widen. "That is bad. Will they be in trouble?"

"Most definitely," Father nodded. "If I can use my tracking skills to locate all of them, the imperial army will arrest them. It is hard though, as clan members are often out on the prowl and hard to find."

"Have they done some very bad things?" I asked, my heart pounding with fear.

"Yes," Father nodded. "We need not concern ourselves with that tonight, though." He pulled me closer, embracing me. "Try to sleep now, okay? We'll need to walk again tomorrow."

"Can I have cuddles?" I asked Father.

"Sure," Father lay back onto the floor, pulling me down with him.

I wrapped my arms around him and rested my head against his chest, listening to the comforting rhythm of his heart beat.

"Here," Father pulled blankets up over us both. "Are you warm?"

"Yes," I nodded, slowly drifting off into a content sleep.

At the break of a new day, my mother and I awoke to a solo, evocative tune. Peering out from behind the trunk of a cedar tree, my eyes fell on my father. He was sitting in the middle of the grassy plain, concentrating on blowing into a flute. It was an instrument he had mastered, having played it since he was a child.

As the sun continued to rise, the tune became more intoxicating, lulling me into a completely relaxed state. I allowed my mind to drift, imagining I was walking through a pretty meadow full of roses. In my mind's eye, I held a rose flower in my hands and sniffed at it, my eyes shining with pure happiness.

In my dreamy state, the air smelled of roses, warming my spirit and coaxing me to stop and rest. Lying back in the grass, I stretched my arms up to the sky, inviting the sun to join me. Warm tingles rippled across my skin and eased the pressure in my head. I was light, drifting through the breeze and letting the wind take me somewhere untouched and soothing.

The flute's evocative sound continued to rise in dynamics, awakening me from my meditative state. Next to me, my mother was swaying her hips and shifting her body through the wind. Her eyes were on my father and he was smiling at her lovingly. My little heart fluttered gently, feeling warmed by my parents' adoration for each other.

Stepping forward, my mother clapped her hands together, adding a grounding rhythm to my father's tune. I smiled, watching them both play together. The pitch of the music rose to a great height, almost soaring above us into the sky.

I spun around and around in full circles, feeling elated. It was a relief to have a break from running and to experience the sheer joy of music.

Meeting my mother's gaze once more, my father blew more softly into the flute, allowing its sound to drift away until it was silent. Placing the instrument down on the grass beside him, he waved my mother towards him.

Swaying her hips gently, Mother moved towards Father and straddled his lap. Stroking my mother's face, my father stared deeply into her eyes. Their lips locked in a passionate kiss for a long time.

Turning to face me, my mother held out her hand for me to reach.

I dashed across the grass, smiling gleefully. Grabbing hold of my mother's hand, I allowed her to draw me closer to her. I felt my mother and father's arms around me in a family hug.

"Adira," Father said softly as he stared into my eyes. "The tune of life surrounds you everyday. Listen to it closely and you will learn how to carry its rhythm as you trek your own journey through life."

My father's message was profound, yet reached me. I made a silent promise that I would begin to listen more closely to the terrain.

As the memory dissipates, I discover that I am standing on top of a tall, grassy hill. A couple of cockatoos squawk and swoop passed me, landing at its base. Pecking at the grass, they savour the seeds that they discover, completely unaware that I am watching them.

I consider my advantage right now. I could crawl up and grab one of the cockatoos with my bare hands. *I can do this*, I tell myself. *Just like*

Mother and Father did many times. In my nomadic lifestyle, I became desensitised to trauma, having watched my parents hunt and kill many a live animal to feed us.

I also watched many a person die at the hands of the Petoys.

My heart pounds wildly and I rub my temples with my fingers. It is so easy for the past and present to collide together sometimes. It makes my brain whirl with dizziness as I try to reground myself and live in the present. Somewhere deep inside, sits the frightened child, Adira, who still searches for her mother.

Rolling onto my stomach, I observe the birds more closely. They are rubbing their beaks together, sharing their joy in feeding. A feeling of love sweeps over me, as I remember my mother feeding me. I can still taste the flavoursome berries she picked from trees and popped into my mouth. *Food brings strength, Adira*, she would say. *And wakefulness. You need to be ready to fight for your life.*

Sitting out here, I feel the rawness of the past wash over me. Reaching for my bag, I retrieve my mother's case file and stare once more at her familiar, troubled expression. I have so many unanswered questions that I wish could be resolved.

Opening the folder, I flick through the papers until I reach the second letter. The jolted and uneven handwriting suggests that Empress Celine may have written this letter with a shaking hand:

> Spring 1998
>
> Dear Maricelle,
>
> The wax of my single tallow candle has melted considerably and only a tiny spark of life remains in its fire. As I sit at this desk, its flailing light bewitches me. My hands are clutched tightly together, trying to summon my energy to regain my composure. Inside my heart, a deep sadness resides, creeping its way through my body.
>
> Lowering my hands to my womb, I feel a great sense of hollow emptiness. Once there sat a precious life, wrestling its way inside my being and sparking my heart with love and hope.

Days would filter their light through the palace windows and I would roam the corridors, rubbing my hands gently across my womb and talking to the precious, growing child within me. I had such dreams and ideas for its life. There was so much that I wanted to show it outside these palace walls.

The afternoon came when my heart did break. I tried all I could but my body could not carry the precious child. A great sadness began to fill my heart and I have carried it since. Two children have I now lost.

The Emperor has not taken the time to console me in this great tragedy. His expectation is that I will reward him with an heir as soon as possible. Upon hearing the tragic news, he punched his fist in the air and yelled with great frustration as he exited the chamber.

Alone, I sit, staring at closed walls, ignoring the beauty of daylight and feeling the darkness of grief creep its way through my very being.

I stand now, resting against the wall of the corridor and staring blankly at the flickering candle light. The silence screams its existence, bouncing off the walls. I am eternally grateful to be able to confide in you, my dear Maricelle. I greatly miss your company.

Blessings to you,

Empress Celine.

A deep sadness fills my heart as I consider how alone Empress Celine was in her trauma. I wonder where Mother sat when she read the Empress' letters and became privy to a world that was as dark as hers as she tried to escape the Petoys.

Standing slowly, I watch as the startled cockatoos jump and fly away.

Descending back to the arid plain, I stare into the distance.

Very soon, I will be immersed in the rhythm of a city terrain
as I makeshift my way across it.

Chapter 5

I return to Girl's hideout the next afternoon and discover that she is dismantling a plywood wall. Girl pushes forcefully and it crashes onto the ground with a loud bang. She glances over at the damage. Plywood planks are scattered across the grass. "Great," she mutters. "A big clean up."

"I can help," I offer kindly. My voice pierces her focus and she jumps, startled.

Girl stares at me, her mouth dropping open in surprise. "Lira! You've come back," her eyes soften. She seems relieved to have my company.

"Lucky I did," I say, picking up a plank of plywood. "I see it really is time to move on." I lay the plank across the ute tray.

"Yes," Girl's eyes narrow. "I'm in a bit of a ... rush," she sounds breathless.

It is hard work, taking apart the makeshift setting. I watch as Girl disconnects the front door from the side wall. She tosses it onto the grass and sighs with relief.

"How far away is the viso?" I ask.

"Viso?" Girl's brows furrow with confusion.

"Sorry," I realise that I must teach her the lingo. "Viso is the code word that we use for a dangerous person on our tail."

"Oh," Girl's eyes narrow and an intense expression crosses over her face. "About ten minutes away. I spotted his silver Mercedes parked behind the trees late last night. He's solo but strong enough." She tears a hand through her hair. "It won't take him long to find us."

There is no time to talk now. I move quickly, packing plywood planks into the ute tray. Girl helps to lift and transport the front door. We lay it down flat on top of the planks.

Running over, we unpeg the groundsheet that Girl was using as the floor surface. I hold it straight while she kneels down to roll it up. Tying it securely, she stares directly into my eyes.

"Final check list?" She asks, focused on the get away.

"The folder with the special papers?" I begin to list.

"You've got it," Girl automatically replies.

"Tent?" I continue, hoping that I can remember all the items.

"Got it," she is quick to respond.

"Your mirror?" I can't help mentioning that one.

"Would never forget that," Girl smiles.

"Your statue?" It's the last thing that I can think of.

"Packed away safely in a box in the ute tray already." Girl smiles. "I completed it last night."

"Congratulations!" I touch her lightly on the shoulder. "I'm sure it looks amazing, you are very talented at sculpting."

"Thanks Lira," Girl is still smiling. "Can you think of anything else?'

"Oh, hair dye!" I announce. Girl will need some to maintain her cover.

"I've run out," Girl replies. "Remind me to pop into a supermarket."

I am silent for a moment, absorbing her comment.

"You are coming with me, aren't you?" Girl is nervous.

I don't know what to say, so I look away. The dismantling was a harsh reminder of the upheaval of life on the run.

I take a sweeping glance at the absence of setting. A small pile of wood shavings lay in the red and green leaf littered grass. They will need to be removed quickly.

"It's really good to meet another woman from Mira," Girl says, meeting my gaze. "How old were you when you came here?"

"Six," I say softly, still focusing on the leaves and trying to block out the memories that flood my mind.

"I've only been here for four months," Girl says as she hoists the rolled ground sheet over her shoulder. She tosses it into the ute tray. "The first month I stayed with Concetta. The last three I have been on my own." She flexes her fingers and stares off into the distance. "It's hard being alone all the time," Girl says. "So dangerous," she lowers her head.

I watch as Girl scrambles on her knees, collecting the wood shavings. She seems strong, yet vulnerable at the same time. I realise that she needs to find closure too.

Girl pockets the wood shavings. "All clear," she declares. "Any more final checks?"

I inhale a deep breath and take the plunge.

"We can't go anywhere without my camera," I say. "It will keep our story alive."

Girl looks at me with wide, excited eyes. "You *are* coming!" She exclaims, clapping her hands in delight.

A small smile of relief crosses my lips as I realise that I have made up my mind. "Yes," I say.

Jumping into the driver's seat, Girl starts the ignition and the ute warms up. "Ready to go now?" She is in the zone. Her eyes are narrowed into slits and her brain is ticking away.

I take a moment to really look at Girl. Intensely focused, she has bewitched me with that brain of hers.

"Yes," I say nervously, suddenly afraid of what lies ahead.
I am shaking as I hop into the passenger seat.

"You okay?" Girl asks, picking up on my anxiety.

All I can do is nod as I sit back in my seat.

"Let's go!" Girl floors the accelerator and we speed away, hoping to escape our tail.

Chapter 6

As the ute roars down the street, Girl takes a quick glance in the rear view mirror. "Oh no!" She cries. "The tail's caught up!"

Peering behind me, I catch a glimpse of a silver Mercedes tailing us. The driver swipes away at his greying curly locks and narrows his piercing grey eyes. My heart pounds wildly in my chest. It is Chief Opula, staring intensely ahead. I hear his tyres squeal as he increases his speed and tries to drive us off the road.

"Hang on!" Girl cries, swerving the ute into the closest exit.

We zoom down the exit ramp and barely make it through the green lights, swerving sharply left and skidding onto Sava Road.

My heart is beating at about a hundred miles an hour and I clutch desperately onto my seat, hoping not to be thrown sideways.

Girl straightens up the ute and peers into the rear view mirror. "Tail lost for now," she says, continuing to drive. "I have to take another route to our destination."

I marvel at Girl's sharpness in the situation. She seems so used to getting away. My heart and head are taking a little while to catch up with each other.

Girl breaks gently and turns right onto Pine Street. She waits until the traffic clears and turns left, continuing down Vision road.

Makeshift Girl: The Secret Heritage Trail

I take this time to catch a breath and to stop myself from shaking.

Girl turns left onto the narrow Watley Street. As she drives, I appreciate the beauty of the green and gold grassland on my left. We are heading into a semi rural area with a number of small houses dotted across the plains.

"We're still clear," Girl takes a final glance in her rear view mirror and slows the ute down. She turns into a small parking area on the left side of the road and presses her foot on the break. Turning off the ignition, she sighs with relief. "Thank goodness we're alright," she faces me, pulling at her blue hair in frustration. "I'm sorry I didn't leave earlier. The tail obviously caught up with me."

"The tail was after *me*," I say, watching as Girl's eyes widen in surprise. "It is Chief Opula, the leader of the Petoy clan."

"Who does he think he is, chasing after you?" Girl's eyes flash angrily.

"He desperately wants to capture me. I've never understood why," I say.

"The Petoys make me so angry," Girl crosses her arms over her chest.

I inhale some deep breaths, trying to calm myself down. My mind is still flicking through the vivid images of the car chase.

Girl stares through the windscreen, her gaze falling upon the sight of the grassland before her. Her eyes light up and she opens the driver's door. "Time for a walk!" She announces as she kicks her shoes off and carries them in her hands.

Opening my own door, I step outside onto the dirt and stretch. It is nice to see a smile on Girl's face.

I follow Girl through the tall blades of grass. She walks slowly, stopping for a moment to enjoy the feeling of her bare feet on the earth.

"This is perfect," Girl stretches up towards the sky. "It's a beautiful day, the sun is so warm," she sounds relaxed. "It's nice to breathe again."

I stand next to her, allowing myself a moment to bathe in the sun's warmth.

After a short while, Girl opens her eyes and reaches for my hand. "Walk with me?" She asks. I let her guide me across the grass, my hand swinging in hers. She stops in front of a patch of dandelion flowers and flops down onto the blades, pulling me down with her. "Dandelions are special," Girl says. "Where I come from, we ask the seeds to bring us luck." Leaning towards a dandelion flower, she closes her eyes, whispers a few words and blows gently. Girl opens her eyes and watches the seeds fly away in the breeze.

We watch the dandelion seeds float until they disappear. Girl leans back onto her arms and meets my gaze. "I've felt like a wilted flower, hiding away for so long."

"I understand," I say. "You need your air and your sunshine."

"Yes," Girl agrees. "My earth, too. It's hard getting used to the city roads and driving a ute all the time. I'm used to walking long distances."

I am quiet as Girl speaks, listening to the gentle tone of her voice. I watch as she stands up and stretches like a cat. "The sun is beginning to lower," she says. "It's time to find somewhere to sleep."

I jump up onto my feet and follow Girl further across the grass until we hit a grove of pine trees. The earth below them is scattered with pine needles and cones.

As Girl picks up a pine cone and studies it, a smile lights up her face. "How lovely," she says. "It's always nice to take a piece of nature with you." She continues to walk, stroking the pine cone.

I keep my eyes peeled to the car park, making sure that there is no sign of the Mercedes from earlier. The darkness is growing a little stronger now and will soon conceal us.

Girl pauses and presses her feet into the dirt. "Firm," she says, nodding. "That's good. We can pitch our tent here."

I study the patch of dirt, checking its perimeters. It seems well concealed from any unwanted visitors. "Looks good," I agree. "We can't stay here for too long though."

"I know," Girl sighs, staring up at the sky. "It'll be nice to just enjoy this peaceful time though before we have to head back to the city."

"Of course," I agree.

Girl inhales a deep breath and turns back towards the car park. "Let's get the tent," she says, taking a few steps forward until she hits the grass again. Her gait is light and floaty. I trudge behind her slowly, my mind allowing itself to enjoy the calm time that we share right now.

Once we reach the ute, Girl hands me the tent poles. I hold onto them with both hands, feeling their heavy weight.

Girl grabs the groundsheet and throws it over her shoulder. She is obviously very used to carrying heavy things for a long distance.

My heart races as we walk back across the grassland. If we don't get set up quickly enough, we may be spotted out here.

Once we reach the dirt patch, I watch Girl bend her legs as she places the groundsheet down onto the earth. "That was good exercise," she says as she flexes her muscles.

I pop the poles down next to the groundsheet and begin to walk back to the ute quickly.

I feel Girl at my heels. "Slow down, Lira!" She calls. "We'll get it done."

"It'll be too dark soon," I say. "We need to hurry."

I reach the ute and open the passenger door. Grabbing my bag, I hang it over my shoulder.

As I close the door, I watch Girl effortlessly lifting the dome inner tent over her shoulders. "Meet you over at the camp spot, Lira," she calls, pressing the lock button on her remote as she heads off across the grassland.

"Okay," I say, reaching into the ute tray to grab the guy ropes, pegs and the fly. They are light to carry and I make it back across the grass quickly.

As I place the gear down onto the ground, I notice that Girl is already laying out the groundsheet. While she works, she sings in a light, spiritual tone:

> *"Take the north trek for you to be,*
> *where the people arrive by sea.*
> *The land shimmers with its view*
> *of my homeland and all that's true.*

> *"Feet print their trails upon the sand,*
> *arriving to sell wares made by hand.*
> *The cloth floats in air, light and free*
> *coloured with dyes of land and sea.*
>
> *"Clutch the cloth close to your heart,*
> *let its creation speak its art.*
> *Share its journeys across the land,*
> *away from the dark horse's hand."*

Girl's eyes are glazed as she stares up at the fading sunlight.

I am silent for a moment, letting her be in her own space.

After a moment, Girl smiles shyly. "A song from Mira," she says softly.

"It's beautiful," I say, smiling reassuringly. "You have a lovely voice."

"Thank you," Girl stares at the groundsheet. "I wonder how things are back home."

It must be so hard for Girl, not being able to return home right now. I know that Redbank is very different to the life that she is used to.

Chapter 7

We sit for a while, listening to the breeze as it coasts across the darkening sky. It lifts the dome up into the air and Girl jumps on top of it, in order to prevent it from taking off.

"Can you help me with the poles?" Girl asks. "We'd better secure them before the dome flies away."

"Sure," I reply, picking up a corner of the dome. I hold it in place for Girl while she threads a pole through the material.

My mobile phone is ringing.

"Let me just check who it is," I say as I retrieve my phone from inside my pocket.

Looking down at the caller identification, I notice that it is my husband Mitch. Inhaling a sharp breath, I close my eyes.

A memory flashes in my mind of Mitch's face smiling tenderly at me as he drew me close on our wedding day. Kissing him, my heart and soul soared to great heights.

Tears well in my eyes and a deep ache burns in my heart. Mitch is the only man I have ever loved, yet I fear that he has betrayed me.

"Lira?" Girl's hand rests upon my shoulder. "Are you okay?"

I am silent, shifting my gaze to the ground, unable to answer her.

Girl kneels in front of me with concern in her eyes. "Do you want to talk about it?"

I shake my head.

Ding!

My gaze shifts to my phone again.

I have a new lead, Mitch's message reads. *Can I meet you?*

It feels strange being so distant from Mitch. I miss him so much, it hurts more than words could describe.

Natural Ways, is all I can manage to message back. It is the code word for our location.

After a short while, Girl's eyes widen as she stares off into the distance. "A van has arrived," she announces.

A white van is heading across the grassland towards us. It stops in front of the ash trees.

The driver's door swings open and out jumps Mitch. My heart skips a beat as I watch him stride across the grass towards me.

Mitch smiles nervously when he sees me, flashing the cute dimple on the left side of his mouth. His blonde, curly hair looks a little dishevelled, as though he has slept roughly. There are lines of fatigue under his blue eyes.

We stare into each other's eyes for a long while. My heart aches so deeply, it feels like a brick in my chest. This is my husband, the love of my life.

Mitch steps closer to me and his eyes are flickering with sadness. "Hi Lira," he says softly. "How are you?"

He sounds so formal. It hurts that we are so close yet so far apart.

"Hi," I reply, placing a hand to my chest.

Reaching out, Mitch grabs hold of my hand and kisses it gently. "My beautiful wife," he says softly. "I miss you so much."

I close my eyes, enjoying the familiar feeling of his hand in mine. In my heart I always believed that I would be holding his hand forever. I never thought that he'd stray.

After a moment, Mitch pulls his hand away and I open my eyes. "Hi there," he says to Girl. "I'm Mitch, Lira's husband."

Girl's expression is serious. "I'm Girl," she says. "It's nice to meet you."

"You too," Mitch smiles weakly. He shifts his gaze until he is staring into my eyes. "What are you doing out here, Lira?"

I stare down at the ground, feeling numb. "Preparing to head into the city."

"The city?" Mitch looks surprised. "That's a very exposed area, Lira. Are you sure?"

"Yes," I reply. "It's something that I have to do."

"You have a lead for us?" Girl senses that I am uncomfortable and is taking charge and moving things along. I am grateful for that.

I feel Mitch's eyes on me and meet his gaze.

"I do have a lead," he says softly. "One I need your help, Lira, to decipher. Would that be okay?" His eyes widen hopefully.

"What's the nature of the lead?" I ask in a shaky voice.

"Communications," Mitch's eyes narrow with concern. "It's not important right now. I am worried about you."

I don't want to be the focus of Mitch's attention right now. "What sort of communications?" I ask him, trying to direct the conversation.

"The banter on the CB radio in the van has kept me up pretty late. Truck drivers certainly know how to chat," Mitch sighs. "It's not easy to understand everything they say."

"Who have you been listening to?" I am interested.

"Local truck drivers," Mitch says. "I was flicking through the channels the other day and stumbled across a conversation between two drivers that I was concerned about."

"Really?" Girl asks. "What were they saying?"

Mitch rubs his forehead. "They're using coded language." He stares at me. "That's where your detective skills come in handy, Lira."

I smile weakly. "How long do we have Mitch?"

"Half an hour," Mitch sighs. "I've got to be back on the road again as soon as possible. Life as a delivery boy is interesting. Some of the stuff you deliver raises the eyebrows."

"I can imagine," I say, staring deeply into his eyes. "Are you okay?"

"Yes," Mitch nods, his gaze softening.

We have connected for a moment. A smile spreads across my lips and my heart flutters in my chest.

Mitch smiles too, his eyes alight with hope.

After a moment, I become consciously aware that Girl is watching us and blush red. "We'd better get the job done," I say, breaking our connection. I wave my hand towards the van. "Lead the way."

Mitch opens the door and steps up into the driver's seat. "Hop in!" He calls as he reaches over and opens the passenger door for Girl and I.

I hoist myself up onto the passenger seat and shuffle over to make room for Girl. She sits next to me, buzzing with excitement.

"I've never heard CB radio chatter before," Girl says.

"Do you have a handle?" I ask Mitch.

"Yes," he smiles. "A few of the delivery guys I've met have given me the nickname Wave, as my hair is so curly."

"Well Wave," I say. "Let's tune in."

Mitch selects channel 17. "I'll just turn the mic gain control up to maximum," he says as he twists the dial.

A female voice enters the radio waves. *"In 3 hands Rapido, Frosties, Over."*

"I don't know who that voice belongs to," Mitch says. "She sounds very superior."

"Yes, she does," Girl agrees.

"More like 10 hands," Rapido replies. *"Busy at Suds. Over."*

"Apparently Rapido is pretty quick on the job," Mitch rubs his chin, thinking. "I think he's been involved in some sort of theft. He's been on the radio a lot lately, chatting in codes."

"Got it! Over and out." Replies the female voice.

We listen a little while longer.

All that can be heard is the scattered transmission of different voices and then silence.

"How far away do you think they are?" I ask him, trying to ascertain their distance.

"The signal metre suggests they are not too far away, say about twenty clicks away from here," Mitch says. "I am guessing they've arranged to meet somewhere in the city."

My mind whirs as it processes what I've learned.

"Any idea what Suds might be?" Girl asks, gaging our attention.

"Not at the moment." I say. "I'm thinking that the men have planned out a specific route," I suggest. "The codes given are probably precise locations along the route."

"That makes sense," Mitch nods, his eyes glazed in thought.

"Our next step is to work out what the codes represent," I say. "They are obviously well accessed by the drivers and therefore will be commonly known. There are also bound to be more locations. We will need to take a close look at a map to work this one out."

"Of course," Mitch sits up on his knees and reaches over the back of his chair. "Here," he says as he grabs a large sheet of paper. "I have a spare map of Redbank. You can have it," he hands it to me.

"Thanks," I say. "Leave this with me. I'll see what I can decipher."

"Lira, the expert detective," Girl smiles.

"You'll let me know what you discover?" Mitch asks uncertainly.

"Yes," I reply a little too curtly.

Mitch inhales a sharp breath.

Thick tension smothers the air.

Mitch opens the driver's door and jumps outside.

Girl places a hand on my shoulder. "Lira," she says. "Are you two okay?"

I sigh, running my fingers through my hair.

"You're doing what I do," Girl smiles. "You're stressed."

"Yes," I nod.

A moment later, Mitch opens the passenger door. "Come for a walk with me," he offers, reaching out his hand and smiling nervously. "It'll be nice to enjoy the fresh air with some beautiful company."

Mitch can certainly have a way with words. He has melted my heart.

"Go on," Girl smiles. "I'll keep building that tent." She jumps through the passenger door, leaving me to face Mitch.

Mitch's eyes widen with hope. Nervously, I reach for his hand and let him guide me down onto the ground. Once I've landed on my two feet, I notice that he is still clasping my hand in his. It feels so familiar that I don't want to let go.

We walk away from the van, heading north across the grassland. It is prettier here with a gorgeous patch of violet flowers. Pinks, oranges, lilacs and whites ... the flowers bring a moment of comfort and peace in the mayhem.

I sit down, running my fingers across the violet petals. They are so beautiful, a bright light in the madness of life.

"This is nice," Mitch says, plonking down next to me.

"Yes," I say softly, avoiding his gaze.

Mitch crooks my chin up with his finger. "Lira," he breathes. "I miss you so much. I need you."

I gaze into his eyes, which glimmer with hope. "You've always had me, Mitch," I say, moving his hand away. "I have always been loyal to you."

Mitch narrows his eyes. "And I to you," he says.

I stand up, needing some space. "Then why did you hold Sophie, Mitch? Was my love not enough?" Tears are welling in my eyes.

"Oh Lira!" Mitch jumps up onto his feet. "You mean the world to me. Please believe me when I say that nothing happened between Sophie and I. She just needed my help, that's all."

"I don't know if I can trust you, Mitch," I try to hold back my tears. "I have given you all of me, loved you with my heart and soul. It hurts me deeply that you would be intimate with anyone else." My voice is cracking.

Mitch's eyes widen. "I guess I deserve that," his tone is serious. "I wouldn't want to see you with anyone else either. It would tear me up inside too."

I can't hold back my tears any longer. They spill freely down my cheeks and my heart feels like it has been ripped apart.

Mitch pulls me into his embrace, holding me tightly. "I love you," his voice cracks. I can hear his heart pounding in his chest. "I don't know how to be without you."

I meet his gaze. It is warm and loving, just as I remember it. Mitch gently wipes my tears away with his hand.

I close my eyes, enjoying the tenderness of his touch.

Suddenly, a loud roar shatters the silence. Spinning around, I see a large truck cutting across the grassland towards the pine needle floor.

"Get down, Lira!" Mitch yells, waving his arm in the air. His voice is wild with panic. "Hide all you can!"

I jump, landing my body flat in the dirt. All I can hear is the loud roar of an engine pulling up in the distance.

I hear Mitch scurrying away.

The engine is very loud. Rolling over onto my stomach, I push violets aside, peering between blades of grass.

A very large truck has pulled up beside Mitch's van.

I spot Girl dashing behind the trees. Thank goodness she is safe.

My gaze darts back to the truck.

Zac jumps out of the driver's side. His jet black eyes are narrowed and he wears a grim expression.

My mouth drops open in shock. What is Zac doing here?

Mitch gulps nervously and his shaking fingers fiddle with the hem of his gold t-shirt. He must be so scared right now.

Zac walks with brisk, long strides across the grass. "So, you are Wave," he snarls, poking Mitch in the chest intimidatingly. "You're late, pretty boy. The delivery was due two hours ago."

"Right," Mitch wipes beads of sweat away from his forehead. "Who are you?"

"Let's just say I'm keeping an eye on you," Zac snickers. "I make sure you get your work done on time. Better me than someone more senior dealing with you right now."

Mitch's eyes widen. "I wasn't given a time, I am on my way there."

"You call this being on the way there?" Zac barks. "Jump right back in that van and make sure you drop those boxes off immediately. No fooling around, got it?"

"Got it," Mitch nods, waving his hands.

"Good," Zac pushes Mitch so forcefully that he lands with a thump onto his bottom. "Well, go on!" He yells, shooing Mitch with both his hands.

Mitch jumps up onto his feet and scampers towards the van. As he hops into the driver's side, he glances in my direction.

I am still hiding in the grass, shaking.

I hear the van begin to rev and Mitch reverses, turning it around and heading out of Pinewood Park.

Zac watches him leave. As he heads back towards the driver's side of his own truck, I zoom in the focus of my mobile phone and take a photo of his profile. Zac is one scary man.

I hope that Mitch is okay.

I watch as Zac reverses his truck and turns it around. He burns across the grassland and out of the park as though he is in a great hurry.

I stay put for a while. Experience has taught me to wait when there is danger.

After what seems like an entire day, I press my hands into the dirt and lift myself up off the ground.

It is very dark now and I need a light to see.

Digging into my pocket, I pull out my mobile phone and switch the torch light onto a dim setting. That's better.

I can't see anything scary to worry about. Ears pricked, I listen for unusual sounds. There is nothing but the chirping and clicking of cicadas. Phew!

Standing slowly, I begin to take a few steps, trying not to make too many rustling sounds through the grassland.

Eventually I reach our meeting place and stop walking.
The abandoned groundsheet flaps wildly in the breeze.

My heart beats wildly in my chest. There is no sign of Girl.

I hope that she is okay.

Chapter 8

I feel a cold chill outside and it is biting through my toes. Stamping my feet, I try to keep warm. Staring into the distance, I remember the last family moment that I had with both my parents in Mira ...

The rain was falling gently that night, a welcome relief from the tropical heat of the day. I cupped both my hands together, catching droplets of water until they formed a pool in my palms. I licked my parched lips, my mouth feeling dry from thirst. Bringing my hands to my mouth, I sipped the water and sighed with relief.

Standing under the shelter of a cedar tree, I stared at the fire crackling as it burned through the fallen logs and twigs that I had gathered earlier with my father. The flames licked at the air, unaffected by the light rain. I was mesmerised by their vibrant red-orange colour, which burned steadily.

The firelight enabled me to view the open plain. A deer dashed across the terrain and paused to nibble at the grass. I watched it munch away, my heart aching to be able to run and play so freely.

A chuckle averted my attention to my parents, who were sitting on the ground, in front of our makeshift tent. My father's arms were wrapped around my mother's waist. She sat in front of him, brushing her long, brown hair with her fingers. Her smile was radiant, warming my heart.

Clip Clop.

Pricking my ears up, I froze. It was the sound of horse hooves, galloping their way across the open plain.

My heart pounded wildly in my chest. I knew that the horses belonged to the Petoy clan.

I felt myself being lifted and my mother began to run, pressing me close to her chest.

Diving behind a bush, my mother lowered me down onto the ground. Meeting her gaze, I watched her place her finger over her lips, motioning for me to stay silent.

I nodded, wide eyed with fear. Peering through the bush, I frantically tried to locate my father.

He was standing right where Mother had left him, tugging at his orange shirt nervously as he watched two men approach him on horseback. One of the horses reared up high into the air as a Petoy man pulled its reigns.

"Whoa!" The Petoy man cried, pulling the reigns more firmly as the horse began to trot. Gradually, it stopped moving, allowing the man to dismount. I watched his head scarf fall into his eyes as he jumped onto the ground and landed firmly on two booted feet.

"Voltan Vivesque," the man spoke with an air of superiority. Pushing his head scarf back on top of his brown hair, he rested his gaze upon my father.

"Good evening Chief Opula," my father's voice shook a little. Crossing his arms over his chest, he met the Chief's gaze with a serious expression.

The Chief bent down, examining the fire. "A cozy meal, I see," he said, kicking away the rabbit carcass. "You are feeding your wife and child well." He stepped closer to my father and grabbed him by the collar of his shirt. "Actually," a twisted smile crossed his lips. "You are providing for a child that will never be yours."

My father gasped as the Chief pulled his collar more tightly. I could hear his rasping breath as he struggled to breathe.

"So, where is she?" The Chief's voice lashed through the air, making me jump.

Mother put her arm around me and held me close. I was shaking, terrified of the Chief. I wanted him to let my father go.

"She's not here," gasped my father, surprising me. "I decided I didn't want the child in my life anymore, so I told her and her mother to leave." His voice was strained as he rasped for breath.

The Chief cocked his head, maintaining his grip on my father's neck. "The woman betrayed you," he hissed, his eyes narrowing. "She has confused your heart, made you weak."

My father's eyes were bulging from the pressure of being strangled. "Please," I heard him gasp. "Let me go!"

The Chief stared into my father's eyes intensely. "It is best you hand over the child to us," his voice was dark, sending a shiver down my spine. "We need her to strengthen our resistance against the empire. You are going to hand her over, aren't you?"

Father's eyes were wild as he struggled to release the Chief's grip. "She is long gone," he gasped.

I reached for my mother's face, shaking and scared. As she met my gaze, I could sense her deep worry.

I waited for an explanation, a reason why my father would say those things about me. There wasn't one. My mother shifted her gaze towards my father and bit her lip anxiously.

The Chief finally released my father, letting him drop onto the ground. "Has she?" His voice was eerie. Stepping back, he faced the other man, who sat silently, watching. "Search his tent," he ordered firmly. "Any female belongings, bring them to me."

The other man dismounted his horse, his eyes dark and menacing as he stared at Father. Passing him, he pushed his way inside our tent.

Mother met my gaze again, holding one of my hands. "Adira," she whispered softly. "In a moment, we are going to run, okay?"

I narrowed my five year old eyes, upset with my mother's suggestion. "Why?" I demanded. "Can't we wait for Father?"

"No," Mother shook her head. Reaching down, she picked me up and I wrapped my legs around her waist.

The man exited the tent. He carried a dried pink rose that I had been keeping on our journey. Handing it to the Chief, he smiled slyly at father. "Seems they were here," he said gruffly. "Not too long ago."

The Chief held the rose in his palm. Lifting it, he smelt its scent. "This rose is dry," he said, tossing it onto the ground and trampling on it. "It would have been picked a few days ago."

My heart fell as the rose shattered into tiny fragments. It had been my friend and I had shared many a story with it as we roamed the earth. My heart ached for my rose, its tiny life had warmed my heart. I began to cry, my heart broken.

Mother's eyes widened and she placed a hand over my mouth. "Sssh," she said. "Adira, sssh."

The Chief's ears pricked up, listening. "What's that?" He demanded, hearing my sobs. "She is here, isn't she?" Reaching into his pocket, he pulled out a knife and waved it into the air, pointing it directly at Father. "We Petoys do not take betrayal kindly," he snarled. "You are helping an asset hide away. Why don't I cut you into tiny pieces right now?" He pressed the knife into my father's chest.

Father inhaled a sharp breath. "I will help the Petoys," he gasped, holding his hands up. "I have been finding a way to bring the asset to you."

"Good," the Chief released my father, who fell down onto his knees. "Find her!" He barked, waving the other man towards us.

Mother clutched me tightly. "Hold on!" She cried. I could feel the vibrations of her feet pelting across the grassy ground.

"Come back!" I heard footsteps thrashing across the earth, a distance away from us. Suddenly the sound ceased, replaced by the clan member's voice. "You won't get too far, we will find you!"

My mother continued to run, pelting across the terrain and heading deeper into the forest. The world around me zapped by like a blur and I closed my eyes, wishing it was all a dream and that I would wake up next to my parents by the tent again.

It wasn't a dream.

Beginning to slow down, my mother walked at a steady pace, cutting through the village and heading down to the sandy shore. The strength in her was admirable as she continued to carry me, even as she struggled to trek through the deep sand.

"Here we are," Mother said as she stopped in front of a boat shed. Kicking its small wooden door open, she stepped inside cautiously, keeping her eyes peeled for any unwanted visitors. "Good, it's empty," she sighed with relief and placed me down onto the sandy floor.
I watched as she shut the door firmly behind us.

A small ray of light shone through a crack in the door, enabling me to see my mother's face in the darkness. She bent down and stared into my eyes.

"We're on our own now, Adira," Mother said softly as she stroked my hair. "Your father has no choice but to do as the Chief commands."

My lips trembled at the mention of my father. "When will we see him again?" I asked.

My mother lowered her eyes, thinking. After a moment, she stared into mine again. "I don't know," her voice shook as she spoke. "We'll try our best to find him, alright?"

"Alright," I sighed, relieved by my mother's decision to help my father.

Mother sat down and patted the ground beside her. I sat next to her and she put her arm around me. She sang to me:

> *"Where the flowers grow you'll be,*
> *dancing among dew dropped petals.*
> *Morning kissed, you awaken free,*
> *twirling with joy across the meadow.*
>
> *"Stay away from the tall, dark trees,*
> *their bodies cast large shadows.*
> *Fractured light brings no sleep,*
> *as dark horses seek your youth."*

As she sang, I let the words sweep over me like a gentle, fluffy cloud. I knew that there was a message in the song but I was too young to understand it.

Mother's voice soothed me. I was safe in the dark boat shed with her. My eyelids began to droop and I drifted off to sleep.

As my thoughts return to the present, I become aware that I am shivering from the cold. Using my phone torch, I seek shelter under a tall pine tree. It seems a little better under here as the wind is not so sharp.

Reaching into my cloth bag, I retrieve my mother's case file once more. Opening it again, I am surprised when the third letter slips out of the folder easily and lands in my lap. Picking it up, I shine the torch light over the writing, scanning it with eager eyes:

Summer, 1998

Dear Maricelle,

The Emperor likes to keep an eye on all mail sent from the palace and so he does not approve of the use of envelopes. So I have learnt how to employ the ancient art of letter locking: delicately folding and slitting sections of the letter and gluing them down with adhesive where necessary. I feel a lightness of life to know that my words in this letter are sealed away and will only be revealed to you.

I have been sleeping outside in the conservatory, so that I may get a breath of floral scent to soothe my nerves. It seems to provide some relief from the darkness that has ventured its way through my veins.

It was last evening that I dozed off while enjoying the scent of fragrant roses and slept with my head pressed against the window. I awoke to the sound of male voices and upon opening my eyes, discovered the Emperor in intense discussion with a youthful man who carried some candles of a different variety.

Listening closely, I heard the Emperor demand that the man begin to sell him the luxurious beeswax candles he had, in exchange for bolts of silk. The youth enthusiastically agreed, handing the Emperor half his load of candles and promising more once the payment was received.

Gazing around the conservatory, I viewed the tallow candles, appreciating once more the work it took to craft such precious light.

The future continues to advance upon us, Maricelle and with it brings rapid and unwelcome change. Already today, some of the tallow candles have been removed and replaced with beeswax ones.

The Emperor bade my company to show me the illustriousness of the beeswax candles. He tells me that they do not have an offensive odour, are of much finer quality and burn longer. The candles are highly sort after by the most distinguished people of the world.

My heart drums its worried note, considering what will happen to tallow for our people who need it to glow their lights of life.

I hope you are keeping safe,

Empress Celine.

The Empress' letter writing empowered her with a new sense of freedom as she make shifted her own way through such a dark and restrictive life. She did so in many ways: whether finding a temporary shelter; eavesdropping on conversations; secretly writing and delivering letters and gifting used candles.

It seems that my mother and the Empress both have something in common: under adversity, they engage with their instincts to fight for their beliefs and survival.

My phone is ringing in my hand. Checking the screen, I note that it is Girl's caller identification. She's okay!

Pressing the accept call button, I hold the phone to my ear.

"Lira?" Girl sounds breathless. "Where are you?"

"Where we last saw each other," my teeth chatter as I speak.

"Oh good," Girl breathes a sigh of relief. "Hold tight, I'll be there in five."

I still feel numb and not just from the cold. Even after Girl's call, I feel a strong, pervading sense of loneliness.

Staring down at Mother's photograph on the front of the case folder, I inhale a sharp, unsteady breath. I am beginning to wonder if I'll ever find her again.

Makeshift Girl: The Secret Heritage Trail

I slot the letter back into the case folder, still staring at Mother's beautiful face. *I wish you were here with me, Mother*, my thoughts flood my mind. *I promise you, I will find you.*

After a few moments, my breathing begins to settle and I take in my surroundings. It is quiet and peaceful here and the darkness is strangely soothing.

It is time to begin searching for clues. I step forward, my arms outstretched and sweeping through the breeze. The phone's torch light enables me to see patches of the pine needle floor. My eyes narrow as they focus on the visuals. I know something will show up. A clue. I can discover even the most discrete clues. Sometimes they land me in a lot of trouble.

Clunk.

What is that sound? I can feel something firm beneath my left foot. Stepping back, I aim my phone's torch light at the object. As the light glows, it reveals a small, silver bulldog clip attached to a folded sheet of paper.

Bending down, I pick up the paper. Removing the bulldog clip, I pocket it and begin to unfold the paper. It flaps in the wind, almost flying out of my hands.

Straightening up the paper, I stare at the message. It is unmistakably raw. *Have you seen this Girl?* Demands the large, black type font. My eyes are drawn to the image accompanying the message. There she is, with her long black hair and green eyes. It is Girl. She is intensely focused on pushing a cart filled with colourful wares across a grassy plain. The photo must have been taken of Girl when she was in Mira.

My heart is pounding in my chest. Girl is in great danger.

Flipping the paper over, I study it for clues. It is predominately white, marked with coffee or tea stains. The edges of the paper are bent and worn down, as though it has been attached to someone's belt or around one's neck on a lanyard for a while.

The back of the paper is blank but I am not fooled by its appearance. Shining the phone light more directly onto the paper, I squint with one eye, searching for the tiny embellishment.

It takes a lot of patience to do this, continuing to glance across the paper in horizontal lines, waiting for that special sign to …

"Ah!" I gasp as my eyes fall on the tiny black lines of letters.

Eyes on Wave, the message reads, almost embedded within the whiteness of the paper.

My hands begin to shake. I hope that Mitch got away okay.

Swish! Swish!

I jump about a foot in the air as the sound bursts through my ears. Forcing myself to stop panting and listen, I identify the sound. Someone is running through the grass.

Switching off my torch, I pocket my phone and dash across the pine needle floor. The tree I hide behind is large enough to conceal my body. Bobbing down, I pocket the paper. My heart is racing.

Stomp!

The runner's feet are loud as they dash across the pine needle floor. The sound ceases directly in front of my tree. Inhaling a sharp breath, my ears prick up and listen attentively for any movement.

Ding!

I jump about a metre in the air. My mobile phone flashes suddenly. I can see the light through my pant pocket. Retrieving my phone, I check the screen. *I'm here Lira*, Girl's message reads. *Meet me when it is safe.*

I sigh with relief. The runner is only Girl.

Standing slowly, I peer out from behind my tree's thick trunk. It is hard to see in the dark but thankfully the moonlight above provides a glow.

It is hard to miss that blue hair. I watch Girl run her fingers through its strands in frustration.

I exhale a sigh of relief. It *is* Girl. She is safe.

Stepping out from behind the tree, I tread across the pine needle floor, approaching Girl who is listening intensely to the noise around her.

"Hello Lira," Girl's voice sends a slight shiver down my spine.

"Hi Girl," I am shaking. "You got here in record timing."

"Yes," Girl nods. She faces me, her eyes narrowed and serious. "Let's go, right now."

I don't ask any questions.

As I follow Girl across the grassland, I feel exposed. Anyone could spot us here. Did the man in the truck park somewhere close by?

Once we reach the ute, I hop into the passenger seat and face Girl. She is sitting in the driver's seat and clasping her shaking hands together.

After a moment, she stares out the window with an intense expression on her face.

"Are you alright?" I ask her.

"I am now," Girl's voice is trembling. "I nearly got discovered back there. Luckily I managed to escape through the trees. I kept running, as far away as I could."

I stare at Girl, absorbing what she is saying. She is in so much danger right now.

"Is Mitch okay?" Girl's eyes narrow worriedly.

"Yes," I nod. "Zac, the man who came looking for him, demanded that he returned to work and delivered the boxes. Mitch left in his truck a while back."

Girl's eyes widen in surprise. "You know Zac? Who is he?"

"Jacquelyn's husband," I say. "He's obviously involved in some shady business. Concetta tells me that Jacquelyn is unaware of his ventures."

"Poor Jacquelyn," Girl looks sad. "We live in such a strange world, Lira. People are pushed beyond their extremes to satisfy human desire, no matter what the cost. I feel the most sorry for its victims." She stares off into the distance, thinking.

After a moment, Girl meets my gaze. "How did Zac know where to find Mitch?" She asks.

"That's a very good question," I reply, my brain racing with possibilities. Somehow, Zac was able to find Mitch here. It was an unplanned, impromptu meeting with us … "Maybe they've pinned some surveillance on him," I suggest. "I'll have to take a closer look at his van."

"Good idea," Girl lowers her head. "I feel so bad that Mitch is in danger. We have to help him."

"Yes, we do," I agree.

Girl tears at her hair. "It's all so scary, Lira. The Petoys are so clever."

"They like to think they are," I say. Reaching into my pocket, I retrieve the paper that I discovered earlier. "I should show you this," I hand it to her.

Girl's mouth drops open as she stares at her photo. "Oh no," she says, pulling at her hair. "The search party has increased." Her eyes are wild as she stares at me. "It's so hard to keep safe, Lira."

"We will outsmart the Petoys," I say confidently, grabbing hold of her arms and pulling her close for a hug. "I am here for you, whatever it takes."

Girl stares at me with watery eyes. "That's really sweet," she sniffles. "Thank you." She pockets the paper with shaking hands.

My mind wonders, flashing through images of the discovery I made on the pine needle floor. I meet Girl's gaze. "I need you to trust me," I say gently.

Girl's eyes widen and she inhales a sharp breath. "What is it?" She is panicking.

"We need to park the ute somewhere close by and discrete," I tell her. "In the morning, I will check the pine needle floor for Zac's footprints. I need to gather as much identification on him as I can."

"Say no more," Girl says, pulling away from me and sitting up in her seat. She starts the ignition and backs the ute out of the car park. Waiting for traffic to clear, she turns left onto Watley Street.

Indicating left again, Girl turns onto Crescent Street and pulls up in front of an empty block of land. Straightening the ute, she presses on the brake and switches off the ignition.

"Thanks for everything Lira," Girl looks at me. "You are amazing."

I relish Girl's compliment. "It's my pleasure," I say, pushing my seat back. "Let's get some sleep."

"Yes, will do," Girl agrees, settling back into her seat.

I stretch out my legs. It is nice to be warmer in the ute. Blocking out the vivid images in my mind, I allow myself to close my eyes and see the black …

I gradually drift off to sleep.

Chapter 9

I awaken as the dawn is rising. Stretching my arms, I peer through the windscreen. The sky is blue and clear. It is going to be a lovely day.

Glancing to my right, I notice that Girl's seat is empty. She is an early riser. I hope that she's returned to the park.

My thoughts drift to my mother and I wonder how she is travelling out on the dangerous terrain of Mira. The Petoys are unrelenting and would not be easy to escape.

Reaching for my cloth bag, I dig into it, retrieving my mother's case file once more. Circling her photographed eyes with my finger, I wonder what secrets she holds so deeply in her dark, mysterious gaze. Maybe her next letter might give me some more clues.

Inhaling a deep breath, I open the file. Flicking through the letters, I locate the fourth one. The Empress' writing is shaky and I soon discover why:

Autumn, 1998

Dear Maricelle,

I rode through the streets of Mira in my carriage tonight. It was a great shock to have many citizens screaming protest at my presence and pressing their very angry faces against the glass windows.

I saw so many hands clutching desperately at the carriage or pulling bodies up over its frame, trying to stop our motion.

While my heart did pound ferociously in my chest, I turned to my courage within, instructing the driver to stop the carriage. Pushing open the door, I placed both booted feet firmly down onto the dirt ground. For a moment, I felt the assailing comfort of fresh air caressing my very hibernated skin.

The pelting of footsteps seemed to fade as I regained focus and glanced around at the scene before me.

In that moment, I realised what great misfortune had been bestowed upon the people. It broke my heart to see so many thin beings who were suffering great anguish and crying for a morsel of food. Some bodies lay fatigued on the footpath, unaware of the events around them.

Staring ahead, I felt my body clutched and clawed at. Strong words of desperation were cried into my ears. I felt a deep responsibility for the people and the situations that they found themselves in. I also felt helpless to prevent the Emperor from causing any more harm.

Meeting the gaze of a young woman in a tattered dress, who clutched my arm, I reached out to connect with her. "I am deeply sorry for the trauma that has befallen you," I said, feeling saddened by her demise, which she had whispered hoarsely into my ears.

Another young woman's dark eyes sparked with anger. "Your husband, the Emperor, has banned tallows candles as he is superstitious of the darkness that their putrid smell brings," she sneered. "He has gone so far as to demand that we must trade two bolts of silk for a single beeswax candle. We villagers cannot afford such an expense. Nor do we wish to part with the silk that we spend such a long time producing on our farms."

My heart froze in shock. "I am sorry for your burden," I replied, feeling shaken.

"Sorry?" A man pummeled his chest with outrage. "Your husband is greedy, preventing us from having the utility of modern electricity as he fears progress so much. Instead, he leaves us to discover a way to be able to afford to light our own homes and streets. To take away the only form of light we have is criminal. Plunged into darkness, our livelihoods and health will greatly suffer."

"I saw beeswax candles being delivered to the palace this morning!" Another young man cried. "Shame on the Emperor, to put his own luxury before the needs of his people!"

I stood still, absorbing the last words that I had heard. They were spoken in the way that I felt as the wife of the Emperor: abandoned and left to fend for my own light of being.

There was nothing more that I could say. Staring ahead, I felt a deep emptiness wash over me once again.

Stepping into the carriage, I stared out the window as it departed, leaving the desperation of the people behind on the streets.

It is so precious, life. It pains me deeply that its spirit and its glow, is beginning to extinguish.

I have a plan to help our people and will discuss it with you when I meet you shortly.

Blessings to you,

Empress Celine.

Closing the file, my mind races with thoughts of the people of Mira. The tallow candle is a major part of their heritage. Candle making gives them a sense of pride and dignity that they can produce their own lights through life. It is the same with the people's abilities to produce and design silk, which provides them with a way to make and sell wares through trade.

Taking the people's independence away from them and demanding unreachable expense is unjust. It is no wonder that they began to protest against the Emperor's rulings.

What an increasingly unstable place for my mother and father to navigate through. How tired my mother must be right now.

It is time to get moving so that I can discover more clues.

Staring at the steering wheel, I discover that Girl has left the keys dangling in the ignition.

Sliding my legs across the glove box, I land my bottom onto the driver's seat. As I adjust the rear view mirror, I check if there are any tails. None.

Turning the key, I start the ignition. The ute tremors awake and begins to rev. I indicate right and drive out onto the road.

There has to be a side street nearby, which leads to the grassland car park …

Let me try Hirately Street.

I indicate left and turn into the street, narrowly missing the parked cars staggered on both sides of the road.

I take the next left down Yola Street, rubbing my eyes as I head towards the end of the road. Sure enough, the entrance to the car park is straight ahead.

As I head into it, I notice that it is empty. No sign of any nasty tails.

I drive through the car park and onto the grassland. As I pull up next to the pine needle floor, I notice that Girl has already arrived. She is busy dismantling the tent. She turns to face me as I park, her eyes shining.

"Hi Lira," Girl says. "Thanks for driving the ute here." She tosses the tent poles into the ute tray.

"Better to be safe," I say as I hop out of the ute. I pick up the dome and toss it over my shoulder.

"Wow, such strength Lira," Girl smiles. "Let me see your muscles."

I toss the dome into the ute tray and flex my right arm. "What do you think?" I ask her.

"Very toned," Girl chirps. "You could lift that ute." She purses her lips as she giggles, trying to stop herself.

"You're in a jovial mood this morning," I say as I pick up the guy ropes. I swing them around as I approach the ute tray. "See if you can catch these ropes." I hold them up high into the air.

Girl jumps up, her hands grasping them on her first try. "Too easy!" She laughs. She tosses the guy ropes into the ute tray.

"Let's see who can pull up the most pegs off the groundsheet," I challenge her.

Girl's eyes light up. "You're on!" She laughs, dropping down onto the ground. Her eyes narrow into slits while she focuses on the task.

I sit on my knees and begin spinning a peg. It takes a while to loosen its grip in the ground. After a short while, I twist it gently and pull it up. My hand is already aching a little.

Glancing at Girl, I notice that she has already pulled up three tent pegs. She works quickly, twisting and pulling at each peg with great ease.

A few more minutes pass and I am still stuck twisting the second tent peg. It has been tacked in so firmly that it is hard to release.

"All done!" Girl calls, holding up multiple tent pegs in her hands.

"You are so fast," I am surprised. "Well done."

Girl smiles. "Can I help you with that peg?" She steps closer to me. I let her take over and watch as she spins the peg, loosening it with ease.

"You must camp lots," I say as I watch her pull the peg out of the ground.

"Yes, I do," Girl jiggles the tent pegs in both hands. "Some journeys I take on the roads go for days at a time. It can be quite remote too, so a tent comes in handy."

"It must be hard work," I empathise. "Especially if you're carrying a heavy load on your back."

"It can be," Girl sighs, handing me the pegs. Bending down, she begins to roll up the groundsheet. As she works she continues to speak: "Sometimes I take a cart with me so that I don't have to carry such a huge load. Other times, the roads are too rocky for a cart, so I take a couple of trekking poles instead."

Standing, Girl lifts the rolled up groundsheet with both hands and tosses it into the ute tray. She stares at me intensely. "Last night, while you were sleeping, I stared at the photograph of myself pushing the cart for a long time. It got me thinking about Mira and just how hard we merchants work." She digs into her pocket and pulls out a folded sheet of paper. "I wrote this poem," she says, meeting my gaze. "Would you like to hear it?"

Makeshift Girl: The Secret Heritage Trail

"Yes please," I say as I search the ute tray. Discovering a small, empty cloth bag, I slide the tent pegs into it and tie the bag securely. Resting my back against the ute tray, I focus on Girl, who is straightening the paper and clearing her throat. She smiles at me and turns her attention back to the paper, reading:

> "The day's heat sears,
>   casting a burnished glow.
>   The sandy granules rise,
>   a dusty haze smears the landscape.
>
> "A sultry place I trek with familiar steps,
>   across the rugged, unmade terrain.
>   A pathway marked with lines of travel
>   undertaken by past merchants.
>
> "The cart I push is old and worn,
>   its planks of wood breaking apart.
>   One of the wheels wobbles loosely
>   as it travels across the shifting terrain.
>
> "The surface is rugged with potholes
>   that I must dodge and swerve passed.
>   Worn cart handles irritate my hands,
>   leaving the stinging pain of blisters.
>
> "Old, yet beloved to my family,
>   the cart is marked with the prints
>   and sweat of our ancestors,
>   who began our journeys in trade.
>
> "I carry our world in this cart,
>   wares we have taken ages to create.
>   Foraging through earth and trees
>   to source our natural ingredients.
>
> "Wares I push with deep pride,
>   along the sloping, uneven terrain.
>   I can travel further with the cart
>   and expand my avenues for trade.

"The market is a long trek away,
   a place of vibrant colour and culture.
   Shaded with rich, historical trade,
   proudly displayed in a myriad of wares.

"Spruiking merchants sell off their wares
   to bright eyes of interest in their heritage.
   Some merchants stand screaming wildly,
   pointing at a thief fleeing into the distance.

"It is the Petoy clan who steal our wares,
   using our heritage to advance their resistance.
   I hope we can work together to stop the theft
   and succeed in saving Mira's precious heritage."

Girl stares at me with a hopeful expression. "Do you think we can do this together, Lira?"

I wrap my arm around Girl's shoulder. "Your poem is powerful," I say to her. "It has resonated deeply with me. As you read, I visualised every merchant in Mira who has ever had to push a cart to trade. It is their life work, their spirit and our heritage. We need to do all that we can to save it."

Girl nods, smiling weakly at me. "I think we'll do well together." Pocketing the paper, she reaches into the ute tray. "I want you to experience something," she says as she ruffles through her belongings.

After a few minutes, Girl cheers. "Here they are!" She retrieves two black poles. "I have to tread such a long way in Mira. Like many other merchants, I take these everywhere with me. I can't live without them. They take a lot of the pressure off my body when I am trekking or hiking." Girl hands one of the trekking poles to me.

I am surprised at how lightweight the pole is in my hands. "Is this made of aluminium?" I ask Girl.

"Yes, it keeps it light," she says. "Try walking with it yourself."

I walk, pressing the trekking pole into the ground. It does take my weight, alleviating some of the pressure off my legs. "This is great," I say, my eyes spotting a footprint on the ground. I stop moving.

"What is it?" Girl steps closer.

"Stop," I point at the footprint. "There's a footprint just here."

"Here's another," Girl points at a second footprint. "And another …"

"Hmm," I nod, bending down. "Mitch's sneaker footprints run across here," I point out another set further away. "I believe these footprints here may belong to Zac. I need to be careful that I don't disturb a footprint. Measuring them with a solid and slightly elevated object would prevent that." An idea hits me. "Can I use this trekking pole to measure the footprint?" I ask Girl.

"Sure," she shrugs.

I place the trekking pole next to the footprint. "I need a marker," I say. "Can you pass my bag?"

Girl dashes over to the ute and grabs my bag off the driver's seat. "Here you go," she hands it to me.

I reach into my bag, locating the masking tape that I carry around for moments like this. Placing the bag down, I grab the trekking pole again. "It is really important to get an accurate measurement from the big toe to the heel," I tell Girl as I take a piece of masking tape and stick it onto the trekking pole to mark the length of the footprint. Reaching into my bag again, I grab a pen and write *length* on the tape.

"Can I help?" Girl is keen to assist.

"Your can measure the width," I hand Girl the measuring tape. "Measure across the widest part of the foot, right here," I show her.

Girl uses her own trekking pole to measure the footprint. She sticks some masking tape onto the pole and labels it with a mark indicating its width.

"Now to measure these properly," I say, reaching into my bag to grab the measuring tape. I measure the length marked out on the pole. "That is 26.4 centimetres," I say, grabbing the pen off Girl and noting the measurement on the masking tape. "He has big feet." I hand Girl the measuring tape. "How wide is it?"

Girl measures the marked width on her own trekking pole. "9 centimetres," she says, making a note of the measurement on the masking tape.

I reach into my pocket and retrieve my phone. "There is a border around the sole along with a clear herringbone pattern. Can you see here?" I show Girl.

"Yes," Girl says, staring at the footprint.

I take a photo of the sole pattern so that I can recognise it again in the future.

My gaze falls upon a second footprint with clear tread marks. Shuffling towards it, I study it closely. "Zac has medial wear on his left shoe. See the stress marks on the footprint? This is evidence of over pronation, where the inward cushioning roll of his foot is exaggerated when he walks or runs."

"Wow," says Girl, her eyes widening. "You can tell all that from a footprint?"

"Yes," I say, staring at her. "We've developed some identification of Zac from his footprints. If he wears these shoes for work, he'll continue to wear them. We may see these exact same footprints elsewhere and know where he travels."

"Oh," Girl's eyes light up. "You are amazing, Lira, truly amazing."

I lower my head, blushing red. "We've got all we need here," I say, pocketing my phone.

"Great," Girl sounds cheery as she grabs my bag and tosses in the masking and measuring tapes.

I place the trekking pole in the back tray of the ute. Girl hands me my bag.

Girl tosses her own trekking pole into the tray. "Let's go," she opens the passenger door for me.

I slide into my seat, feeling surprisingly pumped after my detective work.

Ding!

I retrieve my phone from my pocket. "It's definitely time to head into the city," I say, reading the message. "Concetta has sent us the co-ordinates for a dead drop that she wants us to collect."

"Where is the location?" Girl asks, peering at her screen. "How strange, it's written in code: sub 32, sit 4."

I consider the message. "It will be the subway at Redbank Station," I suggest. "There is probably a number 32 platform there."

"Oh Lira," Girl sighs. "You are so clever. It would have taken me a lifetime to figure that out."

"Let's go," I say. "We don't want to lose the dead drop."

"No, we don't," Girl agrees, turning on the ignition. She pops the gear stick into reverse and presses her foot on the accelerator. Once the ute has backed out far enough across the grass, she turns it around to face the car park. Driving through it, she heads right down Watley Street, taking a zig zag of streets until she reaches Suva Road.

As Girl takes the on ramp and merges onto the highway, I let my tired mind wonder about Mitch. It is too dangerous to message him right now. All it takes is for Zac or someone else to realise where we are.

I drift off to sleep with my heart fluttering in my chest. *I hope you got away safely, Mitch.*

Chapter 10

When I open my eyes, I discover that Girl has driven a long distance down the highway.

I yawn and stretch, adjusting myself upright in my seat.

"You're awake," Girl smiles. "You had a good rest."

"Yes," I say, watching the cars zoom passed us. "I must have needed it." My eyes fall upon a large, green sign up ahead. *Redbank City, 2 kms*, it reads.

"We're nearly there," I say, feeling a little nervous.

"Yes," Girl says. "We'll arrive in two minutes." I watch as she zooms down the middle lane.

Beeping her horn, Girl warns a car, which almost cuts directly in front of her. The driver swerves back into his lane.

Indicating briefly, Girl merges into the left lane. "Here we go," she says, taking the off ramp into Redbank. The ute zooms down the curved road and Girl breaks at the red light. "I'll find a park along Lighthouse Boulevard," says Girl. "It's busy so the ute will remain unnoticed. We'll have to walk a little way to the subway." Girl turns right onto Lighthouse Boulevard. It is indeed busy with people dashing off to various destinations.

We pass numerous cafés where people are sitting outside enjoying the sunshine while indulging on food or drink.

My stomach rumbles. It would be lovely to do that if we could. Right now, it's too risky.

Girl indicates left and pulls the ute into a parking spot outside the front of Harriet's Café. Reaching over, she opens the glove box and grabs her sunglasses.

Putting them on, she stares at herself in the rear view mirror. "Not bad," she says. "I should blend in well."

I reach into my bag and grab my own sunglasses. As I adjust the rims over my eyes, I breathe in, enjoying the smell emanating from the café.

"Smells great," Girl sniffs. She opens the driver's door. "I'll be back in a minute." She dashes bravely into the café.

My heart begins to pound. I am worried about her safety.

A few minutes pass and I fidget with my fingers. Girl is taking a while.

Reaching into my cloth bag, I grab my mother's case file. There is one more letter left and it falls easily into my lap when I open the folder. My eyes scan the Empress' words eagerly, hoping for some clue as to the whereabouts of my mother:

Autumn, 1998

Dear Maricelle,

The terrain bumps incessantly beneath the wheels of the carriage as we journey through the heart of Mira. I am grasping firmly onto my seat, as we rattle through a very loud and violent protest.

I am deeply shocked by the sight of civilians who are slaughtering animals in the streets. It is their visceral stand against the Emperor as they assert their rights to make and use tallow candles freely.

The carriage is being shaken and hit by civilians, causing it to sway off course. I pray silently that the driver can navigate the horses safely through the lashing anger that cuts through the air like a sharp knife.

Susan Marshall

A face presses against the window and I catch sight of the black headscarf on the young man's head. The gold, rearing horse gleams in the daylight, a reminder of the power of the Petoy clan.

Only yesterday, after our meeting, two young male clan members accosted me at the palace gate and demanded that in future I should hand them the beeswax candles that I had begun to provide to you. I was threatened with my life if I did not follow through with their request.

I refuse to submit to the hostile nature of the Petoy clan, whose acts of resistance against our empire have increased tenfold of late. Just now I see the clan's large truck making its way down the street. It is a rare sight in our ancient city, where we still rely on the horse and carriage.

This modern progress seems to excite the civilians, who believe that the Petoys will help them to succeed in the future. Many of them have defected to the clan and some are seated or standing in the cargo tray of the truck, punching their fists in the air in joint protest.

As we finally cut through the ear deafening protest, we are headed out towards the forest area.

It is quieter here and a chance for me to share one final confidence with you, Maricelle. The Emperor is highly superstitious and believes that my loss of both children has been inflicted upon me by the scent of the tallow candles. So he has replaced these with ones made of beeswax, which he believes, in their pure state, will improve my chances of success in fertility.

At the moment, there are also many bee hives scattered across the palace grounds. The Emperor has hired a famous bee keeper, named Carlos Rotaras to care for the bees and to also obtain their specific wax for candle making.

The Emperor has ordered my cook to present me with raw honey to eat every evening before I sleep. He believes that it will heal the impurities of the tallow and help me to blossom with child.

My thoughts are with you right now and I hope you are managing well in your own situation. I sincerely hope that I am helping in some small way as you trek the dangerous terrain carrying your own blossoming child.

While I continue to travel through the forest, I am saddened by the fact that this will be my final letter to you, Maricelle. I am in great danger of having such writing intercepted by either my superstitious husband or a member of the Petoy clan. I am fearful of what the consequences will be if such an event were to occur.

So, as we planned, I intend to provide you with all the used beeswax candles from the palace. It is very unsettling that the candles are only ever used once and replaced with fresh new ones. It is the Emperor's orders, as he wishes to gain the benefits of their purity.

In my time alone, I have walked the length and width of the palace and counted all the candles. There are 4246 of them in total, which are burning every day in order to provide as much light as possible. That many candles should not be wasted, yet used to provide opportunities.

I know that you will read this final letter after our upcoming brief meeting. However, I trust that you will use these beeswax candles to provide yourself and the people of Mira with better chances at life.

May you continue to honour our spirits of life,

Empress Celine.

Closing the file, I consider how frightened both the Empress and my mother are right now. The current resistance movement against the empire of Mira is very strong and I wonder just how many civilians have now defected to the promise of progress that the Petoys offer them.

An idea hits me: *Find the beeswax candles, find my mother.* I know my mother's generous heart. She will still be doing all that she can to help the civilians of Mira to find their feet again.

Placing the file into my bag, I stare out the window, waiting for Girl. There she is, exiting the café and carrying two take away cups and a bag of food. She waves for me to follow her as she passes by.

I open the door and hop out of the ute. Grabbing my bag, I shut and lock the door.

Walking quickly, I lower my head so that I can't be recognised. There are people everywhere.

"I'm with you," I say as I fall into step alongside Girl.

Girl nods, continuing to walk briskly.

I keep up with her, dodging the gazes of people walking passed us.

I am shaking nervously.

Soon we reach Spring Park. Crossing the grassland, Girl's gait becomes much lighter. She plonks down in a secluded area under an oak tree.

I sit next to her, allowing myself to exhale. "We got here safely," I sigh.

"Yes," Girl nods. "Harriet's Café was pretty empty. I managed to buy some food for us both." She hands me the cup and rifles through the paper bag, retrieving her egg and bacon roll.

"Thanks Girl," I smile, peeking inside the lid of my cup. It is a cappuccino. I take a sip. "Oh, that's lovely," I sigh with relief. It feels so good to drink a coffee. It is warming me up.

"That's the least I could do," Girl smiles. She takes a bite of her egg and bacon roll. "That's tasty," she says. "My first time eating one of these. Are they popular here?"

"Yes," I smile. "Especially as a take-away breakfast." I place my cup down onto the grass and dig into the paper bag, retrieving my egg and bacon roll. Unwrapping it, I take a bite, savouring the tasty flavour of the bacon. "Yum," I smile.

We eat quietly for a while, both absorbing the atmosphere. It is a lovely park that is lush and green. Shrubs and trees surround the borders of grassland, providing it with generous shading.

We are sitting a short distance away from the barbecues and play equipment. I can see a boy crossing the monkey bars. Another little girl is soaring high on a swing. She smiles as her mother helps to push her higher. How nice it would be to play so freely without fear.

Once we finish eating, I stand up, grabbing the rubbish and heading over to the bin.

Girl follows me closely. "Keep moving," she says, grabbing my arm as I finish disposing of the rubbish. "We're being tailed."

I glance behind me, spotting the silver Mercedes parked a few metres away from us. Its lights cast a dim glow.

Lowering my head, I keep walking, following Girl across the grass to the other side of the park.

Girl glances over her shoulder. "Tail's gone," she says. "Thank goodness."

I sigh with relief.

Girl glances at the station. "Are you ready to enter the subway?" She asks.

"Yes," I say. "We need to keep a low profile."

"Of course," Girl says. "Let's go."

"Focus," I say, as Girl walks briskly ahead of me. "Take on the persona of an early morning commuter. You are heading towards a specific destination. The people around you are ones to dodge passed as you try to get to your train on time."

"Got it!" Girl calls, keen to arrive at her destination.

As we approach the subway entrance, Girl's mouth drops open when she realises how busy it is. "Lots of people," she says softly, stopping in her tracks. She is paralysed with nervousness.

I realise that I need to take control of the situation.

I hold Girl's hand and begin walking with her, dodging passed the bodies on either side of us.

"Watch out!" A fiery, grey haired man calls, bumping into me as he pushes passed us.

I ignore him, continuing to guide Girl. We reach the top of the steps leading down to the subway. "Keep walking," I direct her.

We descend the staircase, still holding hands.

People push passed us but I ignore them, pulling Girl closer to me in order to save her from tripping or falling.

Once our feet hit the ground, I check the signs above us for platform 32. "This way," I lead Girl down an escalator and onto the platform. There is a train stationed here, being alighted by passengers who jump onto the other side of the escalator in order to exit the platform.

"Is this the platform?" Girl asks softly.

I nod. "We've come at a perfect time," I tell her. "There's lots of distraction."

Girl nods, understanding.

My eyes scan the platform, counting the benches along it: 1, 2, 3 … "Come with me," I say, pulling Girl towards the fourth bench. I sit on it and stare at her. "Work with me?" I ask her.

Girl nods. "Whatever you need."

I pull Girl towards me, letting her straddle my lap.

Girl smiles as she looks into my eyes. "Well," she says softly. "This is different," she reaches out to stroke my hair.

I smile at her, reaching under the bench and feeling around for an obvious drop. There it is! I can feel a firm, smooth card texture.

Feeling around more, I locate the tape that has been used to attach it to the bench. I use my fingernail to remove the tape and lift the card away from the wood. As I do so, my hand knocks against a second dead drop: a folded piece of paper. I feel around its edges, removing the single piece of tape attaching it to the bench.

"I've got two things," I say, holding my discoveries between us. I see that one is a photo and another a letter.

"You have?" Girl stares at the items. "Wow! Look at that photo!"

The photo is of Jacquelyn Botanica, wearing a dress decorated with a modern, green swirl print. She leans against a large truck and peers through the driver's window. Next to her, stands Naricia Petoy, whose lips are plastered into a satisfied smile. In front of them both is a pile of carton boxes, sealed and ready to be taken inside the building behind them.

A building with a large, neon sign that flashes the name: *Botanica*.

My heart freezes with sadness. "It seems that Jacquelyn has agreed to work with the Petoys," I say, wishing it wasn't true.

Yet, it *is* true. Jacquelyn has been brainwashed into the promise of progress that the Petoys have offered her.

"Gee, that was quick," Girl sighs. "Yet not surprising. Naricia has all sorts of places lined up for work so that she can build the Petoys' market. She just needs to find the right recruits. Ones like Jacquelyn, who are promised the world for some shady work in return."

My eyes widen. "What sort of shady work?" I ask her.

"Mostly illegal trade," Girl sighs. "Here, you'd better keep this photo. It's a good piece of evidence."

"Thank you," my is mind whirring. I pocket the photo and meet Girl's curious gaze.

"What's the other item?" She asks, staring at it.

I unfold the paper, noticing that it was originally letter locked. "A letter from Empress Celine of Mira to Concetta," I say.

"Why do you have that?" Girl asks.

"I'm not sure," I reply. "Let me read it aloud." The Empress' familiar, neat handwriting makes my heart skip a beat in anticipation of news of my mother:

Autumn, 2022

Dear Concetta,

Maricelle once told me that if she was missing, I should contact you. I fear for her safety in our dangerous world.

The streets of Mira drum their own savage beats as the Petoys rear their dark horses and threaten to attack. With so many civilians defected to the clan, it has made the streets very dangerous to roam.

My treks out on the roads of Mira are more challenging these days as I continue to grow older. I do my best to avoid the aggressive Petoys. The civilians know my face well and bow in my presence, often clutching at my skirts and staring at me with desperation in their eyes.

My heart breaks with sadness when I see evidence of their demise. Tattered and starving, the civilians are grateful to see the glow of the lantern hanging on my carriage. As the Emperor persists with his ban of the tallow candles, it is the brightest remaining light that they are able to see out on the darkened streets. *Vivo!* They cry, letting the light glow and radiate its warmth across their bodies.

It seems healing, the light, ridding the afflictions of many who arrive at our meeting place. Colds mysteriously disappear as do aches and pains once suffered. My heart warms when I see the civilians' faces relax with relief.

Last evening I handed many blankets and used beeswax candles to the civilians, wishing them warmth and good health in the cold chill of autumn. It is getting darker earlier these days and without light, many cannot engage in the work that they feel obliged to do.

Maricelle did not arrive at our meeting place last evening. I waited for over an hour for her to arrive, checking constantly over my shoulders for followers.

Whispers echoed amongst the civilians, informing me that Maricelle has gone underground. She is determined to keep the lights of life shining in those civilians who are currently forced to seek refuge in the shelters of caves.

The Petoys believe that taking beeswax candles or engaging in the city's major trade of silk making demonstrates unwelcome loyalty to the empire. More recently, civilians' homes have been burned and raided by the clan, who accuse them of betraying their resistance movement. Many families have also had their heritage silk garments stolen. Such ancient garments share the voices and narratives of their ancestors and are proudly marked with their family totems. I fear what the Petoy clan desires to do with the garments.

I am shaking as I sit here and write. I beg for your help to locate the wonderful Maricelle and to return the missing silk apparel to our traumatised people.

Warm wishes to you,

Empress Celine

I inhale a deep breath as I absorb the Empress' words. My mother is officially missing, possibly underground somewhere in Mira. Yet, in such adversity, she continues to help the civilians. I feel a deep sense of admiration for my mother.

"I wonder who Maricelle is," Girl says softly. "I hope she is found soon."

"She is my mother," I announce.

"Oh," Girl's expression saddens. "Are you okay?"

I bite my lip, feeling the enormity of sharing the news with Girl.

"I haven't seen her for a long time," I blurt. "I really miss her."

Girl is silent, giving me time to think. An image of my mother's face fills my mind. She is smiling and laughing as she holds me close. I feel a deep ache in my heart, wishing that I could see her again.

Girl rubs her forehead in frustration. "I can't believe how out of control the Petoys are," her cheeks redden. "They can't force the people of Mira to join their resistance."

"No, they can't," I agree. "We need to do all we can to find those silk garments. They may even show up here in Redbank."

"Yes, they may," Girl agrees. "Should we go now?" She reaches for my hand.

I pocket the letter and allow Girl to pull me up onto my feet. We climb the stairs slowly, the image of Jacquelyn's innocent face planted firmly in my mind.

Once we exit the subway, I pull Girl across the grass and stare into her eyes. "Looks like things are much bigger than we thought," I say.

"Yes," says Girl. "Let's head back to my studio and see if we can work out a plan."

"Good idea," I agree.

We begin to walk, cutting across the grassland back onto Lighthouse Boulevard. Girl grabs my hand and takes on a light jog, weaving her way through the crowd of people.

The faces and bodies just keep coming, pushing and pressing their ways passed us and making my head spin.

When we finally step out of the crowd, I exhale a deep sigh of relief. We are still safe.

Chapter 11

Later that afternoon, Girl drives the ute into the arts precinct on Shade Lane. As she pulls up outside an old, orange brick workshop, she smiles. "There's Sophie," she says.

My heart pounds in my chest. Subconsciously, I slide down in my seat.

"Are you okay, Lira?" Girl is concerned.

"Yes," I lie. Girl does not know about Mitch and Sophie. It is best not to drag up old news, especially about someone that Girl likes.

"Come on," Girl says, reaching over to open my door. "Let's say hi."

I inhale a deep breath and close my eyes. I can do this. Just for a moment I can look passed my hatred for Sophie and be nice.

Pushing open my door, I step outside the ute. My gaze rests upon the exotic beauty of Sophie Yang. Her long, black hair falls in thick strands across her bare, olive shoulders. She pushes it back, her striking brown eyes staring at me.

"Hello Ladies," says Sophie, her thick red lips forming a warm smile.

"H-hi," I stammer, taken aback by her beauty. I watch her adjust her tight fitting, sleeveless orange dress, which clings to her shapely curves and shows off her cleavage.

I can see why Mitch is attracted to her. There is something very come hither about Sophie.

"Hi Sophie," Girl sounds happy. "How are things going at your gallery?"

"Busy lately," says Sophie. "I seem to be getting a lot of new art in for sale."

"That's good for business," Girl says.

"Yes," Sophie's eyes light up. "Very good for business." She meets Girl's gaze. "How is Hidu?" She asks. "Is he treating you well?"

"Great, he is very supportive," a dreamy expression forms across Girl's face.

Hidu is Sophie's older brother. The siblings grew up very close back home in Mira and helped to run their family's small community garden. After they lost their home, Sophie knew that she had to find a way to help the family, so she packed and left for Redbank. She eventually opened up her own art gallery and began to sell and display art.

Girl's eyes are glowing. "I want to show you both my new work," she waves us towards the workshop building.

A big smile crosses my lips as I stare at the orange brick workshop. Girl has added some gorgeous lamps in its front window. They cast a soft, yellow glow on a sculpted forest that she has on display. I admire the intricate detail in the trees and grass. A sloping mountainside provides a majestic background to the forest, its carving smooth and lyrical.

"Your sculptures are so beautiful," I compliment Girl as she carries her box up to the front door.

"Yes, they certainly are," Sophie agrees, standing next to me. Something white shines in her hair and I look closer. It is tallow candle wax. I know that smell anywhere.

Stepping away, I try to calm my racing heart. As I turn my gaze back to the studio window, all I can think about is my mother.

"Thanks," Girl smiles at us over her shoulder. "This one is based on a setting from back home."

"Yes, I see it now. It's the forest of Mira," Sophie's eyes widen excitedly. "It looks as enchanting as it does back home."

"That's good," Girl smiles. "I was aiming for enchanting."

Sophie meets Girl's gaze. "I am so happy that this old workshop has worked out for you," she smiles. "You've brought such a vibrant life to the space. To think that I've only ever used it to repair and conserve art. You've transformed the space into a studio. Girl's studio."

Girl's face softens. "Really? Thank you Sophie, that means a lot. I am so grateful that you have let me use your workshop while I am in town."

"You're practically family," Sophie smiles. "You can use this space for as long as you need." She steps back from the window. "I'd better head back to my gallery," she says. "I've got a lot of work to do."

"Okay," Girl smiles. "See you again soon."

"See you," Sophie waves as she walks away, her striking brown eyes glowing in the light. We watch her turn left down Glass Road and disappear towards her gallery.

After Sophie leaves, I sigh with relief. My shoulders feel sore and I realise that I have been tensing them. I rotate them, trying to loosen their muscles.

"Wow," Girl is smiling. "Girl's Studio, eh? It has a nice ring to it." She approaches the ute tray and lifts two boxes, carrying them in her arms. Approaching me, her eyes light up again. "I have more work to show you," she smiles. "Come and see." Unlocking the front door, she steps inside her studio.

I follow Girl, smiling as my eyes fall upon the range of sculptures that she has on display on her work bench.

"Wow!" I am amazed at the beauty of the birds and the flowers that she has created.

"You like these?" Girl asks, placing her boxes down onto her workbench. "I miss the beauty of home so much, it's nice to be able to recreate it through art."

"They are so precious, so beautiful," I say, bending down to study the detail of a rabbit. "Your sculpture art is like poetry."

"What a lovely thing to say," Girl says softly. "That's really touching, Lira."

Girl opens one of the boxes and takes out her wrapped statue. Once she removes the tissue paper, I inhale a sharp breath of admiration. It is very striking with the deep blue waves of the sea rising and falling at different heights in poetic, smooth lines. On the crests of a few waves, Girl has carved two different totems in white: a claw and an eagle's talon.

A gently rippling body of deep blue water sits at the bottom of the waves. Across it rides a small, grey boat with its white sail hoisted up high into the air. Inside the boat is a person with olive toned skin, dressed in a white linen dress. Her hair is long and black and she is rowing oars and smiling as she stares up at the sky.

"What do you think?" Girl asks, waiting for my reaction.

"It is divine," I say. "So spiritual and rhythmic."

"Thank you," Girl is touched. "This sculpture shares one of my precious memories from home." She strokes the art work and begins to sing:

> *"Where the trees meet the sea,*
> *lies a forest of ancient history.*
> *Here a true love did thrive,*
> *burning its candle through time.*
>
> *"Ages later, here she stands,*
> *a daughter of love's true flame.*
> *She is the future of Mira's trade,*
> *at once loved and betrayed.*
>
> *"Her bare feet kiss the earth farewell*
> *as she steps towards the sea.*
> *Climbing aboard her small boat,*
> *she stares ahead at the unknown.*
>
> *"In the hull she carries wares*
> *that share her story upon land.*
> *A claw and a flying eagle,*
> *carry the spirits of her home.*

"The boat rides choppy crests,
below a fiery, deep red sky.
A warning that danger awaits,
her unique being upon her land.

"She leaves the waters as they be,
to follow her past upon her feet.
Within the red bank of peril
are the answers that she seeks."

Girl's gaze rests upon her sculpture. She presses her hand gently on the rowing girl.

"What an amazing song," I say admiringly.

"Thank you," Girl smiles, her thoughts a mile away.

"You must miss home so much," I sigh.

"I do," Girl nods, her eyes watery. "This sculpture is my connection with home," she says. "I've been working on it since I arrived here."

"Yes," I say, remembering. "Concetta said that she filmed a lot of your work on this."

"What about one last video?" Girl wipes away her tears. "You can document it as work completed."

"Sure," I reach into my bag and retrieve my video camera. Peering through the view finder, I zoom the lens into focus on Girl and the statue. "Ready?" I ask.

"Yes," Girl says, a small smile forming on her lips.

I press record and watch Girl present Beach Crescendo. As she hugs the statue, tears build in my eyes. I know how much it means to Girl to share this piece. She's put her heart and soul into it.

"It's been an honour to have you share your work with me," I choke on my words as I place my video camera back into my bag. "I know how much it means to you."

"Oh Lira, please don't cry," Girl rushes around the table and wraps her arms around me. "You'll make me start again too."

I close my eyes, feeling the warmth of Girl's hug.

After a moment, Girl steps back, wiping away her own tears. "See?" She sighs. "You've got me weeping too."

Once we've both relaxed, Girl reaches for a purple silk bag that lies strewn across the work bench. Digging into it, she reveals a small, bronze coloured book.

"What a beautiful book," I say, admiring the blue, shimmering wave pattern on the front cover.

"Yes, it is, isn't it?" Girl agrees. "It is a journal that belonged to my ancestor, my great, great, great, great, great, great grandmother, Aisha." Girl flicks through the book, her eyes lighting up when she discovers the page that she is after. "Would you like to read an entry?" She asks.

"Of course," my eyes widen in surprise. "It would be a great privilege to read some of your family history, Girl." I receive the open journal in my hands and am met with very elegant writing, making it a pleasure to read:

Winter, 1275

The forest of Mira is beautiful at night. The moonlight bounces off the trees, casting shadows that do not frighten me. Instead, I feel that they are company as I step gently across the tall grass stalks.

Approaching the old cedar tree, I dig into the pocket of my mint green dress and retrieve my white silk scarf. Caressing it gently, I give it a kiss before tying it around the branch of the cedar tree. Closing my eyes for a single moment, I feel my heart swell with love as I remember my betrothed, Kirano's face. If only I could see him now ...

Ahwoo!

Startled, I jump high into the air. Cocking my ears, I listen closely. The sound echoes throughout the forest. I realise that it is the howling of wolves, not too far away in the distance. At this time of the evening, they would be on the hunt for food.

Ahwoo!

The howling sounds more agonised and louder than usual tonight. Something has clearly disrupted the wolves.

Stepping quietly across the grass, I peer through the trees into the distance. I can see lights flashing and a flurry of movement. The tents are being set up for Empress Mira's winter solstice celebration.

The first tent to be erected belongs to the Empress. I see the gold and indigo swirling pattern on it now, the traditional colours belonging to her ancestry. It is decorated with numerous candle lanterns, which are hung on its poles and are swinging gently in the breeze.

Surrounding the Empress' tent on one side are those of the barons and on the other, their wives, the baronesses. It is etiquette for the man and woman to sleep separately. If necessary, the men must be ready to take on combat and the women be prepared to attend to the Empress at a moment's notice.

The household staff rest in tents pitched further behind the Empress' lodgings. At the moment, I see that they are in quite the flurry, preparing food for a celebratory feast.

Each year the Empress arrives here with her entire household to celebrate the end of shorter days and darkness and to welcome the proceeding light of spring.

Tonight is the longest night of the year and the Empress is seated at the head of a long wicker table threaded with leaf and branch trimmings from the surrounding cedar trees. The barons and baronesses who chat excitedly amongst themselves accompany her. Several kindling fires are lit around the boundary of the campsite. Sparking the energy of light across the night sky, the fires celebrate the forthcoming dawn of spring and provide ample light for the celebration.

She is very beautiful, the Empress. Blessed with long, wavy brown hair, she allows it to flow freely in the wind. She smiles a warm smile which lights up her deep blue eyes as she admires the abundance of food and decorations that fill the table.

Looking closely, I see that true to her love of nature, the Empress wears a silver silk jacket with a brocade of ladybugs, birds, trees and flowers. It is buttoned right up to her neck and covers her entire body, down to her ankles.

Snap!

Makeshift Girl: The Secret Heritage Trail

I jump at the sudden, intrusive sound. Pressing myself against a tree, I hold my breath as I hear the footsteps crunching across the forest floor. My heart thumps in my chest as the fear begins to overcome me. I cannot afford to be discovered here. It is forbidden for a young woman to be out in the forest at night, especially on her own.

Pressing my nails firmly into the bark of the tree, I watch as a silhouette reveals itself in the moonlight. Tall and built, the human frame enters the clearing that I stand in. My eyes are immediately drawn to the breathtaking sight of his face. I am familiar with those deep brown eyes, which draw me gently towards him. I let him pull me into his warm embrace.

"Kirano!" I breathe, pressing my head against his regal blue jacket. I can hear his heart beating rapidly with excitement.

"Aisha," Kirano's voice is as soothing as I remember. Looking up, I see his warm, adoring smile. "I see that you tied your favourite silk scarf to the tree."

I smile back. "It helped you to find me," I say softly, my heart dancing with happiness.

For a moment, we stare deeply into each other's eyes. I can see the gold flecks shining in his.

Kirano strokes my cheek gently and crooks up my chin with the nook of his finger. I close my eyes, enjoying the sensation of his lips pressing against mine. It sends a tingle from my heart down to my toes.

Stepping back, Kirano studies me. "You are even more beautiful than any memory could serve," he says admiringly. "Your long, shiny black hair seems to almost dance in the wind and those deep green eyes of yours are quite mesmerising."

Kirano's compliments warm my heart. It is dangerous for him to be here with me. A regal soldier must demonstrate absolute devotion to the Empress and not be distracted by a common villager.

I watch as Kirano steps back and unties the silk scarf from the tree.

"Thank you," I say, as he wraps the scarf around my neck. "I feel warmer now."

Kirano grabs my hands and rubs them together. "You are very cold," he says, staring into my eyes.

Ahwoo!

We both jump at the sudden howl.

I hear a rustle behind the trees. I know that sound very well.

"Stand back!" I command, pushing Kirano behind me. "A wolf has arrived."

There, creeping out from behind the trees is a majestic male wolf with grey and brown fur. Acutely alert, it stares intensely at us with its golden eyes.

"Hello Sinta," I say, meeting the wolf's gaze. Sinta cocks his head to one side, studying me.

"You know the wolf?" Kirano's voice is strong, causing Sinta to arch his back, his ears pricking up and alert. In a moment, the wolf will attack.

"Ssh," I whisper. "Let me tend to this."

Sinta takes a few steps forward, his gaze now focused on Kirano. He licks his lips with hunger and snarls, displaying his strong white teeth.

My heart beats rapidly. I have only seen Sinta this way when he is about to attack prey. He is clearly asserting his dominance over Kirano. I need to think quickly and cause a distraction.

An idea enters my mind. I pull the scarf away from my neck and hold it up high. "Here Sinta," I say gently, waving the scarf through the air.

Sinta looks up at the scarf, his eyes lighting up with excitement. Snatching it in his claws, he pounces on it, scratching the material and sniffing at it.

"Good boy," I say, stepping closer to him and scratching him under his jaw. Sinta looks up at me, his eyes glazed.

Digging into my pocket, I pull out a piece of raw venison. "Here," I say, placing the food on the grass before him.

Sinta pounces on the food and tears at it with his claws. He eats ravenously, his attention completely focused on his meal.

Looking up at Kirano, I see that his mouth has dropped open in amazement.

"Go!" I mouth silently to Kirano, waving him away.

Still in awe, Kirano nods and steps backwards. He blows me a gentle kiss before he disappears behind the trees.

Makeshift Girl: The Secret Heritage Trail

I pick up the scarf and tie it around my neck. Looking down at Sinta, I see that he is still hungry. If I don't feed him more food immediately, he will attack the crowd of people behind the trees.

"Up!" I say, coaxing Sinta to stand. He jumps up onto his feet.

Digging into my pocket, I pull out another piece of venison.

Sinta swipes at it with his claw, his eyes burning with excitement at the sight of the food.

"Not yet," I say, walking ahead of him. "Follow me." Stepping gently, I hold the venison towards him, enticing him to follow me away from the trees and the crowd.

Sinta and I walk silently, keeping each other company and disappearing into the pitch black night.

Looking up from the journal, I feel flushed with excitement. "What a brave woman Aisha was, Girl," I smile. "She was amazing with the wolf."

Girl nods. "Yes, she was," she agrees.

"I can see where you get your determination from," I say, drawing connections between Girl and her ancestor.

"My mother says that too," Girl smiles warmly. "I guess I do."

"Can I read some more?" I ask, keen to know what happens next.

"When the time is right," a thoughtful expression crosses Girl's face.

"Alright," I sigh, handing the journal back reluctantly.

Girl places the journal into her silk bag, which she lays on the work bench. She scratches her head for a moment, thinking.

"Is everything okay?" I ask her.

Suddenly, Girl dashes towards the front of the studio. "That's right!" She calls as she picks up a flyer.

"What is it?" I ask, heading over to join her.

"It's a flyer advertising Botanica, Jacquelyn's new fashion boutique. I saw it inserted under the front door when I opened it." Girl points to the flyer. "It'd be interesting to see what she has on display."

"Definitely," I agree. "It looks like it's on Bloom Street, right next to Spring Park."

"Let's check it out tomorrow," Girl says. "It may give us a new lead."

"Great idea," I say.

Girl opens up a box and pulls out a can. "I know it's not glamorous," she says. "Are you hungry for canned tomato soup? It's all I've got."

"Sounds great," I say. My stomach is rumbling.

Girl opens the can and pours it into a microwave bowl on her bench. She seals the lid and pops it into the microwave. "I ate this soup when I worked here on late nights," she says as she selects the heat level, the time and presses the start button. The microwave whirs into action. "It was safer than heading outdoors."

"Of course," I agree. "You've got to do all you can to keep safe."

Beep!

The microwave has completed cooking.

Girl opens the door and uses a cloth to take the hot, steaming bowl out of the microwave.

"Can you grab that clean mug next to you, Lira?" Girl asks as she places the bowl down onto the bench.

I grab the mug and join Girl as she removes the lid from the bowl. "Place your mug down here," she points to a spot on the bench.

I place the mug down and watch as Girl pours soup into it.

"There you go," Girl says. "Hope that's enough to eat."

"It's perfect," I say as I take a sip of the soup. It has a mild tomato flavour and feels good going down.

Girl sips from the bowl. "Life on the run means no luxuries like cutlery," she smiles, tomato soup smeared all over her mouth.

"Who needs cutlery?" I shrug, smiling at Girl.

"Not me!" Girl laughs, taking another large sip of soup.

Chapter 12

Early the next morning, Girl parks the ute along Flag Road. "A good place to park," Girl says. "Nice and quiet." She adjusts her sunglasses on the bridge of her nose and opens the driver's door.

As I step out of the ute, my eyes fall on a tall, dark blue building with many shiny glass windows. Displayed on the right side of the building is a large billboard advertisement, which reads: *Vote 1: Alexander Rahi for Mayor & Leader who Empowers.*

I study the face of the Mayor. He has dark brown hair and shiny, olive skin. Fine lines crease upon his forehead while he raises his eyebrows and widens his large, brown eyes. His right hand is formed into a fist, which he clutches to his chest. He smiles a firm smile, as though he is demonstrating internal strength.

"A strong advertisement," I say, peering over my shoulder at Girl.

"Yes," she agrees as she steps closer to the billboard. "I wonder what he aims to empower?"

"Good question," I reply, walking around to the front of the building. Two more posters with the same image and message as the billboard, hang from the windows either side of the front door.

My eyes fall upon a single poster stuck to the front, silver metal door and I point to it, drawing Girl's attention. The message reads: *Meet His Honourable Mayor, Rahi Alexander at the Redbank Artists' Market at the Town Square.*

"I'll be there," Girl says decisively. "Do you want to come with me?"

"Sure," I say. "It can only help us."

"Let's keep walking," Girl steps ahead. "We don't want to be caught facing early morning work commuters."

We walk further along Flag Road and turn right onto Bloom Street. Soon we reach Botanica, a rendered brick building, painted a deep green colour. Two large display windows glisten at the front of the store.

"Good," Girl points to the closed sign displayed on the front door. "We're early enough to get a feel for the place before the shop opens."

I approach the shop window on the left and admire the range of fashion on display. There is a mannequin wearing a yellow floral dress. Another mannequin is adorned with a silver blouse and a red leaf printed skirt.

"Oh no!" Girl gasps, pointing at a display. "It can't be!"

"What's the matter?" I ask, my gaze resting upon a number of silk scarves lying on a wooden table in the display window.

Girl inhales a sharp breath and points once more at a design. "See this silk scarf here?" She says, bringing my attention to a beautiful, sheer orange scarf, embroidered with images of the sun. "This totem belongs to the Jandoe family from back home. It has been in their family for generations and is precious to them. They would never want to see it on display in a store like this."

My mind whirs as I absorb what Girl is saying. Why would Jacquelyn be producing works like this? Her works have always been original in the forest.

"The totems of the elephant and lotus on this scarf here, belong to the Vess family," Girl's voice lashes. "They are antique totems from many past generations and are used for specific family and celebration purposes. Someone has obviously appropriated the authentic totems in order to create this replica scarf."

I stare at the scarf. It seems as though it is made of silk too, appearing to be sheer and light.

Girl stamps her feet. "What does Jacquelyn think she is doing?" She begins to pull at her hair. "She can't do this to people."

I let Girl have the space she needs to absorb what she has learned.

My mind is trying to compute what it all means.

A minute later, a blue van pulls up at the front of the store.

I see a flash of dark blonde hair exit from the driver's door. A tall body appears next, wearing a bottle green linen dress with embroidered yellow sunflowers. Facing the store, the lady's light green eyes twinkle and her hair floats gently in the breeze. It is Jacquelyn Botanica.

I watch Jacquelyn tread softly across the footpath in her brown sandals. She has an air of lightness about her and as she reaches us, she smiles a kind smile.

"Good morning Lira," Jacquelyn's green eyes twinkle. "How are you and your friend today?"

"Great thank you," I reply, trying to take the focus away from the very livid Girl.

Jacquelyn's smile broadens. It sets off the healthy peach glow of her cheeks. "Are you shopping for clothing? I'm sure that I can help you find something suitable."

I stare at Jacquelyn, observing her peaceful and kind expression. I have known her for many years and she has always taken such pride and care in her natural threads and materials. Her designs truly come from her heart.

"It would be lovely to see your designs," I say, still feeling confused by the silk display.

Jacquelyn reaches into her dress pocket and retrieves a bundle of keys. "Do come inside and take a look," she smiles gently as she opens the front door.

Huffing, Girl storms into the store.

I follow behind, determined to keep Girl out of trouble.

Once I enter the store, the colours and styles of fashion on display amaze me. Jacquelyn is very passionate about nature and this is evident in her designs. A strawberry printed dress hangs from a rack, accompanied by a button up blouse and skirt of the same design. My eyes fall upon a royal blue evening dress, embroidered with fine golden leaves, displayed on the far right wall.

Suddenly, I feel a presence on my left. It is Jacquelyn. Her smile is broad and welcoming.

"Can I help you with anything Lira?" Jacquelyn asks. "Size? Colour? Material?"

"Do you have anymore of these?" Girl gets to the point, still hiding behind her sunglasses. She points at the silk scarves at the front of the store.

Jacquelyn's eyes narrow and her cheeks redden. "Oh yes, many of them," she drags out a cardboard box lying underneath the bench that the scarves are displayed on. "How many do you need?" She asks as she sorts through the scarves.

While Jacquelyn is preoccupied, I sneak out my phone and photograph the scarves on display. Good to have the evidence.

Jacquelyn makes two piles of scarves, each containing exact replicas of both the sun and elephant and lotus designs. "We have lots of these scarves available," Jacquelyn's voice sounds sad. "They are very popular with our customers. Would you like to feel the sheer material?"

Girl's lips press together. She begins to pull at her hair. "No, thank you," she says through gritted teeth.

I step in front of Girl, protecting her from an outburst. "We're not sure what we're after yet," I smile at Jacquelyn. "We have a couple of birthdays to plan for. We'll let you know when we decide."

"Of course," Jacquelyn smiles, pushing the box back under the bench. "I will let you both browse."

"How much are the scarves?" Girl blurts while pulling at her hair again.

"Two hundred and forty five dollars each," Jacquelyn replies, staring into space. "I'm sure you'll appreciate that they are indeed an exquisite collection." Her voice is unfeeling and monotone.

Girl's hands form into fists and her cheeks redden.

Jacquelyn meets my gaze, her eyebrows raised with concern. "Feel free to browse through the rest of the store," she says calmly. "As you know, Lira, I have handmade all the apparel at the back with local, organic cotton. They are priced reasonably for the customer."

"No thank you!" Girl is livid.

Jacquelyn steps back, startled. She shuffles her feet nervously on the floor.

I place my hand on Girl's shoulder, attempting to calm her down. My gaze shifts back to Jacquelyn who looks sad.

"Are you okay Jacquelyn?" I ask, concerned about her. "You know you can talk to me about anything."

Jacquelyn's eyes light up with hope. "Thank you Lira, I will remember that."

I can't help but launch my question at her. "Are these scarves being distributed anywhere else?"

Jacquelyn stares directly into my eyes. "Plans are being made to have them sold internationally," she says, her eyes darkening. "When, I am not sure," her gaze drifts away from me.

Girl is seething. I can almost see smoke blowing out of her ears.

I grab Girl's arm and pull her towards the front door. "We've got to go," I call out as we exit. "We're running late for a meeting. We'll be back another time."

"Enjoy your day," Jacquelyn's voice cracks as she watches us leave.

Once we hit the street, Girl pulls her arm out of my grasp.

"I am so angry right now," she seethes, her cheeks now a deep red. "This is just not right."

I wrap my arm around Girl's shoulder and direct her back towards Flag Road.

"I'm sorry," I say. "I can only imagine how stressful this is for you."

"Stressful?" Girl lashes. "You have no idea what this all means."

Reaching the ute, I open the driver's door. "Tell me," I say, ensuring that she pops safely inside.

Girl sits down and crosses her arms over her chest angrily.

I jog to the passenger side, pull open the door and jump into my seat. Closing my door, I turn to look at Girl.

"We're in real trouble back home," Girl's eyes narrow. "We need to find out more about these silk designs," she decides. "As they stand, they are counterfeit and their production must be stopped."

"I understand," I say, supporting Girl. "What Jacquelyn is doing is completely out of character for her. Her works are usually very natural and handmade. I don't think she fully realised what she was becoming involved in."

"She should just walk away," Girl huffs.

"It may not be that easy," I say gently, trying to help Girl see reason. "There's often a lot more to the story than what is visible."

My phone is ringing.

"Sorry, I just need to take this call," I say, retrieving my phone from my pocket.

I notice Mitch's name flashing on the screen as the caller identification.

"Hi Mitch," I say, answering the phone.

"Hi Lira," Mitch sounds flustered.

"Is everything okay?" I ask him.

"No," Mitch replies. "I'm stuck in the middle of Clarice Road. Do you know where that is?"

"Yes," I say. "We're not too far away. We'll come and help."

"You'll see my van on the side of the road," Mitch sighs.

"Okay, see you soon." I pocket my phone.

"Is everything alright?" Girl asks.

"Mitch is stuck on Clarice Road. He needs our help." I tell her.

"Let's go," Girl turns on the ignition. She pulls out onto Bloom Street and does a u-turn, heading towards Flag Road.

Turning left onto Flag Road, Girl revs the ute, picking up speed. She brakes suddenly as she approaches Lighthouse Boulevard.

"It's getting busy," Girl says, noting the traffic building around us. She turns right onto the Boulevard and crawls at a snail's pace behind the cars. "Come on!" She calls out. "I could get there faster on foot!"

I believe that she could.

After a few minutes, the traffic clears and Girl turns right onto Clarice Road.

"There is Mitch's van," I say, pointing at it. The van's hazard lights are flashing. I feel my heart flooding with worry for his safety and a desperate urge to be with him.

Girl pulls up behind the van and breaks, turning off the ignition and pulling the handbrake firmly.

I open my door and jump out. Girl is following closely behind me as I dash over to the van.

"Mitch?" I call, jumping up to see if I can spot him through the driver's window.

"Lira, watch out!" Girl pulls me off the road just in time. A red Lexus roars passed us with its horn blaring.

I gasp in shock, my heart pounding. "Wow!" I exclaim. "That was close."

"Yes," says Girl. She wraps her arm around my shoulder.

It takes me a moment to calm myself down.

"Thanks for rescuing me," I say, smiling weakly at Girl.

"Any time," Girl soothes, rubbing my back.

"Lira, are you okay?" Mitch jumps out of the driver's side of the van. His face is etched with lines of worry.

I nod, exhaling a sigh of relief. "You're okay," I say to him. "I –"

"You were worried about *me*?" Mitch asks, a relieved smile forming on his lips.

I nod, still trying to catch a breath.

"That's nice," Mitch smiles. He looks at Girl. "That was really quick thinking back there."

"It's what the city's taught me," Girl says. "Everything happens so rapidly here. I often wonder when things will begin to slow down."

"Never," Mitch says, shaking his head. "The city is obsessed with keeping its wheels churning. Trade rolls around the clock here, to keep it going. People work so hard, they seem to have lost track of what's real." He gazes off into the distance, his mind a world away.

"Are you okay, Mitch?" Girl asks concernedly.

Mitch snaps out of his thoughts. "I don't know," he sighs. "I am working in a very dangerous industry."

"What's happened?" I reach out to touch his shoulder.

Mitch places his hand over mine and smiles weakly. "I got run off the road," he says. "A very large truck tailgated me, its lights were blinding. I could hardly see and wound up spinning out of control across the road. Luckily my fight instinct kicked in and I managed to pull the van onto the side of the road here."

Instinctively, I pull Mitch close, hugging him tightly. "I'm sorry," I say to him. "That must have been very scary."

"It was," he says, embracing me.

"Poor thing," I soothe. Pressing my head against his chest, I listen to his pounding heart.

"I've busted a tyre. I can't drive right now." Mitch sounds defeated.

"Don't worry about that," Girl says. "Have you got a spare?"

"Yes," Mitch nods. "In the boot."

"I'll change it," Girl opens the boot. "You'll be back on the road in no time," she calls over her shoulder.

Makeshift Girl: The Secret Heritage Trail

Mitch shakes his head as Girl drags a large spare wheel out of the boot. "She is amazing," he says.

"I know," I say, stepping backwards. I have an idea. "Do you mind if I inspect your van?"

Mitch raises his eyebrows. "Sure …" He is puzzled.

"Give me a minute before you change that tyre, Girl," I say.

"Okay," Girl steps back, waiting.

Approaching the van, I lie on my back and check the undercarriage for signs of any tracking devices. There is nothing around the front. As I scoot towards the back of the van, I see a small light flashing. Shuffling closer, I check the object.

"Aha!" I call out to my imaginary audience. "A GPS tracker!"

Reaching up, I tear away the adhesive and release the tracker. I catch it in my hands.

Sliding out from under the van, I pull myself up. "All good for you to go now, Girl," I call.

"Thanks!" Girl grabs a jack out of the boot and sets to work.

I approach Mitch and hand him the GPS tracker. "Here you go," I say. "It looks like you're being tracked."

"Really?" Mitch's eyes widen. "That explains a lot."

"I wonder why you're being tracked?" I ask aloud.

Mitch lowers his head, thinking. "That right!" He exclaims. "Follow me!" He opens the boot and drags out a cardboard box. "Strange things have been happening to me since I began collecting and delivering these boxes," he says. "Oddly, there is no identifiable label on them."

"Have you checked what's inside them?" I ask him. "That might give you some answers."

"I don't dare to," says Mitch. "I have a really tight time frame to deliver them. Lateness results in the confrontation by someone from the delivery company, just like the other day. I wouldn't want anyone to believe that I am tampering with the boxes."

"Hmmm," I think aloud. "If I were you, I'd deliver that box like you should. When you arrive there, park the van far away and walk in, so no more tracking can be attached. When you've completed this job, stick to the time frames of the deliveries." I touch his face gently. "I don't want you in anymore danger, my love. I think these truck drivers are involved in a very dangerous and possibly illegal business."

"You are probably right," Mitch sighs. "I will do as you've suggested. Thanks for looking after me, Lira."

I let his words fill my heart with hope.

Mitch's blue eyes twinkle and he stares into mine.

I know that twinkle. It usually occurs just before Mitch …

Leaning towards me, Mitch presses his lips firmly against mine.

I have missed his lips and the thrilling sensation of his kiss. I close my eyes, feeling my heart fluttering wildly in my chest.

Mitch pulls back, staring into my eyes. "I love you," he says softly.

I stare at him, mesmerised by the twinkle in his eyes. I feel warmth nestling into my heart.

I wish I could wipe the memory of his intimacy with Sophie out of my mind.

"Tyre's done!" Girl calls out, causing us to step apart. She approaches the boot, rolling the old wheel. "You're good to go now Mitch!"

"Thanks Girl," Mitch helps Girl load the old wheel into the boot. "I really appreciate it."

"I enjoyed that," Girl smiles. "It was good physical labour. It reminded me of some of the work I used to do back home." She glances at the tracker in my hands. "What have you got there, Lira?"

"A GPS tracker," I say. "It was stuck on the undercarriage of Mitch's van. Someone has been keeping track of his every move."

Girl frowns, her brain ticking.

"We're going to have some fun with this tracker," I say. "Let's leave it behind this daisy bush here. It'd be a great way to see who comes looking for you, Mitch."

"A great idea," says Mitch. He pulls me close and kisses me on the forehead. "Thanks for everything, Lira."

"My pleasure," I smile. "I'll be in touch soon."

"Speak soon," Mitch grins. "Thanks again Girl," he says as he opens the driver's door of his van.

"Not a problem," Girl smiles and waves.

We watch as Mitch starts the ignition and pulls out onto the main road.

My heart pounds with worry as I watch him go.

Once Mitch's van has disappeared into the distance, I face Girl. "We'd better hop into the ute," I say. "Mitch's tracker could arrive at any moment."

We dash back to the ute and I open the passenger door. Sitting upright in my seat, I take a quick glance at Girl, who is resting her head on the steering wheel.

"Are you okay?" I ask her.

"Just really tired," she says, rubbing her eyes. "Life on the run is very difficult."

"I know," I agree. "Let's hope that we get some new leads soon."

"Yes," Girl nods, running her fingers across the steering wheel. "Is this a stakeout?"

"I guess you could say it is," I smile.

"If only we had some donuts," Girl giggles. "Stakeouts can go for a long time, can't they?"

"Sometimes," I say. "However, I think this stakeout will be a short one. Very soon someone will arrive here to kick Mitch's butt back into gear. It'll be interesting to see who it is."

Chapter 13

We sit in the ute, staring out the windscreen for a very long time. I can feel the sensation of pins and needles in both my ankles. I kick them into the air, trying to keep my blood circulating.

The clock on the dash board continues to click over:
10 minutes.
25 minutes.
40 minutes.

Car after car zooms passed us, pricking my ears up for the sound of a truck each time.

No truck yet.

Girl is remarkably patient. She gazes out her window with a thoughtful expression on her face. At one point she jumps upright. Opening her door, she leans outside and stares at the road.

"What are you doing?" I am concerned for her safety.

"Watching something," Girl points across the road. "See that green neon sign in front of Tora's Take Away Noodle store?"

I peer out the open driver's door, my eyes falling upon a bright green neon sign that announces: *Open late for take away, 7 days*.

"Watch how the sign flashes and then blacks out once a truck stops in front of the store," says Girl.

Makeshift Girl: The Secret Heritage Trail

I keep my eye on the sign. One flash ... two ... a truck suddenly pulls into the curb outside the store, its breaks squealing loudly as it comes to an abrupt stop. The neon light blacks out automatically.

Girl slams the driver's door. "The driver is crossing the road," she gasps, shrinking back into her seat.

I watch as a tall man with a stocky build steps onto the footpath ahead of us. His light brown hair is combed over to one side and his fringe flaps wildly in his face. Large yet narrowed, his dark eyes peer at his mobile. Furrowing his eyebrows with deep concentration, he reveals several deep character lines on his forehead. The man could possibly be in his early forties.

As the man continues to stare at his mobile phone, his yellow safety vest loosens itself up and flaps wildly in the breeze, hitting him in the face. I watch him swat away at the vest, taming it under control aggressively. Pulling down the vest, he presses the Velcro back together and flattens it against his zip up brown jumper.

I see the man's mobile phone flashing and watch as his dark, menacing eyes take in the message. Springing into action, his blue jeaned legs take short steps across the asphalt as he looks around for something ...

"That's him!" I grab Girl's arm. "He's looking for Mitch!" I slide down in my seat. "We can't afford to be seen," I gasp.

Girl nods and slides down in her seat too.

I watch as the man scratches his head in confusion. There is no truck or driver to be found.

Reaching into my bag, I retrieve my mobile phone and set it to camera mode. I hold the phone up in the air, waiting until the man faces us ...

There he is. He certainly has dark, spooky eyes. His brow wears the deep creases of hard work and stress.

I snap a quick photo of him and bob back down into my seat. Whoever he is, he is after Mitch.

The man stamps his feet in frustration. "What the ... ?" He calls out to no-one, his voice strong and lashing as his hands cut through the air.

I feel the hair stand up on the back of my neck. This man is not one you would want to get onto the bad side of.

Taking one last glance around him, the man shrugs. He pockets his phone and sighs. Waiting for the traffic to clear, he begins to cross the road in long strides and enters Taro's Take Away Noodle Store.

"Let's see what he exits with," Girl says. "There is something a little strange about this store."

We continue to survey the store for a few more minutes.

Suddenly, the man exits the store and stops in front of the entrance. He examines the contents of a white envelope and punches his right fist in the air with excitement. Peering over his shoulder, as though he is checking for followers, he quickly tucks the envelope behind his safety vest and pats it, smiling contentedly.

Girl looks at me. "Interesting, eh?"

"Yes," I say, keeping my eyes on the man as he jumps back into his truck. As he merges back into the traffic, I quickly make a mental note of his number plate.

"Redfin," I say aloud, noting it down on my phone. "What an interesting registration name."

"Yes," Girl agrees. "Must be his handle or something."

"Perhaps," I mull over the word. "Redfin. Sounds daring and dangerous."

Girl taps me on the shoulder. "Look!" She says, pointing to the green neon light. "It's flashing again."

"Mmm," I mutter aloud. "It seems like the business that Mitch is involved in is undertaking some dark and dangerous work."

"Agreed," Girl's eyes narrow. "I hope Mitch is going to be okay."

"Me too," I bite my lip worriedly.

After a moment, I swing open my door. "I'll be back in a minute," I call.

Dashing across the footpath, I push aside the daisy flowers. There is the GPS tracker, still flashing. Grabbing it, I switch it off and return to the ute.

"We're not going to leave it here?" Girl asks, watching me slide back into my seat.

"No way," I puff, trying to catch a breath. "It will get Mitch into trouble. We've discovered who is after him. We will need to re-install this onto his van as soon as possible."

"I see," Girl's eyes are wide. "The last thing we want is more danger for him."

"Yes," I shudder. "These truckers certainly mean business. They won't hesitate to discard of Mitch if necessary."

"You think?" Girl's mouth drops open. "That's really scary."

I nod, glancing at the man's photo on my phone. "We need to work out who this man is," I say to her. "He seems to be a little higher up in the chain."

It is quiet for a moment as we both ponder.

"What a morning it's been," Girl finally says, sitting upright in her seat and turning the key in the ignition. "Full of shocks and surprises."

"Yes," I agree, my mind flicking through recent events. "I'm glad we're all okay."

"Me too," Girl agrees. "Ready to go?"

"Yes," I nod, holding onto my seat with both hands.

Girl indicates right and waits for the traffic to clear.

Heading out onto the road, she does a u-turn and drives back towards the city.

I am surprised that Girl isn't speeding this time. I let go of my seat and settle back.

While Girl drives, I study the features of the man in the photograph. He is very strong and menacing.

Chapter 14

That evening, Girl and I decide to explore the city. Crossing over to Veta Street, we become immersed in the spectacles of night life. People are out and about everywhere, expelling a vibrant energy that is contagious. The ever cautious me keeps an eye on the road, concerned for our safety on the streets.

An electric guitar twangs its sultry tune across the open air, catching Girl's attention. "Can you hear that?" She asks, her eyes alight with excitement.

"Yes, it's alluring," I smile.

The sound is coming from Nora's Bar and Grill, which is decked out onto a wooden patio. It is a modern place to eat, equipped with bright red chairs and grey marble tables.

A modern rock band is playing on the front patio, facing the seating. The male guitarist's long black hair flicks in the air while he strums wildly at his electric guitar. A young male drummer, who beats madly at the drums, accompanies him. Working up a sweat, the drummer's face is scrunched up in deep concentration.

The lead female singer's long brown hair flicks in the air as she performs a chassé and swings her hips. Her voice is deep, holding the sultry lyrics with conviction and making the audience cheer and swoon.

"Wow," says Girl, her eyes on the singer. "She's great."

"Yes, she is," I agree.

Girl's eyes are wild with excitement. "Let's get a drink," she sounds daring.

I meet her gaze, anxious suddenly. "I'm not sure that it's a good idea."

Girl's eyes widen. "Please Lira? We've got to have some fun. I'm so tired of the stress. I just need to unwind a little."

I stare down at the ground, feeling Girl's angst. "Okay," I say, meeting her gaze again. "Just for a little while though. Any sign of danger, we're out of here, okay?"

"Okay, sure," Girl shrugs. Turning on her heels, she heads towards the bar. "Drinks are on me," she smiles. "What would you like?"

"Oh thanks," I smile with gratitude. "I'd love a glass of sparkling Pinot Noir."

Girl waves her hand, trying to get the bar tender's attention. He turns to face her mid strumming air guitar, his shaved, auburn hair glistening in the light. "Hey," he grins broadly. "What can I get you?" His green eyes shine with appreciation as they rest upon Girl's face.

"A glass of sparkling Pinot Noir for my friend," Girl smiles.

"Sure," the bar tender sets to work, grabbing a large bottle of wine while he bops away to the music. Girl throws her head back, laughing and joining in the dancing. The bar tender's eyes widen in surprise and a wide grin forms on his lips. "I'm Gavin," he calls out. "What's your name?'

"I'm Girl," she smiles.

"Just Girl?" Gavin's eyebrows raise.

"Just Girl," she nods, shimmying away to the music.

"Let's do it!" Gavin calls. As he opens the bottle, the cork flies into the air and hits Girl smartly on the shoulder.

"Whoa!" Girl exclaims, clutching her shoulder and grimacing in pain.

"Sorry," Gavin's cheeks redden. "Please let me dispose of that."

"I'll keep it," Girl says, surprising him. "It'll be a memento of our Girl's night out." Retrieving the cork from the floor, she stares at it.

Gavin nods, a small smile crossing his lips. "Is it a special occasion?" He asks.

Girl's feet shuffle nervously on the floor as she considers a response.

"I've just landed a new job," I lie, taking the focus off Girl.

Gavin meets my gaze. "Congratulations!" He smiles. "What work do you do?"

"I'm a florist," I continue to embellish, my voice straining over the music. "I've just landed a secret contract with a large corporate team. I'll be designing their floral art displays for their main office."

"Right," Gavin nods, accepting my story. Shaking his hips, he proceeds to pour the sparkling Pinot Noir into a glass. My cheeks redden. He is hot. The bubbles sparkle vibrantly in the liquid, making my mouth water.

"Here you are," Gavin's voice is husky as he hands me the drink. "Good luck with that new job."

"Thanks," I say, feeling shy suddenly. Accepting the glass, I take a sip. Closing my eyes, I sway to the music as I enjoy the crisp taste of the wine. It feels great going down.

"Can I get you anything?" Gavin shifts his gaze to Girl who is still dancing. His eyes flash with longing.

Girl is holding the cork in the palm of her hand and twisting it in slow circles. "What?" She looks up, meeting Gavin's gaze. "Oh yes," she leans towards him, trying to speak loudly over the music. "I'd love a glass of sparkling Shiraz please."

Gavin's smile widens. "Good choice," he smiles, grabbing a bottle. He turns around as he opens it this time, avoiding another cork escapade. "You'll love this drink," he says, swaying to the music. The bubbles pop ferociously as he pours the drink into the glass. He places the drink on the bar in front of Girl.

"Thank you," Girl smiles. Holding the glass, she takes a small sip. "This is divine," she sighs.

Makeshift Girl: The Secret Heritage Trail

Gavin winks at Girl. "Let me know if you need anything else," his tone is suggestive.

Girl meets my gaze, her eyes wide with surprise.

"We're right Gavin," I say, dousing out the heat with a wet blanket of protectiveness. "We'll leave you to your work." I swirl my sparkling Pinot Noir in the glass.

Gavin shrugs and withdraws, heading towards another young lady in a red dress, who is leaning against the bar. She has her brown hair tossed to one side and her eyes narrowed, looking a little frazzled. He shimmies his hips again, pouring her a single shot of Vodka and then another.

I shift my attention back to Girl. "Are you having a nice time?" I ask her.

"Yes," Girl nods, still dancing away, her eyes scanning the dance floor. "Look!"

My gaze follows the direction she points and rests upon a disturbing sight. There, on the right side of the dance floor, is Mitch. He has his arms around Sophie, who has her head resting against his chest. They stand still and focused, their bodies wrapped in a tight embrace, oblivious to the dancing around them. The vibe between them is intense with heat, making my heart clench in anger. Why is Mitch doing this? Does he not believe in being faithful to me?

"Lira?" I feel Girl's hand on my shoulder. I shrug it off and thump my drink down onto the bar.

As Mitch walks away from Sophie, I follow him left down a corridor.

My head is soaring with rage. Storming behind Mitch, I watch two waiters burst through the waiter's doors ahead, carrying hot plates of food. They stare at us with annoyed faces as they dodge passed us.

Mitch pauses mid stride to let them pass and as he does so, I slam into his back.

"What the -?" Mitch spins around, concerned. "Lira!" He steps back, very surprised to see me.

"Hello Mitch," I grunt, crossing my arms over my chest. "Looks like I've disrupted your date."

"My date?" Mitch's eyes narrow with confusion. He pulls nervously at his silver tank top. "I don't know what you mean."

"I saw you with Sophie, Mitch," I am slurring as the alcohol begins to kick in. It is hard to think clearly right now.

"Oh!" Mitch's mouth drops open. "Lira, it's not what you think, we –"

"Save your words," I splutter, reaching out to hold onto a wall. I feel dizzy all of a sudden and need to stop myself from crashing.

Mitch's hand rests on my shoulder. "Are you okay?" He asks concernedly.

I shrug his hand away. It takes a moment for the dizziness to finally pass.

Mitch turns me around to face him. "Have you been drinking?" He asks.

"Yes!" I blurt loudly.

Mitch smiles. "Well, it's great that you're having fun."

"I don't need your permission," I snap. It is unlike me, yet the alcohol is enhancing my fierceness.

Mitch sighs, leaning his back against the wall of the corridor. "I care about you," he says softly.

"Hmm," I grunt, disbelieving his words.

Mitch meets my gaze. "It's not safe here, Lira. Naricia is attending a business meeting. You don't want her to discover you here." He grabs my left arm with his free hand and pulls me away, further down the corridor and across the right wing of the balcony. The strong beat of the music shocks me and the lead singer raises an eyebrow at us as we pass her by.

"Ouch!" I yell, as Mitch continues to pull my arm, leading me behind the curtains and into the backstage area.

"Sorry," he says, letting go of my arm. "It's safer outside, I promise." He stands still, waiting for me to decide whether I will exit through the door.

Taking a deep breath and feeling groggy, I lean my full body weight against the heavy metal door and push it open. I nearly fall onto the step outside, yet grab hold of the door frame just in time.

"Are you alright?" Mitch reaches out to assist me.

"I can look after myself," I stumble through my words, asserting my independence.

"Oh, I know that," Mitch says, his eyes boring into me as my feet hit the grass.

Dropping onto the blades, I sit and catch a breath. My eyes scan my surroundings. I am sitting in a small, grassy courtyard, next to a couple of umbrella tables.

"Are you sure it's safe to be here?" I ask, nodding towards the tables.

"It's safe right now," Mitch says. "Naricia will be running a private function here soon." He bobs down facing me, his blue eyes filled with concern.

I avert my gaze away from his, staring down at the ground. I don't think that I can trust Mitch right now.

Standing up slowly, I find my balance and begin to walk away, wanting to be left alone.

"Hey," Mitch says, jumping up and grabbing my hand gently. "Baby, can I have a hug?"

The fog in my head is beginning to clear. I turn sharply to meet Mitch's gaze, releasing his grasp of my hand. "Why are you here Mitch?" I launch into detective mode.

"I had to make a delivery to Naricia," Mitch sighs. "While I'm here, I'm also helping Sophie source information she needs."

"Helping Sophie?" My words are sharp on my tongue. "What could she possibly want, Mitch? You are a sucker for a pretty face," I turn on my heels.

Dashing ahead of me, Mitch turns to stare at me intensely. "Baby," he says softly, touching my face. "Let's not do this. We are stronger than this, aren't we?" I can hear the pleading tone of his voice.

My heart begins to race with anxiety. "I don't know," I say, genuinely unsure. "Are we, Mitch?"

We're both silent for a moment, staring into each other's eyes.

Mitch cups my face in both his hands, his eyes filled with worry. "My beautiful Lira," he says huskily. "Please trust me."

I step back, my mind a whir of confusion. "I don't know what to think anymore," I say, crossing my arms. "You're constantly in Sophie's arms. How can I trust you?"

Mitch nods, understanding. "I'm sorry," he says, lowering his head in shame. "I will leave you be, Lira." Stepping backwards, he takes one last look at me, his mouth open as though he is about to say something more.

My heart feels like it's ripping in my chest. I feel so betrayed. It is probably best that we just give each other some space for now.

After a few moments, Mitch turns away, climbing the steps and facing the door. He takes one last glance over his shoulder at me, his lips parting into a small, sad smile.

I study his expression, my heart falling.

Opening the door, Mitch steps inside, shutting it closed behind him.

There goes Mitch, off to be with Sophie. A single tear rolls down my right cheek. I swipe away at it and inhale a sharp, shaky breath. It is no use crying right now. It is time to move on.

Walking slowly up the steps, I approach the metal door and pull it open. Checking that all is clear, I cut across the backstage area and step onto the right wing of the stage. Inhaling a sharp breath, I dash passed the singing band.

"Hey!" Calls the guitarist, his cheeks red with rage. "Get off the stage!"

My heart is racing as I jump, landing my two feet onto the concrete floor. Dashing down the corridor, I pause, pressing my back against the wall. My eyes peel the dance floor.

At the very back of the building is a small, orange brick office. I watch as the front door is swung open and out walks Naricia, her dark hair billowing out around her face as though she has been caught in a strong gale. A red leather dress wraps itself tightly around the curves of her body, revealing her voluptuous cleavage. Three men in dark blue business suits follow Naricia out onto the dance floor.

Flicking at the strands of her hair, Naricia flutters her eyelashes flirtatiously while she chats animatedly. The men accept the flyers that she hands to them. I watch as one of the flyers drops and flutters amongst the men's black shoed feet. Landing flat on the floor, it displays its hostile message: *Have you seen this Girl?*

My heart thumps with fear. The hunt is continuing to increase. Girl is in so much danger right now.

As Naricia shakes the hand of a business man, I dash across the dance floor and return to the bar. I head straight towards Girl who stares at me while taking a sip of her cocktail.

"You're panting, Lira," Girl's eyes widen and her voice slurs. "Is there something wrong?"

I nod, trying to catch my breath. "Naricia's here," I pant, holding my hips.

Girl's eyes narrow with anger. "That woman," she splutters, stumbling as she stands. "Where is she?" She regains her balance and stands on her swaying tip toes, her eyes scanning the crowd.

"It doesn't matter," I wave my hand dismissively. My gaze returns to Naricia, who has approached a bouncer on the left side of the dance floor. His face is tense as he speaks to Naricia and pulls at his short, brown spiky hair. He is wearing a white singlet and jeans, his bulging muscles rippling strongly in the light as he stretches.

Naricia's eyes scan the dance floor, searching for Girl and I. Spotting us, she points in our direction and instructs the bouncer. Accepting Naricia's instruction, the bouncer places his hand over the mouth piece of his headset and speaks into it.

My eyes dart across the room, landing on another tall, male bouncer with brown hair tied back into a pony tail. He is wearing a green t-shirt and black bike shorts. Pressing his earphone to his ear, he listens intensely to the message coming through.

I face Girl, my heart pounding. "We are in grave danger right now," I say. "We've been found. We need to leave fast."

Girl's eyes widen in shock. Leaning towards me, she slurs into my ear: "Get me out of here, Lira."

I nod, grabbing her hand.

Taking one last swig of her cocktail, Girl bangs the empty glass down onto the bar. "Thanks for the drinks!" She calls.

Gavin gives her a thumbs up, coupled with a flirtatious grin.

I lead Girl across the dance floor, heading towards the corridor. Luckily, Naricia has re-engaged a lively conversation with the business men.

It gives us time to escape.

Girl is drunk and presses her body firmly against me, slinging her arms around my neck. "I can't hold myself up, Lira," she splutters.

"I've got you," I say, grabbing her hand.

"Okay," Girl nods, her eyes glazed.

Pulling Girl's hand, I run, turning right and leading her down the busy corridor. A couple of waiters scowl at the intrusion and press their bodies up against the walls, trying to avoid a collision.

Reaching the end of the corridor, I inhale a sharp breath. "Hold tight!" I cry, pulling Girl's hand and cutting swiftly across the right wing of the stage. The guitarist's eyes are like daggers as we pass by. He waves, grabbing the attention of the brown, spiky haired bouncer and points at us.

We have precious moments to leave before we are caught. Pushing the curtains apart forcefully, I pull Girl back stage.

Girl is panting. "Why all this running, Lira?" She is too intoxicated to focus.

"Ssh!" I turn around to face her. "We have to be quiet now."

Girl stops, almost choking. She begins to cough.

"You've had too much to drink," I tell her. "Let me take care of you now."

"Oh, it's dark in here," Girl giggles. Letting go of my hand, she grabs hold of the curtain and wraps it around herself. "Oooh! I'm a ghost!"

Makeshift Girl: The Secret Heritage Trail

I take a deep breath, calming myself down. We must leave right now. "Come on!" I command, grabbing Girl's hand. "We've got to go!" I pull her towards the back door. Pushing it open, I guide her down the steps and outside into the darkened courtyard. "A few more steps and we're out of here safely," I say.

The back door swings open again, revealing the brown, spiky haired bouncer. He stands on the steps, peering at us across the courtyard. Pointing in our direction, he chats lively into his mouth piece.

"Come with me!" I cry, grabbing Girl's hand. I pull her across the grass, beginning to run.

"Lira! What are you doing?" Girl cries out, flicking my hand away. She stops, placing her hands on her knees and catching her breath.

"Keep moving!" I yell. "We are not safe!"

Approaching a short, black gate, I straddle it with my left leg and jump down onto the grass on the other side.

"Hey!" The bouncer is running across the courtyard towards us. It will only take him a moment to catch us.

"Take my hands!" I cry, reaching for Girl.

She is dazed, the alcohol making her uncoordinated as she tries to hoist herself up onto the gate.

Reaching out, I grab Girl's hands and pull her up. Standing, she sways groggily and releases my grasp. "I can do this, Lira," she slurs. Pushing her feet against the wire, she hoists herself up and straddles the top of the gate.

"Jump!" I cry, watching Girl's legs tense up. The bouncer is still running fast. He has nearly caught up to us. "Quickly Girl!"

"Okay!" Girl takes a deep breath and jumps, landing on her bottom onto the cement. "Whoa!" She sobers, realising what is happening. "That man is chasing us, Lira!" She points at him.

"Yes he is," I say. "Let's go!" I grab Girl's hand again, pulling her up onto her feet. Beginning to run, I drag her along with me.

I can hear the bouncer's feet pounding against the cement as he jumps over the gate.

"Focus Girl!" I yell, dashing across the road into the park.

We cut across the grass and through the small native bushes. I spot the ute a few metres away.

"We're nearly there!" I call, continuing to run. I am panting but it doesn't bother me. I am too focused on the getaway.

"Hey!" I hear the bouncer close behind us. His feet are thumping across the grass.

"Lira, I can't run much further, I'm getting a stitch," Girl cries, beginning to slow down.

I stop in my tracks, turning to face Girl. She is limping across the grass.

I can do this!

Reaching out, I lift her in both my arms. She straddles her legs around my waist and leans her head against my left shoulder.

Girl is heavy but I seem to manage. Finding my inner strength, I support her weight in my arms. My feet continue to pelt across the grass and onto the cement of the car park.

I place Girl onto the ground next to the passenger side of the ute and open the door. "Inside you get!" I grab her hand and lead her inside. Helping her to sit down, I shut the door firmly, running to the driver's side.

The bouncer has reached the car park now and is nearly upon us.

I swing open the ute door, jumping into the driver's seat. Turning on the ignition, I rev the ute. "Hold on Girl!" I yell, popping the clutch into reverse.

Backing out of the parking space, I can hear the bouncer's hands thumping the roof of the ute. "Hey, come back here!" He yells, almost smashing Girl's window.

I ignore him, spinning the ute around. Exhaust fumes billow into the air behind me.

Facing the road, I press my foot firmly onto the accelerator. We zoom ahead, tyres squealing. I watch the bouncer attempt to run after us, becoming a smaller and smaller speck in the rear view mirror as I tear away down the road.

I exhale a deep sigh of relief. We are lucky to have escaped this time.

Chapter 15

As the sun rises, I park the ute in the curb outside Girl's studio. "Here we are," I say, turning to face her.

"Thanks Lira," Girl sighs. "I'm sorry I lost control back there. I don't know what came over me."

"It's okay," I assure her. "We are safe. We just can't afford to do that again."

"No, we can't," Girl agrees, grabbing her silk bag. She opens her door and steps outside onto the footpath. Turning to face her studio, she gasps in horror. "Oh no!"

Approaching Girl, I see what has distressed her. The front door of the studio has been broken into. There is a big hole in it, where the thief managed to jimmy the lock and pulled the door wide open.

Following Girl inside the studio, I feel her tension reverberate through my bones. Scanning the room, I notice that a few of Girl's drawers have been dented after being forced open. Papers and files have been carelessly strewn across the floor.

"Let me get some light in here," I offer, beginning to draw one of the red striped curtains open.

"No," Girl shakes her head. "It's too dangerous. Keep them shut."

I shut the curtains, my hands beginning to shake. Is it safe enough to be here?

I look around the studio. Most of Girl's sculptures are still here, including her amazing tree forest, which has been tossed carelessly onto the ground. I pick up each tree and place them gently onto the bench next to Girl, who has her head down and her back facing me. She is pressing her hands down firmly onto the bench space where her precious Beach Crescendo sculpture once sat.

I approach Girl and place my hands on her shoulders. "Come here," I say, pulling her closer to me.

Girl rests her head on my shoulder and begins to sob. I hold her tightly and stroke her hair. I can only imagine how much pain she must feel right now.

After a moment, Girl steps back with tears still dripping down her cheeks. "My precious sculpture," she says softly. "It's gone forever."

"No, not forever," I say, taking her hands. "We'll find it together, I promise."

Girl's eyes widen incredulously. "How?" She asks. "Where in this maze of craziness do we begin?"

"Where we decide to," I reply, taking her hands. "For now, we need to move quickly. Whoever took your sculpture may come back for something more. Let's pack you up and get you out of here."

Girl nods, her brain beginning to kick back into gear. "You're right," she says.

Girl opens her workbench drawer and takes out her treasured chisel set. She is silent, drawing out one of the chisels and twisting the handle in her palm. "My father gave me this chisel set," Girl says softly.

"It's beautiful," I say, admiring the glistening blade. "He must appreciate your talent."

"He does," Girl says. "My father is very artistic himself." She places the chisel set into her silk bag. Picking up an old milk crate, she begins to pack the rest of her art supplies.

I help her to wrap her remaining red gum sculptures with cloth.

"Can you pass me the foam over there?" Girl is pointing towards a large, wooden table. "It should be right next to my folio."

I spot the foam half dangling off the side of the table. Picking it up, I notice something odd. The folio is not on the table.

Handing the foam to Girl, I approach the topic gently. "Are you sure your folio was meant to be on the table?" I ask.

Girl nods, busily stuffing the foam into a spare box. She gently packs her red gum sculptures away and seals the box with masking tape. "Can you bring it here?" She mutters, busy.

"I can't," my words hang in the air.

Girl stares directly into my eyes. "Why not? It's not that heavy. Should be easy to lift."

"That's not it," I motion for her to glance at the table. "It's not on the table."

"I'm sure I left it there," Girl is confused. "I added the final swatches to the folio and ..." Girl approaches the table.

There is a moment of tense silence as her brain registers what has happened. "It's gone!" Girl yells. "I can't believe this!" She grabs a pencil off the table and throws it across the room. It bounces across the slate floor.

I step back, giving Girl her space to breathe.

After a few moments, Girl settles down. She grabs one last box and begins packing the clay models away. One model catches her eye. She picks it up, her hands shaking. "This is all I have left of Beach Crescendo," she says. "My original clay model. I wish I knew where the real red gum sculpture was."

My heart falls in empathy for Girl. Beach Crescendo spoke the lyrics of her heart and soul.

Girl wraps the model in a cloth and tucks it carefully into the top of the box. "I can't afford to lose the assets I have hidden inside that statue," she says determinedly. "I owe it to my family to get it back."

"Of course," I say, reaching out to touch her shoulder gently. "Things are so difficult right now, you must feel very overwhelmed."

"Yes," Girl sighs, biting her lip. "Unfortunately, the Petoys are unrelenting in their resistance movement against the imperial dynasty of Mira. I believe that the theft of my statue and Aisha's scarf were acts of resistance themselves. The Petoys would know that the totems on the statue belong to my family. They protest strongly against me becoming the new chief of silk. The way they see it, I will continue the ancient silk tradition in Mira and this will keep the silk tax raised quite high."

"That's extreme," I say. "You're not responsible for the silk tax."

"No, I am not," Girl shakes her head. "The Petoys have been after us for years. Poor Aisha was persistently hunted down by them." She digs into her silk bag and retrieves Aisha's journal. Flipping to a page, she looks at me. "This entry will inform you about how dangerous Mira became for Aisha and her father, Sefra in the 1200s."

I accept the journal and stare at its open page. Aisha's elegant handwriting greets me. It reads:

Summer, 1275

The pink and purple hues of twilight shift along the sky, casting a warm glow of light over the rocks I stand upon as I stare out to sea.

I can see the last boat drifting into the harbour, its square–rigged sail flapping wildly in the air as the wind hits it from behind. My heart beats wildly with excitement and I look up at Father, who stands next to me, his grey hair fluttering in the cool breeze. I am about to learn about our silk trade route.

Father taps his hand on the handle of the cart he has been pushing. It is loaded with silk garments that he has designed to sell at the Empress' summer market.

Father is the Empress' private silk merchant. He has produced hundreds of apparel for her over many years. This summer, the Empress is allowing him to sell his silk at a stall at her market, which is being held at her palace.

"Take care to appreciate the hard work of others, Aisha," says Father as he rubs his aching back. "It shows good character in leadership." His chest convulses as he coughs deeply.

"Are you alright, Father?" I ask him, concerned at how unwell he seems. He is the only family I have and I do all I can to look after him as he continues to age.

"Hmm," Father clears his throat. "Pay attention, Aisha," he directs my gaze back to the boat. I watch as a couple of men jump down off its deck and land their feet onto the sand.

As they anchor the boat, I notice that the men's tunics are tattered and their hair is dishevelled from battling the wind. They look weather beaten and fatigued.

Once the boat is anchored, I watch as one of the men jumps back up onto the deck and begins to pass two wooden boxes to another, who stacks them onto the sand. One of the boxes is very heavy and the man struggles under its weight, bending his legs to place it down firmly onto the sand.

"Maritime trade," Father says. "It's tough work, being at sea. Those two men would have spent weeks, even months, getting here. It's a relief to see that they have a couple of large boxes to unpack. Sometimes, one arrives with barely anything at all to sell." Staring off into the distance, Father wears a thoughtful expression on his face.

I stare at the men once more, watching as they drop down onto the ground and sit, catching a breath. One of the men lies back on the sand, knotting his hands behind his head and staring up at the starry sky.

"It is time to go," Father says.

"Is it okay if I accompany you, Father?" I ask him. It is the first time that Father has invited me to attend such a meeting. He often tells me that the routes to the palace are dangerous.

Father stares at me. "Follow my instructions," he says.
"I'll keep you safe."

Wrapping my arms around my body, I try to warm myself from the chill of the cold air. I smile as my Father pats me gently on the head. "It is good for you to learn some things, Aisha," he says.

"Yes Father," my eyes are alight with happiness.

Father reaches out to touch my scarf. "Your mother's scarf," he says softly. "She loved this so very much, you know. I remember her creative streak, how she refused to use the strong dye colours that we usually use for silk design. Instead, she preferred a shade of white, which would not sell as successfully in trade. She loved this scarf, the way it sat humbly around her neck and gave her senses of comfort and peace as she held you tight. You would often beg to wear it, Aisha."

I stroke the scarf subconsciously. A memory flashes in my mind of my mother's shaking hands as she shaped spun silk into this beautiful scarf. My gentle mother, who coughed violently and shook, plagued she was with an illness that had deteriorated her immensely. I spent every moment I could with her, my heart knowing that each might be my last.

"Beautiful Aisha, wear this scarf with your love," said my mother one morning as she tied it around my neck.

I stared at her, my lips wobbling as tears rolled down my cheeks. "I'll wear it, always loving you, Mother," I replied. My mother nodded, her eyes also filling with tears as she realised that I understood how little time we had left together.

Stepping forward into her open arms, I breathed in her special scent as she embraced me, kissing my hair. We stood there a long while, neither of us speaking. Even now, I still feel her embrace and smell her essence. I could never part with this scarf and its memories of her.

Father releases the scarf. "You need to hide this scarf in your tunic, Aisha," he says gently. "Merchants are not to wear silk at all. It would be heart wrenching for us both if it was taken away from you."

My eyes widen. "Of course Father," I say, pulling the scarf gently away from my neck. I tuck it inside the top of my tunic.

Jumping off the rocks, I reach Father as he pushes the cart down the sandy pathway to the shore.

"Now, let me do the talking, Aisha," Father says, pausing for a moment, a metre away from the men. "The men will not expect to be greeted by a young lady."

"Of course, Father," I say. I stop walking and let Father greet the new arrivals. The man who is lying on his back is the first to sense Father's presence and rolls over, pulling himself up onto his feet.

"Good evening," Father says in a warm tone. "Welcome to Mira. I am Sefra, the Chief of silk trade. The Empress has sent me to help escort you to her palace."

The man bows, his white teeth flashing as he looks up and smiles. "I'm Ricardo," he says softly, his gaze meeting mine briefly. He is a young, handsome man, with short blonde hair. "This," he taps his companion on the shoulder and motions for him to stand. "Is my brother."

Scampering to his feet, the man stares at Father. "Good evening, I am Lucio," he says, smiling happily. He pushes strands of black hair away from his eyes.

Ricardo meets my gaze appreciatively. "What a beautiful shore you have here at Mira," He says. "It is very peaceful."

I blush, unsure of how to respond to the attentions of Ricardo.

"It can be," Father's tone is serious, making both the men straighten up. "My daughter, Aisha will check your boxes and ensure that you do intend to bring wares to sell at the summer market."

Tearing my eyes away from Ricardo's intense gaze, I kneel down and attempt to lift the lid of the first wooden box. It is very tightly fitted and hard to remove.

"Let me help you," Ricardo offers, dashing to my side. His hand brushes against mine as he grabs hold of the lid and removes it from the box. I retract my hand, my cheeks blushing shyly.

Ricardo meets my gaze and smiles warmly at me. "What do you think of these?" He asks.

I shift my gaze to the box. Inside it, there is an abundance of lapis lazuli gems in different cuts and sizes.

"Wow!" I exclaim. "They are very beautiful."

"Are they rare where you're from?" Father asks, admiring the jewel.

"Yes, they are very sought after," Ricardo nods as he places the lid back onto the box. "May I place this on your cart?" He asks Father.

Father nods. "Of course," he says, watching as Ricardo carefully moves some of Father's garments in order to make room for his box. "What other wares have you brought with you?" My father asks Lucio, who is opening another box.

Lucio grins. "Come see for yourselves," he waves us both over.

The next box is filled to the brim with almonds and pistachios.

"Taste one, go on," Lucio invites us, his eyes shining.

Father reaches into the box and retrieves a pistachio. Placing it into his mouth, he closes his eyes with contentment as he chews. "These are very good Aisha," he says as he open his eyes. "Do try one."

Reaching into the box, I retrieve an almond and hold it in my hand for a moment, admiring its shape. It tastes slightly bitter and catches at the back of my throat, making me cough.

"Not for you?" Lucio is crestfallen.

I shake my head and look down at the sand. I can't find the words to speak.

Shutting the lid, Lucio places the box carefully onto the cart.

"Ready to go?" Father asks the men.

"Yes Sir," Ricardo speaks for them both.

Father pushes the cart, which is now heavier in weight. I walk beside him, ready to be of assistance if he needs. We leave the shore and its sand behind, stepping back up onto the gravel pathway and heading towards the palace.

Ricardo and Lucio walk behind us, bantering about the highlights of their journey across the sea.

"You couldn't even keep hold of the fish!" Ricardo laughs. "It jumped straight back into the wa –"

"Ssh!" Father's instruction is abrupt and silence fills the air. He steps forward quietly, his ears pricked up as he listens for any noises. He motions for me to bend down with him and place my ear to the ground. "Listen carefully Aisha," he begins to cough and clutches his chest, rubbing it gently.

Listening closely, I hear a thudding sound reverberating through the ground. "Someone's coming," I say. "It sounds like the thudding of horse hooves."

"It may very well be," Father says, placing his ear back down to the ground. "You are right, Aisha," he sits up and smiles at me proudly. "Can you guess which way they are heading?"

I listen once more to the thudding sound. "That's strange," I say. "It has stopped suddenly, close by too."

Father raises his eyebrows. "We need to move quickly," he says, pushing the cart with force across the gravel.

I move with him, keeping up with his pace. I can feel the footsteps of Ricardo and Lucio almost on my heels as we press on, curving our way along the unmade dusty road and beginning to cut across the grass through the forest.

"What happened back there?" Ricardo's voice is strong in the silence.

Father stops pushing the cart. "We were discovered," he says, facing Ricardo. Beads of sweat are forming across his forehead. "If we had stayed any longer, the rebels would have attacked us and taken all our wares."

"Oh," Ricardo's gaze is troubled. "What should we do now?"

"We must keep cutting across this grass," Father says determinedly. There is an invisible pathway through here that we merchants take to meet the soldiers. Follow me closely."

"We will," Lucio is alert and ready to go. "Do you need some help pushing your cart, Sir?"

"I won't turn down some help, boy," Father sounds relieved. He steps aside, allowing Lucio to take control of the cart.

I grab hold of Father's arm with both hands, helping to steady him as he continues to walk. I notice that he is becoming very tired.

As we continue walking, a dark, huddled shape appears in the dappled moonlight. I watch as it steps closer, revealing its furry body. It is Sinta, the wolf, deciding to approach us.

"Whoa!" Ricardo cries. "Watch out!"

"No need to panic," I say, reaching into my tunic pocket to retrieve a piece of venison. I hold it out towards Sinta. He takes it in his mouth and devours it hungrily. "There you go, Sinta, is that better?" I pat his soft, grey fur. Sinta closes his eyes, rubbing his head gently against my leg.

"It would be hard for Sinta to hunt right now," Father says. "There are too many scary soldiers and rebels around, aren't there, Sinta?" He pats him on the head.

"You are friends with a wolf?" Lucio sounds surprised.

"We take care of him," I say, smiling at Sinta. "And he, in turn, takes care of us."

Suddenly, Sinta pounces forward, clawing into the ground. A snarl escapes his lips.

I swivel around, my eyes falling upon a couple of men on horses. They wear black head scarves, emblazoned with the totem of a golden, rearing horse.

It is the Petoy clan. They are masterful trekkers of the earth, establishing their routes wherever their pillages let them rest. It has been rumoured among the villagers that the Petoys have formed an armed resistance to overthrow the Empress as ruler of Mira. They do all they can to disrupt the order and stability of the city and to strike fear in the people, who don't always escape their attacks.

Sinta continues to snarl and I grab hold of his fur, holding him back. "Stay Sinta," I whisper. "Not yet."

I watch as one of the clan strokes his long, brown beard. A thin smile crosses over his lips. "The daughter of the Chief of silk," his voice is deep and haunting as he speaks to me. "I think you should come with us."

Father places his hand on my shoulder. "She is not going anywhere with you," he says firmly.

The other clan member jumps off his horse, stepping forward slowly and staring arrogantly at Father. I feel the hairs begin to stand up on the back of my neck.

"Pretty face," the clan member reaches out to stroke my cheek. His gaze is intense and a smirk is smeared across his thin lips. "You will be a strong asset to us Petoys. You could mother Alzat's children, eh?" He tosses his long black hair back and glances over his shoulder at Alzat.

Alzat's voice is dark. "Yes Yazat, she could. She could also help us trade silk."

These men are ruthless. It is known that the Petoys bed many women. They do not have any laws abiding them to be devoted to one woman for life. I do not desire to be part of their world.

"Hey!" Father is angry. "That's enough. She is not for you."

Sinta sneers once more, his sharp teeth revealed. He is ready to pounce at any moment.

I grab Yazat's hand and forcefully remove it from my face. "Do not touch me," I breathe, staring into his coal black eyes. "I will never go anywhere with you Petoys."

Yazat laughs cruelly. "We'll see about that," his voice is sinister. He grabs hold of my arm and tries to pull me back towards the horse.

Sinta howls loudly and digs his claws into the ground. It startles Yazat and he steps back, letting go of my arm.

"You have exactly five seconds to leave us," I command Yazat in the strongest voice that I can muster. "Or Sinta will devour you for his dinner."

Sinta howls again and licks his lips, attempting to pull away from my grasp. I hold him firmly and stand my ground, staring directly into Yazat's eyes.

Yazat steps back, keeping a careful eye on Sinta. As he mounts his horse, he glares at me. "This is not over," he sneers.

Alzat leans forward on his horse, his dark brown hair falling into his eyes. "We will find you, pretty face and you will come with us. You'll see." His voice is dark and menacing, sending a chill down my spine. He beats the side of his horse with his hand. "Let's go!"

As the men disappear into the distance, my heart pounds with fear. I realise that I am in grave danger.

Sinta stops howling and sits, panting. Reaching into my pocket, I pull out another piece of venison and feed it to him.

"Well done, Sinta," I smile, patting his head. "You were great."

"Aisha," Father's voice breaks as he pulls me close. "I am so sorry that you had to go through all that."

I look up, meeting the gaze of Ricardo. He places his hand on his heart.

"You are so strong, Aisha," he says with admiration. "Those men were scary."

"Yes, they were," I agree, my heart still pounding. I step back. "Where is Lucio?"

"He ran and hid behind the cedar tree over there," Ricardo points. "My brother gets scared very easily." He whistles shrilly. "Hey Lucio, all is clear now. You can come back."

Lucio steps out from behind the bushes, looking embarrassed. "I was afraid," he admits, staring down at the ground.

Father coughs strongly. His tired legs tremble as he struggles to hold himself up. "We'd bet-ter mo-ve," *he gasps.*

I take hold of Father's right arm, trying to help him steady himself onto his feet.

Ricardo rushes to Father's left side. "Please let me help," *he offers, reaching his arms out.*

Father nods, his eyes half closed. Ricardo wraps his arm around Father's left shoulder, enabling him to rest his weight upon him while he walks.

"Aisha?" *Father is groggy.*

"I am right here with you," *I say, taking Father's right hand in mine and squeezing it tightly.*

"The soldier, not too far …" *Father's voice drifts off as he points towards a group of spruce trees.*

I make eye contact with Ricardo. "Keep walking slowly," *I say softly.* "I'll return in a moment." *Letting go of Father's hand, I run towards the spruce trees. My eyes scan the dirt path, trying to locate a presence …*

"Aisha!" *It is Kirano, mounted on a horse in the middle of the pathway. He is dressed in khaki in order to camouflage himself amongst the trees.* "What are you doing here?"

It is a relief to see Kirano. I look up at him, desperately wanting to tell him what just happened but it will have to wait.

"Are you alright, Aisha?" *Kirano attempts to dismount his horse.*

"No, do not dismount!" *I cry.* "You need to ride to Father. He is very weak."

"Where is he?" *Kirano is concerned.*

"Not too far away. I'll show you." *I turn around and jog back the way I came with Kirano riding closely behind.*

Once we reach Father, I notice that he has stopped walking and is resting his weight against Ricardo. His eyes are closed.

"Aisha," *Father is afraid.*

"I'm right here, Father," I grab hold of his hand. "Kirano is here now. He will escort you safely to the palace."

"Yes, Sir, I will." Kirano dismounts and pats the ground, motioning for the horse to lower itself to the floor.

Ricardo walks slowly, gently guiding Father towards Kirano.

"Kirano?" Father's eyes flutter open. "You're here, my boy?"

"Yes, I am," Kirano's voice is gentle. "Let me take care of you now. I will ride you to the palace on my horse."

Father lets Kirano help him mount the horse.

"Hold on tightly," Kirano directs, helping Father grasp the reigns. "I am going to sit right behind you now, alright?"

Father nods, understanding. His knuckles are white from the effort of holding on.

Kirano mounts the horse, holding Father around the waist. "Up!" He calls, commanding the horse to stand. It does so, steadying itself on its feet and shaking its mane. "Steady!" Kirano calls, patting its side gently.

"Aisha?" Father's voice is barely audible.

"I am right here with you, Father, walking beside you," I say as I stroll alongside the trotting horse. "Lucio is still pushing the trolley and Ricardo is scouring the ground. We are safe now."

"Good," Father breathes a sigh of relief.

Kirano meets my gaze, his eyes full of questions.

I say nothing as I continue to walk through the night and I am grateful when we finally reach the tall gates surrounding the Empress' palace.

"Sit!" Kirano commands. The horse drops to the ground immediately. Kirano dismounts and helps my Father step back down onto the ground.

Father rests against Kirano, panting a little. He swipes away at the beads of sweat across his forehead. "Thank you boy," he says.

"It was my honour to help," Kirano smiles. "I know the Empress is expecting you. Should we go inside?"

I turn to face Ricardo and Lucio. "Thank you both," I say. "Without your help, we –"

"Say no more please," Ricardo waves his hand. "We hope your father gets his much needed rest and feels better soon. We thank you for your welcome." Reaching into the cart, Ricardo grabs a box.

"Thank you," Lucio smiles warmly. He grabs the remaining box out of the cart. "Mira must be a wonderful place with such kind people."

"It is," I assure him. "You'll see."

Ricardo's gaze is intense. "Please keep safe, Aisha."

"I will," I smile. "All the best with your trade. Enjoy the summer market."

The men turn and wave one last time before disappearing behind the gates of the palace.

Kirano's gaze is troubled. "Aisha, you know you cannot ..." his voice drifts off.

"I know I cannot enter the palace, Kirano," I say. "Please ensure that my Father is taken care of."

"I will," Kirano is worried. "Please wait right here for me and I will escort you home."

"Aisha?" Father reaches for my hand. "Please remain hidden. It is not safe out here."

"I will Father. Go now," I coax, watching as Kirano pushes the cart with his free hand.

Kirano points to his left. "There are soldiers guarding these front gates." He waves to a tall, dark haired soldier who stands tall and on guard at the entrance. Meeting Kirano's gaze, the soldier smiles warmly.

Kirano places his hand on my shoulder and calls out: "Please ensure that my betrothed, Aisha, is safe out the front here, Hanaro."

"Hi Aisha," Hanaro nods. "Lovely to finally meet you. I will keep you safe until he returns."

"Thank you Hanaro," Father manages to say. "Please, pop by my silk stall and I will gift you a silk handkerchief for your troubles."

"Why thank you," Hanaro smiles. "However, I am happy to help for no reward. Kirano is a very old friend of mine."

Father glances at me one last time, smiling weakly. "I'll see you in a couple of days, Aisha."

"See you soon, Father," I smile encouragingly.

I watch as Kirano guides my Father and the cart through the palace gates.

I turn to face Kirano's horse, who greets me with warm, glowing eyes. "Hello," I say, stroking his mane gently. "You are beautiful, aren't you? It's just you and me for a while. We can watch all the merchants. I wish I could travel far away and see the worlds they come from …"

Closing the journal, I clutch it tightly to my chest and exhale a large sigh of relief. Aisha and her father managed to escape the antagonistic Petoys.

I know that I have a deep strength that lies within me, like Aisha. It drives me to stop at nothing to achieve my desired goal. I am unafraid because of it.

"What a strong person Aisha was," I say to Girl. "It would have been so difficult to be a girl in Mira at that time." I hand the journal back to her.

"Yes, it was," Girl says. "It still is." She places the journal into her silk bag.

"So the Petoys were known as rebels in Aisha's time," I say.
"That's interesting, how long ago they began to take a stand."

"Yes," Girl nods. "As you read more journal entries, you'll be able to understand why the resistance movement began."

"That'll be very useful," I say. "It can only help us to understand the Petoy clan's motivations better."

"That's right," Girl agrees. "I am still so upset about losing Aisha's silk scarf too as it is sacred to my family. My parents are also very distraught at its theft. When I turn 23 in a few weeks time, the Emperor will officially induct me as the new chief of silk of Mira. On that day, it is traditional for me to receive a number of essential items, including my mother's scarf, which I will wear proudly around my neck."

"Wow," I say, surprised at what I have learned. "Concetta told me that you were being inducted soon. I didn't realise that the silk scarf was a required garment for the ceremony."

"Of course it is," Girl says, staring into my eyes. "It bears the eagle talon's totem, belonging to the empire of Mira. It also bears a wolf claw totem, belonging to my family. The scarf proudly displays the connection and unification of my family with the traditions of the empire."

"I see," I ponder aloud. "That means your scarf would be highly valuable to the Petoy clan."

"Yes," Girl runs her fingers through her hair in frustration. "Not only can they manipulate it to falsify a connection with the empire, they can also use it to gain access to the palace. I am afraid of what they plan to do, Lira."

"Yes," I empathise. "So am I."

Girl meets my gaze. "I am determined to be inducted Lira, to ensure that the silk trade continues in Mira as it should. I can't bear to see how the families' ancient silk garments are being stolen and their totems appropriated, all to advance a resistance movement."

"Let's make sure it happens," I say, smiling encouragingly at Girl. "You will be a wonderful chief of silk."

"Thank you," Girl says. "I have a lot of work to do before then," her eyes narrow. "We need to try to locate as many stolen ancient garments as we can, including my scarf, before irreparable damage occurs."

"I couldn't agree more," I say, my heart burning with fury at the Petoys' actions.

Girl inhales a sharp breath. "It's time to leave now."

Sadly, Girl takes one final sweeping glance at her studio. It is one of the most stable places she has. Her studio is where she channels her creative energy through her artistic ventures. Girl lifts the two boxes containing her original clay models and red gum statues. "Goodbye studio," she says sadly as she walks towards the front door.

I pick up the milk crates, following Girl out onto the street. She keeps walking, choosing not to take one final glance at her favourite place. It would be hard to let the studio go.

Girl dumps the boxes into the ute tray. Stacking the milk crates behind the boxes, I watch as she flops down into the passenger seat. She looks defeated.

I give her some space while she copes her own way.

"I'm sorry," I finally say, sitting in the driver's seat. "I can only imagine how hard this must be for you."

Girl nods silently, her eyes closed.

"Ready to go?" I ask.

Girl nods. "Can you take me to the willow trees at Spring River?" She asks. "There's someone there that I've arranged to meet."

"Of course," I say, adjusting the rear view mirror.

Girl retrieves her phone from her pocket and begins to text message.

Switching on the ignition, I indicate right. Once the traffic has cleared, I do a u-turn and begin to drive back towards the city.

I wonder who Girl wants to meet.

Chapter 16

As I drive down Lighthouse Boulevard, I notice how busy it is with commuters heading towards their destinations. There is a queue lining up outside the entry of the subway into Redbank Station.

As it is a sunny day, Spring Park is packed with groups of people having lunch picnics. Continuing to drive, I turn left onto Vista Road and follow its trail away from the heart of the city. Spirit River flows alongside us, its waves glistening in the sun.

After a few moments, we are faced with the poetic views of the willow trees, sweeping their long branches into the river. I turn left onto Heart Road and drive down its slope towards the embankment.

"Wow!" Girl exclaims, mesmerised by the setting. "I am always taken aback by the beauty of this scenery."

"Me too," I say as I park the ute alongside the embankment. I switch off the ignition and stretch. "This is a lovely relaxation spot."

"It sure is," Girl smiles, staring out the windscreen. "There he is!" She calls out as she pushes open her door and jumps out onto the footpath.

Stepping outside the ute, I stretch once more, watching Girl as she runs across the grassy embankment.

A tall, young man with dark, olive skin and black hair stands underneath the sweeping leaves of a large willow tree. He has a calm presence and smiles happily as Girl runs towards him. Stepping forward, he opens up his arms to embrace her.

"Hidu!" I hear Girl call as she embraces him. Hidu closes his eyes and a happy smile crosses his lips.

Stepping back, Girl glances over her shoulder. "Lira! Come over here!" She calls, waving me towards her.

I walk in long strides across the grass, eager to meet the boy who makes Girl so happy. Hidu's dark brown eyes shine with small gold flecks as he smiles warmly at me.

"So you are Lira," Hidu says in a soft, calm voice. Its tone is soothing, making me feel quite relaxed. He steps forward and takes both my hands in his. "It's an honour to meet you." He bows his head slightly as he speaks, showing respect.

A warm smile crosses my lips. "It is lovely to meet you too," I reply.

Hidu releases my hands and touches Girl lightly on her shoulder. "I've known Girl most of my life," he stares at her fondly.

"We grew up together back home," Girl's smile is radiant. "I don't know life without Hidu." She stares into his eyes for a long moment.

Hidu smiles widely, showing off his lovely white teeth. "I have missed seeing Girl around," he tells me. "The silk worms miss you too, Girl."

Girl's eyes widen. "How is the mulberry farm?" She asks Hidu. "Has Father got enough silk supply?"

A thoughtful expression crosses Hidu's face. "It's slow," he says. "Your father is on merchant business, delivering silks to the Governor of Tisu. He will be absent for at least two more weeks, depending on whatever else he is asked to do while he is in residence. Your mother takes care of the silk worms in the evenings, when she doesn't have to manage the market stall." He stares at Girl. "Your mother is very worried about you. She asked me if I knew how you were. I don't know what you want me to say."

Girl nods, understanding. "Tell her that I am very well," she says. "Tell her that her daughter is working very hard to find the scarf and is making good progress."

Hidu's eyes widen. "Is that really true?" He asks, making eye contact with me.

I remain silent, waiting for Girl's reaction. Her face saddens and she drops her head, her eyes fixed on the grass. "No, it's not," she says, her hands beginning to tremble. "I just had my sculpture stolen with the assets hidden inside it." Her voice is shaking as she lowers her head.

"Oh Girl," Hidu says gently. He pulls her to him, holding her tightly in his embrace. "I'm so sorry."

"Thank you," Girl says weakly, burying her head in Hidu's shoulder.

I watch Hidu's face redden as he digests the news. "As if it isn't bad enough that a number of family trades, including ours, has fallen," he sighs. "The Petoys have absolutely no respect for the origins or importance of our resources and trades. We need to get the scarf back for your own family's future, Girl. Look what happened to mine."

"I know," a worried expression crosses Girl's face. "I must have that scarf back. The future of Mira depends on it. I especially must have my statue back too," she sighs. "If the assets inside the statue get into the wrong hands …" her voice drifts off, unable to complete her sentence.

"You'll get it all back, Girl," I say determinedly. "I'll make sure you do. Mira deserves a strong future and we're going to ensure that it has one."

Hidu smiles weakly, his eyes staring directly into mine. "You've filled my heart with hope," he says softly. "Girl's family have become my family too. They have a vision that should be nurtured and brought to life. It will only help our village to prosper once again."

Girl rests her head against Hidu's chest. It is quiet for a little while as we drift into our own thoughts. Breaking the silence, Girl begins to sing in a soft, husky voice:

> *"A bird flies high,*
> *stretching its wings*
> *as it dotes*
> *upon its beach.*

> *"Shaking its plumage,*
> *it adorns the sands*
> *with an array*
> *of colourful feathers.*
>
> *"A rainbow of life*
> *on land and at sea,*
> *arrive to sell silk*
> *of ancient quality."*

Hidu strokes Girl's hair gently. He has tears in his eyes, which begin to fall freely down his cheeks. "I love it when you sing," he says to Girl. "It touches my heart."

"Mine too," I say softly. "That was beautiful, Girl."

Girl smiles softly. "Thank you both," she says. "My father calls me his silk bird." She stares off into the distance, thinking. "I have a big job to undertake, ensuring that the silk tradition continues in Mira."

"I see," I say, feeling for Girl. "It must be very difficult carrying so much weight on your shoulders."

"It can be," says Girl. "So I sing this song to remind me of my important role. My father once told me that the lyrics would mean a lot more to me when I was older. They certainly do carry a lot more weight for me now."

"I will do all that I can to help you, Girl," Hidu says, wiping his eyes. "I am always in the shadows, watching out for you. I will pass on whatever information I can to assist."

Tears glisten in Girl's eyes. "My wonderful man," she says, reaching for Hidu. "You know how I feel about you." She strokes him lovingly on the cheek.

Hidu places his hand on hers. "I do," he says softly, closing his eyes.

Hidu seems so gentle and kind. How lucky Girl is to have found someone who cares so much about her.

It is silent for a long moment while Girl and Hidu hold each other. I feel awkward watching them so I turn around and begin to walk away, heading towards the river.

The sun feels warm against my skin. It bounces off the gently flowing water, making it shimmer. I walk slowly along the small pier, feeling the firm wooden planks beneath my shoes.

Sitting on the pier, I take my shoes off and throw them aside. Placing my feet into the cool river water, I exhale a deep breath. It is nice to take a moment to relax and enjoy the scenery. I kick the water gently, making it splash.

Across the gurgling water, the river red gum trees tower high. They are quite the picturesque scene, making me long to return to the forest they dwell in, to visit Concetta.

Small ripples begin to appear in the waves. Staring down, I spot eels undulating through the water. Their dorsals and fins are elongated as they brush against my legs. It is a strange sensation, yet reassuring. I am here and able to enjoy this moment.

I hear footsteps along the pier and look back. It is Girl and Hidu, they are walking hand in hand, heading my way.

"That looks like a great idea Lira," Girl says as she takes off her shoes. She tosses them aside and flops down next to me. "Oh!" She exclaims as she dangles her feet into the water. "That's cold."

I giggle. "Yes, it is," I say. "You'll get used to it though."

Girl stares at Hidu. "Are you joining us?" She asks, patting the wooden plank next to her.

Hidu smiles and takes his shoes off. He places them down gently onto the pier. "Sounds great," he smiles, sitting next to Girl. "Oh, that's refreshing," he sighs once his feet hit the water.

Girl giggles, kicking her feet. "Those eels are tickling me!" She pulls her feet out of the water and dangles them into the air.

After a moment, Girl looks at Hidu. "Have you had any good leads recently?" She asks him.

Hidu sighs. "Let me think," he says, closing his eyes. "Yes, I had one recently."

"What was it?" Girl asks.

Hidu opens his eyes and stares out at the water. "I'd been watching the trucks leave our village in Mira and wondered where they went. Two nights ago, I jumped into my car and followed a truck all the way across the highway. The driver didn't stop once. Not even to eat or get fuel. I realised that he had to get somewhere urgently and it just made me even more curious. I followed him to the front of the Botanica Warehouse in the Redbank Industrial Estate." Hidu's eyes are narrowed and focused as he reflects.

Girl stares at me and raises her eyebrows. "The Botanica Warehouse," she says. "I never knew that existed. What happened when he arrived?"

"Well, Naricia stepped out of the warehouse and stood in front of the driver's window, waving excitedly at the man as he parked the truck," Hidu waves his hand in the air, re-enacting the scenario. "Once the man stepped out of the truck and handed Naricia a cardboard box, I took that opportunity to grab a photo," he says. "It's good evidence that she is working with him. Would you like to see it?"

"Yes please," Girl peers at the screen on Hidu's mobile. "Take a look at this, Lira," she waves me over.

In the photograph, Naricia's eyes are shining with excitement as she receives the box from the man we staked out earlier across the road from Tora's Noodle Store. He is also grinning, as though he has just won a million dollars.

"Hmmm," my brain sorts through the information that I have learned. "It'd be interesting to see what's in that box," I say aloud. "Hidu, are you able to share the address of the warehouse with us?"

"Sure," Hidu retrieves his phone from his pocket and types some information into it. "I have just texted you the link to a map of the warehouse location," he tells Girl. "Please be careful. It seems like a very dangerous place to go."

"Thank you Hidu," Girl checks her phone. "That's very handy."

I retrieve my mobile phone from my pocket and find the photo I took of the man trying to track down Mitch earlier. "Can I show you a photo too?" I ask Hidu, waiting for his reaction.

Hidu nods, leaning forward to stare at my phone. "What is it?" He asks curiously.

"I have a photo of the same man you saw with Naricia," I say as I point to the photo.

"Yes, it is him!" Hidu is astonished. "How did you get that photo?"

"We were on a stakeout earlier," Girl sighs. "Trying to track down the person who is following Lira's husband, Mitch. Turns out it's the same man."

"Interesting," Hidu is animated. "You'll have to tell me more about this story, Girl."

Girl's eyes narrow and her cheeks redden. "We visited the Botanica store and discovered that Jacquelyn is selling counterfeit silk using the totem designs of families from our village." Girl's hands clench into fists. "I am so angry about all of this."

Hidu turns pale and he sits back, absorbing the information. "Whoa!" He finally gasps. "That is not on!" He stands up and faces both of us. "This is very serious news," he says, his forehead lined with creases of concern. "News we best keep to ourselves for now. There are some very dangerous people after you Girl."

Girl stops pacing and stares at Hidu. "I know," she sighs. "If I make it through all this okay, I'll be able to return home."

"You will make it," I say determinedly. "You have both of us here for you."

Girl smiles at me. "Thank you Lira, you're a great friend. Tell me something though?"

"Yes?" I ask her.

Girl places her hands on her hips. "Where are we going to go now?"

Hidu raises his hand. "A place I should not know about," he says. "For your own safety. That way, if I get caught, I can't give away any location." Standing, he pulls Girl to him, holding her tightly. "I'd better get back to work. I will see you when the time is right."

Girl closes her eyes, snuggling up to Hidu. "Of course," she says. "Thank you my amazing man."

Hidu smiles as he pulls away from Girl. "Bye," he says, waving at both of us. "It was nice to meet you, Lira. Please take good care of her."

Girl smiles at me nervously. "I feel safer when you're around Lira," she says. "You will still help me, won't you?"

"Of course," I say, pulling my feet out of the water. Standing up, I face Hidu. "I will do all that I can to look after her," I promise him.

"Thank you Lira," Hidu's face softens with relief. "I feel better about leaving, knowing that she is in such good hands." He meets Girl's gaze. "Take care," he says to her. "Be sensible."

"I will," Girl grins. She leans against my shoulder as we both watch Hidu leave. "Oh, he is so handsome," she sighs once he has disappeared from view.

I smile warmly. "He seems to make you happy," I say, enjoying seeing the lightness in Girl's steps as we walk back down the pier towards the ute.

"He sure does," Girl smiles. She grabs hold of my hand. "Thank you again Lira, for helping me. It means a lot to me."

"That's okay," I say, feeling my hand swinging in hers. I stop walking and wait for her to face me. "Do you want to check out the warehouse?" I ask her, wanting to help her get to the bottom of what's happening.

"Yes, let's do it," Girl wears a determined expression.

We continue to head back towards the ute. As I sit on the passenger seat, Girl hands me her phone.

"The map that Hidu texted to me is here," she says. "Can you direct me while I drive?"

"Sure," I say, noticing that the warehouse is not too far away. "It will only take us a few minutes to get there."

"It feels good to be doing something constructive Lira," Girl smiles as she starts the ignition. "It gives me hope."

I nod, understanding.

Girl reverses the ute and turns right, heading down Heart Road. "Which way do I go?" She asks as she approaches Vista Road.

"Left," I say. "Keep following this road around the bend. It will become Nouveau Road."

"Okay," Girl's eyes narrow as she focuses on the cars ahead of her. "So slow," she sighs.

Eventually, Girl navigates the ute around the bend and hits Nouveau Road.

I scan the left side of the road, looking for the entrance to the Redbank Industrial Estate. "Take the next left, it's Industry Road," I tell Girl. "Once you enter it, you will see Botanica Warehouse directly on your left."

"Thanks," Girl says as she turns left. "I see," she says, pressing the brakes. She stares at the warehouse. "It's too obvious, parking directly out the front. Let's take a look around the estate and see what else is here." Girl drives down Holdridge Street, passing the Botanica Warehouse. "Nick's Memorabilia Warehouse," she mutters. I make a note of it on my phone.

Taking the next right down Glacier Street, we are faced with two large buildings: A-Z Antiques on the right and another on the left.

"J.F. Snow Globes," I read the front signage. I notice a large truck parked in front of the warehouse. It is dressed with the same string of lights that I saw on Zac's truck earlier. The back doors are open and some men are unloading boxes from it.

"Stop for a moment, please," I request, wanting to get a closer look at one of the men.

"Sure," Girl breaks and follows my gaze, staring at the front of the building. "What are we looking at?"

I lean forward, waiting for the man to turn around and show his face. There he is, retrieving a large box out of his truck and placing it down onto the ground.

"It's Zac," I say, watching as he stretches his arms over his head. "See over there?"

We watch as Zac lifts another box in both arms and carries it into the building.

"Hmm," says Girl, biting her lip. "I wonder what's in that box?"

"Me too," I sigh, waiting to see if Zac returns. He doesn't. "We'll have to find a way into that building," I tell Girl.

"Yes," Girl agrees. "If Zac is delivering boxes in there, especially under Redfin's command, then we must investigate it."

We are both silent, watching the movement around the truck.

After a short while, Girl looks at me. "Should we keep looking around?" She asks.

"Yes," I agree. "Let's see what other clues exist around here."

Girl drives straight ahead, reaching the end of Glacier Street. "This truck depot is very big," she says as we reach the end of the street. "It's conveniently located right next to the docks."

"Yes," I agree. There are quite a few trucks parked in the depot: flatbeds, car transporters, heavy rigids and semi trailers. My gaze rests upon the odd red Land Rover parked in the middle of the depot. "Look!" I exclaim, pointing at the man stepping out of the four wheel drive. "It's Redfin."

"And so it is," says Girl. "I wonder what he's up to?"

Redfin retrieves a remote control from his pocket and unlocks a silver, light rigid truck. The string of lights surrounding its cabin flash a blue light.

Climbing on board the truck, Redfin begins to reverse and a loud beeping sound can be heard across the depot.

Girls' foot revs the accelerator. "Let's follow him," she sounds eager.

We watch as Redfin exits the Truck Depot and swerves to his left, heading down Industry Road. Following him, Girl takes a left down Gear Street and an immediate left again onto Industry Road.

"He's stopping in front of the Botanica Warehouse," Girl sounds surprised. "It must be a regular delivery location."

Girl indicates right and sits idly on Industry Road, a distance far enough away that we can observe what Redfin is doing.

Redfin reverses the truck into the warehouse driveway. It nearly hits a green Commodore, which is parked at an awkward angle.

Jumping out of the truck, Redfin peers over his shoulder before pressing a remote button in order to open the large roller door. The darkness of the warehouse swallows him up as he disappears inside.

"There's nothing in his hands," Girl comments. "I wonder what he's doing in there."

A moment later, Redfin exits, carrying two clear plastic bags. They glow with a myriad of colours. Opening the passenger door of the truck, he throws them onto the seat.

Suddenly, Redfin taps his pocket and pulls out a mobile phone. Holding it to his ear, he disappears back into the warehouse.

"I've got to get into that truck," I open my door.

"What?" Girl looks shocked. "Lira, that's dangerous!"

I stare into Girl's eyes. "When isn't it dangerous?" I ask.

Girl looks flustered. "Please, I don't want to see you hurt."

I touch her gently on the shoulder. "Don't worry," I say. "I'll be fine. Can I ask you a favour?"

"Anything," Girl is worried.

"Tail me," I say. "I'll need you to be there."

Girl's mouth drops open. "Lira, you're not planning to drive that …" She can't finish her sentence.

"Trust me," I say. "I know what I am doing."

Girl nods, her mouth still wide open.

Shutting the passenger door, I dash quickly towards the truck.

It's a very big truck and easy to hide behind. Pressing my body against the side of the tray, I arch up onto my tip toes, peering inside the warehouse. I can see Redfin, waving his hands wildly in the air as he chats on the phone.

Tiptoeing, I grab hold of the handle and quietly open the driver's door. Checking over my shoulder, I pray that Redfin hasn't heard me. He is still chatting on his phone and punching his forehead with his fist.

Taking a deep breath, I launch into action. Jumping up the steps quickly, I land my bottom onto the driver's seat. Bobbing down, I ensure that my frame is not in view and close the door, nearly knocking my head into the dashboard.

Peering up at the passenger seat, my eyes fall upon the plastic bags that Redfin tossed in here moments ago. Reaching up, I snatch at them and watch them slip down onto the carpet.

Suddenly, the driver's door swings open and there stands Redfin. My breath catches in my throat. His glare is menacing, sending shivers down my spine.

"Hey!" He shouts. "What are you doing in here?" He grabs hold of my foot firmly and drags me across the floor of the truck.

My fighting instinct kicks in. Placing my hands firmly down onto the carpet, I stop myself from moving. Kicking my free leg backwards, I land it squarely in Redfin's face.

"Aw!" He yells, clutching at his left cheek in pain as he flies backwards.

Taking advantage of his stunned state, I slam the driver's door and sit forward, searching wildly for the truck keys. Good. He's left them in the ignition.

Turning on the ignition, I listen to the engine chug as the truck bursts into life. Pressing the clutch peddle with my foot firmly, I shift the gear stick into first gear and drive the truck out of the warehouse car park. Full locking the steering wheel, I swerve to the right, feeling the large body of the truck turn itself around onto Industry Road.

"Hey!" I hear Redfin cry. "Come back here!"

Easing off the accelerator, I press down firmly onto the clutch and shift the gear stick, engaging second gear. Taking a sharp left back onto Nouveau Road, I focus on increasing the truck's speed. Flooring the accelerator, I feel thrilled by the loud roar of the engine.

Peering into the rear view mirror, I spot Girl tailing me closely. Redfin isn't too far behind in the Commodore. It will only take him a moment to catch up.

Gritting my teeth with determination, I floor the accelerator again, trying to gain as much distance as I can away from Redfin. Third gear it is! The wind is even stronger now and I feel like my hair is going to fly off my head. A strong whipping sound bursts into my ears as I floor the accelerator one more, engaging fourth gear. Nouveau Road is wide and long enough to take the truck and its speed for a little while.

Approaching the bend, I break and quickly down shift gears to second. Swerving in a sharp circle, I almost veer the truck off the side of the road. Adjusting the steering wheel, I manage to straighten up and engage the sweet third gear as I roar straight down Vista Road.

As I drive, I allow myself to enjoy the sheer thrill of speed and wind, an exhilarating joy I haven't experienced in a long time.

After a short while, I gaze into the rear view mirror and notice that Redfin is catching up.

I need to make a quick decision. Very soon it will be hard to find anywhere to park the truck. I begin braking, reducing the speed and rapidly down shifting to first gear.

Taking one last look at the rear view mirror, I see that I managed to slow down just in time. There is still enough distance between Redfin and us.

Throwing on the indicator, I swerve into the right curb and break firmly until I am stationery. Pulling the handbrake, I switch off the ignition and inhale a deep breath. It's now or never.

Pulling the keys out of the ignition, I push open the driver's door and toss them into the scattered grassland.

Grabbing the two plastic bags, I jump out of the truck and dash towards the ute. Opening the passenger door, I jump into my seat, dragging the bags in with me.

I feel Girl's eyes on me. "Lira!" She exclaims. "You –"

"Let's go!" I cry, spotting the Commodore approaching us.

"Right," Girl floors the accelerator and we speed away, leaving Redfin stumbling out of the Commodore. I smile with satisfaction as I watch him punch the air in anger.

I can feel my heart racing as I sit back in my seat. I close my eyes, trying to calm down.

"That was amazing, Lira," Girl sounds excited. "I never knew you could drive a truck!"

I open my eyes, feeling my heart pounding in the back of my throat. "Mitch taught me how to drive," I smile as a memory of Mitch flashes in my mind. His tone was gentle as he moved his gorgeous muscular arms when teaching me to steer and change gears.
"It's come in handy a few times throughout the years."

"Especially now," Girl agrees. "Where do you want me to park?"

"Just alongside Spring Park," I tell her. "On Veta Street here,"
I point to the right.

Girl turns a sharp right and heads down Veta Street. "Here we are," she says, parking the ute under a canopy of trees. Switching off the ignition, she stares at me. "I can't wait to see what's in these bags, can you?"

"No, I can't," I agree.

Girl grabs hold of a plastic bag and begins to open it.

"Wait," I say firmly, digging into my black cloth bag. I retrieve a box of plastic hand gloves. "Pop these on first, so that your fingerprints aren't all over the evidence."

"Good idea," Girl grabs a pair of gloves and pulls them on over her fingers.

"They're a little tight," I say, as I pull the rim of a glove up over my right wrist. Luckily it still fits.

"Can I look now?" Girl asks eagerly.

"Sure," I say, watching as she opens the plastic bag.

"Oh!" Girl gasps in horror as she retrieves a dress from the bag. She stares at it for a moment, tears building in her eyes.

I bite my lip with concern. The crimson red evening dress that Girl is holding is stunning, embellished with a golden swirling pattern on its bodice. Its crimson red skirt drapes, revealing a series of striking, golden sun totems. It is clear what has happened.

"The poor Jandoe family," tears run freely down Girl's cheeks. "This is one of their original silk dresses. Can you see the precious sun totem?"

"Yes," I say gently, my heart breaking for the Jandoe family.

Girl smacks her forehead. "This dress would have provided the Petoys with the original sun totem that they appropriated when making the scarf that is for sale in Botanica," her cheeks redden with anger.

"I see," I realise.

Girl rifles through the bag. "A Betra family's original silk shirt with stunning dragon totems," her voice cracks. Pulling out an authentic, white silk skirt with twisting, green vine totems, she pulls at her hair. "This one belongs to my dear friends, the Yetla family."

After a while, the two bags have been emptied and a pile of original silk garments lay in a pile on the glove box.

"I can't believe this," Girl shakes her head. "The families will be beside themselves right now, wondering where their precious garments are."

"Yes," I empathise. "How violated they must feel by their theft."

For a moment, we sit quietly, letting our minds absorb what we have discovered.

I open one of the plastic bags. "Let's put these away now," I say. "We'll have to decide on a safe place to store them."

Girl nods, wiping her eyes. She helps me pack the garments away and ties the ends of the bags into knots. Reaching for her silk bag, she digs into it and retrieves Aisha's journal. "This really hurts my heart," she says, tapping her chest. "My family have been helping the local villagers of Mira to preserve their heritage silk collection for centuries." She flips open the journal to a specific page. "Read for yourself," she says as she hands it to me.

I accept the journal, my eyes eagerly scanning Aisha's elegant handwriting:

Winter, 1276

Standing in the dimly lit area of my small living room, I shake my hand vigorously. The burning light from the sulfur matchstick continues to extinguish. Glancing down at the floor, I see several matchsticks that I have discarded. My hands are too cold and shaking to keep them alight, rather they chill and smother the burning flames.

Picking up one last sulfur matchstick, I hold it steadily in my hand. Taking a deep breath, I strike its head determinedly against the wooden table edge. It crackles alive, burning a single, bright flame. I smile, content with my persistence and achievement.

Grabbing a tallow candle, I light it with the match, enjoying seeing it flicker into life. Extinguishing the match's flame, I drop it onto the floor.

Turning my focus to the burning candle in my hand, I smile, admiring the energy of its glow radiating throughout the dark space. Its acrid smell does not disturb me. I can tolerate it in order to be blessed with the company of a candle.

Stepping outside the front door, I hold the candle directly in front of me. Its light pierces through the dark blanket, allowing me to make out the shapes of rocks and grass on the terrain ahead of me.

I begin to walk, taking long, deliberate strides across the earth. The gravel crunches beneath my feet as I venture ahead, through the winding pathway of the village.

The windows of the houses are lit warmly with candle light, enabling people to find their ways back home in the dark. In some windows, there are the shifting silhouettes of bodies, which are unravelling their own stories through time.

Makeshift Girl: The Secret Heritage Trail

Approaching the wooden façade of one of the houses, I knock on its golden door. The sound of shuffling interrupts the silence and the door creaks open slowly.

"Who is there?" Asks a young female voice.

"It is me, Aisha," I reply. "I am here to repair your silk dress."

"Oh, Aisha," A wisp of brown hair flicks around the door frame, followed by two striking blue eyes. "It's lovely to have you here. Please do enter."

"Thank you Mrs Gestari," I say, smiling warmly.

"Please call me Setana," she says as she opens the door more widely and ushers me in. "We've known each other for a very long time."

I follow Setana along her darkened corridor. We enter a small space, dimly lit by a single tallow candle, which burns brightly in its silver holder on the wooden kitchen table.

"I am sorry that I do not have any more light," Setana sighs. "I have not had any time to make anymore tallow candles, as I am so busy with baby Nikira." She turns to face a small crib, in which a little baby girl lays, with a tuft of brown hair and a bright smile, gurgling away. She is rugged up in a warm, woolen blanket.

"There is ample light in here," I say as I place my candle next to hers on the table. "What a beautiful daughter you have."

"Yes, isn't she?" Setana picks up Nikira and rocks her gently, kissing her on the forehead. "Would you like to hold her?" She offers.

"Yes, I would love to," I say, holding out my arms to accept Nikira. She lies calmly as I rock her gently, clenching her hands into tiny fists and staring around her world with her bright blue eyes.

Setana crosses the room to a small table and retrieves a dress. She returns, holding the garment up for me to see. "This was my grandmother's silk dress," she says. "You can see it bears the beautiful totems of my family."

I stare at the dress, admiring it. "The cedar tree totem is beautiful," I say. "It is complimented by the rich turquoise colour of the silk."

"Yes," says Setana, running her fingers across the silk sleeves and bodice. "It is so light, yet carries so much history," she sighs. "I am afraid that it is beginning to fall apart." She reveals a tear in the bodice of the dress.

"Oh," I say. "That is unfortunate. I can fix that."

"You can? That would be wonderful." Setana extends her arms towards me. I glance at Nikira, who is smiling contentedly.

"You are a natural with children," Setana smiles. "Are you planning to have any of your own?"

"One day," I say softly. "If I am blessed enough." I place Nikira gently into Setana's arms.

Reaching into my skirt pocket, I retrieve a small needle. "Can I sit somewhere?" I ask.

"Yes, on the lounge over here," Setana removes Nikira's baby clothes off its seat and drapes them over the side of the crib.

I sit on the lounge, accepting the beautiful silk dress from Setana. It feels sheer and light in my hands, evidently made from the highest quality silk.

Setana grabs my tallow candle from the table with her free hand and places it next to me on the wooden side table. "This should make it easier to see," she says softly. Sitting next to me, she undoes the strap on her own dress' bodice and holds Nikira close to her breast, feeding her.

Threading the needle with turquoise silk, I set to work on repairing the delicate bodice. It takes a lot of concentration to make the silk stitches thin enough so that they appear to vanish within the material.

After some time, I turn the dress over with its under side facing me. Sliding the needle under the nearest stitch, I form a loop with the silk thread. Inserting the needle through it, I form a knot, which I tie off. "Do you have a utility knife?" I ask Setana.

"Yes, at the back," she waves towards the wooden bench at the back of the room.

Standing, I cross the room to the bench, carrying the dress. Grabbing the utility knife, I use it to cut the remaining loose silk thread free from the knot.

"There," I sigh. "The dress is repaired. Where would you like me to place it?"

"Next to me," Setana says as she reties the bodice of her own dress.

I place the silk dress on the lounge and pocket my needle and silk thread.

Setana rubs Nikira's back, helping her to pass wind. She peers over at the dress, her eyes shining with happiness. "Many blessings to you, Aisha," Setana gushes. "You have helped to preserve the Presque family's heritage silk." She passes me a gold coin.

"It is my humble honour," I smile, receiving the payment. "I will take my leave now, Setana. I hope you and Nikira fare well during the increasing cold." I retrieve my burning tallow candle from the side table, feeling the warmth of it in my hand. Its light glows across the room.

"And you," Nikira smiles as she leads me towards the front door. "Bless your generous heart, Aisha," she says as she watches me leave.

Closing the journal, I feel a huge sense of responsibility. "The silk of Mira has such a strong heritage," I say. "We need to do all that we can to protect it."

"Definitely," Girl agrees, placing the journal back into her silk bag. "I appreciate your support, Lira."

I consider our situation. We have nowhere other than the ute to reside in. A place to rest is essential to keep us safe and energised.

"Do you mind if I ask Mitch if he can help us?" I ask Girl. "We are both exhausted and he may be able to find somewhere for us to stay for the short term."

"Sure," Girl sighs with relief.

"Okay," I reach into my pocket and retrieve my mobile phone. Inhaling a deep breath, I dial Mitch's number. It takes a little while for him to answer my call.

"Hello," Mitch's voice sounds sweet on the end of the line. My heart flutters anxiously.

"Concrete," I say abruptly, using our code word for *sanctuary*.

"Oh!" Mitch sounds shocked. "Are you okay?" I can hear his concern.

"I'm okay," my tone is distant. I am still hurt by his betrayal.

"Good," Mitch sounds relieved. "I'll text you some details soon. I'm still on shift but I will try to see you as soon as it's over, okay?"

"Okay," I sigh, unsure if I want to see him. I end the call.

Ding.

It is the sound of Mitch's message coming through.

Girl steps closer to me and stares at the screen of my mobile. "What are you looking at?" She asks.

I meet Girl's gaze. "Mitch has just sent us the address of a motor inn," I tell her. "It's on Destiny Road, the main road out of town. He's finishing work and says he'll have a room organised for us there within the next hour."

Girl's mouth drops open in surprise. "That's so nice," she smiles. "Mitch is being supportive, Lira."

I smile with gritted teeth. "Should we go?"

"Yes," Girl eagerly agrees. "Best we hide somewhere safely before Redfin finds us."

Chapter 17

As we arrive at Journey Motor Inn, I marvel at the L shaped layout of the yellow building. The sun shines on its bricks, making them appear almost golden and speckled.

Girl parks the ute in the bay outside the reception office. "Is this where you're meant to go?" She asks me.

"Yes," I say, popping on my sunglasses. "I've got to collect the keys to our room. I'll be back in a minute." I step out of the ute and approach the glass door into the reception area. A large poster is stuck on it, advertising a pizza delivery service. *One family pizza for the price of a large*, it reads. My mouth drools as I view the ham and pineapple pizza in the image.

Reaching into my pocket, I grab my mobile and take a photo of the phone number on the poster. It will be nice to order a pizza tonight.

Suddenly, the door opens and a middle aged man stands before me. He has shoulder length red hair, which he has tucked behind his ears. His brown eyes widen with surprise.

"Well, hello," he says, looking me up and down. "Welcome to Journey Motor Inn. I'm Shane. How may I be of service to you?"

I avoid eye contact with Shane, feeling uncomfortable by his stare. "I have come to collect the keys for my room," I say, shuffling my feet.

Shane lets go of the door. "Well, follow me," he says exuberantly. He pops behind his desk and leans on his arms. "What name are you booked under?" He asks, staring at me longingly.

I inhale a deep breath and gaze at the desk, avoiding Shane's stare. "Mary Lee," I say, using the cover name that Mitch organised for me.

I can hear a woman's voice in the background. Turning around, I realise that the television is blaring. The woman is wearing a khaki tank shirt and shorts. She is walking across a dry, rugged landscape, looking a little lost. "I should be able to find my way back home," the woman sighs dramatically. Her words strike a chord in my heart.

I feel hands upon mine and look up. Shane stares at me with shining eyes. "There you are lovely," he says. "I lost your attention for a moment."

I withdraw my hand from his and step back from the counter. I feel sick in the stomach and mad at Shane for behaving so inappropriately. "Can I have the keys please?" I demand, my face reddening and my hands shaking. I want to leave the reception area as quickly as possible.

"Of course Mary Lee," he smiles a broad smile and heads to the back wall. "Here it is," he says, grabbing a key ring from the hanging board. "Room 35," he hands me a bundle of keys. "It's up the ramp and off to your right."

"Thank you," I say, snatching the keys from him quickly. I do not want him to grab my hand again.

"Let me know if you need anything," Shane continues to smile. "Dial 126 and you'll have my attention immediately." He ushers me to the front door.

"Okay," I say, walking in long strides across the room. I can't exit quickly enough.

Shane opens the door for me and touches me lightly on the shoulder as I step outside. "Have a wonderful stay, Mary Lee," he coughs, nearly choking on his words. "Oh, I need a drink." He steps back inside the reception area, finally leaving me alone.

Makeshift Girl: The Secret Heritage Trail

I am relieved to get away from Shane. The air is warm and fresh, wisping gently across my face. I exhale a deep breath and allow myself to relax for a moment.

"Jade, watch that ball!" I hear a female voice call out. My gaze falls upon a young woman who is watching a little girl chase after a basketball that she has thrown towards me. The girl's blonde hair flops into her eyes and she bends down, trying to stop the ball from rolling any further with her hands.

I extend my leg, stopping the ball in its tracks with my foot. Bending down, I pick up the ball and look at the girl.

She is puffing, her hazel eyes wide with worry. "I'm sorry Miss," she says. "Can I please have my ball?"

Bending down, I hand her the ball. "That's okay," I say. "You just might want to watch where you are throwing the ball. Cars come through here."

The girl nods, her eyes still wide. "Of course, Miss, I will. Thank you so much for giving me my ball back." She turns and races back to her mother. I watch the woman mouth a silent *thank you* to me.

Stepping forward, I scan the parking bays, looking for the one allocated to room 35. There it is with the number sprayed boldly on the concrete. Turning to face the ute, I wave to Girl, pointing to the parking space. Girl starts the ignition and drives slowly into the parking spot.

I approach the driver's window. "Here we are," I tell Girl. "We are booked into room 35."

Girl steps out of the ute and stretches tall. "Oh, that's better," she sighs.

I approach the ute tray and grab Girl's box of red gum statues. It is too risky to leave them in the ute. Girl joins me, grabbing a large bag herself. "Clean clothes and toiletries," she smiles. "It will be nice to shower and change."

I nod, agreeing. Life on the road is tough. It's nice when you get a chance to take care of your personal hygiene.

I reach into the passenger seat and grab the two bags of silk clothing. "Let's store these inside the clothing and toiletries bag," I suggest. "That way everything is kept together."

"Good idea," Girl nods. She holds open the clothing and toiletries bag and I pop the silk clothing bags inside it. Girl ties the ends of the bag together in a knot to seal it.

I glance at the ute tray. "Is there anything else you want to take inside?" I ask.

Girl rifles through her belongings. "Just this box," she says, pointing to the box of her clay statue models. "We can be sure all is safe then."

I pick up the box and stack it on top of the one that I am already holding. "Guess we're all set," I smile.

"Yes," Girl agrees, falling into step beside me. We walk up the ramp and reach the rooms.

I count the door numbers of the rooms while I pass them. "30, 31 …" I say aloud as I continue to walk.

"We're just here," Girl calls out, having reached our room already. I catch up with her and hand her the key. "Here we go," Girl looks over her shoulder and smiles at me. Unlocking the door, she watches it swing wide open.

We are greeted by a cozy little living room, equipped with a green leather couch and a small television. I place the boxes down on the wooden coffee table and walk across to the small kitchen bench. "Oh, a kettle!" I exclaim, grabbing it and turning on the tap. Once the kettle is filled with water, I return it to its heating element and switch it on.

Glancing towards my left, I see a small greeting pack sitting on the bench next to the kettle. It contains coffee, tea, sugar sachets, milk pods, a stack of plastic coffee cups and a small box of chocolates. "Would you like a tea or coffee?" I ask Girl as I grab a tea bag and a cup.

"Tea please," Girl places a tea bag into her cup.

Once the kettle boils, I pour hot water into our cups. Girl jiggles her rosehip tea bag and looks at me. "Well, it's nice of Mitch to organise this room for us," she smiles. "Don't you think so?"

"Yes," I nod. "He can be good like that."

Girl takes a sip of her tea. "Oh, that's lovely," she says. "All I need now is something to eat."

I suddenly remember the pizza delivery service. Placing my cup down on the bench, I reach into my pocket and retrieve my mobile phone. "Do you feel like a pizza?" I ask Girl as I show her the advertisement.

Girl's smile broadens, showing off her lovely white teeth. "That would be great," she says. "I'd love their super special. It should be packed with flavour."

"Sounds perfect," I say. I punch the pizza restaurant's phone number into my mobile.

"Your order please?" The answer is prompt.

"A family sized super special pizza," I say. "Can we please have it with extra olives?"

The brisk female voice confirms my order. "Anything else?"

"Throw in some herb bread, a garden salad and a large bottle of orange mineral water," I say. I am so hungry. I'm sure that Girl is too.

The woman's voice pipes through the mobile, confirming my order again. "Is that for pick up or delivery?" She asks.

"Delivery," I reply, giving her the address.

"Your name please?" The woman asks.

"Mary Lee," I reply, using my cover name. "I'll pay on delivery with cash."

"Delivery will be about 20 minutes," the woman says. "Enjoy your pizza journey."

I pocket my phone. "We have 20 minutes," I tell Girl.

Girl tosses her cup into the bin and heads into the living area. "Just enough time for me to shower," she says. Grabbing the clothing and toiletries bag, she walks towards the back of the room. "There's the bathroom," I hear her say as she peers into a room at the back.

I stand, sipping my tea for a long while and enjoying the peace and quiet. It is nice to relax and think without having to run.

Knock knock.

I jump a mile high.

"Pizza delivery!" A man's thick accent calls outside the front door. I check the time on my mobile phone. That was fast. He is earlier than expected.

I approach the front door and pull it open. A tall man with olive skin that glows in the evening lamp light, greets me. He cocks his head to one side and strands of his greying hair fall into his eyes. Pushing them out the way, he gazes at me, his grey eyes swirling intensely. It is Chief Opula.

My heart thuds wildly in my chest.

He has found me.

"Hello," says Chief Opula, his gaze softening as he stares at me. "Such beauty stands before me." The rough skin of his thumb scrapes against my cheek. As it does so, his white tunic sleeve falls back over his right elbow and reveals a tattoo of a gold, rearing horse on his arm.

I inhale a sharp breath, which raises the Chief's eyebrows.

Forcing myself to wait, I gage how I should respond.

"Such soft skin," Chief Opula caresses my face, his thumb and fingers feeling like rough sandpaper against my skin. "You are of age now, eh?' Placing his hands behind my back, he pulls me to him firmly, pressing his body against mine. His stench is strong: a mixture of oil and dirt.

My heart is beating furiously but I harness my strength. Grabbing the Chief's hands from around my back, I twist around and free myself. "Don't move," I say, grasping him firmly around the neck in a tight headlock. "Or I will strengthen my grip."

The Chief is coughing and gasping for breath. Beads of sweat are forming across his forehead. He is panicking. Good.

"Please," the Chief gasps, holding up both hands in surrender. "Let me go."

"Let me consider your request," I say, tightening my grip a little. The Chief inhales a sharp breath, his body tensing. "I'll let you go, Chief Opula," I huff as I juggle his weight in my arms. "As long as you promise to leave me be."

The Chief closes his eyes for a moment and his sweat drips down his cheeks. He finally nods.

I release him forcefully, pushing him towards the doorway. "Go!" I command, waving him away.

Chief Opula takes one final glance at me. "You are all I hoped you would be," he smiles smugly. "Beautiful and fierce. I will wait for you as long as it takes and you will join me."

"Never," I seethe, my eyes lashing with anger. "I will never join you Petoys."

The Chief's eyes narrow intensely. "Once you see the riches that you can have, you will," he demands. "We'll meet again soon, Adira." As he turns on his heels, my heart freezes in my chest.

Waiting a few moments, I step outside into the warm night air. Locking the door, I tread lightly across the concrete, as quietly as I can, following Chief Opula down the ramp. He cuts through a fern, heading towards the back of the reception office.

Bobbing behind the fern, I watch as the Chief approaches his silver Mercedes.

Pressing the remote, the Chief pulls open the driver's door. I watch as he settles into his seat and begins to chat on his mobile, pointing back towards the motel rooms.

My heart thuds with fear. It would be safe to say that the Chief is confirming our whereabouts.

Taking a deep breath, I reach into my pocket and pull out my mobile phone. As I take a photo of the Chief's face, my eyes focus on his arrogant smirk.

Pocketing his mobile, Chief Opula sits in his car, staring out the windscreen, waiting.

Dropping down onto my knees, I am determined to avoid being spotted by the Chief.

I crawl slowly back to the ramp and ascend it as quickly as I can on all fours. I keep crawling until I reach the motel room. Grabbing the keys, I fumble with them until I find the right one. Reaching up, I place the key in the front door's lock and twist it until the door opens.

Crawling inside, I retrieve my keys and shut the door, locking it quickly. I am wild with panic, knowing that we only have minutes to spare before we are caught.

Taking a few deep breaths, I try to settle my rapidly beating heart. It is so difficult this existence. My mind reels, considering how so much detail could have been gained about my whereabouts so quickly. Shane, the motel receptionist's face pops into my mind. His over attentive behaviour, greeting me at the door, feeling my hands … was he gathering information on me?

I feel a presence next to me and look up, meeting Girl's gaze.

"Was that the pizza delivery, Lira?" She asks, her eyes wide with hope.

I nod, feeling almost faint with anxiety. I need to pull myself together right now. It is no use panicking. "You're not going to like this," I tell her, unsure of how to approach the situation.

"Try me," Girl eyes narrow and she crosses her arms over her chest.

"Grab your things," I breathe. "We have seconds to leave."

"Right," Girl nods, her eyes widening as she registers what I am saying. She doesn't ask any more questions, just dashes towards the bedroom.

I pick up the box of red gum statues and watch as Girl re-enters the room with the bag of clothing and toiletries.

"Pass me that bag," I say, reaching out for it.

"Sure," Girl places it on top of the box that I am holding and runs across the room. She lifts the box of clay statue models effortlessly.

"We can't return to the ute right now," I tell her. "There will probably already be somebody there waiting for us. It's best that we find a spot to hide."

Girl nods as she opens the front door. "Keys?" She asks, reaching out for them.

I pass the bundle of keys to her and she trials a few different ones before she successfully locks the door.

"A good distraction," Girl says. "They'll assume that we're still inside and it will take them a while to get the door open. It'll buy us some time."

"Great idea," I say, beginning to head towards my right. "We need to go this way. Behind the front office, the Chief is sitting in his silver Mercedes, waiting for us. I think he's called in some assistance."

Girl's eyes widen. "Lira?" She begins to shake.

"We'll be fine," I say firmly. "The dark will help conceal us. Let's go!"

We walk quickly across the concrete, passing the other motel rooms. The lights shining on their doors startle me, exposing our bodies as we shift across the ground. I continue to move quickly, trying to ignore the weight I carry and its impact on my shoulders.

"This way!" Girl's voice is a loud whisper. She turns right, leading us towards the back of the building.

We are greeted with another small glass building with orange, circular tables spilling out the front onto the concrete. It is busy with couples and families chatting and eating. It is far too busy to enter. We will be discovered for sure.

On the front façade of the building, a bright, yellow neon sign flashes its lights: *Journey Diner*.

Girl faces me. "What do you think we should do?" She asks.

I consider the function of the diner. Suddenly, an idea pops into my head. "Follow my lead," I say.

"Okay," Girl cocks her head to one side. "You look pretty determined, Lira."

"Well, I need to see what cover we can create," I say, pointing towards the diner. "We need to find a way out of here."

"Oh," Girl smiles. "This sounds interesting. A bit of improvisation, eh?"

We walk towards the diner, passing the noisy chatter of people engrossed in conversations. I spot a number of empty tables, piled with dirty dishes that haven't been collected.

"I have an idea," I say, heading passed the tables. "There should be a door around the back."

As we head towards the back of the diner, I can feel Girl's energy buzzing beside me. She is super alert, ready to take on anything required to keep her safe.

After a short while, Girl points to a small wooden door with a red door knob. "Over there," she says softly.

I glance over my shoulder, checking that we haven't been followed.

Approaching the door slowly, I press my ear against the wooden stile, listening for any sounds of people approaching. It is quiet.

I make eye contact with Girl and motion for her to stand next to me. She shuffles closely, her nervous energy sparking in the air like live electricity. "It's okay," I meet her gaze and smile reassuringly. "Just follow my lead."

Girl nods, her eyes wide. She inhales a deep breath and grabs onto my singlet. I squeeze her hand tightly, watching as she exhales her breath and begins to settle down.

"Are you alright?" I am worried that I am asking too much of her.

"Yes," Girl sighs. She lets go of my singlet. "Ready when you are."

I turn my attention back to the door. Its location right next to a large dump bin suggests that it is only really used by the cleaning staff. Inside, there should be a room that stores the disguises that we need to leave here safely.

I press my ear to the wooden stile once more. Inside the room, I can hear the sound of wheels screeching across a floor.

"Five more minutes!" I hear a female voice call. "See you out back."

"Yes," a male voice replies. "Looking forward to it."

The female's laughter is light and bubbly and begins to fade, along with the wheels of the trolley as she exits from the room.

I listen for a little while longer. Finally, there is the sound of footsteps clacking across the floor as the man also leaves the room.

I make eye contact with Girl once more and point at the door. She nods, understanding. Stepping forward, I reach for the door knob and twist it gently until the door swings open.

The room inside is small and brightly lit. A mop has fallen out of an open cupboard along the back wall and has left a puddle of water on the ground. Stepping closer to the cupboard, I peer inside it and see a variety of cleaning equipment, including: antiseptic spray bottles, mops, mop buckets, brooms and sponges.

Girl places her box down in the far back corner of the room and rotates her shoulders. "That's better," she sighs.

I follow her lead, stacking my box on top of hers. The bag of clothing and toiletries lays precariously on top of the boxes. I stretch my arms behind my back, thankful to take the weight off my shoulders.

My eyes drift to the shelving next to the cupboard. An assortment of linen has been folded neatly and piled onto each shelf. I spot a used apron and hair scarf strewn across the ground. Someone obviously finished work for the day and discarded them.

I turn to face Girl, who is staring out the room, across the lino floored corridor. She has an intense expression on her face, as though she is concentrating on something specific.

Stepping closer, I wait silently until Girl senses my presence. She turns to face me, her eyes wide with fear. "Be careful, Lira," she whispers. "I've been found."

In the dim light shining down the corridor, stands a tall man, wearing a black, rearing horse headscarf. His dark blonde locks fly out from under the material and fall into his eyes. Green and piercing, his eyes stare intensely at Girl and a devilish smirk crosses his lips. Rolling up the sleeves of his red, chequered shirt, he reveals a rearing horse tattoo on his right arm.

"Vianna," the man's voice is dark and bounces in an echo across the walls. The name strikes the air and makes Girl jump backwards, her hands trembling.

My heart pounds in my chest. I am afraid for Girl's safety right now.

Girl stands tall on her tiptoes and begins to rock her feet. Her body is tense, absorbing the sound of her name. Cocking her head to one side, she meets the man's piercing gaze. "I am not her," she says with conviction.

The man's eyelashes flicker as he lets Girl's response sit in the air between them. "Your steps, Vianna, will always circle back to us Petoys. It's better that you surrender yourself now and accept your fate."

Girl holds her ground, keeping her gaze level and constant. "You seem to have your wires crossed," she says calmly. "I am a mere Girl who feels the solid world beneath her feet. The terrain may be rough and at times hard to trek but I always find a way. You did once too, Dari, remember?" She steps forward, reaching out a hand, which she places lightly on his arm. "It's not your fault, what happened to your family. Your silks were of the finest quality and sought after across the sea. Your totem was taken from you in Mira."

Dari's eyes narrow darkly and he pulls at his hair with frustration. "You think you know what it's like to lose your identity? You, who will control the very trade that was stolen from under us? Try watching your own family members rot away, unable to eat, while the rich become even richer. The Petoys, they've promised us freedom, new riches and a break away from the selfish empire."

Tears pool into Girl's eyes. "I am sorry, Dari," she whispers. "For you and your beautiful family. I have such fond memories..."

It is quiet for a moment, while Dari and Girl contemplate.

After a short while, Girl grabs Dari's hand. "Don't forget what it's like to run, Dari. Do you remember the feeling of the breeze flying through your hair when we used to run through the forest? We were young and freer then, with thoughts of how we'd like our futures to be."

Dari's lips tremble as he meets Girl's gaze. "Yes," he agrees. "We were."

Straightening up, Dari flicks Girl's hand away. "It was foolish to dream. The world of Mira did not allow it. What happened to you, Vianna?"

Girl steps back, raising her arms into the air. "I am a mere Girl now. This Vianna you remember, she has sailed away, across the wide sea and off into the horizon. There is a world she seeks that drifts like a gentle wind into her dreams. It is a place where words heal and caress her soul, which is shattered by endless persecution."

A wicked smirk crosses Dari's lips and he steps closer until his face is level with Girl's. "Break your soul we will," he spits, his eyes sparking and sinister. "You and your empire have no place in this world and will be wiped from living memory." He grabs hold of Girl's arm forcefully. "Come with me now!" He pulls her arm, dragging her out of the room.

As they exit the room, Girl moves quickly, grabbing hold of the door and slamming it forcefully into Dari's face. He stumbles to the ground, grasping hold of his head and moaning in pain. "I'm sorry Dari," Girl's voice is firm as she steps backwards. Glancing around the room quickly, she grabs hold of a long extension cord and approaches him again. "I will not be going with you today." Dropping Dari's hands by his side, she begins to wind the rope around his loose hanging arms and waist, binding them together.

I stand back, my mouth wide open with surprise at the ease with which Girl manages the situation.

"Nice and tight," Girl says, admiring her work. She ties the end of the rope together, making a knot. "A bit hard to move now, isn't it, Dari?"

Dari's eyes flicker with rage. "You'd better watch yourself, *Girl*," he threatens. "You will be found again, by someone even more dangerous than me. What will happen to you then, I wonder?"

Girl places her hands on her hips. "Oh Dari," she sighs. "You've been playing in the darkness for too long. Theft, betrayal, murder … you've become desensitised to the ways of the Petoys. It won't be long until they tire and dispose of you too."

Dari smirks. "Have you seen this Girl?" He asks in a patronising tone. "If only you realised how big the hunt was for you, *Girl*. We won't stop until we capture you."

Girl meets my gaze. "Grab me a cloth please," she points to a shelf along the back wall.

Dashing over to the shelf, I grab a large, blue cloth and hand it to Girl.

Rolling the cloth into a ball, Girl grabs hold of Dari's chin and pulls it down firmly, forcing his mouth open. "Enough," she commands, shoving the cloth ball into his mouth.

Dari's eyes widen in surprise and a muffled groan escapes his lips. He wriggles furiously, trying to escape his entrapment.

"Give me a hand?" Girl's eyes rest on me.

"Sure, I thought you'd never ask," I say, approaching Dari.

Girl places her hands under Dari's underarms. I grab hold of his feet.

"Ready?" Girl asks.

I nod.

We lift Dari together and I step backwards into the cleaning room. His body is moderately heavy and I am thankful that I am not dropping him as he kicks his legs forcefully.

"Keep going," Girl points her head towards the back of the room. "You're nearly there."

I keep stepping backwards and peer over my shoulder. I see what has caught Girl's attention. A second metal cupboard sits at the back of the room. It is closed.

Once we reach the cupboard, Girl releases her left hand, twists open the lock and pulls open the doors. The inside of the cupboard is fairly empty, except for a few large pillows that Girl kicks out with her feet.

"In he goes!" Girl directs. I lower Dari's legs into the cupboard. Girl guides his body inside and we watch as he leans precariously against the back wall. "It will be good for you to think for a while, Dari," Girl says, shoving the pillows back inside. Her hands reach out and grasp the two cupboard doors.

Dari shakes his head and stamps his feet with rage.

"Goodbye Dari," Girl shuts the cupboard doors and twists the handle until it locks. I can hear Dari's muffled whimpers in the background.

"Wow!" I exclaim, staring at Girl. "I never knew you could do that."

Girl sighs. "Being a young girl in Mira, I had to learn self defence," she said. "Lucky I did, it saved me this time."

"For a short time, yes," I agree. "Until someone comes looking for Dari."

"You're right," Girl's eyes widen. "What should we do now?"

I know that we only have a few minutes to spare. Dashing across to the storage shelving against the far back wall, I grab two white aprons and hair scarves.

Approaching Girl, I reach for her hair. "Try to keep calm," I say as I place the hair scarf over her scalp. I twist her blue hair strands into a bunch, letting the remaining material of the scarf cascade down and cover them completely.

"Ouch!" Girl's cry is acute as I tie the ends of the scarf in a knot at the back of her head.

"Sorry," I say as I step back. "Your hair is covered now. Conceal your clothing with this apron."

Girl pats at the scarf on her hair. "Thanks Lira," she says. Grabbing the apron, she guides her head through the neck strap and lets the apron material cascade over her stomach. "Can you help me tie the ribbons?" She asks.

"Sure," I grab the two ribbons dangling on either side of the apron and pull them tightly. "Not too tight?" I ask her.

"Perfect," Girl smiles.

"Great," I tie the ribbons together, forming a bow, which sits neatly on Girl's back. "There you go," I say, stepping back and grabbing my own apron. I work quickly, pulling the strap over my head and letting the apron fall down over my stomach. I tie the straps behind my back.

"Ssh!" Girl nudges me.

My ears prick up. I can hear the click clack of footsteps approaching our room.

Grabbing the head scarf, I toss it over my scalp and ensure that the length of remaining material covers the strands of my hair.

The footsteps sound very close now. We will soon be discovered.

Tying the ends of the scarf into a knot, I inhale a deep breath. It is time to take on a new persona.

"Now come over here," I say, grabbing Girl's arm and leading her towards the shelving unit.

Girl stares at me, clearly confused.

"Work with me," I whisper, turning her to face the shelves.

The footsteps click clack into the room. Out of the corner of my eye I notice a young woman, possibly in her early twenties, dressed in her cleaning uniform: a white apron and head scarf. She approaches the cleaning cupboard and stores her mop and bucket away.

"Great," she mutters as she pushes her black hair away from her face and picks up the fallen mop. "Another mess to clean up." Grabbing some paper towel, she soaks up the dirty water on the floor.

I hear a banging sound in the cupboard. It is Dari, trying to raise attention. The young woman jumps, her black hair flicking wildly across her shoulders. She turns around, her green eyes darting across the space as she tries to locate the source of the sound.

I tap the shelf loudly, trying to match Dari's banging. "All the clean linen, including spare uniforms are kept here," I say loudly, pretending that I am showing Girl her way around the room. "We make sure that they are folded very neatly."

In my peripheral vision, I notice the young woman nodding. She is satisfied that my banging of the shelf was the sound that she heard and is returning to her tidy up.

"Right," says Girl, working with me. Glancing out of the corner of my eye once more, I notice the young woman placing her dirty apron into a cleaning trolley.

"Someone has been very messy here," I say, picking up the apron and hair scarf that lie strewn across the ground. "Please make sure that you place your dirty uniform into this trolley at the end of your shift."

"Of course," Girl says, watching me toss the uniform items into the trolley. She nudges her head towards the left, directing my attention to another man entering the room.

"Seb!" I hear the young woman greet the young male cleaner. He is stockily built with short, light brown hair with a long fringe that flops into his eyes.

A dull banging noise fills the room, startling us all. I know that it is Dari, stamping away in the cupboard.

"What was that?" The young woman has turned pale.

"The cleaning room ghost!" Seb makes a scary face, his bright blue eyes flashing.

"Don't say that Seb!" The young woman crosses her arms over her chest in annoyance.

"Shift's over!" Seb's voice sounds dramatic as he rips off his apron and hair scarf. He throws them across the room and the hair scarf lands strewn over my arm. "Sorry," Seb says, his eyes a little mischievous.

I hear the young girl inhale a sharp breath. "Seb!" She exhales anxiously. "She's a manager."

Staring directly into my eyes, a flash of worry crosses Seb's face. "My most sincere apologies, Ma'am," he says. "I will never do that again."

Something in Seb's voice suggests that he is used to a very aggressive management style at this bistro, so I ensure that I follow through with it. "Place your dirty uniform into the trolley properly," I say firmly. "Next shift, you can work ten minutes later, collecting everyone's uniforms and ensuring that the load is ready for washing. Is that clear?"

"Yes Ma'am," Seb lowers his head. "I'll do as you say." He removes the head scarf from my arm and places it carefully into the trolley. Stepping back, he stares down at the ground.

"That's better," I say, maintaining the control in my voice. "You may leave now."

The young girl stares at Seb worriedly. "Let's go Seb," she says softly, motioning towards the door and throwing her bag strap over her shoulder.

We watch as the two young cleaners exit the room and step outside into the open air.

Stepping forward, I press my back against the frame of the door. Girl huddles up next to me.

"I'm glad that shift is over," Seb sounds annoyed. "I'm getting sick of being told what to do by such strict management. I think it might be time to consider something else to do for work."

"Really?" The young girl is surprised. "What will you do?"

"I don't know," Seb's voice has flattened. "I'm not sure any other employer would hire me. I've only ever cleaned. I hope I might be able to do something else."

"I'm sure you could," the young girl consoles. "Any employer would be lucky to have you."

"You're so sweet, Zera," Seb's voice is gentle. Reaching out, he pulls her closer to him and they kiss gently.

After a moment, Zera pulls away. She pushes her long, black hair away from her face. "It might be a good time for you to leave your job," she says, narrowing her brown eyes. "Rumour has it that this motel is being sold."

"Really?" Seb raises his eyebrows and runs a hand across his spiky, brown hair. "Do they know who the buyer is?"

"No-one has been named," Zera sighs. "I wonder if it has something to do with the Petoy business. Every night I seem to land one of these flyers. What do I want with their trucks?" She flicks the flyer into the air, letting it float gently to the ground.

Girl stares at me with wide eyes. "The Petoys!" She whispers strongly.

I place my finger to my lips, motioning for her to be quiet.

"I guess I'll start looking for that new job, then,' Seb sighs.

It is silent for a moment, while Seb kicks some loose stones around the concrete, lost in his thoughts.

"Walk me to my car, Seb?" Zera's voice fills the silence.

"Of course," Seb's voice softens. "I'll take care of you, Zera."

"I know you will," Zera smiles broadly, showing off her lovely white teeth.

Seb reaches out his hand and Zera takes hold of it. The couple walk away, disappearing into the darkness.

Girl grabs hold of my arm, turning me to face her. "They're everywhere, the Petoys," she whispers hoarsely. "Even here at the motel." Letting go of my arm, she steps through the doorway and outside. I watch her bend over and retrieve the flyer that Zera discarded. Girl stares at it silently.

My gaze darts to the back of the room, where we have stored our belongings. An idea pops into my head. Grabbing an empty trolley, I push it towards the boxes.

Pulling open the white curtains that fringe the bottom level of the trolley, I reveal a steel storage shelf. Picking up the first box, I place it onto the shelf, followed by the second box. Finally, I store the bag of clothing and toiletries. Pulling the white curtains shut across the shelf, I smile. All is well concealed.

Time to organise the cleaning equipment. Dashing towards the cleaning cupboard, I stop and scan the shelves for spray bottles of disinfectant. There is one, waiting to be grabbed. I place it on the top shelf of the trolley, along with a roll of cleaning squares. I may have discovered a way out of here.

Spinning the trolley around, I wheel it towards the door and push it outside into the open air. Closing the door behind me, I turn to face Girl. She is crouched on the ground, still staring at the flyer.

"Girl, are you okay?" I ask, pushing the trolley aside and sitting next to her.

Girl stares at me and shakes her head. I notice that her hands are trembling.

I put my arm around her shoulders. "Do you want to talk?" I offer, knowing that I may be pushing it a little.

"Nar-ic-ia Pet-oy," Girl stammers. "She is un-stopp-able." She passes the flyer to me.

Holding the flyer in both hands, I read its eye catching message in bold, red font: *Petoy Delivery Service: Your Business is our Business.*

Below the typeface, is an image of Naricia, with her trademark, bright red lipstick, standing next to a truck strung with blue neon lights flashing over its cabin. Naricia wears a skin tight, purple dress that reaches her knees. With both hands grasping her hips, she looks fiercely determined.

On the bottom of the poster, the viewer is invited to: *call Naricia Petoy and her team for prompt service, 24 hours a day, 7 days a week.* A phone number is provided as the only way to contact the business.

Girl rests her head against my chest and begins to cry softly. I hold her for a long while, letting her release her stress.

When Girl has calmed down, I stand slowly, pulling her up onto her feet. "Naricia Petoy is fierce," I say, pointing to the flyer. "A very strong personality."

Girl nods, swiping away at her tears. "Yes, she is," she sighs. "She and my family have quite the history."

My eyes widen in surprise.

Girl meets my gaze. "Please get me out of here safely, Lira. If Naricia finds me, it's all over."

I jump into action. Naricia *cannot* find Girl. Pocketing the flyer, I grab Girl's hand and head towards the trolley. "Pop in here," I say, opening the white curtain.

"Really?" Girl's eyes widen in surprise. "You came up with this idea? You're a genius, Lira."

"I've watched too many classical movies," I smile. "This may work, if we play it just right."

"Give me a hand?" Girl asks, placing her right foot onto the steel shelf.

I grasp Girl's hand and help her crawl onto the shelf. She just fits between the stacked boxes and the clothing and toiletries bag.

"I will stop a few times, pretending to clean," I tell Girl. "Wait until I say the words: 'I'm so tired' and you can jump straight into the ute. Okay?"

"Okay," Girl smiles with relief. "Thanks so much for putting yourself on the line for me, Lira." Her eyes narrow into slits. "I feel so bad that it has to be this way."

"It's fine," I grin. "We're a team, remember?"

"A team," Girl repeats, her smile returning. "Yes, a team." She closes the curtains, leaving me to focus on my task ahead.

I push the trolley across the cement, heading back towards the motel rooms. Turning left, I head down the corridor, aware that I may now be under the gaze of Chief Opula. Stopping in front of each room, I spray the windows with the disinfectant and wipe them clean with a square wipe. I continue doing this, so that I become a monotonous part of the landscape of the motel. *I am nothing exciting to watch, Chief Opula.*

I clean the window of our room and a couple more before I reach the end of the corridor. *Here we go*, I mouth silently. *We're on the way out now.*

Pushing the trolley down the ramp, I approach the front reception office. There is only a small, dull light shining on the front window. The inside of the office is closed and unattended.

Reaching for the disinfectant bottle, I spray the glass on the front door. As I wipe the glass with a square wipe, I study the tiny logo on the right hand corner of the pizza advertisement. It belongs to the Petoy Delivery Service.

Reception area cleaned, I spin the trolley around and head towards the ute. My heart begins to pound in my chest. I know that I only have a couple of minutes to get us out of here.

In the dim light shining from the outdoor lamps, I notice that the ute has remained untouched. There is no-one around or near it. Stopping the trolley at the ute tray, I reach down and pull open the curtains. Girl looks up at me, her eyes raised in anticipation. I remain focused, picking up the two boxes and stacking them in the ute tray, along with the bag of clothing and toiletries.

Taking a deep breath, I stretch up high. "I'm so tired!" I exclaim, placing one hand over my fake yawning mouth.

Jumping out of the trolley, Girl bobs down and dashes towards the passenger door of the ute. Pressing the remote, she unlocks the door and pulls it open. She jumps inside so quickly that no-one would notice that she had.

Pushing the trolley aside, I walk slowly towards the driver's door and open it, plonking myself onto the seat. Shutting the door, I ignore Girl, who is crouched on the floor of the passenger area.

Starting the ignition, I peer into the rear view mirror. All is clear behind me. I reverse the ute slowly out of the parking bay and turn it around to face the exit.

My hands shake a little as I head towards the main road. Hopefully I've fooled the Chief enough that he didn't even notice the ute leave.

Turning right onto Destiny Road, I inhale a sharp breath, waiting for the worst to happen. It doesn't. There is no-one tailing us.

I keep driving, turning a sharp right down Crescent Road and right again onto the Boulevard.

We've returned to Redbank's main city area. Still no tails.

"We did it!" My voice cracks with surprise.

"You are amazing, Lira!" Girl sounds relieved.

As far as the Petoys are concerned, we are still somewhere in that motel complex. It won't take them long to realise that we have both left and then the hunt for us will be unstoppable.

I know where we need to head right now.

Chapter 18

The darkness of night sits like a thick blanket, making it difficult to see ahead as I venture off Vista Road and head into the forest. A beam of light shines from a thin slither of moon. It bounces off gnarled and distorted shapes, grabbing my attention.

Pressing the brake, I stop driving and inhale a sharp breath as I realise what I am seeing. The shapes are completely severed tree stumps, which are the remnants of the once living and breathing red gum trees that inhabited the forest floor.

My heart falls as my eyes scan the forest, taking in the sight of many severed tree stumps. Poor trees. Such beautiful life, destroyed for human desire.

Suddenly, I spot a shape shifting across the bank of the river. Squinting, I see long, dark blonde trestles of hair flowing in the wind. It is Jacquelyn, embracing one of the severed tree stumps.

"Wait here," I tell Girl as I open the door. "I'll be back in a minute."

"Okay," Girl sighs, settling back into her seat. "Take care Lira."

"I will," I smile reassuringly at her as I close the driver's door.

The ute headlights make it easier for me to see as I step across the fallen debris on the ground.

Crunch!

My foot crushes a beer can that someone has thoughtlessly discarded in the forest.

Jacquelyn jumps, startled by the sound. Holding onto the tree stump, she shields her eyes with her hand as she stares into the headlights. "Hello?" She asks in a shaky voice. "Can I help you?"

I step into the light, allowing Jacquelyn to see me. "It's me, Lira," I say, placing my hand on my heart. "I saw you there and wanted to check if you were okay."

Jacquelyn's eyes are streaming with tears. "I- I don't understand wh- what's hap- happened," she stammers.

I step closer towards her and open my arms. She lets me embrace her, burying her head into my shoulder. I hold her for a long while, letting her release her pain.

"Thanks Lira," Jacquelyn steps back, wiping away her tears. "How could anyone do this to our beautiful red gum trees? All our wisdom and guidance is gone."

I am silent, letting Jacquelyn express how she feels. As the custodian of the Redbank forest, she has worked hard to preserve its cultural heritage. She has also worked with the local villagers to nurture the forest and tend to its needs. The way the red gums have been so brutally severed would hurt her. It hurts me too. My eyes are welling with tears.

Jacquelyn strokes the trunk of a remaining red gum tree. Her voice cracks as she begins to recite:

> "Light wind, ripple yourself
> across the precious, gentle gems
> that reach beyond me
> and crumple and ripple and toss.
>
> "Leaves taken by you, wind,
> as they fall upon autumn's trek.
> Green and furling, swaying wisdom
> that no words could speak.

Makeshift Girl: The Secret Heritage Trail

"Unfurl my body, wind,
  lift me up into the branches
  of a majestic beauty that guides
  a people through life.

"I would sway with you, branches,
  taking that journey across the ages.
  Tossing my own mane of leaves
  through the quiet, awaiting air.

"Silently, I choose to engage
  with your wisdom."

Jacquelyn continues to stare up at the red gum tree and presses her hand firmly against its trunk. "I could swear I feel its heart beat," she says softly.

Stepping closer, I place my hand next to hers on the trunk. "I feel its energy," I say as its vibrancy zings through my heart.

Jacquelyn meets my gaze. "We must do all we can to save these remaining precious red gums," she says. "Will you help me Lira?"

"I will do all that I can to help," I say, taking hold of Jacquelyn's shoulders. "Do you have any idea how this may have happened?" My heart is wringing with remorse.

Jacquelyn sighs. "A couple of days ago, Petra, one of the villagers, said that she heard some heavy sounds up in the north area of the river bank. I didn't think much more of it, believing that it was probably a party hosted by one of our camping families."

I nod, understanding. "You have a difficult job," I empathise. "It must be hard to keep track of everything going on in the forest."

"It is now," Jacquelyn stares off into the distance. "This new job at Botanica, it's got me distracted from all this." She lowers her head sadly.

"Is everything okay?" I am concerned for her safety.

Jacquelyn shakes her head. "I wish I'd never taken that job," she sighs. "I was naive, thinking that I was going to be able to sell my designs on a bigger scale." She stares into my eyes. "Naricia is not interested in my designs at all. Instead, she has me designing a new silk range, which I know is not right." She places her hand over her heart, clearly stressed.

"What's not right with the range?" I ask, feigning ignorance.

"A number of things." Jacquelyn's gaze drifts off into the distance. "Firstly, the material I am meant to design is a light polyester, not silk. It makes me so sad to know that I am working with an oil based textile, which contains very high levels of micro plastics. The toxic chemicals in polyester are damaging to our rivers and oceans once they are released.

"A lot of the material has been wasted, as it falls apart when I try to manipulate it into a design. I try my best to dispose of it through recycling, however Naricia often passes by to collect the wasted bits and pieces, letting me know that she is disposing of it secretly at the Redbank landfill station so that no-one else can use the material."

"I am so sorry," I say. "This practice goes right against your very nature."

"Yes," Jacquelyn bites her lip. "There's something else odd too."

"What's that?" I ask gently.

Jacquelyn sighs. "I can't work it out but something isn't right with the silk patterns that I am receiving."

"I agree," I say.

Jacquelyn's eyes widen in surprise.

"Let's head over to the ute." I encourage her. "I think that it is time that you heard what Girl has to say."

"Girl?" Jacquelyn raises her eyebrows. "Is she the woman that accompanied you the other day?"

"Yes," I say.

"Will she be okay to speak with me?" Jacquelyn bites her lip nervously, probably remembering the anger that Girl displayed at Botanica.

I place my hand on her shoulder. "She'll be fine," I say. "Happy to let you know the facts."

"Okay," Jacquelyn nods. "Let's talk to Girl."

Grabbing Jacquelyn's hand, I lead her towards the ute and open the passenger door.

"Hi Jacquelyn," Girl's eyes narrow. "You're out late."

Jacquelyn tenses her body, uncomfortable with Girl's demeanour. I clench her hand more tightly, reassuring her.

"Girl," I say gently. "All is not as it seems. Jacquelyn is worried about the range of scarves that she is selling at Botanica. It is something that Naricia has forced her to do. I thought you might like to tell her about the totems."

"Totems?" Jacquelyn looks confused. "What totems?"

Girl studies Jacquelyn's expression. "How do you conceive your initial silk pattern?" She asks.

Jacquelyn sighs. "That's the thing. I never get to design the silk patterns myself. Someone always delivers the design to me and I have to work with what I am given."

Girl's eyes narrow. "Hmm," she says. "What is delivered to you?"

Jacquelyn rubs her forehead, deeply in thought. "Usually a roll of material already printed with a silk pattern. I have to use it to create a number of design concepts for a scarf, shirt, skirt, robe or dress, whatever is requested."

Girl stares down at her hands, which are clenched tightly together. I realise that she is trying to keep her emotions in check.

Jacquelyn stamps her feet, breathing out cold air and trying to keep warm. She wraps her arms around herself and meets Girl's very steady gaze.

"I'll be direct," Girl says. "Can I trust you to treat this information confidentially?"

"Yes, of course," Jacquelyn nods, her eyes wide.

"The silk patterns you are receiving have been created using traditional totem designs that belong to specific families of Mira. The totems represent their heritage, beliefs and culture. Unfortunately, the families' original silk garments have been stolen and their totems are being appropriated for counterfeit design and commercial sale."

Jacquelyn drops my hand and steps back, covering her mouth with her hands. "Oh no!" She gasps. "How awful! Those poor families of Mira!" Her eyes widen in horror. "Please believe me when I say that I had no idea about this."

"We do," I reassure her. "This is not something that you would consciously do."

"No," Jacquelyn shakes her head. "I care deeply about people and their heritage. I wouldn't be the custodian of this forest if I didn't." She wipes away her tears. "I am afraid I can't get out of this one," her voice crackles with strain.

"Why do you think that?" I ask, knowing that something else is brewing in her mind.

"Naricia has blackmailed me," she sighs. "When I first began working for her, I told her that I didn't think that the job was for me. She told me that I had better design what she demanded or she would expose both my and Zac's involvements in illegal trade to the police. Now I know what she means by illegal trade."

"Zac's involved too?" I ask, knowing very well that he is but wanting to gain more information from Jacquelyn.

"Yes," she sighs. "They've got him delivering their top secret parcels."

"Do you know what's in them?" Girl's eyes widen with curiosity.

"No," Jacquelyn sighs. "I know that Zac is always stressed. He can't miss a deadline or there are serious consequences."

I nod, understanding. Zac confronted Mitch the other day. It seems that they are both under a lot of pressure.

"Typical Petoy behaviour," Girl grits her teeth. "Naricia, like many Petoys who acquire perceived power, like to stranglehold it. In reality, they are afraid of losing the control and riches associated with what they do. Naricia is only as powerful as people let her be."

"So why is she doing this?" Jacquelyn's cheeks have reddened. "Why hurt people?"

Girl inhales a sharp breath and stares at the windscreen.

"The Petoys have formed a resistance movement against the Emperor of Mira," I tell Jacquelyn. "They want the dynasty to crumble. Their resistance has been persistent for centuries. Destroying the core silk trade, which brings the most revenue to Mira, is part of their stand against the empire."

"That's huge," Jacquelyn's voice is shaky and her eyes dart from side to side. "I don't want to support their resistance."

I reach for her, putting my arm around her shoulder. "There is always a way out," I say soothingly. "You've just got to work out how you want to play it."

Jacquelyn meets my gaze with confusion in her eyes. "What do you mean?" She asks.

"Well," I say. "What do *you* want to do about this?"

Jacquelyn scratches her head and stares at me again. "I want to walk away from the store and return to creating my handmade designs in this forest. I don't want my name associated with any unnatural textiles or illegal design work or trade, Lira."

"I hear you," I say softly. "Go home now. You need to get some rest before tomorrow's shift. When you do go to work, I want you to compile evidence, be it recordings, paperwork or photographs of any conversations that you have; materials you receive or products that have been created. Keep a record that we can use for your benefit and to build evidence."

"I see," Jacquelyn nods. "I can help expose the Petoys' shady work."

"Yes," I say. "If you're up for it."

"I am," Jacquelyn says decisively. "I don't want to see anyone or anything else hurt."

I nod, understanding. "I'll walk you to your van," I say, falling into stride beside her.

"Thanks Lira," Jacquelyn smiles weakly at me as she opens the door of her blue van. "You've given me some hope," she says softly as she sits in the driver's seat.

I smile and wave as Jacquelyn drives off, feeling relieved that I have helped her in some small way.

Heading back to the ute, I open the driver's door and wiggle into the seat. "Well, I guess we have an informant," I say. "I've known Jacquelyn for a long time. Her response was truly genuine."

Girl nods. "Yes, I saw that too. It angers me that someone so special has been manipulated by Naricia."

"Jacquelyn's very upset about the red gum trees too," I say. "It is a tragedy for the people of Redbank. Those trees held a special guidance and wisdom that can never be replaced."

"Yes, they did," Girl nods. "It is the same in Mira. Our trees and plants are part of our psyche. We work with their natural states to provide resources while ensuring that they live a long life."

"How?" I ask. During my short time in Mira, I never had the privilege to become aware of the significance of nature for its people.

Girl's expression is thoughtful. "Well, we might use the bark, leaf or fruit of a tree or plant to make dye for silk. We try to acquire our resources from a range of plants so that we are not hurting a single natural resource too much. They are a strong part of our culture and deserve to be treated with respect."

Reaching into her silk bag, Girl retrieves Aisha's journal. "Let me read you Aisha's entry on making silk dye," she says.

I sit back in my chair, listening as Girl shares Aisha's story:

Summer 1276

> As the morning light drifts through the wooden doorway, it lights up the small room that we have designated to silk design.
>
> My father is talking to Kiara, a tall, olive skinned woman, with dark brown hair, which falls in a long cascade down the back of her tunic. Kiara is our head dyer and she uses a traditional water extraction method to produce dyes.
>
> "The tropical weather has been kind to us," Kiara heads over to a bench and retrieves a plant cutting. She smiles, her brown eyes sparkling as she

hands it to Father. "We have been able to harvest an abundant amount of this Indigofera suffruticosa plant. The straight fruits on the Indigofera tinctoria have also been very plentiful and robust this year."

"That's wonderful news," Father smiles. "Have they steeped well?" He approaches the wooden vat.

"Yes," smiles Kiara. "Hirta worked late three nights ago, stirring the steeped mixture with lime powder to oxygenate it thoroughly. I often wonder how she manages to stir so vigorously and never seems to tire."

"Hirta is very energetic," I smile. "One time she encouraged me to keep working, even though I believed that I couldn't complete a silk dress. She has a fighting spirit in her, it keeps her going."

"Thank you Miss Aisha," I am startled by a voice behind me. Spinning around, I face Hirta, who has entered the room. "I am very grateful that you appreciate my work."

"I certainly do," I smile at Hirta, whose short, black hair appears wet and windswept. "Is it windy outside?" I ask her.

"Yes, Miss Aisha, a tropical storm has hit." Hirta wraps her arms around herself, her lips trembling. Her light blue tunic is drenched from the rain.

I unravel my shawl from its comfortable position on my shoulders and wrap it snugly around Hirta's. "Please warm yourself with my shawl," I offer. "We don't want you to become unwell."

Hirta smiles warmly, her brown eyes sparkling. "Thank you Miss," she sounds relieved. "I couldn't sleep. I wanted to arrive early to check if the blue sediment has formed yet." She bends down and places a plank of wood over the top of the wooden vat, leaving a small gap. Tipping the vat over, Hirta pours the oxygenated water into a small drain hole dug into the ground. "It has!" Her voice is excited. "Look!" She holds up the vat, her eyes shining as she shows us the blue paste that has settled on the bottom. "Isn't it beautiful?"

"Yes, it is," Father smiles, taking in the sight of the rich, blue paste. "Indigo paste," he says. "Blue gold." Suddenly he coughs violently, clutching at his chest.

Kiara pulls out a wooden stool and helps Father to sit. "There you are, Sir," she smiles warmly.

"Thanks Kiara," Father is still rubbing his chest.

Suddenly, a loud banging sound bursts through the air.

Father looks up, alarmed. "What was that?" *He splutters, glancing around nervously.*

Dashing to the window, I peer outside. A tall young man, wearing a black headscarf is slamming his body with full force against the front door.

"It's a Petoy!" *I cry.* "He is trying to burst through the front door! Grab a table, quickly, so that we can form a barrier."

Hirta and Kiara each grab an end of a medium sized table and rush over to the front of the room. Pushing the table firmly against the door, they secure it either side with empty vats.

The loud banging continues and then gradually ceases. I hear footsteps shuffling away. The man has given up and left.

Kiara is shaken. "Let us just hope that the Petoys never discover our methods for producing this indigo dye. I think they may want access to our equipment and techniques."

Father shakes his head. "I'm sure they do," *his voice croaks.* "If they get their hands on our traditional silk making techniques, all will be lost to us and the empire. So no-one can know about this," *he gasps, struggling to speak.* "Aisha, you promise you will keep this a secret?"

My eyes widen. "Of course, Father."

Father inhales a couple of deep breaths, trying to settle his chest. After a moment, he stares deeply into my eyes. "The Empress relies on our secret indigo dye to make her the most vibrant and rarest indigo apparel. It represents the identity of her new dynasty. She once told me that a dress that we created for her was worth a substantial amount of money in the silk trade."

"Wow," *I am amazed.* "Your secret will rest in my heart, Father. There it will be locked away, ensuring the prosperity of our work in helping to sustain the Empress' dynasty."

"Good," *Father smiles warmly.* "Aisha, your maturity is to be admired. You will make an excellent chief of silk one day." *He coughs again and swipes beads of sweat away from his forehead.*

My heart flutters with happiness. It is an honour to be given such a compliment by my Father. I only hope that I will be able to fit his very big shoes in my future role as the chief of silk.

Girl shuts the journal and stares out the windscreen. "I feel the same way," she says softly. "I don't know if I'll ever be able to do what my father does."

My heart reaches out to her. "You will be an amazing chief of silk," I encourage her. "Girl, your life experiences have helped you to gain wisdom. You will be a leader who not only respects and continues your family's silk traditions. You will also know how to make silk trade relevant and successful for Mira right now."

Girl meets my gaze and smiles shyly. "Thank you for believing in me, Lira."

I bite my lip thoughtfully. "The Petoy clan were already using force to gain access to your family's silk traditions in Aisha's time," I reflect.

"Yes," Girl nods. "They will not stop until they completely dominate the silk trade."

"Interesting," I say. "If they are that interested in your family's techniques then we should play it to our advantage. Do you or your family have access to any of the indigo silk apparel that was made for the imperial dynasty?"

Girl shakes her head. "Not anymore. It's all stored away in the palace." Her eyes light up. "That's an idea, Lira," she says. "If only we can get our hands on one of those silk garments, we could set those Petoys off on the wrong track."

"Exactly," I smile. "I am going to do all that I can to ensure you step into your new role safely," I tell her. "We both know that it's time to visit Concetta for some advice."

Girl nods. "Yes," she agrees. "She might be able to help fill in some blanks." She settles back into her seat.

"Yes she might," I say, easing my foot off the break and accelerating. I drive in silence for a while, my hands shaking from the vibrations of the bumpy, dirt track.

Redbank forest is eerie to drive through at night. There is no clear road to follow, so I rely on my headlights to shine through the pitch black darkness.

"Whoa!" I cry as I swerve passed a tree stump. "Sorry Girl, I didn't see that coming."

"That's okay," Girl says. "What's that?" She points ahead.

The headlights shine upon an old, gnarled elm tree ahead. I brake, slowing the ute right down. "It's just the tree I'm looking for," I smile. Stopping the car, I pull up the handbrake. "I'll be back in a minute," I say as I push my door open.

The cold air hits me sharply. I stamp my feet, trying to keep warm. Gazing at the stars, I take a moment to appreciate the night sky. It is nice how some things don't change. There is Orion, the constellation that Mitch and I would stare at for an age.

I close my eyes for a moment, remembering the comforting feeling of Mitch's arms wrapped around my waist and his head against mine. *Let's make a wish*, he said one night.

We wished for our own family. I will always remember that night, our fervent promises to love each other deeply and to commit ourselves to having our own children. Promises that I have always kept nestled deeply in my heart. Do those promises still mean anything to Mitch?

Tearing my gaze away from the stars, I inhale a deep breath, refusing to cry. I miss Mitch so much. I wonder if he misses me too.

My gaze falls upon the old, gnarled elm tree and I step forward, my fingers tracing its bark. "Hello old friend," I say. "Where is that dead drop?" I bend down and stretch my hand inside the tree hollow. My fingers knock against a small, hard object. Retrieving it, I stand up and smile. "Here it is," I say, glancing at the mobile phone.

Red Night, I type the code words for absolute danger and press send.

Ding!

A message instantly appears on the phone's screen. *Green door*, it reads. They are the code words for all clear.

Sliding open the back of the phone, I rip out the sim card. Pulling open the driver's door of the ute, I reach inside and grab my bag.

"What do you have in your hand?" Girl asks me.

"Something that should be destroyed," I say as I dig into my bag. Retrieving a lighter, I step outside and flick its wheel until it generates a spark, followed closely by a bright, yellow flame.

Girl jumps out of the ute and rushes to my side. "Lira, what are you doing?" She is rattled.

I hold the sim card over the flame, watching as it begins to burn and melt. After a short while, black ash floats through the sky.

Girl stares at me, her eyes wide with fear. "Lira, why did you just do that?"

"To keep us safe," I tell her. "It was a one use prepaid phone. I contacted Concetta and destroyed the sim so that we can't be found."

"Oh," Girl sighs. "Is she okay to have us around?"

"Yes," I say. "First, I need to destroy this phone." I throw the phone onto the ground and dash to the back of the ute. "Is it okay if I use your trekking pole?" I ask Girl.

Girl nods, her eyes wide. "I've never seen you like this before, Lira," she says.

"You haven't had to until now," I say, smashing the trekking pole into the phone. It feels good, releasing some stress. I smash the phone again and again until it has been reduced into tiny pieces.

"Wow!" Girl exclaims. "You've done this before, haven't you Lira?"

"Yes," I sigh, stepping back to admire the damage. "In my world, you can never be too safe."

"I know the feeling," Girl agrees. "Pass me the trekking pole."

I hand her the object, curious of what she is about to do. Girl walks a few metres away and uses the pole to form a hole in the dirt. She presses the pole firmly, making the hole larger.

Returning the pole to the ute tray, Girl bends down and pockets the toxic battery. "I'll dispose of this carefully," she says, smiling at me. "Let's bury the phone pieces," she directs as she collects them.

I help her to collect the phone pieces and we throw them into the hole. Girl covers them up with dirt.

"There," Girl says, smoothing the dirt with her hands. "Now we definitely won't be discovered."

"Time to go," I say as I head back towards the ute. I jump into the driver's seat and shut the door.

"You are so organised, Lira," Girl says admiringly as she rubs the dirt off her hands. She hops back into the passenger seat and closes the door.

"I have to be," I say as I release the handbrake and press my foot on the accelerator. The ute lurches forward and begins to rattle again as it crosses the bumpy dirt ground.

I am grateful when I reach the turn off onto the gravel driveway. It is nicely hidden, curving away through a path of elm trees.

Chapter 19

A short while later, my eyes rest upon the wooden log house at the end of the driveway. It is small and dimly lit by a single lamp in the front window.

I turn off the ignition and the headlights. "We are here," I announce. "We should keep our visit short and sweet."

"I know," Girl's eyes are narrowed and focused. "Let's go."

Opening the driver's door, I step outside and stretch. It is good to release the tension in my back. Grabbing my bag, I sling it over my shoulder.

"Give me a hand, please," Girl says, her silk bag swinging on her arm as she attempts to pick up the couple of boxes containing her art.

"I'll take them," I say, feeling the heavy weight of both boxes as she loads them into my arms.

"Thanks Lira," Girl grabs the clothing and toiletries bag and locks the ute.

We walk slowly up the short flight of steps and onto the porch.

Knock, knock, knock, knock, I do as I have been asked, almost too exhausted to knock against the front window.

The front door opens and Concetta greets us with her shoulder length blonde hair tied back into a pony tail. She looks lovely in a blue linen dress that compliments her deep blue eyes. Concetta smiles, her face youthful for her age. She looks no older than her mid thirties. It always amazes me that she is actually in her fifties.

"Hello Lira," Concetta steps forward and pulls me into her strong embrace. I feel a big, wet kiss on my cheek. "How are you?"

"Hi Concetta," I smile as I step back. "Tired and a little stressed. We could do with your help right now."

"Of course," Concetta smiles. "Girl! Lovely to see you too!" She hugs her. "It's been a while."

"It has," Girl says, her face softening at Concetta's warm welcome.

"Come inside," Concetta waves, motioning for us to follow her.

I wait for Girl to venture up the front porch steps. Checking over my shoulder one last time, I breathe a sigh of relief.

Definitely no tails.

Entering the small hallway, I hang my bag on the wooden coat stand.

Glancing at the white walls, I notice that they are bare. Concetta does not have a hall stand or any art on display. It is easier to leave suddenly and without a trace that way.

It is the same in her small living room, which only contains a two seater, red leather couch facing a small television that sits on a bench.

I place the boxes on the floor, stacking them up against the back wall. Standing and stretching, my eyes fall on the small fireplace on the opposite side of the room, which is lit and roaring away.

Approaching the fireplace, I face my back to it and wrap my arms around my body, enjoying the toasty warm feeling.

Concetta may not have any displays on her walls, yet she cannot resist photos. Sitting upright on the mantelpiece is a single photo displayed in a walnut coloured wooden frame. It shines in the light that glows from the fire.

I remember when Concetta took that photo of Mitch and I. We were snuggled up on our couch in our home on top of the milk bar. *I hope you're both happy here for a long time*, Concetta said after she took the photo.

Concetta let us stay there, knowing that it would be a safe place for us to be together. She worked downstairs in the milk bar itself, under cover as a shop owner. Every day Concetta would keep her ear to the ground, listening to the leads that would come from customer chatter.

Leads that helped her to locate Vianna, also known as Girl.

I glance at Girl now. Placing the clothing and toiletries bag down in the corner of the living room, she stretches. "It's really nice to see you again, Concetta," Girl says softly. "I'll never forget all that you've done for me."

"I'd do it all again in a heart beat," Concetta smiles. "We've known each other for a long time, Girl. I still remember how I met your mother. I arrived in Mira for a holiday and didn't know where to stay. Your mother was so kind to invite me to lodge with your family while I was there. How is she?"

"Good," Girl sighs. "Worried about me." She runs her fingers through her hair.

Concetta sits down on the couch. "Come, join me," she waves us over. Girl sits next to her and Concetta makes eye contact with me while I sit on the far end. "Have you been compromised?" She asks me.

"Yes," I reply, staring back at Concetta. "Chief Opula found me at the motel room that Mitch organised for us tonight."

"Oh Lira," Concetta's face falls. "That must have been scary. Are you alright?"

"Seeing him brought back nightmares," I gulp. "I practiced my stranglehold technique and scared him away for a little while. I'm not sure how long I can hold him off, though."

Girl's mouth has dropped open. "You used a stranglehold on the Chief?"

I blush shyly. "Yes, I did," I shudder. "He suggested that I was of age now." I feel sick to my stomach when I remember his creepiness.

Concetta nods. "He has a future mapped out for you, Lira. He will want you to become intimate with him and to rear his children."

I cover my face with my hands. "Rear his children," I sigh. "Why me, Concetta?"

Concetta stares into the distance, thinking. After a moment she meets my gaze. "Your story will reveal itself when it should," she says. "When you are ready."

I stare at Concetta, realising that she is protecting me. It is not a story she wishes to share with me right now. I place my hand on my chest. My heart is racing with anxiety and an ugly feeling sits heavily in the pit of my stomach.

"Are you okay Lira?" Girl wraps her arm around my shoulder.

I nod, unable to speak.

"Lira," Concetta says softly. Meeting her gaze, I see that her eyes are filled with worry. "We've both known that this time would come. The Chief has found you. You need to work out if you are ready to take that next difficult step."

I think about all that Concetta has taught me. I know that I have been prepared well physically and have learned to create a strong cover story. What I am not prepared for is my own mental state as I have to grapple with the Chief's demands. I feel ill.

Noticing how uncomfortable I am, Concetta changes the subject. "How's Mitch?" She asks me.

"Okay," I reply. "He is just surviving."

"Hmmm," Concetta sighs. "That sounds like Mitch. Fiercely determined and always wanting to help others." She meets my gaze with a worried expression. "When did you last speak to him, Lira?'"

"Earlier in the afternoon," I reply. "Girl's studio had been robbed and her statue stolen."

"Really?" Concetta looks surprised. "That's not good, Girl."

"No, it's not," Girl sighs sadly. "I am so worried about the assets I've stored in it. If they get into Petoy hands ..."

"Let's make sure that they don't," Concetta says firmly. "I've promised the Emperor of Mira that I will do all that I can to protect the city's integrity and trade."

"You have?" Girl's eyes widen with surprise.

Makeshift Girl: The Secret Heritage Trail

"Yes," Concetta nods. "Those assets need to return to your hands as soon as possible, Girl." She meets my gaze again. "Did you get discovered during the theft?" She asks.

"No," I say. "The theft had occurred long before we arrived. Girl cleared out all her remaining art works and belongings and we fled to Spirit River to meet Hidu."

"Good. What did Hidu have to say?" Concetta sounds interested.

"He let us know about a strange shipment of silk items being delivered to the Botanica Warehouse. We drove out to the Redbank Industrial Estate and discovered Zac making a delivery to J.F. Snow Globes."

"Hmm," Concetta ponders. "J.F. Snow Globes. I'll get Hidu to look into that."

"Thanks Concetta," Girl smiles. "I'm sure Hidu will discover exactly what's going on."

"I'm sure he will too," Concetta smiles.

Girl stares at me. "Tell her what else happened at the Industrial Estate, Lira. You were pretty brave."

Concetta meets my gaze. "What did you do?" She asks.

I relay my story of discovering the stolen garments in Redfin's truck and my narrow escape.

Concetta's mouth drops open in surprise. "Well Lira, I am impressed," she smiles. "You have used your instincts well today and survived two very dangerous situations. As you know, the Petoys are not always easy to escape."

"Thanks Concetta," I smile gratefully. Standing, I walk to the back of the room. Reaching into the clothing and toiletries bag, I pull out the two bags of silk garments. "These are the garments that we discovered," I say, handing them to Concetta.

Standing, Concetta grabs a pair of gloves off the mantelpiece. Returning to her seat, she pulls the gloves over her hands. Opening the first bag, she retrieves the crimson silk evening dress.

"Wow!" Its beauty blows Concetta away. "This is just beautiful," she breathes.

"Yes, it really is," Girl agrees. "It belongs to the Jandoe family back home. Their sun totem is sacred to their ways of life."

Concetta meets Girl's gaze. "They deserve to have this garment returned to them," she says firmly. "And they will. As soon as we are able to prove its theft by the Petoy clan."

"Good," Girl sighs with relief. "Not only will the Jandoe family be very grateful, they will also feel that justice has been delivered to the thieves."

"That's right," Concetta smiles. "Later I will ask you to tell me which families these other silk garments belong to, Girl," she says. "How would you feel if I kept them locked securely away, so that they are being protected?"

Girl meets my gaze, unsure of how to respond.

"It's your decision," I tell her. "You are about to lead these silk makers and merchants. How can their silks be best kept?"

"Somewhere locked," Girl sounds decisive. "I don't want them travelling around with anyone or they'll be rediscovered by the Petoys."

"I know just the place," Concetta smiles. "I have access to a large safe nestled in the heart of the Redbank forest. You are welcome to come along with me Girl and we can store them away together. I will let you know the code to open the safe and you can do so any time."

"Sounds good," Girl nods. "Let's do it tonight. I will rest easier knowing that the garments are safe."

"That is understandable," Concetta's expression is serious. "I know how much the people of Mira mean to you and we will do our best to ensure that we can help restore some of their faith and confidence in their silk traditions. I know that the Emperor desires to see the restoration of the silk trade in Mira. This is something we are all working towards achieving."

Girl and I nod, agreeing.

"Did you go anywhere else today?" Concetta asks.

"Just the motel," I sigh. "Which we narrowly escaped."

"I ran into a person from my past, his name is Dari," Girl says, running her fingers through her hair. "He used to be a wonderful boy and we would play together in Mira. He has since joined the Petoys' resistance movement and tried to capture me."

"My goodness," Concetta's eyes widen. "That would have been scary, Girl."

"It was," Girl nods. "However, I fought back and tied him up."

Concetta raises one eyebrow. "Where is he now?" She asks.

"In a cupboard in the cleaning room of the motel bistro. That is, unless he was released by a Petoy." Girl exhales a frustrated sigh. "Once they defect to the Petoy clan, it is hard to bring them back or to help them see reason. Dari, like others, believes he has joined a worthy cause. Nothing I would say could change his mind."

"That's often the way," Concetta nods. "The Petoys have been able to justify their acts of resistance and win over new followers for a long time now."

"Yes," Girl says. "It seems that the Petoys also run a serious delivery business." Digging into her pocket, she retrieves the flyer and shows it to Concetta.

"Naricia Petoy," Concetta sighs. "It's no surprise that she's in charge of their delivery service. She has just the right level of aggression to take it to the next level."

"Yes, she has," Girl agrees, her eyes darkening.

"It's okay, Girl," Concetta grabs her hands and rubs them gently. "You will get through all of this fine, we'll make sure of it." Concetta meets my gaze.

I bite my lip with worry for Girl.

"I know," Girl's voice cracks. "It's just so hard, life on the run."

"So gain control of it," Concetta advises. "Form a home base for yourself. One you know that you are safe in. This will give you more time to anticipate the next moves of the Petoys."

I nod, understanding. "That's good advice, thanks Concetta."

"No problems," Concetta smiles. "I'm always here to help." Concetta's eyes narrow in thought. "Did Mitch visit you at the motel?" She gazes into my eyes again. I can see that she is worried about him.

"No," I reply. "Which is odd, I know."

Concetta reaches into her pocket. "I'm going to call him in," she says as she retrieves her pager. "I hope he's alright."

While Concetta types her message, I meet Girl's gaze. She looks sad. "This is so hard," she sighs.

I put my arm around her shoulders. "We'll work this out, you'll see."

Concetta's pager beeps and she checks her message. "Mitch will be here in fifteen minutes," she says. She stands up. "Now, excuse my poor manners. You must both be very hungry. Would you like some beef stew?"

"Yes please," Girl smiles. "That would be wonderful."

"Well, how about you settle in while I warm up the stew?" Concetta offers.

I am surprised. "Do you think that it's wise for us to stay?" I ask.

"Definitely," Concetta smiles warmly. "It will give you time to refocus. Girl, you can have the guest room you stayed in previously."

"Thank you so much Concetta," Girl stands slowly and heads towards the back of the room. She lifts the two wooden boxes in her arms. "Lira, you take this bag of clothing and toiletries. It's your turn for a shower."

"Thanks Girl," I smile as I watch her leave the room. "She is truly amazing," I tell Concetta.

Concetta nods. "Yes, she is," she begins to head towards the kitchen and I follow her. Opening the fridge, she takes out a large container of stew and places it onto her wooden bench. "How have you been coping with things, Lira?" Her eyes are filled with concern.

I bite my lower lip and consider what to say. "It's been quite the learning experience," I say carefully. "My instincts in detection have kicked in when they've need to."

"Good for you," Concetta smiles as she takes the lid off the container and tips the stew into a large pot. "You are a great detective Lira. I've always admired your ability to uncover information, even in the most difficult circumstances." She places the pot onto the stove and stirs the stew with a wooden spoon while it cooks.

"Thanks Concetta," I am touched by her compliment. I wait for her to meet my gaze before I ask my heart felt question. "Has there been any news of my mother?"

Concetta bites her lip and her eyes narrow. "Not specifically," she says, reaching into her pocket. "There is, however, some news of the state of Mira from Empress Celine." She hands me a letter. "Can you store this in your mother's case file?"

"Sure. Thanks Concetta," I take the letter and pocket it.

Knock, knock, knock, knock.

"That must be Mitch," Concetta smiles. "Are you okay to stir this stew please Lira? I'd better greet him."

"Of course," I take the wooden spoon from Concetta and stir away at the stew. It smells so delicious that it brings comfort to my pounding heart. Picking up some stew with the wooden spoon, I taste it. Perfect.

Turning off the stove, I grab a ladle and begin serving the stew into four bowls that have been placed onto the bench.

"Mmm, is that stew?" I hear Mitch's voice and look up to see him standing on the other side of the bench.

He is so handsome with his curly golden locks falling into his face. I watch as he smiles, revealing the cute dimple in his right cheek.

"Y-yes," I stammer. I inhale a deep, nervous breath and try to speak once more. "It is."

"Hi," he says, crossing over to my side. He touches me lightly on the cheek and I blush.

"Hi," I can't seem to find my voice.

Mitch grabs hold of my shoulders and turns me around gently to face him. "Are you okay, Lira? Concetta told me you had several narrow escapes today."

"Yes," I nod, releasing myself from his grasp. I try to sound brave. "Girl and I are both lucky to have got away. It seems like the Petoys have also infiltrated that motel."

"Oh hell," Mitch's face reddens. "I am so sorry for putting you both at such risk. I had no idea."

I stare into Mitch's eyes for a moment. He runs his fingers through his hair and bites his lip anxiously.

"It's okay," I say. "We're both fine. Girl is getting comfortable in her room right now."

Mitch sighs with relief and cups my face in his hands. "Lira," he says. "I don't know what I would have done if you –"

"Well, just look at you two," I turn to see Concetta standing in the doorway. She is beaming with pride. "Seeing you both standing there warms my heart. It's just like old times."

I step back, my face flushed with stress. I am not ready to face Mitch yet. Deep in my heart, I am wounded. "The stew's ready," I say, averting the attention away from Mitch and I. "We should eat it now before it goes cold." I pick up two bowls and place them on the wooden circular table that is positioned in the centre of the kitchen.

"I'll just go and round up Girl," Concetta winks at me before she turns and walks away.

"Let me help you Lira," Mitch approaches the table with the two remaining bowls of stew. He watches as I return from the cutlery drawer and begin to lay out the spoons and forks next to the bowls.

As I place the final spoon down, I feel Mitch's arms around my waist. "Lira," he breathes.

I inhale a sharp breath, dropping the spoon. It bounces on the wooden table, almost matching the beat of my pounding heart.

"Lira," Mitch turns me around to face him and stares into my eyes. "I miss you –"

"Oh, isn't that sweet," I hear Girl's voice and meet her gaze, beginning to blush again.

"Don't mind us," Concetta smiles knowingly. She approaches the table and sits on a seat. "Make yourselves at home."

Girl sits next to Concetta. "Wow, this stew looks and smells delicious."

Mitch touches my face gently. "Time to eat, eh?" He holds out his hand for me to take.

Reluctantly taking Mitch's hand, I let him guide me to my chair.

"Here you are, Lira," Mitch pulls my chair out from under the table.

"Thanks," I say. "You don't need to fuss, Mitch. I'm fine." I can sense that Concetta has picked up on the tension that I am feeling towards Mitch. Her concerned eyes stare at me as I sit down.

"This looks great," Mitch settles into the chair next to me and begins to dig his fork into the stew. "Mmm," he sighs, closing his eyes as he chews. "Concetta, your stew is always so amazing."

"Thanks Mitch," Concetta sounds touched.

"It is really lovely," Girl says, swallowing a mouthful and picking up a piece of carrot with her fork." I love the flavour." She pops the carrot into her mouth and chews.

I can't eat much right now as a nauseas sensation is churning away in my stomach. I can still feel Concetta's eyes on me and it makes me feel even more anxious. I want to escape through the imaginary hole in the floor.

I stir the stew around my bowl, picking up a single piece of beef with my fork and placing it into my mouth. I chew slowly, enjoying the strong burst of garlic and cloves on my tongue. If only I could just block out the anxiety I am feeling right now …

Concetta's eyes are almost burning a hole into me. Suddenly, she pushes her chair back. "Mitch, can you help me organise some drinks?"

"Of course," Mitch pushes his chair back and follows Concetta over to the bench top. I hear the sound of the kettle beginning to boil and Concetta laughing at Mitch's light hearted jokes.

I sigh with relief. It is nice to have some space to eat. Picking up my spoon, I load it with vegies and beef and begin to eat properly. I am hungrier than I realised.

"I'd almost forgotten what it was like to be here," Girl says as she places her fork down onto the table. "Now I remember the warmth, the feeling of family …"

I nod, swallowing my last mouthful of stew. There have been times throughout my life in Mira and Redbank when I have been able to stop running and to experience the luxury of such feelings. The moments seem impermanent and fleeting as I continue to makeshift my way across the terrain.

"Hot chocolates everyone?" Concetta's voice pipes through, interrupting my thoughts.

"Yes please!" Girl smiles.

"Lira?" Concetta asks.

I meet Concetta's gaze and manage a small smile. "Yes, that would be lovely, thanks."

Concetta holds my gaze for a moment, studying me. "Right," she says, finally turning away. "They'll be ready in a moment."

Girl yawns and covers her mouth with her hand. "I'm so tired," she sighs. "It's nice to relax for a little while."

"This should help with that relaxation," Concetta grins as she hands Girl her cup of hot chocolate.

"Oh, thanks," Girl smiles as she takes the cup. "Mmm," she sighs as she tastes the drink. "Just what I needed, thanks Concetta."

"You're welcome," Concetta beams as she sits at the table.

"For you, Lira," Mitch places a cup of hot chocolate in front of me on the table.

"Thanks," I say, staring at the cup. I can smell the wonderful aroma of chocolate. Taking a sip, I sigh with relief. It's lovely to unwind a little.

"It's nice, isn't it?" Mitch asks as he sits back in his chair and swirls his cup. "Good to just stop for a while."

"Yes it is," I agree, unable to meet his gaze.

"After the horrible experience I had earlier today, it's nice to relax," Girl places her head in her hands.

"What happened?" Mitch jumps up, concerned.

"My studio got broken into," Girl runs her fingers through her hair in frustration. "Someone stole a very important red gum statue that I have created." Her face falls as she shares the news.

"I'm sorry Girl," Mitch says. "That is terrible." He steps forward, reaching his arms out towards her.

"Thanks Mitch," Tears begin to fall down Girl's cheeks as she steps into his embrace. Mitch's worried gaze meets mine. It is hard seeing her like this. I want to do all that I can to help her.

"I'm sorry," Girl finally says as she steps back and wipes her eyes. "I didn't mean to –"

"It's okay," Mitch cuts in, smiling gently at her. "I'm here for you."

Girl nods, unable to speak.

Mitch glances at me. "Do you need some help?" He asks me. "I'm happy to do whatever needs to be done."

I smile, appreciating Mitch's offer. Grabbing my bag, I dig into it and retrieve the city map that he gave me. "You can help us do some mapping," I say as I discover a pen hidden in the depths of my bag.

"Sure," he says as I lay the map out on the table.

"That sounds like a great idea," Concetta says. "A great way to regain group focus."

The map is well detailed, marked with the major sources of trade in Redbank. My eyes fall on Girl's studio and I circle it, writing *statue theft* and the date that it occurred.

Girl grabs the pen out of my hand and circles the Botanica store. *Counterfeit silk*, she writes, marking the date.

"Counterfeit silk?" Mitch repeats, his eyes widening.

"Naricia got her way with Jacquelyn," I say, meeting Concetta's gaze.

Concetta nods. "Just as we suspected. What has she got Jacquelyn doing?"

"Naricia has presented Jacquelyn with her dream, a chance to sell her own handmade designs in a store named after her: Botanica."

"Yes," Girl says. "Jacquelyn has been blackmailed into assisting with the development of counterfeit silk apparel for the Petoys while she is there. They are designed by appropriating totems that belong to families back home."

Concetta's eyes narrow. "Do we know how Jacquelyn is?" She asks. "If she will assist us?"

"Yes she will," I say. "I spoke to her tonight. She is on board to help expose the Petoys' theft and counterfeit trade activities."

"Great," Concetta smiles. "I knew she'd come through."

I grab the pen and circle J. F. Snow Globes. "Jacquelyn's husband Zac made a delivery here," I say. "We're yet to work out what was in the box."

"J. F. Snow Globes," Mitch says. "I've never delivered anything there, nor have I heard of it. It sounds interesting."

"There may be a reason why you haven't delivered anything there yet," says Concetta. "I told the girls that I'll get Hidu to look into the place. I'll see if he can organise a map of its internal layout and let us know about any activity taking place there."

"Okay," Mitch nods. "Sounds good."

Girl's eyes continue to scan the map. "There is the Botanica Warehouse, where Lira discovered the silk garments. See?" She circles the location.

"Yes," Concetta points to the map. "It's conveniently located not too far away from J. F. Snow Globes. It is also positioned very closely to the Truck Depot and the Redbank Docks, too. That's interesting."

"It is?" I ask her.

Concetta meets my gaze thoughtfully. "Well, it's in prime position to receive any type of deliveries, be it via road or ship, very quickly."

"Who knows how the silk garments arrived there," Girl sighs. "Someone had to pick them up from Mira originally. I wonder who?"

"That's a good question," I reply. "We know so far that Redfin is the one who is sneaking them out of the warehouse." I reach into my pocket and pull out my phone. "This is Redfin," I say, showing Mitch and Concetta the photo of the man we staked out.

Mitch's eyes widen in surprise. "That's Nick Farago!" He exclaims. "He owns Nick's Memorabilia on Minute Street. I've collected the odd delivery from him here and there."

"Nick's Memorabilia …" Girl repeats as she searches for it on the map. "There it is!" She circles it.

"Nick also drives a truck," I say, remembering Nick kissing the white envelope. "He seems to be gaining riches from his work."

Mitch's forehead creases with confusion. "What do you mean?" He asks.

"Nick is the man who came looking for you after you left," I tell Mitch. "He didn't succeed in locating the GPS tracker. I have that here with me."

Mitch's eyes narrow as he absorbs the information.

"Tora's Take Away Noodle Store …" Girl circles the location. "Envelope collection."

"What envelope?" Mitch asks curiously.

"Nick entered the noodle store and exited with a white envelope," Girl says. "It's probably some sort of payment."

Mitch's mouth drops open. "I've heard a couple of the delivery guys mention getting noodles," he says. "They've never really told me where from. That must be what they are referring to." He looks at me. "You've both been very busy," he says. "Things are starting to make a little more sense."

"They are?" I ask curiously.

Mitch runs his fingers through his hair. "I had to make one of my unusual deliveries at Red's Laundromat yesterday," he says. "It is always creepy. I was instructed to type a code into a specific washing machine and place the box I showed you the other day inside it.

"Once I closed the machine, it beeped four times. I looked around the room and spotted a camera on the opposite wall. I couldn't help feeling a little scared."

My heart pounds with worry for Mitch. "That does sound scary," I say. "Was there anyone around?"

"No," Mitch says. "I didn't feel right leaving the boxes there. I'm used to someone signing off for my deliveries." He shrugs. "Maybe it's linked to all of this somehow."

"Where is the Laundromat?" Girl asks.

"On Lighthouse Boulevard," Mitch points to the map. "Right here."

I step closer, watching Girl circle the location. "Conveniently located for a quick exit out of the city," I say.

Mitch looks up at me. "Where are you going with this?" He asks.

"Suds," I say, repeating the code words shared by the mysterious voice on the CB radio channel. "I think we might have discovered a very significant location."

"You are amazing, Lira," says Girl. "Truly amazing."

"Indeed you are," Concetta beams.

"What would we do without you?" Mitch says admirably.

I lower my head, blushing. "Thanks," I say shyly.

"Well team," Concetta says. "You have found your new focus. I believe it's time to stake out Red's Laundromat."

"Yes," I agree. "Do you want to help me, Girl?"

"Definitely," Girl nods. "I'll be there with you."

"Let me know what you discover," Concetta says. "Now Mitch, I need you to pay very close attention to the deliveries that arrive at Red's Laundromat. We need to track where they go."

"Will do," Mitch says. "I'll let Lira know if something suspicious arises."

"Great," Concetta smiles.

I point to the map. "There is one more location to note. The Journey Motor Inn, which has been infiltrated by the Petoys." I circle the location on the map. "We were lucky to have escaped from there."

"I'm so sorry, Lira and Girl," Mitch looks sad. "I had no idea."

"That's okay," Girl waves her hands. "We know you didn't mean to put us in danger, Mitch." She smiles warmly. "Concetta, do you think we could store the silk garments away soon? I am starting to feel very tired."

"We can do it right now," Concetta stands.

"Great," Girl collects the bags of silk clothing and turns to face Mitch and I. "See you in the morning, you two. Have a great rest."

"You too," Mitch smiles. "Keep safe."

"Will do," Girl smiles.

"Let's go Girl," Concetta leads Girl down the corridor.

Mitch meets my gaze. "I guess we'd better retire, too," he smiles, reaching his hand out for me to take.

I stare at his hand nervously. "Okay," I eventually concede. Picking up my cup of hot chocolate, I follow Mitch down the corridor to my childhood bedroom on the left. It was a secret and safe place to stay with a woman who had opened her home and heart to me.

I feel the fluttering of nervous butterflies in my chest.

It is just Mitch and I.

Alone.

Chapter 20

My childhood bedroom hasn't changed at all. A large, queen sized bed still takes up most of the space. It is covered with a quilt decorated with pink roses, which are my favourite flowers.

On the walls are numerous photos. My eyes are drawn to a favourite photo of Mitch and I standing outside our tent on our camping trip at the Nestle Camp Ground. I am trying to snatch Mitch's hat off his head and we're both laughing.

There is another photograph of Concetta and I, making cupcakes in her kitchen. My face is covered with flour and I look amazed as I watch Concetta decorate her cupcakes so beautifully with flowers made of icing. The remaining posters are of nature: roses in bloom in a cottage garden, a gorgeous waterfall and a parrot in flight. I still smile every time I look at my display. The images help me to reground myself by reminding me of who I am and what I like.

On the far side of the room is a wooden cupboard and next to that is a small chest in which I keep some of my favourite things. Swirling the hot chocolate in my cup, I walk over to the chest and pull open the drawer, retrieving the crystal star that Mitch gave me.

"Do you remember this?" I ask him, my hands shaking as I show him the star.

"Yes," Mitch nods, his face softening. "I remember our wishes, too."

I inhale a sharp breath, trying to stop myself from crying. Those wishes meant everything to me.

Mitch reaches out to stroke my cheek. "I still want what we wished for, Lira," he says, staring into my eyes. "Do you?"

I take the last sip of the hot chocolate and place the cup and star on the bedside table. My head is spinning with confusion. "I do," I say. "If we have a loyal relationship, Mitch."

"We do," Mitch nods, his eyes widening. "Lira, please believe me. I have no interest in Sophie whatsoever. She is with Nick Farago."

"Nick Farago?" My mind reels.

"Yes," Mitch sighs with frustration. "Apparently Nick's not treating her right. She often calls me to help her return home. She's moved in and out of Nick's place so often, I've lost track."

"Oh," I sit on the bed, surprised at the news. "That's not good at all. How often is it happening?"

"About once a week," Mitch sighs. "On the rare occasion, twice a week. I don't know when she's going to come to her senses and leave him."

I stare at Mitch, surprised by his statement. "Love is hard," I say. "Sometimes, deep inside, you hope that everything will get better, that it will be alright." I choke on the last words, feeling a deep ache in my heart. I know what it's like to hope.

Mitch's eyes widen and he drops down onto the floor in front of me. "That word hope," he says. "I feel it too, all the time." Placing his hands on my knees, he stares deeply into my eyes. "I really miss you, Lira," he says sadly.

I feel a tug of pain in my heart and it brings tears to my eyes. "I miss you too," my voice cracks. "It was hard seeing Orion tonight without you." Tears begin to roll down my cheeks.

"Oh Lira," Mitch's voice shakes as the tears well in his eyes too.

We stare into each other's eyes for a long moment, connecting through our ache, our longing for each other. I feel a tremendous pull towards him and a longing to be held close. Sliding down onto the floor, I feel him embrace me tightly and I place my head against his chest.

I can hear Mitch's heart pounding strongly. "My beautiful wife," he says softly, stroking my hair. "I love you with all my heart."

My heart is brimming with warmth from his words. Looking up, I stare into Mitch's eyes. The tears are rolling down his cheeks.

"I'm here, Mitch," I say softly, holding his face in both my hands. "Always. I love you."

Mitch manages a small smile through his tears. I see a light of hope sparkling in his eyes.

Leaning closer, I kiss Mitch softly on the lips. As he kisses me back, I feel the ache in my heart dissipate and be replaced by deep love. It sits there, nestled comfortably while I continue to kiss his soft, warm lips.

Our kiss grows more passionate and I am being lifted and placed on the edge of the bed. Mitch sits next to me, stroking my face and gazing into my eyes. His tears have dried and his blue eyes are sparkling.

I smile at him, pulling him close and locking my lips with his again. I feel like I am floating in the air, way up high above the madness of the world. I am safe in Mitch's arms.

I feel Mitch's hand travelling up underneath my singlet and tracing my belly button. I moan, letting him pull my singlet up over my head and toss it gently onto the bed.

"You are so beautiful," he says, his eyes shining. His gaze drifts across my body and he smiles appreciatively.

I pull at the hem of Mitch's tank top and his smile widens. Raising his arms, he lets me remove it. Throwing it onto the bed, my heart flutters wildly at the sight of his gorgeous, muscular torso.

I trace Mitch's abdominal muscles with my finger, feeling a stirring in my loins. Pushing him back gently onto the bed, I kiss him all over his chest and stomach.

Mitch is smiling and his eyes are shining with love. "I've missed this so much, you so much," he murmurs, cupping my breasts in his hands and stroking them gently.

I moan, aching for him so deeply, I feel as though I might faint.

Mitch rolls me over onto my back gently and continues to caress my stomach and thighs. I close my eyes, wanting him to touch me deeply, to show me his love.

I feel his lips rain soft kisses across my shoulders and my breasts. As his tongue teases my nipple, I cry out in sheer ecstasy. Only he knows how I like things. Just like the way his tongue is circling my nipple now, arousing me to the point of explosion.

Lifting Mitch's head with my hands, I stare into his eyes. Raising my hips off the bed, I pull down my pants and underwear and toss them aside.

Mitch sits back and his gaze drifts across my body, drinking it in. He exhales a deep breath of appreciation. Reaching for my hand, he places it over his heart. I can feel it beating rapidly.

Sitting up, I pull him close to me, pressing my bare chest against his. Our lips lock again and we kiss deeply and passionately, our tongues grazing.

Reaching down, I unbuckle Mitch's jeans and pull down his zip. I can feel his manliness through his boxer shorts and I am burning with desire.

"Oh Lira," Mitch moans as I reach into his boxer shorts and stroke his penis. Rolling him over gently onto his back, I pull his jeans and boxer shorts down over his legs and toss them onto the carpet. Kissing his legs, I make my way up to his hips and meet his gaze once more.

Mitch is panting, his eyes shining with anticipation. "You are so sexy," he breathes, stroking my buttocks with his hands.

"Don't stop," I whisper, taking hold of his hand and rubbing my clitoris against his fingers. I moan, arching my back as he strokes me in gentle circles.

Pulling Mitch's hand away, I clutch it against my pounding heart. Staring deeply into his eyes, I straddle him, guiding his penis deeply inside me and rotating my hips in gentle circles. I can feel the bed rocking beneath my legs and it makes me feel dizzy.

"Oh!" Mitch moans, grasping my buttocks firmly. I can feel him throbbing inside me.

My body is searing with a strength and energy that I never knew I had. I thrust myself firmly against him, enjoying the tingling sensation that I feel in my loins. It is getting stronger and stronger, working me up into a frenzy. I am about to explode at any moment now.

"Oh!" Arching my back, I cry out in pure ecstasy. Powerful waves are shooting through my loins as I reach the peak of my climax.

I feel Mitch grab hold of my waist firmly. "Oh Lira!" He cries out, thrusting his hips. I ride out his climax with him, closing my eyes as I feel the sensation of his seed spurting forth inside me.

Tears well in my eyes. I feel so loved.

"Are you okay, Lira?" Mitch reaches for me, pulling me down next to him onto the bed. He strokes my face and stares deeply into my eyes.

Tears are rolling down my cheeks. "This is so beautiful, Mitch. I feel so loved, thank you."

Mitch's gaze softens. "It meant the world to me too," he smiles gently. "Thank you." He pulls me into his embrace, wrapping his arms tightly around me.

A few moments later, I begin to shiver.

"Are you cold?" Mitch asks, pulling me closer.

I nod. My teeth are chattering.

"Here, let's get under the covers," Mitch rolls off the bed and rushes to my side, pulling the sheet and quilt over me.

I open up my arms, inviting him to join me. "Snuggle with me?" I grab his hand and pull him back down towards me.

"Sure," Mitch slides under the covers and pulls me closer to him.

"This is nice," I say, feeling the warmth of his tight, muscly torso against mine. "I've missed this."

"Me too," Mitch strokes my hair.

I rest my head against his chest, listening to the solid, reassuring rhythm of his heart beat. My beautiful husband is here with me at last.

My eyes feel heavy and begin to droop. I smile with happiness as I drift off into a very content sleep.

Chapter 21

I wake as the sun rises the next morning and turn on my side to face Mitch. He is smiling blissfully in his sleep with his hands clasped together over his chest. Leaning forward, I kiss him gently on the cheek and slide my legs down until my feet hit the carpet.

Putting on my singlet and pants, I step into my runners. Grabbing my bag, I take another glance at Mitch and smile. He is still here. Stepping into the corridor, I close the bedroom door gently behind me.

All is very quiet inside the house as everyone is still sleeping. I open the front door and step outside onto the porch, grateful for the cool breeze against my skin. Sitting on the front step, I dig into my pocket and retrieve Empress Celine's letter. Unfolding the once letter locked paper, my eyes scan the narrative:

Autumn, 2022

Dear Concetta,

This evening I am sitting in the conservatory of the palace with the door wide open. The stark, black night encroaches upon the space, leaving only a single beam of moonlight streaked across the marbled floor.

I refuse to burn the beeswax candles that decorate the walls. My heart cries uncontrollably at the significant death of my people, who have been greatly neglected by the Emperor. Even in his old age, he has not ceased his desire for illustriousness. Filling the palace with wealthy wares of trade, he still refuses to engage in the wheels of progress. Denying people the modern utilities of electricity, machinery and transport, he has little care for their lives.

I keep my chamber door locked in the evenings, listening acutely for the sound of the Emperor's footsteps outside my door. When the door knob twists, I often hear him calling my name drunkenly. I am fearful when he stumbles into the room, his eyes burning with desire.

I am tense in our love making, gritting my teeth and grasping the bed firmly. He is an impatient man, demonstrating no attentiveness to my needs and completing his duty quickly and forcefully.

When he leaves, I sit up and hug my legs tightly to my chest. My ripped clothing brings a chill to my bones and I shiver. I feel used and discarded at once, my light shrinking and wavering in the turbulent sea of wifehood.

I never gave the Emperor a child. Deep in my heart, I never wanted to.

The Emperor has a number of children, all born to his mistresses whom he houses in the palace. In contrast, I have been his greatest challenge. His deep desire for an heir has never been fulfilled in his life with me as his wife.

I know that I am also his deepest regret.

My work is incomplete. My heart rests with my people who desperately need strength and support right now. I do not have Maricelle to help me as she is still missing.

Last evening I decided to walk the long trek to the meeting place in order to experience life as a civilian does. Holding a headscarf around my hair, I strode across the dirt terrain, hearing the crunching of gravel beneath the flat heels of my shoes.

The air was warm and abuzz with the sound of cicadas chirping loudly and accompanying me on my journey. My arms felt bare beneath my tattered, grey dress, which fluttered against my legs in the gentle breeze. Pausing for a moment, I bent down, grabbing handfuls of dirt and smearing it across my face, arms, legs and dress. It felt strangely soothing and cathartic. I was transforming myself into a person that I cared for. My role as the Empress was diminishing into a mere speck.

Weaving through the forest of Mira, I ran my hands across the textured bark of the trees, feeling their energy and lives. I was grounded and in tune with the earth.

It was not long until I reached the cliff facing out to the sea. Peering out at the shore, I noticed its welcome emptiness.

Stepping my feet across the sand, I felt the warm granules tickle my toes. My heart did smile with contentment as I continued to mark my footprints across the sand. *You are here*, I told myself. *You are Celine and you are alive.*

As I approached the water's edge, my eyes fell upon the sight of the Emperor's ship. Recently bought and titled the *Extravaganza*, its decadent yet sickly structure elicited anger within me. It would be a nightmare to be confronted with such intimidating richness as a civilian. One would feel so small and insignificant in its presence, as though their life and needs were completely irrelevant.

At least twenty guards protected the ship, keeping watch constantly for trespassers. As I watched the men in action, I gasped in horror. A group of Petoy men crept up silently behind the guards and slit their throats, discarding their bodies ruthlessly across the sand. Under the beams of the moonlight, pools of blood seeped their way across the golden granules.

Falling to the ground, I clutched at my chest, silently lamenting the guards' deaths.

Life is merciless in Mira.

Moments later, the Petoy leader hoisted himself up onto the deck of the ship and reached down to help the other men to climb up. The clan set to work, unravelling the mooring ropes and hoisting the mast. The leader took control of the helm, initiating himself as the captain. Spinning the wooden spikes on the axle, he cried out in delight: *For our riches! For our progress!* The other men chanted along with him, pumping their fists in the air.

The leader set sail, heading east across the great sea. I watched the ship gradually diminish in size as it continued its course across the water.

I did not feel any loss for the ship. Instead, I sat for a long time, staring at the vacant eyes of the men who had lost their lives. Watching their blood continue to pool across the sand, I felt a tremendous ache in my heart.

Mira has suffered much destruction and I do not know how to begin to help it to recover. I fear the ship is headed your way, Concetta and dread what the Petoy clan wishes to inflict upon the city of Redbank.

My heartfelt prayers for your safety,

Empress Celine.

Staring up at the rising sun, I feel a deep sadness wash over me. Too many people have suffered in Mira at the hands of ignorance and greed. I consider how the Empress must feel, to wish to run away from her role and be free out on the terrain.

My heart pounds in my chest as I consider my mother's situation. She must be exhausted and fearful right now. I can only imagine that she must also be very hungry without the support of the Empress' candles. *I hope you are safe and well, Mother.*

Placing my hand on my stomach, I feel it churning wildly with dread. The Emperor's ship may soon arrive here in Redbank waters. What do the Petoys hope to do with it? I know that it has something to do with the illegal trade operation that they are engaged in.

Pocketing the letter, my eyes fall on Mitch's van. I stand slowly on my feet. I must focus and get some work done. Time is closing in on us.

Reaching into my bag, I pull out the GPS tracker. Placing my bag down onto the concrete, I lower myself down onto the ground and slide under the van. I position the tracker in its original location, so it never raises suspicion. The adhesive still sticks well onto the undercarriage. I ensure that the tracker is still switched off and slide back out from under the van.

"Hi Lira, what are you doing?" Mitch reaches out his hand towards me.

"Reinstalling the GPS tracker onto your undercarriage," I grab hold of his hand. "I've left it switched off. Turn it on when you are ready to be tracked."

"Okay," Mitch is smiling. "Thank you Lira." He pulls me up onto my feet. "You are so hot right now, smeared with grease."

"I am?" I ask, taking a look at the grease marks on my skin.

Mitch nods and leans closer towards me. I close my eyes as he kisses me, feeling his passion and his tongue against mine. Suddenly, his hand is pulling the strap of my singlet down over my shoulder.

"Wait," I say, grabbing his hand. "There's one more job I want to complete this morning."

"What is it?" Mitch asks, reaching for me. I can see the desire burning in his eyes.

Reaching into his pocket, I grab his keys and press the button on the remote to unlock the van. "I want to listen to the CB Radio," I say. "Early in the morning is a good time to hear trucker plans for the day."

"Okay," Mitch sighs in defeat. "I'll wait." He heads over to the driver's door and pulls it open.

Sitting in the passenger seat, I watch as Mitch selects channel 17 and turns the mic gain control up to maximum.

Static fills the air, followed by a man's voice.

"Rapido, check in please, Rapido! Over."

"Checking in Redfin, how can I help? Over."

"You're running late, Rapido! Deliver rags from Suds in 30. Over."

"Work still in progress, Redfin. More like 70. Over."

"I'll hold you to that. Over and out."

Mitch switches off the signal and turns to look at me. "Wow!" He says. "Seems like the pressure is heating up for Rapido. I wonder what the rags are?"

"Me too," I agree. Pushing open the door, I jump out of the van and head towards my bag. Retrieving the special papers, I lay them out on the bonnet of the van.

"What are you looking at?" Mitch asks, wrapping his arms around my waist and kissing my neck.

I try to ignore the fluttering sensation in my stomach. "The record we've been keeping of your deliveries," I sigh, pointing to the time line. It is hard to ignore Mitch's hands travelling underneath my singlet and stroking my stomach. "It seems that you've been delivering boxes to Red's Laundromat every second Wednesday."

Mitch tilts his head to the side, thinking. "Yes, come to think of it, I have."

"Have they always been delivered the same way, inside the washing machine?" I ask him.

"Yes," Mitch nods, releasing me. "They have. Where are you going with this?"

"Let's take a step back to basics," I say, turning around to face him. "Girl and I are heading to Red's Laundromat this morning. We'll track the trade route of the box that you delivered yesterday. Can you send me a photo of the box so that I will know if we've found the right one?"

"Sure," Mitch says, retrieving his mobile from his pocket. He presses a few buttons on the screen. "There you go," he says.

Ding!

Opening the message, I check out the photograph of the box. "Great," I say. "This photo will be very helpful." I pocket my phone.

"That's good," Mitch smiles, staring into my eyes. He takes the special papers out of my hands and places them back into my bag. Slinging the handle over his shoulder, he reaches for my hand and leads me back inside the house.

"Good morning you two," Concetta smiles as she passes us down the corridor. "Did you sleep well?"

"Yes, we did," Mitch smiles as he hangs my bag on the coat stand.

Concetta's mouth drops open in surprise. "Why are you covered in grease, Lira?"

"Undercarriage work," I smile. "I've just got to clean up."

Concetta smiles knowingly. "I'll see you two love birds soon. I'll cook some pancakes for you all to take away with you."

"You don't have to do that," I say, touched by Concetta's motherly nature.

"You're family, Lira," Concetta smiles. "I will always look after you." Turning away, she disappears into the kitchen.

"Concetta is so caring," I say as Mitch pulls me into my childhood bedroom.

"Yes, she is," Mitch smiles, closing and leaning his back against the door. "She cares about you."

I rest my hand on my heart, touched. "I care about her too," I say.

Mitch steps closer and places his hands on my shoulders. "My gorgeous wife," he breathes, lowering the straps of my singlet so that they fall over my arms. My breasts fall out of the singlet and my nipples are erect. I feel excited tingles across my skin.

Mitch tugs at my singlet and lets it drop to the floor. Bending down in front of me, he circles my nipples with his fingers, making me burn with anticipation. "The future mother of my children," he says in a sexy voice, pulling my pants down. I feel his finger stroking me in gentle circles around my clitoris.

"Oh," I moan, circling my hips. "That feels so good."

Staring into my eyes, Mitch stands and removes his singlet and pants. He tosses them onto the carpet.

We are both naked now. I am burning with desire.

Taking my hand, Mitch leads me into the small, cerulean blue and white tiled ensuite. It has a single, separate shower with room enough for us both to stand in.

Mitch opens the sliding glass shower door and guides me into the shower. Shutting the door, he turns on the tap, feeling the water temperature as it heats up.

The water feels lovely against my skin, like the gentle pitter patter of rain. Closing my eyes, I allow myself to enjoy the sensation.

"Mmm," sighs Mitch as he smells the coconut scented body wash. "My favourite scent." He pours a drop onto his hand and places the container back onto the shelf. Mitch stares into my eyes and smiles lovingly at me. I smile back, my heart fluttering with adoration.

"You are so beautiful," Mitch says softly, his eyes drinking in my body. Dotting body wash on my breasts, he gently rubs it in with his fingers.

I moan, closing my eyes at the gentleness of his touch.

Mitch continues to rub the body wash across my skin. I feel his hands grasp both my buttocks gently and my eyes flutter open, meeting his gaze. My breath catches in my throat as he pulls me closer and presses his body firmly against mine.

"Mitch …" I caress his face and kiss him gently on the mouth. He kisses me back softly and strokes my buttocks in circles with his fingers.

"Oh!" I cry out, feeling a strong stirring in my loins. Mitch picks me up and I straddle him, pressing my back against the tiled wall. I meet his gaze once more, my heart burning with passion. "I want you," I breathe.

Mitch eyes glow and sparkle with happiness. I feel him press his firmness against me and I spread my legs, allowing him to enter me.

"Oh Mitch …" I gyrate my hips, desperately wanting him to fill me.

My climax is sharp and strong. I clutch tightly onto Mitch, crying out and thrusting firmly as I ride out the waves of ecstasy.

"Oh!" Mitch shakes as his seed spurts forth inside me. "I love you," he gasps, pulling me closer for a tight embrace. I bury my face in his shoulder and sigh with contentment.

After a while, I step back into the shower water and rub my hands gently across my body, rinsing the body wash away.

"Look at you," Mitch's eyes are full of appreciation and he pulls me closer, embracing me tightly.

I suddenly feel a wave of dizziness and grasp Mitch's shoulders. "I think I need to sit down," I say.

Mitch turns the shower tap off and lifts me up. He carries me into the bedroom and grabs a towel, which he places onto the bed. Lying me down on the towel, he wraps it around my body. "Are you okay, Lira? Did I hurt you?" Mitch is standing at the end of the bed, wrapping his own towel around his waist. He is staring at me with concern.

I shake my head. "That was amazing," I smile as the dizzy spell ceases and I finally muster the confidence to sit up. "It's been so long since we've made love like that." Standing slowly, I wipe my body and let the towel drop to the floor.

"Too long," Mitch sighs, looking me up and down. "My beautiful wife, if only I could be with you every day."

"You will be," I smile as I reach into the clothing and toiletries bag. I grab a white tank top and put it on. "As soon as we complete our mission." I step into a short, crimson skirt, enjoying the sensation of it fluttering against my skin.

"No underwear?" Mitch asks, reaching for me.

I shake my head, smiling seductively as I lift my skirt. "Not yet …"

"You are so sexy," Mitch smiles, reaching for me once more. "I am so lucky …"

Chapter 22

Concetta smiles as Mitch and I enter the kitchen. "Hello you two love birds," she coos.

"Hi Concetta," Mitch smiles. "Thank you for letting us stay last night. We really needed it."

"Yes, we did," I agree, smiling happily.

"Good for you both," Concetta smiles. "Here are both your pancakes. Lira, Girl has packed and is waiting for you in the ute. These pancakes are for her."

"Thanks for breakfast," I smile, retrieving the food parcels from Concetta. "Girl seems eager to go. We'll be in touch soon."

"Yes, we will," Concetta nods, guiding us to the front door. She pulls me towards her for an embrace. "Beautiful Lira, be safe."

"I will," I say, so touched that I feel tears forming in my eyes.

"Bye Concetta," Mitch smiles. "Thanks for the yummy breakfast."

"My pleasure Mitch," Concetta smiles. "Keep your wits about you and make sure you're there for Lira when she needs you. She is your wife, Mitch."

"I always will," Mitch's smile widens as he grabs my hand. I hear the front door close as we walk down the front steps.

Mitch pulls me close and I breathe in the coconut scent of his skin. "It was lovely to shower with you this morning," I say softly, reaching out to stroke his golden locks. "Just like old times."

"It was, wasn't it?" Mitch agrees. He nuzzles my neck. "Maybe we should just return to the room." His voice is sexy, turning me on.

"Girl's waiting for me in the ute," I say, staring into his eyes. "I can't just leave her there."

"No, definitely not," Mitch nods. He leans towards me and whispers in my ear. "I'll be thinking about you all day."

My smile is warm with gratitude. "What a lovely thing to say," I stroke his gorgeous face and circle the dimple on his cheek. "I will miss you."

"Me too," Mitch smiles.

"Really?" I joke, grabbing hold of his shoulders. "I didn't realise that you had the hots for yourself."

"I can't keep my hands off myself," Mitch cracks a cheeky smile and strokes his chest. "Or you either," he reaches out and tickles me in the ribs.

Mitch knows my ticklish spots very well. I am laughing so hard that I have tears rolling down my cheeks. I wait for the right moment and grab hold of both his hands, clasping them tightly. "I got you," I say firmly.

Mitch's cheeky smile flashes across his lips again. "And what do you plan to do with me?" He asks, raising an eyebrow. "I am at your disposal."

I laugh loudly and tighten my grip on his hands. "Your body won't be so easy to hide away," I say, my voice taking on a husky tone. The sight of his firm, taught biceps is turning me on.

"Really?" Mitch feigns innocence. "Please, my Lady," he pleads playfully. "Tell me why you can't give me the hideaway I deserve."

My heart is pounding as I pull him closer to me. "Let me just confirm what I have discovered," I say seductively.

"Of course, my Lady," Mitch jests. "Whatever you need."

I let go of Mitch's hands and grab hold of his biceps. I run my hands firmly across his taught muscles. "Mmm," I sigh.

"What have you discovered?" Mitch's voice is huskier now. He clasps my face with both hands and stares intensely into my eyes.

I inhale a deep breath, mesmerised by his deep blue gaze. "I-I-" I stutter, flustered and unable to speak properly. I feel my words jumbling in my head.

"Let me help you find your words, my Lady," Mitch says in a sexy tone. He kisses me on the neck.

I moan, closing my eyes.

"Does this help?" He asks.

"Somewhat," I tease. "I need a little more evidence."

"Is that right?" Mitch smiles. He grabs hold of my hands and places them under his tank top. I run my fingers along the smooth, firm muscles of his torso. "Is this helpful?" He asks.

I nod, feeling weak at the knees. Taking a deep breath, I finally grasp my words. "This is perfect evidence that you are just too hot to hideaway. I definitely can't keep my eyes or hands off you either." I pull Mitch closer to me, staring deeply into his eyes.

Mitch smiles a sexy smile. "Well," he says softly. "You won't mind then if I kiss you, my Lady?"

"That will be fine," I say in a mock serious tone. "It will certainly help me to complete my investigation." I am shaking with anticipation, waiting for him to make his move.

Mitch leans towards me and kisses my upper lip. It sends a jolt of electricity through my body. He licks my lower lip softly, making me open my mouth to receive his tongue. It feels warm and soft as it caresses mine. After a few moments, Mitch pulls away, bowing slightly. "Glad to be of service, my Lady."

My body is still shaking, burning for him. I step forward and grab hold of his face. Mitch's eyes widen in surprise. Leaning towards him, I kiss him firmly on the mouth. Mitch kisses me back, grabbing me around the waist.

I pull away suddenly, stepping back and wanting Mitch to feel the same ache that I feel when he is absent, that burning deep inside.

"Come back here," he sighs, reaching for me.

I shake my head, continuing to step back. "Lady's orders," I say in a surprisingly firm tone. "Meet me at our lodgings on Friday night. We need to close this case officially."

"Yes, ma'am," Mitch is panting. His eyes are filled with longing. "I'll definitely report to our lodgings on Friday evening."

I can feel my heart soaring with love. "See you then," I say, staying strong and maintaining my mock serious tone. "Don't forget to turn on your tracker."

"Yes, right, of course," Mitch smiles. "See you then."

As I walk away, I feel Mitch's eyes on me. I smile, relishing his longing for me. He still loves me!

As I reach the ute, a broad smiling Girl greets me. "Nice to see that you two have sorted things out," she says, staring at me through the driver's window.

"Thanks," I say, feeling a little drunk with longing for Mitch. Not long now, only one more night and then I get to hold him again.

"Lira?" Girl waves her hand in front of my eyes, trying to gain my attention.

"Y-yes," I stare at her, my eyes regaining focus.

"What's that yummy smell?" Girl asks.

"Oh, this is for you," I say, handing Girl her food parcel. "Pancakes made with love by Concetta."

"How sweet," Girl smiles. "She is such a caring person."

"Yes," I nod. "She definitely is."

Girl opens her food parcel and stares at its contents. "Wow!" She smiles. "I feel so spoiled, she's put a small raspberry jam sachet in here too. She knows it's my favourite jam. Look, there's also a folded piece of paper." Unfolding the paper, Girl reads the message. *"Be courageous Girl. The road is yours."* She stares at the paper a little longer, taking in the words. "How supportive," Girl finally says. "What a lesson, too, to take control of my road."

"Concetta's great like that," I smile. "She has a way of making you feel like you can achieve anything."

Girl nods, her gaze drifting out through the windscreen.

I head over to the passenger's side of the ute and open the door. As I slide into my seat, I notice that my bag is lying on the glove box and that the special papers are spread out across the dashboard. "Have you been documenting?" I ask her.

"What?" Girl's eyes follow my gaze. "Oh, yes," she says, realising that I am referring to the papers. "I thought I'd might as well make notes of times and places."

"Any patterns yet?" I ask her.

"Yes, only one pattern so far," Girl replies, turning in her seat to face me. "Every third Monday, Nick visits Taro's Take Away Noodle Store to collect a white envelope."

"Interesting," I reply, grounding myself again. My brain is finally working. "He's a regular."

"Yes," Girl agrees. "I can only imagine he's being paid for his work for the Petoys."

"That sounds about right," I agree. "He's obviously in charge of something very significant. We just need to figure out what."

"Sure do," Girl nods. She places the special papers in their folder and slots it into my bag. "Are you ready to stake out Red's?"

"Certainly," I nod, sitting back in my seat.

Girl starts the ignition and gently backs the ute. "It was nice to sleep in a warm bed last night," she says as she turns the ute around to head back down the driveway. "I bet you slept well too," she smiles a cheeky smile.

"Yes, I did," I smile dreamily. My mind floods with memories of my night with Mitch. His hands all over my body, his kisses … I miss him already.

It takes twenty minutes to arrive at Red's Laundromat. Girl parks the ute in front of the Redbank Newsagent so that we are a little distance away.

I hope that we have arrived in time to see Rapido before he leaves for his delivery.

I peer at myself in the rear view mirror. My light brown hair is a little dishevelled, so I lick my fingers and smooth the static strands down. My cheeks are pink and glowing. It's been a little while since I've seen them like that. It is wonders what a night of love can do for the mind and body.

My hazel eyes are shining with happiness. It seems a shame to cover them up with sunglasses. I adjust the arms over my ears and loosen my hair up so that it falls naturally over my ears, right down to my shoulders.

Opening the passenger door, I step outside. As I adjust my crimson skirt, my eyes gaze rests upon a large oil mark on the road in front of the ute. I retrieve my phone from my bag and photograph it.

"What are you looking at?" Girl joins me.

I peer over my shoulder, checking that no one is watching us. "This oil mark," I whisper. "It's fresh. I'm guessing that it's probably from a pretty run down truck." I stare at Red's Laundromat. "I'm sure that there's a car park out the back," I share with Girl. Stepping up onto the nature strip, I pause, my eyes spotting a familiar footprint. "Look," I point. "It's Zac's footprint again."

Girl stares at the footprint, her eyes widening. "It looks pretty fresh," she says. "Do you think it was his truck that was out the front here?"

"Possibly," I nod. "Let's go see if he's here."

I walk ahead, turning left onto Clarice Road and heading through the entry into the car park behind the laundromat.

"There's the Petoy delivery truck," Girl nudges me. I look up, my eyes falling on a familiar sight. It is the old, grey truck that rocked up at Pinewood Park the other day. Zac's truck.

I glance around the car park, my gaze resting upon the back door of the laundromat. It is wide open. "We only have a few minutes," I tell Girl. "Zac will exit the laundromat very soon."

"What should we do?" Girl's energy is searing. She is ready to take on what needs to be done.

"Dash behind the side of the store," I tell her. "On 3. Ready?"

Girl nods, a determined expression crossing her face.

I begin to count: "1, 2, 3!"

We bolt across the car park, pressing our bodies up against the side wall of the laundromat. Peering into a large, glass window, my gaze rests upon Zac, who is opening a box identical to the one that Mitch showed me in his truck. Retrieving a silver silk dress, he holds it up towards the light, squinting at the detail of its small, mint green raindrops.

Glancing closer at the skirt of the dress, Zac rubs his gloved finger over something and shakes his head. Grabbing a wet cloth, he wipes away at a mark or stain and checks the material once more in the light. A smile of satisfaction crosses his lips and he steps closer to the window and peers outside at the car park.

"Get down!" I pull Girl down with me and shuffle across the ground, moving further across the wall, away from the window.

"What is it?" Girl is alarmed.

"It's Zac," I say. "He is cleaning the ancient silk garments in the laundromat."

"Really?" Girl sounds surprised.

"Yes," I nod. "He's standing by the window now, waiting for someone."

Suddenly, I hear the sound of wheels. Looking up, I watch as Nick pulls up in his red Land Rover. Stepping out onto the concrete, he raises his arms up and stretches. Heading into the laundromat, he shuts the door behind him.

"Wait here," I instruct Girl in a low voice. Digging into my bag, I grab a GPS tracker. "Keep this safe for me," I smile, slinging the strap of my bag over Girl's shoulder.

"Sure," Girl's expression is curious as she watches me leave.

Turning, I dash towards the Land Rover and drop down onto the ground, sliding under the vehicle. I pull off the adhesive and stick the GPS tracker onto the undercarriage. I switch it on so that I can keep track of Nick's ventures.

I hear a beeping sound as the truck is unlocked. I only have seconds to spare. My heart pounds as I slide out from under the Land Rover. The electric blue running lights begin to flash over the cab, right down along the side of the tray.

Taking a deep breath, I dash back to Girl. "Phew!" I say, leaning against the wall and gasping to catch a breath. "That was close."

A moment later, a familiar figure exits the Laundromat. It is Zac with his brown hair floating freely over his shoulders as he carries three large boxes over to the truck. I notice that one of the boxes is the one that Mitch delivered. It holds the ancient garment.

"Oi, Rapido!" A voice barks. Nick storms out of the laundromat, carrying a box. "You forgot this one." Nick bangs the box down on the truck's cargo tray. He stands back, scratching his head. "What's got into you?"

"Lots of things," Zac rubs his nose in frustration. "I don't like what you've got me doing."

I stare at Girl, my eyes widening with surprise. "Zac is Rapido," I whisper.

Girl nods, her gaze returning to the scenario playing out before us.

Nick's eyebrows raise in surprise. "Well, someone's got to clean the ancient garments, eh? Remove those fingerprints. Better you than we all get caught."

"When's it going to stop?" Zac's eyes flash with anger. "It's wrong, this stealing. You know it is, Redfin."

Nick crosses his arms over his chest and raises an eyebrow. "Now Rapido, it's not the time to get all flaky on me, okay? The cash is coming in, isn't it?"

Zac slams his fist onto the cargo tray with such force that Nick jumps. "What cash? I'm not seeing any of it." He turns to face Nick, the character lines on his forehead creased with annoyance. "Look Redfin, you still owe me for the last run. I need cash on delivery. I've got a wife to support and a truck to maintain."

Nick cuts his hands through the air. "Okay, okay, settle down. Cash will be on its way soon."

Zac's eyes flash with determination. "It better be," he says gruffly.

Nick sighs. "Rapido, if we don't get these garments delivered before the meeting tomorrow night, Naricia will unleash her wrath and we both won't be here to receive anymore money."

"Is the meeting still at Chaud et Froid Café?" Zac asks.

"Yes it is," Nick tears his hair. "Enough chatter Rapido. Just get the garments delivered right now."

"Okay, okay," Zac steps up into his truck and slams the driver's door. He turns on the ignition, letting the truck warm up for a moment. As he slams the truck into reverse it almost jumps back, billowing out a cloud of exhaust fumes into the air.

Nick coughs, his eyes watering from the fumes. He waves his hands in front of his face, trying to swipe the billowing fume cloud away.

"We need to follow Zac," I say. "Let's go!" We dash back up Clarice Road. I can feel my sandalled feet striking firmly against the footpath. My crimson skirt makes it hard to jog too fast but I push on ahead, following Girl around the corner onto the Boulevard.

Girl jumps into the driver's side of the ute and pushes the passenger door open for me.

"There he is!" I cry as the truck turns right onto the other side of the Boulevard. I slam my door, settling myself into my seat.

"He's heading back into the city," Girl says, turning on the ignition and pulling out onto the road. "Out of my way!" She yells at a car who zaps passed her. She swerves the ute in a u-turn and roars into the left hand lane, catching up with Zac's truck. It has stopped at a red light, indicating a left turn onto Flag Road.

"It seems like the operation's pretty local," I say to Girl. "I wonder where Zac's heading?"

"We'll soon find out," Girl's teeth are clenched as she swerves left onto Flag Road. The traffic is not too bad this time of the morning. We move with a consistent flow, passed the Mayor's office. The truck indicates right, intending to turn onto Harmony Road.

"Interesting," says Girl. "I wonder what's up here?" She follows Zac, keeping her distance as she turns right onto Harmony Road. Swerving right, the truck heads down Shade Lane.

The truck suddenly breaks, stopping outside Sophie's Art Gallery.

"What's he doing here?" Girl pulls into the curb, parking a few metres away from the Gallery. Switching off the ignition, she turns to face me. "How odd," she says, crossing her eyebrows.

I am not surprised when I see Sophie step outside her gallery in order to retrieve the box from Zac. She smiles and winks as he turns on his heels and heads back to the truck.

Girl stares out the front windscreen for a long while after Zac's truck has left.

When Girl finally looks at me, her eyes are flashing with anger. "I can't believe that Sophie's involved with the Petoys," she says crossly. "How can she do this?"

I shrug. "Easily," I say. "All it takes is for the right opportunity to present itself."

Girl looks at me. "What sort of opportunity?"

"That's what we need to work out," I tell her. "We need to keep a close eye on her."

Girl nods, absorbing what she has learned. "Okay," she agrees. "Should we enter the gallery now?"

"Not now," I shake my head. "It's too risky. We'll work out a plan."

"Thanks Lira," Girl smiles weakly. "You always know just what to do."

"Speaking of knowing what to do," rifling in my bag, I retrieve my mobile phone. I view the GPS tracking app. "Nick's Land Rover is stationary on Harmony Road. We're just around the corner. Should we see what he's up to?"

"Yes," Girl sounds relieved to focus on something else. She starts the ignition, turning the ute around and heading to the end of Shade Lane. Indicating right, she waits for the traffic to clear before entering Harmony Road.

There is only one major location on this road. It is a vibrant, yellow building. Glancing out my window, I see a large sign displayed across the top of it, which reads: Happy Beats Music Store.

"He can only be in that store," I say, pointing to it.

"Okay," Girl pulls into the curb, parking a few metres away from the music store. Turning off the ignition, she swings open her door and jumps outside.

I open my door and pull my skirt up above my knee caps. Lowering my feet onto the ground, I stand, slamming the door behind me.

"Let's go!" Girl calls, beginning to jog.

I walk as fast as I can, keeping up with her.

Girl waves towards the right side of the building and I nod in encouragement. Reaching the wall, we press our bodies up against it, glancing out at the car park.

A tall woman with shoulder length brown hair is leaning up against Nick's Land Rover. She has a solid build with gorgeous round cheeks that glow a warm pink as she laughs heartily. Bending down, she pats a small beagle, who is jumping up on the skirt of her fluorescent green dress. "Here you go, Chuckles," she says, feeding the dog a treat. "Good boy!"

Chuckles barks in excitement, gulping down the food. After a moment he releases his grasp of the woman and begins to run across the car park towards us.

"Oh no!" Girl panics, pressing up against the wall. "He'll give us away!"

I grab Girl's hand and pull her backwards, towards the front of the store. "Behind here!" I call, pulling her down behind a small hedge bordering the property.

Peering above the hedge, we watch as Chuckles dashes onto Harmony Road and continues to run towards Veta Street.

Once Chuckles has disappeared, I stand up. "Should we see what Nick's up to?" I ask Girl, reaching for her hand.

Girl nods, letting me pull her up onto her feet. We return to our stake out spot, leaning against the right wall of the store.

Nick hands the woman a large red gum frame. Her eyes shine with a vibrant amber sparkle of happiness as she receives the object. "Led Zeppelin!" She shrieks, hugging the frame to herself. "You're amazing, Nick Farago! How did you get your hands on this?"

Nick smiles, his eyes wide with happiness. "I have my connections," he says. "I'm glad you like it, Tonya."

Tonya's eyes widen. "I *love* it!" She exclaims. "I can't wait to hang this on the wall inside the store. It'll add to the ambience."

Nick fidgets with his blue polo shirt. "I'd better leave you to it then," his smile has faded a little. "I've got more errands to run."

"Of course!" Tonya steps away from the Land Rover. "I'll see you next Monday with the big order."

Nick frowns for a moment, thinking. "Oh yes," he finally says. "Of course. I'll call you when it's ready to be delivered." He hops into his Land Rover, starting the ignition. Tonya steps back, waving as he leaves.

I grab Girl's arm, pressing her back against the wall. "Stay still," I say. "Until Nick's left."

Girl nods, staying put. I watch the Land Rover zap passed us on Harmony Road and disappear into the distance.

"Phew!" I exhale a deep breath, relieved that we are still safe.

Girl nudges me. "Tonya's heading back towards the store," she whispers. "Let's go before we're discovered!"

I follow Girl down Harmony Road towards the ute. My mind is whirring as I open the passenger door and settle back into my seat. "We need eyes inside that store," I tell Girl as she starts the ignition.

Girl looks at me. "Right," she agrees, her eyes wide. "You think it might help us?"

"Definitely," I nod. "We need some surveillance set up in there so that we can keep an eye on Nick's work."

"Agreed," Girl taps her legs in frustration. "There's just so much to do," she says through clenched teeth. "How do we begin?"

"I have an idea," I say. "I know just how to work our way into the music store."

"You do?" Girl looks at me. "How?"

"Befriend Chuckles," I say confidently. "And we'll befriend his owner."

Girl shakes her head. "You are so clever, Lira. Phenomenal."

I laugh, putting my arm around Girl's shoulders. "Not phenomenal," I say softly. "Just well trained, that's all."

Girl smiles warmly. "What would I do without you, Lira?"

Chapter 23

Later that afternoon, I park the ute alongside Spring Park. "Ready to put our plan into action?" I ask Girl.

Girl nods, a hopeful smile crossing her face. She pushes open her door and begins to rifle through the back tray of the ute.

A few moments later, she returns with an orange sport shirt and black Lycra track pants. "I hope these fit you," she shrugs.

"Let's see," I smile warmly, reaching for the clothes.

Girl turns away, keeping an eye on the road while I change. It is challenging to change clothes in a ute seat, however I seem to manage, removing my tank top over my head and putting on the orange sports shirt. I knock my legs against the dashboard as I remove my skirt. Pulling up the Lycra track pants, I feel them cling snugly to my skin.

"How are you going?" Girl asks.

"Great," I say. "The clothes fit me well." I step out of the ute, spinning around for Girl to see my disguise.

"Mmm," she says, digging into the ute tray. She pulls out a black wig. "Put this on, too." She helps me to pin the wig down onto my head.

"Let's see what I look like." Checking myself out in the rear view mirror, I am happy with how snugly the wig sits on my scalp. I complete the disguise with a pair of red framed sunglasses. "What do you think?" I ask.

"You look very sporty," Girl says, smiling. "Well done on the disguise."

"Thanks," I am relieved that the disguise works. Opening the door, I hang my bag strap over my shoulder. I can smell the pancakes nestled in there and waiting to be eaten. "Text me when you arrive at your destination," I say as I step outside.

"Of course," Girl smiles. "See you soon."

Taking a few steps away from the ute, I look behind me. No tails.

It will be nice to run for enjoyment and not away from someone.

Tying my black wig up into a pony tail, I am pumped. I have to stretch my aching arms and back.

Knotting the laces on my runners, I jog on the spot, gaining momentum.

Glancing over my shoulder, I check that all is clear.

Not so lucky this time. I catch site of the silver Mercedes a couple of metres away, idling. Exhaust fumes billow out the back. It is hard to miss. The Chief is stalking me again.

My heart pounding, I try to focus on the task at hand. I begin jogging around the park slowly, increasing my distance away from the Mercedes and warming myself up. My legs hurt a bit and I am out of breath quickly. I press on, cutting across the grass and through the tree-lined pathway.

Dashing behind a tree, I catch my breath. I am panting hard and sweat is dripping down my face. I am so unfit. Wiping my eyes, I glance over at the road and sigh with relief. I think I've lost my tail for now.

Ding!

Reaching into my pocket, I grab my mobile phone, glancing at the message from Girl. *In 30 dots. Back of wall.*

I pocket my mobile. Taking a quick glance around me again, I sigh with relief. Still no tail.

Time to jog.

I take off again at a steady pace. I have thirty seconds to get to Veta Street. I cut across the grass and check once more for any tails. Still clear.

Jogging onto the footpath, I head down Veta Street. I can smell breakfast emanating from the doorway of Café Chaud et Froid. Yum. I'd love to grab something to eat. I wonder if they serve breakfast all day?

My heart beats with excitement as I notice Chuckles, the beagle, sniffing his way around the chairs outside the front of the café. He is nibbling on some food scraps left behind. He was very easy to find.

I slow down and come to a stop. Chuckles jumps up onto my leg and sniffs at my bag. He can smell the pancakes.

"Hello Chuckles," I say, reaching into my bag and grabbing the food parcel. "Great detective work. You can share some of these pancakes with me." Opening the food parcel, I break off a small chunk of pancake and hold it up.

Chuckles barks in excitement, his eyes gleaming.

I feed him the pancake. He gobbles it down quickly.

"Very hungry, aren't you?" I ask. "The rest of these pancakes are for me." I pocket them, glancing around me. "Where is Tonya?"

Chuckles looks up at me expectantly. He is still very hungry. I reach down and stroke his long, floppy ears. "Poor thing," I coo. "You can follow me for now." I can't believe my luck. Chuckles is on his own and I get to take him home.

I stretch my arms and legs, taking a moment to breathe. I am not used to jogging. It is taking a lot out of me. Once I've flexed up, I begin to jog again, this time towards Harmony Road and the music store.

As I reach the car park behind the store, Chuckles yaps in excitement. Tonya is grabbing boxes from the boot of her green, MG Roadster. The car is a stunning classic, its bodywork glimmering impressively in the daylight. For a brief moment, I visualise myself sitting in the driver's seat and feeling the breeze whip through my hair as I coast along the open road.

"There you are, Chuckles," Tonya's voice snaps me out of my daydream. I watch as she stacks the boxes onto the footpath and bends down to pick up the beagle who is jumping up onto her legs. "Where did you get to?"

"Café Chaud et Froid," I say. "Hi, I'm Stephanie."

"Tonya," she smiles at me kindly as Chuckles licks her face. "Thanks for looking after him. How did you know to return here?"

"I just followed him," I lie. "He seemed hungry and I wanted to make sure that he got home safely."

Tonya is silent as she absorbs my story. "Thank you. How kind of you," she says, patting Chuckles.

This beagle story may prove to be very useful indeed.

I take a moment to scan the perimeters of the store. *Where is Girl?* There she is, standing behind the left side wall of the music store. She gives me a thumbs up.

"Can I help you with these boxes?" I ask Tonya, finding a reason to enter the music store.

"What these?" Tonya stares at the boxes. "Sure, that would be great. I just need to take them into my store."

I pick up one of the boxes.

Grabbing the other box, Tonya leads the way. Unlocking the door, she steps inside her store.

The shop is small with CD and vinyl racks scattered across the floor. A range of music, including: rock, classical, dance, jazz and heavy metal decorate the racks.

"Pop the box down here," Tonya taps the top of her counter.

I stack the box on top of a few others. It looks like there is a backlog of unpacking and sorting to do. Maybe I could offer to help.

"Thanks again," Tonya says, watching Chuckles head over to his food bowl. He scoffs the food down hungrily. "I appreciate all your help. I wouldn't know what to do without Chuckles."

"Not a problem," I smile. "It looks like you might need some more help."

I am prolonging my stay. Long enough for Girl to rifle through Tonya's car and discover what she needs.

"With these boxes?" Tonya seems to be grabbing the opportunity. "Oh would you? I'm short of a sales assistant at the moment. She is away on holidays overseas. Actually, I could do with an extra hand for a work shift. Are you free?"

Gee, Tonya does not waste any time. Nor will I.

"Sure," I say, not believing my luck. "I have some time free at the moment."

"Great! I will pay you for your work," Tonya says. "You let me know what hours you can do."

"I can work for about three hours on Monday," I offer. Working here will help me to gather more information about Nick's work.

"So from 9 til 12 on Monday?" Tonya's eyes are sparkling. She is eager to reach an agreement.

"Sure," I nod. "I can do that."

"Sounds great!" Tonya reaches out and shakes my hand, grinning enthusiastically. "Welcome to Happy Beats Music Store. Glad to have you on board, Stephanie."

"Thank you," I say, smiling warmly.

"Feel free to take a look around," Tonya waves her hand towards the shop floor. "Always good to become familiar with where you will be working."

I grab the opportunity. A set of shelves display a large collection of rock music that shouts out for attention. I study the artists and try to get a feel for Tonya's interests.

Behind the shelves, I spot a large painting on display on the back wall. It is an image of a restaurant with groups of people sitting on leather upholstered seating and eating at wooden tables. A dance floor spills out towards the right, busy with a flurry of dancers dressed in shiny 70s gear. It would be a great place to hide a surveillance camera behind.

"I have to go now," I say. "I'll see you on Monday."

"See you then!" Tonya rushes over, opening the shop door for me as I leave.

Once outside, I walk quickly, dashing across Harmony Road, turning right onto Veta Street and running straight ahead.

As I reach the corner of Seek Alley, I glance over my shoulder. I can see the silver Mercedes parked a short distance away on Veta Street, its dim lights shining. I want to head down and confront the Chief and demand that he leaves me alone. I am not brave enough to do that. Instead, I pop down and begin to retie my shoelaces.

After a short while, the Mercedes pulls out and indicates that it wants to turn. When the traffic clears, I watch it take a u-turn and disappear back up the street and out of my vision.

I wait a couple more seconds. No sign of the silver Mercedes.

Turning left, I head down Seek Alley. My brain feels like it is in a fog as I take on a light jog, almost tripping over the uneven concrete.

I dash passed the back doors and fences of shops and notice a gate open with a car reversed into its driveway. A young man stops unloading his boxes in order to take a long sweeping glance at me as I pass by.

"Baby, looking great!" He calls, wolf whistling.

I blush with embarrassment. *Keep focused, Lira!* I dash passed the dump bins, further down the alley way.

Where is Girl? My eyes scan the ground and the walls. There she is, leaning against a stone wall towards the end of the alley way. She is staring at her phone intensely. I slow down to a walk, panting. I need to stop for a minute to catch a breath. My heart is beating so hard that it feels like it's going to burst out of my chest.

Girl feels my presence and looks up. Her eyes are glazed with concentration. It takes her a moment to realise that I have arrived. "You're here," she smiles. "Safe and sound."

"Yes," I gasp, smiling back. "What a morning it has been."

Girl's eyes widen with curiosity. "Have you been running?"

"Yes, escaping a tail," I say, holding my hips as my breathing begins to settle.

"Are you okay?" Girl's eyes narrow with concern.

"Yeah fine, just catching my breath." Eventually my breathing settles to a more comfortable pace and I meet Girl's gaze. "How did you go?" I ask her.

Girl looks at me sheepishly. "I took some photos of the interior of Tonya's car," she says. "I didn't take anything, I just looked." It isn't Girl's style to steal.

"What did you find?" I ask curiously.

"Rock albums," she says. "A lot of them."

"Let me guess," I add. "Lots of rock from the 70s."

"You bet," a small smile passes Girl's lips.

"Anything else?" I ask her.

"A lot of receipts for expensive items bought from Nick Farago," Girl's eyes narrow. "It seems that she is a regular customer of his."

"Interesting," I say. "What sort of pieces has she bought?"

"One off collector items," Girl says, her expression thoughtful. "Like a statue of Blondie and a crystal disco ball. Nothing unusual. Nick does sell memorabilia."

"Yes, he does," I say. "I've scored myself a temporary job at the music shop. I will set up some surveillance in there so that we can keep a closer eye on things."

"That's great Lira," Girl meets my gaze. "Are you sure you're okay to take on the job? It might put you in danger."

"I want to," I say. "What's happened to you is beyond terrible. You need support. I am happy to help."

Girl lowers her head shyly. "Thanks," a small smile spreads across her lips.

"Firstly," I say. "We need energy. Let's eat."

"Sounds great," Girl smiles as she falls into step beside me.

We turn into Hatter Lane, which branches off from the alley. Better to eat in a hideaway like Oakwood Café than out in the open. You never know who could be watching us.

Chapter 24

I am super alert this evening as we walk back to the ute. We take the quiet Sole Street across to Kiry Street. My ears have adjusted to the sound of Girl's shoes striking the footpath and the occasional snap of a twig.

It is silent. No-one is around as all the shops are closed. An occasional car zooms passed us as we continue to walk and our heads both turn each time to check that it isn't a tail.

After a while, Girl leans against the wall of the Redbank Chemist. "I just need to stop for a moment," she says, sighing. Sliding down, she sits on the cement with her back against the wall.

I sit down next to her. My bottom feels cold against the asphalt. "I'm tired too," I say, glancing at her.

Girl stares ahead, her eyes glazed in thought. "Well Lira," she says after a moment. "I've been thinking about Concetta's advice. Being out on the streets like we are has proven to be too dangerous. We need to establish that base."

"Where?" I ask, my heart beating fast. "We have to be careful not to expose ourselves."

Girl stands. "Come with me," she says, grabbing my hand and pulling me up onto my feet. She leads me towards a grey brick shop front. I read the signage displayed on the front window. It reads: Lucca's Real Estate Agency.

"I glanced at this window earlier today," Girl says, looking at me. "Currently there is an apartment available for lease." She points to the apartment image.

I study the advertisement of a small, one bedroom apartment, conveniently located on the boulevard in the heart of the city.

"I've been running for too long Lira," Girl says, placing her hands on her head. "Lately I've realised that trying to hide has got me into even more trouble. It's time to blend in with the crowd a little more."

"You want to stay in this apartment?" I ask her.

Girl nods. "Sure," she says. "I'll give it a go for a while. I need to begin to take control of this situation." She stares ahead, a thoughtful expression crossing her face. "It's something I've learnt from Aisha," she smiles. "She also had to find the strength to take on leadership too." Reaching into her silk bag, Girl retrieves the journal and flicks through the pages. "Here," she hands it to me. "Read this entry."

Summer, 1276

Reaching the age of 68 during summer, my father begins to feel very tired.

"Aisha," he whispers hoarsely as he settles himself into his wicker chair. "We must speak about the future."

Turning to face my father, I notice the deep lines of age across his loving face. My dear father who reared me the best he could on his own. He stares into my knowing eyes now, not speaking but silently making me aware of his fate.

I shift uncomfortably on my feet, feeling unprepared for this discussion. I am the daughter of the Chief of silk of Mira. My father has traded silk in countries very far away and has returned with produce such as: nuts, grains, wheat, salt and spices to keep us going.

"Is it that time, Father?" My voice is shaking. I wring my hands together, trying not to cry.

My father nods, still staring into my eyes. "Please Aisha, do not be afraid. I have had a long and prosperous life. I wish to know that you are happy and settled before I go."

Tears well in my eyes and cascade down my cheeks. Bobbing down next to my father, I take his hands in mine. "My loving father," I say to him. "I will always be grateful for the sunlight that you have bestowed upon my life."

My father pats my hands. "My light will always follow you, dear daughter. Even in your darkest moments. I hope you can find comfort in that knowledge." He chokes on his words, coughing violently.

Standing, I hand my father his cup of water. He drinks in large gulps, sighing with relief as his chest settles. "Thank you," he says, returning the cup to me. "My caring daughter, always here to help me. You will be a wonderful wife to Kirano."

"Thank you Father," I say, appreciating his approval. I swirl the remaining liquid in the cup. "Is there anything that I can do to help you feel more comfortable?"

My father sits upright in his seat and reaches into his pocket. He pulls out a small book covered with pig skin. "I leave this with you," he says. "It has all the information needed to keep our family's silk business running. Most importantly, it contains the Empress' seal. She presented it to me as an official licence of her approval for me to run this business and its trade in Mira." My father shuffles in his seat. "You are of age now, Aisha. It is time for you take over the business."

I nod, accepting my duty. It is the way that trade works in Mira. Once a child reaches a mature age, like I am at 15, it is time for them to step up and take on the duties required to help the city. All my life, I have known that this day would arrive. Right now it seems surreal, as though I am not sure of what I am supposed to do. In reality, I have been assisting my father with the silk business for years, even helping him to create garments for trade.

Placing the cup down on the wicker bench, I step forward and accept the book. "I will do my best, Father," I promise him as I pocket the book inside my tunic. "I hope you can find peace in knowing that."

My father nods, his eyes shining with relief. We stare at each other a while longer, finding comfort in the silence that sits between us. My heart sinks with sadness, knowing that I will miss these quiet moments with my father.

Father coughs and taps his chest. "It will take some time for the Empress to become used to you," he smiles. "She needs to learn to trust you. You have one thing in common, you are both women and leaders. This is rare in Mira and scorned upon by some. You will find comfort in supporting each other."

"I see," I say, staring into the distance. "I will try my best to connect with the Empress, Father."

"Good," Father smiles, sitting back in his chair. He eyes begin to droop.

"Speaking of the business," I say, taking my cue to leave. "I'd better dismiss Tiata from her duties for today."

My father's eyes flutter open. "Of course," he coughs and clears his throat, waving me away.

I walk quickly towards the front door and push it open. The warm night air greets me as I step outside, enabling me to inhale large, grateful breaths. I know that I am in shock. I can't imagine my life without my father.

After a few moments, my breathing settles and I begin to walk towards the small room designated for rearing silk worms.

"Good evening, Aisha," Tiata's warm voice greets me as I step into the dimly lit room. Her beautiful black hair is unwinding itself out of plaits and falling into her deep brown eyes. She wears a light blue tunic and pulls the long sleeves back, exposing her wrists. Tiata places a bundle of mulberry leaves into a wooden tray that sits in front of a tall wooden trellis inhabited by silk worms.

"The silk worms are keeping you busy," I smile.

"Yes," Tiata smiles, her cheeks flushed red. "They're fully grown and ravenous right now. I am feeding them three times a day."

I listen to the sound of the silk worms munching on the leaves. It sounds like the gentle pitter patter of rain.

Tiata waves her hand in front of her face to cool down. "Can I help you with anything, Miss Aisha?" She asks, staring into my eyes.

It is hard to hold back my emotions with Tiata. I have known her most of my life. My father hired her to nurture and feed the silk worms when I was a child. She is 6 years older than me and can read me like a book.

I muster my courage to speak. "It is time for you to go home." My voice cracks on my last sentence and I bite my lip to prevent myself from crying. Retrieving the pig skin book from my tunic pocket, I stare at it, trying to hide the tears that have begun to fall down my cheeks.

Tiata approaches me and places her hand on the book. "Oh Aisha," she says softly. "It is time?"

I can't speak. More tears spill down my cheeks and I swipe at them with my free hand.

Tiata draws me into her embrace. "It will all be fine," she says in a soothing tone. "You will be a great chief of silk. The works I have seen you produce are beautiful."

"Thank you," I say, a small smile forming on my lips. "I will need your help, Tiata. There is still so much I need to learn about silk making."

Tiata smiles proudly. "Well," she says, standing tall. "I have some time now." She steps across the room and picks up the distaff, which lies on the table next to the hand spindle. "You have made many silk garments over the years," she smiles. "It will help you to know how to thread silk fibre so you are aware of all the stages of silk production."

I am humbled by Tiata's offer to teach me a new skill. "Please do teach me," I smile. "Such a skill will be very beneficial to have."

Tiata retrieves a mass of silk fibre from the table and holds it out in her palm. "At the moment this is raw silk fibre," she says. "The first step we need to take is to bind this fibre to the distaff. Would you like to try?"

I step forward, eager to learn. "Yes I would," I say, taking the distaff and the silk fibre from Tiata.

I hold the silk fibres against the distaff. Tiata helps me to tie some blue ribbon around the fibres in order to hold them firmly in place.

Tiata secures the distaff firmly in my left hand. "Now you need to find a piece of silk filament fibre that you can pull," she says, pulling at the fibre. "See what I am doing?" I watch as Tiata narrows her eyes and pulls carefully at the filament fibre so that it forms one continuous thread.

"How beautiful," I smile. "To think of how hard the silk worms work to produce this."

"Yes," Tiata nods. "Take this thread," she hands me the thread in my right hand. I keep pulling it, watching it grow longer in length.

Tiata approaches the table and grabs the hand spindle. "Now," she says as she returns to me. "Let me show you how to wind the thread." She takes the end of the silk thread and begins to wind it around the spindle. I can feel the thread tightening in my right hand.

"What do I do now?" I ask her.

Tiata places the hand spindle in my right hand. "Turn the handle of the spindle in a clockwise motion, like this," she helps me turn my hand. "You will notice the silk thread twist slightly as it emerges from the distaff and wraps itself around the spindle. It helps to form a softer thread." She steps back, letting me continue to spin.

As I spin, a childhood memory of my mother flashes in my mind. She is spinning silk on a spinning wheel and I am watching her.

It is not painful, this memory. When my mother passed, she left a burning hole in my heart, one that I have always found the need to fill with a suitable purpose. For the first time, I feel I have found it. Maybe I can learn to make silk as exquisitely as she did.

"Wonderful," Tiata's eyes are shining. "You are spinning well."

"Thank you Tiata," I smile, happy to be learning. "I appreciate what you have taught me. You head home now, your husband will be wondering where you are."

Tiata stares at me with a concerned expression. "Are you sure?" She asks. "I am still able to keep you company."

"Yes," I continue to smile. "I am happy to keep spinning for a while. Keeping busy takes my mind off other things. Go before it is too dark. I will see you in the morning."

"See you in the morning," Tiata smiles empathically. As she leaves, she closes the door gently behind her.

I continue spinning until the silk thread has wound itself completely around the hand spindle. Placing the hand spindle and distaff on the table, I rotate my shoulders, which are aching. Closing my eyes, I allow myself a moment's rest.

I see a vision of my father's face smiling at me. He appears calm and peaceful. "Aisha," he breathes gently. "I feel so light, so free, like silk in the wind."

I jump at the distressed cry of Kiara, which cuts through the night air.

I feel numb, unable to move.

It is time.

My father smiles at me for one last moment before he fades away.

My eyes glisten with tears. I feel a heavy weight in my heart as I return the journal to Girl. "How sad," I say softly. "It is heart breaking to lose your father, I know that myself."

Girl stares at me sympathetically. "I'm sorry, Lira," she says. "That would have been a very difficult time."

"Yes," I nod. "I think about my father all the time. He still has a big place in my heart."

It is quiet for a moment while we both drift into our thoughts.

Girl finally speaks: "My family has always had a strong relationship with the imperial dynasty," she says. "Aisha knew that it was her responsibility to continue the silk trade for the family, just as I accept mine."

"It's a very big responsibility," I agree. "A base will be good for you. You need to regain purpose and control of the situation."

"Yes, I also need to keep safe and aware of what is happening," Girl says. "This apartment will give us a stable place to plan and gather information."

I nod, understanding.

Girl meets my gaze. "Can you book the tour of the apartment?" She asks me. "It'll be safer if you do."

I consider what Girl is requesting. "Of course," I say, smiling with reassurance. "I will book it in as soon as possible."

Girl smiles warmly and touches me lightly on the shoulder. "Thank you Lira," she says. "I appreciate your support."

We continue walking towards the ute, kicking the stones across the footpath.

We are both silent, our minds considering what we are yet to face.

Chapter 25

I meet the real estate agent, Vicky Kerling, outside the Lighthouse Apartment Complex the next morning.

Vicky is tall with brown hair and bright hazel eyes. She wears a pair of black rimmed glasses, which she keeps moving up and down across the bridge of her nose. She projects a studious presence as she flicks through her paper work and straightens up the skirt of her snug grey suit.

"Stephanie?" Vicky asks in a formal tone as she spots me standing tall and straight. I am in disguise, having borrowed one of Girl's button up, knee length dresses. It is dark blue with gold polka dots. On the collar it has a bow, which makes it look quite formal.

On my feet I wear a pair of silver high heels. My black wigged hair is tied back severely from my face into a pony tail. My face is covered with thick foundation and strong streaks of dark blue eye shadow accentuate my eyes.

As I turn to look at Vicky, I am happy with my disguise decision. As a successful business woman, I should get along with her quite well.

"Yes," I reply, speaking in an eloquent tone. "Nice to meet you Vicky." I smile and turn on the charm, readied with my cover story. "I only have a short while. I have arranged a meeting with a very important business man from Nynia in an hour."

"Well, we'd better begin our tour then," Vicky smiles, peering at me over the rim of her glasses. I note that she likes to study her clients and really take them in. I'd better maintain consistent with my cover.

Vicky takes small steps, heading towards the large, glass rotating doors. "We need to make our way through here."

I follow Vicky through the revolving glass doors and onto the corridor on the ground floor. She leads me to the elevator and presses the button.

"Work must be very busy," Vicky says, attempting to engage me in conversation. "Do you have many international clients?"

Bing! The elevator doors slide open.

Vicky steps into the elevator, holding her arm out to prevent the doors from closing.

"Thank you," I say, stepping into the elevator. It is empty except for the two of us. I stand tall and straight, using one hand to hold onto the steel bar to steady myself as the elevator begins to rise.
"I have many international clients, Vicky," I say, returning to our conversation. I decide to elaborate further, so that my story becomes even more believable. "At the moment I am lucky to stay in one place for a while. I don't need to travel so much as my clients are visiting Redbank for a change." I look at Vicky. Has she bought my story?

"Good for you," Vicky says, smiling. Her eyes narrow slightly as she studies me again. It makes me feel nervous.

Bing! The elevator has reached the first floor. The doors open and Vicky waits while I step outside and into the corridor.

"Wait until you see this beautiful apartment," Vicky says, approaching its front door. Reaching into her pocket, she grabs a bundle of keys. While she fumbles through them, I take a look around the corridor.

Small lamps hanging on the walls dimly light the corridor. It gives it a homely, intimate feel. A large window lets in streams of bright day light and draws my attention to the view of the park and art precinct across the other side of the road. Girl and I would be quietly concealed here.

"Stephanie!" Vicky's voice is animated. "Step inside the apartment!"

I turn to face Vicky. Her eyes are shining as she holds open the front door.

I step into the apartment and stop in the middle of the living space.

A light gold, plush carpet lies beneath my feet, filling the living area. To my right is a bright blue modular couch, facing a wall mounted television. At the back of the room are three large, empty white shelving units, which can be used to display an assortment of things.

"This is the living area," Vicky says, her arm sweeping across the room. "Nice, isn't it?"

"Yes," I agree, appreciating the view. "I see there is a lovely kitchen on the far right." The copper granite stone island bench is stunning.

"Oh yes," Vicky says. "Should we have a look?" She leads me into the kitchen and I admire the small silver stove and dishwasher. They are luxury after life on the run.

"A very generous sized kitchen," Vicky says. "You can store a lot in these cupboards." She opens one of the overhanging, brown cupboard doors. "See?"

I nod, smiling. It is nice.

"You even have a big fridge," Vicky opens its door. "In case you feel like stocking up on groceries."

"If I have time," I say. "I'm often grabbing take away as I work so late."

Vicky nods, smiling. "Let me show you the bedroom," she says, beginning to walk across the light gold carpet and towards the back of the apartment.

I follow Vicky into the bedroom and smile excitedly. It is lovely to see a queen sized bed, well dressed with a floral doona cover and two pillows. I could lie down right now and have a nap.

On the right side of the bed is a small bedside table with a lamp. Across the side wall is a sliding door mirror. Opening it, I discover shelving and hanging space.

"Lots of room for all your clothes," Vicky comments, studying me again.

She is clearly waiting for my reaction.

"Good," I say, maintaining my formal tone. "I see there is a small ensuite?"

"Yes," Vicky says, walking across the room. "As you can see, it is equipped with a toilet and a large shower."

The ensuite is adorned with a floral tiled pattern, which covers the floor and walls. The shower is a generous size and is enclosed with a screen and a large glass door. It would be great to have a long, indulgent shower.

"Let me show you the balcony," Vicky says, exiting the bathroom. I follow her through the bedroom and living room, across to the very left hand side of the apartment.

We stand in front of a large, glass sliding door, which closes off the entry to the balcony.

Vicky fumbles with her keys again, locating the one to the balcony. As she unlocks the door, I step back and allow myself to enjoy the moment.

The balcony is small with wooden decking. A glass parapet encloses its edges.

Stepping onto the balcony, I breathe in the welcome fresh air. It is a lovely view here out onto the park, the major shopping strip and the art precinct.

I feel Vicky's eyes on me and turn to meet her gaze. "So what do you think?" She asks. I notice that she's inhaled a deep breath. She's more nervous than I thought. That means she wants my business.

"It's lovely," I say. "Just the right size for me right now." I smile broadly at her. Reaching into my dress pocket, I retrieve my mobile. "Should we make a time to organise the paperwork?"

"You mean the lease?" Vicky asks, smiling. She ruffles through her papers. "I just happen to have it here. You are more than welcome to take it with you and return your application when you can."
She hands the papers to me.

"Best I do it right now," I say, flicking through the papers.
"I'm so very busy."

Vicky sighs with relief. "Great!" She exclaims, handing me a pen. "Here, let me help you."

We approach the small oak table next to the kitchen. Vicky pulls out a chair for me sit on.

"Thank you," I say, giving her a warm smile. Vicky moves her chair next to me and sits down. It is hard to write with her eyes on me. There is quite a bit of information that I need to make up, like my name and previous addresses. I lower my head, hoping that she will take the hint to leave me alone for a while.

"I'll just make a phone call," Vicky says, standing and grabbing her phone. She walks across the living room and exits through the front door.

Now, for work, what do I do? I know, I'm a business executive at … Let's say Dily International, the famous and successful corporate building in the heart of the city. I know that Girl will provide a great fake reference.

Satisfied, I sign the lease application form and bundle the papers together.

That was not easy. I hope my fake existence proves credible.

Standing, I pick up the papers and walk out the front door. Vicky is standing in the corridor, chatting on her mobile. She ends the call when she sees me and pockets her phone.

"How did you go, Stephanie?" She asks, her eyes shining.

"Great," I say. "All completed." I hand her the papers.

"Thank you," Vicky says, thumbing through the pages. "Well, Stephanie Zera, you will hear from me in the next day or so." She meets my gaze and smiles warmly.

"Great," I grin. "I'll hear from you then. Thank you for the tour, Vicky."

"My pleasure," Vicky says, touching me lightly on my arm as she walks away. "Best of luck, Stephanie."

"Thank you," I say, keeping the smile plastered on my face as Vicky walks further down the corridor. I watch her disappear down a flight of stairs.

I did it! Girl will be so proud of me.

All we need to do now is wait.

Chapter 26

That afternoon, Girl and I step through the automatic glass sliding doors into Sophie's Art Gallery. We are greeted warmly at the front reception desk.

"Good afternoon Ladies, would you like to store your bags in the cloak room?" The receptionist has her red hair tied up into a pony tail. She smiles a warm, gracious smile.

"No thank you," Girl shakes her head. "Can we please purchase two tickets for entry?" She digs into her pocket and pulls out some change.

While Girl pays for the tickets, I step forward through the entry door into the main section of the gallery.

The floor is dressed with a dark grey carpet, scattered with light grey, square plinths with rounded edges. Sophie has a strong passion for curating local artworks and this is evident in the diversity of ceramics and sculptures displayed on the plinths. My eyes are drawn to a tall, pastel blue vase decorated with tiny pink roses. Its flared rim is lyrical, cascading down the side of the vase in a gentle, sweeping motion. It is so beautiful that it touches my heart.

"What a lovely vase," Girl stands by my side. "I could see you filling that with many flowers, Lira."

"Yes," I sigh. "I can too. Unfortunately I cannot afford a vase like this right now."

Girl nods, understanding. "It's good that it's filled your heart with warmth," she says, putting her arm around my shoulder.

I glance around the gallery, my heart beginning to race a little. Where is Sophie?

I raise my eyebrows in surprise when I notice that the large, white walls surrounding the gallery are decorated with tallow candles in silver holders. They are the only form of additional light available in the room and I wonder where Sophie is able to source the candles.

Many paintings are displayed across the walls. Some works on canvas are ultra modern, such as the deconstructed traffic lights precariously dangling on a balancing pole. I don't usually favour modern art but this work gels with my experiences of life on the run.

I often have dreams where I am paralysed at the traffic lights, even though they are green, unable to keep running.

I know that I am exhausted.

There is Sophie. She is standing in front of a small crowd of people, who are seated on light grey lounge chairs. They have gathered to view a multimedia display on a large screen. Squinting, I see that Sophie is wearing a bright yellow t-shirt, emblazed with the portrait of a young, female artist. Vetra Undi, is her name, displayed in bold, white letters underneath her portrait.

Vetra herself, is standing in front of the screen. She has very short, spiky brown hair and her bright blue eyes narrow with concentration as she flicks through the channels on her remote. Vetra's short, black and white chequered dress flutters against her dark olive skin as she moves. The light that is seeping in from the windows bounces off the sheer, three quarter length sleeves that cuff with large black buttons at her elbows. Vetra subconsciously strokes the white collar of the dress while she continues to flick through the channels, finally stopping at a slide containing an image of herself, along with the statement: *Vetra Undi: Street Alight.*

Turning on the heels of her black stilettos, Vetra approaches Sophie and whispers into her ear.

"Oh, are you ready to begin?" Sophie eyes are alight with excitement.

Vetra nods, allowing Sophie to lead her towards the small microphone set up on a stand in front of the screen.

"Ladies and gentleman, boys and girls, I welcome Vetra Undi to this art gallery," Sophie beams. Vetra is a contemporary professional photographer, who enjoys capturing images of life on our streets. Please enjoy her presentation."

Vetra smiles and rests her eyes upon the audience who are clapping. "Thank you for your warm welcome," her voice is gentle. "And thank you Sophie for letting me present at your gallery today. It's been fun to explore and capture the life of the streets of Redbank in my new artistic project: *Street Alight*." Vetra pauses for a moment, turning to face the screen. She begins to press the buttons on her remote and flick through the pictures.

Vetra points to the screen. "In these photographs, you can see how the dawn light announces a new day with a fresh softness. The light was able to enhance the liveliness in the portraits of many a subject. It was lovely to photograph Chelsea, waiting for a train on a platform at Redbank Station. She snuggles her jacket tightly to her chest and the light gently kisses her face, emphasising her silent happiness."

A cheerful hum ripples through the audience.

Vetra flicks to the next photograph. "I also particularly enjoyed photographing the actions of Tonya Birano, dancing away without music in front of the Happy Beats Music Store. The increasing daylight bounced off her body, allowing emphasis of her movement. It also accentuated the sheer joy that she was expressing in that moment." Vetra pauses and takes a sip of water.

The audience giggles and chatters amongst themselves.

As Vetra flicks to the next image, I glance around the gallery. My eyes fall upon a partitioned off area in the back right corner. Dashing across to the plinth on my right, I hide behind the very large truck sculpture sitting on it.

Girl catches up with me, her eyes widening. "It's a Petoy truck!" She whispers, pointing at its lights. She reads the label displayed underneath it: "Sculpture commissioned by Naricia Petoy." Girl pulls at her hair in frustration. "The Petoys will do all they can to dominate Redbank."

Suddenly, Sophie looks up, her eyes narrowed. She has heard Girl's voice and is checking to see whether she can locate the visitor. I pull Girl down with me, so that we are crouched down low behind the truck on its plinth.

Looking up, I keep an eye on Sophie. Eventually she shrugs and returns her gaze to Vetra.

Vetra's eyes light up with excitement as she flips to the next slide. "Capturing the sunset on camera was my favourite time in Redbank. Its glorious glow was able to accentuate the gorgeous ripples of water in Spirit River, giving them a romantic spirit." Vetra smiles, her eyes gazing off into the distance.

As she flips to the next slide, Vetra faces Sophie. "Sophie was unaware that I was able to capture this wonderful picture of her standing on the pier with her romantic partner. Is it Nick?" Vetra asks.

Girl's mouth drops open. "Romantic partner?" She whispers.

I gaze at the photograph. Sophie is holding a cardboard box that she is peering into.

Vetra clears her throat. "See how the dusk light provides a warm glow on Sophie and Nick's faces, adding that feeling of intimacy as she receives the gift? I bet I know what the audience wants to know, Sophie. What was in that box?"

Audience members cheer and clap their hands.

Sophie blushes a deep red. "A personal gift," she says, lowering her head shyly.

Vetra continues to pry, seemingly unaware of how uncomfortable Sophie is. "If I gaze closely, Sophie, it appears that you were given a lovely dress. Am I right?"

While Sophie takes a deep breath and gathers her words, I begin to dash across the carpeted floor, until I reach the partitioned off area of the gallery. I can hear Girl shuffling closely behind me. Hiding behind the partition, I pull Girl down next to me behind the desk.

I don't dare to look up, for fear of being spotted. Listening carefully, I catch the shakiness of Sophie's voice.

"Yes," Sophie smiles. "Nick bought me a lovely pink mermaid style dress so that we could go out to dinner to celebrate my birthday."

"Oooh!" An audience member gushes in the background.

"How sweet!" Another audience member sighs.

"That's not a gift from Nick," Girl's voice is filled with rage. "I know that silk dress, I can see its bear totem on it clearly. It belongs to the Salander family in Mira," she whispers to me.

I rub Girl's back, trying to soothe her rage.

After a moment, Girl exhales a long held breath and rests her head against my arm. "Thanks Lira," she sighs.

"That's okay," I whisper. Staring over at Sophie, I notice that she has moved behind a display table filled with merchandise supporting the *Street Alight* project. Vetra is helping her to sell t-shirts, mugs, books and other merchandise to audience members.

While Sophie is engaged in selling, I raise my head up high enough to peak at the desk surface.

I inhale a sharp breath.

On the desk, lies the ancient silver silk dress with mint green raindrops that Zac delivered to Sophie the other day. Next to it is a piece of white paper, on which Sophie has sketched the totems evident on the dress.

Standing, Girl's eyes fall upon the dress and she covers her mouth in shock. Glancing across the desk, she places her hand on a long roll of material, which has been printed with the totems in a clear pattern. "How can she do this?" She whispers strongly. "How can she turn such important, ancient totems into a commercial pattern like this?"

I am in shock myself. Glancing over at the left side of the desk, my eyes fall upon a large card decorated with three dress designs. The card has the Botanica logo on it and a message from Jacquelyn: *Which dress do you like best, Sophie?* A large, blue circle has been drawn around the long evening gown.

The audience has begun to leave. I hear them chatting excitedly as they head towards the exit doors.

We only have a couple of minutes to leave before Sophie discovers us. I need to move quickly. Ignoring the rage in my heart, I grab my phone and photograph the evidence before me.

Sophie has a lot to answer for.

Pocketing my phone, I turn to face Girl. Her cheeks are bright red and her fists are clenched.

"Let me get my hands on her," Girl seethes, beginning to head towards Sophie.

"No," I say gently, grabbing Girl's arm and pulling her back. She fights against me, trying to escape. "That would be the worst thing you could do," I try to reason with her. "We have the strong advantage of being aware of what Sophie is doing without her knowledge. Let's not spoil this opportunity to be ahead of her game."

Girl stops resisting my grasp and exhales a large breath. "You're right as always, Lira," she says. "Thank you for helping me see sense."

Glancing over the top of the partition, I notice that Sophie and Vetra are in deep conversation as they stare at the photograph of Sophie and Nick.

Dashing away from the desk, I pull Girl's hand and merge us within the departing crowd of people. We walk quickly, blending in with the moving bodies and heading towards the exit.

Once we step through the automatic glass doors and our feet are firmly on the footpath, I release Girl's hand.

Girl stops, holding onto her legs and taking deep breaths. "I feel so defeated Lira," she sighs. "What do we do now?"

I check the front door for the opening hours. The gallery closes in half and hour's time. "We wait," I say. "Sophie will leave the gallery soon and when she does, we'll follow her and discover what else she's up to."

Girl stands taller and her eyes shimmer with hope. "Oh Lira," she says. "You always know the best thing to do." She leads us back towards the ute.

A short while later, Sophie exits the gallery and heads towards her bright orange BMW, which is parked out front.

"Let's go!" I exclaim, nudging Girl. "We need to follow Sophie."

Girl starts the ignition and revs the accelerator. Swerving into a u-turn, she accelerates down Shade Lane, tailing Sophie closely.

Once on Vista Road, the BMW slows down and indicates left onto Bloom Street.

"Surprise, surprise," mutters Girl as she follows Sophie around the corner. "Botanica it is," she announces as Sophie parks outside the Botanica store.

Girl pulls the ute into the curb a few metres ahead of Sophie's vehicle and turns off the ignition. "What does Sophie think she is doing?" Girl's face reddens as she turns back to watch Sophie carry her role of fabric into Botanica.

"We'll soon find out," I say, opening the passenger door and stepping onto the curb.

We walk slowly towards the store, giving Sophie time to settle in. I can feel an angry energy radiating from Girl as she stomps beside me.

After a moment, Girl stops walking and stares down the side of the Botanica building. Noticing something important, she motions for me to follow her.

I walk quietly, trying not to crunch the gravel too loudly beneath my shoes.

Girl presses her nose up against the glass of a small window, which is slightly ajar and peers into the store. "Come here," she whispers loudly, waving me towards her.

Approaching the window, my gaze rests upon Sophie, who is showing the role of material with the totem patterns on it to Jacquelyn.

"What do you think?" Sophie asks Jacquelyn as she unravels some of the material. "Will this totem pattern suit the evening gown that you've designed?"

Jacquelyn flicks her long hair back from her face. She squints as she feels the material and studies the totem pattern. Stepping back, she rubs her chin in concentration. "I'll do my best," she sounds stressed. "The material is weak and falls apart so I am limited as to what I can produce with it. Is there a way to improve its quality?"

Sophie shakes her head. "No, I am afraid not. Naricia doesn't want to spend too much on resources or production. She's pretty set on this cheap material. We've just got to make it work for us."

"Okay," Jacquelyn sighs and shrugs in defeat. "I just feel wrong trying to pass this off as silk when it's clearly not."

Sophie stares at Jacquelyn and sighs with frustration. "You'll get used to it," she says. "It is what it is."

I inhale a sharp breath, shocked at Sophie's reaction.

Jacquelyn is staring at the floor and shuffling her feet uncomfortably. "Okay, you might as well let the team know to go ahead and print more of this material," she says weakly.

"The team?" Girl whispers. "Who else could be involved?"

"I will," Sophie says, re-rolling the material. "We're still waiting on a large shipment of the base material to arrive on the truck. It's already a week late. I'm hoping it will arrive tonight."

Jacquelyn stares at Sophie intensely. "Naricia popped in yesterday, querying about this dress. I told her that it would be ready as soon as possible." Her hands begin to shake. "Naricia firmly reminded me that it had better be ready quickly or I'd have to answer to someone more senior." Jacquelyn clasps her hands together firmly, trying to stop shaking. "She is scary.'

Sophie's eyes narrow and she places her free hand on her hip. "Yes she is," she agrees. "My advice to you would be to work as quickly and efficiently as possible." Sophie stares into Jacquelyn's eyes "And don't ask anymore questions or it will lead to trouble for you." She places the roll of material on the counter. "I'll see you again soon, Jacquelyn," she says, her eyes dark and distant. "Hopefully with some product."

As Sophie leaves, the front door slams shut behind her.

Jacquelyn leans her back against the door and inhales a sharp breath. It only takes a moment for the tears to fall freely down her cheeks.

My heart reaches out to Jacquelyn. I want to do all that I can to help her.

Stepping back from the window, I walk quickly down the side of the Botanica building to Bloom Street. There is Sophie, hopping into the driver's seat of her BMW.

Turning around, I meet Girl's gaze. "We must continue to follow Sophie," I tell her. "It's the only way to discover more about her role in all of this."

"Right," Girl nods. "What are we waiting for? Let's go!"

We dash down the road, passing Sophie's car as she starts the ignition. Looking back, I see her checking her phone, completely unaware of our presence.

"Quickly!" Girl calls, opening the driver's door and hopping into the ute. She opens the passenger door for me.

"Thanks," I say, sliding into my seat. "Ready when you are."

Girl peers into the rear view mirror. "Here she goes, driving passed us now," she says, pulling out onto the road. She drums her fingers on the steering wheel as we stop at a red light at the end of Bloom Street. I can see the BMW a couple of cars ahead of us, indicating left.

The lights change to green and Girl turns left, following the BMW onto Veta Street. Sophie takes a sharp left once more, turning onto Minute Street. Girl follows slowly, keeping her distance.

"I wonder where she is heading?" Girl asks aloud.

Suddenly, Sophie pulls up outside a blue brick building. Looking up, I read the sign: Nick's Memorabilia Store.

"I'll just park here," Girl says, pulling into the curb a couple of metres away from the store. She turns off the ignition and stretches. "My shoulders are aching," she sighs. "I'll have to catch up with Hidu for a nice massage."

I smile, feeling happy for Girl. "You're very spoilt," I say. "What a lovely guy to give you massages."

"He is," Girl's gaze is dreamy. After a moment, she returns her attention to me. "Should we go and investigate?" She asks.

"Disguises first," I say. Reaching into my bag, I grab my black wig and stare into the rear view mirror. It only takes a minute to pin it down onto my head.

"Can you help me pin my wig down?" Girl asks, adjusting a red wig onto her head.

"Sure," I say, grabbing a couple of pins out of her hand and pinning her wig into place. I keep working away, adding more pins until I have secured the wig onto Girl's head. "There you go!" I exclaim. "What do you think?"

Girl studies her appearance in the rear view mirror. "I certainly look different," she tosses the long, red hair strands over her shoulder. "Thanks Lira."

"No worries," I say, placing my sunglasses over the bridge of my nose.

"Good idea," Girl pops her own sunglasses on. "Ready now?" She asks.

I take a moment to look at Girl. She is so determined to be part of it all, no matter what the risk. I feel a need to protect her.

"What is it, Lira?" Girl sounds nervous.

I bite my lip, considering how to tell her. "Your bravery and determination are amazing," I say. "However, this time, we are entering a dangerous territory. Nick Farago is very strong and I don't want you to be captured."

Girl nods, understanding. "Thanks for caring about my safety, Lira," she says softly. "What do you suggest I do?"

"Keep a low profile," I say. "It is best that you stay out on the footpath so that you don't get caught."

"Alright," Girl sighs. I can see that she doesn't really like the idea.

Pushing open my door, I slide out of my seat and feel my feet hit the cement footpath. Girl falls into step beside me and we head towards Nick's Memorabilia Store.

The electric blue, rendered brick building is split into two sections. On one side are large windows that display a range of memorabilia: signed posters of celebrities, figurines and musical instruments.

A single window is positioned on the left side wall of the building. Bobbing down, Girl and I peer through the window.

The room inside is large and dimly lit. Brown gold, wooden parquetry covers the entire space and travels in a chequered pattern throughout the room. Across the back wall rests a large fridge and situated next to it is a small sink. A stack of plates, bowls and cups lie precariously on the sink bench, waiting to be washed.

A few cardboard boxes are stacked next to the sink. One of the boxes looks identical to the one that Mitch showed me and has the pink silk dress Sophie was gifted by Nick strewn across it. Next to that lies an open pink suitcase, in which lie dresses, tops, skirts and underwear. The suitcase must belong to Sophie.

In the middle of the room lies a double mattress. Sophie is lying upon it and the top half of her body is naked. She is arching her back and moaning while Nick kisses her stomach.

Girl and I step away from the window, staring at each other.

"That was intense," Girl says.

"Yes," is all I can manage to say.

"Do you think they are living in the store?" Girl asks.

"I think so," I nod. "It looks set up for basic living."

I hear Sophie moaning again and I blush red. "I think it's time to go," I tell Girl.

"Yes," Girl nods. Her cheeks are bright red too. She follows me to the front of the store.

I turn to face Girl. "It's best you stay out here," I tell her. "It'll be quicker if I just dash in and out."

"What are you going to do?" Girl's eyes widen.

"Take a look inside the store and see if anything stands out." I begin to walk towards the front door.

"Okay," Girl nods, her eyes narrowing with worry. "Please take care, Lira."

"I will," I smile reassuringly. "I'll be back before you know it."

Approaching the front door, I reach for the metal door handle and press it down gently. Bracing myself, I wait for a large creaking sound as the front door opens. Luckily, it remains silent.

Leaving the door ajar, I tiptoe quietly into the store and gaze around. Many posters are scattered across the walls, displaying images of iconic artists and performers throughout time. Each one of them has a signature etched across the canvas.

Across the floor, lie a number of arcade gaming tables, which flash away with multi-coloured lights. There are also a couple of classic juke boxes and some old floor lamps.

A few tables are scattered across the room, displaying different items. One table is dedicated to soccer cards, balls and jerseys that represent different professional teams and players.

Stepping towards the front of the store, my eyes fall upon an open box lying on the counter. Peering inside, I see that it is packed with many used beeswax candles. What are they doing here?

I hear the sound of footsteps and dash behind a juke box. My ears prick up as I listen intensely to the sound.

"Nick!" It's Sophie's voice. "You are not listening to me!"

"What do you want me to do, Soph?" Nick is exasperated.

"Don't deliver those beeswax candles," Sophie pleads.

"Why not?" Nick's voice is gruff. "I'll get paid for it. I need the money to continue to pay the rent for this place. Business here is very slow and rent is way too high. You want to continue to live here, don't you?"

"Yes," Sophie places her hands on her hips defensively. "I can't believe that you're supporting the Chief's crazy delusions of grandeur."

"What?" Nick's voice is fierce. "How about you get on with your work and I'll get on with mine?"

"What are we doing, Nick?" Sophie sounds frustrated. "We both know that this relationship we have isn't going to last."

"Why? Because I don't meet your standards?" Nick's voice is thunderous. "I'm not rich, Sophie."

"Is that what you think of me, that I desire wealth?" Sophie retorts. "You seriously don't know me at all."

"You seem to be making more than I am," Nick whines. "In fact, in your position, you owe me cash and a lot of it."

"So I do," Sophie agrees. "And when the Chief decides to hand down some of his profits, we can all be paid." She waves her hand in the air and sighs in defeat. "Let's not confuse this relationship, eh? It's purely business." Her voice wavers.

"Fine. I've got to get back to work," Nick sighs, unaware of Sophie's sadness. "You'd better head down to Frosties."

"Yes, Frosties," Sophie says bitterly. "See you around Nick." I hear her footsteps shuffling across the shop floor. The front door slams shut behind her as she leaves.

Nick approaches the sales desk. He slams his hand on the table and sighs with frustration. I jump, startled by the aggression he exudes.

Nick's mobile phone rings. He reaches into his pocket to retrieve it.

"Hello?" He says gruffly as he answers the call. "Oh Rapido, what is it?" He sounds frustrated. "You're running late? The Chief will go crazy, he's waiting for his candles. You'd better hurry up."

My leg begins to ache and I shuffle a little, banging my foot into the juke box. It sets off a ringing tone, which draws Nick attention.

"I've gotta go," Nick says, pocketing his phone.

Curling up, I hide the best I can behind the juke box.

Suddenly, I feel Nick's gaze boring a hole into me. "What are you doing behind here?" He asks.

I tap the floor, pretending to search for something. "I dropped my money," I say. "I was looking for it." I hope that Nick can't recognise me through my disguise.

Nick searches with me for a moment. "Too bad," he finally says. "Money certainly has a way of slipping through our fingers, doesn't it?"

"Yes," I nod, silently acknowledging his personal situation in his question.

"Do you need a hand?" Nick asks, reaching out his hand towards me.

I let him grab my hand and pull me up onto my feet. He stares at my face intensely, as though he is trying to work out who I am.

"You have such a beautiful store," I smile. "I was wondering if you had any jewellery boxes? I love the old fashioned wooden ones."

"Hmm," Nick scratches his head. "Yes, I think I do have one. Follow me." He leads me to the back of the store and points at a small bench. A brown, wooden jewellery box sits on it. Inside it, sits a pretty ballerina, carrying a bunch of flowers.

"Can I wind it up?" I ask Nick.

"Sure," Nick nods.

I wind up the spring as tightly as I can. Letting go, I watch it begin to unwind and listen to the music play. It is a gentle, bittersweet tune that pulls at my heart strings as I watch the ballerina spin around in a slow circle.

The song reminds me of my mother. Suddenly, my mind is flooded with a memory of her singing her special song to me:

> *Where the flowers grow you'll be,*
> *dancing among dew dropped petals.*
> *Morning kissed, you awaken free,*
> *twirling with joy across the meadow.*
>
> *Stay away from the tall, dark trees,*
> *their profiles cast large shadows.*
> *Fractured light brings no sleep,*
> *as dark horses seek your youth.*

Inhaling a sharp breath, I step back from the music box with tears welling in my eyes.

"Is everything alright?" Nick asks. "If this is not suitable, I can help you find something else to buy."

"No, that's okay," I reply, swiping at my tears. "It is really beautiful. I'll come back soon with enough money to purchase it."

"I understand," Nick nods. "Money is hard to come by these days." He leads me towards the front door. "Hopefully you'll be able to pop in again soon."

"Yes hopefully," I smile as I step out onto the footpath. Nick waves as he shuts the shop door.

Turning to face the main road, I watch as Girl steps away from the window facing Nick and Sophie's home. She has a worried expression on her face.

"Is everything okay?" I ask her.

"I'm worried about Sophie," Girl says, scratching her head.
"I watched her storm out of the store with tears in her eyes."

"Sophie's quite stressed," I say and relay what I've learnt about Sophie and Nick's relationship to Girl.

"That's hard," Girl sighs as she falls into step beside me. "Poor Sophie, I'm sure that she didn't realise what she was getting herself into."

"No," I agree.

My mind still rings with the sound of the jewellery box and I feel a small tug in my heart. It has helped to bring back some precious memories of my mother.

Chapter 27

That evening Girl rushes across the embankment of Spirit River. "Hidu!" She cries, running into his open arms.

I smile as I watch Hidu greet her with his loving embrace.

"Hi," Girl smiles into his eyes.

Hidu pulls her close and kisses her gently on the lips.

"Mmm," Girl sighs, reaching up to touch his face. "Let's do that again." Leaning towards him, she presses her lips firmly against his.

Hidu closes his eyes, enjoying the sensation. He kisses her back firmly, drawing her even closer to him.

I feel a warm tingle in my heart for Girl and Hidu. It is so lovely for them to have found love in each other.

Turning away, I gaze at my mobile phone.

Fish eve, the message reads.

Stepping ahead, my feet cut across the grass and land on the pier. In the distance I see a silhouette standing on the wooden planks, facing the water.

I know her frame anywhere. Approaching the silhouette, a fond smile crosses my lips. There she stands, wearing a red hooded jumper, which covers her blonde hair neatly. She clutches a fishing rod in her hands, which has been cast into the river. Blowing out steam from her mouth, she shuffles on her green cargo legs to keep warm.

I stand next to her, facing the river. "Nice eve for fishing," I say, letting her know that I have arrived.

"Yes, the eels are thriving," Concetta replies, handing me a fishing rod.

I cast my rod into the water, still staring ahead. It is important that I keep as low a profile as possible, otherwise we may both be discovered.

After a few moments of silence, Concetta leans towards the river, peering closely at the water. "Look!" She points at the thrashing movement in the waves.

Peering closely at the watery depths, I see an eel undulating near the surface of the water. Watching it move gracefully, a sigh of relief escapes my lips. It is nice to stop for a moment, away from all the madness of life.

"Nice cover," Concetta says quietly as she studies my clothing.

I run my hands across the organic cotton of the embroidered lilac blouse. As I do so, my grey, pleated skirt flutters in the air, nearly taking me with it.

"Whoa!" I say, pushing back onto my feet to reground myself. I have nearly toppled into the river.

"Are you okay?" Concetta asks, retrieving the fishing pole from me.

"Yes," I nod.

Concetta places the rods down on the ground. They remain cast with their lines floating visibly in the water.

Turning to face me, Concetta grabs me gently by the shoulders. "Life can hit us so hard sometimes," she says, staring into my eyes.

"It does," I agree. "I always wonder what hope I will find across the terrain. It changes all the time. Right now, the wind plays with it, tossing its dirt in the air, challenging the terrain to ground itself. I remind myself that in fierceness, there is also a delicate beauty. You just have to look in the right place to find it."

"Wise words," Concetta smiles warmly. "There is an admirable strength in you, after all you have endured. Hold onto that, it will keep your feet firmly on the ground."

"I will," I cock my head sideways. My face feels heavy underneath my makeup. "Do I look old enough?" I ask Concetta.

"Yes, very," Concetta smiles. "Let me fix your hair," she pats my grey wig and tucks loose strands behind my ears. As she does so, she hums under her breath.

"Drifting Lullaby," I say, smiling. "So beautiful. You used to sing this song to me when I needed comfort."

Concetta nods, smiling. She knows when I am nervous. The song is soothing my nerves.

"Your makeup and grey wig have certainly aged you," Concetta says as she steps back. "Now for your shoes," She bends down and retrieves a pair of shoes lying next to her on the deck. "It is important that they are ones you would never wear. The last thing that one changes is their shoes and that's one of the easiest way to identify a person. This pair should fit you. I've barely worn them myself."

I slot my bare feet into the pair of black flat shoes. They are so comfortable and soothing. "Thank you," I say appreciatively. For a moment I just stand there, enjoying the relief my feet feel. It is wonderful.

"Keep those shoes," Concetta smiles. "You may need them again in the future."

"Okay, thank you," I smile.

Concetta takes hold of my shoulder again and stares intensely into my eyes. "Are you ready?"

"Yes, fire away," I say, inhaling a deep breath of focus.

"Your name?" Concetta's question is blunt.

I thought of a name last night, while I tossed and turned in my seat in the ute. It is a name that I can easily remember.

"Anne," I say, ready for the string of questions that I know will be forthcoming.

"Accent?" Concetta fires through the questions.

"English," I reply, looking at her.

"Anne will work," she says, smiling. "A nice English name. Your story?" Concetta is on a roll.

I pause for a moment, remembering the feeling of working with Concetta. The swift, sharp answers, the preparation …

"Too slow," Concetta snaps. "Cover blown and you're in grave danger –"

"For my life, I know, I know." I say, looking at her. "Just give me a moment," I say.

"You won't have a moment out there," Concetta warns. "We need to keep you safe."

I'm starting to warm up now. It's taking a little while but I'm getting my groove again.

"My name is Anne. I was born in Yorkshire, to a farming family. I grew up with a busy father, who worked hard to marry me off to a loving husband –" I stop talking, lowering my head and staring at the ground.

"Don't worry," Concetta touches my right shoulder. "Mitch will find his way back. He always does."

"I hope so," I say softly. "Mitch is being tracked by members of the Petoy clan. He can't afford to have his cover blown or he'll be hurt."

Concetta sighs and looks up at the darkening sky. "Time has a way of propelling us, Lira. It makes us feel unsettled and urgent at times. Mitch will find a way to navigate himself through all of this. He has to in order to keep safe."

"Agreed," I say. "He's in a dangerous place right now. I can feel it. I hope he is okay."

Concetta meets my gaze again. "Take care of yourself too, Lira. You are surrounded by more danger than you realise. The hunt for you has increased. The Chief is determined to have you for himself."

"Really?" I begin to tremble. "How do you know this?"

"I have my eyes," Concetta says softly. "They keep watch for me. The Chief has delegated a young male clan member with the job of tailing you. His name is Felibo," Concetta digs into her pocket and retrieves a photo. "This is him, see?"

In the photograph, Felibo is leaning against a wall, chatting on his mobile. He is running his fingers through his spiky black hair and an intense glow burns away in his brown eyes. A small shiver runs down my spine.

"Thank you for letting me know," I say, feeling my heart beginning to pound. "I will keep an eye out for him."

"So will I," Concetta says, retrieving a surveillance camera from her bag. "Let me help you pin this on." She attaches it under the collar of my blouse. "There," she says. "I will see everything that you see."

"Good," I smile nervously.

Concetta straightens my collar. "Keep safe, Anne. We'll catch up again soon."

"Yes, we will," I say in my English accent.

"Great accent," Concetta smiles as she reels in her fishing rod and tosses it over her shoulder. Grabbing the spare rod, she smiles at me one last time. "See you soon," she says.

I watch her walk away, her body shrinking into a small speck in the distance.

Staring out at the river, I take a moment to absorb what I have learned. The night is dominant now, its sharp blackness smeared across the sky. I had better move quickly before I miss the meeting.

Turning on my heels, I walk back down the pier, passing Girl and Hidu, who are lying wrapped in a tight embrace under the willow tree. I feel a sense of comfort knowing that Girl is safe with him and not about to enter the lion's den with me.

Cutting across the embankment, I pull open the driver's door of the ute and hop inside. Turning on the ignition, I listen as the ute sparks with life. *I can do this*, I tell myself as I drive down Heart Road and turn right onto Vista Road.

I barely notice the drive to Café Chaud et Froid. Pulling up in the car park at the back of the building, I switch off the ignition.

I step out of the ute, landing my feet onto the concrete. A dim glow emanates from the café, a welcome presence in the ink black night.

I walk slowly, shuffling across the concrete and portraying an elderly woman who needs to stop and sit for a moment because she is very tired.

Her seat happens to be the back step of the café.

Plonking my bottom onto the step, I sit and survey the area for a moment. It is too quiet.

I note the mess strewn on the concrete step. Half eaten sandwich and fruit platters have been dumped in a pile on the ground.

So there was a function on tonight. What for? Hmmm. It does not bother me to sift through the food rubbish and take a closer look. It is in trash that treasure often lies ...

Buried underneath the rubbish lays a pile of glossy, colourful flyers, decorated with the image of Girl pushing the cart. *Have you seen this Girl?* My heart stops at the confronting message. Poor Girl. The hunt for her has definitely increased.

I check the time on my phone. It is 8 p.m. The Petoy clan aren't due to arrive for another half an hour. That gives me time to settle in.

I shuffle slowly towards the front entrance of the café. Pushing open the heavy door, I hear it rattle as it shuts firmly behind me. Inside I am greeted with the warm buzz of family and friends spending time together. I feel a stab of longing for those special times when I could have coffee so openly with Mitch.

Shaking my head, I will myself to remain strong. I can smell freshly served coffee and it leads me towards the counter. The owner and barrista, Monsieur Fontin is standing behind the coffee machine, drinking a cappuccino.

Monsieur Fontin is a tall man with dark, receding hair. His face is tense as he drums his fingers on the counter. I can almost hear his thoughts marching a beat: 1, 2, 1, 2. Coffee now, coffee now ...

I can't imagine how stressful it would be to serve at such a busy café.

I wait patiently behind a young couple who are retrieving their take away lattes from the counter. As they turn away, carrying their drinks, the young woman nearly walks into me.

"Sorry, Ma'am," the young woman's blue eyes narrow with concern. "Are you okay?"

"Fine," I nod, happy that she believes that I am old. The disguise is working. I shuffle aside, letting the couple pass. The front door rattles again as it slams shut.

After a moment, Monsieur Fontin glances up and notices me standing there. His hand stops drumming across the counter and he pulls it away subconsciously as though he is slightly embarrassed.

I pretend not to notice, keeping my eyes on the menu written in white chalk on the blackboard behind him.

"Bonjour, Madame," Monsieur Fontin says kindly, his amber eyes shining. "Comment vous-appelez vous?"

"Je m'appelle Anne," I say, a small smile beginning to form on my face. I feel like I am stepping into character right now.

"Belle française, Anne," he smiles, looking pleased. "What will I serve you today?"

Now is the time to try my English accent. "A latte, please," I reply, with a little too much emphasis.

"Of course, Madame." Monsieur Fontin seems ignorant to my faltering accent. He sets himself to work, grabbing the milk from a small fridge and pouring it into a jug. Turning on the steam wand, he uses it to warm the milk.

There is something about the rush of a café that makes me feel at home. It may be the fact that I know that I will be served with delicious food and drink in a warm and welcoming place. This café is a treat for me right now. I haven't had a nice coffee in ages.

I watch as Monsieur Fontin prepares the latte by pouring the hot milk over the coffee. "Would you like a sprinkling of chocolat on top?" He seems to like mixing his French and English words together. It makes the café visit a charming experience.

"Oh yes," I say, nearly forgetting my English accent. I cover my mouth with my hand. *Stay focused, Lira.*

"Are you okay Madame?" Monsieur Fontin is concerned.

I nod. "I am just excited," I say, making myself smile. "The latte looks lovely."

"Oh merci!" Monsieur Fontin is chuffed. "Can I interest you in a croissant, an escargot or a palmier? They are very fresh this evening."

"I'd love an escargot please," I say, smiling. "Do you mind if I eat in?"

"Bien sûr! Of course!" Monsieur Fontin jumps into action. "Follow me! I will show you to your table. Where would Madame like to sit?"

"Next to a back window please," I say.

"Not a problem," says Monsieur Fontin.

We weave through the empty tables towards the back window.

"Here you go," Monsieur Fontin places my latte and escargot down onto the table. He pulls out a large, cushioned chair for me to sit on.

As I sit, I take a moment to close my eyes, enjoying the comfort.

"Are you okay, Madame?" Monsieur Fontin sounds concerned. He probably thinks I am about to faint. "Are you chaud? Warm? Can I take your shawl?"

"Non, merci," I say, shaking my head. I need the attention taken away from my disguise. "Je vais bien." I can speak a little French, so I use it as a distraction.

"Oh, vous parlez Français!" Monsieur Fontin is excited, flicking out a serviette with great gusto. "Une serviette, Madame." I let him place the serviette over my lap. He seems happy to be communicating with someone else in French.

"Oh merci," I smile, warmed by his kindness. "Vous êtes très gentil."

Monsieur Fontin stares at me appreciatively. "Thank you for sharing a moment of Français with me, Madame. I miss ma famille. They are all overseas en Provence. Je travaille to make money to see ma famille." He lowers his head, thinking.

It must be so hard for him, not seeing his loved ones. I know what it's like.

"I understand," I say gently. "I'm sure they all miss you too, Monsieur."

Suddenly, the door swings open and Naricia and Nick enter the café, their boisterous chatter filling the room. My heart begins to pound in my chest.

Monsieur Fontin springs into action, heading towards them. "I must serve these customers," he turns to smile at me. "Let me know if you would like anything else, Madame." Monsieur Fontin bows slightly and walks away, heading towards the front counter.

Taking a sip of my coffee, I sigh with relief at its comforting warmth. Lovely!

I watch Naricia as she pulls up the straps of her navy and white floral dress. "A cappuccino and a chocolate croissant," she gushes. She tosses some cash onto the counter. "Keep the change."

Monsieur Fontin looks up from steaming the hot milk at the coffee machine. "Merci, Madame, that is very generous of you."

Naricia shrugs, turning her attention to Nick. "What are you going to order?" She asks, stroking his shoulder flirtatiously.

Nick's expression is thoughtful. "Just a vienna, please," he says, digging deeply into his pocket. He retrieves a small amount of change and stares at it intensely for a moment before placing it onto the counter.

The front door swings open again, this time bringing a shivering Sophie inside from the cold. She raises her eyebrows at the sight of Naricia flirting with Nick.

"Bonjour Monsieur Fontin!" Sophie calls out as she pops her bag down onto an empty table. Taking off her large, black trench coat, she hangs it on the coat rack. She stands smiling at Monsieur Fontin. Her off the shoulder, ruffled top with a gold and red floral print, clings tightly to her skin, revealing her cleavage. A short, light blue skirt wraps snugly around her gold, high-heeled legs.

"Bonjour Sophie, Vous veux un chocolat chaud?" Monsieur Fontin smiles warmly.

"Oui, merci," Sophie looks up, smiling. "That would be wonderful."

Picking up a sample of material, Sophie approaches the window that I am sitting at.

I shrink back into my seat. Sophie would be able to recognise me for sure. A newspaper lies strewn across the table and I grab it, flicking it open to a double page spread. While I hide behind it, I can still see Sophie in my peripheral vision. She is testing coloured material samples against the window.

"Voici votre chocolat chaud, Sophie," it is Monsieur Fontin's voice. I can see his hand passing Sophie her mug of hot chocolate.

"Oh merci, Monsieur," Sophie smiles warmly. Placing down her samples, she takes the mug and sips her hot chocolate. "This is delicious," she sighs contentedly. As she lifts the cup again, a set of copper bangles jangle together on her left arm, reminding me of the sound of maracas. "Just what I needed."

"Je vous en prie," Monsieur Fontin is beaming. He picks up the material samples. "These couleurs are nice," he says. "What are they for?"

Sophie swallows her sip and places the mug down onto my table. She sways her hips, peering at the samples. I notice that Monsieur Fontin's cheeks are turning red. Sophie is stunning.

"These are colour sample ideas from the *A Touch of Silk* range for your new curtains," Sophie says, looking at them. "Which one do you like? This blue or orange?"

"Bleu," says Monsieur Fontin decisively. "Très chaud," he says, admiring Sophie. Realising what he has just said, he shakes his head. "Très sophistiqué."

Sophie raises an eyebrow. "Bleu it is then," she smiles. "I'll order the material tomorrow. We should have the curtains in a couple of weeks. The windows will look great!"

"Yes, they will!" Monsieur Fontin beams. "Merci Sophie."

"Not a problem," Sophie says, turning to grab her mug of hot chocolate from my table.

Bang! I feel her smash into my arm as she falls flat onto her chest on top of my table.

Tossing the newspaper down, I jump up, grabbing Sophie around the waist and helping her to stand once more.

"Thank you," she says, sighing with relief. "I am so sorry." She cocks her head to the side, studying my face.

Shaking her head, Sophie finally looks away.

I exhale a tiny sigh of relief. My disguise has succeeded.

"That's okay," I reply in a perfect English accent. I can feel hot chocolate dripping on my leg.

"Let me clean this up,' Sophie offers, grabbing a serviette and bending down. She tries to soak up the liquid on my leg, her bangles jingling away.

"Sophie Yang!" The voice is menacing and fired across the room.

Looking up, I see Nick standing in the middle of the café with a serious expression on his face.

Sophie begins to shake while crouched on the ground. She tries to settle her hands down by clasping them together. The bangles rattle ferociously, making her a conspicuous vision in the room.

I gulp as Nick steps forward, his eyes staring fiercely at Sophie. The silence is so intense that it makes me shake too.

"Who are you?" Monsieur Fontin bellows at Nick. "We have no room for rudeness here. If you can't be nice, then leave."

"I am one of her suppliers," says Nick. "Aren't I, Sophie?"

Sophie looks up at Nick. "Yes, you are, Nick."

"Nice of you to show up," Nick says. "I've been waiting for you to pay me for my deliveries. Two months later and still no cash."

"I'm sorry Nick," Sophie looks defeated. She drops her serviette and begins to fiddle with her skirt. "You know I can't just hand money to you. Not now, anyway."

"What do you mean?" Nick bellows. "I deliver, you pay, easy as that!" He places his hands on his hips. His expression is menacing.

Sophie inhales a sharp breath, her chest rising and falling. She stares into the distance, considering what to say.

After a moment, Sophie stands up, meeting Naricia's gaze.

"Let's sit down," Naricia gushes, ushering them both to a table. She meets Nick's gaze as he thumps into his seat. "Calm down now, please," she says between gritted teeth.

"Why?" Nick is flustered. "Sophie owes us both money. She knows that."

Sophie steps confidently towards the table. "There is so much more we have to do," she tells them. "The products are taking too long to produce."

Naricia's eyes widen. "I thought the *A Touch of Silk* range was coming along nicely," she says, panicking slightly. "You haven't suggested otherwise, Sophie."

Looking up, my gaze rests upon Monsieur Fontin. His mouth has dropped open in shock.

Sophie presses her hands down firmly on the table, leaning towards Naricia. "I don't have to say anything," she says. "It's the Chief you need to please, not me. I suggest you speed up the process as quickly as possible. It's fast fashion he's after, not ancient and authentic."

"How's the team going down at Frosties?" Naricia asks Nick. "Have they produced much of the range?"

"Some," Nick sighs. "There's been a lot of waste. The material's not holding together very well."

Naricia sighs. "You get what you pay for," she says "Synthetics aren't going to be as strong as real silk. The idea is that we make profits off it as quickly as possible." She meets Sophie's gaze. "I have some exciting news," she lowers her voice.

I sit forward, biting into my escargot and chewing frantically as I strain my ears to listen.

Sophie plonks into a chair. "What is it, Naricia? I hope it's not another crazy idea that you want to try out."

Glancing at Monsieur Fontin once more, I notice that his attention has been averted to a young girl who is ordering coffee at the front counter. I shift my gaze back to the group meeting.

"It's not an idea," Naricia says. "It's a fact." She leans forward, her eyes lit up with excitement. "Our clan has made great progress in our resistance movement against the empire of Mira," she smiles wickedly. "I heard news just this morning that they are planning to raid the palace very soon."

"Really?" Nick's eyes widen. "What do they hope to find?"

"Assets," Naricia's smile broadens. "Ones that will help us destroy the silk trade of Mira once and for all."

I sink lower in my seat, fearful of the power in the room. These ruthless people will not stop at anything to destroy Mira's silk trade.

Nick nods, meeting Sophie's gaze again. "What do you want me to do?" He asks her.

"Ensure that *A Touch of Silk* range is being produced and readied for dying," Sophie says. "The synthetic dyes will be here soon. We did our best to ensure that they match the original garment colours."

"I'm sure they'll be fine," Naricia shrugs. "A little difference shouldn't be too much of a problem."

"That we'll have to see," Sophie sighs. "Naricia, how's the advertising campaign coming along?"

"Great," Naricia smiles. "The range is creating quite the stir in the media."

"Good," Sophie smiles knowingly. "The more hype, the better."

"Got it," Naricia smiles.

"Meeting's over," Sophie sighs. "We've all got things to do."

"Yes," Naricia agrees, standing up. "Walk me to my car, Nick?"

"Sure," Nick smiles, his gaze resting upon Sophie. His lips thin into a smirk. "See you soon."

The door slams shut behind Naricia and Nick, rattling away loudly in the now quieter café.

Swallowing the last mouthful of my escargot, I watch as Sophie turns to face me. It takes her a second to reach my table.

Gaging eye contact with me, Sophie's eyes are full of recognition. "Can I help you clean up, Madame?" She asks firmly, pointing to the toilet.

I stare at her. She is such a strong woman.

"That would be great," I say, determined to discover more about Sophie and her role in this mess. "Lead the way."

I follow Sophie, weaving around the café table and heading towards the back of the building.

Approaching the ladies' toilets, Sophie pushes the door open with great force. Heading towards the sink, she turns on the tap. Water bursts into the sink, splashing everywhere. She ignores it, stepping towards the towel dispenser and snatching at many squares of paper towel. Her hands are shaking.

"Are you okay?" I ask tentatively, unsure if she wants to talk.

"Fine," Sophie's voice is abrupt as she soaks the paper towel in the blasting tap water.

After a moment, she shuts the tap firmly and turns to look at me with soaking wet, dripping paper towel in her hands. "I'm tired of this," she sounds frustrated. "Everyone has something to hide in this world, even you in your disguise. It is hard to know what's real and what isn't."

I gage her eye contact. She looks intensely angry.

"I understand how you feel," I say. "I wish I didn't have to be in disguise right now." I realise that I am opening up my feelings to Sophie as I speak and it feels somewhat therapeutic. "I am so tired of running. I would rather be at home, continuing life as normal."

"Why can't you?" Sophie asks, placing her hands on her hips determinedly. "You do have a choice, don't you?"

"I wish it was that easy," I say, taking in her somewhat naïve will. "It's too dangerous." I watch Sophie's eyes widen as she hears my words.

"Dangerous?" She laughs, throwing her head back. "Don't I know that?"

"I guess you do," I study Sophie's movements. She has wrapped her arms around herself protectively and is staring down at the tiled floor.

Sophie bends down next to me. "Here, let me do this," she dabs the paper towel on my leg. She works intensely, her copper bangles jangling a steady beat on her arm.

"Thanks," I say, my mind racing with many questions as she works.

Sophie smiles a knowing smile. "I never forget a face. It wouldn't matter what disguise you wear. You are Girl's friend and that makes you someone to watch."

I jump, my heart pounding. "Watch?" I ask her. "Why?"

"Because you may carry valuable information that others need," Sophie says, tossing her black hair back behind her shoulders. "That makes you very sort after."

I step back, staring at Sophie who is still kneeling.

"Don't worry, your secret is safe with me," she says, staring deeply into my eyes. "You play an old woman well too."

After a moment, Sophie tears her gaze away and stands up, reaching out to touch my hair. "It won't be long until I'm grey too, with all this stress," she sighs.

I watch her carefully. There is something jittery and fragile about Sophie. A lot has happened to her. She is scared. She needs to know that she is safe with me.

Sophie bites her lip nervously. "You don't know who you are mixing with. The Petoys are very dangerous. You just saw Naricia and Nick."

I nod, still observing Sophie. She is now biting her fingernails and staring off into space.

"How well do you know Nick?" I ask her, curious about their relationship.

"A little. Why?" Sophie begins to pace the tiled floor. She seems wired, as though there is a set of springs under her feet.

I can understand that. It is hard to trust anyone.

Turning around, I check the toilet cubicles. There is no-one in there. It's just Sophie and I. Studying her movements as she paces, I wonder how much she knows. It's time that I gained her trust. I decide that some reverse psychology is needed right now.

"How do we know we can trust *you*, Sophie?" I ask her. "You could blow our cover at any moment." I am playing with her own fear, making her confront it from a different perspective.

Sophie sighs, leaning against the wall. "I could," she says, rubbing her arm. "I don't want to though. It's not in my best interest."

Her response surprises me. "What really happened Sophie?" I attempt to reach out to her. "Let us help you."

Sophie stares down at the ground and then up at me. "It's a cruel world," she says, frowning. "You've got to go with your gut." She steps forward, staring at me. "My gut says I can talk to you, so I will."

"You can trust me Sophie," I reply, touching her gently on the shoulder. "I am listening."

Sophie reaches out and touches my cheek. "You Lira, underneath that disguise, why don't you swing by my art gallery for a visit? We can chat there."

I am slightly uncomfortable but also know that I must go ahead with her suggestion. Sophie has information that may assist Girl and I.

"Sure," I say, smiling reassuringly. "I can meet you in half and hour."

"Great," Sophie says, stepping back. "I will see you then."

I watch as Sophie pushes the door open and steps outside.

As the door closes behind her, I sigh with relief. I seem to have gained Sophie's trust.

After a moment of silence, I swing open the door and step back into the café. My eyes scan the street outside the window. There is Sophie, hopping into her orange BMW.

It is time to go.

"Merci Monsieur Fontin!" I call out as I head towards the front door of the café. Pushing it open, I step outside, inhaling a large, grateful breath of fresh air.

Chapter 28

Relax, I tell myself. *You'll be fine.*

Turning to face Sophie's art gallery, I walk slowly towards the glass doors. They slide open and I step inside. "Sophie? Are you in here?" I call.

"Lira? You made it!" Sophie greets me with a lively smile and a swing of the hips. "Come in!" She ushers me onto the main floor of the gallery.

"Wow!" My mouth drops open in surprise when I see the tallow candles alight across the walls. "That candle light is really something," I breathe, enchanted by the burning flames.

"Yes, isn't it?" Sophie appears next to me. "I've even become accustomed to their strong smell. That's the nature of tallow candles, though."

I turn to face her. "Where do you purchase them from?" I ask.

Sophie frowns. "I used to buy them from a woman in Mira once a month," she sighs. "It was a secret business, as the Emperor has banned tallow candles and it is one of the only ways that many people can have light and make money. I would meet the kind woman down at the pier of the beach and buy as many candles as I could, knowing the funds went back to the people who made them."

My heart is beating ferociously in my chest. "Who was the woman?" I ask, trembling slightly.

Sophie doesn't notice my nervousness. Retrieving her mobile phone from her pocket, she flicks through some photographs until she pauses at one. There, standing on the pier is a beautiful woman with dark brown hair, flying in the wind. Her kind, brown eyes smile as they face the camera. She is rugged up in a colourful shawl and her dress is in tatters. Yet, she still smiles.

"This is the woman," says Sophie. "She never told me her name. I think it must be a beautiful one seeing that she is so kind."

"It is beautiful," I say. "Her name is Maricelle Vivesque."

Sophie's mouth drops open. "You know her?"

"Yes," I stare into Sophie's eyes. "She's my mother."

"Oh!" Sophie places her hand on her chest. She stares at the photo once more. "I see it now, the similarity in your eyes and cheek bones. You both seem like such lovely people too."

I smile, grateful for Sophie's compliment. "You said you used to see her," I say. "Where is she now?"

"That's a good question," Sophie frowns again, thinking. "She didn't show up at the pier last time which is very unusual for her. I was left to visit the houses of the people who usually sell their candles and bought as many as I could. The beeswax candles that they are expected to use are very expensive. I pay them a little more than I should for the tallows so that they can also put food on their tables."

"That is very generous," I smile, touched by Sophie's efforts. "I am sure that the people of Mira are very grateful."

Sophie sighs. "I don't feel like I am doing enough," she says. "Between the harsh ban that the Emperor has imposed and the current theft of their heritage silks, the people of Mira have no legs to stand on."

"I know," I say, surprising Sophie. "I wish I could do more too."

"Well, there's something we both have in common," Sophie smiles.

Staring at the floor, I notice Sophie's sleeping bag lying in the middle of the space. "Have you been staying here?" I ask her, staring at the food wrappers and clothing on the ground.

"Yes," Sophie says. "I have nowhere else to stay right now so I sleep here each night."

"I'm sorry to hear that," I say. "It must be hard."

"It can be," Sophie says, looking sad. "The room echoes with thousands of haunting voices every night. It keeps me awake and ready to defend." She looks up at me and a tear rolls down her right cheek.

I reach out and touch her left shoulder. "You're at war with yourself, aren't you?" I ask gently.

"Yes," Sophie nods. She grasps my hand. "It's nice to be able to express how I feel with someone."

I nod, understanding. Sophie must be very scared right now.

After a moment, Sophie swipes away at her tears and sighs loudly. "Would you like a drink?" She asks, grabbing a bottle of wine off a bench.

"What is it?" I ask curiously, stepping forward to check out the bottle.

"It's a Cabernet Sauvignon," Sophie strokes the bottle, her hair falling into her face. "One of my favourites. So good after a stressful day." She sculls from the bottle and offers me some.

I accept the bottle and swirl it gently. Here goes! Taking a big swig of the red wine, I feel it flow down the back of my throat. It is nice. Maybe too nice.

"Great, isn't it?" Sophie smiles, grabbing the bottle and taking another swig of the wine. As she swallows it, she places the bottle down onto the bench and meets my gaze. "I'm dying to see your real face," she says, strutting towards me.

I feel Sophie pulling the bobby pins and the grey wig off my head. She tosses them onto the floor. "Such lovely light brown hair," she says, stroking my hair. "So soft …" her last word drifts for a while as she continues to play with the strands of my hair.

"Thank you," I say, my heart beginning to pulsate. I am so nervous right now. Can Sophie see my hands shaking?

Sophie stares into my eyes and strokes my face. "Under that make up," she says softly. "There is the beauty of you."

What a nice thing to say. I've lost touch with who I am lately. "Thank you," I say. "I feel like a jigsaw puzzle, shattered into bits and pieces right now. I don't know who I am anymore." I reach out for the wine bottle and take another swig, sighing with relief as I feel the warmth of the liquid going down.

I watch as Sophie retrieves a pack of make-up wipes from her bag. "These come in handy a lot," she says, pulling out a handful of wipes. Taking my hand, she leads me towards the wall mirror in the art gallery. "Take these Lira," she coaxes me gently. "Let yourself breathe again."

I take the makeup wipes and stare at my heavily made up face in the mirror.

I am feeling a little dizzy and my brain seems to be playing tricks on me. I could swear that the old woman staring back at me is warning me to leave her be.

"You can do it, Lira," Sophie places her hand on my shoulder. I watch her toss her black hair back in the mirror. "It's time to let yourself just be."

"You're right," I say, holding up the makeup wipe. "I want to be myself again."

I rub the makeup wipe against my skin and watch the foundation disappear.

There is my golden tanned skin with my small freckles across my nose. As I wipe away the eye shadow and mascara, I sigh with relief at the sight of my hazel eyes.

I am my raw, natural self.

I feel tears building up in my eyes. They roll down my cheeks and some hit the ground.

"Hello gorgeous Lira," Sophie says, turning me to face her. "Welcome back."

I let Sophie pull me close to her and rest my head on her shoulder. My tears just keep falling and falling …

I never realised how much I needed this moment.

Sophie holds me the entire time I cry.

I sob, *really* sob. It feels good to release the tension and the stress of everything.

As my breathing settles, I pull back, staring into Sophie's eyes. "It's been so long since anyone has ever taken the time to speak to me like that," I say.

Sophie smiles, wiping the remaining tears away from my face. "You deserve to be, Lira," she says. "We all do. The maze we're in will just keep continuing to run its obstacles. We need to take the time to reconnect with ourselves and to remember who we are. Otherwise, what's the point of continuing if we have nothing left?" Sophie's eyes are deep and thoughtful. She seems so wise after all that's happened to her.

"You are so strong," I say, touching her bare shoulder. "You've been through so much, yet manage to still know how to be."

Sophie stares into my eyes. "Yes, I have," she sighs, swaying a little.

"Is there something you need to tell me, Sophie?" I ask.

Sophie takes my hand, leading me away from the mirror. "All is not as it seems, Lira," she says, gazing into my eyes. "The Petoys must be stopped. They've taken a vast number of people from Mira, promised them progress and placed them into forced labour at Frosties." She approaches her sleeping bag and retrieves a folded piece of paper tucked into it. "I received this letter from one of the citizens, Caray, who I used to buy tallow candles from in Mira. She had no idea what she was getting herself into by joining the Petoys here in Redbank. Would you like to read this?" Sophie offers me the letter.

"Yes, I would," I say solemnly.

Taking the piece of paper, I unfold it and allow my eyes to scan the rushed handwriting:

Makeshift Girl: The Secret Heritage Trail

Autumn, 2022

Dear Sophie,

It is dark inside this building. The woman in charge has boarded up the windows with thick, wooden planks. As the days pass, I have lost all awareness of night and day and feel as though I am living an eternal nightmare.

My hands are raw from the amount of stretching, cutting and dyeing I have had to undertake. The synthetic material I must work with is hard to manipulate. It bunches, refusing to flow with the finesse I am expected to achieve. My hands are raw and blistered from so much exposure to the material's toxic chemicals.

At night times, the woman in charge exits the building, bolting the door firmly behind her. As soon as she leaves, I dig into my tattered skirt pocket and retrieve my hidden tallow candle. My hands shake painfully as I strike a match and try to light the cotton wick. It takes a few attempts, yet eventually I am rewarded with a single, flickering flame that gives me comfort. It is a candle I made secretly, back in Mira, even though it is forbidden to do so. As you know, I cannot afford to purchase the beeswax candles that the Emperor demands that we use.

Glancing around me, I see a lot of wasted material. It sits in piles at the feet of the workers, who also seem flustered with the polyester synthetic and would rather rid of it than continue to try to manipulate it. I often wonder what happens to that waste and pray that it doesn't cause irrecoverable damage.

I feel the woman leader or her guards' eyes on me frequently, ensuring I am working hard all hours of the day. I dare not meet the gaze of another worker, for fear of accusation of distraction.

I once saw Mrs Piranto, you know the famous shell artist from Mira? She fell asleep at her work bench.

The woman in charge strode towards her, with narrowed dark brown eyes. "Get up!" She yelled, slamming her fists on the older woman's bench.

Mrs Piranto jumped out of her chair, landing firmly onto her bottom on the cement floor. "I'm sorry Miss," she could barely form her words. "I am just so tired."

The woman leader's bright red lipstick spread into a menacing smirk. "If you don't resume working immediately, I will make that call and your husband will be severely hurt," she threatened.

Mrs Piranto placed her hand on her forehead, nearly passing out. The colour drained from her cheeks, leaving her pale. "Whatever you say, Miss," she managed to gasp and returned to trimming her material.

My stomach quenched with nausea as I felt Mrs Piranto's fear. A warm, generous spirit, she had begun to gain international trading opportunities for her shell art before she was enticed with the promise of progress.

I was promised progress too, as I completed my latest tapestry work on my front porch in Mira. I foolishly bought the woman leader's story of having the opportunity to work in a shop that would help improve my trade.

I did not realise I would land myself in this "shop." It is a small, unsanitary building, where I am forced to work, eat and sleep. There is a tiny area dug into the back of the room, where we may excrete at our will. Every morning one of us is forced to cover the hole with fresh dirt in order to rid of some of the offensive odour.

One night, we workers formed a circle around the tallow candle as it burned, allowing each other to bond by holding hands. It felt strange to connect with fellow people from Mira again. We have all become estranged from each other as we slave away for the woman leader.

In our circle, we closed our eyes and prayed. I pictured the streets of Mira, adorned with the rugged rawness of our original footprints. We once stepped together or passed each other by, busy but comfortable with our work in various trades. Now we are anonymous, our identities stripped away from us. Men, teenage children and we women are now under the rule of a menacing clan.

Like many of us, it is my most fervent wish to return to my life in Mira, no matter how dark it now is. I pray that you will be able to help us all escape this never ending nightmare.

My soulful prayers for your safety during this time,

Caray.

My hands are shaking as I pass the letter back to Sophie.

"Shocking, isn't it?" Sophie frowns angrily.

I nod, unable to speak.

Sophie meets my gaze. "We need to find a way to stop the counterfeit trade," she says firmly. "The Petoys are out of control."

"Agreed," I nod. "Somehow, those workers will be freed," I promise her. "We'll need your help to make it happen."

"I'll do everything in my power to help," Sophie sounds determined. "We need a good plan."

"Yes, we do," I agree. Bending down, I pop my wig into my bag and pick up my shawl. "Let me think about it."

"Okay," Sophie agrees.

"I'd better go," I say, heading towards the exit. "See you soon, Sophie."

"Bye Lira," Sophie's voice is small.

I feel Sophie's eyes on me as I exit the gallery. As my feet hit the footpath, a deep ache swells its way through my heart.

Chapter 29

As the sun rises, I walk across the embankment at Spring River. My heart falls at the sight of Girl standing in the tall grass blades, her eyes streaming with tears.

Hidu stands behind her, next to the willow trees. He is staring into the distance with an angry expression on his face.

I stop walking, absorbing the tension in the air.

Girl spots me and stares directly into my eyes. I can feel her pain and her need for comfort. My instincts push me forward and I walk towards her, opening up my arms.

Hugging me tightly, Girl buries her head into my shoulder. I hold her for a long time while she cries.

Girl stands back and rubs her eyes. She looks very tired. "I've asked Hidu to give me some space for a while," she says softly.

I glance at Hidu. He is still staring off into the distance and clenching his fists.

I remain silent, letting Girl take the time to process her feelings. She stares down at the ground, fidgeting with her fingers and thinking. After a long moment, she meets my gaze. "I feel so betrayed, Lira."

I touch Girl's arm lightly. "Why is that?" I ask her in a gentle tone.

Girl looks up at the sky for a moment, considering her words. Her gaze darting downwards, she stares into my eyes and grabs my hands. "Let Hidu speak for himself," she finally says, pulling us towards him.

As we approach Hidu, he senses our presence and my gaze locks with his. A look of guilt crosses over his face and his cheeks redden.

"Hi Hidu," I say, reaching out to him. "Are you alright?"

Hidu shakes his head and runs his fingers through his hair in frustration. "All is for nothing," he says.

"That is my greatest concern," Girl sighs. "I see now that I made a big mistake in confiding in you, Hidu. I got you too worked up, too emotional. It's best you don't know so much."

"We love each other," Hidu pleads. "Am I just a fool for thinking that?" He grabs Girl by the shoulders roughly. "Tell me, is anyone ever good enough for the esteemed Girl?"

"Let go of me!" Girl squirms out of Hidu's grasp. She stares at him in disbelief. "There is a madness in you, one that is out of control. It's making you do crazy things."

Hidu laughs deliriously. "I've been mad for a long time, Girl. It was bad enough that my family lost their home at the hands of the Emperor of Mira. I can't bare to watch the Petoys rip you and our beloved city, Mira to shreds too." Tears spring forth in his eyes and he swipes at them in frustration. "Maybe I am a fool for loving you, Girl," he sighs. "But I am not sorry for what I did."

I step closer to Hidu and touch him lightly on the shoulder. "What did you do, Hidu?" I am concerned.

"Tell her, Hidu," Girl says, a fire sparking in her eyes. "Lira deserves to know what we're all about to face."

I inhale a sharp breath in anticipation of Hidu's announcement.

Hidu shrugs before turning to face me. "Well you should know," he is revved up, angry. "I broke into Frosties and stole a box of the counterfeit silk scarves."

The news hits me like a sharp slap. I gasp in shock.

"Show her the box," Girl demands in a distressed voice.

Hidu reaches behind the trunk of a willow tree and retrieves a cardboard box. He plonks it down onto the ground it front of him, spilling the scarves out onto the grass.

There are scarves in a multitude of colours, each with different totem designs. I watch Girl clench her fists and begin to seethe.

Hidu eyes flash with anger. "I have surveyed Frosties like Concetta asked me to. It is the epicentre of the Petoys' counterfeit silk production. It broke my heart to see the forced labour taking place there. Some people looked thin and worn out, barely fed after days of work. Others had fallen asleep at conveyor belts while the print run occurred."

"Gee," I say. "That's horrific. The Petoys have gone way too far."

"Yes, they have," Hidu agrees. "I took this box for all that is still decent in this world and all that needs to be nurtured and protected, just like our poor people who need a way out of forced labour."
He pauses, staring at Girl who has her back to him. "I hate seeing you so angry, Girl," Hidu is exasperated. "It tears me up inside."

Guilt flashes across Girl's face. "I let you become too close to me, Hidu," she breathes. "Confided in you too much. I know what you saw was painful but you believed you had certain liberties. I never thought you'd steal from the Petoys and put us in such grave danger."

Hidu's eyes flash in defiance. "If they want to take from you and hurt people, then I will take from them."

Girl runs her fingers through her hair and sighs. "Hidu, trade war has existed for aeons. The resistance movement the Petoys have formed against the empire of Mira began a long time ago. My ancestor, Kirano, helped to ward off the clan's attacks against the reigning Empress of his time.

Nowadays, the Petoys are distressed at the cost of land and silk tax in Mira. The Chief of the clan is on a vengeance path, doing all he can to destroy the authentic silk trade and to pass off counterfeit silk as genuine. It is in this way, that he hopes to finally destroy the authentic silk trade and its economical value in Mira. He desires to see the empire fall apart so that the Petoys can step in as the new leadership."

Hidu steps forward, his cheeks burning. "Part of his vengeance is to destroy you, Girl. Without you and your future leadership, the authentic silk trade will not survive in Mira. Do you think I am going to stand by and let that happen?"

Girl inhales a deep breath and stares up at the sky. "I am not afraid anymore," she says. She shifts her gaze to Hidu. "I am tired of running. It's time for me to settle down and face this issue head on. If I am to become the new chief of silk for Mira, then I need to set a good example. In my eyes, that does not involve putting everyone in danger."

Hidu lowers his head in shame. "I'm sorry," he says softly. "I never meant for this to happen."

"Yet it has," Girl stamps her feet. "To think of all that Lira, Mitch and I have done to maintain a low profile and to keep out of danger. In one crazy action you have put us all in the firing line." Girl stares at me concernedly. "What did Concetta have to say, Lira?"

"Concetta informed me that the Chief has ordered a male Petoy clan member to keep a close eye on me," I relay the information that I have gleaned.

Girl's eyes widen in shock. She is quiet for a moment, absorbing what she has learned.

Hidu steps forward, reaching out to us with his open arms. "Please hear me out," he pleads. "I have a plan. I am going to take these scarves back home to Mira. My friend Gashri majored in sericulture. He will be able to analyse the material of these scarves and confirm whether they are made of genuine silk or not."

Girl's eyes widen in surprise. "These scarves are not yours to take, Hidu," she asserts. "You must return the box to Frosties today, before anything terrible happens."

"Okay," Hidu sighs in defeat. "I will." He stares into Girl's eyes for a long moment, his gaze softening. "I'll head off now," he finally says as he reaches down to pick up the box. He retrieves a sheet of paper from his pocket and hands it to Girl. "I'll leave this map of Frosties' floor plan with you. All the best, Girl."

I stand next to Girl, watching her eyes well with tears as Hidu leaves.

After he has disappeared, Girl turns to face me. "I'm so sorry," she says. "I accept most of the blame for this. I should never have confided so much information in Hidu."

"Everyone needs a confidant," I say gently. "You fell in love with Hidu. You trusted him. You can't help how he handled the information."

"Some space from him is vital," Girl's voice cracks. "He is reckless and will only put us in more danger."

"I support your decision," I say. "Let me know if you need anything."

My one use mobile phone is ringing. It is the real estate agent.

"Hello? Stephanie speaking," I answer in a business like tone.

"Hello Stephanie, it's Vicky from Lucca's Real Estate Agency. Are you free to discuss your recent application?"

"Yes, of course," I say. "Was it successful?"

"Oh yes," Vicky replies in an excited tone. "I am very pleased to inform you that your application to lease the apartment at the Lighthouse Boulevard Apartment Complex has been successful."

"That's wonderful news," I can't help smiling. It's nice to have succeeded at something in this mayhem.

"Great," Vicky is buzzing. "The apartment is ready for you to move into as soon as tomorrow morning. You will need to pop by our agency to collect the keys. Make sure you bring some photo identification."

"Okay," I say. "Thank you Vicky. I will collect the keys in the morning."

Ending the call, I meet Girl's gaze with a smile on my face. "It seems that we have a safe place to stay for a while," I tell her.

"The application was approved," Girl's eyes light up with hope.

"Yes it was," I say. "Thanks for helping out with the reference."

"Not a problem," Girl smiles broadly. "We finally have a base to work from," her voice sounds bright.

"Yes we do," I nod. "I'd better get rid of this phone." I scan the grass for a place to bury the phone. As I do, a feeling of anxiety washes over me. Deep in my heart, I am afraid of the dangers we are yet to face.

Chapter 30

Staring through the window of our new apartment, I take in the visual of the wide, concrete pathway of the boulevard.

There is a flurry of movement this morning. Cars, joggers and bus commuters fill the streetscape. It is a place you can blend into easily. Good to know.

Turning around, I nearly slip on the tiled flooring of the bathroom. Reaching for the glass wall of the shower, I stop myself from skidding any further and take a deep breath. *It's time to indulge a little*, I coax myself. *You deserve it.*

Opening the glass door, I step inside the shower, feeling the firmness of the tiles beneath my feet.

Turning the tap on, I adjust the water temperature to very warm and stand under the spray of water, letting it soothe my body.

It is so nice to have this treat and to relax for a little while.

I rub some milk shampoo onto my scalp and as it foams up, some of it drops into my eyes. They begin to sting. Swiping at my eyes, I turn to face the shower water and let it run across my face and hair. The shampoo washes away, leaving me with a slight sting in the eye that I know will eventually disappear.

What can I use to wash my body with?

I see that Girl has placed some pomegranate scented body wash on the shelf.

Opening it up, I take a sniff. It smells divine.

I pump some body wash into my hand and rub it gently onto my stomach. It feels so smooth, giving me a slight zing feeling. The massage and body wash also soothes some of the tension in my shoulders and back.

Rinsing off, I turn the tap off and exhale a deep breath of relief.

It is nice to feel cleansed and soothed.

What a lovely mini escape.

Wrapping myself in my blue bath towel, I walk into the bedroom. I had the bed to myself last night and Girl slept on the couch.

Removing my towel, I let it drop onto the floor and stand in front of the mirror door, taking a look at myself.

My body is a little more toned than I remember. I can see my biceps flexing on my upper arms.

Rubbing my stomach, I admire its flatter appearance, which is new for me. I haven't been able to eat large meals on the run so I've lost a bit of weight.

Golden tanned and glowing, my skin compliments my light brown hair, which falls in long strands down my shoulders.

My face is glowing, highlighting the freckles bridging my nose and my pronounced cheek bones. My hazel eyes shine a little, accentuated by dark grey lines of fatigue.

I still can't sleep properly. Even in a comfortable bed.

I'm too stressed.

Sighing, I reach for the tank t-shirt I had set out to wear. Putting it on over my head, I watch the lime green material fall over my chest and stomach, revealing a sign on the front of the t-shirt that screams: *Music Rocks!*

A small smile forms across my lips. At least this time the disguise is more fun.

Makeshift Girl: The Secret Heritage Trail

I pull on my underwear and reach for the pair of dark orange 70s flares that are sitting on the bedside table.

Stepping into the pants, I feel them cling to my bottom and thighs as I pull them up. They will have to do.

Running my fingers through my hair, I try to rid myself of the knots I feel stuck in its strands.

I don't have the convenience of a brush.

Satisfied, I pin on my black wig and part my hair in the centre. I bunch the strands of my hair into two pigtails, which I tie with rubber bands. Pigtails were a common theme that I noticed in Tonya's restaurant painting and will reassure her that I share her passion for the 70s.

Time to take one last look in the mirror.

Very 70s!

Leaving the bedroom, I step into the living area and spot Girl on the couch. She is curled up in a blanket.

"Good morning," she smiles, rubbing her eyes. "You look very nostalgic in that gear."

"Thanks," I return her smile. "I was going for a 70s vibe."

"It works," Girl nods. Her newly blonde hair cascades down her shoulders as she sits up.

"Your hair looks great!" I say.

"Thanks Lira, it will be harder to recognise me now," Girl smiles.

She looks so different with blonde hair.

My tummy is rumbling so I head towards the kitchen to prepare some breakfast. "Do you want some toast?" I ask her.

"Yes please," Girl is preoccupied, tossing the blanket aside and standing up. "Sounds great." She stretches her back like a cat and yawns.

"How did you sleep?" I ask as I pop four slices of bread into the toaster.

"Okay," Girl rotates her shoulders and stretches her arms out. "I must say it is more comfortable than sleeping in the ute."

"Of course," I look at her. "You get to have the bed tonight."

"Yay!" Girl cheers, her voice slightly groggy. She approaches the kitchen bench and turns on the kettle. As it warms up, she leans with her back against the bench.

"Raspberry jam?" I ask Girl as I spread butter on the toast.

"Lovely," she says, her face etched with lines of deep concentration.

I take the plates of toast and mini jam jars over to the oak table and sit down, still admiring Girl's hair.

"Would you like some tea?" Girl finally asks as she pours the boiling water into a cup.

"What flavour is it?" I ask, hoping it is something that I like.

"Peppermint," Girl replies. "It's all I've got."

"Sounds great," I smile, watching her pour water into the second cup. Peppermint tea is tasty.

Girl approaches the table and places the cup of tea down in front of me. "Here you go," she says, staring at me with a concerned expression.

"What is it, Girl?" I pause in the middle of biting my toast.

"I'm worried about you working at the music store today,"
Girl bites her lip as she sits down.

"Why?" I ask. "Tonya's harmless. It is only one last shift. I should be fine."

"It's not Tonya that I'm worried about," says Girl, crossing her arms. "Nick is due for that large delivery today, remember? Be careful."

"I will," I say. "I'll even set up some surveillance. We can keep track of what Nick is delivering and ensure that it is all above board. If Tonya's one of his biggest clients then there will be a tonne more deliveries on their way."

"Surveillance sounds good," says Girl. She stares directly into my eyes. "Please be careful Lira, you don't know how powerful Nick actually is."

'I will," I say, appreciating Girl's concern. "I'll get out if it gets too hard to handle."

"Call me and I'll come get you," Girl says, her expression serious.

"Okay," I say, standing up. I pat my pant pocket, checking that the surveillance camera is still in there. It is. "What are you up to today?" I ask Girl.

"Working on plan b," Girl says. "Best to have another place to go to if things don't work out here."

"Yes," I agree. "I look forward to hearing your idea," I retrieve my fluoro bag from the kitchen bench.

"Good luck," Girl bites her lip anxiously.

"I'll need more than luck," I smile. "I will need to work brilliantly undercover." Stepping into a pair of orange sandals, I tighten the straps, ensuring that my feet are comfortable. "See you soon!" I call as I head out the front door.

As I venture down the corridor, my outfit catches the attention of tenants who are leaving for work. The pair of 70s flares flap against my legs as I step into the elevator with the mayhem of a crowd of people, blending in as best as I can.

I can feel sets of eyes staring at me and keep my head down, trying to look preoccupied. The last thing I need is for someone to recognise me.

Bing! I am grateful when the elevator finally arrives at the ground floor.

Stepping out into the corridor, I walk quickly, trying to beat other bodies to the exit.

I manage to arrive at the revolving glass doors quickly and push my way through them. My pony tails flap their way in the wind as I exit the doors and begin to run towards Veta Street.

I am late.

Reaching the doorstep of the music shop, I am greeted by Chuckles. He jumps up onto my legs and barks with excitement. I seem to have bonded with him.

Patting Chuckles' head, I smile. "Nice to see you too," I say.

Tonya steps out to greet me. "Good morning Stephanie, I am so glad you made it today. You look amazing!" She is bubbly this morning with a happy smile spread across her lips.

"Thanks Tonya." It was nice of her to greet me like that.

I follow Tonya inside the store.

"Cool bag," Tonya grins.

I stitched the bag together using fluorescent orange and green cloth. It hangs loosely over my shoulder, screaming 70s.

"You can put your bag down over here," Tonya points to a shelf underneath the sales desk.

"Thanks," I say, tucking it in. I'm not worried about leaving the bag there. It only contains my spare wallet with some cash for lunch.

Inside my flare pocket sits a tiny surveillance camera.

"Ready to begin work?" Tonya asks. She is holding a box of vinyl records.

"Of course," I smile, reaching for the box. "Do you want me to sort these?"

"That would be great," Tonya grins. "Can you sort them by artist and place them on this shelf here?"

"Leave it with me," I say, peering into the box. There is a variety of music in there. Mostly rock, along with some pop and dance compilations.

The phone rings on Tonya's desk. She heads over to answer it.

I listen as I sort through the records.

"Hello Nick," Tonya sounds excited. "You have it? I'll meet you out the back in the car park." She grabs some cash from the register. "I'll be back in a minute!" She calls excitedly as she heads towards the back of the store.

Nick Farago is outside.

A cold shiver of anxiety runs down my spine. I pat my head, checking that my black wig is securely on my scalp.

Once the jangly back door closes, I stand and wait. It is quiet, except for the sound of Chuckles chewing on his toy. He looks up at me as I walk passed him.

Stay there Chuckles! I beg silently.

Not so lucky. He is following me across the store.

Approaching the painting, I glance over my shoulder once more. No-one has entered the store. It is still quiet. I will have to work quickly.

Digging into my pocket, I grab the tiny surveillance camera.

Chuckles barks excitedly and jumps up onto my legs. He must think I have a treat to give him.

"Down Chuckles!" I hiss, trying to shake him off.

He is staying put, staring at me with bright, hopeful eyes.

It is awkward trying to hook up a surveillance camera with a dog attached to my legs.

Holding up the bottom left corner of the painting's frame, I peer at the wall behind it. Besides the chips of paint peeling away, it is quite smooth.

I feel Chuckles' paws beating against my legs. It is hard to balance myself but I stand firm, determined to complete my task.

I need to tune the dog out.

I remove the backing off the adhesive on the camera's circular base. Juggling the painting in my left hand, I hold its corner up while leaning forward to press the camera against the wall.

Not so lucky.

Chuckles pummels my legs so hard that I topple backwards, landing onto the floor. The tiny camera flies through the air and bounces across the ground.

"Aw!" I am winded for a moment. Chuckles jumps up and presses his front paws on my shoulders. He licks my face.

"Chuckles," I say, staring at him. "You need something to chase." I spot a toy bone lying against a rack of vinyl records.

Slowly standing on my two feet, I allow myself a moment to catch my breath.

My ears prick up, listening for sounds.

Silence.

I need to move quickly. There's no knowing how soon Tonya will return. Grabbing the toy bone, I hold it up high.

Spotting it in my hand, Chuckles barks excitedly.

"Fetch!" I call, throwing the bone down the aisle.

Chuckles runs after the bone and pounces on it, chewing away. He is distracted for now.

I retrieve the surveillance camera and rush back to the painting.

Lifting up the bottom of the frame, I expose a large area of wall to work with. I stick the camera onto the wall and angle it so that it captures a sweeping view of the front door and sales desk.

Perfect.

Flipping the toggle switch to video mode, I step back, admiring the work that I have completed.

Suddenly, I hear the sound of the back door jangling open.

"Woof! Woof!" Chuckles barks in excitement.

Letting go of the frame, I stand back and head straight towards Chuckles. He is almost eating the toy bone.

"Are you hungry?" I ask Chuckles as Tonya approaches me.

"Of course you are, aren't you Chuckles?" Tonya coos, patting him. "Here, have a biscuit."

Chuckles barks excitedly, jumping up to grab the biscuit in his teeth.

"Good boy, Chuckles," Tonya pats his head as he chews.

The back door opens again and there is Nick Farago, wheeling in a large, heavy trolley. Stopping to catch a breath, he adjusts his sports cap, which has fallen lopsidedly on top of his brown-grey, receding hair. His gaze is serious, holding the weight of many a dark story.

Stepping back, I cringe at the power that Nick exudes.

Reaching over to grab the trolley again, Nick's yellow safety vest catches on the side of the glimmering juke box, which he is struggling to push along.

"Come on!" He mutters gruffly, ripping the safety vest free. The vest continues to rustle and glimmer over the top of his brown and blue zip up jacket as he pushes the trolley across the shop floor.

"Where do you want this, Ton?" Nick grunts, his forehead marked with deep lines of concentration.

"Right here, Nick!" Tonya gushes, running over to the back corner of the shop. "I am so excited!"

"Right-y-o!" Nick bends his jeaned legs and pushes the trolley forward, heaving it with all his might. It sends the juke box sliding down towards the shop floor.

Crash! I cringe as I hear it thump onto the ground.

Nick meets my gaze, his eyes lighting up as he recognises me. "Hi there," he says. "I didn't know you worked here."

"Yes," I say, exhaling a nervous breath. "Just for this shift."

"She's filling in for Nicolette," Tonya smiles. "I really appreciate your help, Stephanie."

I feel eyes on me and meet Nick's gaze. He is staring at me intensely. After a moment, he tears his gaze away from my face and lifts the juke box so that it stands upright.

Tonya doesn't seem to notice. She is so excited that she is dancing away to invisible music.

Chuckles snuggles up at her feet, peering up at her with loving eyes.

"Ready to go," Nick sighs as bends down to plug in the jukebox. Standing, he uses his safety vest to wipe the sweat away from his brow.

"Thanks Nick!" Tonya is bursting with excitement. "I'll see you next week," she bubbles.

Nick takes one last glance at me. "The music box is still available if you want it," he says. "I'd get in quick though, before someone else grabs it." He begins to turn the trolley around.

"I'll pop by soon," I say.

Nick nods, concentrating on my face. After a moment, he turns around, pushing the trolley towards the back door. As he does so, a folded sheet of paper falls out of his jean pocket and floats down onto the ground. Oblivious to what has happened, he exits the store.

After I hear the back door slam shut, I place my hand on my heart, willing it to stop beating so fast. Nick is gone now. I am safe.

Glancing at Tonya, I see her eyes lit up in amazement. She is staring at the copper coloured juke box, which flashes away on the floor. It is a definite collector's item. Tonya definitely has a bit of cash to burn.

Stepping forward, I bend down and pretend to tighten the straps of my sandals.

Glancing one more time over my shoulder, I am satisfied that Tonya is still mesmerised by the juke box. She selects some music. The large speakers blare with the tunes of a 70s rock song.

Reaching out, I grab the paper and slip it into the pocket of my flares.

"What do you think of this music?" Tonya asks, spreading her arms widely.

"It's great," I say. "Adds a lovely ambience."

"Exactly," Tonya grins. "This is heavenly!" She dances away with Chuckles at her heels.

I am not sure what to do, so I just watch. Tonya is in her own world, dancing up and down the aisles.

The phone rings.

"I'd better answer that," says Tonya, walking towards her desk.

I work slowly for the rest of my shift, placing records and CDs on the shelves.

Tonya approaches me at midday with a big smile on her face. "Thanks for all your work Stephanie," she says, grabbing a disco album. "It's great to see the racks looking fresher."

Approaching her front desk, Tonya opens the till of her cash register. She rifles through it, retrieving a bundle of cash, which she offers to me. "Please accept this as payment for your work," she smiles.

Makeshift Girl: The Secret Heritage Trail

"Thank you Tonya," I say, accepting the cash. "That is very generous. Let me just pop this box on your desk before I go." I place the box down on the smooth, wooden surface.

I begin to walk towards the front door with Chuckles at my heels. I feel him pounce up on my legs and bend down to pat him. "See you Chuckles," I smile. I feel a little tug of sadness in my heart at having to say goodbye.

"Thanks again Stephanie!" Tonya calls, selecting a song on her juke box. I wave casually and can't help smiling as I watch Tonya jive away to her rock music.

Chuckles howls along with the song.

I push open the jangly shop door and step outside into the fresh air. I can feel the paper burning a hole in my pocket.

Walking briskly down Harmony Road, I stop in front of a tall, grey corporate building. Digging into my pocket, I retrieve the paper and open it eagerly.

It is a consignment note. Reading the details, I notice that a number of authentic silk garments, described by their type, colours and totems, are listed, including ones that Girl and Concetta have hidden away. They are priced well into the thousands of dollars.

At the very bottom of the list is Girl's silk scarf. *Silk scarf, white, claw and talon totems.* It is priced at $4500. I feel nauseas in my stomach. Poor Girl and her family. Their precious silk scarf is being sold off. No price could ever replace the importance that the scarf plays in her family's history.

My eyes scan the bottom of the sheet. The consignor is listed as Nick Farago, who has organised the sale independently from the Petoys. His signature is scrawled in large strokes across the dotted line. Nick has arranged the sale of the silk garments to an international buyer: Kita's Fashion Museum in the city of Vilessa. The current order is due for delivery by the end of the month. Nick would certainly be feeling tremendous pressure to find the missing silk garments.

I feel anger rising in my throat. Nick Farago is out of control. It is time to investigate him.

Chapter 31

I kick stones across the concrete as I walk down Minute Street. My mind is flooded with emotion. As my eyes fall upon the deep red leaves falling from the maple trees, my head reels with the last memory I have of my mother ...

The autumn I turned six years of age, my mother and I were still running across the terrain of Mira and trying to escape the Petoy clan.

Exhausted, my mother suddenly stopped running. Panting, she grabbed hold of my hand. "It's time to stop running now, Adira," she sighed with defeat.

I turned to face her, feeling relieved. "Really? That's good, Mother." I felt a yearning to explore and play. "Can I play now?"

My mother's eyes filled with sadness. "I want nothing more than for you to play and enjoy your life," she said, stroking my hair and face. "You deserve that chance, Adira." She pulled me gently by the arm, leading me towards the tall maple trees.

I sat on the ground, wriggling my bottom into the dirt until I was comfortable. Staring up, I watched my mother begin to pace back and forth in front of me.

Suddenly, Mother bobbed down and stared into my eyes. "Adira," she said gently. "You know that I love you very much."

"Yes, Mother," I smiled happily.

Mother froze and stared intensely into my eyes. The deep red leaves of the maple tree fell gently, landing on her shoulder, her head and the floor surrounding her. "I want the best for you." She rubbed my shoulder gently. "This is hard to say but it is time for us to part ways for a while now," she said softly. "Do you remember our talk?"

My breath caught in my throat. "No!" I cried out, tears welling in my eyes. Just like the maple leaves, which abandoned their tree, my mother would abandon me too.

Mother's eyes also welled with tears. "This is hard for me, Adira. If you stay with me, you will certainly be caught. I need to keep you safe." She inhaled a shaky breath before speaking again. "Concetta has agreed to take care of you in Redbank and keep you safe."

"Mother," I sobbed, clinging to her top. "I want to stay with you."

"You will," Mother smiled gently, yet her eyes were still sad. "As soon as it is safe, we will be together again, just like I told you."

I lowered my gaze, staring at the dirt sweeping through the air. I knew nothing but to makeshift my way across the earth with my Mother. It had been my waking existence all my tiny life.

My world was suddenly about to change and it scared me deeply. I could feel my little body shaking with fear.

"Stay there quietly," Mother said. She removed her shawl from her shoulders and placed it over mine. Reaching around her belt, she unclipped a small parcel and handed it to me. "Here is some food to keep your tummy full."

I took the parcel, barely able to hold it in my shaking hands. It terrified me that I was going to be left behind.

Stroking my face, Mother said softly: "This is the safest place for you be right now. The clan won't find you here. Wait for Concetta, she will be here soon." Leaning closer, she kissed me on the cheek.

I felt cold in the shawl. Blasts of air struck against my neck and legs under my long sleeved dress. My shivering increased and I couldn't tell if it was from the cold or my fear. My tears continued to fall, rolling in a constant stream down my cheeks.

"Adira?" My mother's voice crackled. Staring up into her hazel eyes, I saw her deep sadness. It set my heart beating fiercely and my little body trembled. Reaching up, I grasped my mother tightly around the waist, burying my head into her chest.

Mother held me close, singing her special song to me:

> *"Where the flowers grow you'll be,*
> *dancing among dew dropped petals.*
> *Morning kissed, you awaken free,*
> *twirling with joy across the meadow.*
>
> *"Stay away from the tall, dark trees,*
> *their profiles cast large shadows.*
> *Fractured light brings no sleep,*
> *as dark horses seek your youth."*

I closed my eyes, letting her voice linger in my heart and mind. When my eyelids fluttered open, I was met with her serious gaze.

"It's time for me to go now," Mother's voice cracked and tears spilled down her cheeks.

The twigs began to snap, startling me. I stared up at my mother and snatched wildly at her hand, wanting to go with her, to escape. Taking my hand in hers, my mother squeezed it tightly, the tears running like a river down her cheeks.

"I love you, Adira," Mother choked on her final words. Letting go of my hand, she trampled the leaves and twigs beneath her feet loudly, setting off the scattered shouting of voices across the forest.

Wild eyed, Mother turned and fled as fast as she could, away from the mad horsemen, deep into the treescape.

It was piercingly silent.

My little heart was racing with fear.

There I sat, huddled against the trunk of the cedar tree. Placing the food parcel in my lap, I wrapped myself more tightly in my shawl.

As the cold night air surrounded me, I stayed awake, my heart pounding at the sounds of wolves howling in the distance.

I waited a long time, hoping my mother would return.

As the early morning light shifted its way across the sky, my little body trembled again and I cried and cried.

No Mother.

I was alone.

As the memory dissipates, I become aware of my long strides across the footpath and clutch at my aching heart. I feel a desperate need to hear the tune of the music box again and to feel a connection with my mother. I am also very determined to locate the missing ancient silk garments. These thoughts drive me as I continue to trek senselessly towards Nick's store.

Ding!

It is a message on my mobile from Mitch.

Looking forward to seeing you tonight, Lira. Is 7p.m. Okay?

I check the time. It's 5:30 p.m.

I'm out and about, I reply, intensely focused on my goal. *Maybe 7:30 p.m.?*

Where are you? Mitch's reply is prompt.

Heading towards Nick's Memorabilia. Undercover work. I send the message back, sighing.

Ding!

Not a good idea, Lira. You need back up. It's too dangerous.

I ignore the message, pocketing the phone. As I continue to walk down Minute Street, I begin to feel rage churning in my stomach. This man, Nick has taken too many liberties. If I don't work quickly enough, precious ancient garments, including Girl's scarf will be lost forever.

Stopping in front of Nick's Memorabilia Store, I inhale a sharp breath and release it forcefully. The shop closes in half an hour. I will have to work quickly.

Swinging the shop door open, I step inside and my gaze rests upon Nick. He is playing an arcade game intensely, his brows furrowed in deep concentration.

As the front door slams shut behind me, he looks up and meets my gaze.

"Hello again," he says, stepping away from the game. "You've come back."

"Yes," I say, my determination pushing me ahead. I approach the jewellery box and open the lid. Winding the spring tightly, I release it and close my eyes as the bittersweet tune begins to play again. Images of my mother's face flash through my mind. Her beautiful smile, her embrace, her hand reaching for me …

Once the music stops, I open my eyes and see Nick standing before me.

"You like the music?" He asks, studying my face.

I nod, my head in a fog. "It brings back a few memories," I say.

Nick's eyes widen. "You've heard that tune before?"

"Yes," I say, feeling overwhelmed and dizzy. I hold onto the shelf, steadying myself and push my hair away from my face. As I do so, the wig I am wearing tumbles off my head and falls to the floor.

Nick raises his eyebrows. "I thought I knew you," he says, his eyes darkening. "You are the Chief's protected species, Adira."

I clutch onto the shelf firmly. "I don't know what you're talking about," I say. "My name is Stephanie."

"Liar!" Nick's voice is thunderous, making me flinch. "What do you think you're doing here, spying on my store?" He grabs hold of my arm forcefully.

I acknowledge Nick's size. He is not someone I would be able to wrestle. I will have to use another tactic to get him to let me go.

"Why do you think I'm spying on you?" I ask him. "Have you got something to hide?"

Nick's eyes flash with anger. "You're coming with me!" He yells, pulling me towards the back of the store. Opening the doorway to a small office, he pushes me inside the room.

Makeshift Girl: The Secret Heritage Trail

My heart is pounding with fear. Nick's rage is uncontrollable and scary. I realise quickly that it would be better if I use my connection with the Chief to my advantage.

"I'd be very careful if I were you," I I warn Nick as he turns to face me. "You wouldn't want to harm me, otherwise you will have to answer to the Chief."

Nick inhales a sharp breath and settles himself down. "Has he asked you to check on me?" He sounds paranoid.

"Yes," I lie. "To make sure that you are getting on with everything like you should."

"I am," Nick says, punching his forehead. "I've got a box of those traditional garments to collect from Mira tomorrow evening. Tell the Chief that, okay?" Beads of sweat are forming across his forehead.

"Right," I say. "What the Chief really wants to know is what you are doing with them."

Nick's eyes widen. "Nothing," he waves his hands, his gaze fearful. "I hand them over to be used for design, that's all."

I can't believe how gullible Nick is right now, passing on information to me so readily.

"Let me out now," I demand. "You don't want me to let the Chief know about your little operation on the side, do you? We're all over it, Nick Farago."

Nick steps back, his eyes wide with horror. "What?" He stares up at the ceiling, his mind racing. "How?"

I stand still, keeping my gaze fixed on him. Even though I am terrified, I demonstrate that I am in control.

Suddenly, Nick stares at me again. "I am tired of this," he throws his hand in the air. "If the Chief wants to bring me down, then he will lose out too." Stepping forward, he takes hold of my shoulders forcefully. "Protected species or not, I'll have you first." Grabbing my t-shirt, Nick tears away at it aggressively until it rips apart and tosses it onto the floor. He stares at my body with his mouth open and his tongue licking his lips.

I begin to shake. My stomach feels nauseas.

"You are quite the beautiful woman," Nick says, running his fingers through my hair. He presses his lips against my cheeks, moving down to my neck. I feel his hands pulling down my flares. They drop to the floor, covering my sandalled feet.

"Mmm," Nick moans, pulling me to him tightly. He stinks of sweat and bad breath. A wave of nausea churns in the pit of my stomach and my heart is almost bursting through my chest. *Please get me out of here!*

Suddenly, I hear the sound of the shop door opening.

"Stay right there," Nick says, staring appreciatively at my body as he steps back. "We'll continue this very soon." He leaves the room, shutting the door behind him.

After he leaves, I pull up my flared pants and search the office wildly. There is a white cloth covering a computer and I grab it, wrapping it around myself.

I discover a long bundle of rope on the floor. Picking it up, I begin to unravel it, waiting for Nick to return.

"Where is my wife?" I hear Mitch's voice booming in the store.

My heart soars with hope. Mitch is here to save me!

"Your wife?" Nick sounds surprised.

"Mitch!" I bang on the office door, desperately trying to get his attention.

"Lira!" Mitch rushes to the door. "Baby, are you okay in there?"

"Managing okay," I call back. "Please get me out."

"You'll do nothing of the sort!" Nick yells.

"Back off!" Mitch yells back.

Suddenly, I hear Mitch scream in horror.

Thud.

Silence.

My heart beats wildly in my chest. *Please let Mitch be okay ...*

Moments pass and my heart nearly bursts through my chest with worry.

"Stand back, Lira!" It's Mitch's strained voice. I exhale a deeply held breath, relieved.

Something hard is thrown through the door's window, shattering the glass into tiny pieces. Looking down at the floor, I watch a large, novelty gold coin land on the ground next to my feet.

Mitch jumps through the hole in the door and drops to the ground. He is clutching his left arm in pain. "Aw," he groans.

"Are you okay, Mitch?" I ask. He has been wounded.

Mitch nods, wincing. Suddenly his mouth drops open in shock. "Lira, are you okay?" He is staring at my discarded t-shirt, which lies in a bundle on the carpet. His gaze drifts upwards and he discovers that I've wrapped myself in a cloth.

"I'm fine," I say. "You arrived just in time. It stopped him from –"

Mitch stands, meeting my gaze with his sad eyes. "I'm so sorry," he says, reaching for me with his uninjured arm. I let him pull me to him. His heart is pounding wildly in his chest.

Stepping back, I show Mitch the rope. "This should come in handy," I say. "It will stop him from going anywhere for a while."

"Yes, great thinking," Mitch says. "Here, let me take care of this."

I follow Mitch out of the office. Nick is lying on the floor, slowly regaining consciousness.

"I'll get you," he mumbles, clutching his head. "You just wait."

Mitch grabs hold of Nick's arms with his right hand. "More to the point, I've got you," he says, placing Nick's arms down by his side. Wincing in pain, Mitch wraps the rope around Nick's arms and waist, binding them tightly together.

"What do you think you're ..." Nick's voice drifts off. He is still very dazed and confused.

Using one hand, Mitch rolls Nick over onto his side and ties the rope in a secure knot. "There," he gasps strongly. "That'll teach you to keep your filthy hands off my wife." He steps back, his eyes flashing angrily.

"Your wife?" Nick chuckles deliriously. "Adira, never ... Petoys ..."

Mitch raises his eyebrows. "It's *Lira*," he says. Kicking his leg hard, he aims for Nick's crutch.

"Aww!" Nick groans. "That hurts!"

"Good," Mitch exhales a sharp breath.

"Mitch," I grab hold of his right arm. "That's enough now, okay?"

Mitch turns to face me, his cheeks red with anger. After a short while, he begins to calm down. "I'm sorry," he says, reaching out to touch my face.

"How is your arm?" I ask him.

"Fine," he clutches at his wounded left arm.

I realise that I only have a few moments to grab what I need. "Can you stay here for a minute?" I ask him. "I need to collect something."

"Okay," Mitch looks puzzled.

Dashing out towards the back of the store, I run like mad down the corridor and push firmly against the door into Nick and Sophie's home. It swings open immediately and I fall inside, landing on my legs onto the floorboards.

Scanning the room quickly, my gaze rests upon the pink mermaid silk dress strewn across the box at the back of the room. Crossing the floor, I collect the dress and cradle it in my arms. I have one more heritage silk garment to return to its rightful owner.

I leave the room, closing the door behind me. Sprinting down the corridor, I return to the store, discovering Mitch sitting on the floor next to Nick, who has passed out. Mitch is clutching his arm and rocking, his face tense with pain.

"Are you okay?" I whisper, bending down next to Mitch.

"Okay," Mitch nods. He stares at the dress. "What have you got there?"

"An ancient garment from Mira," I whisper.

"Oh," Mitch shakes his head angrily. "This man is a law unto himself." He bites his lip frustratedly.

"Yes," I nod. "He plans to sell the garments off to make money."

Mitch's eyes flash with anger. "Why don't we just call this in right now?"

I touch his shoulder gently. "We need to gather as much evidence as we can first." Staring at Mitch's left arm, I notice blood dripping down his bicep.

Reaching for the cloth around my waist, I tear off a large piece. "Here," I say. "Let me wrap this around your arm."

Mitch holds out his arm and I see the severe gash wound. I say nothing, not wanting to worry him. Wrapping the cloth around his arm, I tie it gently.

"There you go," I say, touching Mitch's face gently. "It will do until we can treat it, my love."

"Thanks Lira," Mitch smiles weakly. "Help me up?" He stretches his right hand towards me.

I grab hold of Mitch's hand and pull him up onto his feet. "Let's go," I say, leading him towards the front door.

Turning the lock on the inside barrel, I step outside and listen as the front door slams shut. "Locked in," I say. "Until someone discovers him."

"That'll probably be Sophie," Mitch says, falling into step beside me as we head towards his van.

"I'm driving," I say firmly, reaching into Mitch's pocket and retrieving the remote. Opening the passenger door, I help him up inside.

Lying on the ground, I shuffle under the van's undercarriage and check the GPS tracker. It is still switched on. I switch it off and slide out from under the van.

Climbing up into the driver's seat, I glance at Mitch. He is looking paler than before, his eyes closed. "Don't worry, my love, we'll be home soon," I say, reaching out to touch his face. "I'll help you feel better, I promise."

Chapter 32

It is late when Mitch and I arrive at our makeshift home. Pulling up in the parking bay outside the front of the milk bar, I switch off the ignition and the head lights.

"Mitch, we're here," I shake his right shoulder gently.

"What?" Mitch's eyes flutter open. He is groggy.

Opening the driver's door, I grab the silk dress and my fluoro bag and jump down onto the concrete. Dashing to the passenger side, I open the door and reach my free hand out towards Mitch. "Take my hand, Baby. Let me help you out."

Mitch takes my hand and I guide him slowly down the steps and onto the concrete.

"Thanks," he manages to whimper, swaying dizzily.

I place his arm over my shoulder and take his weight, leading him to the front door of the milk bar.

The lights shine at the front of the building, penetrating like a haunting halo through the shop window glass.

Stepping forward, I peer into the windows. I can see the shelving displays, stocked with sweets, toiletries and canned food. There are no signs of life in the building.

I exhale and wait for my breathing to settle. It's impossible. I am panting so rapidly, I think I am about to faint. My hands are shaking now, too.

"Is everything okay … ?" Mitch's voice fades out.

I take a few deep breaths. Good, I have stopped shaking. Darting glances over both my shoulders, I check that all is safe.

No tails.

"All is fine," I say brightly, trying not to worry Mitch. A strange feeling has settled in my stomach. I know we are not safe here. We need to get inside quickly.

Reaching into my bag, I grab my bundle of keys. They jingle loudly in the silence. My heart is pounding like a hammer in my chest. We could be discovered here at any moment.

Taking one last glance over my shoulder, I spot the flash of a car's headlights against the shop windows across the road. The light is metres away, yet still close enough.

My hands begin to shake. *Tune it out*, I tell myself. *The driver could be going anywhere.*

The flash of light has finally … disappeared! Phew!

Sorting through the keys, I discover the one I need and insert it into the keyhole. Twisting the key to the right, I hear it click. I'm in.

Pressing down on the door handle, I step back, bracing myself. The door swings open, revealing the darkness of the shop floor.

Standing outside again, I check the street once more. I swear I can hear the sound of shoes striking against the footpath. Have we been followed here? No one walks these streets this time of the night. Everything is closed.

Click, clack, click, clack … the sound is approaching quickly. Someone is heading towards the milk bar.

Slamming the front door behind me, I dead bolt it shut. Taking a deep breath, I tighten my grip around Mitch. "We're going to move quickly now, okay?" I can hear the anxiety trembling in my voice.

Mitch's eyes widen nervously. "Okay," he says groggily.

Harnessing my energy, I run through the dark, taking Mitch with me. I know my way across the shop floor with my eyes closed. I've lost count of the amount of times I've had to plunge the milk bar into darkness to save Mitch or myself.

Making my way to the stairwell ignites a few more memories of Mitch and I dodging the heavy banging of doors and flashes of lights out the front. We'd escape up the stairs, like we are now, into the home we lived in up top.

Jiggling my bundle of keys, I discover the right one and unlock the door to our home. "We're here now," I say softly, guiding Mitch inside. I shut and lock the front door.

We are faced with the comforting sight of our tiny makeshift living area, which is decorated with a pale blue carpet. A two seater, beaten, green vinyl couch sits in the middle of the space, accompanied by a wooden crate that we use as a coffee table.

I guide Mitch into the living area. He flops onto the couch.

Tossing the cloth bag and silk dress on the coffee table, I crouch next to Mitch. "Let me take a look at your arm," I say. Red blood is soaking its way through the cloth. "Let's take this cloth off," I try to sound cheerful and to mask the concern in my voice.

I unwind the blood soaked cloth and place it onto the floor.

"Aw!" Mitch grimaces in pain.

Examining Mitch's left arm, I notice just how deep the gash is.

"Oh Baby," I say softly, my heart pounding with anxiety. "Should we go see a doctor? You may need stitches."

Mitch shakes his head. "Too risky," he blurts. He looks at me with tired, hopeful eyes. "Could you help me?"

"Of course," I reply. "Let me get what I need."

As I walk into the bathroom, I pause a moment, letting myself shake. Mitch has been badly injured. I hope I can help him recover.

Filling a bowl with warm water, I place it down onto the bench. Pulling open the medicine cabinet doors, I grab some antiseptic, a cloth, cotton balls and bandages.

Carrying the bowl of water and medical supplies is tricky but I manage to place them down onto the coffee table in the living room.

Turning to face Mitch, I notice that he is shaking. Grabbing the throw rug off the couch, I wrap it around him gently.

"Thank you," Mitch says, his shaking beginning to dissipate. He reaches out to stroke my hair with his right hand. "That's better." His voice is weak with fatigue.

My heart soars with love. I need to be strong right now, to help him recover. "You're doing great," I say in a surprisingly shrill voice. "You're going to be fine, Baby, you'll see."

Crouching next to Mitch, I use the water and cloth to wash away the blood from his wound. "Take a deep breath," I say, pouring some antiseptic on some cotton wipes. "This may sting a little."

"Aw!" He winces as I treat his wound with the antiseptic.

I pause, looking up at him. "You okay, baby?"

"I think so," he says, trying to sit up as I wrap the bandage around his wound and pin it into place. He is completely exhausted.

Bobbing in front of Mitch, I grab hold of his right hand. "You must be starving," I say.

"Yes," Mitch says weakly. "Very." He stares into my eyes. "I love you taking care of me."

I kiss his hand gently. "I love taking care of you," I smile. "Let me get you something to eat."

Mitch grins. As I stand up, he pulls me towards him until my face is level with his. Leaning closer, he kisses me softly on the lips. "Thank you. I feel so loved," he says.

My heart soars with happiness. "My pleasure," I say. "I'll be back soon."

Walking towards the kitchen, I feel a little lighter. It is wonderful to take care of Mitch. I've missed him so much lately.

Opening the freezer, I discover some left over lasagne from one of my cooking marathons. Popping it into the microwave, I set the timer to fifteen minutes to give it enough time to defrost and reheat.

It feels good to be back home, even if it's only for a short while. This place holds so many memories for Mitch and I. We've built our lives here, grown together and shared many loving moments within these walls. It is hard to imagine not living here.

Beep! The microwave is ready.

Grabbing the oven mittens, I remove the baking dish from the microwave. The aroma of the lasagne makes me salivate with hunger as I serve it onto two plates.

Grabbing a couple of clean forks out of the drawer, I head back into the living room.

"That smells divine," Mitch smiles as I approach him. "My favourite!" His eyes light up when he realises that it is lasagne.

I place my plate down on the coffee table and sit next to Mitch. "Here," I say, feeding him a mouthful of lasagne with a fork. "This should give you some energy."

Mitch chews slowly, closing his eyes as he savours the flavour of the food. "It's so nice to be home with you," he smiles weakly. "I am so lucky to be spoilt with your cooking."

I beam with happiness. What a nice thing to say.

I continue to feed Mitch, watching him slowly regain some strength.

Swallowing his final mouthful of lasagne, Mitch reaches for me. "Come here," he says, his eyes shining.

I put the plate down on the coffee table and step closer to Mitch, letting him pull me to him.

Mitch hugs me tightly. "Thank you my amazing wife," his voice is hoarse. "This means so much to me. You mean everything to me."

I nod, understanding.

Mitch settles back onto the couch. "Can I feed you now?" He asks, a cheeky smile forming across his lips.

"Sure," I smile, reaching over to grab my plate. "Are you okay to use a fork with your right hand?"

"Definitely," Mitch smiles, feeding me some lasagne.

As I chew, I savour the tomato, salami and cheese flavours. It is wonderful to taste an old favourite.

"Whoa!" Mitch's mouth drops open as he realises that he has dropped a heap of lasagne on my cloth body wrap. "I'm sorry."

I look at him, my eyes shining. "I'm not sorry," I say, my lips forming into a smile. Placing my plate onto the coffee table, I stand and unwrap the cloth, letting it drop onto the ground.

"Look at you," Mitch inhales a sharp breath of admiration as his gaze drinks me in. "The woman of my dreams."

Kicking my sandals off, I straddle Mitch on his lap and cup his face in my hands. "The man of my heart," I say softly.

Mitch presses his lips firmly against mine. As we kiss, I feel his hand move across my arm like butterfly wings and slowly caress my breast.

I moan, arching my back and closing my eyes.

Mitch leans in closer, pressing his lips against mine again. I kiss him back firmly, my heart beating wildly with love.

Pulling back, I smile into his eyes while I pull his t-shirt gently over his head.

"Aw!" Mitch winces in pain as he left arm stretches too far.

"Sorry Baby," I say, tossing his t-shirt onto the floor.

Mitch meets my gaze with shining eyes. "That's okay," he says softly. His gorgeous torso makes me burn with desire.

Mitch pushes me back gently onto the couch. "You are so beautiful," he says, staring into my eyes.

"You are too," I say, reaching for him.

Mitch smiles and slides down, kissing me passionately across the breasts. I moan as his tongue tickles my nipple.

I feel his left hand sliding my flares down. He traces the hem of my underwear.

A jolt of electricity spasms through my loins as Mitch removes my underwear and tosses it onto the carpet.

I want him so badly I think I might burst.

Mitch stands and kicks off his sneakers. He undoes the buckle of his belt. Unbuttoning his pants, he pulls them down, letting them fall onto the floor. My heart stops in my chest at the sight of his very erect and firm penis.

The stirring in my loins amplifies, sending multiple electric shocks through me. "Come here," I say, reaching out to him.

Mitch smiles, lowering himself back onto the couch. Kissing my legs, he moves up and I feel his lips caress my inner thighs.

"Take me," I moan, raising my hips into the air.

"With pleasure," Mitch says, smiling into my eyes. Gently, he guides himself inside me.

It is amazing, feeling Mitch move inside me. As he thrusts, I feel erotic spasms shoot through my body.

"Oh!" I cry out, grabbing hold of his firm buttocks and pressing him even more deeply inside me. "Don't stop!"

"Oh Baby!" I feel Mitch climax, his seed spurting forth inside me.

"Oh!" Clutching his buttocks, I gyrate my hips harder and faster, riding out the waves of my climax. It feels *so* good.

"Welcome home," I say softly. "I love you."

"I love you too," Mitch sighs, placing the throw blanket over us. He snuggles up, spooning me.

I drift off to a very content sleep.

Chapter 33

Bang! Bang! Bang!

I jump up, startled by the intrusive noise.

"What's that?" Mitch sits up and swings his legs over the side of the couch. He throws on his pants and buckles up his belt. Stepping into his sneakers, he reaches for his t-shirt.

"Here, Baby," he passes his t-shirt to me.

I put the t-shirt on, straightening it out against my skin. It is loose and comfortable. Picking up the flares, I step into them, pulling them over my waist. The sandals slip onto my feet easily.

Bang! Bang! Bang!

The sound is urgent, making my heart pound with fear.

I stand silently, waiting for the sound to dissipate. It doesn't.

Smash! Is that broken glass?

"We need to move quickly," Mitch jumps up and pulls on his pants. Stepping into his sneakers, he glances at the window on the far wall. "Pass me that chair," he points to a wooden chair sitting next to a small bookshelf.

I grab the chair and place it next to the window. "Baby, what are you doing?" I am anxious.

"Getting us out of here," Mitch is very focused, his eyes narrowed. I watch as he opens the window. "We should be able to fit through here fine," he says.

I can hear a set of footsteps click-clacking up the staircase. Whoever it is, they are only a few seconds away from discovering us.

"Come on!" Mitch reaches his hand out towards me.

"Wait!" I call, grabbing my bag and stuffing the silk dress into it. Swinging the bag over my shoulder, I dash back to Mitch.

Jumping up onto the chair, I let him hoist me up onto the window sill. Sitting on the ledge, I stare down at the ground below. It is not too high and a simple jump should land me onto my feet.

"You can do it," Mitch encourages me.

Yes, I *can* do it.

Taking a deep breath, I grasp onto the ledge. *I can do this*, I tell myself. *It's not that far to the ground.*

Staring down at the ground, I lean forward and propel my body into the air.

It feels strange as I fall, as though time has stopped. I seem able to control how I move. I place my legs out in front of me, ready to land flat on my feet.

As I hit the ground, I jump a couple of times from the impact and land flat on my stomach onto the grass.

After a moment, I press my hands into the grass, pulling myself up to a standing position. I unwind the bag strap from around my waist and let the bag hang loosely over my shoulder.

My eyes dart across the ground, madly trying to locate Mitch. There he is now, landing firmly onto his bottom.

"Ouch!" Mitch yells, clutching his bottom.

I bolt like lightening, reaching Mitch and placing my hand on his shoulder. "Are you okay, Baby?" I am worried that he has caused more injury to himself.

Mitch nods, his eyes glazed.

I wrap my arm around his shoulders. "Can you stand?" I ask him.

Mitch nods, allowing me to hoist him up onto his feet. He stretches his legs and stamps, sighing with relief. "That's better," he smiles. "Thanks Baby."

"Let's go," I say to him. "We'll be discovered at any moment."

"Yes," Mitch agrees. "Are you okay?" He asks as he grabs hold of my arm.

"Yes, fine," I say.

We smile into each other's eyes for a moment. Mitch strokes my hair gently with his free hand. Suddenly his body tenses as he stares over my shoulder.

I spin around, my gaze falling upon the silver Mercedes. Its headlights gleam brightly in the night as it approaches us.

Mitch pushes me ahead of him. "Run, Lira, run!" He cries.

I dash across the footpath, my heart beating frantically in my chest.

Kneeling behind a hedge, I look up frantically, trying to locate Mitch.

He is running away from the silver Mercedes, which is keeping pace with him.

"Where is Adira?" I hear the Chief's voice bellow from the open window of the car. "Hand her over now!"

Mitch continues to run, ignoring the voice. I can hear the slapping of his feet against the concrete.

Suddenly, he stumbles over the root of a tree and falls to the ground.

I spot the Mercedes pulling into the side of the road. It will only take a moment before Mitch is caught.

Jumping to my feet, I run to Mitch's aid. "Grab my hand!" I call, reaching for him.

"Go, Lira," Mitch grunts. "He's after you. Run now, while you can."

I am not leaving without the love of my life. "I will run with you, right now," I grab Mitch's hand firmly and pull him up onto his feet.

Mitch jumps up and stares at me with wide, terrified eyes.

"We can do this," I encourage him. "Let's go!"

Running, we are, as fast as we can. I can barely feel my sandalled feet striking the concrete pathway as I head towards Mitch's van.

It takes a moment for the Chief to realise that he needs to turn the car around to continue following us.

Suddenly, he is tailing us again.

"We're not going to make it, Lira!" Mitch yells.

"Yes we are!" I call back, surprised at my bravery. Usually Mitch is the one who encourages me to continue.

Cutting across the road, we arrive outside the front of Gus' Green Grocer.

There is the van, parked about a metre away.

"Hand her over!" There is the Chief's voice again, bellowing across the night air.

Mitch is livid. His fists clench and he stops for a moment, ready to launch at the Chief.

"Ignore him!" I cry. "Keep moving, we're nearly there!"

Mitch spins around and charges as quickly as he can, reaching the driver's door of the van.

Jumping up the steps, he pulls the driver's door open. Once inside, he reaches over and opens the passenger door for me.

The van begins to rev as Mitch prepares for take off.

"Wow!" I gasp as I jump onto the passenger seat and close the door. "We've made it!"

"Not yet," Mitch says with a determined expression on his face. "Hold tight, Baby!"

Mitch floors the accelerator, doing a sharp u-turn and roaring down Tinker Street. I am amazed at how he manages to drive so sharply with one arm injured.

The Mercedes zooms into vision in the rear view mirror. It is tailing us closely.

Mitch swerves into the right lane and merges onto Vista Road. The landscape whips passed us like a blur. I check the rear view mirror. It is hard to shake the Mercedes off our tail.

"Are you okay, Baby?" I am concerned at the pain Mitch must be in.

Mitch nods, sweat dripping down his forehead as he concentrates on getting away.

Swerving right, he takes Veta Street and a sharp left onto Kiry Street. The Mercedes is no longer tailing us. We have a couple of minutes to really lose the tail.

I marvel at Mitch's magic as he cuts through as many side streets as possible. As he stops at the lights at the intersection on Lighthouse Boulevard, my heart pounds anxiously.

Still no Mercedes. Phew!

Swerving left down Clarice Road, Mitch takes a final glance in the rear view mirror.

No tail.

"That was close," Mitch sighs with relief.

"Too close," I sigh.

"Yes," Mitch nods in agreement. His hands are shaking as he grasps the steering wheel.

Turning left onto Wester Street, Mitch pulls into the curb. Switching off the ignition, he exhales a deep sigh of relief. "Thank you for rescuing me back there, Lira," he says, turning to face me.

"Oh Mitch," I say, reaching out to touch his face. "You would have done the same for me too."

Mitch smiles lovingly at me. "Of course," he agrees. Suddenly, his eyes narrow and he grabs my hands in his, holding them tightly. "It's become quite dangerous, this existence, hasn't it?"

I nod, relieved to finally have Mitch express my own inner turmoil.

"Baby," a concerned expression crosses his face. "Please be safe. I can't imagine –"

"Sssh," I say, placing my finger to his lips. "You don't have to imagine anything horrible. I will do all I can to keep myself safe, I promise."

"I will too," Mitch says, squeezing my hand. "I can't wait until this is all over."

"Me too," I agree, staring into his eyes. "I love you so much."

"I love you too," Mitch smiles.

Releasing Mitch's hand, I kiss him gently on the neck. "There's so much I want to do with you," I murmur, continuing to kiss him across his bare chest.

Mitch moans and pulls me closer to him. "I can think of something we can do right now," he murmurs, reaching under my top.

"And what would that be?" I tease.

"Let's go wild," Mitch says cheekily as he strokes my stomach.

"Yes, let's do that," I smile.

Closing my eyes, I submit my heart to my husband as he presses his lips firmly against mine.

Chapter 34

Later that night, I awaken to the pelting of heavy rain on the roof of the van. My ears prick up, listening to the fierce whistling of the ferocious winds outside. Sitting up slowly, I peer outside the window. I can see the rain teaming down sharply through the light of a distant street lamp. It would not be fun to be outside right now.

I glance at Mitch who is still sleeping peacefully, his body stretched out across the back seat. Leaning towards him, I kiss him gently on the cheek.

Reaching for his strewn t-shirt, I pull it on over my head and straighten it over my stomach.

"Mmm, hello beautiful," I feel Mitch's arms around my waist. "Come back here."

"Oh hello," I say, reaching up to stroke his hair. I close my eyes, enjoying the sensation of his lips against my neck.

Mitch pulls me back down next to him and strokes my face gently. "It's so great to be with you," he says softly, staring into my eyes. "Even if there is a storm howling outside." He cuddles me tightly.

I smile gently, letting myself get lost in his deep blue gaze.
It is comforting to be around Mitch again and to feel so loved.

Mitch's mobile is ringing. He reaches into his pocket to retrieve it. "It's Sophie," he says, showing me the caller identification. His eyes narrow with concern.

"Take the call," I say, relieved by his honesty.

"Okay, I'll put it on speaker," Mitch says. He accepts the call.

"Mitch?" It's Sophie's voice. "Can you please help me?"

Mitch meets my gaze with uncertainty in his eyes.

I nod reassuringly.

Mitch smiles at me and touches me lightly on the face. "I love you," he mouths.

I feel a warm tingle in my heart.

Mitch turns his attention back to the phone call. "I'm here with my beautiful wife, Lira," he says. "She'll be able to help you too. Where are you Sophie?"

I sigh with relief. Mitch is happy to take me along with him.

"Hi Lira," Sophie says, her voice a little lighter.

"Hi Sophie," I reply. "Are you safe right now?"

"Not really," Sophie says. "It's dark, it's raining heavily and I'm freezing. I have been locked out of Nick's shop. Can you come get me?"

"We'll be there as soon as possible," I reply, suddenly concerned for Sophie.

"Let's go," I say to Mitch as I climb into the passenger seat.

Mitch reaches around the back seat of the van and finds a spare t-shirt. He winces in pain as he threads his arms through the sleeves. Straightening the t-shirt over his stomach, he takes a deep breath, trying to settle the pain. "Okay, I'm ready," he says, meeting my gaze. Grabbing the back of the driver's seat with his left hand, he pulls himself up and crawls over the glove box and into the seat. Mitch starts the ignition and warms up the van.

I keep Sophie on the phone, knowing that company is vital for her right now. "Keep talking to me Sophie, while we drive."

A sudden outburst of rain pelts down, making it impossible for me to hear Sophie. I keep the line active, letting her know that I am still here. It would be very scary out in that storm.

As the rain settles into a light pitter patter against the windscreen, I watch Mitch turn left off Lighthouse Boulevard onto Veta Street. The moonlight bounces off the cat eye reflectors, which mark the edges of the road. Mitch turns a sharp left down Minute Street. I squint, trying to locate Sophie in the dappled light.

Moments later, I see the shape of a human silhouette, standing on the curb of the road outside Nick's Memorabilia Store. Patches of moonlight bounce off her dark hair and highlight the rain teeming down across her body.

"There she is!" I call out, pointing towards Sophie.

Mitch brakes suddenly and the tyres skid across the road, spinning the van.

"Are you okay, Mitch?" My heart is pounding as I wait for him to regain control of the steering wheel.

"Yes," Mitch says, straightening the van. He pulls over carefully into the curb. "I'm sorry, Baby," he says as pulls up the handbrake. "It's hard to drive through the rain and the dark with an injured arm."

I touch him gently on the shoulder. "It's okay, we're fine. We made it."

Pushing open the door of the van, I jump down onto the curb. I am hit with a strong slap of very cold air. The rain slashes against my skin, making me wince in pain.

"Sophie!" I call out as I run towards her. She is hunched over with her hands over her head, trying to protect herself from the teeming rain. I wrap my arm around her shoulders. "I've got you," I say, leading her towards the van.

Opening the back door, I help Sophie to step inside the van. She collapses onto the back seat, her breathing erratic.

"Thanks Lira," Sophie gasps, her body shivering.

"We need to get you dry," I say, searching the back of the van. One of Mitch's tank tops lies on the floor carpet. I pick it up and use it to dry Sophie's drenched skin.

Sophie's shivering begins to dissipate. She smiles a weak smile. "Mitch has said so many wonderful things about you, Lira. I can see why. You are a truly amazing woman." She stares deeply into my eyes.

"Thanks," I inhale a sharp breath, feeling uncomfortable by the intensity of her gaze. Averting my eyes, I begin to dry Sophie's long black strands of hair.

"Thank you," Sophie smiles. I notice her teeth are still chattering from the cold. She unzips her green dress and pulls her arms out of her sleeves.

Staring into my eyes once more, she reaches around her back and undoes the clasp on her red lace bra, revealing her voluptuous breasts. I gulp, taken aback by her beauty. "That's better," Sophie sighs. "No more drenched clothes. Do you like what you see?" Her voice breaks at her final words.

Tearing my gaze away, I look back at Mitch. His eyes are focused on the road as he drives, unaware of the exchange between us.

I can feel Sophie's hand stroking my hair and look up at her. She traces my lips with her finger. "You are so beautiful, Lira," she says softly. "A real woman. One who should be cherished and safe. This world is so crazy." Tears are forming in Sophie's eyes. She is vulnerable and a little disoriented.

Checking the back seat, my eyes fall upon another one of Mitch's spare tank tops. Reaching over, I grab it. "Let me help you get dressed," I offer Sophie.

"Okay," Sophie sighs. Tears are dripping down her cheeks.

I pull the tank top over Sophie's head and help her slide her arms through the sleeves. Sophie kicks her legs up as I pull her dress down. I throw it onto the back seat. Grabbing a pair of Mitch's spare track pants, I pull them up over Sophie's legs and tighten them around her waist.

Sophie swipes at her tears and smiles weakly. "You are very sweet, Lira," she says. "It's nice to be treated with care."

I grab Sophie's hand. "You're welcome," I say. "I'd like to think we are starting to become friends."

Sophie nods, a warm smile crossing her lips. "Yes," she says. "That would be great, Lira." She tightens her grip on my hand. "I feel so lost right now."

I stare into Sophie's eyes. They look troubled, as though they store a dark secret.

"Do you want to talk?" I ask her.

A long moment passes as Sophie stares out of the window. Finally, she inhales a deep breath and turns to face me again. "I've known Nick Farago for a while now. He helped me find my feet when I arrived in Redbank." She scratches her head and sighs. "Nick developed quite an attraction for me. He would pop by my art gallery often, bringing me gifts and wooing me and, well, eventually he won me over." Sophie places her hand on her chest. "Nick is a very demanding lover and I know that his attraction to me is purely physical," she stares off into the distance. "Tonight things got pretty hot and heavy …" her voice drifts off.

"Are you okay, Sophie?" Mitch asks. "He didn't hurt you, did he?"

"No," Sophie shakes her head. "Nick is strong but not aggressive towards me."

It is silent for a moment, while Sophie reflects. I meet Mitch's gaze in the rear view mirror. His eyes are narrowed and concerned.

Sophie lets go of my hand. She pushes her hair back from her face and sighs. "I was a little silly tonight," she breathes.

I touch her lightly on the shoulder. "I'm sure you weren't," I say gently.

"Yes, I was." Sophie thumps backwards into the seat. "I waited until Nick was sleeping and crept slowly out of the room to the store. I was desperate to find any information that would lead me to understand more about his secret delivery work. Moving quickly, I pulled open a desk drawer and discovered a consignment note."

"A consignment note?" Mitch asks. "What was being delivered?"

Sophie's eyes narrow. "Boxes of ancient silk garments," she says. "Ten in total. Set for delivery in a few days' time."

"Oh no!" I can't help but call out. "That is not good."

"Did you see who will receive the delivery?" Mitch asks.

"No," Sophie's eyes widen. "I didn't have time. I took a quick photo of the note with my mobile and sent it to you, Mitch. Did you receive it?"

"I'll have to check," Mitch says. "Wait, I'll just pull over."

Mitch pulls into the curb on the side of the road. He reaches into his pocket and retrieves his mobile phone. "Yes," he says. "I did receive it. The shipment is to be delivered to the Vilessa Fashion Museum, which is across the sea. You can only arrive by water vessel and must cut across the waters of Mira to get there. I wonder how he's organising that?"

"Beats me," Sophie sighs.

"What happened, Sophie?" I ask her. "Did Nick find you?"

"Yes," Sophie nods. "He saw me photographing the consignment note with my mobile phone camera. He told me to keep my nose out of his business and ripped my phone out of my hands." She inhales a sharp breath, her eyes narrowing intensely. "Nick grabbed my arm, pulling me outside the store and onto the street. He stared at me with cruel eyes before spitting out: 'nosy slut' and threw my phone at me. I stood there in shock, watching as he stepped back into the store and slammed the door behind him."

"Damn that Nick Farago!" Mitch punches the dashboard. "That man needs to be stopped."

"Agreed," Sophie sighs. "He has become very involved in the Petoys' counterfeit trade. He helps to run the operation down at Frosties. He knows what he's up for if he gets caught."

"He was probably scared," I say as I realise what is happening. "Nick obviously doesn't want you to be too aware of his involvement in the counterfeit silk trade."

Silently, Sophie absorbs the news. "I am involved in part of the operation," she admits. "Chief Opula saw some of my design work at my gallery and managed to convince me to start designing patterns for his new *A Touch of Silk* range. He asked me to take charge of the silk production and to ensure that the range was ready for trade as soon as possible. I was told that it would boost my artistic reputation and I would make a lot of profit from the work.

"I was naïve to take on the work. I began to receive beautiful silk garments from Nick and I recognised their designs from Mira, especially their totems. The Chief demanded that I copy the totems and reproduce them in garments that were to be made of synthetic material. It hurt me deeply that I had been tricked into counterfeit trade production.

"I am worried about the families of Mira and what it means to them to have their heritage ripped out of their hands. So I have been creating patterns but altering the style of the totems so that they don't look exactly the same as the authentic ones." Sophie clenches her hands into fists and stares at the floor. "I don't know how to get out of this mess," her voice is strained.

"You are in a difficult position," I say, touching Sophie's shoulder gently. "Nick is a very dangerous man."

Sophie stares at me with wide eyes. "Yes, he is," she says. "I've seen first hand how he treats the workers at Frosties."

"Where is he now?" I ask her.

"Gone," she says. "He got into his four wheel drive and left a short while ago. He didn't seem to care that I was standing out in the freezing cold rain." She stares ahead, her eyes sad. "I'm such a fool," she says.

"No you're not," Mitch shakes his head. "Nick's the fool."

"Let's see where he is now," I say, retrieving my phone from my pocket. I open the GPS tracker app. "Oh, he's stopped in front of Happy Beats Music Store," I say.

Suddenly I remember the surveillance camera I set up in there. "Let's take a look at what he's up to." I invite Sophie to join me in viewing the live surveillance footage on the app.

"You have a camera in the store?" Sophie sounds surprised. "Lira, you are truly amazing."

"Isn't she?" Mitch smiles. "That's my talented wife."

I am flattered and can't help smiling as I turn my attention to the surveillance app and press the record button.

Nick is holding Tonya around the waist and kissing her on the neck. "You are wonderful, my love," he says to her.

"Am I?" Tonya beams. "Thank you Nick."

Sophie's hands fly to her mouth in shock. "That two timing bastard!" She yells.

I place my hand on her shoulder. "I'm sorry," I say gently.

Sophie swipes at her eyes and inhales a sharp breath. "He's not worth a single tear," she declares.

"No, he's not," I agree.

"Look!" Sophie points at the phone screen.

I stare at the footage. Nick is opening a cardboard box and pulling out several ancient silk garments.

"Aren't these beautiful?" He beams at Tonya. "You know, these old fashioned things are worth a lot of money."

"I bet they are," Tonya nods. "They look amazing."

Nick places his hands on Tonya's shoulders. "Are you still okay to hold onto these for me?" He asks her. "Very soon, I will sell them to that fashion museum out in Vilessa and we'll have a heap of cash to spoil ourselves with."

Tonya rubs her hands together with excitement. "Ooooh, I'm thinking a luxury boat …"

"We'll see," Nick says firmly. "Money like this only comes once. We should spend it wisely."

"Sure," Tonya nods, her expression serious. "Where would you like me to keep these?"

"In your storage room," Nick smiles. "Out of sight until we need to send them off."

Tonya tosses the garments back into the box. Grabbing packing tape off her desk, she seals the box shut. "Consider it done," she says, picking up the box and heading towards the back of the store.

I stop the recording and stare at Sophie. "You won't have to deal with Nick any longer," I say gently. "He is about to be arrested."

"Really?" Sophie's mouth drops open.

"Yes," I nod. Opening my message app, I begin to type: *Video evidence attached. For your action at Happy Beats.*

I send the message to Concetta and await her reply.

Now, is the response that I receive.

"It will all be over in a few minutes," I say. "Nick won't be able to sell off any ancient silk anywhere."

"I want to see the arrest," Sophie begs. "Please?"

"Okay," I reluctantly agree. "Can you drive us to Happy Beats Mitch?"

"Are you sure about this Lira?" Mitch's eyebrows furrow with concern.

I glance at Sophie. Her eyes are alight with anticipation. "Yes," I say. "Let's go."

Mitch takes a right down Flag Road and a right again onto Harmony Road. As we pull up outside the Happy Beats Music Store, we see Hidu and his partner in imperial operations jump out of an unmarked, red car and enter the store.

Parked at the curb, we watch as Hidu's partner exits the store a few moments later, escorting Tonya with her head lowered in shame, to the unmarked car. Guiding her onto the back seat, he locks the door and sits in the passenger seat, waiting.

Hidu exits a few moments later, escorting Nick and the box of ancient silk garments towards the red car.

"You've got nothing on me!" Nick is yelling, his voice belting through the rain.

Digging into my bag, I retrieve the consignment note that Nick left behind at the music store.

"Stay right there!" I tell Sophie. "I have to give Hidu something."

"I'm coming with you!" Sophie jumps out of the van, followed by Mitch who grabs hold of her arms, restraining her. "You cheat, Nick! You thief!" Sophie yells, trying to release Mitch's grasp.

Nick's eyes widen in surprise. "I knew there was something not quite right about you Sophie," he wiggles his arms, trying to free himself from Hidu's grasp. "Did you do this to me?"

Sophie laughs. "No," she shakes her head. "You've done this to yourself. So eager to please women, you wind up exposing yourself in the process. I hope you rot in jail." She spits at him, her eyes flashing angrily.

"That's enough Sophie," Hidu warns. "Into the car with you, Nick." He pushes Nick towards the back door.

Nick's eyes narrow as he realises that I am here. "You!" He yells. "It was you, wasn't it? Keeping an eye on both Tonya and I, pretending to be helpful at the music store. You were spying on us, reporting back to this idiot."

"Watch your tongue!" Hidu's voice is firm. "I am an Imperial Operative of Mira, thank you. You've been under my watch for a long time."

"You ain't got enough to arrest me!" Nick scoffs. "How do you know I have anything to do with this box of pretty stuff?"

"We've got footage," Hidu says firmly.

"And we've got this too," I say, waving the consignment note that Nick left behind at the music store. "It is proof of Nick's arrangement to sell authentic ancient silk garments at a set price to the museum of Vilessa. It is even signed off with his signature." I hand the note to Hidu.

"Thank you Detective," Hidu's eyes meet mine, shining brightly with gratitude.

"Detective?" Nick sighs with defeat, staring out at the sky. "This game of life is cruel," he sighs. "It plays with you, makes you believe you can have riches. You can never control life, though as it's always a step ahead of you, waiting to catch you in the act."

"In you go," Hidu says, guiding Nick into the back of the car. Locking the door, he turns to face us. "Well done Detective," he says. "Great job."

"Thanks," I smile weakly.

"See you soon, bro," Sophie smiles. "You make a great Imperial Operative."

Hidu smiles warmly at Sophie. "See you soon," he says. Opening the driver's door, he hops into the car and pulls out of the curb, disappearing down the road.

"Let's get you home," I say, wrapping my arm around Sophie's shoulders.

Sophie looks up at me, her eyes relieved. "You are amazing, Lira. Thanks for everything."

"It's not over yet," I smile. "We still have a counterfeit trade operation to stop."

"I'm happy to help," Sophie smiles. "Just let me know what you need me to do."

Chapter 35

The distressed call rings later that morning, while Mitch drives me back towards my apartment. I answer my mobile phone, listening acutely to the disturbing sounds of a pleading people.

"Lira!" Jacquelyn is terrified. "Please help us! We're under attack!" I can hear a voice screaming in the background.

I inhale a sharp breath. "Where are you?" I ask, worried for Jacquelyn.

"At the north end of the forest!" Jacquelyn's voice shrieks in horror.

"Mitch and I will be there soon!" I exclaim.

Ending the call, I turn to face Mitch whose eyes are wide with worry. "That was Jacquelyn, she's under attack at the north end of the forest." My heart is thumping wildly in my chest.

Mitch's mouth drops open. "Oh no!" He gasps. "It's getting ugly."

"Yes," I nod.

Mitch grabs my hands. "Stay close to me out there, okay Baby?" His eyes are narrowed with concern.

"Of course," I say. "In fact, I'll just message Concetta now, so that we can have some back up organised."

I text Concetta the code words: *Black Day. North Canopy.*

Concetta's response is immediate: *Race car.*

"Back up is on its way," I tell Mitch.

"Good," Mitch nods. He kisses me gently on the cheek. "I love you, Baby. My priority is you, okay?"

"That's very sweet," I smile, feeling touched by his care for me. "We'd better go, Mitch."

"Yes," Mitch lets go of my hands and starts the ignition. As he drives, I notice that his hands are shaking.

After a short while, we pull into a parking bay at the north end of the forest. Mitch reaches into his glove box and retrieves a knife.

"Seeing things have been so dangerous lately, I've been keeping this knife with me," he shares. "Please take it Lira. It'll protect you if you need it."

I stare into Mitch's worried, yet loving gaze. "Thank you for taking care of me, my love," I say, reaching out to stroke his cheek. Receiving the knife, I pocket it into the waist band of my flares.

"Are you ready?" Mitch asks.

"Yes," I inhale a sharp breath and push open the passenger door. As I step outside, I hear another scream piercing the air. It sends a cold shiver down my spine.

Bending down, I dash across the grass. "Follow me," I instruct Mitch. The autumn leaves swirl across my feet, drawing me into the world of the forest. I feel my heart warmed with love as my mother's face enters my mind. She is here with me in spirit, encouraging me to continue.

The continued screaming rips at my heart as I trample across the terrain. The gold, green and red fallen leaves at my feet remind me of the fighting nature of Mother's life.

Even under adversity, a spirit will still find a way to breathe and exist.

My heart catches in my throat. Even here, under the wise, river red gum tree, do people continue to fight for justice. A number of villagers have handcuffed themselves to the tree and sit, surrounding it, refusing to move.

Jacquelyn is also handcuffed to a branch, yet stands facing a couple of Petoy men. One of them is aiming an axe at her.

"Move now!" The Petoy man wields his axe in a large circle in the air. As he does so, his black, curly locks of hair fall into his brown eyes. He glares through them at Jacquelyn, his lips forming into a threatening smirk. "Or I'll hurt you like I hurt that man over there."

I stare into the distance, my gaze falling on Mr Petrosis, a village elder, who is clutching his leg and writhing in pain on the dirt ground. His cries are heart wrenching, filling the night air with a pervading sadness.

Mitch grabs hold of my shoulder. "Lira," he whispers. "We should wait for back up, it's too dangerous here."

I shake my head. Back up is too far away. I must help Jacquelyn immediately. Retrieving the knife from my flares, I clutch it tightly in my fist. Its blade gleams brightly in the moonlight, encouraging me to harness my bravery and step forward.

"You wouldn't want to hurt Jacquelyn," I say, drawing the man's attention to me as I hold the knife out towards him. "She is a friend of mine."

The man throws his head back and laughs cruelly. "So?" He shrugs, turning to face me. His pupils are like dark, black bullets.

"Do you know who I am?" I command, standing tall.

The man shrinks back, suddenly afraid of my power. "No," he shakes his head.

"I am Adira Cazon," I harness the strength of my voice. "Wife of Mitch Cazon and daughter of Maricelle and Voltan Vivesque. I have been hiding here in Redbank, away from you evil Petoys, since I was a child." I can feel the autumn leaves piling up around my feet, grounding my stance. I inhale a deep breath, feeling my mother's love surge through my heart.

"You are Adira," the man pushes his black locks away from his eyes and he stares at me admiringly. "The Chief's favourite. I can see why. You are more beautiful than any words could ever describe." He steps forward and his eyes narrow with desire. "You would make a man very satisfied," he says, reaching out to grab hold of my chin. I feel his thumb stroking my cheek roughly.

"You let her go!" Mitch yells, stepping beside me.

I place my hand on Mitch's arm, holding him back. "I am not afraid of this man," I say, cocking my head to one side. "He is very young, searching for a way through life." I meet the man's gaze. "You were once a villager of Mira yourself, weren't you? You lost something dear to you and it affected you deeply. The Petoys' chants of progress were just too good to refuse, weren't they?"

The Petoy man's face is solemn, reflecting.

"You didn't expect to turn against your own, did you? Here or in Mira, people are the heart of a city. Without them and their wisdom, a place cannot breathe or exist."

"Wisdom?" The man seethes. "That word tonight, it's getting on my nerves. These people, they preach that this tree is full of wisdom and that it needs to be preserved."

"It does!" Jacquelyn cries. "This tree has guided generations of Redbank people through life."

The villagers hum in agreement, staring up at Jacquelyn.

Jacquelyn points towards the river. "This tree also plays an important role in the Spirit River system," her eyes flash with determination. "It strains the water and shifts important nutrients across the flood plains. This helps the native animals, like the eels and the growling grass frog, have chances at continuing to breed and survive in a well cared for habitat."

The villagers begin to sing, their voices a welcome relief in the thick tension of the air. It is a song that I learned as a child, as I familiarised myself with the terrain. A song that I now hold close to my heart:

> *"I gave my heart to the red tree*
> *that breathes the light of day.*
> *In return it blessed my spirit*
> *with the strength and will to be.*

Susan Marshall

*"Its red spirit accompanies me
along my trek of earth's plight.
Giving me the voice of wisdom
to reason with the dark of life."*

"You are about to inflict great trauma by logging this tree," I accuse both men. "Do you wish to carry that guilt around with you for the rest of your lives?"

The other Petoy man throws his head back, his red locks falling upon his shoulders. "No guilt here," he snarls. "Now, get out of our ways, all of you, otherwise we will force you to." Retrieving a knife from his pocket, he jumps forward and aims it at the neck of a young woman, causing several other villagers to gasp in horror.

"That's enough!" Mitch cries, jumping behind the man and grabbing him around the arms. "Drop the knife, now!"

The man looks back, his eyes wide with surprise. Shifting his gaze to his knife, he wields it in his hand. "Why should I?" His tone is defiant.

I step forward, aiming my own knife at the man. "Drop it now!" I command. "Or you will face the wrath of *my* blade." I press the knife into his chest.

The man inhales a sharp breath and drops the knife. I pick it up and hand it to Mitch.

"Do not move!" Mitch cries, aiming the knife blade at the man's neck. "Or I will cut you!"

Suddenly, I hear a scream and turn swiftly to face Jacquelyn, who has been accosted by the man with the axe.

"Let me go!" Jacquelyn screams.

The dark haired man laughs menacingly. "You are all voice, no strength," he says to Jacquelyn. "You think you are so smart, chaining yourself to this tree. It won't save you now. One hit from this axe and you will not see the light of day."

Jacquelyn meets my gaze, her eyes full of fear. "Adira," she begs. "Please help me."

I nod, reassuring her that I will.

Staring down at the terrain, I watch a trail of autumn leaves drift and scatter themselves across the familiar marks on the earth that I have skirted passed since childhood. The marks are a way out of this mess. Inhaling a deep breath, I muster my courage to lure the dark haired man's attention. "Before you hurt Jacquelyn," I say to him. "Why don't you come over here? You are really turning me on right now, you, with all your strength."

"Adira!" Mitch is astonished. "What are you –?"

"What do you care?" I lash, waving my hand behind me. "You leave me alone too much. It makes me seek other sources of attention."

I don't look back at Mitch, knowing that I will buckle. I need to keep focused right now, to get the man with the axe to believe and approach me.

The man lowers his axe and turns to face me. "Well," he says. "What a nice interlude of entertainment." He takes a step towards me.

"Yes, that's it, you are making me so hot right now," I sigh, encouraging him to continue to step closer.

The man takes another step and I inhale a sharp breath of anticipation. "Are you making me wait?" I cock my head to one side. "I don't think I can wait much longer now."

"Mmm," the man sighs, stepping forward once more. As he does so, the earth gives way beneath his feet. I hear the man scream as he drops down into its large hole.

"Not so clever now, are we?" I say as I peer down at him. "You've been caught in a fox trap. If you even knew the ways of this terrain, you would have worked that out."

"Let me out!" The man cries. He clutches at his arm, which has been injured.

"Oh, so you feel pain, do you?" I feel no empathy. "Sit with that for a while and think about how much pain you readily inflict upon others."

The man looks up at me with a mixture of anguish and guilt in his eyes.

Stepping away, I approach Jacquelyn. "Are you okay?" I ask her.

Jacquelyn nods, her eyes glazed with amazement. "You are really something, Adira," she smiles. Reaching into her pocket with her free hand, she retrieves a key. "Well done everyone!" She calls as she unlocks her handcuffs. "We have saved the wise river red gum!"

A cheer erupts amongst the villagers and they unlock their handcuffs.

"I've got you, Mr Petrosis," Jacquelyn says, resting the man's weight against her chest. Reaching into her pocket, she retrieves her mobile and dials frantically. "We need an ambulance," she instructs the operator at the end of the line.

Suddenly, the ringing of an alarm pierces the night air.

"Back up has finally arrived," I announce.

A moment later, Hidu and his colleague push passed the tree branches and enter the space.

"Good evening Detective Cazon," Hidu nods towards me.

"Good evening, Imperial Officer Hidu," I say.

"What have we got here?" Hidu approaches Mitch who is still grasping the Petoy man tightly.

"A dangerous man who intended to harm as many villagers as possible," I say. "He also aimed a knife at Jacquelyn."

"Why did you do that?" Hidu asks the man who is now rolling his eyes.

"They were in the way," the man stares at Hidu determinedly. "Me and my buddy," he points to the trap. "We were requested by our boss, Naricia Petoy, to log this mighty fine river red gum. These stupid people handcuffed themselves to the tree and refused to let us cut it down."

"There's another man in the trap!" Jacquelyn calls.

Hidu gazes into the trap. "And so there is," he rubs his thumb across his chin.

"That man wielded his axe directly into Mr Petrosis' chest!" Jacquelyn cries.

Hidu shakes his head, still staring at the man in trap. "You Petoys," he seethes. "You are out of control!" He turns to face the red haired man. "These *people* are local villagers," his voice is fierce. "The river red gum tree means more to them than a dark heart like yours could ever understand." He turns to face his colleague. "Jastar, please arrest this man and take him to the car."

"Yes boss," Jastar nods. Grabbing hold of the Petoy man, Jastar handcuffs him. "You are under arrest," he says firmly. "Now walk!" He pushes the man towards the car.

Hidu faces me. "I need to grab a rope and a harness from the car," he says. "Could you keep watch over things here until I return?"

"Of course," I smile as Hidu walks away.

"Detective Adira Cazon," Mitch's hand grasps my shoulder. "You are phenomenal."

"Thank you," I meet Mitch's gaze. "You were so brave!"

Mitch looks puzzled. "Those things you said about me earlier, did you mean them?"

"Of course not!" I grab hold of Mitch's face and kiss him firmly on the lips. "I said what I did to capture that man. I love you."

Mitch sighs with relief. "I love you too," he smiles, pulling me tightly into his embrace.

Moments later, the paramedics arrive and tend to Mr Petrosis. Jacquelyn stands next to me while we watch him be carried away on a stretcher.

"He'll be fine," she says, her eyes teary. "He has to be."

"He *will* be," I say, pulling Jacquelyn close for a hug. "You will be too, you know. This event will force the Mayor to take a bigger stand against logging. The Petoys need to be stopped."

"I hope so," Jacquelyn wipes away at her tears. "Thank you both for all you've done," she says, smiling weakly.

Mitch smiles empathically. "We'll do it all over again, if we have too," he says. "Life is so precious and needs to be protected."

"Agreed," Jacquelyn sighs. "Our villagers deserve to tread their native forest freely without fear. Instead, they have been hiding away in their homes. I hope things begin to change soon."

"I hope so too," I say. "Are you all okay to return home?"

"Yes, I think so," Jacquelyn smiles.

"We'll see you soon," I say, hugging her one more time. "Take care."

"You too," Jacquelyn sighs. "Thanks again."

"Bye Hidu," I call as I watch him scale down a rope into the trap's hole.

"Bye!" Hidu calls. "Thank you both for all your efforts."

"You too!" I call.

"Come here," Mitch says, slinging his left arm around my shoulders as we walk. "My amazing wife, you have had quite the adventurous evening."

"And so have you," I say.

Mitch stops walking and stares deeply into my eyes. "You have such a big heart," he smiles. "It's one of the things that I love about you."

"Oh Mitch," I sigh, feeling his lips against my cheek. "Kiss me."

"With pleasure," Mitch smiles, his eyes twinkling. I close my eyes as he presses his lips gently against mine.

Chapter 36

The next morning, I return to the apartment to see Hidu crouched on the sofa with his head buried in his hands.

Girl is pacing across the floor and wringing her hands together. Once she notices me, she stops in her tracks, looking flustered. "Lira, would you believe that Hidu took a counterfeit scarf all the way to Mira?" She stares at Hidu. "Are you crazy? You could have put yourself in great danger."

Hidu lowers his hands and looks up at her. "I didn't though," he sighs. "It was only one scarf, Girl. I returned the rest to the Botanica Warehouse like you asked me to."

Girl runs her fingers through her hair. "Was your friend, Gashri, trustworthy?" She asks.

"Yes," Hidu nods. "He is very discrete." Digging into his pocket, he retrieves a piece of paper. "I have the results of his test of the scarf material here," he says, unfolding the sheet. "Have a look for yourself." He offers the paper to Girl.

Girl stares at the fluttering paper. "Okay," she finally concedes, stepping forward and taking it. As she reads the details, her eyes narrow intensely. "Not good," she finally says. "The scarf is made of a highly micro plastic polyester, made sheer enough to pass off as silk." She runs her fingers through her hair in frustration.

"Synthetics!" She fumes. "So toxic and pollutant. It would hurt the people of Mira deeply to discover how their totems are being appropriated and sold this way."

"Now you see why I had to get the scarf tested," Hidu sighs, rubbing his forehead with his fingers. "It's my job, Girl. I have to investigate any suspicious activity in order to help prevent the loss of Mira's silk trade."

"I know," Girl sighs. "This confirms what Jacquelyn suspected about the material. We need to handle this information rationally and safely otherwise we'll put ourselves in danger. I also want to see justice achieved properly for the people of Mira." She lowers her head, staring at the ground.

"Of course," I say gently, stepping closer to Girl. "We need to handle this right."

Guilt flashes over Hidu's face. "I'm sorry Girl," he says. "I didn't mean to make you feel that you were in danger. I won't do anything reckless, I promise."

"Won't you?" Girl is still staring at the ground. "Can I trust you?"

"You can," Hidu stands, approaching her. "Please look at me."

It is silent for a moment. The suspense hangs thickly in the air.

"Girl?" Hidu's voice cracks. "I just get so angry with the Petoys, I'm sorry …" His voice drifts off.

Girl is still staring at the floor.

"Why won't you look at me, Girl?" Hidu chokes on his words. "It hurts me so much." Tears begin to fall down his cheeks.

Girl glances up, her eyes narrowed with concern. "Oh, please don't cry," she begs, stepping forward and caressing his cheek.

Hidu sniffles and swipes at his tears. "I love you," he says softly. "I can't imagine life without you."

Girl's eyes soften. "I've been too hard on you," she realises. "I'm sorry, Hidu. I have been so scared that you had betrayed me somehow, that you were deliberately leading the Petoys to us. I know now that my fear isn't rational."

Makeshift Girl: The Secret Heritage Trail

"I could never betray you," Hidu drops to his knees onto the carpet. "You know, yesterday I arrested Nick and Tonya for their theft and conspiracy of the illegal trade of the ancient silk garments."

"Yes, he did," I say. "He was amazing."

"You did?" Girl's eyes widen with surprise. "Why didn't you tell me Hidu?"

Hidu meets Girl's gaze. "It was the last thing on my mind," he sighs. "All I could think about was how I was going to sort things out with you."

"That's great news, Hidu," a smile crosses Girl's lips. "You too, Lira," she stares at me. "I hope Nick and Tonya both receive the sentences they deserve."

"They will," Hidu nods. "The Emperor of Mira will grant them just sentences for sure." He faces me. "We discovered that Nick and a couple of other delivery workers were stealing the ancient silk garments from Mira and delivering them initially to Taro's Take Away Noodle Store. Upon delivery and completing their work, they would receive a payment from Naricia Petoy."

"That makes sense," I say, remembering Nick kissing the white envelope.

"Naricia is working at the noodle store?" Girl's mouth drops open in surprise.

"Was," Hidu emphasises. "Not anymore though. The store's been shut down as it was purely a front to their illegal trade operation. It's been hard to link Naricia to the operation as we have no evidence."

"That woman!" Girl seethes, crossing her arms. "She is heartless."

Hidu stares into Girl's eyes. "Forget Naricia for now," he says gently, reaching for both her hands. "Here I am, Girl, asking you to forgive me. If I can't be with you, it would calm my heart to know that you don't resent me."

Girl's eyes widen. "I don't resent you," she says, stroking his hair. "Right now, you have reminded me of the traits I love about you," she says. "Your big loving heart, your honesty and your bravery to accept what life throws at you." She drops down onto the floor, meeting his gaze at eye level. "I was foolish to ask you to leave," she admits. "It is you I ask to forgive *me* for my brashness. Will you?"

"Yes," Hidu says, relief sweeping over his face. "I do."

Girl and Hidu stare deeply into each other's eyes.

"Hold me," Girl breathes, shuffling into Hidu's arms.

Pulling Girl into his embrace, Hidu sighs with relief. "Vianna," he says softly, caressing her face. "Here you are, raw and real, the girl of my heart. I have missed you so much," he kisses her softly across the cheek.

Girl closes her eyes, smiling with contentment. "You've always known me," she says softly. "You are the one who keeps me grounded and helps me to find my way." Opening her eyes, she places her hand on her heart. "I feel you so deeply in my heart."

"That is so sweet," Hidu smiles. "I will always be here for you, Vianna."

Girl's eyes light up with happiness. "Kiss me," she says, cupping Hidu's face in her hands.

Hidu's smile radiates through his eyes. Leaning towards Girl, he kisses her softly on her lower lip.

"Mmm," Girl sighs, parting her lips and kissing him back.

I feel awkward watching Girl and Hidu, so I head into the kitchen and turn on the kettle.

I hear the scuffle of footsteps on the carpet and look back, discovering Hidu and Girl holding hands and smiling at me.

"Tell her, Hidu," Girl nudges him.

"What is it?" I am intrigued.

Hidu's gaze meets mine. "We've had some serious news. Concetta asked me to let you both know that the Petoy clan has attempted to raid the palace of Mira."

"Oh no!" I am shocked. "That is horrible. Did anyone get hurt?"

"There was one casualty," Hidu's eyes narrow. "The Petoys managed to accost the Emperor and his guard outside the antiquity room.

"The guard was killed and the Emperor escaped with a severe knife wound in his abdomen.

"Once the clan burst into the room, they attempted to steal a historical, indigo silk garment from the Emperor's heritage display cabinet. The two guards in the room managed to fight them off and retrieve the precious garment. The clan members staggered out of the space, wounded and threatening another attack."

"I don't know what to say," Girl says shakily, staring off into the distance. "The Petoys, they are unstoppable."

"That's just it, they *think* they are unstoppable," says Hidu. "It has led to them acting recklessly and making mistakes. "He meets my gaze. "Concetta wants you to text her so that she can organise a brush pass for you tonight. A contact will hand you an asset urgently. It is one that will help you both succeed in your mission."

"Right," I say, meeting Girl's gaze. "Are you okay if I do this tonight?"

"Yes, of course," Girl nods. "Please be careful Lira."

"I will. Can I ask you a favour?"

"Sure, anything," Girl nods.

"Please call me Adira from now on," I say decisively.
"I am not hiding behind Lira anymore."

"Adira Cazon, eh?" Girl's smile is radiant. "What a beautiful name."

"Thank you," I smile appreciatively. "Now, I'll just text Concetta and see what she wants to do." I retrieve my phone from my pocket. My hands shake with anticipation as I type my text message: *Walk by.* Pressing send, I feel my heart pound as I wait for a reply.

Ding!

The response is rapid. Staring at my phone, I read the message:
Sub 4, 14 rotations.

I know what Concetta's code means. She wants me to engage in a brush pass at 2 a.m. on platform 4 at Redbank Station. It is now 1:15 a.m.

"Brush pass is organised," I announce, pocketing my phone. I retrieve my black wig from my bag.

"Here let me help you," Girl pins the wig down onto my head. She grabs hold of my shoulders and stares into my eyes. "This is all happening way too quickly," she sighs.

"It always does," I smile warmly. "Momentum has a way of forging ahead, you've just got to do your very best to keep up."

"Yes," Girl nods. "You do."

"It's time to go," I say, picking up my bag.

"Take care," Hidu says softly. "We'll be thinking of you."

"I will," I smile reassuringly. "See you both soon."

Chapter 37

It is eerie walking across the platform at Redbank Station this evening. The white lights cast a hazy glow, illuminating the shifting bodies of commuters who are waiting for the train.

Looking up at the arrival and departures schedule, I make a mental note that the next train is due to arrive in four minutes. It heightens my anxiety and I stop for a moment, inhaling a deep breath.

To my left, an old man stands, leaning against a pole. He looks up at me as I pass, his green eyes gleaming almost crazily in the white light. "Hello Miss," his voice rattles and his teeth gnash together. "Got some spare change?"

I ignore him, continuing to walk across the platform. My gaze rests upon a young mother with a boy around six years of age. The mother is wagging her finger at him as he runs across the seats of the benches. "Get down Kris!" She cries.

The little boy ignores her, continuing to dash across a bench.

"I know it's late," the mother sighs. "Come on Kris, sit down with me here." She plonks down on the closest bench, waving her son over to her.

Kris glances at his mother, his eyes lighting up with happiness. Jumping off the bench, he runs towards her, wriggling his bottom onto the seat next to her. Resting his head against her arm, his eyes close automatically.

Watching the family has warmed my heart. One day I may be able to love my own child, too.

Two minutes before the train arrives.

A cold chill creeps across my arms and into my heart. I know that I am being watched.

Glancing out of my peripheral vision, my eyes fall on Felibo, leaning with his back against a brick wall next to the news stand. He is puffing on a cigarette and the smoke wafts in a large wave through the air.

I am shaking now, knowing that I am under surveillance.

Walking passed Felibo, I stop at the news stand and grab a Fire Street Newspaper. As Felibo approaches me, I can feel his body heat radiating from him. He inches closer and his intense gaze almost burns a whole into me as I place my change onto the counter.

"Adira," the cigarette fumes are strong in his breath as he whispers hoarsely. "Step back now, before it's too late."

I close my eyes, feeling my heart pounding wildly. I can hear the sound of the train pulling into the platform.

Screech, the train brakes suddenly. Sparks of light ignite as its wheel bearings strike against the metal rails.

My eyes shoot upwards, staring at the arrivals and departures schedule. It is exactly 2 a.m.

Gazing to my right, I notice the train door sliding open and the passengers alighting onto the platform.

I swallow firmly, feeling a lump descend down the back of my throat. I know what I have to do.

The whistle sounds. I have seconds to spare. "Felibo," I whisper, feeling him retract back in surprise at the mention of his name. "It's always too late, isn't it?" I step passed him and approach the stationery train.

Felibo falls into stride beside me. "You can't do this," his voice is gruff. "You can't leave Redbank."

I step one foot onto the carriage. "No, I can't," I say, as Felibo pushes passed me and jumps onto the carriage. "But you can."

Stepping backwards, I ensure that my feet return onto the platform.

"All clear!" The station master waves.

A sly smile crosses my lips as I watch the train doors shut firmly.

Felibo's mouth drops open in surprise. As the train begins to take off, I watch him bang his fist fiercely against the window.

I have no time to enjoy my victory. There is no telling who else is on surveillance here.

It is 2:04 a.m.

The white light strikes my eyes, making me feel a little disoriented. Glancing to my left, I see her.

She is a young woman with long brown hair, braided into plaits. They swing rhythmically as she raises her knitting needles high into the air.

Click, click, click, is my signal.

I check over my shoulder for any tails.

There are none.

It is eerily silent here now, except for the occasional burst of voices in animated conversation.

Glancing again at the young woman, I see her begin to stand. She wraps her loose strand of red wool around her knit work. Stepping forward, she begins to walk across the platform towards me.

It is now or never.

Striding across the cement floor, I stare straight ahead and peer from left to right, as though I am trying to locate someone.

As I walk passed the young woman, I step closer to her and reach out my hand slightly, feeling her place something soft and slippery within it. Scrunching the asset in my palm, I keep walking, heading towards the escalators.

I ascend quickly, taking the steps two by two. One commuter elbows me in frustration as I step in front of him. I ignore the reaction, continuing to ascend until my feet land firmly onto the footpath outside.

The cool air is refreshing, brushing against my skin and increasing my alertness. Peering over my shoulder, I check one last time for any tails.

I swear I can see the silver Mercedes parked in the curb on the other side of the road.

Breaking into a sprint, I run across the footpath and cut across the grass at Spring Park. Hiding behind a small bush, I check once more for tails.

There are none. The Mercedes is gone.

Opening my palm, my mouth drops open in shock. In a small, sheer silk bag I hold an indigo blue sash, which glistens in the dim lamp light.

My hands begin to shake and I step back, still staring at the sash. As I do so, the world around me begins to tremor with the heavy stamping of feet.

"No more bans! No more taxes! Yes to progress!" It is the Petoy clan, their shouts of protest ringing through the night air.

Stepping backwards, I retreat into the shadows, standing with my back against a large shrub.

The sound grows louder, almost deafening. The protest leader holds up a handful of the Mayor's campaign posters. "Rahi is a monster!" He cries. "If he takes away our chance at progress then we'll bring him down!"

"Bring him down!" The other clan members chant. "Bring the monster down!"

The protest leader's eyes light up with a devilish gleam. A twisted smile crosses his lips and he sets the flame upon the papers, filling the night air with a bright red and orange fire.

Dropping down onto my knees, I hide behind the shrub, my eyes transfixed onto the fiery flames. I am faced with the fire of the past ...

On the open grassland of Mira, the flickering embers of the fire pit mesmerised my young eyes, drawing me into its deep red and orange spark of life. It was warmth that I had not experienced since being parted from my father.

Makeshift Girl: The Secret Heritage Trail

I felt Mother's hand grasp my shoulder and she pulled me closer to her. "We should go, Adira," she said softly, trying to lead me away from the flames.

I shook my shoulders firmly, releasing Mother's grasp. "It is beautiful," my eyes were alight with excitement. Stepping forward, I let the heat from the fire warm my cold, shaking hands and body.

Once the chill evaporated, my gaze shuffled across the grassland to a body lying on the ground. Stepping closer, I dropped down, rocking on my knees. Tilting my head to one side, I stared at the man, whose mouth was wide opened in shock. His open eyes stared up at the red streaked sky.

"Hello," I felt strangely calm around the man. He had a story to tell, lying there and letting the sky wash over him. "What can you see up high?" I was curious as to what vision he had.

There was no answer. The man remained still, silently saturated by the vista of the endless sky.

Realising that he could not speak, I felt a sad tug in my heart.

Mother knelt down beside me and placed her hand upon my shoulder. "He is sleeping, Adira," she said softly.

I nodded, understanding. "He is having dreams about the sky," I said, touching the man's khaki tank top and lowering my face towards his. "I hope you have sweet dreams," I whispered softly into the man's ear. "Maybe you will find some light in all this dark."

Mother reached out to touch the indigo silk sash that was tied around the man's neck. "He was a member of the imperial army," she sounded sad. Turning to face me, her eyes narrowed with concern. "We must leave now, Adira. It's not safe to be here."

My heart pounded in my chest, yet my head told me to wait a moment, to glance around me.

Shifting my gaze to the right, my eyes fell upon a small, orange piece of cloth, strewn across a couple of blades of grass. Shuffling across the earth, I could feel my knees scraping against sharp stones. I ignored the stinging pain in my skin, determined to reach my destination.

As I approached the cloth, I stared at it for a moment, studying its familiarity. Picking it up, I breathed in its comforting, male scent. "Father!" I announced, turning to face Mother. "Father's shirt!"

Mother dashed to my side and gasped at the sight of the cloth. "So it is," she breathed, clasping her hands over her heart.

It was silent for a moment, as we both drifted into our thoughts. I remembered Father's warm, loving face smiling at me. It made my heart ache with desire to hold him close again.

"The Petoys must have found him," Mother's voice was shaking. I inhaled a sharp breath of fear at the news. Mother met my gaze, her eyes concerned. "He would have been out trekking the earth with this other soldier. By the looks of it, your father got away."

I sat still, letting Mother's words wash over me. Father was in danger, trying to escape the Petoys. My heart pounded with fear for his safety.

As the memory dissipates, I discover that I am staring at the silk sash, which is crumpled tightly in my fist. Relaxing my hand, I study its detail. It is decorated with an eagle talon totem, marking it as an official asset belonging to the Emperor of Mira. A smile forms across my lips as I realise the luck that we have been blessed with. This sash is an asset for our situation right now. We could use it to our advantage and bring the whole silk trade operation to its knees.

Glancing out at the protest, I watch as burning papers float through the night air and disintegrate into ash, which falls in sparks upon the grass.

The Petoys think that they are strong, yet they are reckless. They do not know what is about to hit them.

Chapter 38

The indigo silk sash burns a hole in my pocket as I hop into Sophie's BMW the next morning. I am feeling a little nervous about an important job that Girl and I will undertake at Frosties. The back seat is super comfortable and I close my eyes for a moment, letting my arm, back and thigh muscles release their tension.

Girl smiles as she flops onto the seat next to me. "Thanks for agreeing to help us, Sophie," she says.

"There is nothing I would rather do more," Sophie's expression is sad. "It's been so emotional working my shifts at Frosties. The people are under such oppressed conditions. I sneak food into them every time I work." She gestures towards the passenger seat, which holds a box full of pre-made sandwiches and fruit.

"That's really generous of you," I say, feeling worry churning in the pit of my stomach. "I hope that we can release our people from Frosties as soon as possible."

"Me too," Girl agrees. "We need to empower them to fight back."

"Yes," I agree.

"Agreed," Sophie says. "Their beautiful spirits deserve to be free again."

I stare out the window, my mind drifting as Sophie drives. My people once treaded the world freely in Mira, their spirits soaring across the land. I would do anything to help them return home to their families, comforts and familiarities.

After a short while, Sophie pulls into a car park outside J.F. Snow Globes, also known as *Frosties*, the final destination mentioned on the CB radio.

"Wait here," Sophie says as she grabs the box of food and opens her door. "I need to relieve Naricia. She undertakes her management jobs for an hour each day. Once she has left, I will be able to let you in."

"Thank you," I smile, grabbing my fluoro yellow safety vest off my lap. I slide my arms through the armholes and stretch the front, sticking it together with the Velcro adhesive. Rotating my arms and stretching my neck, I mentally prepare myself for my role.

Sophie steps out onto the concrete, shutting the driver's door gently behind her. I watch her disappear through the front door of Frosties.

"Are you nervous Adira?" Girl's hands are shaking a little as she attaches the Velcro together on her own safety vest. "I am a little," she admits. "I'm not used to taking on undercover roles."

"A little," I say, scratching my scalp. The black wig has made my head feel hot and itchy. "Don't worry," I reassure her. "The security vest will make you look like a worker. Our job today is to inspect the security cameras and to fix them."

"Of course," Girl nods, understanding. A moment later, she meets my gaze. "I hope that everyone is okay in there."

I meet Girl's gaze and we stare into each other's eyes silently. Nothing more needs to be said. We both feel our care and concern for our people.

Digging into the pocket of her pants, Girl retrieves Hidu's map. "Apparently there are a number of security cameras throughout the building," she says. "Hidu tells me that there is one in the main working room." She points to a large area on the map, labelled 'work room'. "There is also a security camera attached to the wall located next to the bottom of the stair well, close by the front door."

"Hmm," I say. "That will be a tricky one to bypass. I'll see what I can do."

Girl stares at me thoughtfully. "Yes," she agrees. "It will be the first camera to pick up any footage of us and send an alarm bell to security."

"Are there anymore cameras?" I ask.

"Yes, one more," Girl says. "It is upstairs in Naricia's office." She points to a large floor area on the map. "I wonder what she gets up to in there."

"We'll soon find out," my mind reels through what I have learned. Firstly, I need to sort out the security camera by the front door so that we are not seen.

I meet Girl's gaze once more. "When the front door opens, stay put here in the ute for a short while," I tell her. "I'll reposition the security camera so that we are not seen."

"Okay," Girl nods, her eyes widening. "Lucky you're here to keep us safe, Adira."

I reach out and squeeze her hand. "I'll do what I can," I say. "When I am done, I'll open the door again and that will be your cue to step inside."

"Sure," Girl claps her hands together. "We've got this, Adira."

"Yes we have," I say, encouraging her.

The front door of Frosties flies open, swinging in the breeze. It is my cue to enter the building.

As I step onto the footpath, a strong burning smell assaults my nostrils, making me gasp and cough. My throat burns and my eyes sting, releasing hot tears that rain down my cheeks.

A thick, black fume cloud billows into the air. Something is burning at the back of Frosties.

My eyes fall upon the front display window. Glittering on a steel shelf are many transparent spheres of snow globes. One details a picturesque scene of a train steaming puffs of snow as it travels down a track. Another scene details a small garden frosted with the snowfall of winter. I sigh with frustration, pulling at my hair. J.F. Snow Globes is a business being used as a front to cover up an illegal operation.

Following my instincts, I dash to the right side of the building and lean against its grey brick wall. Peering around the corner, I see a small courtyard bordered with box hedges. Standing there is Naricia, who is wearing a face mask. She is digging into a large, white rubbish bag and retrieving offcuts and scraps of polyester material with counterfeit totem patterns displayed on them.

Towards the right is a grey 44 gallon drum, which burns alight with a roaring flame. I watch in horror as Naricia approaches the drum and throws in the polyester material. As it burns, another black smoke cloud billows into the air. The stench is deadly, overwhelming my eyes and throat. Stepping back, I double over, coughing violently. My eyes sting again and release a flood of tears, which roll profusely down my cheeks.

Naricia is officially insane. Burning such a toxic material is hazardous to the environment and to the health of others. I make a vow right then and there to compile enough evidence to have Naricia arrested.

Retrieving my phone from my pocket, I place the collar of my t-shirt over my nose and mouth to protect my airways from the toxic fumes. Dashing back to the corner, I take photos of Naricia in action.

Satisfied with the evidence, I turn and head back towards the front of the building. It is dangerous being out here for too long.

Lowering myself onto the footpath, I stare upwards, peering through the font door's window. From this vantage point I can study the viewing range of the security camera inside the building. It is pointing straight ahead in order to capture footage of anyone entering or exiting the building. I realise that there is an opportunity to enter at the very left hand side of the doorway, where the camera would probably only capture one's arm or the right side of their body.

Crawling, I stick to the left, grasping firmly onto the door frame and landing my knees onto the lino flooring of the building entrance.

I kick the front door shut behind me and scan the floor to the left of me quickly. My gaze rests upon a large, sealed cardboard box displayed with an *A Touch of Silk* range sticker. Digging into my pant pocket, I retrieve my mobile phone and zoom the camera lens in, taking a photo of the sticker on the box.

Makeshift Girl: The Secret Heritage Trail

Tapping the top of the box, I acknowledge that it is firm, indicating that it is full of product. The Petoys are gaining momentum now and very soon their range will be delivered across the sea. The knowledge of this pushes me to work faster so that I can help prevent the upcoming delivery from taking place.

Pushing the box against the wall, I step on top of it and approach the security camera. Grabbing hold of it, I readjust its positioning upwards so that it faces the top of the doorway and the roof. That will do for now. It will enable Girl and I to enter and exit the building without being seen.

Jumping off the box, I push it back into its original location and stretch my arms. I could do with a massage from Mitch right now. Just the thought of his hands against my back and shoulders makes me feel warm and fuzzy inside.

Approaching the front door, I swing it open again and wait. Girl arrives a moment later, gingerly stepping into the entrance.

"Well done!" She whispers hoarsely and clears her throat, irritated by the fumes outside.

I smile, very pleased with the result. Girl is safe.

Girl takes hold of my hands and stares into my eyes. "Are you ready to meet our people?"

"Yes," I say decisively. "Let's go."

I trek beside Girl, listening to the wind slapping against the building. The outside world is announcing itself, inviting us to step outside and be. A venture I know that each oppressed person from Mira would long for as they battle through the horrors of their entrapments here each day.

Entering the work room, my nose is assaulted with a strong odour. It is the stench of defecation that reeks through the building. My stomach churns with nausea and I block my nose with my fingers.

"Terrible, isn't it?" Sophie joins me. She waves towards the people who are seated in a circle on the floor, eating sandwiches and fruit.

"Our poor people have to live in such squalor. It makes me so angry. We have to get them out of here, Adira."

"Yes," I agree. My eyes sweep the walls of the room, locating the camera. It is positioned on the back wall and primarily focused on the small, aluminium work tables laid out in two lines across the space. The camera's main purpose is to survey the work activity of the people.

The work tables themselves are scattered with scissors and scraps of polyester material designed with counterfeit totems. The tables echo with the pain and suffering of my people who have been forced to work at them. I feel empathy for them as they suffer such oppression and witness their very own heritage being abused.

My eyes continue to scan the room, assessing our safety. The area that my people are sitting in is out of viewing range of the surveillance camera. My heart falls as I notice the tattered and unwashed states of my people. Many are thin and frail, not having been fed enough under such oppression.

A young woman who carries a burning tallow candle, steps away from the circle. The candle light flickers wildly in the semi darkness of the room and shines a ray of hope.

The young woman wears a purple tattered dress, which is ripped and smeared with dirt marks. Her long, dishevelled brown hair falls into her face and she pushes it out of the way, revealing a pale complexion, dotted with freckles, which are scattered across her cheeks and the bridge of her nose. Her eyes are a dull grey green and they carry the weight of the world.

"Hello, I'm Caray," the young woman says, meeting my gaze. "You must be Adira."

"I am," I say, smiling warmly.

"Sophie has told us all about you," she smiles. "She said that you'll arrive soon and help us."

"I want nothing more than to help all of you," I say. "Do you know Girl?"

"Yes," Caray nods. "Once before in Mira, Girl, you went by another name."

Girl nods. "Yes, a name that has floated away across the sea. I am called Girl now, fleeing all I can from the Petoys and their endless persecution."

"I'm sorry to hear that," Caray's eyes water with tears. "The Petoys have taken from us all in horrific ways."

"Yes, they have," Girl agrees.

Caray shines her candle light upon her people. "I know that you both have to work," she says. "But take some time to speak to us. It might just give us all the hope we need."

"Of course," I say, following Caray towards our people. Sophie is rubbing the back of an old woman who is sobbing. My heart wrenches as I hear her cries pierce the air. Her pain and suffering touches my soul and raises my fighting spirit.

"Attention everyone," Caray says softly. "This is Girl, who many of you know from Mira."

Eyes light up around the room once they recognise Girl.

"Your hair is yellow," an old man says. "I remember it being black."

"Yes," Girl says. "It keeps me well disguised. The Petoys are dangerous."

Nods ripple across the room.

"It is well known amongst us that I am to be inducted soon as the new chief of silk of Mira," Girl says thoughtfully. "All this time I have trekked the earth, trying to flee the Petoys and to bring back what rightfully belongs to my family.

"Now I stand here, facing all of you. You help me remember my ancestor, Sefra's beliefs in the spirit of silk and how its energy flows through space and time, even after it has been designed. It is your spirits and stories that I am here to save. Let's work as a team to return you home to Mira. Together we can save our stories and our heritage."

"Save our spirits! Save our heritage!" The people cry, pumping their fists in the air.

Girl waves her hand towards me. "I'd love for you all to meet my friend, Adira," she says proudly. "She is the brain behind our plan. You can trust her, she will do all that she can to help you."

Eyes stare intensely at me, radiating with hope. I inhale a deep breath, calming my nerves. I need to step up now, to lead our people. "I am from Mira too," I say. "I too have seen much horror at the hands of the Petoys. From the moment I was born, my parents and I fled their wrath. At the age of six, my mother sent me here to Redbank as she worried that I would not survive. All my life I've wanted to see her again and to hold her close.

"We all have our own anguish with the Petoys. It unites us with a common bond. We are people of Mira who deserve to trek the earth freely without fear of harm."

"Here! Here!" The people cheer.

Digging into my pocket, I retrieve the indigo silk scarf. "I have managed to obtain a very important traditional silk garment," I say. "Empress Celine trusts us to use it our advantage."

I am met with wide eyed, curious gazes.

"This indigo sash is worn by the military of Mira and is highly sort after by the Petoys. They recently broke into the imperial palace of Mira and tried to steal it. This works to our advantage. Together we can make the Petoys believe that they are creating indigo silk. If we fool them enough, we will destroy their entire *A Touch of Silk* range."

"How do we do that?" An old man asks.

"We will alter the dye colour," Girl replies.

Various heads nod, understanding.

"I see," says a young man. "We'll trick them into believing they own riches, yet destroy their range."

"Exactly," Girl smiles. "Does that sound like a plan?"

"Yes!" The people cry, crawling towards Girl and I. I feel hands clutching at my pants and safety vest, grateful people who feel that they have discovered a way to bring down the very people who have hurt them.

"We have much to plan," I say, rubbing an old woman's hands gently. "When the time is right, we will break you all out of here so that you can return home to Mira. That, I promise."

It warms my heart to see smiles of hope flicker across our people's faces.

"You have 20 minutes left," Sophie stares into my eyes. "Naricia will return soon."

Sophie's warning propels me into action. "We have to go," I say. "We are setting things up to help you leave."

"We will see you soon," Girl says, squeezing the hands of the last few people who have reached for her.

"We'll need our passports!" A man cries. "They've taken them from us so that we can't return home or travel anywhere."

"We'll find them," I promise. "And return them to you."

The man points upwards. "Try upstairs," he says. "The woman leader is sure to have locked them away in her office somewhere."

I nod. "Thanks for the lead," I say. "First, I must complete a task here." Locating a small step ladder, I place it against the back wall and climb it. Reaching the security camera, I dig into my pocket, retrieving my own small surveillance camera. Peeling the backing off the adhesive on the camera's circular base, I aim the surveillance camera towards the lower right hand corner of the camera and stick it down. Flipping the toggle switch to video mode, I step back and check that the surveillance camera has enough viewing range.

Satisfied with my work, I descend the ladder, landing my feet firmly onto the ground. "This camera is secret," I tell the people. "It will help us to get you out safely."

Heads nod vigorously and mouths drop open in amazement.

"Take us with you now!" One woman calls as we exit the room.

"We will soon, we promise," Girl chokes on her words, her heart breaking with empathy.

Leaving the work room, we trek quickly back down the corridor to the flight of stairs at the front door. A whiff of toxic black smoke seeps its way through the window next to the security camera. Peering outside, I see Naricia dashing passed with a handful of the polyester material.

"Naricia is working outside," I whisper to Girl. "She's burning the scrap polyester material."

Girl's eyes narrow. "So that's what the toxic, burning smell was outside." She shakes her head. "Does that woman have no sense? She's polluting the air with toxins."

"Yes," I say. "She is," I meet Girl's gaze. "We've only got a small window of time left before Naricia re-enters the building," I tell her. "We need to move quickly now or we'll be caught."

"Right, let's go," Girl ascends the stairs two at a time. I follow, almost jogging up the stairs and meeting her on the landing.

As we reach the top of the stair case, a guard steps across the landing, listening to his walkie talkie. I grab hold of Girl's hand and drag her back to the stair case banister. Bending down, I shake it, pretending to check its safety. "This one needs some work," I say.

"Let me see," Girl follows my lead, rubbing her fingers over the wood to check for damage. "You're right," she pretends to agree.

Glancing at us, the guard shrugs, obviously believing that we are undertaking maintenance work on the building.

Once he leaves, I exhale a sigh of relief and reach for Girl's hand. She pulls me up onto my feet and we step up onto the landing and dash across the white tiled floor.

Soon we reach a large room, decorated with casement windows, which provide a sweeping view of the office inside it.

Girl approaches the front door and rattles the door handle. "It's locked," she sighs, rolling her eyes. "Yet another obstacle to overcome."

"Not really," I say, noticing that one of the windows next to the door is slightly ajar. I pull at its frame with all my might until it swings open.

"Is there anything you can't do, Adira?" Girl smiles appreciatively. "Nothing seems to daunt you."

I blush shyly. "I can't design silk," my voice is small. "We all have different skills."

"You're right," Girl smiles. "However, your heroic prowess is amazing."

I lower my head, blushing more deeply. "Thank you," I allow myself to accept her compliment. My gaze drifts back to the window. "Wait here," I tell Girl. "I'll check out the surveillance camera."

"Thanks Adira," Girl smiles.

Placing my right leg over the window sill, I hoist myself up and through the open window. I hit the blue carpet on two feet and balance myself, standing straight.

My eyes scan the office, checking our safety. There is no one here, just the video surveillance camera on the back white wall. It casts a sweeping view over a large desk in the right hand corner of the room.

Keeping out of its viewing range, I grab a black leather chair from the red gum conference table in the middle of the room. Carrying it, I lean it against the back wall and stand on its seat, staring up at the surveillance camera. Using both hands, I swing the camera around until it is facing the back wall.

Jumping down off the chair, I land on my left foot, stumbling as I try to regain my composure. Once I am standing straight, I pick up the chair and return it to its place at the conference table.

Dashing back to the window, I wave Girl inside. "All is clear," I say. "Come in."

Girl clambers over the window sill and jumps into the room. She shuts the window firmly behind her. "No one will suspect anything," she says. "Which is just how it should be. I don't want anyone downstairs to be blamed for this forced entry."

"Point taken," I acknowledge. "We'll have to work quickly."

"Yes we will," Girl agrees, her eyes falling upon the red gum desk at the right hand corner of the room. "What the -?" She heads towards the desk and stares at a black leather book that is lying on top of it. "It's my art folio!" She exclaims. "Naricia has had it all this time!" She stares at me.

A wave of relief washes over me. "Thank goodness you've found it," I say. "I'll photograph its location as evidence of theft."

"Oh, sure," Girl steps back, giving me room to approach the desk.

I retrieve my mobile phone from my pocket and photograph the folio, ensuring that I capture the desk. As I do so, my gaze rests upon a framed photo of Naricia sitting on top of two Petoy clan members' shoulders. She is pumping her fist in the air, exuding a love for fame and power that is gut wrenching.

As I take more photos of the evidence, I notice a couple of smudged fingerprints on the front cover of the folio. Zooming in, I also take some close up shots of them for further evidence of Naricia's theft.

"All done," I say. "The folio is now yours to take."

"Thanks Adira," Girl retrieves the folio and flicks through it. "Naricia's drawn circles around my statue model sketches," she shakes her head. Suddenly her mouth drops open. "She's taken my statue, I know she has!" Girl cries. "I shouldn't be surprised. That woman has had it in for my family for a long time!"

"I'm sorry, Girl," I say, feeling overwhelmed by her wave of reactions.

"No need to be sorry," Girl places her free hand on her hip. "We're going to find my statue Adira, no matter what. Naricia will not be allowed to get away with what she has done."

"No, she won't," I agree.

Girl tucks the folio under her left arm. "Take a look at this," she says, pointing to a framed black image on the back wall.

Stepping closer, I see a photograph of a couple of Petoy men unloading wooden crates from an old truck. The caption accompanying the image reads: 'Petoy Progress, 1896: making deliveries in the revised edition of the first truck designed by Gottlieb Daimler.'

The truck was very different to the ones of today and looked like a cart with a two cylinder engine positioned at the front. It also had iron wheels. A Petoy clan member sat up the front on an open driving seat, much like that which is found on a carriage.

"Paving the way to progress," I say. "I can imagine that owning that truck made the Petoy clan more efficient in their trade and delivery services. They could carry more wares and travel longer distances with a lot less hassle."

"Yes, they most certainly would have been able to," Girl smiles. "It looks like they've been advancing their delivery service for a long time. She points to a second image. "See this one here of the wooden boat? Is that anchored in Spirit River?"

"Yes," I say, reading the caption: 'Petoy Progress, 2022, launching maritime trade with small wooden boats at Spirit River, Redbank.'

Girl shakes her head. "The Petoys expect to extend their delivery service across the ocean to other countries." She meets my gaze. "There is no way that their counterfeit silk garments will be sold overseas, Adira."

"Certainly not," I agree. "We should keep moving. Let's find those passports and get out of here before we're discovered."

We approach a filing cabinet at the back of the room. Luckily it is unlocked. Pulling open the top drawer, Girl rifles through the files.

I am on lookout, checking over my shoulder to see if anyone is entering the room.

All clear so far.

Girl opens the second drawer and rifles through more files. "There they are!" She cries, retrieving the passports. Holding them in both hands, she kicks the drawer shut and runs towards the conference table. I watch as she picks up an empty plastic bag and places the passports inside it.

Twisting the bag tightly, Girl stuffs it inside the waist band of her pants. "Hopefully I can conceal this well," she says as she straightens her tank top over her waist.

"It looks fine," I say. "Let's go." Turning on my heels, I catch up with Girl, who has opened the front door, which unlocked easily from the inside.

Once outside in the corridor, Girl and I both sigh with relief.

"Now to escape," I say. "Follow me."

We dash down the staircase, listening for any conspicuous sounds. Just as we reach the middle step, the front door opens and Naricia storms inside the building.

I bob down and press myself up against the banister, trying to remain out of sight. I can feel Girl's erratic breathing behind me. I know that she is fuming right now and most certainly wants to confront Naricia. I place a hand on her leg, trying to settle her fury.

Naricia saunters towards the work room and is swallowed by its darkness.

"Let's go!" I cry, running towards the front door.

Girl stands still on the step, staring after Naricia. Her cheeks are flaming red and her fists are clenched. "I want to sort that woman out," she seethes.

Retreating back up the steps, I grab Girl's hand. "Look at me," I say.

Girl meets my gaze furiously. "I'm so angry, Adira."

"I know," I say gently. "Please remember that we have come this far. Let's not spoil our discoveries by confronting Naricia right now. We need to build even more evidence against her, like the theft of your statue."

Girl exhales a deep breath, relaxing her body and unclenching her fists. "You're right as always, Adira," she says.

Pulling Girl's hand gently, I guide her down the stairs and out the front door.

Once we step outside Frosties, the lingering toxic fumes assault my lungs. I turn to face Girl, shaking my head. "Naricia is insane," I tell her.

"Yes, she is," Girl nods. "She has been for a very long time."

We are both silent for a while, staring up at the black, toxic cloud gradually dissipating in the sky.

Chapter 39

The next morning, Girl and I visit the Redbank Artists' Market in the hope of discovering more clues as to the location of her stolen statue.

Wooden trestle tables spill out across the Town Square and are dressed with the wares and creations of local shop owners and artists. It is a colourful and vibrant celebration of art.

"This is great," says Girl, smiling broadly. She tucks a strand of her blonde hair behind her ear. It is hard to read her facial expression beneath her sunglasses but I get the feeling that she is feeling at home here.

I push up my sunglasses, adjusting them across the bridge of my nose. My scalp is itching a little. It takes all my concentration not to scratch it for fear of my red wig falling off.

The market is very busy. There is a general buzz of excitement as visitors discover new art pieces and wares. Girl grabs my hand and helps me to swerve passed groups of people visiting stalls.

I follow her towards a stunning white marquee, embroidered with silver stars.

Whoever owns it has exquisite taste in design.

"I know whose stall this is," Girl smiles slyly. "It's Sophie's."

As we draw closer to the entrance of the marquee, I hear the sound of tribal music playing inside. It has an upbeat rhythm and Girl begins to dance.

"Dance with me, Adira," Girl smiles.

I groove along with the beat and we bump our hips together, laughing happily.

"I thought I heard your voices," I turn sharply to see Sophie standing at the entrance to the marquee. She is wearing a pair of glasses and her hair has been parted into pigtails, which swing above her shoulders. Her gold midi dress wraps around her body snugly, showing off a little cleavage. I can't help but be mesmerised by her beauty. Feeling my stare, Sophie turns her gaze towards me, a small smile forming on her lips.

Girl is still dancing, her arms waving in the air. "Hi Sophie!" She calls out. "The music is great!"

Sophie breaks her gaze, shifting her attention to Girl. "I'm glad you like it," she smiles. "Hidu and I grew up dancing to this music. We used to play it during the summer festival, once we had gathered our harvests."

"How lovely," I say. "What did you harvest?"

Sophie's eyes widen in surprise at my interest. "A range of things," a thoughtful expression crosses her face. "We had a communal garden at our place in Mira and the villagers shared in its bountiful harvest each season."

Girl stops dancing. "Sophie and Hidu are avid gardeners," she smiles at Sophie. "They both have green thumbs. The fruits and vegetables they grew back home were really something. I remember one year Hidu won an award for the best watermelon at the summer festival."

"Yes, he did," Sophie smiles warmly. She waves us towards her. "Come and have a look at my display."

We follow Sophie inside the marquee and are greeted with a cozy, star lit room. On small benches, Sophie has placed single works of art: a pineapple sculpture, a felt hat, a gold and blue striped ceramic vase ... the works are beautiful.

"Wow!" Girl exclaims, running her fingers across a small cat sculpture. "These works are amazing!"

"Aren't they?" Sophie agrees. "The artists are happy for me to sell them at this stall."

I scan the tent quickly, spotting a small bench, which holds Sophie's bag and an EFTPOS machine. Underneath it, sits a cardboard box.

Girl meets my gaze and I point my head towards the bench. Spotting the box, she nods, understanding.

"Tell me more about this cat sculpture, Sophie," Girl says. "Are you okay if we take it outside so I can view it in clearer light?"

"Sure," Sophie smiles, her eyes lighting up at Girl's interest. She faces me. "Feel free to keep looking around Adira, we'll return soon."

"Thanks, I will," I say.

Sophie smiles at me. "Yay! Great to hear you're going by your real name again, Adira." She follows Girl outside the marquee.

I wait a couple of seconds, keeping an eye on the tent entrance. All is clear. Taking a deep breath, I dash over to the small bench and drop onto my knees. Pulling the cardboard box out from under the bench, I unfold the open flaps and gasp in surprise at the content.

It is a gorgeous, emerald green evening dress, which feels so soft to touch as it is made of fine silk. Two golden arm straps contrast beautifully against the deep green of the bodice, which flows into a long skirt exquisitely designed with a silk brocade of swirling golden cloud and wave totems. It makes the dress appear as though it has stepped out of a fairy tale.

Laying the dress out onto the small bench, I feel a twang in my heart. This dress would have been a precious garment to the person who made it. It is obviously another dress that Sophie is expected to create counterfeit totem patterns from.

Retrieving my phone from my pocket, I zoom in and take photos of the dress. It will upset Girl terribly when she sees that another garment has been stolen from a family in Mira.

I hear laughter outside the tent and lift the dress gently, popping it back into the box. Just as I kick the box under the table, I spot Girl entering the marquee. She has one eyebrow raised and I nod, confirming that all is clear.

Glancing across the marquee, I am drawn to a painting of a garden displayed on a small easel. Walking towards it, I take in the gorgeous, naturalistic sunflowers and azaleas in the foreground of a small, grassy garden with a duck pond.

"Here we are," Sophie says as she enters the marquee. "I'm glad you like the cat statue, Girl."

"Yes, I do," Girl smiles. "It's given me some ideas for my own work."

"Good," I feel Sophie's presence and turn to stare at her. She is stroking the cat statue and staring at the painting of the garden. "It's a lovely concept, isn't it, the garden?" Sophie points to the small, wooden cottage in the background of the picture. "Imagine being able to live somewhere that peaceful for as long as you like," she says, mesmerised by the image. "With no one to take your life away from you." Her eyes become intense and she tightens her grip on the cat.

I study Sophie in this moment. She is very troubled, as though she has a dark story wrestling in her heart. She just needs the right amount of coaxing to be able to talk …

I inhale a deep breath. "I would love to live somewhere like that," I speak from my heart. "Mitch and I have always imagined having our own peaceful place to raise our family."

Sophie stares at me with wide eyes. "It's a dream that isn't always easy to achieve," she sighs. "My parents had to pay a very expensive fee to the Emperor every year in order to obtain land use rights of a modest patch of land in Mira. I grew up watching my mother and father work on the land every day, from sunrise to sunset. They were avid gardeners and grew a range of fruits and vegetables that they would serve at our table. I grew up spoilt with such healthy and beautiful food, nurtured by their hearts and hands.

"I spent a lot of time on the land with my parents, preferring to be outside than confined to our home. It was a tiny, makeshift wooden log cabin that my father built by hand. It provided the barest of shelter, especially during severe weather conditions. It was also too small to fit our family, especially as Hidu and I grew older.

"We were a poor family and my parents aged quickly, trying to put enough food on the table. We heard stories of other families within the village who also struggled to live each day and my mother preoccupied herself with trying to find a solution.

"When I was a teenager, my mother built a small garden plot, bordered with some cedar wood logs. Hidu and I helped her to plant a range of fruit and vegetable seeds, such as: tomatoes, lettuce, cucumbers, beans and watermelon.

"Once the produce had grown, my parents enabled the villagers to access the garden plot and to donate a small amount of money to purchase produce. The garden plot became known as a communal one, which serviced the needs of the people of the village who would have otherwise remained in starvation. It felt good to provide relief for men, women and children and to watch their health begin to improve.

"A year later, my parents' land use rights reached its maximum time frame of 25 years. I had just turned 23 and had committed myself to looking after the garden and ensuring that the villagers had enough to eat. I felt that nurturing others was something that I was born to do and couldn't imagine not doing that.

"One morning, a messenger arrived on our doorstep and handed my father a sealed letter from the Emperor. My father's eyes widened as he shut the front door and ripped open the seal. As he read the letter, tears formed in his eyes and his hands shook. Unable to speak, he handed the letter to my mother and dropped to the ground on his knees.

"I still remember my mother reading the letter. It said:

> "*Dear Mr Gway and Mrs Saria Yang,*
>
> "*I write this letter to order you and your family to evacuate the land you have leased on Yeva Road. The land will be presented as a gift to my cousin, who will use it as he so wishes.*
>
> "*Your committed upkeep of the land is appreciated. I wish you well on your future endeavours.*
>
> "*Emperor Laynton of Mira.*

"My mother gasped in shock and the letter fluttered slowly to the floor. Hidu and I ran to her aid, helping her to sit on the wooden chair.

"As the night progressed, my mother became ill, gaining a fever that made her delirious. My heart pounded with fear as I pressed wet cotton cloths over her forehead, desperately trying to cool her down. She cried out and pushed me away, afraid of the stranger who was helping her. It hurt me to see her so confused and disoriented. My mother was everything to me and I couldn't imagine life without her.

"The next morning, my mother's fever had settled. While my father held my mother's hand, she stared at him deeply in the eyes. "Gway," she said with strain in her voice.

My father reached out to stroke her hair. "What is it, my love?"

My mother waved her hand in the air. "Bring my children to me."

"My father waved Hidu and I closer and we sat with him. My heart cried while I stared into my mother's life drained eyes.

"Mother's voice was fighting for its strength. "The world will keep changing," she gasped. "Find a way to ground yourself and fight to live." Her last words drifted away and her eyes began to close.

"My father stroked my mother's face lovingly. "Saria?" He stared at her. "Are you with us?" My mother was very still, unable to respond. "Saria!" My father shook my mother by the shoulders, trying to wake her.

"Hidu grabbed Father gently by the arms. "Father," he pulled him away.

"Placing my ear to Mother's chest, I listened carefully. There was a heart beat but it was weak. Tears fell like a river down my cheeks as I realised that she didn't have much longer to live.

"Hidu's eyes were wild. "Is she okay?" He asked.

"My own eyes widened with shock. "Her heart is faint," I gasped, holding onto the bed frame.

"Hidu jumped erratically. "I'll get the doctor!" He dashed across the floor, almost tripping over my father as he fled from the room.

"It took a long time for Dr Jexa to arrive. He was one of the local villagers who had been purchasing our produce and had dedicated his care to those who were impoverished.

"I removed the cloth I placed on mother's forehead and stood up, letting Dr Jexa tend to her. He checked her alertness with a torch light and got no response. "Hmmm," his tone was serious. "She is unconscious."

"My father began to sob and his pain lashed at my heart. I stared down at the ground, trying to come to terms with what was happening.

"Dr Jexa checked Mother's heart with a stethoscope and shook his head. "A very weak heart," he said softly, turning to face my father. "Mr Yang, I am afraid she does not have long now."

"My father nodded, unable to speak.

"Hidu paced the ground, inhaling and exhaling short, sharp breaths. "She's got to be alright," his voice was strong. "I blame the Emperor for this. He can't take her away from us."

"My heart burned with rage. "No, he can't," I agreed, "He has no right to her life."

"My father's eyes widened. "Please," he begged. "Keep your anger in check, both of you. This is not the time or place to express it. It would hurt your poor mother to hear you speak that way."

"Making eye contact, we both lowered our heads in shame. I could still feel anger radiating through my body and walked outside to get some fresh air.

"It wasn't until the early hours of the next morning that I felt a hand on my shoulder. Looking up, I met my father's traumatised gaze. "I'm sorry," he barely whispered, shaking with shock.

"I sobbed with all my heart, throwing my arms around my father in a tight embrace. "I'm sorry too," I blurted, sensing his vulnerability.

"My mother had a solemn cremation, attended by many villagers who had become fond of her over the years. Later, Father, Hidu and I visited the forest and sprinkled mother's ashes over the roots of her favourite cedar tree. *This tree grounds me*, Mother would often say. *It reminds me that I am alive in this uncertain world.*

"After covering the ashes with dirt, I reached for my father and brother's hand. We prayed together for mother's spirit to find peace.

"Afterwards, I stared at Father and Hidu. "What now?" I asked them both. "What do we all do?"

"Father stood tall. "Ground ourselves," he replied.

"Hidu punched his fist into the air. "Fight to live," he said passionately.

"Standing, I embraced them both. "Mother would be proud of us," I said softly. "Let's pack our things and work out what comes next."

"We dismantled our home. It broke my heart to watch it become reduced to a scattered pile of plant matter.

"Grabbing my bag, I stood with my father and brother, breathing in my last breath of our land. *Farewell, the only home I've ever known.*

"My father grabbed both our hands. "Let's go," he said. "Let's find that ground."

"We walked away, not looking back, our hearts and minds considering what future we were left to face." As Sophie completes her story, she stares down at the ground sadly.

"I'm sorry Sophie," says Girl. "It would have been so hard."

"It still is," Sophie sighs. "The Emperor has continued to increase the land use tax and this has made it very difficult for people to live in Mira." She scratches her head. "I fear for the lives of many who cannot support themselves adequately. Hidu tells me there has been no replacement of our communal garden with anything that may support villagers who are in great need of help."

Girl runs her fingers through her hair in frustration. "No wonder the resistance is growing stronger," she sounds annoyed. "The people are desperate to see justice prevail." She throws one hand in the air. "It's just a pity that many of our people believe that the horrid Petoys are their saviours from all of this."

Sophie's gaze is distant, staring ahead. "Yes," she agrees. "Some believe the Petoys will help save them. That is, until they discover what is involved in joining their resistance."

I study Sophie, who stands with her arms wrapped around herself. I can feel her inner torment radiating from her as she frowns and bites her lip.

"Good afternoon market vendors and visitors," a male voice calls over a loudspeaker. "Please gather around the centre of the Town Square for the reveal of this month's feature art work. This special event will be taking place in five minutes."

"Let's go," Sophie turns to face us. "Something positive to see."

"Sounds great," Girl falls into stride beside us as we head towards the display.

A decent sized crowd has gathered in the centre of the Town Square. They are pointing at a display, which is covered by a large black cloth. A buzz of anticipation erupts as people try to guess what sort of art work will be revealed.

I feel eyes upon me and turn to face a tall man with bronze toned skin and dark brown eyes. It is Felibo. The hood of his grey jacket falls back from his black, spiky hair.

Realising that I am watching him, Felibo turns away and disappears into the crowd.

An alarm bell rings in my head. Felibo has found me again. I will need to stay alert and ensure that he doesn't catch me.

Suddenly, a bright, happy tune blasts through the loud speaker. It is dominated by the loud screeching of feedback. I cover my ears and grit my teeth as the noise is grating on me.

I feel a nudge from Girl and look up. A tall man is approaching the art display. Two guards flank him as he walks, which emphasises that he is a very important person. The man's dark brown hair is shining in the sun and there is a glow of excitement in his olive complexion. As he approaches the crowd, I identify the man as Mayor Rahi. He is wearing a dark blue suit and a silver shirt. The outfit is complemented with a dark blue bow tie, which is tied crookedly, adding an element of humour to his presence. Smiling charismatically at the audience, the Mayor stops in front of the display, waving his guards away into the background. This is his moment in the spotlight.

Waving at the crowd, Mayor Rahi's smile spreads even wider across his lips. "Hello," he says. "It's lovely to be here at the Redbank Artists'

Market." He flutters his eyelashes and smiles for the cameras, which are clicking madly around us. He knows just how to play the media.

Once the buzz has died down, Mayor Rahi's face switches to a solemn expression. He steps closer to a lectern on which hangs the same poster we saw at the Mayor's office the other day. *Vote 1 for Mayor Rahi. A Leader who Empowers*, screams the sign.

Mayor Rahi clears his throat and launches into his speech. "I have enjoyed being out on the streets and chatting to so many of our wonderful people recently. I heard their inspirational stories and their needs to express their identity. It is no secret that the blow to our red gum commodity has affected many deeply." He places his hand on his heart, his commercial gesture. I glance around me. Many of the people are sucked in.

I inhale a deep breath of anticipation. In only a matter of seconds, Rahi will unleash his political jargon.

Mayor Rahi smiles charismatically and rants on: "Here in Redbank, we do all we can to empower the people. The feature art work that we have chosen to display this month highlights how creative our natural commodity can be." Rahi turns to face the display. As he does so, a drum roll bursts through the loud speaker briefly and cuts short. Rahi lifts the black cloth dramatically, revealing a statue enclosed in a glass case.

I feel Girl crash against me. She is shaking uncontrollably. "Oh no!" She gasps, nearly falling over.

It takes me a moment to register that there, displaying itself conspicuously, sits Girl's red gum sculpture.

I grab hold of Girl, holding her protectively. What a shock this must be for her right now.

Mayor Rahi gestures proudly towards the statue. "This art piece speaks of identity, of life. The girl in the boat continues to sail, even through the crashing waves." He inhales a deep breath and raises his hand in the air, forming a fist. "We will thrive!" He pledges as he thumps his chest with his fist. "Our wood has not diminished yet. This artist has taken its rarity in our city and revealed its soul." He pauses and stares out at the sky, appearing to be thoughtful and reflective for a moment in time.

Audience members cheer, pumping their fists into the air.

After a moment, Mayor Rahi turns to face the audience. "We need to do all we can to protect our fading, red gum resource," he says. "This decision has not come easy. Due to the violence exhibited down at the forest towards our villagers the other day, we have passed a legislation to ban all existing logging of red gum in Redbank." Mayor Rahi clutches both hands to his chest. "We hope that this action will help us save our last trees and begin a replanting program in order to restore our forest and Spirit River to their former states of glory." His eyes peel the audience, awaiting their reaction.

Suddenly, a chant bursts through the audience. "No more bans! No more taxes! Yes to progress!" A number of men and women wearing Petoy head scarves step out of the crowd and march towards the display cabinet.

Mayor Rahi's face whitens and he steps back, unsure of what to do. The two guards grab hold of his arms and escort him away from the danger. I watch as they usher him into a long, black limousine.

"No more bans! No more taxes! Yes to progress!" My attention is turned back to the chanting. The protesters are flocked together in front of the cabinet and are raising their fists in the air. "Mayor Rahi is another leader who is holding back progress. We must resist his ban! Join us!"

Several members of the audience cheer and jump up to join the protest group. Two Petoy men slap large white stickers labelled with bright red statements: *Fight against tax! Support Progress!* on the display cabinet.

"It's the resistance," Sophie whispers. "It's here now, too."

The chanting stops and a young Petoy man steps forward. His dark eyes are narrowed and piercing. "Have you seen this Girl?" He asks in a foreboding voice as he holds up the pamphlet displaying the image of Girl pushing her cart in Mira.

Voices raise in the audience as people turn to face each other, to ask if they know of the Girl in the photograph.

Girl leans firmly against my side. Her hand shoots across her mouth, stifling her terrified scream.

"Take a deep breath," I say softly. "We need to keep you safe right now."

I am in a state of shock myself.

The Petoy man's face twists into a devilish expression. "This statue has been created by the girl in this photo. If you do see her, let us Petoys know. We cannot let her become the future chief of silk in Mira. She will maintain a high silk tax tradition and that will kill us all off."

There are shocked gasps from the crowd.

The man sticks the pamphlet down in the middle of the display and joins the protesters.

"No more bans! No more taxes! Yes to progress!"

Girl is inconsolable right now. She is shaking and tears are dripping down her cheeks.

The shock dissipates and I realise the danger that we are in. Grabbing Girl's hand, I stare into her eyes. "We are going to leave now, okay?"

Girl nods. She appears very small and vulnerable right now.

Putting my arm around Girl, I meet Sophie's gaze. "Take care," I say to her. "Keep as far away from the Petoys as you can."

Sophie lowers her head. "I will," she says softly. Looking up again, she touches Girl gently on the shoulder. "I am so sorry, Girl," she says, looking worried. "Please hide away the best you can."

Girl nods, unable to meet Sophie's gaze.

"Come on," I say, beginning to lead Girl away from the crowd. "Let's get you out of here safely now." She is too weak to move on her own, so I hold her against me, dodging passed the scattered bodies.

My heart pounds wildly in my chest. Girl is in grave danger and I hope that I can keep her safe.

Chapter 40

Sitting on a grassy patch in the forest, Girl stares at me sadly. "It breaks my heart that the Petoys are doing this," her voice cracks. "Silk is the heart of Mira. My mother showed me how beautiful the simplicity of life was when I watched her harvest silk from a silk worm. It was amazing to watch the silk fibre unravel from its mouth.

"My mother was against the traditional methods of soaking the silk worm's cocoon into boiling water in order to separate the silk thread. She valued the life of the blessed, tiny creatures that gave her the exquisite fibre and loved to nurture and watch them grow.

"Such loving care for the silk worms led to a high quality silk fibre and I would be mesmerised as I watched my mother spin and weave it into exquisite cloth.

"I would help my mother to design garments with the silk cloth and was amazed at the beautiful dresses, sashes, shirts and scarves that would evolve. She taught me how to prepare the indigo dye for the Emperor's silk and I would enjoy watching the cloth eventually transform into a rich blue colour.

"As a young child, to me silk was magic. It was an ever changing fibre, that seemed to survive no matter what happened to it. You could spin it, weave it, dye it, manipulate it and it would always remain strong as silk. It taught me that change was not scary and that at times, it required resilience to survive it. It is a lesson I have always carried with me throughout life." Girl smiles through her tears. "I miss my mother so much," she says softly. "She has been my source of strength and comfort for so long that I feel lost without her."

I hold out my arms, drawing Girl into my embrace. "I understand," I say softly, feeling the warmth of my own mother in my heart. "No-one can ever replace your mother, it is a truly special bond."

Girl nods, wiping away her tears. "You know," she says, sitting back in her seat. "I think of all the women who have been producing silk for centuries in Mira. It is not an easy task, you know, in fact it is very laborious.

"Women in Mira are poorly recognised for their roles in silk production. Men are predominately the merchants of silk and are often complimented for the quality of the silk product created by women.

"I used to watch my mother hand over her silk designs to my father. She would greet him farewell at the front door when he left for merchant business. I could see how hard it was for her to remain a silent partner, unable to share what work she had done to complete the silk garment or to be present to experience the joy of its trade."

"That's hard," I say, feeling compassion for Girl's mother.

"In Aisha's time, things were a little different," Girl says. "Empress Mira ruled Mira and she was a little more supportive of women in leadership." Digging into her pocket, she retrieves Aisha's journal. "Would you like to read an entry?"

"Yes please," I say, accepting the journal from Girl. Aisha's familiar writing is scrawled across the page. It reads:

Autumn, 1276

The days pass, ringing a long, loud sound that deafens my ears. I try to block out the noise, to make it go away but it persists. I know that it is the sound of my aching, broken heart.

My dreams are fretful and I wake up panting. Staring silently across the room, I believe that I see my father, sitting in his favourite chair. My heart clenches with pain as I realise that it is only a memory. One that I wish would never fade.

Makeshift Girl: The Secret Heritage Trail

Many days pass where I shuffle through the house and cuddle my father's favourite blanket, breathing in his special scent.

Until finally, one evening I wake up and realise that I am alone.

The loud noise begins to dissipate, fading away into silence. Standing slowly, I wrap myself in my father's blanket and swing open the front door.

The night air is cool with a gentle breeze. I inhale large, grateful gulps of fresh air.

A strange shape sitting on the patio startles me. It moves suddenly and I jump high into the air.

"Who's there?" I ask, stepping back and dropping the blanket. I form my hands into fists, ready to defend myself.

The shape stirs and awakens. It is Kirano, leaning against the wall of the hut. His eyes shine as he realises that it is me.

My heart fills with love as I watch him sitting there. His voice had journeyed its ways through the holes in the hut for a number of days, trying to reach me in my mourning. I could hear his words, yet they sounded distant. My mind was too plagued with the persistent noise of heart ache.

Bending down, I reach out and touch Kirano gently on the cheek. "Hello," I say gently. "You waited for me."

Kirano nods, sitting up slowly. "Yes," his voice is gentle. "I've been so worried about you. I'm here, willing to help you in any way you need."

My eyes brim with tears. "Thank you," I manage to say. "It is good to see you."

"Aisha," Kirano stands and takes my hands in his. "I will always care for you." He pulls me closer into his warm embrace.

I close my eyes, enjoying the feeling of his arms around me. I have been isolated in the hut, shutting myself away from the world. I savour his warmth and his care. It soothes my heart.

Kirano crooks my chin up with his finger and stares into my eyes. "Are you alright?" He asks concernedly.

I stare at him, feeling the sadness sweep over me again. It makes me tremble and tears begin to spill freely down my cheeks. "I miss my father," I choke on my words.

Kirano pulls me into his embrace again and I cry and cry. After a short while, I feel myself being lifted and realise that he is carrying me outside, towards the forest.

I hear the sound of horse's hooves, galloping in the distance.

"Kirano!" I look back, my eyes falling on two Petoys who are riding their horses towards us.

Kirano drops me onto the ground. "Run, Aisha, run!" Reaching into his belt hook, he withdraws his bow.

I am still for a moment, staring at him. "I can't leave you, Kirano."

"You must," Kirano's voice is firm as he retrieves an arrow from his quiver and prepares to fire. "I will fend them off."

Picking up the hem of my long skirt, I run. The ground is firm and I can feel my feet striking against it. My heart feels as though it is going to burst through my rib cage.

I can hear the sound of galloping and turn quickly, my heart stopping in my chest. My gaze falls on one of the Petoys, charging on his horse.

Turning away, I stumble and my feet slip out from under me. I am too tired to move now. Sitting on a patch of grass, I inhale short and sharp breaths.

It takes only a few seconds for the Petoy man and his horse to reach me. As their gait slows to a trot, I recognise his familiar face.

"Well hello again," Alzat smiles slyly. Dismounting his horse, he takes long, confident strides towards me. "No wolf this time, eh?"

I meet Alzat's gaze, my heart weighing heavily in my chest. He has found me.

"Have you lost your voice, pretty face?" Alzat's voice creeps into my very being, making the hair stand up on the back of my neck.

I say nothing, watching him.

Grabbing hold of a strand of my hair, Alzat pulls my head back firmly. I inhale a sharp breath, yet still I do not speak.

"Speak, pretty face, tell me your desires," Alzat pulls me up onto my feet.

I meet his gaze and stare silently into his eyes, which burn with intensity while he waits for my reply.

All I can feel is the pain of loss eating away at my heart. If I wait long enough, I may find a way to walk away from this mad man.

"I want to see the sunrise," I say, trying to appeal to his human spirit. "It will be a break from the darkness and ash that I see all around me. Can you see it too, Alzat?"

Alzat nods, his gaze becoming distant as he stares out at the sky. "Everywhere," *he says hoarsely, loosening his grip on my hair and lowering his head.* "I buried my brother yesterday."

I cross my eyebrows, feeling a stab of pain in my heart. "I am sorry for your loss," *I say softly.* "Mira is not what it used to be."

"No," *Alzat shakes his head.* "Blood seeps its way through the veins of the city now. It shows no care or remorse. Instead, the empire continues to chew its own fat, taking money from the people who cannot afford to live here." *His eyes flash menacingly as he faces me again.* "You are the new Chief of silk, yes?" *His voice is dark again, penetrating my brain.*

"Yes," *I shake, knowing my fate.*

Alzat grabs me forcefully around the waist. "You are an asset to us Petoys," *he breathes.* "You have links to the wealth of the empire. You will help us gain riches." *He grabs hold of the button on top of my tunic.* "That is, after I've had my way with you first."

As he tears at the buttons of my tunic, a single tear rolls down my cheek. It is hard to say what I feel the most sorry for: the people of Mira or myself?

Alzat stands back, staring at my naked body with appreciation. "You will make beautiful children," *he says, stepping forward.*

I inhale another sharp breath and close my eyes. I feel my stomach churning with fear.

"Ahhh!" *I hear Alzat scream suddenly.*

My eyes flutter open and I watch as Alzat clutches his chest, which has been hit by an arrow. He falls to the ground.

Pulling my tunic over my body, I peer over my shoulder.

There stands Kirano. He lowers his bow, staring at me with concern.

Bobbing down next to Alzat, I check his neck for a pulse. There is none.

More tears begin to fall down my cheeks. All I can feel is deep sorrow. Another man has died in Mira.

"Aisha," *Kirano steps slowly towards me and reaches out his hand.* "You are safe now, come with me."

Standing, I begin to step back, holding my tunic tightly around me. I do not wish to go anywhere with Kirano right now.

"Aisha?" *Kirano sounds surprised.*

"No more death," *I say, stepping back further. I am shaking and my head is spinning.*

Kirano grabs hold of my arms and rubs them gently. "Aisha, you are not thinking clearly right now."

I stare directly into Kirano's eyes. "Yes I am," *I say firmly.* "Leave me be."

"What ... ?" *Kirano's eyes widen with shock.* "Let me take you home, Aisha. I will look after you."

"No," *I shake my head firmly. Turning around, I stumble away, across the dirt ground and head towards the grassland.*

I button up my tunic as I walk, my hands cold and fingers stiff. My mind is plagued with a darkness that I am not sure will ever leave me.

Suddenly, I hear a piercing scream. "Stop them!" *A female voice cries.* "Bring my falcon back to me!"

I stop in my tracks, staring at the tall woman with long brown hair that is floating through the wind. Her blue eyes are narrowed intensely as she points at two men angrily. It is the Empress of Mira.

Gazing behind her, across the grassland, my eyes fall upon two men who are sipping drinks from a flask and swaying about, clearly intoxicated. One of the men holds a shot gun in his hands, which he is aiming up into the air.

There, above us all, flies a bird. Its bluish grey wings are spanned beautifully as it soars through the sky.

The man with the gun laughs and fires a shot into the air.

"No!" *Cries the Empress.*

The bird is startled in flight and flutters its feathers. Swooping down, it tries to locate a safe place to land. As it approaches, I hear the powerful beating of its long tapered wings. It is a majestic peregrine falcon, exuding a strength and vitality that makes my heart soar with admiration.

"I've got you, falcon," the man with the gun snarls, aiming to fire at the bird.

The falcon meets my gaze, its yellow eye rings widening in fear at the sound of the man's voice. I raise my arm silently, willing it to land on me, to save it from its tragic fate.

In one small, precious moment, I see the falcon's dark eyes flicker with relief. Lowering its black hooded head, it swoops down low and lands upon my arm.

I inhale a sharp breath of surprise. The falcon has trusted me. Staring at its face, I admire its beauty.

Adjusting its sitting position, the falcon's sharp talons press into my skin. It begins to preen its creamy white breast feathers with its precious yellow beak.

I feel eyes upon me and turn to see the Empress with her hands on her knees and her mouth dropped opened in shock. Beginning to move, she stumbles towards me. "You have saved beautiful Gira," the Empress gushes as she reaches me. Holding out her hand, she helps the falcon to perch on her fingers. She meets my gaze with an appreciative smile. "How can I repay you for this blessing?"

I cock my head to the side, studying the Empress. "Put a stop to the madness of death," I request.

The Empress' gaze softens. "My most fervent wish," she nods. "My barons over here have decided to betray me. They let out Gira without my permission and set her out to hunt."

"It appears as though Gira was being hunted too," I say, staring at the barons.

"Yes," the Empress is angry.

I make eye contact with the baron who holds the gun. I am not afraid of his misplaced aggression. "You are intoxicated," I tell him. "You nearly made a very grave mistake."

"Yes, you did, Tyrol," the Empress' voice is stern.

Tyrol narrows his gaze and raises his gun, ready to fire once more. "Well, I am about to make an even bigger one, crazy bird ladies. Maybe I should shoot all of you?" His laugh is sinister, making my blood crawl.

The Empress places her hands on her hips. "You will be punished for this," she seethes.

"We are already punished, Empress," Tyrol says aggressively. "What are we in Mira meant to do with the likes of you, a woman leader? You are weak, taxing us so harshly for land and silk trade. You also deny us the privilege of using the falcons for sport and trade. Bring back the days your father was the leader of this city and the world was a more just place to live in."

The Empress' eyes flash with rage. "Hold your tongue," she says firmly. "Any more words from either of you and I will have you beheaded."

Tyrol snickers. "We'll see about that," he snarls. "What do you think, Lyle?" He asks the other baron.

Lyle's long, red hair falls into his eyes, making it hard for him to see. He rubs his chin with his hand, thinking. "It's time for justice," he says sternly. "You, Empress, are losing favour with your people. Your city is slowly turning against you. It won't be long before there will be armed men outside your palace walls."

The Empress stands tall, her gaze strong and focused. "I know all about the resistance that is forming," she says, raising her eyebrows. "Those who are foolish enough to try to destroy my empire will be severely punished. That does include both of you, should you choose to do so." She waves her hand dismissively. "Lock them away, Bitano," she commands her guard. "Tomorrow I will enforce their punishment."

"It will be my pleasure, your Imperial Majesty," Bitano steps forward and grabs hold of Tyrol, snatching the gun from his hands. "Don't move!" He orders, tying the baron's hands behind his back.

Lyle dashes, trying to escape the guard. In five strides, Bitano reaches him and pulls his arms firmly behind his back. "Stay still," he orders as he ties the baron's arms together with rope.

"Walk now!" Bitano orders, commanding the barons to walk ahead of him. Two soldiers who are riding horses accompany them.

Makeshift Girl: The Secret Heritage Trail

After the men have left, the Empress lifts her hand until her gaze is level with the falcon's. "Are you alright, Gira?" *She seems genuinely concerned about the bird.*

Gira presses her head against the Empress' chin. I watch as the Empress closes her eyes and a content smile crosses her lips. Warmth kindles in my heart as I witness the precious beauty of this moment of love.

The Empress' eyes flutter open and she meets my gaze. "I have banned falconry in Mira," she says. "Only four of my father's falcons have survived the sport and the demand for their trade. I treasure them with all my heart. I do not wish to see anymore die."

I nod, understanding. "Life is precious," I say. "My father passed away recently."

"Your father?" The Empress raises her eyebrows. "I am deeply sorry for your loss. Do you mind telling me who he was?"

"Sefra, the Chief of silk," I say, my voice catching in my throat.

The Empress places her free hand on my shoulder. "A much loved man," her eyes fill with sadness. "He will be greatly missed."

"Yes, he will," I choke on my words and tears fill my eyes.

The Empress rubs my shoulder, trying to console me. "Sefra's memory will always be alive in the heart of Mira, Aisha," she says softly.

"Thank you," I smile weakly and swipe away my tears. I am surprised that she knows my name.

"It is late," the Empress stares up at the sky. "We have much to discuss about your new role as the Chief of silk. I also need some help taking care of my falcons." Her tone is direct and decisive. "Can I invite you to stay at the palace for a couple of nights? You will be safe there and cared for. It is dangerous for a young woman to be alone at any time in Mira now." The Empress glances at me, her eyes filled with concern.

I exhale a deep breath, relieved at the Empress' offer of care. "That would be wonderful," I smile. "Thank you for your kindness, your Imperial Majesty." I curtsy with appreciation.

"It's the least that I can do," the Empress smiles warmly. Turning around, she commands her footman: "Marti, dress two horses for return to the palace."

"Yes, your Imperial Majesty, I will," Marti replies, his grey eyes shining.

Meeting my gaze once more, the Empress' smile is bright. "Take Gira," she smiles, placing the falcon on my shoulder. "She really likes you and will keep you company on the way back to the palace."

"Thank you," I say, touched by the Empress' faith in me.

"The horses are ready, your Imperial Majesty," Marti leads two horses towards us.

"Let's go!" Empress Mira commands.

I feel warmth nestling in my heart as I step forward with Gira on my shoulder. I have some beautiful company for a while. It makes me feel less alone in this dark, mad world.

A small smile crosses my lips as I realise that I have gained the trust of the Empress. My father would be very proud of me.

Shutting the journal, I stare down at the ground. Aisha's story resonates strongly with me right now. I have spent most of my life fleeing from the Petoys.

"Are you okay, Adira?" Girl asks.

"Yes," I manage to say. "I'm just absorbing Aisha's story."

It is silent for a moment, each of us drifting into our own thoughts.

"Let's make a wish," Girl says, picking a couple of dandelion flowers. She hands one to me. "It will help us to continue through this madness."

Holding the dandelion flower in my hand, I consider all that I wish for. Deep in my heart, I know the fundamental thing that I desire. Closing my eyes, I blow gently. The wish escapes my lips in a silent whisper: *I wish for us all to be able to tread confidently through our lives danger free.*

Chapter 41

Later that afternoon, I discover Jacquelyn and Zac sitting on the forest ground, surrounded by a trail of severed red gum trees. Tears are falling down Jacquelyn's cheeks as she strokes a discarded tree branch.

When Zac meets my gaze with his troubled eyes, he jumps up, ready to defend them both. "Who are you?" His voice bellows.

Jacquelyn glances up, her eyes softening when she meets my gaze. "Adira!" She sighs with relief. "I'm so glad that you've come to see us."

"You know her?" Zac steps back, shifting his gaze back to Jacquelyn.

I sigh with relief. He is not going to attack us after all.

"Yes," Jacquelyn smiles warmly, her eyes shining. "Zac, this is my dear friend, Adira, who I have known for a long time. We used to play hide and seek in the forest together when we were children."

Zac stares at me with a serious expression. "Have we met somewhere before?" He asks me, his mind churning through the possibilities.

"No," I shake my head and exhale a deep, brave breath. "You've been too busy threatening my husband, haven't you Zac?"

Zac's gaze shifts away uncomfortably. "Your husband?"

"Mitch Cazon," my words hang in the air. "I believe you call him Wave."

Zac jumps and fidgets with his fingers. "Wave!" He sounds surprised. "Yes, I have had a few strong words with him recently. What's it to you?"

"Zac!" Jacquelyn gasps incredulously. "Show some respect."

I walk around Zac in a slow circle. "You are one scared man, aren't you Zac?"

"Scared?" I can sense Zac's tension as his hands begin to shake.

"Yes, so scared, you won't even tell your wife what you are up to." I stand before him, meeting his gaze.

Jacquelyn spins around and faces her husband. "Is this true, Zac?" She asks.

Girl steps out of the shadows, an eerie presence in the dim light. "Say yes, Zac," she says softly. "Tell her what you are really after, go on …"

"You!" Zac jumps up and grabs Girl's shoulder. "I could hand you in right now," he breathes menacingly.

"Zac … ?" Jacquelyn is shaking. "What's got into you?"

"You can't and you won't," Girl says, pushing Zac's hand away firmly. "I am far more valuable to you than your clan friends." Her voice is calm and in control.

Zac stands his ground. "Yes, you are valuable," he sneers. "You are my ticket out of this mess. If I just hand you in, the Petoys will finally destroy you and put an end to all of this."

Girl laughs harshly, her voice bouncing off the surrounding trees. "You think I'm scared of you?" She seethes. "Or of any of the Petoys?" Girl lowers her gaze, staring darkly into Zac's eyes. "I have trekked the terrain for thousands of miles, fleeing persecution and hoping to find a way to use my future power to save the heritage of Mira's silk trade." She exhales a deep breath. "What I have discovered along the way is much devastation." She takes another step closer, pointing towards Jacquelyn. "Suffering that now extends itself from Mira to the people and precious resources of Redbank, too."

It is quiet for a moment as we all stare at Jacquelyn. She has dropped to her knees and is hugging a severed tree trunk. Her sobs cut through the stillness of the air, striking my heart with remorse.

"You want to put an end to all of this, Zac?" Girl's voice is strong. "Then help us to stop the thefts, the loggings and the counterfeit trade. The Petoy clan is tiny in a world filled with so many wonderful, living spirits who deserve to live free of trauma and fear." She steps forward and places her hands on Jacquelyn's shoulders. Staring back at Zac, Girl's eyes are glazed. "Life is so short, Zac. If you can help anyone, then help Jacquelyn."

Zac steps back, staring at his wife. He bites into his fist as he watches her cry. "I will do all I can for Jacquey," he sighs. "She is my whole world. I feel so responsible for the pain she is in right now."

"Good," Girl says, surprising Zac. "Let that guilt drive you to make the right decisions."

"How?" Zac shrugs. "I am so caught up in the Petoys' brutality that I can't work out how to walk away from it. If I try to, I will lose Jacquey."

It is silent for a moment as we absorb Zac's words. His fear hangs in the air between us all, engulfing the space. I know this fear, it was in my father, too, pushing him to make all the wrong decisions. He thought he was keeping my mother and I safe. The price he paid for his involvement with the empire was devastating.

Staring at Zac, I consider his situation. He is scared of losing his wife. That fear has consumed him, causing him to make reckless decisions. He is finding himself becoming more deeply involved in the ruthless actions of the Petoys. I need to help him to find a way out of this mess, for both he and Jacquelyn's sakes.

"Zac," I say softly, drawing his gaze towards me. "Let us help you."

Zac's eyes shine with hope. "I wish I had never got involved in all this," he sighs. "Naricia made me an offer that sounded too good to refuse. I had no idea what sort of work it would land me in."

"Your situation is like many other recruits," Girl says. "The Petoys are masters at manipulating people to engage in their resistance movement. They make you feel that your life will be better and safer if you join their cause."

Zac nods, his face relieved. "Yes," he says. "That is exactly what happened. I was promised a handsome salary to support my family. Turns out I am barely paid anything and am threatened with Jacquey's life if I refuse any extra forced labour they impose upon me."

"I am threatened too," Jacquelyn sniffles, staring up at me with teary eyes. "With our arrest for involvement in illegal trade. This is obviously not a charge that I can refute, as I am now involved in designing counterfeit apparel." She sits up, wiping the tears away from her eyes. "I saw some Petoy men logging these trees the other day," she says. "I ran towards them, begging that they stopped. They climbed into their truck and began to chase me. I was nearly run over. Jumping backwards, my heart pounded in my throat as I watched them roar away towards the north end of the forest."

"You didn't tell me that, Jacquey," Zac looks concerned. "I'm sorry I wasn't here for you."

Jacquelyn sighs as she meets Zac's gaze. "You have to go soon, don't you?"

Zac checks his phone. "Yes," he says. "I begin my shift in half an hour."

"Let me tail along," I say. "I can observe you at work and take some photos. It will help us to work out our next steps."

Zac nods, absorbing what I am saying. "Okay," he sighs. "If you think that will work, I would appreciate your help."

"I ask you for one thing in return," I say, my gaze serious.

"What's that?" Zac inhales a sharp breath of uncertainty.

I stand tall, holding Zac's gaze. "You will treat my husband, Mitch kindly and ensure that he is safe at all times, won't you?"

Zac's mouth drops open in surprise. "Of course," he nods vigorously. "I will do all I can to look after him, I promise."

I meet Girl's gaze. "What do you think, should we believe him?" I ask.

Girl shifts her gaze towards Zac. "If we get a single message that Mitch has been harmed in any way while on your watch, we will ensure that you pay the consequences," she commands.

Zac lowers his head. "I hear you," he says. "I understand."

"Good," Girl says. "Now, Jacquelyn, I believe you can help me. I would like to use some remnant red gum bark and branches to create a replica of a statue that Naricia stole from me. Would it be possible to salvage some?"

Jacquelyn's eyes light up. "Yes, I'd love to," she smiles. "It will be nice to see some good fortune result from this tragedy. Let me help you gather what you need," Jacquelyn reaches for Girl's hand.

"Thank you," Girl smiles as she helps Jacquelyn to stand. "I will stay here with Jacquelyn," she says to me. "I have a statue to build and I am sure she can help me."

"Of course," Jacquelyn's lips form a small smile. She seems relieved to be doing something to help. "Lead the way."

Zac and I watch as Girl and Jacquelyn gather red gum tree branches and bark.

After a short while, I hear Zac's voice: "Thank you for agreeing to help us," he says. "You've picked up Jacquey's spirit and mine too. I will let you know my movements in the future so that you can work out a solution."

"That sounds good," I say.

"I am heading north right now, to the Petoys' makeshift lumber yard," Zac narrows his eyes. It's probably best you come along with me in my truck. Your ute will stand out like a sore thumb."

I consider Zac's offer. "Okay," I agree. "I'll go with you."

Zac heads towards his truck. The electric blue lights flash when he unlocks the door. "Hop in!" He calls as he opens the door for me.

I step up into the passenger area and sit down. As Zac settles into his seat, I grab his attention. "I am happy to keep watch," I say. "However, it is important that you pretend that I am not around so that I am not spotted by any Petoys."

"Of course," Zac agrees. "Ready to go?"

"Yes," I say, settling back into my seat. Zac starts the ignition and the truck sputters into life. As he begins to drive, I feel my heart pounding anxiously in my chest. I hope that we might finally discover a way to stop the Petoys' madness.

Chapter 42

When we arrive at the north end of the Redbank forest, the receding evening sun is dappling its light over the land, casting an eerie glow over the severed tree stumps.

"Stay here," Zac says as he opens his door. "It's not safe out there."

"Thanks for the heads up," I reply, watching him step outside and shut the door firmly behind him.

I wait for a few minutes, peering out the front windscreen to check if there are any Petoys lurking about. There are none. Opening the passenger door, I step out of the truck and land on the ground.

Lowering myself down, I feel my knees sink into the mud. I have done this before, long ago in Mira …

Crouching amongst the winter debris, I hid behind a bush, watching my mother tug roughly at the skirt of her dress. Her stress was silent, yet revealing itself to me through her wild eyes, which frantically surveyed the earth for fresh footprints.

After a few moments, my mother nudged me, pointing at the ground. There lay a single set of footprints, winding itself through the treescape and disappearing within the forest.

In my heart, I knew that we were close to finding my father. We had been in hiding for almost two weeks, trekking through the cold winter air and leaving our trail marks behind. We slept under stark trees, staring up at the stars as the night announced itself. Stars that were constant and shone regardless of the danger or fear that we faced. They soothed my young, terrified heart and gave me hope that one day we would be safe again.

Standing, my mother's hair spilled over her shoulders. She faced me, reaching out her hand for me to take. As I stood, I studied her expression. She was a master at concealing her feelings, hiding them deeply within herself. I learned how to read her small expressions: a twitch of the nose when she was scared; the tightening of the corners of her mouth when she was sad and the softening of her eyes when she held me close and let me escape the cruel world by breathing her comforting existence in.

Clutching my mother's hand, I felt a powerful wave of anxiety ripple through me. I could sense her fear and her hyper alert state. Narrowing my eyes, I let go of her hand and stepped backwards, my gaze staring way off into the distance.

As I continued to retreat, I began to see. The winter bitten forest was waking. The crackling of a red hot fire was warming the chill in its bones. Sparks of light shot through the air and the chatter of human voices could be heard in the near distance. There was a gathering close by.

Drawn to the sound, I turned and began to tread towards it. I felt my mother grasp my hand and try to pull me back. Turning to face her, defiance lashed in my eyes. I didn't want to be alone anymore.

"Adira," my mother pleaded in a hoarse whisper. "Come with me, now please."

I shook my six year old head, mesmerised by the red hot heat. I wanted to join the gathering. Pulling my hand away from my mother's, I ran, dashing behind a cedar tree.

My heart pounded with excitement as I scanned the forest floor, trying to locate human bodies and faces.

That's when I saw him, his arms smeared with the dirt lashed from the earth. His orange shirt was ripped and tattered at the sleeves, exposing his taught, muscular arms. His indigo silk sash cascaded over his right shoulder, flapping wildly in the breeze. Lifting his mud soaked pant legs, he raised his head, his hair fluttering in the wind and his eyes narrowed with worry.

My father took his last few steps. He was met with the piercing, grey eyes of Chief Opula, whose lips twisted into a menacing smile as he raised his gun, ready to fire at Father.

I began to shake, terrified by the vision that confronted me. I could not speak or call out to my father.

My mother reached my side and huddled close, wrapping her arms around me. I felt her body tense as her eyes fell upon my father. "Adira," she whispered hoarsely. "It is best to leave now."

I shook my head, refusing to leave. There was my father, in great danger. Somewhere in my child heart, I believed that maybe by watching him, I could wish him away, towards us and that we could all leave together.

Raising his hands, my father dropped to his knees, surrendering himself. Chief Opula smiled a cruel smile and lurched forward, ripping the sash from my father's shoulder. "You have betrayed us!" His voice bellowed. "Assisting the imperial army to track us down and hiding Adira from us!" Dropping the sash to the ground, he aimed his gun and shot at it, obliterating it completely.

I jumped, startled by the loud noise. The remaining ash rose and floated through the air and I felt a huge wave of panic sweep over me.

"Now you will suffer the consequences," Chief Opula's terrifying voice rang into the air. "Say your last prayer."

For a moment, all I could hear was the fervent whispering of my father. I did not dare look up, terrified of what I might witness.

As the second shot pierced through the night air, I passed out, the darkness sweeping over me like a thick blanket of night.

When I awoke, I was greeted with Orion, twinkling at me in the night sky. Wrapped in my mother's shawl, I huddled up close to her, feeling her pull me into her embrace. I felt warm and safe.

My mother sang to me, her voice cracking with pain and tears streaming down her cheeks. Stroking my hair, she tried to comfort me even when her own spirit was lost.

The tears spilled down my cheeks and my heart weighed heavily with the grief of losing my father. In my childhood mind, I couldn't understand why my father could not return to us. We had journeyed a long way, trying to find him and return him to safety.

All my mother and I had left was each other, sheltering under a cedar tree and feeling the cold night air slap harshly against our skin.

"Adira," my mother said softly, turning me to face her. "The steps we take are hard but are keeping us safe, do you understand?"

I nodded, staring into her eyes. "We keep walking," I said, pointing to the untrodden path ahead.

My mother nodded. "Yes and sometimes we will run too," she grasped my hands in hers. "I am doing all that I can to protect you from the Petoys."

A small shiver rippled its way down my arms and settled into my chest. Wrapping my arms around my mother's neck, I pressed my face against hers and sighed with relief. I felt safe in her arms.

Standing, my mother began to walk, carrying me with her. The dark night shielded us with its black cloak, allowing us to trek a long distance away from the madness.

As we walked, Orion shone brightly. I closed my eyes and fervently wished for a way to make the horror go away.

Staring up at Orion now, my mind begins to regain its focus on the present. There is the constellation, my constant companion throughout all this mess.

"Hello Orion," I say softly. "Walk with me."

Standing, my legs feel weighed down by the thick mud. Peering up at the sky, I wave for Orion to follow me as I tread across the moonlit floor.

Croak, Croak.

Looking down, my gaze rests upon a growling grass frog, who is stationary and staring up at me. Peering closely, I notice that it is struggling to hop. Bending down, I pick up the frog and hold it in my palm, patting it gently. I can feel its heart beat slowing down as it begins to relax. "Hello Frog," I say, staring into its eyes. "You are all alone, like me."

I continue walking, my feet squelching across the muddy ground. Passing the severed tree stumps, I reach the edge of Spirit River.

My mouth drops open as I notice the change in the river water. It was once abundant with vegetation: pond weeds, running marsh flowers, reeds, spike rushes and milfoils. My heart falls as I see that the vegetation has dried up and died off. Some of the plant debris is drifting away across the current of the river. The loss of the terrestrial habitat provided by the red gum trees and their fallen branches and logs has led to disastrous results for the growling grass frog that relies upon it and its surrounding, shrivelling vegetation, to survive.

I gaze down at the frog in my hand. "You must be very hungry," I say, stroking it lovingly. "Let me see if we can find you something to eat."

Treading along the edge of the river bank, my eyes skim across the streaming water. After a short while, my gaze rests upon some tall, emergent spike rush, bordering the river bank.

Stepping forward, I show the frog the plant. "Do you like this?" I ask. The frog lurches forward, clinging to my fingers. Its heart is beating in excitement. "You'll be protected here," I tell the frog. "Your predators won't find you." Dropping to the ground, I place my hand down, letting the frog dismount. It jumps across the river bank, entering the water and hiding behind the spike rush.

I sigh with relief. The frog is safe. As I step back, my gaze rests upon a tiny patch of grass cover and a couple of small shrubs on the river bank. My heart fills with hope. At least the frog can acquire insects to eat in the grass and shrubs and hide when it needs to.

There used to be many growling grass frogs here. I remember jumping along with them as a teenager and watching them bask in the warm sun. It saddens me deeply that I can only see one this evening.

Staring up at Orion again, I sigh. "Thank you for showing me this," I say. "I wish I could know who is responsible for this brutal logging."

As if in response to my wish, the visceral sound of a chainsaw cuts through the silence. I jump, startled by the sound and nearly slip into the river water. Balancing myself onto my feet, I step backwards, returning to the forest floor. I stand still, waiting for the sound to return.

The chainsaw roars again, drawing my attention to the north side of the river bank. I begin to tread, covering ground quickly.

As I reach a cluster of severed red gum trees at the very north of the bank, I jump at the violently loud sound of the chainsaw. It is very close by.

Blocking my ears, I hide behind a shrub and push some leaves aside. Staring ahead, my eyes fall on two Petoy men who wear black head scarves emblazoned with a rearing horse. One of the men is attacking a red gum tree with his chainsaw. I watch as he cuts through the remaining section of the trunk, which falls cleanly away from its roots. Standing back, the men watch it fall with an earth shattering thud.

I feel as though my life has been drained from me as I witness the trunk bouncing heavily across the forest floor. So many years of life and wisdom, gone just like that.

Staring into the distance, I notice that a makeshift sawmill has been established. It is housed within an open shelter, which is held up by wooden posts. Across the back, red gum wood panels form a wide wall, providing it with protection from the wind and rain. The same wood panels deck the roof of the shelter, which is decorated with hanging lanterns to give it much needed night light.

There, in the dim light shining in the sawmill, stands Zac. He is running his hand over a log of red gum wood sitting on a metal stand. After a moment, he looks up and shakes his head at a figure stepping out of the shadows.

It is Naricia, her face forming a sly smile at the sight of Zac. Approaching the saw mill, she stands next to him and places her hands on her hips. "What a strong man you are Zac," She breathes, lightly stroking his right bicep. "Can I take a photo of you in action? You've debarked that log already, I see."

Reaching into my bag, I grab my video camera. It feels bulky in my cold hands but I manage to manoeuvre it into a comfortable viewing position. Pressing the power button, I zoom in the lens and begin to record the conversation between Zac and Naricia.

Zac shrugs Naricia's hand away. "Strength has nothing to do with it," he grunts. "The new mechanical ring cutter has done a good job."

Naricia runs her fingers across the log. "Yes," she says seductively. "It is definitely very smooth, this log." She arches her back and tucks her dark brown hair behind her ears. "Just like your skin. You would shine on our promotional material for maritime trade, Zac."

Zac steps back, uncomfortable by Naricia's advances. "Quit it, Naricia. My work is not an advertising opportunity for you. To be honest, I don't see why your boss feels it is necessary to force us to destroy so many trees." He shakes his head in frustration.

"We are building boats, Zac. They will be our launch into maritime trade. A route towards a larger, more extensive audience to sell our new silk range to."

Zac crosses his arms over his chest. "That's ambitious," he says. "How many boats are you aiming to build?"

"Three in total," Naricia smiles as she runs her fingers through her hair. "One is already built. Zac, you make sure you keep these logs as smooth as possible. The Chief likes his assets to be exquisitely polished."

"I'm sure he does," Zac mutters. "Now, if you'll excuse me, I have to use the head rig saw now." Grabbing hold of the log, he begins to clamp it onto a conveyor.

"Of course," Naricia smiles, fluttering her eyelashes as she steps away. "I don't want to stop your progress, Zac."

Placing my camera back into my bag, I watch Zac feed the log forcefully into the head rig saw, which begins to cut its blades lengthwise through the log, slicing it into planks.

No longer able to gain Zac's attention, Naricia saunters away, heading towards the Petoy men, who are heaving the fallen trunk onto a large logging truck.

"Work faster!" Naricia snaps. "We need more wood planks as soon as possible. The Chief needs all his boats in operation!"

"Where?" I ask aloud. Stepping back, I feel two firm hands on my shoulders. It has caught me by surprise. Using my foot, I kick backwards, landing its sole squarely between my captor's legs.

"Aahh!" He cries out as he drops to the ground. Spinning around, I face Chief Opula, who is clutching his pelvic region in pain.

I feel my hatred for him rise into my chest and it sends my mind spinning. "You again," I seethe. "What do you want?"

Chief Opula raises an eyebrow. "I could ask you the same thing," he says calmly. "Here you are, spying on us Petoys. Were you looking for me, Adira?" A creepy smile spreads across his lips.

I consider my situation. All it will take is one call out by the Chief and the Petoy men will help him capture me. I will have to play it smart.

"Yes," I lie, placing my camera into my bag. "I couldn't help but film your team's magnificent progress in action."

The Chief's lips spread into a satisfied smile.

My approach is working. I force myself to return his smile. "I also couldn't resist seeing you again. I kept searching for you until I located you here."

The Chief's grey eyes burn with desire. Scrambling to his feet, he approaches me. "I knew you'd come to your senses, beautiful Adira," he says, looking me up and down. "I can make you very happy. Much happier than you'll be in the imperial palace in Mira." He pulls me close and strokes my neck with the rough skin of his fingers. "We nobles, we have desires," he says, reaching under my singlet. I feel his hands cup my breasts and he moans, pressing his lips firmly against my neck.

The Chief's manliness hardens against my thigh. He moans again, stroking the nipples of my breasts. I feel sick to the stomach, yet more in control than I thought I would be. The Chief's weakness is *me*. I just have to play my cards right.

Cupping the Chief's face in my hands, I step back, releasing his grasp of my breasts. "Oh Chief," I sigh, harnessing my seductive voice and staring deeply into his eyes. "You make me feel things I cannot find the words to describe. It is best we wait until we can be somewhere more private and fitting for we nobles to express our desires for each other." I trace his lips with my finger and he takes it into his mouth, sucking on it.

"You're right," he says, releasing my finger. "A noble woman like you deserves the very best." He stares intensely into my eyes. "I would like you to visit me on my ship, which sits not too far out at sea. I have a beautiful cabin with a sky deck, which opens up to reveal the night air and the stars. It is there that we can finally submit ourselves to our deep desires."

A noble woman? I'm not sure what the Chief means. I watch as his eyes spark with lust. I can feel his burning attraction for me and am going to encourage it so that I remain safe. "That sounds very romantic," I smile. "However, it is very important to me that we are both dressed divinely."

The Chief's eyes widen in appreciation. "I agree," he smiles. "It appears we are very similar in our urges." He reaches for my hand. "Adira, my body yearns deeply for you but I can wait. I will organise for one of my ladies to design indigo silk attire for me to wear. It is the most distinguished silk a man could ever own." He squeezes my hand firmly and kisses it. "I will see you again very soon, beautiful woman."

"Hopefully as soon as possible," I wink at the Chief. "Life is too short to wait."

"Indeed it is," he agrees, placing his hand on his heart. His eyes narrow and his expression becomes intense. "Soon I will make you mine."

In that moment, I realise what I must do with the indigo silk sash. I need Girl's help to use it to create the illusion of indigo. It will bring down the quality of the counterfeit silk trade and the Chief's reputation with it.

I exhale a deep breath as the Chief steps back and acknowledge the nauseas feeling which is now rising from the pit of my stomach. I feel violated by him and it makes me angry. No-one but my loving husband is allowed to touch me like that. What am I going to tell Mitch?

Chapter 43

Mitch pulls the van into the curb along Vista Road. Jumping out, he runs to my side and grabs hold of my arms.

"Adira," he sounds worried as he notices my dirt and mud soaked skin and clothing. "What happened?"

I meet Mitch's gaze and touch his face gently. "It's so good to see you, my love," I say, toppling sideways.

"I've got you," Mitch catches me and wraps his arms around me in a tight embrace. "Let's get you sitting down."

I let Mitch guide me up the steps and into the van. Sitting back in the passenger seat, I sigh with relief. It is nice to take the weight off my feet.

Mitch shuts my door and runs to the driver's side. Jumping into his seat, he stares at me. "Oh Adira," he says, his eyes narrowed with concern. "Did you nearly get caught?"

"Yes," I say, wanting to be honest with him. "I visited the forest this evening. I discovered that the Petoys have built a makeshift sawmill on the north bank of the forest. They are logging red gum trees illegally and using the wood to build boats."

Mitch's eyes narrow as he absorbs the information. "Boats?" He asks. After a moment, his eyes widen. "Maritime trade," he says.

I nod appreciatively. "You're right," I say. "It is their next big venture in trade. Apparently the Emperor of Mira's large ship is sitting out at sea, recently stolen by the Petoys."

"Interesting," says Mitch, staring out the window. "I wonder who commands the ship?"

I inhale a deep breath and release it slowly. It's now or never. "Chief Opula," I say.

Mitch faces me with confusion in his eyes. "That man will stop at nothing to get what he wants, will he?" He clenches his fists angrily.

"He killed my father," I blurt out, clutching my chest.

"Oh Adira!" Mitch pulls me close and holds me while I sob. It calms me down and my tears begin to dry. He is my husband, my home. I don't know what I'd do without him in my life.

Looking up, I grab hold of Mitch's face and pull him towards me urgently, locking my lips with his. I need to feel his love, his comfort right now.

Mitch kisses me back, sensing my urgency. Pulling away, he crooks my chin up with his hand and stares into my eyes. "You're very stressed," he says, reading me accurately. "What happened out there, Adira?" His voice is gentle and concerned, making my heart pound with love.

I bite my lower lip, considering how I might tell Mitch what happened. There is no easy way around it, so I take a deep breath and launch into telling the story. "You know that Chief Opula has been hunting me down all my life," I say. "For some reason he believes I have noble blood and desires me. Tonight he touched me in ways he shouldn't have." A large dizzy spell sweeps over me and I fall back onto my seat.

"Adira? Are you okay?" I can feel Mitch stroking my face gently. Gradually, the dizzy spell stops and I meet his gaze.

"I'm sorry," I say to him. "I promise I didn't encourage him."

"I believe you," Mitch's cheeks are flaming red with rage. "How dare he," He lashes out, punching the steering wheel. "I want to kill him."

I place my hands on Mitch's shoulders. "Deep breaths," I say, trying to calm him down. "Killing the Chief won't be any use to us or Mira at all. I need you to focus now."

Makeshift Girl: The Secret Heritage Trail

Mitch stares at me, his eyes wide. "What do you want me to do?" He asks.

"Help me bring down his counterfeit trade," I say decisively. "Without trade, the Chief's power will no longer exist. The shame itself will send him to his grave."

Mitch's face is still red and for a moment he stares down at the carpet, absorbing my request. Seconds pass before he meets my gaze again. "Okay, let's do it," he says decisively.

I smile, taking hold of his face. "My love," I say gently. "I married you with my heart and soul. No-one but you could ever have the privilege of touching me so deeply …"

Mitch presses his lips firmly against mine. I kiss him back with all my heart. Pulling back, he meets my gaze.

"Thank you for telling me," he says. "I love you too, more than any world could exist. I will do anything to keep you safe Adira. Chief Opula doesn't know what's about to hit him."

I nod, letting Mitch work his own way through the news. It would be hard for him to realise that another man wants his wife.

"Let me drop you back to your apartment," he says, turning on the ignition. "We both need to get some sleep before tomorrow."

"Agreed," I smile, settling back into my seat.

Mitch drives silently, his mind mulling over what he has learned. Pulling into the curb a metre away from the apartment complex, he turns to look at me.

"Stay with me tonight," I say, reaching for his hand.

Mitch shakes his head. "I'd better not," he says. "I need time to chew through all you've told me, Adira."

My heart begins to race. "I understand," I say, staring at Mitch. "Please believe me, I have no interest in Chief Opula."

Mitch drums the steering wheel, his eyes intense. "That I do not doubt," he says. Reaching for my door, he opens it and watches me step outside. "I just need to get passed this anger," his eyes are flashing with rage.

"Okay," I say, feeling helpless as I watch Mitch shut the passenger door forcefully. He meets my gaze intensely one more time before waving goodbye.

Flooring the accelerator, Mitch speeds off down the Boulevard, leaving me staring at the trail blaze of smoke behind him.

I clutch my chest, feeling pain. Mitch is angry, I know. His pride has been hurt deeply. Hopefully he will settle down and not do anything reckless.

Walking through the front gate of the apartment complex, I push through the glass revolving doors and approach the elevator.

Bing!

The elevator doors open and a young boy and his mother enter the ground floor.

I watch the young boy run passed me, his black fringe falling into his face as he bends down to pick up his fallen diamond kite.

"Silly kite!" He is frustrated at its heavy weight, which he can't seem to lift on his own.

"Don't worry, Harry, I've got it." His mother, tall and brunette, bends down to pick up the fallen kite. As she lifts it, she feels my eyes upon her and turns to catch me staring at them both.

"Hello," I say. "It looks like you've both had a fun day."

"Yes!" Harry's smile is radiating. "Do you like my kite? It can fly really high!"

"It looks lovely," I say, feeling a stab of longing. If only Mitch and I could have our own child …

The concrete is not the most exciting thing to stare at for a long period of time. You begin to notice all the cracks and discolouration. When I look up again, Harry and his mother have ventured right down the other end of the corridor and are opening the door to their apartment.

I focus on the elevator and wait in suspense for it to return to my floor.

Bing!

The elevator door slides open and I step inside, greeted by the intense gaze of Felibo. His black spiky hair and brown eyes are striking, highlighting the chisel like cheek bones on his face.

Pulling the hood from his blue jumper over his head, Felibo looks down at the elevator floor. He seems to be intensely in thought. He presses the button to close the door firmly and it slams shut.

Stepping back and leaning against the elevator wall, I shake nervously as I wait for it to stop at the first floor.

Felibo stares at me, studying my face. I can see that he is deciding how to handle me. I inhale a sharp, fearful breath. *Come on elevator, stop!*

Bing!

The elevator doors slide open again. I exhale a large breath of relief.

Stepping outside, I meet Felibo's gaze again. It sends a shiver down my spine. Reaching out, he presses the button to shut the elevator door.

Breaking my gaze away, I step outside and let the elevator door slide closed.

I am still shaking as I turn to walk down the corridor and approach the front door of the apartment.

Felibo knows where I live now. It terrifies me.

Fumbling for my keys in my bag, I retrieve them and unlock the front door. Shutting and locking it firmly behind me, I lean my back against it and exhale a huge sigh of relief.

I am home now. Safe.

Girl is sitting on the sofa, strumming on a guitar. Hidu sits next to her, smiling happily.

"Are you ready?" Girl asks Hidu.

"Yes!" Hidu exclaims in excitement. "I can't wait to hear your new song."

"Here it goes," Girl strums the guitar strings with ease and sings:

> *"Steel and grease pave the way*
> *to escape the stormy streets.*
> *I rev in haste along endless roads,*
> *my heart seeking rusted dreams.*
>
> *"The road of my run.*
> *The road of my run.*
> *It burns and fuels*
> *my wakeful sleep."*

Girl's voice has the edge of steel, like the ute she likes to rev and burn. Her lyrics are a sharp reminder of her life on the run. It is a life that Girl approaches with fierce determination and vigour.

"That's just great!" Hidu smiles warmly, clapping his hands. He touches Girl's face gently. "You are so talented."

"Yes, you are," I say, my voice startling Girl. Her gaze darts up, meeting mine.

"Thanks Adira," she smiles. "A new song inspired by life on the run."

I nod, unable to speak anymore. I can feel my heart pounding fiercely in my chest. I am stressed.

"Hi Adira," Hidu says. His voice sounds a mile away. The room is beginning to spin.

I feel two arms around me, catching me as I fall.

"Adira!" Girl holds me still and strokes my hair. "You poor thing. You look like you've been through hell."

I nod, unable to speak.

"Can I help?" Hidu's voice is echoing.

"Yes," Girl sounds flustered. "Please help me take her to the bedroom."

Hidu bobs down next to me. "Rest Adira's weight against me, Girl," Hidu directs, opening his arms wide. Girl pushes me gently into Hidu's arms until my head is resting against his chest. He lifts me up. "I've got you Adira, okay?" He says softly as he carries me towards the bedroom.

My lips tremble at his kindness.

"Oh, you are crying," Hidu says as he lies me down onto the bed.

Girl kneels down at the side of the bed and reaches for my hand. She squeezes it tightly while I cry.

"I'll just be outside," Hidu says softly, leaving the room.

After a while, the dizzy spell passes and I try to sit up.

"Slowly, Adira, slowly," Girl guides me gently, helping me up. She looks at me as I dangle my legs at the foot of the bed. "Are you hungry?" She asks.

I shake my head. "No," I manage to say. "I feel sick in the stomach."

Girl's eyes narrow with worry. "Let me get you some peppermint tea," she smiles. "It might help settle your stomach down."

"That would be nice," I smile gratefully.

Girl leaves the room, shutting the door quietly behind her. Standing slowly, I take a look at myself in the mirror. My mouth drops open in surprise. I am covered in mud and dirt.

The door opens again and Girl enters, carrying a cup. "Here you go," she says, handing it to me. "Do you want me to keep you company?"

"Oh, that's okay," I say, feeling bad at interrupting her. "I wouldn't want you to miss your time with Hidu."

"Hidu will be fine," Girl says, waving her hand in the air. "I am here for you Adira." She stares at my mud soaked skin and clothes. "What happened to you?"

"It's a long story," I say weakly.

"I'm listening," Girl says, gazing determinedly into my eyes. My heart settles into a calmer beat. Girl wants to help me. It is a nice feeling.

Taking a sip of peppermint tea, I sigh with relief. It feels good going down. "Well, this evening I discovered a saw mill ..." I begin, sharing my story with the very attentive Girl.

Chapter 44

I can't sleep that night, thinking about the Chief's mention of my noble background. His lusty gaze haunts my dreams and I jolt awake several time, fevered and ready to attack ...

Awakening at the crack of dawn, I discover that I have slept on the floor with my head half hidden under the bed.

Rising, I bang my head on the bed frame. Clutching at my sore head, I slide out from under the bed and stand slowly.

There I am, looking at myself in the mirror.

My light brown hair is very dishevelled and sticks up in the air. I have dark grey lines under my eyes, which are evidence of exhaustion. Rubbing my cheeks roughly, I try to wake myself up.

It is no use. I'm still tired.

Knock, knock.

The sound startles me and I jump about a metre high into the air. Grabbing hold of Girl's trekking pole, I hold it out in front of me, heading slowly across the living room carpet.

It is silent. No one is here. Girl must have gone out somewhere with Hidu.

My gaze drifts to the front door and I step carefully, trying not to make a sound. Peering through the peep hole, I see Felibo standing outside. A black head scarf with a rearing horse is tied onto his head.

Makeshift Girl: The Secret Heritage Trail

I gulp, stepping back from the door. I have seconds to leave.

Grabbing my phone, I text Girl frantically. *Apartment compromised. Stay away!*

Pocketing my phone, I dash into the bedroom and throw on my runners. Tossing my black cloth bag over my shoulder, I sigh. Somehow I am going to have to take our belongings with me.

I grab the two boxes containing Girl's statues and models. Balancing the bag of clothing and toiletries and the trekking pole on top of the boxes, I take a deep breath.

Ignoring the pain of the weight I am carrying, I dash towards the balcony. Balancing the load in one arm, I flick open the lock and slide the door open.

I can hear a strange clicking sound behind me and look back. Felibo is trying to pry open the front door lock.

Stepping out onto the balcony, I grab my bundle of keys. Fumbling through them with one hand, I find the one that I need and lock the door behind me. That will buy me a little more time to escape.

The top of a large privet hedge protrudes into the left side of the glass parapet. It is highly useful right now. Placing my load down at my feet, I pick up a single box and place it on top of the hedge. I do the same with the next box, followed by the bag of clothing and toiletries. Finally, I gently place the trekking pole on top of one of the boxes and watch it balance precariously. It will have to do for now. I will collect them later.

Approaching the parapet, I muster my courage. Placing one leg over the glass structure, I aim for my foot to hit the concrete ledge on the other side. Grasping tightly onto the parapet, I inhale a deep breath as I raise my other leg. I exhale with relief once it also lands safely on the ledge.

Shuffling along the thin, concrete ledge, I approach the brick wall on the side of the apartment complex. A steel fire escape staircase mounts the building and sweeps in a flight of zig zag steps.

Grasping hold of the staircase hand rail with both hands, I take a deep breath. It takes a lot of strength to lift my body weight off the balcony and swing it across to the staircase. Somehow, I succeed, landing my feet successfully on a single step. Toppling, I nearly fall and grip even more tightly onto the hand rail in order to balance myself.

Glancing back up at the balcony, I see Felibo's face peering through the locked door. He is punching the glass, his eyes flashing with anger as he stares at me.

Dashing down the steps to the bottom of the staircase, I run towards the large, steel gate at the front of the apartment complex.

There it is, towering high above me.

I punch the code in and wait for the gate to open.

The code doesn't work. That's odd. Maybe I got it wrong.

I try again.

It still doesn't work. Hmmm.

A small alarm bell rings in my head. Someone has changed the security code. Residents will not be able to enter or exit the front gate. Why? I wish Girl was here to help me figure this one out.

Staring at the gate, I take in its height. It is tall. I am tired. I will still have to climb it.

My mother taught me how to climb gates. We had to do so many times in the past. Usually at full bore speed, running away from whatever snapped at our heels. This time I will have to climb the gate on my own.

Taking off my runners, I aim high and throw them over the top of the gate. I hear them land with a thud on the concrete. I am still a good aim.

I pull my skirt up above my knee caps. That's better, more flexibility to move.

I am not going to throw my bag over the gate. It has too many important things inside it. I leave it swinging over my shoulder.

Grabbing a steel picket in each hand, I pull myself up. Blindly, I aim my right foot towards the bottom rail.

I hit and miss.

Hit and miss again.

I succeed. A silent cheer!

Hoisting myself up the picket even higher, I aim my left foot towards the middle rail. I know it's there, somewhere...

There it is! Phew!

I am out of breath. The bag strap has wrapped itself in a loose chain around my neck.

Holding onto the picket with my right hand, I lean against the gate. Gently, I move my left hand up towards the bag's strap and unravel it slowly from around my neck. Finally, it hangs freely again, over my shoulder.

I can't take too much longer to leave. Felibo will catch up with me any moment now.

From memory, I know that there is a top rung, not too far away from the fancy finials on the picket tips. I made it my business to know every detail of where we were staying, including the steel gate, for a moment just like this.

It takes all my energy to hoist myself up to the top rail of the picket. My feet dangle in the air, trying to land.

Hitting and missing.

Hitting and missing.

I have to try one last time. I owe it to us. To me.

Success!

Pulling myself up, I place both my feet onto the rail. I pant. Sweat is dripping from my brows. It is making it even harder to see.

I am nearly there.

I wipe my eyes with the back of my hand. That's better. I can see again.

Reaching for the tips of the pickets, I run my hands over the finials. They are sharp. Probably rusted too. I feel for a couple of smooth sections that are easier to grab. There they are. Just one more hoist ...

I am surprised at my strength, pulling myself up higher. Up I go, over the tip to the other side of the gate. Somehow I instinctively land on my two feet onto the top rail.

I am happy to jump down from here. I have done so many times in the past. Silently hoping that I don't land too hard on my bare feet, I close my eyes. I let go of the pickets and drop more than jump.

Time seems to go very slowly as I fall through mid air. It catches up very quickly once I land with a thud onto my two bare feet.

Ouch! Concrete is not fun to land on.

I stand shakily on my feet. It was a big drop. It takes me a moment to recover.

I am more than okay though. I've done it! Got over that gate. Escaped the danger … temporarily.

Finding my shoes, I step back into them and head left down Lighthouse Boulevard until I hit Firework Road. Turning a sharp left, I dash down the alleyway, following the side walls of the apartment complex. Where is it?

There it is: the tall privet hedge. It sits behind a small fence, which borders the apartment complex.

It is an easy fence to climb. I step up both the rails quickly, holding onto the tips of the pickets to steady myself.

I can see the trekking pole from here. If I reach high enough I can …

I've got it! Silent cheer!

Balancing myself on the rail, I stretch up high and nudge the bag of clothing and toiletries with the trekking pole. I watch as the bag falls from the hedge and lands onto the concrete behind me.

One down. Two to go.

Taking a moment to rebalance my feet, I stretch up high again and nudge one of the boxes very gently. It slips down from the top of the hedge and as it falls, I jump into the air and catch it, wobbling as I land onto my two feet.

Steadying my feet, I balance the box in my hands. It is safe. Phew!

Climbing the fence rails one more time, I stretch out even further and nudge the final box with the trekking pole. It takes a while to move this box as it seems stuck in the hedge. Finally it breaks away from the plant and sails through the air.

I jump off the fence and land solidly onto my two feet. Running with all my might, I reach out to catch the box as it nearly hits the concrete.

As the box lands in my arms, I am bowled over, landing on my bottom on the ground. I sit for a moment, panting and trying to catch a breath.

Standing slowly, I feel a sharp pain shoot through my bottom. It paralyses me for a moment and I place the box that I am carrying down onto the ground.

After gently stretching my legs, the pain begins to subside and then fade away. Thank goodness it wasn't a serious injury.

It is time to move.

Stacking the boxes on top of each other, I breathe a sigh of relief. I've managed to escape successfully with our belongings.

I use my last bit of energy to lift the boxes. Stacking the clothing and toiletries bag and trekking pole on top of the load, I carry all of it. It is challenging to see passed the load in my arms as I walk further down the alleyway and passed the backs of many tall corporate buildings.

Entering the large, underground car park of one of the buildings, I pop the load down onto the concrete ground next to me and stretch my arms, trying to relieve the tension in my biceps.

Loosened up, I take a look around the car park. It is virtually empty, except for a single Ford Falcon parked near the sliding door entrance to the corporate building. It will be safe enough to wait here, as long as it takes.

Digging into my pocket, I retrieve my mobile phone. *I am safe,* I message Girl. *Please come get me.*

Chapter 45

I feel a gentle nudge of my arm and groan, shaking it off. It is nice to get some sleep.

"Adira? Are you okay?" The voice sounds distant, as though it is a thousand miles away.

Turning over onto my side, my head bumps into something hard and I wake up.

"Aw!" I groan, sitting up and rubbing my eyes. It takes me a moment to realise that I have fallen asleep on the concrete.

Girl is staring down at me, her eyes filled with concern. "Are you injured?" She asks me.

"No," I am groggy. Sitting up slowly, I allow myself to wake up. "We were found," I tell Girl. "I got away safely with our belongings."

"I can see that," Girl looks impressed. "Getting away would have been no mean feat."

"No," I shake my head.

"I'm glad you're okay, Adira," Girl says softly.

"Thanks," that was a nice thing to say. I relish the moment.

"Want a hand up?" Girl offers, extending her arm out towards me.

"Sure," I grab hold of her hand and let her pull me up onto my feet.

Makeshift Girl: The Secret Heritage Trail

Girl picks up the boxes and begins to walk towards the road. "Come on," she says. "It's time to move onto plan b."

With one hand clutching the clothing and toiletries bag, I use the other to lean against the trekking pole as I shuffle across the footpath outside the car park.

My mind whirs. *Plan b*. Girl had mentioned something about that the other morning at the apartment. I wonder what that involves?

Stacking the boxes into the ute tray, Girl smiles. "We are going to be fine, Adira, you'll see."

"Okay," I say, placing the trekking pole into the ute tray, followed by the clothing and toiletries bag.

Settling into the passenger seat, I watch Girl as she begins to drive down Lighthouse Boulevard. Stopping at a red traffic light, she turns briefly to look at me.

"How did you get out?" She seems intrigued, her eyes wide.

"I jumped from the balcony onto the fire escape stairs. After that, I climbed over the steel gate." I am pleased with my efforts.

"Wow!" Girl is astonished. "Good on you, Adira." Her eyes narrow.

"The lights are green," I say gently, hating to break her train of thought.

Girl turns to face the road. "So they are, thanks." As she drives, her hands grip the steering wheel tightly.

Turning right down Veta Street, Girl pulls into the curb. Switching off the ignition, she faces me. "I need your help, Adira," she pleads with her eyes.

"What is it?" I ask, a nervous feeling settling in my stomach. I have a feeling it is going to be something big.

"Come see," Girl jumps out of the driver's seat and dashes to the ute tray. Reaching inside it, she retrieves a replica of her original Beach Crescendo statue.

"Wow!" I exclaim. "You created that very quickly!"

"Yes," says Girl. "It is nowhere near as detailed or as special as the original statue but it will do as a replacement."

I stare at Girl in surprise. "You are planning to switch your original statue with this one?"

"Yes," Girl says decisively. Her eyes widen hopefully. "Do you think you can help me do this, Adira? I'd appreciate your expertise."

I look up at the sky. The morning sun has risen higher, yet it is still early.

"Okay," I say, my mind forming a plan. "We will have to work quickly and efficiently, before the early morning commuters pass through the Town Square."

Girl checks her watch. "I see," she nods. "It's only 7:30 in the morning. We have about half an hour before people will pass by."

I rifle through the ute tray, discovering the cleaning uniforms and head scarves that helped us to escape the motel bistro. "Put this on," I say, handing Girl a uniform.

"Great idea," Girl says, placing her apron over her head and tying it around her back. I help her wrap the head scarf around her hair and pin it into place.

"We are here to clean the display cabinets," I direct Girl as I finish tying my apron and place my head scarf over my head.

"We're cleaners," Girl confirms as she helps me pin my head scarf into place. Stepping back, she stares at me. "You look very professional," she smiles.

"You too," I grin.

Girl rifles through the clothing and toiletries bag and retrieves a cardigan. "This conceals the statue well," she says as she wraps it around the wood. Placing the bundle under her right arm, she locks the ute with her remote and falls into step beside me.

We walk quickly down the end of Veta Street and stop at the traffic lights. There, across the road on Lighthouse Boulevard, is the Town Square. My eyes fall upon a family of pigeons, pecking away at crumbs on the concrete. It is so quiet at the Town Square that they can actually relax and enjoy eating. I would appreciate such luxury.

As the green light flashes, Girl dashes across the pedestrian crossing and sprints across the concrete of the Town Square, scaring off the pigeon family, who squawk and flutter up high into the air.

I walk quickly, maintaining my calm. If there is one thing I know, it is to never, ever fluster when you are on a job. It's how you make drastic mistakes.

As I reach the display cabinet, I see Girl punching the glass ferociously. "Smash, you stupid glass!" She wears a pained expression on her face as she stares at her precious statue.

Taking hold of Girl's arms, I pull her towards me gently. "It's alright," I console, hugging her tightly. "I've got this, okay?"

Girl stares into my eyes for a long moment, her own eyes flashing with anger. Her tension vibrates through my body and I continue to hold her tightly until she calms down.

Finally, Girl exhales a deep breath. "Okay," she says, stepping back. "Lead the way."

Reaching into my pocket, I pull out a piece of cloth. "I need you to clean the other side of this display cabinet," I say to her. "Keep an eye out for anyone walking by and whistle if they do."

Girl takes another look at the statue. "What are you going to do, Adira?"

"Pick the lock," I say.

Girl's eyes widen in surprise. "Oh," she nods. "Of course. You need me to help buy you as much time as possible."

"That's right," I nod. "Are you okay if we handle things this way?"

"Yes," Girl nods decisively. "It's the best plan. No glass will be smashed in the process so it won't raise any suspicion."

"You've got it," I smile. "We need to move quickly now, okay?"

"I'm onto it," Girl says. Turning on her heels, she dashes to the other side of the cabinet and begins wiping down the glass.

Allowing myself to focus for a moment, I consider the training that Concetta taught me many years ago. That's right, there was that old trick …

Reaching up, I pull two bobby pins out of my hair. The head scarf begins to flap into my eyes, but I push it away, so that I can see more clearly. As I do so, I drop a bobby pin.

Susan Marshall

My eyes scan the concrete desperately, trying to locate the black bobby pin. It takes a little while …

There it is!

I pick it up and hold both bobby pins tightly in my right hand.

Nearly there …

Hearing the click clack of high heels a short distance away, I tense up. Peering into the glass, I see a young woman dashing across the Town Square, determined to get to her destination. Grabbing a cloth from my pocket, I begin to wipe down the glass.

The woman vanishes down the Boulevard and I exhale a deep sigh of relief.

All clear.

Pocketing the cloth, I turn my attention to the lock on the display cabinet. It is simple and should be easy to open.

Grasping one bobby pin in the fingers of my right hand, I peer into the barrel of the lock, carefully guiding the bobby pin into position inside it.

Tap!

I hear the bobby pin make contact with the pin inside the barrel.
Too easy.

Holding the first bobby pin in place, I peer once again inside the barrel. There is just enough room in there for me to insert the second bobby pin.

As I push it into the barrel carefully, I inhale an anxious breath as I wait to hear it connect with the second pin.

Tap!

Yay! We're ready to go!

Holding both bobby pins in place inside the barrel, I begin to jiggle them frantically, waiting for the sound.

Click!

There goes the first pin. Great!

I keep jiggling the bobby pins, beginning to sweat. *Come on last pin!*

Makeshift Girl: The Secret Heritage Trail

There is an eruption of laughter in the distance, startling me again.

My gaze darts over my shoulder and falls upon a young couple walking across the Boulevard. Phew!

Regaining my focus on the lock, I take a deep breath and continue to jiggle the bobby pins. It's so tricky! *Please just …*

Click!

Yay! The last pin!

My heart is racing as I try to open the cabinet door. *Please open!*

The door swings open and there sits Girl's statue. I am mesmerised by its beauty.

"You got the cabinet open, Adira!" I hear Girl's voice beside me.

I break my focus, meeting Girl's gaze. "Time to swap over," I say, dashing to the other side of the cabinet.

While Girl swaps the statues over, I keep a close eye on our surroundings. A tall man suddenly steps across the Town Square.

I whistle loudly, startling Girl. Wrapping the original statue tightly in her cardigan, she positions it under her arm.

Click clack!

The man is approaching rapidly. He is humming a tune while he crosses the concrete.

Girl is intensely focused. Placing the replica statue into the cabinet, she positions it neatly, before shutting the glass door firmly. Grabbing hold of her cloth, she begins to clean the glass, just as the man passes by.

"Morning," the man sounds chirpy. "You might want to move on. There's a protest group on its way down here."

Girl nods, beginning to shake. Lifting her arm slowly, she continues to wipe the glass.

After the man has disappeared into the distance, I dash to Girl's side. "Well done!" I say, smiling at her.

Girl beams, her eyes alight with happiness.

"No more bans! No more taxes! Yes to progress!" The shouts boom through the air. Glancing up, I see a group of Petoys flocked together and punching their fists into the air. They are heading in our direction.

"Let me clean up here," I say.

"Sure," Girl steps back, keeping watch.

Removing the bobby pins from the lock, I pocket them safely away. Shaking the cabinet door, I check that it doesn't swing open.

It is shut firmly. Good.

"Have you seen this Girl?" The Petoys thrust the flyers into the hands of people crossing the Town Square. The clan begins to advance towards us. It is a large, intimidating group that will be difficult to escape.

Girl looks up at me, shaking. "Adira," she says weakly. "Help me out of here, please!"

Grabbing hold of Girl's free hand, I begin to jog further down the Town Square, towards the other side of Lighthouse Boulevard.

Clutching her statue under her arm, Girl struggles to run with me.

Once we hit the Boulevard, I stop at the curb, waiting for traffic to clear.

"Oh no!" Girl cries, her eyes falling upon a scattered pile of flyers fluttering across the concrete. It is very confronting seeing her image displayed across them, along with the big, bold question: *Have you seen this Girl?*

Girl is in great danger. We can no longer stay in the city. It is time to flee.

Once the traffic clears, I grab Girl's hand and run across the road. We reach the ute in no time and Girl jumps into the driver's side, pulling open the passenger door for me.

I flop into my seat and stare at Girl. "Are you okay?" I ask, noticing that her hands are shaking as she places the wrapped statue down onto the floor next to my feet.

Girl nods, starting up the ignition. "Time to get out of the city," she says, revving the accelerator. Pulling out of the curb, she roars down the street.

Chapter 46

After a while, Girl turns left off Vista road and the ute tremors over a gravel surface. Pieces of gravel fly at the windscreen, making it harder to see.

Girl flicks on the high beams and drives slowly. She seems very familiar with where she is going, not even showing the least bit of worry.

I am scared. I have never been on this road before.

Girl hits the breaks suddenly, throwing me forward. "Sorry!" She calls as she switches off the ignition.

I slide down into my seat instinctively. I know that I can't be seen but I feel exposed. We are out in the middle of nowhere. Nowhere that I am familiar with.

"I'll be back in a moment," unbuckling her seatbelt, Girl stretches. Pushing open the door, she jumps out of the ute and disappears. What is Girl doing? Is she going mad?

I am staying put. I've had enough adrenalin pumped through me for one day.

Taking some deep breaths, I try to relax. It's too hard to, so I hunt around the interior of the ute. Girl has left the keys in the ignition. That's good. It means that I can still drive if I have to.

Five minutes pass and still no Girl. Time to move.

I grab my cloth bag and the keys. Pocketing my phone, I swing the passenger door open. Walking carefully, I take small steps, stumbling over soft tufts of grass.

Suddenly, I stumble over a large rock. I land with a thump onto my knees. Ouch!

Winded, I stay put for a moment, catching a breath and rubbing my knees.

Grimacing, I stand, testing my weight on my right leg. It throbs with the stress of a mild sprain injury. Relieving it of its burden, I shift my weight onto my left leg and feel some of the pain subside. Limping ahead, I avoid tripping over another rock.

I can only take a few more limps before I am stopped in my tracks, faced with a barbed wire fence. A sign hangs precariously from the wire. It reads: *Bownie's Timber Mill. Permanently closed.*

The sign hasn't prevented someone from entering. I notice that a hole has been cut into the wire. It is large enough for a person to pass through. Did Girl cut the wire? There is only one way to find out.

Ducking through the hole, I step into the yard and am faced with a gravel area scattered with piles of wood.

I navigate my way through the piles, still limping. My knee is throbbing with pain. I need to rest again.

Sitting on a wood pile, I raise my right leg. It is best to keep it elevated.

My gaze sweeps across the yard. A flash of platinum blonde hair flickers in the wind. Girl is here.

Standing slowly, I stretch. What is Girl doing here? As I draw closer, I notice that she is talking to a tall man with a broad frame and dishevelled, short brown hair. He has a long beard, which he strokes gently while in conversation.

I limp slowly towards her. The pain in my knee is worse than before. She senses movement and turns quickly.

A sigh of relief escapes Girl's lips when she realises that it is me. "Oh it's you, Adira," she looks at my knee. "You've hurt yourself?"

I nod, rubbing my knee.

"Hi Adira, I'm Ben Bownie," the man says softly. "Please have a seat here," he drags a wooden chair towards me.

"Thanks," I say, feeling the weight taken off my leg as I sit down.

Girl turns her attention back to Ben. "It's sad what's happened to this timber mill, Ben," Girl sighs. "I used to enjoy coming here to get my red gum wood."

"Yes, I am sad too," Ben sighs, staring into the distance. "Jacquelyn and I had to take a stand against the logging. The Mayor has chosen to turn a blind eye to the Petoys' actions after their recent protest at the Artists' Market. He is afraid of their power and doesn't want a resistance formed against him during election time. In the mean time, we are losing our precious, sacred trees."

"Yes," Girl lowers her head. "It is really sad. Surely the Petoys have abused their logging permits?"

"Well and truly," Ben nods. "Yet the Mayor makes no move to stop them. The clan's even swarmed in here recently, demanding more wood pieces in order to add an extravagant embellishment to the bow of their big ship, which is sitting out at sea."

"Their ship?" I can't help asking.

"Yes, it is what the Chief resides in," Ben smiles. "He likes it to look illustrious. I heard the Petoy men discussing the goods that the ship will deliver in a few days."

"What sort of goods?" Girl asks.

"A new range of silk," Ben says, scratching his head. "I believe it's called *A Touch of Silk*? The Petoy men were gloating about how it was going to make the clan a lot of money in trade."

"Can you get me on that ship?" Girl asks. "I can pose as a sculptor and help design an illustrious sculpture to display on the bow."

"Are you sure you want to do that?" Ben asks. "It could be dangerous."

"Yes, I do," Girl says decisively. "I need to be on that ship when it takes off."

"Okay," Ben says. "You'll need to make sure that you are disguised well. The last thing you want is to be discovered."

"Adira will help me take care of that side of things," Girl smiles.

"I sure will," I agree.

Suddenly, I hear the sound of footsteps and voices in the distance.

Ben's gaze darts over his shoulder. "The Petoys are here again!" He exclaims. "You'd better go!"

"Let's go!" Girl slings her arm around my shoulders and helps me limp faster across the ground.

"It's that Girl!" I hear a man's voice shouting behind us. "That one from the flyer! Grab her!"

Feet smack across the ground behind us rapidly.

"We're nearly there!" Girl encourages me to keep moving.

The pain in my leg is agitating. I ignore it and push ahead. We reach the fence and Girl gently pushes me through the hole.

Once outside, I take a moment to rest my leg while I wait for her.

"Keep moving!" Girl yells as she jumps through the hole. "They're right behind me!"

"I don't know if I can," I whimper in defeat.

I can hear rustling through the fence hole. A voice is shouting directly behind us.

Girl puts her hands under my arms and lifts me up! I am astonished. She is so strong!

She runs towards the ute carrying me, like a superhuman in the middle of a civilian rescue.

Once we reach the ute, Girl pops me down.

Bending down, she gasps for air.

"Thanks for rescuing me," I say, grimacing in pain.

I can still hear feet pelting across the ground behind us. The man's voice is even louder now. "I'll get you!" He yells aggressively.

Girl dashes to the driver's door and jumps in. "Get inside!" She cries, pulling open the passenger door.

"Thanks," I mutter, hopping into the seat and slamming the door behind me.

Gritting my teeth, I try to ignore the throbbing pain in my leg. It will have to wait.

Girl turns the key in the ignition and the ute revs. Her foot plants firmly onto the accelerator. "Stupid handbrake!" She cries. I've never seen her quite so panicked before. Her hands are shaking.

Releasing the handbrake, she floors the accelerator.

I am thrown backwards and my head hits the seat.

"Sorry," Girl is intensely focused on her driving.

I settle back into my seat. My heart is racing.

Girl is frantic, her blonde hair flying in her face as the cold breeze blasts through her window.

"Are you okay?" I am worried about her.

Girl shrugs.

The ute tremors roughly once it hits the gravel. The throttling is hard to bear. I can feel my teeth gnashing together. I don't complain. The pain in my knee is much worse.

A couple of minutes later, we hit the contrasting smooth bitumen of Vista Road. It is good to see light bouncing off the cat eye reflectors, a welcome relief from the darkness.

Girl lets out an exasperated sigh and her driving slows down. Her hands are still shaking and she is gripping onto the steering wheel.

My knee is throbbing badly. I continue to keep myself distracted from the pain. Glancing around, I take in the familiar street signs:
Dabby Street.
Glime Street.
I know these streets. I know where they will take us.

Girl turns left onto Rickard Street. There it is with its wrought iron welcome sign: The Nestle Camp Ground. It is secluded, with plenty of camping spots in hidden places.

Driving around the winding pathway and across the grass, Girl heads deep into the treescape.

She steps on the brake, stopping the ute in front of the oak tree hidden way out back. Girl switches off the ignition.

Hitting her head on the steering wheel, Girl groans. "Today did not go as planned," she says.

"It's getting tough," I look at her. "We knew it was going to be."

Girl nods. "Tonight you were very brave," she smiles. "How's your knee, Adira?"

"Throbbing badly," I grimace.

"Let me have a look," Girl rolls my skirt up and stretches my leg out straight.

"Ouch!" A sharp pain shoots through my knee. "I think I've sprained it," I gasp.

"Sorry," Girl mutters. She tears a strip of material off her t-shirt and lies it on my lap. Reaching into her glove box, she retrieves a bag. Unzipping it, she digs inside and reveals a first aid kit and a water bottle. "Firstly, I need to clean up your wound. It may sting a little," says Girl, taking out the antiseptic and pouring it onto the material. She cleans my wound with the antiseptic and rinses it with the water bottle. The wound does sting, yet also feels a little better.

I look at my knee. "It's swollen," I say.

"Yes it is a little," says Girl. She digs into the first aid kit again. "Let me bandage it up to stop any further swelling or injury." She wraps the bandage around my knee cap tightly and pins it into place.

"Thanks," I say, relieved. "It means a lot."

"No worries," Girl smiles at me.

I yawn. I am fatigued.

"Let's sleep in here tonight," Girl suggests. "You need to keep your leg elevated."

"Good idea," I agree.

Settling back into my seat, I get as comfortable as I can. The pain is starting to ease a little, thank goodness.

I shut my eyes. The dark is soothing and sleep is very welcome.

Chapter 47

A shrill chirping sound awakens me from a restless sleep. Glancing across, I see Girl huddled in the driver's seat, her mouth open while she sleeps. I smile. It's good to see her resting.

Staring outside my window, I spot a bluebird fluttering around the oak tree. I stretch and admire the beauty of the bird, whistling such a lovely sound.

I could just stay here forever. I am enjoying nature in all its finery.

Grabbing my bag, I sling it over my shoulder. Reaching for the door handle, I swing the door open quietly. Raising my injured leg, I turn myself in the chair and step carefully onto the ground. I stand up slowly.

Aw! There is still pain in my right knee. I can't rest too much weight on my leg.

Outside, the cool, morning air is relieving. My lungs are thankful.

Girl stumbles groggily out of the ute, pushing her blonde hair out of her eyes. "Morning," she smiles gently. "How's your leg?"

"Still a little sore," I say as I limp towards her.

"I'm sorry to hear that," Girl smiles empathically as she retrieves her wrapped statue and her silk bag from inside the ute. "I want to show you something," her smile widens. "Are you okay to walk a little?"

"Sure," I follow Girl across the grass to an open area of land. Girl stands in front of a coastal blue caravan with the calmness of a seascape.

"This is plan b," Girl announces. "Our new place to stay. Do you like it?"

"Wow!" I am impressed.

"The wreckers were kind to me," says Girl as she leads me around the caravan. "I was lucky enough to pick up this caravan and its parts. It has a steel chassis, which makes it sturdy enough and long lasting. It will make a great home away from home one day."

I nod, understanding. It will be a great home on the move too.

Girl pats a caravan wall. "It needed some repairs on its hardwood body. Can you see where I had to patch it up?"

"Only slightly," I say admirably. "It looks amazing. You've painted an awesome seascape on it!"

Girl shrugs. "Guess I got a bit creative," she says, popping the wrapped statue under her left armpit. She picks up a paint brush that is bobbing in a pot of paint. "I forgot to paint this section here," she streaks some blue paint in a wave across the wall. "That's better," she sighs, popping the brush back into the pot. Girl is happy when she is being artistic. It is nice to see her eyes shining again.

Reaching into her pocket, Girl grabs a large bundle of keys. She ascends the caravan steps and unlocks the front door. I follow her, limping behind. We step inside.

The interior is very beachy. A sandy yellow wall embraces a small kitchen, equipped with shelving, benches and a sink. Girl holds her hand up for me to stop.

"Don't step any further," she warns. "You'll trip over the lino."

I can see the lino peeling away on the plywood floor.

"It's the last major thing I need to fix," Girl says, placing her wrapped statue and silk bag down onto the kitchen bench.

"Let me help you," I offer.

Girl's eyes widen. "Thanks," she is surprised. "Just watch your poor knee."

"Let's get started," I say, rolling up my sleeves.

Girl hands me a Stanley knife. We cut away at the lino stuck to the base of the cupboards. It is so old that it crumbles at the edges.

Peeling away the lino is easy. Girl rolls it up and tosses it outside the front door.

We inspect the plywood floor. It has a few minor water marks but no repairs are needed.

"Lucky," Girl sighs. "Less work than I thought it was going to be." She stretches like a cat.

After a moment, she looks at me. "Time to remove the glue," she directs, grabbing two scrapers off the bench. She hands one to me.

We work away, scraping at the old glue on the floor. It takes a while. My knee is aching but I don't mind. The physical work is a nice distraction.

"Time for the lino," Girl says. "It's got its own adhesive so it should stick fine."

We carefully remove the backing on the adhesive, little by little, smoothing out the lino from the centre so there are no bubbles or bumps. It is hard work but rewarding.

Once complete, we both stand back, admiring the view.

"It looks great," I say. "Such a nice yellow colour, like sand."

"That was the look I was going for," Girl nods. "Thanks for the help."

"It's the least that I can do," I smile at her. "You've done such an amazing job. The caravan looks great."

Girl lowers her head shyly and a small smile crosses her face.

"I need a drink after all that," says Girl.

"Sounds like a great idea," I agree.

A small kettle sits on the bench, ready for use. Girl fills it with water and switches it on. She grabs two paper cups and some peppermint tea from the shelves.

While we wait for the kettle to boil, she faces me, animated. "Follow me," she says, walking ahead.

I follow Girl passed the makeshift living space, with a box for a couch and a tiny television. There is an old take-away chip wrapper lying on the floor next to the box. It seems like Girl managed to eat a little and keep entertained while working.

We stop in front of a separate space at the back, in which lies a single bed.

"Welcome to the guest area," Girl smiles.

I look around the space. "Do you have a surveillance camera set up yet?" I ask her.

Girl shakes her head. "No, do you have a spare one?" She asks.

"Of course," I say. I reach into my bag and retrieve the surveillance camera. "We need to place it somewhere inconspicuous," I say.

Girl walks to the back of the room and points to a small table, which holds a vase of dried flowers. "How about behind this?" She asks.

"Too obvious," I say. Approaching the table, I bend down, wincing at the pain throbbing in my leg. Removing the backing of the circular base, I stick the camera down under the bottom edge of the table. "Leave it slightly sticking out like this," I say as I lie down to check the camera's view range. "Perfect. Have a look yourself."

I sit up, watching as Girl lies down to check how the camera has been positioned.

"I see," says Girl, squinting. "The camera is well hidden with a broad sweeping view of the room."

"That's right," I say, smiling. "You're learning fast. Now, flick the toggle switch here to video mode," I instruct her.

"Looking for video mode … there it is!" Girl flicks the switch.

I lean towards the camera, checking the switch. "Well done!" I say, crawling backwards and rising to my feet.

Girl crawls out from under the table and stands. "Will we be able to get vision on our phones?" She asks.

"Yes," I nod.

"Okay," Girl smiles. "Thanks so much Adira. We're all set!"

"We are," I grin. We clap our hands together in a high five.

Leaving the room, I limp down the corridor behind Girl. She stops in front of a back door painted with a beach mural.

I hold onto the wall, stretching out my right leg, which is feeling better. "How lovely," I say. "I didn't know you could paint with such detail."

Girl is shy for a moment. "Thanks Adira," she leads me back towards the kitchen. "Sophie and Jacquelyn will arrive later this morning," she says.

"You have organised this already?" I am intrigued.

"Yes, I didn't want to waste any time getting started on creating the replica of the indigo sash. Hidu will arrive soon too with some silk making equipment."

"Great," I say. "How are you planning to dye the replica?"

"Easily," Girl smiles. "I've had a lot of practice in Mira."

A small, pine wood table sits in the dining space at the side of the kitchen, accompanied by four built in seats.

I edge around the table and sit down, flexing my right leg. The pain seems to have disappeared.

The kettle is boiling. Removing it from its heat element, Girl pours the tea and hands me a cup.

We sit quietly for a while, drinking and contemplating.

"Thanks for all the work you have done," I say. "The caravan looks amazing."

Girl smiles shyly again. She obviously isn't used to receiving compliments.

Knock, knock.

Girl stands and heads towards the front door. "Hello my love," Girl embraces a bright smiling Hidu.

"Hello beautiful," Hidu closes his eyes, relishing Girl's embrace. After a moment, he steps back. "The caravan looks amazing. Did you do all this yourself?"

"Yes," Girl nods, a smile spreading across her lips. "Thanks," she grabs Hidu's hand and leads him towards the dining table. "Would you like a cup of tea?" She asks him.

"Yes please," Hidu smiles as he places a small box on the table and sits across from me. "Hi Detective Adira," he says, his eyes alight with happiness.

"Hello Imperial Operative Hidu," I grin. "I see you have a box of goodies."

"Yes," Hidu says, reaching into the box. "I have brought some pieces of silk fabric that your mother created by hand, Girl." He lays the fabric out across the table.

"Wow!" Girl's eyes well with tears. She grasps the table with her free hand. The other one shakes as it holds the tea cup.

Hidu jumps up onto his feet. "Oh Girl," he retrieves the cup from her hand and places it onto the table. "I'm right here with you," he says softly, standing behind her and wrapping his arms around her waist.

"Thank you," Girl breathes. Reaching out her shaking hands, she picks up the silk gently and smells it. "I can smell Mother's scent on this," she says softly. "I miss her so much." She holds the silk close to her chest, embracing it. The tears fall freely down her cheeks.

"It's all going to be fine," Hidu says, turning Girl to face him. He crooks her chin up with his fingers. "It won't be too long now before you can see your family again."

Girl's gaze drifts to the silk fabric. "Mother is here with me," she says. "She is giving me the strength to put an end to the Petoys' madness." She stares into Hidu's eyes. "Have you got the vat?"

"Yes," Hidu grabs Girl's hand. "It's in the boot of the car. Do you want it out right now?"

"Yes," Girl faces me. "Are you able to grab the statue and my bag, Adira?"

"Sure," I say, heading into the kitchen. I retrieve the wrapped statue and the silk bag from the bench and follow Girl and Hidu outside.

Makeshift Girl: The Secret Heritage Trail

Stepping lightly across the grass in her bare feet, Girl clutches the silk close to her chest. Suddenly she stands still, staring up at the sky. "It's so beautiful out here," she says. "There is the sun, the blue sky and the solid earth beneath my feet." She sinks her feet into the earth. "I spent so long in hibernation, trying to hide away from it all." She turns to face me, her eyes shining brightly. "You've helped me find my confidence, Adira. I now know that I can face this head on. I am no longer afraid to sit out here in the open and be who I am." She raises the silk up into the air. "I am Vianna Bereni, an artist and the upcoming chief of silk of Mira." She closes her eyes, letting her words and thoughts fill the space.

"You are the most fiercely beautiful girl I know," Hidu says, dropping onto his knees before her.

Vianna's gaze meets his. "I'm all the more stronger with you by my side," she says, stroking his cheek gently.

Hidu clears his throat. "While I was in Mira, I had the honour of speaking to your father," he smiles gently. "I asked him for his permission to marry you, Vianna."

Vianna's eyes widen with surprise. "Oh Hidu!"

Hidu's eyes well with tears. "Your father reminded me that you were a silk bird, still flying your way through life. He said he gave me his blessing, as long as Vianna wanted to be married right now."

Vianna's lips form a wistful smile. "My father knows me very well," she says. "When I fled Mira, I feared further persecution and hid myself away. I became Girl, anonymous and unsure of who I was. I was driven by a mad desire to get my family's scarf back." She takes Hidu's hand and squeezes it tightly. "Along the way, I have had your love, Hidu, like a ray of light lifting me high above the darkness. You have given me strength and the hope of a future with you. I can't imagine stepping any further without you by my side."

Hidu exhales a deep sigh of relief. Reaching into his pocket with his free hand, he retrieves a ring. "One day, when I was a young boy, I discovered a small nugget of gold in the creek of Mira," he stares at the ring, turning it gently in his palm. "I could not bare to part with it, even when things got desperate for my family." He looks up at Vianna. "After time, I met you and fell in love with you and knew what I wanted to do with that gold nugget." He smiles gently. "I had Antra, the blacksmith of Mira, forge the gold into this precious ring. I asked him to engrave a grass and flower pattern around the inside of it, as I know how much you love the feeling of the earth beneath your feet." He shuffles closer and reaches for Vianna's hand.

Vianna's eyes are streaming with tears of happiness. "That is so touching," she says. "I feel so loved by you." She squeezes Hidu's hand.

Hidu's eyes shine. "Vianna Bereni, I love you with my heart and soul. I promise to continue to walk the earth with you, no matter how difficult the path is to cross. I want to be here, right beside you for the rest of my life." He smiles brightly. "Will you bless me with the honour of becoming my wife?"

"Yes!" Vianna exclaims, her eyes shining with happiness as she receives Hidu's ring on her finger.

Hidu stands, staring deeply into her eyes. "You have made me the happiest man in the world," he says, stroking her cheek and pulling her closer to him. Embracing Vianna in his arms, he leans towards her and kisses her gently.

After a short while, Vianna steps back and stares at her ring. "This is enchantingly beautiful," she says. "I never want to take it off. That way I know that you'll always be here with me."

"That's right," Hidu smiles, his eyes shining brightly. "My fiancée, I love the sound of that."

Vianna turns to face me. "We're engaged, Adira! Can you believe it?"

My heart is radiating with happiness. I step forward and hug them both. "Congratulations," I say. "May your continued journey together be one filled with great love and happiness."

"Thank you," the couple say in unison. I watch as Vianna draws Hidu close in a tight embrace.

Chapter 48

As the morning fades into the afternoon, Vianna's gaze falls upon the statue. She stares at it, running her fingers across the waves. "No more drifting away Vianna," she says softly. "You've finally found your feet."

Hidu sits next to Vianna and places his hand on her shoulder. "Yes, you certainly have," he says. "You are a fiercely brave woman."

"Ha!" Vianna laughs. "I've never thought of myself that way." She turns the statue around. "Can I have my bag please, Adira?" She meets my gaze.

"Sure," I hand Vianna her bag.

Digging into the bag, Vianna retrieves one of her chisels. She strokes it gently, twisting it in the palm of her hand. "Hello baby," she says, smiling. "I need your help right now." Tapping the chisel against the wood panel, she cracks it open.

"Drum roll," Hidu taps his knees. "Ladies and gentleman, Vianna is about to reveal …"

Reaching inside the statue, Vianna retrieves a small, brown paper bag. Opening it, she pulls out a blue cake-like formation.

"A natural indigo dye cake!" Hidu smiles. "That's very fortunate. You'll be needing that right now."

"Yes," Vianna smiles. "This cake is made from my family's secret indigo dye recipe and I have carted it around with me for a long time. I plan to use it now, in our time of need."

"What are you going to do with it?" Hidu asks her.

Vianna digs into the statue again, retrieving another green dye cake. "I will use some of this dye cake to help alter the indigo colour," she says. "I will dye the replica sash in the alternative shade and trick the Petoys into believing it is a genuine indigo colour."

"Isn't it a great idea?" I ask Hidu.

"Genius," Hidu nods. "It will certainly diminish the quality and value of the Petoys' silk range."

"That's the plan," Vianna smiles. She digs into the statue again, retrieving a small piece of white card. She bites her lip nervously. "This asset is extremely delicate. It is the seal that the Empress gave to my ancestor, Sefra, many centuries ago. It is proof of my family's strong connection with the imperial dynasty."

I step closer, admiring the gold, eagle talon seal. "It's very striking," I say. "So precious too, I imagine."

"Yes," Vianna nods. "I can't afford to lose it." Digging into her silk bag, she retrieves Aisha's journal. "I will keep it in here, just like Sefra kept it in the pig skin notebook." She smiles as she places the seal into the journal, which she returns into her silk bag.

"Good idea," I say.

Digging into her statue once more, she retrieves a small wooden object. "This small stamp here," she continues. "Is what Aisha used to add the Empress' eagle talon totem to any silks that she made. We have continued to use it centuries later in our silk designs. We will mark the replica sash with this authentic stamp totem."

"You're lucky to have the original totem," I say. "It wouldn't feel right to copy it."

"No, it wouldn't," Vianna nods. "The Emperor trusts my family with his totem and I plan to ensure that we use it respectfully. He will understand that we used the stamp in an attempt to save Mira's heritage."

I nod, respecting Vianna's approach.

"I'd better get to work," Vianna sighs, picking up the silk cloths. "Hidu, are you able to grab the vat?"

"Sure," Hidu stands and stretches his legs. "I'll be back in a minute," he says as he heads towards his car.

"Adira," Vianna touches me lightly on the arm and I meet her gaze. "I have another journal entry written by Aisha. It will help you to understand how the resistance originally formed in Mira. Would you like to read it?" She retrieves the book from her bag.

"I would love to," I smile, accepting the journal in both my hands.

"Here we go," Hidu has returned with the vat. "Where would you like this placed?"

"Next to me, please," Vianna smiles. "I can work right here."

Hidu places the vat on the grass next to Vianna. "Do you need some help?" He asks her.

"That would be great," Vianna smiles. "Can you half fill the kettle with cold water and bring it here? We need to fill this vat with a little water to liquefy the dye."

"I can do that," Hidu smiles. He jogs towards the caravan, dashing up the steps and disappearing inside.

Vianna breaks the natural indigo dye cake in half and drops the pieces into the vat.

"Here's some water," Hidu has returned with the kettle.

"Pour it straight in," Vianna directs.

Hidu pours the water into the vat. "Is that enough?" He asks.

"Let's see," Vianna reaches into her silk bag and pulls out some large gloves. Putting them on, she grabs a large stick off the grass and uses it to stir the water, which has turned blue. "More than enough," she smiles. "Thank you."

"Okay," Hidu smiles. "I'll just take this kettle back inside."

Vianna continues to stir the mixture. She points to the vat. "Soon we'll have an alternative indigo shade," she smiles mischievously.

"Sounds great," I say, admiring her talent.

Hidu returns and plonks down onto the grass next to Vianna. He watches her continue to mix the dye.

"Perfect!" Vianna calls out after a long while. "Now, for the slight alteration to colour, "I'll just add this quarter of the green dye cake to the mixture," she says as she throws it into the vat too. She continues to stir, mixing the dye colours together.

"Wow!" Hidu exclaims. "That looks glossy."

"Yes," Vianna says. "The colour is perfect. It is a slightly greener indigo shade. The Petoys won't even notice the difference." Reaching out, she grabs one of the silk cloths off the grass. "Time to dye!" She announces.

I watch Vianna dip the cloth into the dye and swirl it around gently. Pulling it out, she checks its saturation. "It needs more dye," she says, dipping the cloth into the dye again and checking it a couple more times.

"Perfect!" Vianna announces, holding up the dyed cloth. It looks stunning, gleaming its gorgeous, green indigo shade.

"Wow!" Hidu smiles. "Vianna, it is so great to see you working your silk magic again."

"Is that so?" Vianna murmurs, leaning forward to kiss Hidu gently on the lips. "It is great to have you right here beside me."

Hidu smiles broadly, his eyes glistening happily. "I love being with you," he strokes her hair gently.

Vianna smiles and returns her focus to the dyed cloth. Standing, she heads towards the side of the caravan, where one end of a washing line is jammed underneath a closed window sill. The line of rope leads out across the grassland and is tied in a knot around the branch of an elm tree.

Grabbing a couple of pegs off the line, Vianna hangs the dyed silk cloth. It flaps gently in the breeze, radiating its indigo gloriousness through the air.

Returning to the vat, Vianna repeats the process with two more silk cloths. "Back ups," she smiles as she hangs the last cloth out to dry.

"They look stunning," I say, admiring her work.

"Thank you," Vianna smiles gratefully. "It's nice to know that I haven't forgotten my skills." She rips off her gloves and carries them in one hand. "Time to tidy up." With her free hand, she pops the stamp into her silk bag and slings its strap over her shoulder.

"I'll take this," Hidu says, grabbing the statue. "It will be safer if it stays with me."

"Agreed," Vianna says. "No Petoy man would want to mess with an imperial operative of Mira." She elbows him jokingly.

"Don't I wish that was true," Hidu sighs. "Rank doesn't seem to intimidate them in the slightest. Not even the Emperor himself."

"That is scary," Vianna says.

I hear the sound of wheels against the terrain and look up. Jacquelyn has arrived with Sophie sitting in the passenger seat of her van. She parks in front of the caravan.

"Hello!" Sophie calls as she steps out onto the grass.

"Hi Sophie," Vianna smiles, twirling her engagement ring with her finger.

"What's this I see you're wearing?" Sophie's eyes widen with surprise as she approaches Vianna. "Hidu!" She calls out as he returns. "Do you have something to do with this ring?"

"Yes," Hidu says, wrapping his arms around Vianna's waist and kissing her cheek. "Vianna and I are engaged."

"Oh, that's the best news I've heard in ages!" Sophie cries. Rushing up, she embraces Hidu and Vianna. "We're going to be sisters," she touches Vianna's cheek. "Isn't that amazing?"

"I've never had a sister," Vianna smiles. "It will be lovely to have that connection, Sophie."

Jacquelyn steps out of the van with a mobile phone pressed to her ear. "You can do it, Zac," she says, placing her hand on her hip. "I'm here with Adira right now. You should come over and speak to her," Jacquelyn sighs. "Okay, love you too, bye." Placing her mobile into her bag, she steps across the grass towards us.

"Hi Jacquelyn," I say, meeting her gaze.

"Hi Adira," Jacquelyn pushes her long, dark blonde hair out of her eyes. She pulls at the skirt of her pastel orange maxi dress.

I stare at her a moment longer, waiting for her to meet my gaze. "Does Zac need some help?" I dare to ask.

Jacquelyn's cheeks redden. "Oh, did you hear my conversation on the phone?" She is embarrassed.

"A little," I nod.

"Zac's discovered something important," Jacquelyn rubs her forehead. "He is not sure if he should share it with you as he is worried about you getting hurt."

"I understand," I say. "Let's see if he decides to visit, okay?"

"Okay," Jacquelyn looks relieved. Digging into her bag, she retrieves a green folder. "This folder is for you," she smiles. "It contains my documentation of all that I have been forced to do at Botanica. I hope it helps to bring some justice."

"Thank you Jacquelyn," I say, accepting the folder. "I will hand this over to Hidu later. He is compiling all the evidence against the Petoys' illegal operation."

"Okay," Jacquelyn smiles with relief. "I trust your decision, Adira."

Jacquelyn shifts her gaze to Vianna, who is showing Sophie her ring. "Oh Girl, did you and Hidu get engaged?" Her eyes shine with anticipation at the news.

"Yes!" Vianna smiles.

"Congratulations!" Jacquelyn steps forward, embracing Vianna and Hidu. "I am so happy for you both."

"Thank you," Hidu grins. "Vianna and I are very excited."

"Is that your real name?" Jacquelyn is surprised.

"Yes," Vianna nods. "From now on, I wish to be called Vianna. She is alive again."

"And a beautiful woman she is too," Sophie smiles. "So caring and thoughtful."

"Thank you Sophie," Vianna smiles. "I'm so happy you both could make it here." She reaches into her silk bag, retrieving the original indigo silk sash. "This is the sash I was telling you both about. It is a piece that belongs to the Emperor's collection in Mira and its totem is displayed here," she points.

"How did you get your hands on that?" Sophie asks.

"The Petoys attempted to steal it from Mira," I say. "We've been given permission to use it to bring down their illegal trade operation."

"Right," Sophie nods.

Vianna stares at Jacquelyn and Sophie. "I need help from both of you, please. Jacquelyn, Hidu has gathered some authentic silk from my parents in Mira, which I would love for you to try to create an identical replica silk sash from. Can you see it hanging back there?"

"Yes," Jacquelyn smiles. "What a stunning colour that dye is," she is impressed.

"Yes," Vianna smiles. "I have created an altered natural indigo dye, which is slightly greener. It should fool the Chief into thinking that he has a real indigo silk sash in this hands."

"I love that it's natural," Jacquelyn's gaze turns dreamy. "Better than the synthetics that the Petoys dye their fake silk range with." Grabbing the original sash, she stares at Vianna. "Do you have a plain silk cloth? I can use that to create the original pattern and then relay it onto the dyed silk later."

"Yes, of course," Vianna retrieves a plain silk cloth off the grass and hands it to Jacquelyn. "That's the last one."

"Right," Jacquelyn nods. "I'd better do my very best then." She gazes around the space. "I just need a solid surface to work on."

"I'll take you inside the caravan," Hidu offers.

"Is that your caravan?" Jacquelyn looks amazed.

"Yes," Vianna smiles.

"It is beautiful," Jacquelyn smiles. "I bet you painted that coastal scene yourself, Vianna."

"She certainly would have," Sophie agrees. "She is gifted when it comes to art."

Vianna blushes. "Yes I did," she smiles.

"Amazing," Jacquelyn breathes with admiration. "Lead the way, Hidu." She follows him inside the caravan.

Vianna reaches into her bag and retrieves the eagle talon stamp. She meets Sophie's gaze. "I would love it if you could ensure that this totem is placed on the sash," she says. Reaching into the statue, she retrieves a black dye cake. "I'll prepare this dye to help you."

"Thank you," Sophie smiles. "Do you want the totem altered slightly?"

"No," Vianna shakes her head. "There's been too much altering of heritage totems already. This totem will be stamped proudly on the sash, marking the empire of Mira's fighting spirit against all this mess."

"Sounds great," Sophie looks relieved. "I will add the totem once the dye is dry."

"Perfect," Vianna smiles. "Thank you Sophie." She begins to lead her inside the caravan. "Let me get you a cup of tea." She turns to face me. "Do you want one too, Adira?"

"No thank you," I smile. "I am happy to stay out here and read. It will be very crowded in there."

"Okay," Vianna smiles. "Enjoy."

"You let me know if you need any help," I offer.

"Will do," Vianna smiles warmly. Turning on her heels, she disappears into the caravan with Sophie.

Stretching out my right leg, I am pleased that I no longer feel pain in my knee. Picking up Aisha's journal, I flip the pages open to the next entry. It is lovely to see her familiar, poetic writing style again:

Makeshift Girl: The Secret Heritage Trail

Spring, 1276

It is Spring, the time of bustling trade in Mira. As I step across the unmade road this evening, the light of my tallow candle creates eerie shadows across the trunks and leaves of cedar trees.

As I push my cart along the winding path of the forest, a haunting glow emanates from the burning flame. The tree branches appear gnarled and twisted, lurking in the background and stretching out towards me, waiting for a chance to attack.

It is not peaceful to walk along the trade route at night. I glance over my shoulders constantly, ears pricked and listening acutely for the sound of horse hooves. Attacks are often swift and sudden, leaving very little chance to escape the dark, rearing horses.

As I approach the end of the winding pathway, the candle light reveals a dark haired man sitting atop a horse. I stop moving, clutching tightly at the handle of my cart, ready to run.

Squinting, I study the man's familiar figure. My heart begins to beat rapidly and I clutch my chest.

Hearing a rustling behind him, the man turns sharply, discovering me standing still in the shadows. A warm smile spreads across his lips as he recognises me.

"Aisha," Kirano breathes. "It is wonderful to see you again."

"Hi Kirano," I say, feeling a fluttering sensation in my stomach. "How are you faring?"

Kirano dismounts his horse and stands before me. "Better, now that you are here," he smiles sadly. "I've missed you."

I lower my gaze, studying the light patterns shifting across the dirt as the candle flame flickers in the wind. It has been a long time since I last saw Kirano and while my heart feels drawn to him, my head is afflicted with the turmoil of confusion.

Kirano steps closer and his shadow looms before me on the earth. I step back, feeling afraid of his power.

"I am sorry," Kirano clutches his chest. "I do not intend to scare you. That is the last thing I want to do."

I look up, meeting Kirano's gaze. His deep brown eyes look sad, as though they are searching for a way through the complex maze of our world.

"I am fine," I say, standing tall and straight. "You need not concern yourself with me."

Kirano's eyes widen incredulously. "Not concern myself with you? Aisha, I made a solemn promise to you that I intend to keep. You are my betrothed and I want nothing more than to be your husband."

Tears are building in Kirano's eyes and he swipes at them in frustration. "It is so difficult being the Empress' soldier," he grumbles. "I am ordered to protect the city of Mira at any cost." He stares at the candle flame, flickering in my hand. "This light you burn, it radiates your beautiful spirit," he smiles weakly. "It carries you across the pitch black, giving you light and guiding your way out of the mess of this world." He meets my gaze. "Keep burning that candle, Aisha, it will bring you hope."

I stare at Kirano, feeling empathy. What he must have endured during his dangerous ventures as a solider. I know what it is like to be alone and afraid.

"Sometimes the light stops my nightmares," I say wistfully. "I keep seeing Alzat's body, lying lifelessly on the ground. The image startles me awake, making me tremble with fear that I am exposed, vulnerable and about to be shot myself."

Kirano's eyebrows furrow with concern. "I am angry at myself for making you feel this way," his voice is deep. "There are things that you do not know, Aisha. Alzat was a member of the Petoy clan, which was founded by the barons who tried to steal the Empress' falcons. They were angry with her decision to take away their privilege of falconry, as they had always partaken in it as a sport with her father. They set about forming a resistance movement against her empire, pledging for hastened progress to bury the Empress' ancient traditions. As part of their resistance movement, they show no mercy to anyone who shows support for the Empress' rule. As you are her Chief of silk, Aisha, you would have eventually been murdered by the Petoy clan."

Kirano's words surround me, smothering me with their conviction. I drop to the ground. "You were trying to protect me?" I ask, trembling with fear.

"Yes!" Kirano exclaims, dropping onto his knees and cupping my face in both his hands. "I love you, Aisha. I will do anything to keep you safe."

I nod, absorbing Kirano's words. My heart is pounding and I acknowledge it, allowing it to feel the warmth that now sits comfortably between us.

"Aisha," Kirano strokes my hair and cheek. Leaning towards me, he kisses me gently on the lips.

I sigh, letting my panic dissipate into the night air. His lips feel warm, familiar and comforting against mine. I treasure the moment, letting my heart soar with the love I feel for him.

After a short while, Kirano stands and offers me his hand. I accept it, letting him pull me up onto my feet.

Stepping closer to my cart, Kirano peers at its contents. "You have completed designing the silk sashes?" He asks with admiration.

"Yes," I say. "All 1,500 of them. Ready for your army. I am on the way to deliver them to the Empress."

"I will accompany you there," Kirano offers. "If you don't mind?"

"That would be lovely," I smile.

As we trek across the open grassland, my candle light flickers across the frame of Ricardo, who is standing beside a cypress tree. He is staring into the distance, as though he is waiting for someone to arrive.

Suddenly, a shadow shifts across the earth behind Ricardo. I jump, grasping onto Kirano's arm.

"What is it?" Kirano's eyes dart across the grassland, falling upon Ricardo, who is struggling under another man's grasp. He has a knife pressed into his neck. "Stay here," Kirano says, releasing me gently.

Dashing across the earth towards Ricardo, Kirano stops. He stands tall, drawing the sword from his scabbard. "Let go of him!" He commands the attacker. "Or you'll face the wrath of my blade."

The dangerous man steps back, raising his hands in defeat. His black, rearing horse head scarf falls off his head, floating aimlessly to the ground.

"Go!" Kirano orders, shooing the man away. "Before I change my mind."

The Petoy man spins wildly on his feet and dashes away into the darkness.

Stepping forward, I reach Ricardo who is gasping to catch a breath. He rubs at his sore neck, which has a deep, red gash.

"Aisha," Ricardo smiles weakly. "It's good to see you."

"You too, Ricardo," I smile warmly. "I am so pleased that we were here to help you."

"Yes, me too," Ricardo sighs with relief. "Thank you for rescuing me, Kirano."

Kirano smiles, touching Ricardo's arm. "I would consider very carefully whether I should be waiting out here in the dark again," he warns. "There is a vicious clan on the prowl and they will not hesitate to harm you."

"I realise that," Ricardo sighs. "I was waiting to receive the silk shirt that I had ordered from the Empress. She requested that I meet one of her soldiers at this message post, where she had organised for the trade exchange to occur.

"I had waited a long time, earning enough money off trade of the lapis lazuli to be able to afford the shirt. I had my money ready and the thief demanded that I hand it over to him or that I would be killed."

"Hmm," Kirano pauses, considering the situation. "This is definitely the message post point," he says. "I am meant to hand you the shirt here." Approaching his horse, Kirano reaches up and unties a wrapped bundle from the bridle. "Here is your shirt, Ricardo," he says as he hands it over.

"Thank you," Ricardo smiles. "I will feel as though I have stepped up in the world in this shirt. I will look so distinguished that I might even sell more trade." He hands Kirano some paper money as payment. "I'd better head off tonight," Ricardo sighs. "Safely back across the sea to home. I might steer clear of Mira for a while."

"Good idea," Kirano nods. "Our city has become a very dangerous place."

Ricardo meets my gaze. "Farewell Aisha," he says. "I wish you all the best."

"You too, Ricardo," I smile warmly. "I am sure that you will succeed in your future trade."

"Thank you," Ricardo smiles. Turning on his heels, he disappears into the pitch black of night.

Kirano's gaze drifts back to the message post. "Interesting," he mutters. "It appears that the Petoy clan is infiltrating the Empress' message service. We must see her immediately."

"Agreed," I say, falling into step beside Kirano. He grabs the stirrup of the horse and guides it to trot gently beside him as we make our way towards the palace.

The palace is tall with a bronze tiled roof that is decorated with tall turrets. On one turret flies the Empress' flag. On each side of the building, there are gold painted walls, which glisten enchantingly. The Empress has had the interior walls decorated with images of the falcons that have been bred in her empire for centuries. The falcons soar high in flight, giving the rooms inside an uplifting energy.

Towards the east of the palace, there are six rooms that the Empress has designated as shop fronts for trade. In these rooms, she has hired artists with the most excellent skills and they use materials from the land around them to create fashion or crafted objects. Every summer, the Empress opens her gates to the surrounding cities and lets them peruse and purchase the wares that are stocked in these rooms.

We meet the Empress in one of the trade rooms, where she is sorting orders of silk garments to be sent to merchants who have purchased them.

Empress Mira greets us with sad eyes. "Greetings Kirano and Aisha," *she sighs.*

"Good evening, Your Imperial Majesty," *I say as I curtsy.*

"Our empathy is with you, your Imperial Majesty," *Kirano's voice is solemn as he bows.*

The Empress meets Kirano's gaze. "Thank you Kirano. Trade is not progressing as well as I would have hoped," *she clarifies.*

"There would be a reason for that, Your Imperial Majesty," *says Kirano. He shares the story of what happened at the message post with the Empress.*

"Well, that explains a lot," *the Empress sighs.* "I've been sending out messages to local and international buyers so that we can increase our silk trade. While I have had a lot of interest in the silk garments, I have not received any payments from the buyers. It seems that the Petoys have outsmarted our message and delivery service. I will need to work out another way to organise trade exchange." *The Empress paces back and forth.* "The lack of funds received for silk trade have left me no choice but to raise the silk tax," *she declares.* "It is going to upset the Petoy clan even more and I dread what they will do to our city."

"We will do what we can to stop them," *Kirano places his hand on his heart.* "It will be my honour to protect you and your empire, Your Imperial Majesty," *he bows.*

"Thank you Kirano," the Empress smiles. Her gaze falls upon my cart. "You have completed making the silk sashes, Aisha," she says admirably.

"Yes," I nod.

The Empress retrieves a sash and admires it. "How lovely it is to finally have an indigo sash with our imperial totem displayed on it," she gushes. "Kirano, I would like to place you in charge of the army and trust that you will guide them out safely tomorrow to where the Petoy clan resides. All soldiers should wear one of these sashes in order to assert the power of our empire over the dangerous clan."

"It would be my honour to serve you, Your Imperial Majesty," Kirano bows.

"Thank you both for your support," the Empress smiles. She stares at us both for a moment, pondering. "Our world has become cruel," she smiles in defiance of her statement. "Yet there is always room for the joy of love. You have both waited a long time for my blessing of your marriage. Right here, in this moment, I, Empress Mira, give you both my heartfelt blessings to marry as you will."

"Thank you, your Imperial Majesty," Kirano bows.

"Thank you Empress Mira," I bow too.

Kirano reaches out and grabs my hand. I smile as I feel him squeeze my fingers excitedly.

The Empress faces me. "Aisha, while Kirano is taking care of our army's mission, I will help you to plan for your special day."

"Will you?" My eyes light up happily. "Thank you, Empress Mira."

Empress Mira's eyes shine. "You have watched silk being designed for a long time and probably always desired to wear it yourself," she says.

I nod, biting my lip in anticipation.

"Well, you have my permission to design your own silk dress for your wedding day. You can also design a silk shirt for Kirano too, if you wish. I will fund the expense of the silk production."

"I humbly thank you, your Imperial Majesty," I bow, smiling excitedly.

"Aisha and Kirano, I wish to extend the land allotted to Aisha's leased silk farm so that the silk business can continue to grow. I gift the land and all structures upon it to you both as your married home and as a recognition of our special bond together. I hope it brings you both many years of love, growth and family."

My eyes well with tears. "That is more than we could ever ask for," I say, feeling the tears roll down my cheeks. "Thank you from the bottom of my heart for your generosity, your Imperial Majesty."

"I will leave you both with this wonderful news," the Empress smiles. "Tomorrow, Aisha, we will discuss plans for your silk farm. I want to ensure that it is structured exactly as you need it to be, including any renovations that may need to occur." She turns to face Kirano. "Once you return from your mission with the imperial army, Kirano, you and Aisha will be wed." The Empress steps backwards, smiling radiantly at both of us as she exits the room and shuts the door quietly behind her.

"We're going to be married," I breathe, grabbing hold of Kirano's hands. "Isn't that wonderful?"

"Yes, it is," Kirano smiles, pulling me close. I close my eyes, enjoying his warm embrace.

My thoughts turn to my caring father, who was always there for me. *You will be proud of me, Father*, I ponder silently, closing my eyes. *I have a future set out for myself with a man who cares deeply for me. We will live together on the silk farm, which we will own, continuing its ancient heritage way into the future.*

Opening my eyes, my mouth falls open as I see my father appear before me, smiling a warm smile. As his precious image fades, I know that his spirit is content and it makes my heart soar with happiness and love.

Chapter 49

I am being shaken and stir, awakening. Vianna is sitting in front of me with an amused smile on her face. "Looks like you needed a rest," she smiles.

"Yes," I say, sitting up. Aisha's journal jostles in my lap as I retrieve it and hand it to Vianna. "Aisha's journal entry was really something," I say. "It is lovely to have had the privilege to learn about your family, Vianna."

Vianna's smile radiates. "I take after Aisha," she smiles. "She has been quite the inspiration to me through all that has happened."

"Now I understand why the Petoys formed their resistance movement against the empire," I say. "It must have been very challenging for the Empress. It is impossible to please everyone when you are the leader of an entire city."

"That's true," Vianna smiles. "No matter what leader you are. I have my own battles to face back home when I become the chief of silk."

"You will be a great leader," I say. "You will take good care of our people."

"Yes I will," Vianna agrees. Turning to face the caravan, she waves. I watch as Sophie and Jacquelyn head towards us.

"We made the sash," Jacquelyn smiles. "Do you want to see it?"

"Yes please," I say. I watch as Jacquelyn opens up her palm, revealing the replica indigo sash. It is sheer and light and enchantingly colourful. "How beautiful," I breathe.

"They're almost the same colour but not quite," Sophie says, showing me the original one.

The replica has a tiny shade of green, which lessens the quality of the indigo. "It is very difficult to spot the difference," I smile. "You've all done such a great job. You should be proud."

"We are," Jacquelyn smiles. She steps forward, touching me on the shoulder. "I hope the sash helps you," she says softly. "I heard that you will need it on the ship."

"Yes, I will," I say. "Thank you for all your efforts, Jacquelyn."

"I'm happy to help," Jacquelyn smiles. "You've been a great friend to me, Adira. I should go now. I have to tend to the forest."

I stand up, hugging Jacquelyn. "Thank you for being there for us," I say appreciatively.

"Always," Jacquelyn smiles, her eyes watery with tears. "I will miss being part of this final chapter but I do not have the skills to undertake the very dangerous work that you're all about to be involved in," she says. "The villagers also need me to look after the forest." She faces Vianna. "Hug?" She asks.

"Of course!" Vianna opens up her arms, embracing Jacquelyn affectionately. "Thanks for everything," she says. "Hopefully this will all be over soon."

"Hopefully," Jacquelyn agrees. "See you Sophie."

"Come here," Sophie smiles, opening her arms widely. "Cuddle time!"

Jacquelyn giggles as Sophie hugs her tightly. "I feel very loved by you all, thank you." Stepping backwards, she waves as she heads back towards her van.

"Good bye Jacquelyn!" Hidu calls as he descends the stairs of the caravan.

Jacquelyn waves one last time before sitting in the driver's seat. We watch as the van reverses and drives away, becoming a small speck in the distance.

"Jacquelyn is so lovely," Vianna smiles. "And so talented with textiles."

"Yes she is," I agree, staring at the sash.

Ding!

It is a message. Reaching into my pocket, I retrieve my mobile and stare at the words: *Deep Red*, it reads, which indicates that Concetta is in danger.

"Is everything okay?" Vianna asks, noticing my troubled expression.

"It's Concetta," I say. "She needs my help."

"Should I come with you?" Vianna asks.

"No," I say. "It is best that you stay here with Hidu. A message like this one should only be tended to by one person."

"Okay," Vianna smiles and hands me her ute remote key. "Take the ute and please let us know if you need assistance."

"I will," I say, stepping backwards.

"Best of luck, Detective," Hidu smiles while he waves at me.

"Thanks," I say, grabbing my bag and slinging it over my shoulder.
"I will see you all again very soon."

Reaching the ute, I plonk down into the driver's seat and shut the door. My mind is reeling with worry for Concetta. Clenching my teeth, I start the ignition and release the handbrake. I press my foot down onto the accelerator immediately. The ute rolls forward gently across the grass and onto the gravel.

Reaching the exit of the camp ground, I press my foot down onto the brake and my hands shake with nervousness. I am going solo to help Concetta. *I can do this!*

"Yes, I can and I must do this," I say aloud to the invisible audience.

Switching on the indicator, I wait for a couple of cars to zoom passed before I turn right.

Heading down Nouveau Road, I can see the tall city buildings looming ahead. Turning right onto Tinker Street, I drive slowly, feeling as though I've stepped straight back into my past. There is the local patisserie and green grocer.

Driving passed a few more shops, I see the building that I need. The old milk bar.

I do not park the ute out front as it will be exposed.

Turning left onto Beka Street, I drive passed the side of the milk bar. There is a small car park tucked into the back of the building, which is a more discrete place to park the ute.

I switch off the ignition and sit for a moment, catching a breath. Staring into the rear view mirror, I check if there are any tails.

All is clear.

Opening the driver's door, I step outside, swinging my bag over my shoulder. I can feel my body shaking with trepidation. I do not know what to expect.

Locking the ute, I stand for a moment, taking in the sight of the old milk bar.

The rear windows are dusty as they haven't been cleaned in a while. That's unusual. Concetta Mancini always keeps a clean shop. I'd better take a closer look.

Heading towards the back door of the building, I notice that it is unlocked. Next to the door lies a pile of crates filled with milk and ice-creams. There is a strong, yucky smell emanating from the stock. I wave my hand over my nose, gagging. It has clearly been here for a while. Something is not right.

I consider whether I should take the risk to enter the milk bar. Who knows who is inside there?

Taking a deep breath, I harness my strength. I'm going to need it right now.

I take small, quiet steps, entering the building. Once inside, I am faced with a mess. Bottles, jars, cans and you name it, have been tossed upon the ground.

Someone has trashed the milk bar.

Susan Marshall

By the putrid smell of off milk, it seems that the intruder was here days ago.

The fluorescent tube lights flash like a disco ball. I feel dizzy but try to ignore it. I need to focus on what is happening right now. Time to take a closer look.

I trek across the room and my feet crunch through the broken glass. Newspapers are strewn across the ground and some broadsheets hang off the shelves. Checking the dates on them, I note that they are three days old. Hmmm.

A faint sound grabs my attention:

Bang, bang.
Bang, bang.

It is the sound of an object on a wall or door. Ears pricked up, I listen acutely for the noise again.

Bang, bang.

It is coming from the back of the milk bar.

Taking careful steps across the broken glass and spilled milk, I walk quietly towards the back of the store.

My eyes peel the room for a something to protect myself with … just in case. I notice a broom, leaning up against a shelf.

Reaching out, I collect the broom and carry it with me, further across the floor.

Bang, bang, bang.

The person can hear my footsteps. Their banging is more insistent, trying to get my attention.

I know where they are now. They are in the store room and the door is shut.

Reaching the door, I grab the handle and twist it. It is locked.

Looking around, I see if I can spot the key. No such luck.

Bang, bang, bang.

"Save your energy," I say softly. "I am here to help you."

It is quiet. The banging has ceased for now.

Suddenly, I hear a small cry behind the door. The voice is soft, yet audible. "No trouble, take what you want," says the female voice.

"Concetta, is that you?" I am concerned now.

"Lira?" The voice is a little stronger now, more hopeful.

"It's me, Adira," I say. "I have come as myself, to rescue you."
It breaks my heart to think of how long Concetta has been locked away in here. "Don't worry Concetta, I'm going to get you out!" I say, keeping my voice cheerful and light.

"The keys!" Concetta says in a hoarse voice.

"I can't find them Concetta," I say, feeling defeated. How am I going to get her out?

"They're in the cash register," Concetta's voice is renewed with determination. "You know the code, Adira."

I did know the code a while ago.

"Of course Concetta," I say. "I'll be back in a moment. We'll have you out in no time."

Carrying the broom for protection, my feet crunch on the glass as I move across the floor. I have almost become an expert at jumping over spilled liquid.

As I reach the front counter, I inhale a deep breath. There are large windows behind it, reflecting the light of the afternoon sun. I can see right outside onto the street.

Directly across the road is Pierre's Patisserie. I have fond memories of that place. The owner, Pierre, always gave me the freshest pies and pasties for lunch. His wife, Claire would make the most delicious soups. I remember tasting a divine pumpkin soup with their crusty olive pain for lunch.

It is odd that the couple haven't noticed what has happened to the milk bar. Claire used to pop in regularly to visit Concetta.

Turning back to face the register, my brain ticks. I remember when Concetta first set the code on the register. She proudly said that it was ... Mitch's date of birth.

Let me think ... Mitch's birthday is in May. What day is it again ... ? We celebrated it together many times. I remember it was early in the month too. Was it the sixth?

I type 0605 in the cash register. No, that code doesn't work.

That's right, it was the fourth. I remember ordering a chocolate mousse birthday cake from the patisserie in the shape of a four for one of Mitch's birthdays. My mouth waters as I remember the taste of that cake. I am hungry.

Approaching the cash register again, I type in 0405. Yes, it worked! The till springs open.

Digging among the coins in the cash drawer, my hand feels the sharpness of the skeleton key. Grabbing it, I absorb its familiarity. I used it many times to access the back store room as a detective. It was there that I would set up the surveillance for inside the building. The milk bar was our front. It was the perfect venue to hear the chatter of people who would pop in to buy their goods and incidentally provide us with current news.

Such important information led to us being able to protect or track down someone much faster.

Taking a deep breath, I stare out of the large, open windows behind me. I can see Pierre across the road, opening the bi-fold doors of his bakery. He has aged a little since I saw him last, huddling over to lift the stands he uses to sell cakes at the front of his store. I want to rush over and help him but I can't. I have to remain unseen. Our lives depend upon it.

Just down the road from Pierre, I spot the silver Mercedes. It is idle and parked on the main street.

Reaching into my bag, I grab my phone and check the time. It's four o'clock in the afternoon. Did the Chief follow me here? I don't have much time.

My gaze returns to Pierre. He is restocking his stand. He stops to catch a breath, placing his hands onto his knee caps. I hope he is alright.

After a moment, Pierre's gaze darts up, as though he can feel eyes upon him.

Dropping onto my knees, I hide under the window sill. I can hear the shuffle of footsteps across the road. They are growing louder as they approach the front door of … our milk bar!

"Madame Mancini!" I can hear Pierre's strained voice out the front.

After a moment, Pierre's fist bangs against the locked glass door. "Madame Mancini, es-vous là?"

It is hard not to unlock the door and let Pierre in. He is such a kind and thoughtful man who has always looked after Concetta. It pains me to leave him stranded out the front.

"Je voudrais un litre de lait s'il vous plaît!" Pierre calls out. "Lorsque vous êtes prêt!" I can hear the shuffle of his footsteps as he walks away.

Phew! That was close!

I'd better move quickly now. It will only be a matter of time before Pierre realises what has happened. The last people we want to deal with is the police. They ask too many questions.

Crawling across the floor on my knees, I use the broom to sweep the broken glass aside. Chips of glass press against my legs, leaving small cuts that sting. I ignore the pain.

It takes a long time to dodge the spilled liquid this way, yet ensures that I remain out of sight.

Finally, I reach the store room door. It is very quiet now.

"Concetta, are you okay in there?" I ask, worried about her.

"Just," Concetta's voice is faint. "Have you got the key?"

"Yes, I do," I reply, reaching up and inserting the key into the lock. "Stand back, okay? I'm going to open the door now."

I can hear the smallest shuffle of footsteps as Concetta steps back from the door.

Turning the key, I unlock the door and slowly open it. I am scared of what state I might find her in.

There is Concetta with her long blonde hair swept up in a bun and loose strands flying in front of her eyes. Her soft, youthful skin is a little dull, yet she still hardly looks a day passed thirty.

Concetta sits on top of a stack of crates, her strong biceps flexed as she clutches onto a heavy black bag.

"Concetta!" I am relieved to see her. "Thank goodness you are okay."

"Of course I'm fine, Adira," Concetta waves her hand. "I've been in here for three days and two nights. It's hard to get air in here but there's plenty to eat." She sighs an exhausted sigh.

"Come on," I say, putting my arm around her shoulders. "We'll talk later. It's time to get you out now."

"Not without these," Concetta holds up the black bag. "I have a video camera and cords in here. Over there is the computer from your office upstairs. I stored them in here a while ago, when I first knew the milk bar was under surveillance. Fortunately I did so, as the Petoy clan had no luck in finding them when they broke in." Concetta's eyes narrow and her expression is worried. "I have some news for you though, Adira."

My heart thumps wildly in my chest. "What is it?"

Concetta leans forward, her expression solemn. "Chief Opula was here," she says. "He told me to pass on a message to you."

"What is that?" My cheeks burn with rage at the thought of the Chief being in the milk bar again.

"You have exactly until midnight in two day time to visit him on his ship, otherwise he will hurt Mitch," Concetta says, her eyes narrowing with empathy.

"Wow," I stare down at the ground. "The Chief will stop at nothing to have me, will he?"

"No," Concetta sighs. "I'm here to help Adira, you just let me know what you need."

"Thanks," I reply, meeting Concetta's gaze. "I'm glad you're okay. You had me worried."

Concetta pats me on the shoulder. "Don't worry, Adira. Let's just get out of here as quickly as we can before we're discovered."

"Of course," I say, glancing up at Concetta. "Are you okay to carry the video camera?"

Concetta nods.

Standing, Concetta stretches her arms and legs and begins to walk slowly out of the store room and onto the shop floor. "Well," she sighs in resignation. "This is quite the spectacular break in. Pity they've gone to so much effort for absolutely no reward. There was nothing to be found." Concetta does not seem the least bit surprised. "I've seen a lot worse than this," she says. "It's lucky that no-one, not you, Mitch or I, got hurt."

I nod in agreement.

Poor Concetta, the mixed feelings that must be rushing through her heart right now. It must be so hard seeing the milk bar like this. She has owned the shop for a very long time.

Concetta begins to film the setting with the video camera. "It's always good to have evidence of a crime," she says, capturing every angle of the room. "You never know when it could come in handy."

My dear Concetta, always the detective.

"All done," Concetta says as she stops filming. She stares directly into my eyes. "Let's get out of here now," she says seriously. "We need to forget about this place."

I nod again, understanding.

"Are you okay to keep walking?" I ask her, checking in.

Concetta flicks her hand into the air. "I'm always able to stand and walk myself out of these situations," she says proudly.

Dashing into the store room, I pick up the heavy computer. "I'm parked out the back," I tell her. "The ute."

Walking slowly, I follow Concetta out the broken back door of the milk bar.

The computer is heavy. Grunting, I lift it up high, placing it into the back tray.

"We've definitely got everything?" I ask her.

"My darling Adira," she replies. "There is nothing else left."

Concetta opens the front passenger door and sits on the seat. "This is comfortable," she says, sighing in relief. She leans back, closing her eyes for a moment.

I close her door and run to the driver's side. Opening the driver's door, I jump into the seat. "Ready to go?" I ask her.

Concetta nods, half asleep.

Switching on the ignition, I rev the ute until it warms up.

Stepping onto the accelerator, I back the ute out of the parking bay and head out towards Tinker Street.

As I turn onto the street, I check my rear view mirror. I am relieved to see that the silver Mercedes has gone.

Continuing to drive, I glance at Concetta. She is dozing off to sleep peacefully.

My heart swells with gratitude.

I am thankful that Concetta is alive and well.

Chapter 50

I drive into the Nestle camp ground while the sun is starting to set with gentle flickers of golden star light. It is so beautiful outside, a peaceful world away from the crazy mayhem.

Driving up to the caravan, I notice a warm light glowing inside. I rang Vianna earlier and asked her to prepare the caravan for an important visitor.

Glancing at my rear view mirror, I check that I have no tails behind me.

All clear.

Parking outside the caravan, I pull on the handbrake and switch off the ignition. It is quiet, except for the soft snoring of Concetta, who has fallen asleep in the ute.

She must feel safe with me to do that. Concetta is usually always on high alert.

What trauma she must have experienced, being locked away. She will talk if she wants to. That is Concetta Mancini's way.

Hopping out of my seat, I step out onto the grass. It feels good to be on solid ground again. For a moment I enjoy the sky, admiring the electric flashes of yellow light. What a beautiful sight.

It is a relief to stretch my body and release the tension in my muscles. I reach up high towards the sky. How lovely it would be to fly freely through the pink-red hues of dusk.

Feeling content after my nature escape, I grab my bag from the ute and walk over to the passenger side. Opening the door, I gently tap Concetta on the shoulder.

Concetta jumps up, startled and awake. Her hands form a fist, ready to fight.

"I'm sorry Concetta," I say.

"Oh Adira," she says, looking a little embarrassed. "*I'm* sorry. I forgot where I was. Did I fall asleep? You should have woken me up."

"You looked so peaceful," I smile. "I couldn't disturb you."

Concetta smiles gratefully. "I didn't thank you. That was mighty fine detective work of yours, finding and rescuing me, Adira."

"I learnt from the best," I say. "Come on, let's get inside."

"Inside?" Concetta raises an eyebrow. "Where are we?"

"At your new hideout," I say. "Come with me."

Concetta swings her legs out of the ute. Standing, she stretches up high into the sky. "*That's* my new hideout?" She admires the coastal caravan. "How beautiful."

"It is," I say, directing her up the stairs. I hold open the front door. "Wait until you see who designed it."

Concetta follows me into the kitchen area, where Vianna is standing over the stove, cooking.

"Hi Adira," Vianna says. "I'm so glad you're both okay," she smiles empathically at Concetta. "Adira explained what happened, Concetta. It must have been very scary."

Concetta waves her hand dismissively. "I am fine," she says, looking around the room. "What a lovely caravan," she smiles. "Did you design all this yourself, Girl?"

"Yes," Vianna grins. "I am glad that you like the design. By the way, please call me Vianna now. I have reclaimed my proper name."

"Wonderful," Concetta smiles warmly. "I am so happy for you both, Adira and Vianna. It seems that both your senses of self confidence have grown."

I feel a warm glow of happiness radiating through my heart. "Thanks Concetta," I smile.

Concetta's gaze rests upon Sophie who is seated at the table. "Hi Sophie," she touches her lightly on the shoulder.

"Hi Concetta," Sophie smiles. "It's lovely to see you again."

"You too," Concetta smiles. "I hope you've been holding your own against the wrath of those Petoys."

"They don't know what's about to hit them," Sophie smiles. "Adira and Vianna have organised an amazing operation."

"You'll both have to tell me all about it," Concetta rubs her hands together. "I do love hearing your plans."

"Hi Concetta!" Hidu enters the room, carrying a wrapped gift.

"Hi Hidu," Concetta smiles knowingly as she stares at the present.

"Where would you like this, Vianna?" Hidu asks, searching for a place to store the gift.

"Pass it here please," Vianna smiles. "I'll keep it on the bench. We're just waiting for someone else to arrive."

"We are?" I ask, confused.

Knock, knock.

"I'll get it!" Hidu smiles as he heads towards the front door.

"Hi everyone!" Mitch enters the caravan with one hand behind his back. His eyes meet mine. "Happy birthday, my beautiful wife, Adira." He retrieves his hand from behind him, revealing a bunch of pink roses, which he offers to me.

"Oh thank you Mitch!" I accept the roses, breathing in their wonderful fragrance. "These are just divine," I say, meeting his gaze. I am touched that he remembered my birthday.

Mitch pulls me close, embracing me tightly. "You deserve so much," he says. "We're all here to help you celebrate this special occasion. You've done so much for all of us."

"Here! Here!" Vianna punches her fist into the air. "You're an amazing friend, Adira. I don't know what I'd do without you." Stepping forward, she hugs me. "Happy birthday."

"Thanks Vianna," I feel a warmth nestling into my heart.

"Happy birthday!" Hidu and Sophie shout in unison.

"Thank you," I smile, my eyes twinkling with happiness.

"Happy birthday gorgeous Adira," Concetta cuddles me tightly. "I can't believe that you are 24 already. You have become quite the remarkable young woman."

"Thank you Concetta," I smile. "Your support and guidance have helped me to grow."

Concetta pulls away, staring into my eyes. "I'm sure your mother is thinking of you today," empathy washes over her face. "She must miss you terribly."

"I miss her too," I say, my heart feeling heavy all of a sudden. "I can feel her here with me right now."

"That's lovely," Sophie says gently. "Your mother seemed like such a caring person. I could just see her holding you close in the warmest hug."

"She would," I nod, tears filling my eyes. "I want nothing more than to find her."

"You will," Mitch says, grabbing hold of my hands. He stares directly into my eyes. "I am sure that you will find her very soon."

"I hope so," my voice cracks and tears drip down my cheeks.

"It's okay," Mitch holds me close. "Everything is going to be fine. We're all here to support you."

The smiling faces of all the people I care about surround me. "It is so wonderful to feel so loved," I say, feeling the ache dissipating. "It gives me the strength to continue."

"Speaking of strength," Vianna says gently. "I made a special stew tonight for us all to share together in celebration of your birthday. Should we eat?"

"Yes please," I smile, taking my seat at the table.

Mitch sits next to me and places his hand gently on my lap. "Are you okay?" He asks softly.

"Yes," I smile. "Much better."

"Let me take these roses," Vianna says. "I've got just the thing to store them in." Grabbing the roses, she heads into the kitchen and opens a cabinet. Taking out a recycled jar, she fills it with water from the tap and pops the rose stems into it. "That'll keep them fresh," she smiles.

"Thank you," I say.

Vianna pours hot water into six cups and places tea bags into them. Hidu helps her to place the steaming bowls of stew and tea cups onto the pine wood table.

I grab my fork and taste the stew. "This is delicious, Vianna," I say, smiling. "I love the lamb and the spices." I savour the taste. It is heavenly after such a tough day.

Nods and smiles of agreement scatter across the table.

"Thank you," Vianna smiles. "I'm no cook, really. I tried my best to make this special dinner for you. No words can express how special you are, Adira. You are my friend for life."

"Oh, what a lovely thing to say," I breathe. "You are my friend for life, too, Vianna."

Vianna smiles warmly. "I have a special something for you from Hidu and I." Standing, she approaches the kitchen bench and grabs the gift.

"You shouldn't have," I say as I accept the gift.

"Yes, I should have," Vianna's eyes shine brightly.

I open the pink wrapping paper, which is carefully designed with painted roses in a myriad of colours. "Did you make this wrapping paper?" I ask Vianna.

"Of course," Vianna smiles.

"It is so beautiful," I say, being careful not to rip it as I peel the tape away. As the paper falls open on my lap, a gorgeous scarf is revealed.

It is white in colour and decorated with stunning pink roses. Tears fill my eyes and I meet Vianna's gaze. "This is so special," I say, my voice cracking. "You made this, didn't you?"

"Yes," Vianna nods, tears filling her eyes too. "With real silk. I tried to think of a totem that would represent you. I remembered how much you love pink roses and so that is what I decorated it with. I hope it brings you joy and peace."

"Thank you," I gasp, standing up and embracing Vianna. "I will treasure this forever, knowing that you made it with your heart." I wrap the scarf around my neck. It feels soft and comfortable to wear, bringing a smile to my face.

"It looks beautiful on you," Vianna smiles.

We return to our seats and eat a while longer, chatting amongst ourselves and enjoying the happy spirit at the table. It is very welcome after all the hard times that we have endured.

My mind begins to consider our plans moving forward. I feel a huge sense of responsibility to make sure that everyone feels comfortable with what they are about to do. "I hope everyone doesn't mind a short interruption to the festivity," I say.

"Not at all," Vianna smiles. "What is it, Adira?"

"I just feel that, seeing we are all here, we should discuss our final plans. Is that okay with everyone?"

Everyone nods in agreement.

"Okay," I reach for my bag and retrieve the folder with the special papers. "Let's do it," I say.

* * *

After much planning and discussion, I sigh with relief. "I think we're all prepared, team. Please keep safe. Remember to alert Vianna or I with a text if you are in any danger."

"Well done Adira," Concetta smiles. "What a great plan. I wish you all the very best of luck."

"Thank you," I say, embracing her. "Best wishes to you, too."

"I'm very tired," Concetta sighs. "I think it's time for this aging lady to sleep."

"Let me take care of you," Vianna stands. "I've prepared a room for you. Hidu, come along and I'll show you the surveillance camera."
She leads Concetta and Hidu out of the room.

"I'd better sleep too," Sophie pulls me into her embrace. "I'll crash in the living area if that's okay?"

"Of course it is," I smile. "Grab whatever blankets you need to keep warm."

"Thanks Adira," Sophie grins. "I hope your night is truly special," she winks.

"Thank you Sophie," I say, my cheeks reddening as I watch her leave the room.

Mitch stands. "I'm heading out to the forest now," he says. "Will you meet me there at our favourite camping spot in half an hour?"

"Wow," I smile. "That's sounds great. I will see you there."

Mitch embraces me tightly and kisses me gently on the lips. "You are amazing," he says softly. "See you soon." My heart pounds with excitement as he exits the caravan.

Suddenly, a body appears at the caravan door. My eyes meet Zac's intense gaze.

"Hi Adira," Zac says. "Have you got a minute? I need to speak to you."

"Sure," I say, stepping back and letting him in. "What is it?'

"I should have made you aware of this earlier, I know," Zac scratches his head. "Since Nick disappeared, I have had to take full responsibility of the delivery of a strange item to the Chief himself."

"What is that?" I ask, offering him a seat at the kitchen table.

Zac shakes his head. "It's okay," he says. "I'd rather stand. I've got to return to work very soon before I'm missed." He bites his lip nervously. "I'm not sure what the fascination is but the Chief likes to have beeswax candles, used ones at that. Once a week I have to make sure that hundreds of them are stacked on a small boat, which I ride out to deliver to his ship out at sea."

I stare at Zac. "Who collects them?" I ask.

"An arm reaches out through the doorway," Zac says. "I hand the candles over, never having the privilege of seeing who it is."

"How odd," I say, meeting Zac's intense gaze. "That deserves further investigation."

"Yes, it does," Zac agrees. "Just be careful Adira, the Chief's a little cuckoo."

"I know," I nod. "Thank you for letting me know, Zac."

Zac exhales a deep sigh. "I feel relieved to have finally told you. Thanks for all the support you've given Jacquey and I. All the best, Adira."

"You too, Zac," I smile.

I watch as he heads out the door, his steps a little lighter.

Chapter 51

As I trek through the forest, the wind blows gently, picking up fallen autumn leaves and lifting them lightly into the air. They circle gently around my feet, drawing my attention to their vivid russet and orange colours. I no longer feel sad when I see them. They are the leaf prints of life, in various shapes and textures. Fractured or whole, I notice how they remain steadfast as they continue to shift along the terrain of time.

I dig my bare feet into the earth, letting the dirt sift between my toes. A deep sense of solace fills my heart. My spirit soars and I feel as though I am floating in the air.

I have missed these quiet moments, where I am at one with nature. It is a deep, primal need I have, to allow my body to blend in with the earth.

As I stare at the ground, I feel my body shifting gently in the wind like a soft whisper. My feet press lightly across the terrain, my toes gently caressing the scattered stones and patches of grass that adorn it.

A familiar scent fills the air and I pause. Warm and sweet, the fragrance tickles at my heart, reminding me of the comfort of my childhood. The sole of my foot is pricked by something and I gasp, staring down at the obstacle. It is a beautiful, fresh picked, deep pink rose.

Bending down, I pick up the rose, bringing it close to my nose and inhaling its gorgeous fragrance. Closing my eyes, I allow the scent to soothe my heart.

Continuing to shift across the forest floor, I discover a second fresh picked rose, which is burgundy in colour. I collect this one too and admire the two roses I now hold in my hand. Caressing their delicate, flouncing petals, I appreciate their unique beauty.

Glancing around me, I wonder where the roses have ventured from. As I do so, my gaze falls on a tall figure, standing tall and smiling. His warm, blue eyes melt my heart.

"Hello beautiful Adira," Mitch says, stepping forward and grabbing both my shoulders. "It's great to see you feeling the earth beneath your feet." He kisses me softly on the lips. "Happy birthday."

"Thank you," I smile. "The roses are beautiful."

Mitch's smile radiates, lighting his eyes. He grabs one of my hands. "I want to show you something," he says. "Walk with me?"

"Sure," I smile, letting him lead me across the forest floor. As we walk, my gaze falls upon a tent resting under an elm tree. It is decorated with a string of lights in the shape of flowers.

"What do you say to a romantic, peaceful evening under the stars?" Mitch asks.

"Sounds wonderful," I smile. "Like a holiday." I sit on the earth in front of the tent. Staring up at the sky, I see Orion shining brightly and it brings tears to my eyes. "This is so romantic, Mitch," I say, my voice cracking. "Truly special."

Mitch plonks down next to me and wraps his arm around my shoulder. I rest my head against his chest and listen to the strong sound of his heartbeat. We gaze at the stars for a long time, enjoying their light and energy sparking across the atmosphere.

Grabbing hold of my hand, Mitch stares into my eyes. "Adira Cazon, I wish from the bottom of my heart that we will be strong together for the rest of our lives."

"What a lovely wish," I say, touching his face. "Mitch Cazon, I love you with my heart and soul. It is still my most fervent wish that we could be blessed with a child of our own."

Mitch smiles, stroking my hair. "Oh Adira," he murmurs. "I wish for that too." Leaning towards me, he presses his lips firmly against mine.

I close my eyes, revelling in the sensation of deep love.

I am being lowered and my body lands on its back on a soft surface. Opening my eyes, I glance around me and realise that I am laying on a soft mattress inside the tent.

"Are you comfortable?" Mitch caresses my cheek gently. Gazing into his eyes, I see that they are glistening with love.

I nod, immersed in the moment and allowing myself to feel the love soaring in my heart. Reaching up, I pull Mitch down closer to me, feeling his strong energy as he presses his body against mine.

"I love you," I say, staring deeply into his eyes.

Mitch rains kisses across my cheek and neck. As his lips meet mine again, I feel an electric spark shoot its way through my body.

I raise my legs, pulling him even closer to me and lifting up the hem of my tank top. "Touch me," I breathe, feeling live-wired.

Mitch caresses me gently across my stomach. Lifting my tank top a little higher, he reveals my breasts.

As his tongue caresses my nipple, I cry out, grabbing hold of his hips. Undoing the buckle of his belt, I pull his shorts down firmly, revealing his gorgeous, firm penis.

I am burning in my loins. As Mitch kisses my thighs, I moan, raising my hips higher.

Reaching under my skirt, Mitch runs his fingers across the edge of my underwear, making me crazy.

"Oh Mitch!" I cry out. "Take me!"

Mitch crawls up closer to me, staring into my eyes. "I love you so much," he breathes. Pulling down my underwear, he tosses it aside.

Lowering himself, he pulls my skirt up over my hips. I raise my legs, helping to guide him inside me.

It feels amazing having Mitch's energy pulsate inside me. It only takes me a few precious moments to reach the heights of my ecstasy. I cry out, riding the electric waves of my climax and enjoying hearing the sound of Mitch reaching his peak too.

Afterwards, I lay in Mitch's arms, snuggled in a blanket.

"Are you comfortable?" Mitch asks.

I nod. "That was so beautiful," I say, enjoying the sound of his strong heart beat.

After a long while, Mitch touches my face gently. "I have a gift for you," he smiles.

I sit up, giving him the space to roll over and retrieve a small gift sitting in the corner of the tent. It is dressed in a shiny blue wrapping paper with white stars.

"Wow," I smile as I receive the gift. I rip open the wrapping paper and gasp in surprise. There in my hand sits the rose vase that I admired in Sophie's Art Gallery. I hold it in both my hands, stroking it gently. "This is so beautiful," I say. "Thank you so much," I kiss Mitch softly on the lips.

"I'm glad you still love it," Mitch smiles. "A little bird told me about this vase a while ago. I bought it and hid it away for today."

"Of course I love it," I say. "It is so beautiful, decorated with my favourite flower."

Mitch's smile widens and his eyes glisten with happiness. "I am the luckiest man in the world," he says. "I often pinch myself, wondering how I got to marry the most wonderful woman in the whole world."

I smile, relishing his compliment. "Thank you," I say. "You mean the world to me, too, Mitch."

"Thank you," Mitch smiles. "Your love means everything to me."

Sitting up, I pull down my tank top and slip on my underwear. "Let's go see the stars again," I say, reaching for Mitch's hand.

"Sure, just give me a minute," Mitch pulls up his shorts and tightens his belt.

We crawl outside the tent, placing the blanket over our shoulders.

"There's one more small surprise," Mitch says, handing me a rectangular gift adorned with blue star wrapping paper.

"You're spoiling me," I smile. Ripping open the paper, I discover a box of milk chocolates. "Oh yum! Thank you!" I open the box, offering Mitch a chocolate. "Would you like one?"

"You go first," Mitch smiles.

I select a round chocolate and pop it into my mouth. "Mmm," I sigh. "Chocolate caramel. Very indulgent." I hand Mitch the box.

"This is very yum," Mitch agrees, sucking on his chocolate. He places the box down next to him and opens up his arms. "Come here," he says.

I shuffle closer to him, letting him embrace me. We stare up at the sky, watching it darken as the sun disappears.

As the evening dapples its remaining light across the forest floor, Mitch nods off to sleep. Pressing his shoulders gently, I lay him onto his back in the tent. Placing a blanket over him, I kiss him goodnight.

Exiting the tent, I stand and press my bare feet into the earth. The air swirls around me, caressing the fallen leaves and sending them tumbling across my feet.

If I listen closely enough, I can hear a breath.

It is far away, many footprints from here, expelling a rhythmic energy, a sign of life.

I used to watch Mother wring her hands together while she sighed. Her eyes were dark and intense as they darted around her. Her ears were pricked and alert to any dangerous sounds.

In our hyper vigilant states our hearts did wrestle, determined to live and fight. We were willing to sacrifice contentment for that single, valuable breath.

A sign of existence.

A sign of life.

Now I inhale the air, the microcosmic particles of the earth and all that I tread upon. I keep inhaling, drawing in the fragments of time that we have both make shifted our ways through. Their presence, their fleeting moments, their courage, their truths, cannot ever be captured in a single breath.

Exhaling, my breath is strong, trekking an age of light, which glows dimly in the distance. Light that bounces across the earth, flashing images of familiar, warm faces, tallow candles, silk and red gum trees. Moments of precious heritage that should be treasured and prolonged.

Continuing to bounce, the light lands upon a small, wooden boat that is approaching the river bank.

Squinting, my gaze rests upon a figure rowing the oars of the boat. Her dark brown hair flies wildly in the breeze and falls in long strands over the sheer material of her crimson red dress.

It is her lips that make her identity obvious. Painted a bright red that glares across the gushing river water, they belong to Naricia Petoy.

I watch Naricia guide the boat into the river bank. Jumping out, she stands knee deep in the water and ties the boat's mooring rope to a pole jutting out along the embankment.

Stepping closer, my gaze falls upon a single beeswax candle lying on the boat's deck. Its wick glows dully as its flame fades away.

I consider the weight of this single candle. Its overarching promise of an heir for a disgruntled Emperor. Its role in banishing the pulsating heart of life in the tallow candle. It has become a ticking time bomb for the fragile lives of the citizens of Mira.

Reaching into the boat, Naricia retrieves a white scarf that she ties around her neck. My heart pounds wildly in my chest. I need to take a closer look at that scarf.

Sensing a presence, Naricia turns sharply and meets my gaze. Startled, she jumps and topples backwards into the water. "Help me out!" She demands, desperately treading water and reaching for my hand.

I step forward, feeling inner conflict. Part of me wants to leave Naricia there to fend for herself. Yet, the other more curious part of me wants to know more about the white scarf that she wears.

The curiosity wins and I step forward, reaching out to grab Naricia's hand. She kicks her legs, letting me pull her towards the embankment. Landing on her feet, she steps onto the grassy terrain, shaking her body dry.

"Thank you," Naricia smiles, her bright red lipstick smudged across her mouth. "It was quite the battle out there."

"Yes," I say, her words resonating with me in a deep way. "So many battles are inappropriate, aren't they?"

Naricia raises her eyebrows in surprise. "You've got to fight for what you want in this world," she says firmly. "Otherwise opportunities will just pass you by."

Naricia's energy radiates an impatient fire that strikes against the landscape, exuding her ambition. Stamping her feet firmly, she tries to shake off the last drops of water from her clothing and hair. While she shakes, I peer closely at her scarf and spot the two conspicuous totems on it: the wolf claw and the eagle talon.

While Naricia is preoccupied with drying herself, I reach into my pocket and message Vianna. *Found scarf. Drive caravan to river bank at the forest now!*

Pocketing my phone, I meet Naricia's gaze as she runs her fingers through her wet hair. "You must be cold," I say.

"Yes," Naricia's teeth are chattering. "Luckily my scarf is dry, it's giving me some warmth."

"It's a nice scarf," I say. "Where did you get it?"

Naricia bites her lip nervously. "It was a gift …" her voice drifts off.

"A generous gift," I say. "It looks like it is made of silk."

"It might be," Naricia avoids my gaze, staring down at the grassy terrain.

A short while later, I hear the sound of wheels against the earth and turn to see Vianna parking the ute next to the river embankment. The caravan is attached to the ute, its coastal art work shining in the dappled light.

Opening the driver's door, Vianna steps out of the ute and meets Naricia's astonished gaze. "Hello Naricia," she sounds in control.

"Vianna, what are you doing here?" Naricia's mouth has dropped open. "You look different."

"I am blonde now," Vianna runs her fingers through her hair. "I've had no choice but to disguise myself after the persecution I have suffered by you Petoys."

"Me?" Naricia plays with the white scarf, her cheeks reddening.

"Yes, you," Vianna says, a thin smirk crossing her lips. "How about you step inside my caravan and we can have our long awaited conversation?"

Naricia sighs with defeat. "Okay," she reluctantly agrees.

I follow behind her, stepping up into the caravan.

"Are you coming too?" Naricia is surprised.

"Yes," I say. "I am a friend of Vianna's."

Naricia's eyes widen in shock as she registers what has happened. "I knew there was something strange about you," she says.
"You waited for me to arrive."

"I am very patient," I say as we enter the spare room. "You were returning from Chief Opula's ship. He seems to have swept you up in his delusions, hasn't he?"

Naricia smiles smugly. "The Chief does not have delusions, darling. He is a man of progress and will take us Petoys far."

"Will he?" I ask. "Or is that the fairy tale he shares with you as he embraces you?"

Naricia's mouth drops open. "My relationship with the Chief is none of your business."

Vianna stamps her foot. "It *is* our business!" She cries. "You are so caught up in his delusions that you are hurting others to gain your own desires." She grabs hold of the white scarf and pulls it away from Naricia's neck. "How dare you take my family's precious scarf," she seethes.

Naricia clutches at the scarf desperately. "This is my ticket," she panics. "My way into the Chief's world. He loves that I own something that has links to the Emperor. It makes me his special lady."

Vianna pulls firmly, retrieving the scarf. "You took this from us, Naricia, didn't you?"

"Yes," Naricia's eyes are fixed on the scarf. "Without remorse. Your father betrayed me long ago, Vianna, choosing your mother as his wife. He had a chance to be with me and we would have run the silk farm together and established a brilliant trade network. The least he can do is let me have this scarf. I deserve access to the imperial palace."

"No you don't!" Vianna yells. "This scarf is not something that just anyone gets to wear. It is an important heritage garment that displays my family's special bond with the empire." She clutches the scarf to her chest, her breath rising and falling sharply with anger.

Naricia meets my gaze and cocks her head. "Is this entertaining you?" She asks me. "Watching Vianna take away my chance at riches?"

I shake my head, realising how gullible Naricia is. "No garment, be it genuine or fake, will ever gain you ultimate power," I say. "You've been delusional, assisting the Chief by creating the *A Touch of Silk* range, which is actually polyester designed with counterfeit totems and poisonous dyes."

"Those silly symbols?" Naricia throws her head back and laughs. "I find it ridiculous that the people of Mira care so much about their ancient silk garments. What are they but clothing decorated with silly little drawings? They've been so easy to copy and reproduce."

"Have they?" Vianna grits her teeth. "Trapping the people of Mira into forced labour is horrific, not to mention illegal. They are desperate to escape Frosties and your demands that they produce the counterfeit silk garments."

Naricia's eyes shine. "Those people have been easy to manipulate," she smiles insanely. "I just threaten them with no way out and they will eat out of my hands. They've managed to produce the entire *A Touch of Silk* range under my orders."

"How far will you go?" Vianna tears at her hair with her hand. "You stole my statue too and put it on public display in the town square. It is you who organised the flyers too, wasn't it? *Have you seen this Girl?* You will do anything to persecute me and destroy me."

"Yes, I did do all those things!" Naricia's eyes flash. "Do you think I am going to let you become the next chief of silk of Mira? That role is mine to take. I will tread on you and destroy you completely, rather than let you rise to power."

"It's over, Naricia," Vianna sighs.

"It's only just beginning," Naricia retorts. "Wait until you see what else I have planned for you, *Girl*."

"You won't have a chance," Vianna is in control. "Hidu!" She calls. "Naricia is all yours."

Hidu enters the room, meeting Naricia's gaze. "Naricia Petoy, with the power granted to me by the Emperor of Mira, I place you under arrest for your crimes," he says, grabbing hold of her arms and handcuffing them behind her back.

"You can't do this!" Naricia cries. "Where's your evidence?"

"Right here," I say, retrieving my phone and replaying the surveillance video of our conversation.

Naricia eyes widen as she views the incriminating footage.

"Can you send it to me please, Detective?" Hidu asks as he guides Naricia out of the room.

"Sure, it's all yours," I send the video to Hidu and pocket my phone.

Turning around, I meet Vianna's tormented gaze.

"That woman," Vianna shakes. "What she has done to us all is unspeakable."

I open up my arms, embracing Vianna. "It's over," I say. "She won't have a chance to plan anything evil anymore."

Vianna stares up at me with tears glistening in her eyes. "I don't know how I feel right now," she says. "It's a mixture of pain, relief and sadness." She rests her head against my chest.

"You've been through a very difficult time," I say. "It can stop here for you, right now, if you wish."

Vianna meets my gaze. "It's not over yet," she says. "I still have fight left in me." Her eyes narrow intensely. "It's time to free our people."

"Yes it is," I say. "You should get some sleep. We have a big job to undertake tomorrow."

Vianna nods, stepping back. "I will," she says. "You'd better return to Mitch. It's your birthday night, Adira. He was so excited about his plans to celebrate with you."

"Okay," my eyes narrow. "As long as you're okay."

"I will be fine," Vianna smiles gently, cuddling her white silk scarf. "My parents are here with me in spirit. See you tomorrow, Adira."

Chapter 52

I awaken in Mitch's warm embrace the next morning, my eyes adjusting to the light seeping through the holes in the tent.

Reaching up, I stroke Mitch's face gently.

"Mmmm," he murmurs, his eyes fluttering open. "Morning beautiful."

"Morning," I smile. Sitting up, I weave my arms into the sleeves of my tank top. As I pull on my skirt, I sigh. "I have to go now. Vianna's returned to the camp ground."

"Right," Mitch nods groggily. He sits up, rubbing the sleep from his eyes. "Let me drive you there," he offers as he pulls on his t-shirt.

I grab my bag, placing my gifts inside it. Crawling out of the tent, my lungs welcome the fresh air.

Pulling on his shorts, Mitch stares up at the sky. "What a lovely morning," he smiles. "The sun is shining for you, Adira."

I smile at his sweet words, yet deep inside my heart is thudding with the anxiety of all that I have to accomplish.

Mitch grasps my hand and leads me towards the van. He opens the passenger door for me and I sit down, staring out the windscreen.

"Are you okay, Adira?" Mitch places his hand on my shoulder.

I shrug, meeting his gaze. "I'm nervous," I admit. "I hope that we can do this."

"We can," Mitch says confidently. "You've prepared us well."

A smile of gratitude crosses my lips. "I love you so much," I say, kissing him softly on the lips.

Mitch kisses me back, pulling me into his warm embrace. I close my eyes, treasuring this moment with my love.

Staring into Mitch's eyes, I feel myself shaking. "I don't think I can do the last part without you," I say, my lips trembling.

Mitch's eyes widen. "I will be there, every step of the way," he assures me.

"That gives me more confidence," I smile. "You are my life, my future. I can't imagine living without you."

"You won't have to," Mitch cups my face in his hands. "There is no way I will let anything horrible happen to either of us out there, okay?"

"Okay," I nod, feeling stronger with Mitch's love.

Mitch starts the ignition and begins to drive. I stare out the window, letting my mind drift and appreciating this calm moment before the mayhem begins.

Mitch drives slowly through the forest, his eyes intense as he stares out the windscreen. Soon enough, we arrive at the Nestle Camp Ground.

As Mitch pulls up outside Vianna's parked caravan, he meets my gaze. "Take care out there," he sounds concerned.

"I will," I say. "You too."

Mitch nods. "I will." He embraces me tightly and I feel his heart pounding.

"I'll meet you at the boat tonight," I say, staring into his eyes.

"See you then, my loving wife," Mitch kisses me gently on the lips.

Grabbing my bag, I open the passenger door. My gaze falls upon Vianna, who is sitting on the front steps of the caravan. She is wearing a pair of silver overalls with a pink, geometric printed t-shirt.

"Hi Adira," Vianna stands. Her feet squelch in her large black boots as she approaches me. She waves goodbye to Mitch as he drives away.

"Morning Vianna," I smile, admiring her outfit. "You look very artistic."

"I do? Thanks," she smiles. "I just need some help with my hair."

"Sure," I say, grasping Vianna's long hair and parting it on the left side. I divide the strands into three sections and begin crossing them over and braiding them together. "There," I say as I complete the plait. "What am I tying this with?"

"This green ribbon," Vianna hands it to me and I tie it around the end of the plait. "Thanks Adira."

"No problems. You look very unique," I compliment her.

"Unique or strange?" Vianna chuckles, a smile forming across her lips. "It's good to laugh," she says. Her eyes look tired. She must have been awake for most of the night.

"Just unique," I smile warmly. "I love your outfit," I admire her overalls.

"Thanks," Vianna grins. "I even picked up some makeup."

I smile, watching as Vianna opens the powdered foundation.

"I need your help," she looks at me. "I'm not sure what to do with all this."

Vianna never wears makeup. This experience would be very new for her.

"Here, let me." Vianna hands me the foundation and I grab the sponge, coating it with the powder. "How much coverage do you want?" I ask.

"Coverage?" Vianna shrugs. "Make me look completely different."

"Okay." I apply the foundation liberally over her face, smoothing it out with the sponge. Her face now has a darker tone. "That's plenty," I say. "Have a look in the mirror."

Vianna peers at her complexion in the hand held mirror. "Thanks," she says. "I do look different. That's important."

"I know," I nod. "Let's continue." Digging into the makeup bag, I retrieve the pink blush.

"Okay," Vianna shrugs, sitting down in the grass. "Go for it."

Using the small blush brush, I accentuate Vianna's cheeks with pink streaks. It gives her a healthy glow.

Retrieving the eyeshadow, I look at Vianna. "Do you have any favourite colours?" I ask.

"These two," Vianna points out the bright mauve and green shades.

"Okay," I say, coating the applicator with mauve. "Close your eyes now."

Shutting her eyes, Vianna waits while I apply the eyeshadow in a mauve streak across the bottom of her eyelids. I use the darker green to accentuate the shape of her eyes and to create a contrasting shadow above the mauve.

"There you are," I say. "What do you think?"

Vianna peers at herself once again in the rear view mirror. "Perfect shading," a smile forms across her lips.

"Great," I smile too. Reaching into the makeup bag once more, I find the mascara. "Some mascara will add some edge to your look," I say as I coat the brush wand black.

"Edge sounds good," Vianna agrees, turning to face me. I brush the mascara across her eyelashes, darkening them. They take on a natural curl as they bounce back from the brush.

"Wow!" I say, stepping back. "You look very artistic now."

Vianna chuckles. "I've never had anyone wow me before."

"Take a look," I say.

Once she catches sight of herself in the mirror, Vianna gasps in surprise. "Wow!" She exclaims. "Irsha Ricky, the artist with edge."

Vianna begins to strut across the grass with her hands on her hips. "Hello I'm Irsha," she sounds confident. "I'm here to create a magnificent sculpture for the bow of your ship, Chief Opula."

"Hello Irsha," I say. "Do you think you might need an accent?"

"Yes," Vianna says. "I've just stepped off a plane all the way from England!" Her voice takes on a perfect English accent.

"Good choice of accent," I say. "You're ready."

Vianna is touched. "Thanks for all your help, Adira, you are such a great friend."

"I'll always be here for you," I smile. "We've got this together, eh?"

"Yes," Vianna nods. "In fact, I have something for you." She reaches into a small cardboard box and retrieves a folded silk dress. "My mother asked Hidu to deliver this dress to you." As she unfolds the dress, its beauty reveals itself. The bodice is a rich, indigo blue silk. It is contrasted by the radiating gold of the skirt, which is decorated with gorgeous leaf and floral totems in indigo and gold colours.

"Wow!" I exclaim. "What a beautiful dress."

Vianna's smile radiates. "Mother made this dress herself. She is allowed to wear it to the palace when she attends special occasions with my father. She trusts that you will wear this dress when you visit the Chief, in order to support the silk tradition and its true indigo colour."

My mouth drops open. "I will be honoured to," I say. "I will take very good care of this dress, I promise."

"I know you will," Vianna nods. "Do you want to take it now?"

"No," I say. "Hold onto it for me. If I wear it too early, our plan will fail. I will collect it from you when we arrive in Mira."

Vianna nods, agreeing. "That sounds sensible," she says. "I'll have it ready and waiting for you." She folds the dress and places it gently into its box.

Sophie steps outside the caravan, wearing the emerald green silk evening dress that she was hiding at the Redbank Artists' Market. Once again I am mesmerised by the deep green colour of the bodice, flowing gracefully into a long skirt exquisitely designed with a silk brocade of swirling golden cloud and wave totems. It takes my breath away.

"Hi Sophie, what a beautiful silk dress," Vianna says admiringly.

"Thank you," Sophie smiles warmly. "It belonged to my great grandmother who used to design silk. My mother handed it down to me once I became an adult and asked me to continue taking care of it, so I have."

"What an honour," I say, approaching Sophie. "It is such an exquisitely beautiful dress."

"You must have hidden this dress well," Vianna smiles.

Sophie's eyes narrow intensely. "I hid this dress away from Nick. If he had discovered it, I wouldn't have it now."

I am silent for a moment, letting Sophie's words trail through my heart. Her story is a strong reminder of the importance of heritage silk and its place in the community of Mira. It boosts my determination and I step forward, ready to do what is needed.

"Are we ready to go?" Sophie asks.

"Nearly," Vianna smiles at Sophie. "We need to hand over a few things first." She digs into her pocket and retrieves her ute keys. "Are you still okay to drive the ute and caravan to Mira?"

"Definitely," Sophie smiles, retrieving the keys.

"Do you mind taking my bag too?" I ask. "I don't want to risk losing what's in it."

"Of course," Sophie retrieves the bag and slings it over her shoulder. "I'll keep it in the ute while we're at Frosties this morning. It will eventually arrive safely in Mira, I promise."

"Thanks Sophie," I smile.

"Let's go!" Vianna calls as she presses a button on her remote.

I open the door and slide into the passenger seat, shuffling over to make room for Sophie.

"A tight fit," Sophie giggles as she flops down next to me on the seat.

"It is," I nod.

As Vianna drives, I take my last glances at the scenery of Redbank, appreciating the tall trees and flocking birds that radiate their lives across the landscape. Very soon, I will leave all this and re-enter the dangerous terrain of my past in Mira.

"We're here," Vianna announces as she parks outside Frosties.

Opening the ute doors, we step outside and face the grey brick building. Its dark, foreboding presence sends a shiver down my spine.

"Are you okay?" Vianna asks.

"Yes," I shake my body, trying to rid myself of the creepy feeling that has formed in the pit of my stomach.

Vianna slings her arms around both of us. "We've got this, team," she smiles.

"Yes we do," Sophie agrees.

"We sure do!" I exclaim.

Releasing us, Vianna reaches into the ute tray and retrieves a large roll of silk. It has a green tinged indigo hue, coloured so expertly that it would fool the untrained eye into believing it was pure indigo.

I glance at the building again, noticing a guard walking passed the front display window. His figure looms hauntingly behind the sparkling snow globes.

"Wait here," I say. "I have to deal with a guard."

"What?" Sophie sounds shocked. "Please be careful Adira, they're really strong."

"I'll be fine," I say, stepping ahead.

"She really will be," I hear Vianna's voice behind me. "She is amazing, Sophie."

I press my body up against the façade of the building, Peering passed the sparkling snow globes in the display window, I watch the guard pace up and down the corridor. He is tall and muscular but not too strong. His dishevelled red hair flops into his brown eyes and he yawns as he paces, clearly exhausted. He will be easy to manipulate.

Inhaling a sharp breath, I tuck my hair behind my ears and plaster a smile across my face. Opening the front door, I step into the entrance. "Hello?" I attempt to appear lost. "Is anyone there?"

The guard spins around and meets my gaze. "Hello," he says, his eyes blinking hard as he tries to stay awake. "How can I help you?"

Makeshift Girl: The Secret Heritage Trail

I run my fingers through my hair, pretending to be distressed. "I'm lost," I fret. "Naricia told me to meet her here but she hasn't shown up. I must have got the wrong day."

The guard shakes his head. "No," he says. "Naricia hasn't been in this week. She usually works on her marketing jobs today. Can I help you?"

"Perhaps," I say, plastering a playful smile across my lips. I lean against the wall, stretching one leg out and placing my hand on my hip seductively. "That is, if you know anything about marketing." My voice is husky and seductive.

The guard's eyes widen with appreciation and he blinks frantically, waking himself up. Strutting forward slowly, he approaches me. "Well," he says in a sultry tone. "I do know a thing or two about marketing," he strokes my cheek with his hand. "Like how to win over the customer."

"You do?" I ask encouragingly, letting him take hold of my face in both of his hands.

The guard stares intensely into my eyes, and shifts closer towards me. "You've got to point out the attractive features of the item," his voice is deep.

I run my fingers across his neck and down the front of his torso. I can feel a heat searing from him that I know he desperately wants to relieve.

"Come with me," I say seductively. "I'll show you my attractive features."

The guard licks his lips and lets me pull him by the shirt. I lead him upstairs towards Naricia's office.

"This room looks good," I say, peering through the windows. "It is empty."

The guard glances over his shoulder, checking that we are alone. Digging into his pocket, he retrieves a key and unlocks the office door.

I lead the guard inside and he kicks the door closed behind him.

"Now," he says, grabbing hold of me around the waist. "Show me."

Caressing the guard's thigh, I hear him moan. He presses his body against me, kissing my neck.

Continuing to caress his thigh, I reach out with my free hand and grab the keys from inside his pocket. Tucking them inside my skirt pocket, I step back and take hold of his face in both my hands.

"There's more to come," I say suggestively. "Close your eyes while I remove my clothing."

"Ooh," the guard bites his lip, burning with desire. "That I cannot wait to see." He closes his eyes and bites his lip excitedly.

Spinning around, I dash towards the front door.

"Hey!" I hear the guard cry. His footsteps thump across the carpet. "Come back!"

I shake my head. "No," I say. "It's definitely time for you to cool down." Stepping outside, I slam the front door and fumble with the keys, pressing my body against the stile. I feel the guard pushing against the door, trying to burst through it.

Attempting a number of keys, I finally discover the one that fits the lock. I twist it, locking the door.

"Let me out!" The guard cries, banging against the door.

"Not in your wildest dreams!" I call as I turn on my heels and dash back down the staircase.

Approaching the security camera at the building entrance, I check that its view is still averted away from the front door. It is. The silly guards are unable to keep watch over their own surveillance.

Pulling open the front door, I wave at Sophie and Vianna. "Come in!" I call.

"What did you do?" Sophie appears astonished as she steps foot inside the building.

"Let me guess," Vianna smiles. "You tied him up."

"Not quite," I smile. "I've locked him upstairs in Naricia's office."

"You are amazing, Adira!" Sophie exclaims.

"I told you so," Vianna grins. "Well done Adira." She slogs the roll of silk material over her shoulder. "Let's go and meet our people!"

"Let's go!" Sophie cries.

"Wait a minute," I say as I retrieve my phone from my pocket. "I just need to check the video surveillance." Opening the app, I gain eyes on the work room. The people are flocked in a bunch on the ground, looking worried. "Something's wrong," I say concernedly.

We dash down the corridor, ready to take on whatever needs to be done.

Reaching the work room, my heart falls at the sight of an old man who has collapsed. He is lying flat on his back on the floor. A group of our people surround him.

"Mr Yarrin!" Sophie cries, dashing to his side. She shakes the man gently and he stirs, opening his eyes.

"Sophie," his voice is faint. "Are you an angel, here to save me?"

Sophie places her hand over her heart. "Up you get, Sir," she says softly as she sits Mr Yarrin up. "Here, lean against me." She plonks down onto the ground next to him and rests his weight against her.

The people sit next to her, their gazes curious.

Sophie smiles warmly at the people. "Today is the day that you all leave this building and return home." Her voice is bright and encouraging.

"Yay!" A cheer ripples through the group.

"We have one last task," Sophie says. "Do you remember how Vianna promised that she would alter the indigo dye?"

Heads nod.

"Well she has," Sophie retrieves the roll of green tinged indigo silk from Vianna. "As we all know, the Chief has only requested one special indigo outfit and it is to be for himself. He wants a silk shirt and pants to wear tonight on board his ship." She unrolls a section of the silk material. "Here is the indigo silk," she says. "It is real silk but with green tinged indigo."

A buzz of excitement erupts amongst the people.

"Let's split into two teams," Vianna suggests. "We have two patterns here. One team can work on designing and cutting the shirt, the other the pants. Does that sound okay?"

"It sounds great!" Caray calls. She stands up, letting the light of her tallow candle flicker in the semi darkness. "I'm happy to work with you, Sophie."

"Okay," Sophie smiles. "I have the shirt pattern." Stepping aside, Sophie gathers a small group of people around her and lays the pattern out in front of them.

I turn my gaze to Vianna, who is surrounded by the remaining people. She is unravelling the cloth and cutting it.

"The remaining cloth is for you Sophie!" Vianna calls, rolling the material towards her.

"Thanks!" Sophie grabs the roll and begins to unravel it. "Time to cut out the pattern," she tells her group.

I shift my attention back to Vianna. She is working with members of her group to pin the silk cloth down onto the pattern.

"Can I cut it?" A young man asks keenly.

"Sure," Vianna hands him the scissors.

The man cuts the silk cloth confidently, following the pattern.

"Wow!" Vianna exclaims once he stops cutting. "You've done a great job! Your silk design skills are sharper than ever, Alex."

"Gee, thanks Vianna," Alex stares down at his feet, smiling shyly. "It's such a pleasure to work with real silk again."

It warms my heart to see Vianna encouraging our people. I know how important it is to her to empower them.

After some time, both the garments have been stitched by members of each group.

Vianna and Sophie stand next to each other and hold the shirt and pants up, side by side.

"What a great job you've all done!" Sophie grins. "This silk is our stand against the Chief!"

"Bring down the Chief!" The people yell.

"I will deliver these garments to him personally this morning," Sophie smiles as she retrieves the silk pants from Vianna. "Along with the silk sash. He will be over the moon."

"The Chief is delusional," Caray mutters. "He thinks that he is going to replace the Emperor."

"He's nuts!" An old man cries. "Let's bring him down!"

"Bring down the Chief!" The people cry, punching their fatigued fists in the air. Staring closely, I see eyes shining with hope and passion and it makes my spirit soar to great heights.

"It's time for us all to leave together now," Vianna smiles. "I have your passports tucked into my overall pockets."

While Vianna and Sophie distribute the passports, I sneak towards the side door and peer outside the window to the front of the building.

Zac is carrying a stack of brown boxes and their *A Touch of Silk* range labels glisten in the sunlight. He is loading them onto the cargo tray of his truck.

Next to Zac's truck, stands a guard, keeping a look out.

"I'll be back in a minute!" I call out. "I just have to deal with an obstacle!"

Vianna nods, understanding. "No worries!" She calls. "Take care."

Stepping out of the work room, I trek down the corridor, listening for sounds of anyone entering the building.

Zac steps through the front door, his eyes widening in surprise when he sees me. "What are you doing here?" He asks.

"Getting the people out of here," I say. "Now is the time for you to do your bit."

"Sure," Zac straightens up, meeting my gaze. "I'll do anything to help those poor people."

"I need you to distract the guard," I say. "While you are doing that, I will board the people onto the cargo tray."

Zac's eyes widen nervously. "Right," he shakes a little.

"You can do this, Zac," I touch his shoulder and smile warmly.

"Yes, I can," Zac stamps determinedly. "Leave it with me, Adira."

I watch as Zac exits the building and approaches the guard. "There are some more boxes upstairs," he says. "They are stacked up high on a shelf in the storage room. Would you be able to help me get them down? You are much stronger than me."

An arrogant smirk crosses the guard's lips. "Of course," he agrees. "Too easy."

I press my body against the wall as Zac and the guard enter the building and make their way up the stairs. My heart is pounding ferociously and it propels me back down the corridor towards the work room.

There is an excited buzz in the air the people stand waiting to leave. Sophie is balancing Mr Yarrin's weight against her.

Vianna raises her eyebrows, waiting for the verdict.

"We have precious moments to leave," I say, heading towards the side door. Digging into my pocket, I retrieve the bundle of keys and try them out, attempting to unlock the door. After a short while, the door unlocks and I push it open. I shield my eyes as a bright light radiates through the darkness of the work room.

"Wow!" Several people exclaim.

"Daylight!" An old woman cries.

The people head towards the door in amazement. Some people's eyes shine with tears.

"I never thought I'd see the light of day again," Mr Yarrin's voice quivers.

For a moment, our people stand, shuffling their feet against the concrete, breathing sighs of relief and staring up at the sky.

"We are free!" Caray cries, waving her passport in the air.

"Not yet," I say, stepping forward. "We need to move quickly now. Hop onto this cargo tray here. I will drive you to the Redbank forest, where you will be cared for and safe."

The people follow me, approaching the back of the truck. Vianna and I hold people's hands, helping them step up. Sophie helps Mr Yarris up onto the truck and sits with him, balancing his weight against her arm.

Caray is the final person to approach the truck. "Thanks so much for helping us all," Caray smiles as I take her hand.

"It is my honour," I smile.

Just as Caray hoists herself up onto the cargo tray, the guard bursts through the front door, his arms loaded with boxes. He is followed closely by Zac.

"What is going on here?" The guard cries, dropping the boxes. They fall with a thump onto the ground and some burst open, spilling the counterfeit silk contents across the concrete. "You can't do this!"

Vianna gasps at the sight of the material. Its loud presence is a reminder of the need to fight for our cause. "Oh yes we can!" She cries.

Caray meets my gaze with terror in her eyes.

"You'll be fine," I tell Caray. "Trust me." I lift her up onto the truck.

Caray nods, plonking down next to another young woman on the cargo tray.

"Get on board!" I yell at Vianna.

Vianna nods, tearing her gaze away from the counterfeit silk. Jumping on board the cargo tray, she pulls up the tail gate.

The guard is advancing towards us with his fingers pointing at me. "Stop right there!" He yells.

I ignore him, dashing to the front of the truck. Pulling open the driver's door, I jump up the steps and plonk into the driver's seat.

Suddenly, Zac opens the passenger door and sits on the seat. He stares at me with wide eyes. "Go!" He yells, kicking the guard squarely in chest. A stunned expression crosses the guard's face and he falls backwards, landing with a thump onto the concrete.

Zac slams his door and stares at me with a mixture of fear and anticipation. "Are you right to drive?" He asks me. "This truck has been giving me a lot of trouble recently."

"Let's see," I turn on the ignition and am welcomed with silence.

"Tessie is getting old," Zac sighs. "These days she finds it hard to start."

I smile reassuringly at Zac. "Tessie will be fine," I say. "She's a true battler."

"Yes, she is," Zac smiles.

Starting the ignition again, I hear the engine chug and splutter as the truck bursts into life.

"Well done Tessie!" Zac sighs with relief.

Pressing the clutch peddle with my right foot, I shift the gear stick into first gear and reverse the truck back out onto Glacier Street. Full locking the steering wheel, I swerve to the left, allowing the truck's large body to turn itself around and meet the intersection at Holdridge Street.

Peering in the rear view mirror, I spot the guard on his feet, dashing towards the back of the truck. His arm is outstretched, attempting to grab hold of the tail gate.

Turning left, I merge onto Industry Road. My heart pumps nervously as I hit Nouveau Road. The guard has grabbed hold of the cargo tray and is trying to climb it.

Flooring the accelerator, I increase my speed, engaging second, then third gears. As the truck roars, the guard's body tremors as he tries to retain his grasp. Soon his left hand loses it grip, leaving him with one arm swinging in the air.

Approaching the bend, I break and quickly downshift gears to first. Swerving tightly in a circle, I watch as the guard wrestles against the force of the motion. He clutches the cargo bed desperately with his right hand, yet the momentum overcomes him. Suddenly, his left hand slips off the tail gate and he screams as he flies through the air and lands on his side on the road.

"Wow," Zac gasps with amazement. "You are phenomenal, Adira."

"Not phenomenal," I smile. "Just well trained, that's all."

Adjusting the steering wheel, I straighten the vehicle. It is a thrill to pick up speed and to engage second and third gear as the truck roars straight down Vista Road.

For a moment, I stick my head out the window, allowing the wind to blast across my hair and face. It is re-invigorating, keeping me focused on the last stretch of driving.

After a short while, I turn left onto Viva Road and continue to drive the truck across the wide bridge over Spirit River.

We arrive at a large car park in the forest, which is filled with a number of other light rigid trucks and buses.

I break, downshifting to first gear and pulling into a car park. Switching off the ignition, I exhale a sigh of relief.

"Well done, Adira," Zac pats me on the shoulder. "You did well coping with Tessie."

I meet Zac's gaze, smiling. "Tessie is lovely," I say. "She was a true heroine today. She carried us all safely here."

Zac nods, his eyes shining. "You are truly something, Adira," he smiles with gratitude.

"Thanks Zac," I say, watching him push open his door.

"I'll call Jacquey," Zac says. "She'll organise some food and medical treatment for the people." He steps down onto the cement, shutting his door behind him.

Descending the steps of the truck, I land my feet firmly onto the dirt. The air is fresh and cool on my skin. Autumn leaves float through the air and pile around my feet. I smile, remembering my mother's beautiful face. *We did it, Mother. We rescued our people.*

Vianna drops open the tail gate of the truck. She and Sophie help the people down off the cargo tray. Mr Yarris rests against Sophie's shoulder as she leads him across the grassy embankment into the forest.

I smile as I watch a young man and woman drop down onto the grass and roll across it. Their cheers radiate through the air as they relish their freedom from the horrific world of Frosties.

A short while later, Jacquelyn arrives with her van full of food. "Hello everyone!" She smiles warmly. "Welcome to the forest. It is truly a wonderful privilege to have you all here. Please help yourself to the food at the back of my van."

Vianna and I help Jacquelyn hand out the paper plates of sandwiches, salads and fruit to our people.

Paramedics arrive and tend to a number of people who need treatment. Mr Yarris is placed on a stretcher and taken onto the ambulance.

"Take care Mr Yarris," Sophie clutches his hand tightly as he passes her. "I'll be thinking of you."

"Thank you Sophie," Mr Yarris' voice is faint. "I might see you in Mira soon."

"Yes you might, Sir," Sophie's eyes fill with tears of worry.

Once the ambulance has left, Sophie turns to face Vianna and I. "Well, I'd better get going," she smiles. "Zac has offered to drive me back to the ute. I'll head out to Mira this afternoon."

"Okay," I say, reaching out to hug Sophie. "Thanks for everything."

"That's more than okay," Sophie smiles, pulling Vianna close. "You two be careful okay? We have a wedding to look forward to soon."

"Yes we do," Vianna smiles. "You'll see Hidu in Mira. He's heading there too."

"Great," Sophie grins. "I will see you two beautiful ladies, safe and well in Mira soon."

We wave as Sophie steps up into the passenger seat of Zac's truck. Zac begins the ignition and backs the vehicle out of the car park. Heading towards the bridge, the truck shrinks to a small spec in the distance.

I feel Vianna's hand on my shoulder and meet her gaze. "I'd better go too," she smiles. "Ben Bownie has permission to row me across the water on one of the Petoys' small boats. He will introduce me to Chief Opula and I will set to work on making him a statue that will satisfy his delusions of grandeur." She shakes slightly and I can tell that she is nervous.

"You will be great," I say to her. "You are a natural at sculpting. I can't wait to see that statue."

Vianna's eyes light up. "I can't wait to show it to you," she grins happily. "You are the best friend I have ever had, Adira. I will never forget all that you have done to help me. I treasure every moment in the depths of my heart. Please take care out there. I will see you and our people very soon." She hugs me tightly.

"You are my best friend, too," I tell Vianna. "I have learnt so much from you and your ancestors. I will carry those lessons with me all my life. I promise you that we will all see you very soon."

We step back, clutching tightly onto each other's hands.

"See you," Vianna's voice is shaky as she releases my hands and turns away.

I watch as she heads towards the river bank without looking back. My heart flutters nervously. I hope that Vianna manages to escape the violent insanity of the cruel Chief Opula.

Chapter 53

The terrain's heart beats a solid pulse that radiates through my feet. Swaying with the rhythm, I am entranced, my gaze piercing through the fog that has settled across the landscape. Pushing passed the sheer veil, my eyes fall upon the bleak truth.

There, stacked on the deck of the red gum boat are the boxes, labelled with the *A Touch of Silk* range stickers. They are ready to be delivered across the river and out to Chief Opula's ship at sea.

My heart burns with rage at the sight of the boxes and what it means for the silk heritage of Mira. Clenching my fists, I inhale a sharp, focused breath. Justice must be served and I am going to see that it is.

Staring up, I am swept into the red streak of night. It engulfs my mind, pulsing with the blood of every life from Mira who has trekked their journeys out here to Redbank, freely or not.

As the sky pulses, its rhythm saturates my very being, igniting my body and setting me alight with energy and a determination to carry the people's load.

My father is with me here in spirit. I see his face, smiling reassuringly, helping me to submit myself to the rhythm of life and its fight to breathe.

A single breath, it is all that is needed. In that breath is the soul laid bare: in its joy, its sorrow, its hardship and its very being.

It is the lesson that I have learned from the terrain as I battled my way across it. At times ferocious, it made me face past nightmares and forced me to fight to survive. I am at one with the terrain, embracing its highs and lows. I have discovered my strength through all that I have endured.

The leaves shuffle against my feet, keeping up the rhythm of breath, of life. As the wind catches beneath the leaves, they propel into the air, twisting, turning and fighting against the force of the breeze. Drifting ahead of me, they push me to press forward and to take the next steps towards the red dappled light of the shore.

Gazing through the sheer haze, I exhale a darker breath, which wraps its life around me, smothering me. I know that it is the deep manifestation of fear that I have built up over a long time.

Once I was afraid to face the unknown. Now I am ready to fight.

My gaze lifts sharply, facing the horizon. My eyes are saturated with the deep red streaks of sunset.

It is a warning, a sign of danger, I know. Yet my heart beats with wilful determination.

The terrain shuffles around me, echoing with the approaching sounds of feet that move their way towards the river bank. Arriving is Caray, leading the other citizens of Mira. They carry their fatigued bodies with pale and angry faces and dig their feet into the muddy dirt. Caray leads them and their rhythms of life escalate as they stamp out their anguish and punch their fists into the air. "We will be free!" The exhausted people from Mira cry in raw, shrill voices.

Their cries fill the red of night, saturating it with their heat, their pain and their desperation. It is the first time that they have breathed in the air of Redbank and felt its terrain beneath their feet since being locked away at Frosties.

A lighter sparks its flame in the air, clutched in Caray's brave fist. Eyes burning with rage, she sets the flame upon the boxes sitting in the red gum boat, sparking them alight. The fire engulfs the entire *A Touch of Silk* range, scattering its ashes through the air and across the water. The other people stand back, witnessing the red gum boat being swallowed by the vicious flames that emit a black, toxic cloud of smoke into the air.

There is silence as the people digest the event. Some wrap their arms around one another, comforting each other as they release their sorrow. Others pump their fists into the air, cheering with relief.

Coughing and spluttering, I wait for the black smoke to dissipate. My throat burns from the impact of the toxic fumes. Summoning my energy, I step towards our people.

"Adira!" Mitch has arrived. He grabs my arm.

I turn to face him, my eyes sparking with life. "Follow me," I say. "Soon we will all be free from this madness."

Mitch's eyes widen in surprise. He releases me, his eyes staring intensely at me while I continue to step forward, into the crowd of people.

"People of Mira!" I call. "Now is our time! To our freedom!"

"To our freedom!" The people respond, pumping their fists into the air.

"Swim with me!" I call. "I will lead the way to the ship."

Heads nod and bodies run forward, rushing along with me to the water's edge.

Peering over my shoulder, I check that Mitch is still with me.

There he is, smiling reassuringly, willing to follow me too.

Grabbing his hand, I clutch it tightly and hold it to my chest. Mitch's smile is warm, like a comforting hug.

Releasing Mitch's hand, I turn and face the water. It is choppy, unsettled and covered by a raging red sky.

That does not deter me. It is one more terrain that I must battle.

Raising my arms up high, I step slowly into the water, letting it pool around me. I can feel the rhythm of the waves, cold and slapping against my skin. They are angry and wilful, inviting me to ride with them, to press forward.

Lowering my body into the water, I let it carry me. It pulls me along and I thrash my arms, swimming frantically across the crests of swelling waves.

Focused on reaching my destination, I have no time to feel tired. I swim sharply, cutting through water and reaching the ocean.

Makeshift Girl: The Secret Heritage Trail

The waves are larger here, roaring high above my head. Diving deeply, I swim underwater, streamlining my body through the power of its life. The sound of the swelling waves comforts my heart and surges me ahead. The water carries me with it, propelling me forward, until my eyes rest upon the ship.

Treading water, I stare up at the mighty ship, which towers above us all. It is a foreboding presence, decked to all its glory and gloating with wealth that is insulting for the people of Mira.

A single, bright white light glows on the ship, a sign of life. Inhaling a sharp breath, I dive into the waves and thrash my body across them, swimming with all my might.

Reaching the ship, I swim around its perimeter until I face the beam that protrudes from the shining light. Its glow is powerful and vibrant, suggesting a journey of life that is free of burden.

Treading water once more, I inhale some more deep breaths, harnessing my strength. It is time to board the ship.

Grasping onto a rope dangling from the side of the ship's huge wooden hull, I hoist myself up and scale it, bouncing my feet against it in order to gain momentum. Kicking my legs against the bowsprit, I grab hold of its metal handrail with both hands and hoist myself up and over it. Throwing myself forward, I land flat onto my stomach on the bowsprit.

Winded, I pull myself up, beginning to shiver in my drenched clothing. Ignoring the cold bite, I lay on my stomach and wrap my legs tightly around the pole connecting the bowsprit to the bow. It takes a lot of focus to maintain my balance, yet I persist.

Reaching out my arm, I clutch hold of Caray's hands as she climbs over the hand rail, landing her successfully onto the bowsprit.

Caray smiles at me, her eyes shining. "Wow!" She exclaims. "You are so focused, Adira,"

I smile, struggling to maintain my balance. "Step carefully down to the bow," I tell her. "I will send the others down to meet you."

"Okay," Caray agrees. "Thanks Adira, you are truly amazing."
I watch as she treads carefully, balancing herself along the pole.

Summoning my strength, I reach out my arms and begin to help more people clamber over the handrail and land onto the bowsprit. I am met with smiles of gratitude as I land them safely. Even when fatigued, our people find their will to continue, treading the careful steps they need across the long pole to the bow to meet Caray.

Mitch soon arrives, grasping hold of my hand strongly. His eyes are full of admiration as I help hoist him up over the handrail.

Balancing with me, Mitch helps more people by guiding them safely onto the bowsprit.

After some time, no more people arrive. I face Mitch, my eyes burning with determination.

"Let's keep moving," I direct.

Mitch places his hand on my shoulder. "I am here for you, Baby," he says softly. "You just let me know what you need."

I stare into Mitch's eyes, my heart soaring with love. "Thank you," I smile. "Let's go."

Balancing myself, I outstretch my arms and place one foot carefully in front of the other, treading across the pole. My heart is drumming a solid beat, propelling me to continue to lead the way.

Taking my last steps, I jump safely onto the bow. Exhaling a large breath of relief, I turn and watch Mitch as he treks the pole. He has his hands outstretched and is gritting his teeth as he crosses. Suddenly, he loses his footing and stumbles, nearly falling.

My heart pounds rapidly and a silent scream catches in my throat. Remarkably, Mitch lands safely on his two feet and manages to take the last few steps across the pole.

"Baby, you made it," I say, drawing him close into my embrace. "You had me worried for a moment."

Mitch's heart is thumping as he holds me close. I wait for his nerves to settle before I step back and meet his gaze.

"Let's go," Mitch says, guiding me across the bow. As we approach my people, he takes hold of my hand to support me.

I stare at my people, my eyes sparking with passion. "Here we stand as one," I say, reaching my arms out towards them. "A people who have the fight to carry on and save our heritage."

The people nod and cheer, standing tall and proud.

"We will take this ship!" I cry. "Let's head home!"

"To home!" Our people shout, pumping their fists into the air.

"Do what you must," I tell them. "We need to ensure that we stop any Petoy from capturing us."

"To Mira!" My people are still chanting and stomping across the deck bravely, ready to confront the Petoys.

The Petoys burst through the cabin doors and storm across the deck, ready to attack. Fists clench and eyes spark with rage as the clan members advance towards my people.

Harnessing their energy, the people of Mira stand their ground and fight, their strength and determination admirable. I watch as Caray knocks out a Petoy clan member with a single punch between the eyes. He staggers across the deck and collapses onto his back, out cold.

My eyes dart across the deck, falling upon Mitch. He is attempting to rescue Alex, who has been captured by a clan member. Wielding a punch, Mitch lands its squarely between the Petoy man's legs. The clan member screams, clutching his groin and releasing his grasp of Alex.

Mitch takes advantage of the moment, tearing the Petoy man's hands behind his back and pushing him forcefully towards the handrail. Combatting the resistant squirming, Mitch lifts the clan member by his legs and tosses him overboard into the watery depths of the unforgiving sea.

Suddenly, my hair is yanked harshly, almost ripping out of my scalp. I turn to face a savage, bearded Petoy man whose eyes are flashing with insanity. Bobbing down, I twist my body around so that my back faces him. The clan member cries out in surprise and grabs hold of my shoulders, as I anticipated that he would.

Reaching behind me, I grab hold of both the man's arms and throw him over me in a somersault. He screams as he is propelled into the air and lands, bouncing on his bottom. Forming my hand into a fist, I punch him firmly in the temple, knocking him out senseless. His body sways and topples sideways, unconscious on the deck.

Mitch approaches me, his eyes wide with surprise. "I never knew you could do that, Adira," he says admiringly. "What strength you have."

I smile warmly, grabbing hold of Mitch's hand. "It's great to have you here with me," I say. "My shining light in all this madness."

Mitch's eyes scan the deck. "It's settled," he says.

It is silent now, our wrath evidently scattered across the deck. Still bodies meet the gaze of the red fiery sky. Pools of blood seep from a few bodies and glisten in the moonlight.

Inhaling a sharp breath, I try to calm my pounding heart. My gaze drifts up towards the sky. It is burning brightly: a narrative of life, blood and loss.

The cabin door swings open again and out steps Chief Opula, his arms strangling the neck of a woman.

I watch the woman shuffle across the deck, her long, greying brown hair flying wildly in the breeze. Her dark brown eyes are deep and wistful, silently expressing her pain.

I can't take my eyes off her, watching as the hem of her long white dress catches under her feet. She stumbles, dropping a beeswax candle onto the ground. It rolls across the deck, yellow white, conspicuous and drawing gasps of disgust from our people.

The woman shudders, yet her eyes meet mine determinedly. "I refuse to light any more beeswax candles for the Chief," she gasps.

"Quiet woman!" The Chief orders, pressing the knife firmly against her neck. A small drop of blood rolls down her skin and my heart pounds with fear for her safety.

"You are delusional!" The woman gasps. "No matter how many beeswax candles you burn, you will never be the Emperor of Mira."

The people of Mira stare open mouthed at the woman, amazed at her bravery.

"Nonsense!" The Chief barks. "No one will stop me from taking down the empire, especially not a peasant like you!"

The woman's eyes flicker and her gaze meets mine. Her eyes are deep and soulful, full of pain and mystery, yet they still spark with life. I feel a rush of emotion surge through my heart as I face the rugged beauty of my mother.

"Adira," my mother chokes, her eyes brimming with tears. "Run right now, away from this mad man, before it's too late!"

My mind whirs with flashes of memories from the past. Running away frantically with mother, across the terrain of Mira, wanting to stop, to play or to ground myself.

"I will not be running away this time," my voice is strong. "I am not afraid of this man." Watching the Chief, I notice how old and feeble he has become. Brash and reckless, he will be easy to manipulate and outsmart.

"Not afraid?" The Chief's sinister laughter echoes across the deck. "What will you do now, Adira, knowing that your mother's life is in my hands?"

I gaze upwards and allow the red heat of the sky to sear its way through my body, fuelling me with a power that propels me forward.

I am ready.

"Nothing," I say solemnly, my eyes sparking with fire. Turning, I step across the deck and bow and balance myself as I tread across the bowsprit pole. Once I reach the handrail, I clutch onto it, staring out at the sea. It is my life the Chief is after and I am going to make him fear losing it.

"Adira!" Mitch cries, reaching for me across the bowsprit pole. "No!"

A fiery strength radiates through me as I meet Mitch's gaze. "Commandeer the ship," I mouth.

Mitch nods, his eyes moist, yet amazed. Stepping back, he retreats towards the helm.

I stare into the Chief's eyes determinedly. "I am here now, Chief Opula, the girl you've always wanted to have. You have one choice. You either let my mother go or I will throw myself into the depths of the unforgiving sea." Reaching behind my back, I grasp the handrail, feeling a power surge through me. I am in command now and am aware that the Chief is flustered.

"You don't want to do that, Adira," the Chief's voice is shaky. "Noble people like you and I, rise above this pointless waste of life. We desire wealth and riches beyond measure. Nothing that these common peasants would ever have the privilege of owning." He nods his head towards the bow. "Peer down, Adira, at the bow, you will see quite the illustrious vision."

I look down, my eyes falling upon a large, dark brown horse head statue. It has been secured to the bow. A foreboding sight, it sends shivers down my spine.

The horse head of Petoy madness.

Polishing the horse head is Vianna, who meets my gaze with a reassuring glint in her eyes. Flicking a switch on the statue, she sets the horse's eyes alight. They radiate a soaring, golden light that beams and bounces across the ocean water.

Vianna's work is magnificent. She has produced just the right amount of opulence for the Chief. I smile at her proudly.

"You're smiling Adira," the Chief sounds relieved. "I knew you would appreciate this magnificent display of grandeur. The light far exceeds the dismal candles that the Emperor cherishes so dearly. It spans across space and time, gracing we Petoys with a mighty power to pave the way for the future progress of trade. Come with me, Adira, rise above these peasants and join me in leading the Petoy empire and its triumphs over Mira." The Chief's eyes glisten with anticipation.

I ground myself, listening to the sound of the waves slapping against the sides of the ship. There is the rhythm of life, rippling its beat persistently through all this madness. For a moment, I sway, allowing myself to connect with those waves and to harness their flow.

"Your progress is hindered," I say solemnly. "Your silk range has been burned to ashes on the embankment of Spirit River."

The Chief sucks in a sharp breath as he registers the news. After a moment, he meets my gaze arrogantly. "I have the best silk of all," he says. "Dyed with indigo." He grasps Mother more tightly. "I also have you, Adira. You will bring me much wealth and prestige with your nobility."

Makeshift Girl: The Secret Heritage Trail

I acknowledge the Chief's dark, unfeeling nature. It is dangerous when he holds my mother's life in his hands. I need to step up and take control of the situation. "This ship will sail," I command, meeting the Chief's gaze. "If any harm comes to my mother or any other citizen of Mira, I will abandon ship."

The Chief's lips spread into a thin smile. "Good," his voice still shakes. "You've come to your senses, true noble that you are."

Again, that word: *noble*.

"I am not noble," I stand my ground. "I am a mere citizen of Mira and Redbank."

The Chief's eyes widen. "You do not know who you are?" Grabbing my mother's face, he stares intensely into her eyes. "You have not told her, have you?" He probes, making my mother shift uncomfortably on her feet.

My mother lowers her gaze, staring at the deck floor. "We have much to discuss, Adira, when the time is right …" She gasps as the Chief tightens his grip around her neck, almost choking beneath his strong grasp.

I raise my right foot, placing it over the top of the hand rail. "I have warned you," I alert the Chief, preparing to jump.

"Adira! No!" Mother's cry is strangled and desperate.

I ignore her, hoisting my body until I am straddling the hand rail.

"Alright! Alright!" The Chief loosens his grip, still clutching Mother.

Mother exhales a sigh of relief, her body shaking.

Time is of the essence right now. The Chief's insanity is unpredictable.

"Sail!" I command, waving at Mitch.

Momentarily, the ship begins to stream through the water. My eyes rest upon the lights which protrude from the horse's eyes and flash towards the horizon.

My gaze drifts upwards towards the sky. The wind is shifting rapidly and heavy clouds are streaming across it, cutting through the deep, red streaks. A storm is on its way.

So much blood has been lost as a result of the Petoys' barbaric actions. The sky flashes its strong warning. How many more lives will be lost tonight?

Staring down, I meet Vianna's gaze again. She points towards the deck. Lying flat on her stomach, she crawls across the bow, heading towards it.

I need to work fast and provide a distraction.

"Oh Chief," I say, lowering myself onto the bowsprit. I begin to shuffle back across the pole, my gaze meeting his.

"Yes Adira?" The Chief's gaze is intense, focused on my movements towards him.

"You are right," I breathe, entertaining his desires. "This is the most extravagant experience. I can visualise the Petoys' future progress."

"You can?" The Chief's eyes light up. "That makes me a very happy man, Adira. Having you by my side will provide a strong stance of resistance against the empire of Mira."

"Yes," I nod, spotting Vianna in my peripheral vision. She pulls herself up onto her feet and dashes across the deck. Ushering our people into a corner, she begins to treat their wounds.

I exhale a sigh of relief. Vianna and the citizens are safe. It is Mother that I need to save now.

"There is just one thing, Chief," I say, reaching out to touch his shoulder.

"What that, Adira?" He is salivating, drinking me in with his intense gaze.

"Well, you are not wearing the indigo silk attire that you promised. Without it, you can hardly be considered noble." I jump onto the deck and stare directly into his eyes.

The Chief bites his lip, considering my request. "You are right," he finally agrees. Releasing my mother, he lets her fall onto the floor of the deck.

Mother gasps, inhaling large breaths of air.

I meet the gaze of the Chief and raise an eyebrow. "Well?" I say with expectation. "You shouldn't keep a noble woman waiting now, should you?"

The Chief nods, his eyes sparkling with hope. "I will return very soon," he promises. "In my indigo attire, as illustrious as it is."

"Wonderful," I breathe, smiling as I watch him retreat and exit behind the cabin doors.

I drop onto the ground, landing on my knees. My mother stares up at me, mesmerised.

"Adira," she sighs, reaching out to touch my face. "My beautiful daughter, so brave and strong."

"Mother," I grab hold of her hand. "I can't believe that you're here with me."

"Help me up, Adira," Mother allows me to pull her up onto her feet. I guide her towards Vianna and our people.

"Hello Maricelle," Vianna smiles. "I am Vianna, Adira's friend."

"Hi Vianna," Mother smiles gently. Meeting my gaze, her eyes flash with determination. "You have him in the palm of your hand, Adira. Keep feeding him his delusion and he will do whatever you ask." Her eyes narrow. "Please stay safe. If there is any chance you will be hurt, then run."

I stand tall, my heart beating bravely. "I will be fine, Mother," I say.

Mother nods, understanding. "I know this is something you must do," she says.

"Yes," I agree.

Mother pulls me into her embrace. I breathe in her familiar scent, my heart racing with the joy of having her here with me.

"I love you, Adira," Mother smiles. "When you are ready, meet me at our hiding spot in Mira and I will tell you all about your past."

"Okay Mother," I say, watching as the cabin doors open. "I must return to the Chief now."

"Yes," Mother nods, releasing me. "Bless you, Adira."

I carry Mother's loving words with me as I trek across the deck. The clouds are shifting even more rapidly across the sky now, preparing to unleash their wrath.

I close my eyes, letting the pending storm fill my heart with courage. It washes over me, soaring through my veins and making me stand tall. "Hello Chief," I say, watching him strut confidently across the deck in his green tinged indigo silk shirt and pants. The silk sash is tied loosely around his neck. "I see you have dressed decently for the occasion," I smile encouragingly.

"Oh yes," the Chief's smile is broad and his eyes spark madly. "I even wear the symbols of the empire," he points to the sash. "What about you, Adira? Do you need to change your clothing too?"

"I will very soon," I say, waving towards the horizon. The ship slows down as it reaches the pier that juts out of Mira's beach.

"We have arrived," I say. "Once you take me to your illustrious home in the mountains, to meet your people, I will be able to dress proudly in my own indigo attire."

The Chief's eyes widen and he licks his lips lustfully. "Yes," his voice is strong. "It will be my honour to bring you home with me. You can help me rule in the mountains."

"Yes I can," I smile wildly and wink at the Chief. "Quite a fitting place for we nobles to express our desires, too."

The Chief is salivating.

I feel the stillness beneath my feet. The ship has stopped moving.

"People of Mira," I say. "It is time to help anchor the ship. Help Mitch all you can."

Guided by Vianna, Mother and my people stand and descend the stairs of the ship, landing safely on the pier.

I exhale a deep sigh of relief. They have escaped the ship and the Chief's madness.

I feel eyes upon me and turn to meet Mitch's gaze. He is worried. I nod reassuringly, waving for him to help anchor the ship. He descends the steps reluctantly, taking one last glance at me over his shoulder before he disappears.

Chapter 54

Turning to face Chief Opula, I am determined to propel ahead.

"We are finally alone, Adira," the Chief's smile is wide. Stepping forward, he grabs hold of my waist firmly. I feel his lips upon my cheeks and neck.

"Now, now," I say, pulling back. "If you really want me, then take me home with you."

"Right, of course," the Chief smiles. Extending his arm, he offers to guide me down the steps and onto the pier.

"I can walk by myself," I say, standing tall.

"The voice of a true leader," the Chief smiles.

Descending the steps, my feet land onto the pier. My eyes peel the beach. To my left, on the sand, I spot a makeshift tent. Outside the front, Mother embraces a tall woman dressed in tattered, citizen clothing.

"Empress Celine!" I hear Mother exclaim, her lips forming a grateful smile.

Empress Celine steps back, pushing her brown hair out of her eyes. "Let's get you treated," she says as she checks my mother's neck. She leads her inside the tent.

Hidu assists an old man who can barely stand. "It's okay, Mr Peers," Hidu says. "Rest your weight on me, that's it. We'll have you feeling better in no time." He guides Mr Peers inside the tent.

Cries of excitement scatter upon the shore and my gaze darts to the right. There stands Vianna with a number of open cardboard boxes lying at her feet. "People of Mira!" She cries. "Here are your beloved heritage silks, returned to you safely!"

A huge cheer ripples through the crowd of people and they rush forward, retrieving their silk attire from Vianna.

Stepping off the pier, I feel my feet sinking into the sand. I head over to Vianna and meet her gaze. "Where is my silk?" I demand.

Vianna smiles as she digs into the box. "Here it is," she says as she retrieves her mother's beautiful silk dress. Once again I am breath taken by the sight of the long, golden skirt, which is adorned with gorgeous leaf and floral totems in dotted indigo and gold colours.

"Thank you," I say, gathering the silk dress in my arms. "This dress is fit for a ruler."

"I can't wait to see you in it," the Chief's tone is seductive.

My stomach churns with nausea at the Chief's advances but I ignore it, tucking the dress under my arm and continuing to step forward passed the happy spectacle.

As we leave the shore and step onto the dirt ground, I peer over my shoulder once more, spotting Mitch lowered and scampering through blades of grass. He is right here, with me, ready to step in when needed.

Exhaling a huge sigh of relief, I throw my shoulders back, continuing to step forward and cut across the grassland. The terrain seems to chatter beneath my feet, unleashing past voices that echo through my mind. This ground holds a narrative of hiding, fleeing and just existing. It is raw and confronting to be here again. Drawing upon the voices, I harness my courage and push ahead until I reach the base of the mountain.

The drumming overtakes the voices, its rhythm vibrating through my body. The Petoys are not too far away now, beating their rhythms of protest and angst against the backdrop of the fiery red sky.

Setting my right foot onto the trail that winds it way up the mountain slope, I tests its stability. It is not slippery and can safely take my weight. I continue to step across the trail, hearing the shuffling of the Chief's footsteps directly behind me.

"Keep following the trail, Adira," the Chief pants. "Once you reach the ledge you are there."

I begin to feel the slipperiness of the dirt beneath my feet. The wind smacks against the terrain, sending dust and rocks scattering across the surface. Some rocks strike my arms and legs, leaving abrasive scrapes and cuts that I ignore. I am determined to reach my destination.

It does not take long to reach the ledge. Staring up at the red sky, I see the giant, heavy clouds ready to unleash a downpour.

The wind has increased in its strength now and smacks against my body, making me sway. I feel the Chief clutch onto the material at the back of my tank top, trying to steady himself.

Once the wind settles, the Chief releases his grasp and I rotate my shoulders, preparing to climb the ledge. I tuck the silk dress inside my skirt's waistband, ensuring that it is safe while I continue to move.

Raising my right foot, I place it onto the rocky surface above me. Reaching up, I grab a protruding rock on the mountain slope with my left hand and raise my left leg onto another secure rock. I continue to climb, shifting across the rocks until my hands are placed securely on the mountain ledge.

Inhaling a sharp breath, I press my hands firmly onto the ledge and hoist my body up. My knees scrape against the edge of the ledge and my body propels forward, landing me flat onto my stomach on the ledge's rocky surface.

Scrambling to my feet, I watch the Chief climb up effortlessly with experience. "Well done Adira," he says as he stands on the ledge and dusts himself off. "You have arrived safely."

"It is wonderful to be here, Chief," I say.

"Quade!" The Chief calls. "Present yourself!"

I hear a scuffling of footsteps amidst the fierce drumming. As the first rain drops begin to fall, my gaze rests upon the fiercely handsome sight of Quade. Tall and muscular, his golden tanned skin glistens in the dappled light. Quade's long red hair sweeps down his back, half tied back in a plait. A pair of deep, amber eyes stare intensely at me.

A warning bell sounds in my head as the rain pelts against my skin. This man, Quade, exudes a power that makes my heart race.

"Your Opulence?" Quade's voice is deep. "I see you have returned with Adira."

"Yes," the Chief smiles. "She is here to help lead us Petoys to victory." He faces me, his eyes flashing with excitement. "You will work with Quade here and make sure that the clan follows orders, you understand? Your nobility will help guide the way."

"Of course," I nod, noticing that Quade is shuffling his feet uncomfortably. He most certainly wasn't expecting to share his power with me.

I hold my silk dress in both hands. "If I am to lead, then I should dress appropriately," I say. "Could you please show me somewhere private that I can change?" I ask Quade.

"Follow me," Quade steps ahead, guiding me into a dark, cave like structure built into the mountainside.

"Thank you," I say as he steps outside.

Placing the silk dress down onto the ground, I remove my tank top and toss it aside. The cool air slaps against my torso, making me shiver. Kicking off my sneakers, I pull down my skirt, leaving it lying on the ground.

Holding the silk dress tightly to my chest, I inhale a deep breath. *Please help me through this madness*, I silently pray.

The dress is silent, glistening in the dappled light that journeys its way into the cave.

Pulling the dress over my head, I thread my arms through the arm holes. The silk cascades down over my torso and legs, floating lightly in the air. For a moment, I stand, feeling the gorgeous, sheer lightness of the silk. It caresses my skin, soothing some of the fear that I am feeling.

Stepping into my sneakers, I harness my courage once more. It is now or never.

Makeshift Girl: The Secret Heritage Trail

Running my fingers through my hair, I step outside the cave. The wind picks up my light brown strands, flickering them through the breeze.

Quade is still standing outside on the ledge. His eyes widen with appreciation, shifting their gaze across my body.

"Let's go," I say, stepping ahead of him. "We can't keep the Chief waiting."

Taking the short trek back to the open ledge, I am greeted by the Chief, who stands in front of his people. His eyes light up with desire at the sight of me. "Oh Adira," his voice is yearning. "You make a man faint with longing." His gaze shifts across my breasts and torso, drinking me in.

"Hello Petoy men," I say, shifting my gaze across the gathering. "It appears that your Chief has failed you dismally."

Gasps of shock scatter through the crowd.

"I, Adira Cazon, have trekked the earth my entire life, longing to find a place to finally rest my noble being. I was promised a life of illustriousness by your leader, yet he has not delivered." I meet the gaze of the shocked Chief. "Here you stand, Chief Opula, in a silk garment that is not dyed with pure indigo, yet tarnished with a horrible shade of green."

A roar of laughter ripples through the crowd.

I beat my chest bravely. "I am the wearer of pure indigo, as one as noble as I should be. Do you see the difference in class, clan?"

The Petoy men nod and wolf whistle. I meet Quade's gaze and his eyes flash with surprise at my courage.

"That's enough!" The Chief is shaking with anger. "How dare you betray me, Adira? I have brought you here to give you a life of opulence and riches."

"Hardly," I say, stepping forward. "You are a mere peasant, who wouldn't understand the first thing about nobility."

"You bitch!" The Chief grabs hold of my shoulders.

"Foul language, too," I say, a smirk forming across my lips. "I will be a much better leader of your clan than you are, Peasant Opula."

The raucous laughter ripples through the clan again.

"You shut your mouth!" The Chief orders, tightening his grip on my shoulders.

"Let go of me!" I command.

"No!" The Chief shakes his head, his eyes wild. "You must be brought back into line."

"Is that right?" I retort. "Just like the way you brought my father back into line, Chief? Did it feel good aiming your gun at him and firing? Did you enjoy watching his last gasps of life?"

The Chief's eyes glimmer insanely. He pushes me forward, towards the edge of the ledge. "You will not take my resistance away from me," he growls, poking my chest. "I can do this without you."

My heart is racing. In only seconds, I will topple over the edge of this ledge and my life will be over.

Peering across the crowd of faces, my eyes rest upon Mitch. There he is, with me, his eyes narrowed and flashing with anger.

I let his anger sweep over me, harnessing my courage once more. Shifting quickly on my feet, I work with the terrain, letting it spin me around on its slippery surface. Kicking up loose stones, I let them strike the Chief's legs and he cries out, releasing my shoulders and stumbling as they strike against his skin.

Taking the chance, I grab hold of the Chief's shirt collar and push him backwards so that he is leaning over the edge of the ledge. "You do not frighten me," my voice is harsh in the fiery night air.

The Chief kicks his legs in protest and suddenly loses his balance. Flying backwards, he grabs hold of the edge of the ledge with both hands. "Help me Adira!" He cries, clutching desperately as his body swings in the air.

I shake my head, staring at him intensely. "No," I say. "Now you know what it is like to stare death in the face."

The Chief screams wildly as his right hand is released from the ledge. "Help me, please!" His cry is acute and its echoes bounce across the mountainside.

I continue to stare, watching as the Chief struggles to support his own weight. Gradually, his left hand finally loses its grip. The Chief's scream is shrill and horrific as he sails through the night air and crashes at the foot of the mountain.

It is silent for a moment as I stare, taking in the lifeless body of the Chief. A pool of blood surrounds his torso, glistening a deep red in the night. It is the same shade of red as the sky and its vast landscape of life and death.

Swinging around, I turn to face the Petoy clan.

"Adira, lead us!" They shout, pumping their fists into the air.

My head is whirring with emotion and a sense of dizziness grips me. I was not prepared to win the favour of the Petoys. Now that I have, all I want to do is flee.

The Petoy men step towards me, reaching out to touch my skin and my face.

Lowering my body, I dash across the ledge, reaching Mitch.

"I've got you," he says, grabbing my hand.

I let him lead me across the ledge. We are faced with a narrow, winding pathway down the slope and I trek it gingerly, trying not to slip over the edge of the mountain.

I can hear the Petoys' scattered footsteps behind us. It sets my heart racing with fear.

I begin to slip down the slope, feeling the sharp sting of small rocks cutting into my legs. My heart races with fear. Stretching my arms out, I try to balance myself, willing my feet to stop slipping and to cease their rapid momentum.

"Take my hand, Adira!" Mitch cries, reaching out behind him.

I grasp Mitch's hand firmly and smack into his back, pushing him forward. He begins to slip too, his feet sliding down the slope.

"No!" I cry.

Suddenly, Mitch throws his hands out in front of him and presses firmly onto the slippery surface. It stops him skidding. He stays there, steadfast and strong, wincing as I slam once more into his back.

We have stopped moving. We are safe.

Standing, Mitch stares into my eyes. "Small steps now, Adira," he says. "We're nearly at the base."

"Okay," I pant, following him slowly.

It takes a few more steps to finally reach the base of the mountain. Once my feet hit the flat grassy ground, I sigh with relief.

"Time to run!" Mitch cries, pointing upwards. "They're right behind us!"

Staring up, I see two Petoy men descending the slope with ease. It will only take them a short while to reach us.

Turning on my heels, I run with all my might across the grassy terrain. Mitch jogs beside me, keeping pace.

The Petoys' cries are wild and desperate, their feet stamping across the earth as they try to reach us.

As we reach a dirt road, I witness a marvellous sight.

It is Sophie, driving Vianna's ute with the caravan towed at its rear. "Get in!" She cries, screeching the brakes in the middle of the road.

"Take us to the beach!" I yell as Mitch guides me into the caravan. Shutting the doors, I peer through the window, watching the Petoys throw their fists into the air with anger as we drive away.

Mitch bobs down next to me. "Adira," he says gently. "Are you alright?"

I stare into his concerned eyes, still feeling shaken. I can't speak right now.

Mitch sits with me, holding my hands. He is here for me and that's all that matters.

The ute screeches to a stop and Sophie runs to the caravan door. "We're here, Adira," she announces as she pulls it open.

Standing up, I meet Mitch's gaze. I only have a short time to spare before the Petoys find me. "Wait here, please," I say.

Mitch lowers his gaze. "This is something you must do yourself, isn't it?"

"Yes," I say. "There is a story I've been waiting to hear my whole life."

Makeshift Girl: The Secret Heritage Trail

Mitch nods, understanding. "Okay, Adira," he says. "I'll wait right here for you."

Approaching the caravan door, I descend the steps and place my two feet upon the sandy terrain. As I trek, my feet sink into the sand and I sway viciously in the breeze. Rain teems across my skin, yet I find it soothing. The rain is shedding its tears, mourning the loss of many lives in this unrelenting madness.

It is a battle to trek across this terrain. In the wild and stormy darkness my visibility is poor but I still continue to press on, knowing my way instinctively.

"Adira," my name reaches me like a soft lullaby. Closing my eyes, I listen acutely. All I can hear is the fierce rage of the wind and rain.

I await the sound of my name again.

"Adira, open your eyes." My eyelids flutter open and my gaze falls upon a dark silhouette flexing in the storm. Peering closer, I notice a warm light flickering in her hand.

"Mother?" My heart beats ferociously, this time with anticipation, not fear.

"Yes, I am here." As Mother reaches her hand out towards me, the flickering light seems to beckon, inviting me to step closer.

While the stormy rain strikes me, I stumble across the ground, battling its strength. I feel the cold air strike against my frame and it blows me sideways, landing me flat onto my bottom.

I stare up, gasping and shivering in the cold. Sand particles force their ways into my eyes. Rubbing my eyelids, I blink, waiting for the grit to clear.

As my vision returns, my gaze falls upon the silhouette. Light and floating, it shifts closer towards me, seemingly unaffected by the turbulent wind and rain.

For a split moment, time stops as I am faced with the rugged beauty of my mother. There she stands in her tattered, long white dress, her bare feet almost completely buried in the sand. In her hand, she carries a single, tallow candle, which sparks its fire into the sky, refusing to extinguish. It is a sign of the steadfast endurance of life.

I stand shakily on my two feet, meeting my mother's gaze. "Mother," I am relieved to see her and to know that she is safe.

"Follow the light, Adira, come to me," my mother's voice is gentle and reassuring.

I stare silently at the flame, allowing it to soothe my pounding heart. It is light, it is life and it is connected to my mother.

Stepping forward slowly, I let my mother draw me into her arms. The scent of her is familiar and comforting.

Mother smiles as she strokes my cheek. "You were very brave," she says to me. "You battled the terrain and the Chief all alone."

"I did," I agree.

My mother smiles soothingly. "See, now the storm is relenting, just like your fear is."

I watch as the gusts of wind and rain dissipate slowly, transforming into a much lighter breeze.

"Take my hand, Adira, let's head into the boat shed. I have a story to tell you."

I grasp Mother's hand, allowing her to guide me towards the shed.

Staring up at the night sky, I notice that it is now saturated with a deep blood red.

I am shaking now and not from the cold. Fear is churning its way into my stomach.

Deep inside, I dread the narrative of danger and bloodshed that is about to unfold.

About the Author

Susan Marshall is an Australian author of plays, poetry and fiction. In 2020, she founded *Story Playscapes*, her writing and publishing business. Susan is renown for delving into her playscapes when developing her writing and the readers enjoy seeing her engagement with the world around her and gleaning insights into how she gains inspiration. Her written works are highly respected by a dedicated global audience.

Susan has completed a Bachelor of Arts (majoring in English, Theatre and Drama) at La Trobe University and a Bachelor of Teaching (Primary and Secondary) at Deakin University. She has taught professionally in primary and secondary schools for more than a decade. Susan has also written a number of articles for academic publications; presented at state and national conferences in drama and literacy education and has worked as an executive committee member for Drama Victoria.

As a writer and educator, Susan brings a wealth of knowledge to Story Playscapes. She is passionate about empowering literacy development in her global readership. Susan is also big hearted in her discussions on social media, where she fosters a love for reading and discovery in her readers.

Susan has produced a range of professional publications, including her play: *Broken World*, which was published by RMDesigned in 2013. The play was launched at the AATE/ALEA National Conference and positively reviewed by the Children's Book Council of Australia. RMDesigned also published Susan's second play, *Indigo's Haven* in 2016.

Susan has also written a range of poetry and fiction, which have been published at Vocal Media. Most notably, her short story: *Peonies for Masha: Her Journey Home* was shortlisted as a finalist in the Vocal+ Fiction Awards in 2022.

Susan is a recipient of an *Award for Special Civic Service*, which was presented to her by the Mayor of Richmond, Victoria, for her work in the community.

Makeshift Girl: The Secret Heritage Trail is Susan Marshall's debut novel for adults.

About the Book Designer

Ryan Marshall is a graphic designer, photographer and illustrator, with more than 20 years of experience in designing a broad range of monographs, trade and fiction publications for world-leading professionals in the arts, design, photographic, automotive, landscape design and architectural industries.

Ryan has applied his unique technical skill set to the design and creation of hundreds of titles and includes significant contributions to international bestselling publications and series.

Ryan's most treasured work so far has been the design contribution to Susan Marshall's debut novel *Makeshift Girl: The Secret Heritage Trail*.

About Story Playscapes

Story Playscapes, established in 2020, is an Australian writing and publishing business founded by Australian Author, Susan Marshall.

The business is dedicated to promoting positive approaches to literacy development. It nurtures a global readership by actively sharing Susan Marshall's diverse range of written works on its website and via print and ebook publications.

Susan also communicates regularly with her readers via social media, encouraging them to develop a love for reading and discovering the story.

Story Playscapes is proud to celebrate its premiere print publication: *Makeshift Girl: The Secret Heritage Trail* in this paperback edition. A literary fiction, it is the exciting first book in the mysterious and uplifting *Makeshift Girl* series for adults.

Story Playscapes

DISCOVER THE STORY

🌐 www.storyplayscapes.com

Ⓕ Facebook: /storyplayscapes

📷 Instagram: @storyplayscapes